More to William Morris

Other Books from Inkling

Untangling Tolkien
Michael W. Perry

Here is the book Tolkien fans have been waiting for—a detailed, day-by-day, book-length chronology of *The Lord of the Rings*. Whether you are a serious Tolkien fan or simply someone who enjoys reading the story over and over, this is the book for you. It is the first new type of reference to be released since the 1970s.

Paperback: 1-58742-019-8

Celebrating Middle-earth
Edited by John G. West Jr.

In speeches first given at Seattle Pacific University in November 2001, six Tolkien scholars describe the literary, political and spiritual background to *The Lord of the Rings*. Contributors are John West, Peter Kreeft, Janet Leslie Blumberg, Joseph Pearce, Kerry Dearborn, and Phillip Goggans.

Paperback: 1-58742-012-0   Hardback: 1-58742-013-9

On the Lines of Morris' Romances
William Morris

In a 1914 letter to his future wife, Tolkien noted that he was working on a story "on the lines of Morris' romances." Here, in one inexpensive volume, are two of the best known of his tales of great quests much like those undertaken by Bilbo and Frodo: *The Well at the World's End* and *The Wood Beyond the World*.

Paperback: 1-58742-024-4

Single Volume Editions of William Morris

Inkling also has single-volume editions of several William Morris books, newly typeset in both paperback and hardback editions.

The House of the Wolfings	Paperback: 1-58742-025-2	Hardback: 1-58742-026-0
The Roots of the Mountains	Paperback: 1-58742-027-9	Hardback: 1-58742-028-7
The Wood Beyond the World	Paperback: 1-58742-029-5	Hardback: 1-58742-030-9
The Well at the World's End	Paperback: 1-58742-031-7	Hardback: 1-58742-032-5

Across Asia on a Bicycle
Thomas Gaskell Allen Jr. and William Lewis Sachtleben

When they graduated from college in 1891, the authors set out to make the first journey around the world on a modern bicycle. Two years later they arrived back in the U.S. after biking 15,000 miles, at that time the "longest continuous land journey ever made around the world." This book describes the most difficult and dangerous part of that journey, their 7,000 miles of travel from Constantinople to Peking, as they biked alone across lands few outsiders ever visited. Along the way, they became the first Americans to reach the top of Mount Ararat, and in China, they were the first to introduce the bicycle to a nation that now has 300 million bicycles. This book is back in print for the first time since 1894.

Paperback: 1-58742-020-1   Hardback: 1-58742-021-X

Bookstores can order from Ingram or Baker & Taylor (U.S.) and Bertrams (Europe). Also available online.

More to William Morris

Two Books that Inspired J. R. R. Tolkien

The House of the Wolfings
and
The Roots of the Mountains

by

William Morris

Inkling Books   Seattle   2003

Description

More to William Morris contains the complete text of two historical novels by William Morris: *The House of the Wolfings* and *The Roots of the Mountains*. It provides fans of J. R. R. Tolkien with an inexpensive edition of two of the tales that influenced *The Lord of the Rings*. It includes a Foreword that explains the literary links between William Morris and J. R. R. Tolkien.

Copyright Notice

Publisher's Note

The House of the Wolfings was first published in December 1888 by Reeves and Turner. A 1904 edition by Longmans, Green and Co. was used to prepare this text, which was then checked against the 1912 edition of *The Collected Works of William Morris* (Volume 14) by that same publisher.

The Roots of the Mountains was first published in November 1889. The 1896 Long, Green and Co. edition was used to prepare this text, which was checked against that in the 1912 edition of *The Collected Works of William Morris* (Volume 15).

As Morris' daughter, May Morris, noted in the 1912 edition, there was inconsistency in how her father handled "proper names and place-names" in both books. She corrected some of those inconsistencies and left others intact. This book has followed a similar policy. As she explained, the tales were written with a "slight hurry and inattention to unessential things, and a sure touch and deliberation in the graver moments."

Dedication

This new edition is dedicated to the many Tolkien fans who long for more books like *The Lord of the Rings*.

Library Cataloging Data

More to William Morris: Two Books that Inspired J. R. R. Tolkien—The House of the Wolfings and The Roots of the Mountains.
By William Morris (1834–1896)
With a Foreword and Introductions by Michael W. Perry (1948–)
251 pages, 7.5 x 9.25 in. 235 x 191 mm.
Includes 90 chapters, a Foreword and two Introductions
Library of Congress Control Number: 2003113118
ISBN 1-58742-023-6 (alkaline paper)

Publisher Information

Inkling Books, Seattle, WA, U.S.A. Internet: http://www.InklingBooks.com/
Published in the United States of America on acid-free paper
First Edition, Second Printing, December 2003

Contents

FOREWORD: WILLIAM MORRIS AND J. R. R. TOLKIEN

In her introduction to the fourteenth volume of *The Collected Works of William Morris* (1912), Morris' daughter May said that, "In *The House of the Wolfings* and in *The Roots of the Mountains* my father seems to have got back to the atmosphere of the [ancient Northern European] Sagas. In that it is part metrical, part prose, the *Wolfings* may be held experimental, but in this tale of imaginary tribal life on the verge of Roman conquest—a period which had a great fascination for the writer, who read with critical enjoyment the more important modern studies of it as they came out."

The impact of those "modern studies" must have been great, for May Morris went on to note with amusement, a "German professor who, after the *Wolfings* came out, wrote and asked learned questions about the Mark, expecting, I fear, equally learned answers from our Poet who sometimes dreamed realities without having documentary evidence of them." The hot-tempered Morris' own response to that professor was amusing. "Doesn't the fool realize," he shouted, "that it's a romance, a work of fiction—that it's all lies!"

As Morris well knew, we know almost nothing about the day-to-day life of these brave and intelligent, but typically illiterate European tribes. In the Middle East, a dry climate, the widespread use of stone and clay, and the early spread of a written language preserved much. In a region that J. R. R. Tolkien would also make such a prominent part of his Middle-earth, a wet climate, the limited use of writing, and the common use of wood and leather left little for future generations to study. What little we do know has as its source the far from objective remarks of their foes, such as the Romans, and the fragments that have come down to us across the centuries, preserved in poetic sagas about great heroes and their accomplishments.

Both Morris and Tolkien drank deeply from those ancient literary wells of "Northerness." Morris did so as part of a wide artistic genius that included the translation of ancient tales—as in his 1870 *Volsunga Saga: The Story of the Volsungs and Niblungs*. Tolkien did so as part of a long professional life as an Oxford professor and a leading expert on the ancient languages and literature of Northern Europe.

These two men knew either much (Morris) or most (Tolkien) of all that was known about these people and their lives. They used that wealth of knowledge to create "dreamed realities" (Morris) or an "imaginary history" (Tolkien) about what it *might* have been like to live in those days. While what they wrote wasn't necessarily true in a strict sense, both knew enough about the past and were talented enough as writers that what they wrote creates a strong sense that they describe what might have been.

Their readers certainly sense this. One wrote Morris that his tales, "convey the impression of your having lived in the time to describe what you have seen." The effect of Tolkien is even more startling. Friends of his fans often complain that those who drink deeply of Middle-earth act as if Tolkien's created world were more real than the one in which they live. In his *Rehabilitations*, Tolkien's close friend C. S. Lewis said much the same when he noted of Morris, "All we need demand is that this invented world should have some intellectual or emotional relevance to the world we live in. And it has."

Without a doubt, both Morris and Tolkien achieved that most difficult of all tasks for an author. They imagined a world with such skill that those who inhabit it seem as real as our next-door neighbor. Morris made clear that was his intent in a July 1889 paper in which he discussed romantic literature and said that, "As for romance, what does romance mean? I have heard people miscalled for being romantic, but what romance means is the capacity for a true conception of history, a power of making the past part of the present." Both Morris and Tolkien were geniuses at doing just that.

Of course there are also differences in how the two men wrote. Morris was relatively indifferent to the broader picture. In *The House of the Wolfings* it is enough for him that his tale resembles the battles that Germanic tribes once fought with encroaching Roman armies. He has no desire to link his tale to actual battles fought on certain dates with specific Roman generals. The same is true of geography in *The Roots of the Mountains*. His description of the *local* geography and its forests is as marvelous as anything in Tolkien and that geography plays a major role in his story. But we are left uncertain about what would seem to be an important fact, which particular mountain range provides a backdrop for the story. May Morris believed the story was set in "the wonderful land at the foot of the Italian Alps" that her father loved so dearly. Others, with perhaps more an eye on history, place it in the German Alps or even in the Carpathian Mountains of Eastern Europe. Even more surprising, although we are left with the impression that the people in *Roots* are descendants of those in *Wolfings*, the actual ties between the two was left unclear. For Morris those things simply did not matter. It was enough for him that his tales can be fitted, however loosely, into European history.

In contrast, as his readers know, Tolkien did not place his tale within the *recorded* history of Europe. The events he described are assumed to have taken place in a past so distant that no independent history or artifacts from the age remain. Only the faintest echoes of what happened then have been preserved in extinct languages and ancient tales about dwarves, elves and dragons. In fact, so much (imaginary) time has passed that even the geography of Middle-earth only loosely resembles that of the Western Europe on which it is modeled.

Tolkien saw this historical vacuum as an opportunity. Into that vast gap, he thrust his own history for a world that, by his account, was just over seven thousand years old when the main events of *The Lord of the Rings* took place. He gave his Middle-earth a history and geography so complex, that numerous books have been written to describe it. In fact, I was able to write a 251-page chronology (*Untangling Tolkien*) in which I describe, typically to the year, the complex and quite plausible chain of events that led to Frodo acquiring the Ring, as well as a precise and detailed, day-by-day account of Frodo's quest to rid Middle-earth of the Ring, aided by his friends. Morris, although almost as talented a story teller, did nothing on that grand a scale.

That said, what Morris and Tolkien had in common was far more important than their differences. May Morris expressed it when she said that her father's writings were "experimental." In biblical language, he was trying to see if the 'old wine' in the ancient Northern tales that he loved so well—tales that were typically told in poetic forms that were no longer popular—could survive being put into the 'new wineskins' of a modern prose novel, with only an occasional burst of poetry. In that he proved quite successful, although much of his success would come through others, such as Tolkien, and through a new form of literature called fantasy that he helped to create out of ancient folk and fairy tales.

Of course, the fact that Morris was building on those tales, does not mean he slavishly followed them. C. S. Lewis readily admitted that, "Morris invented for his poems and perfected in his prose-romances a language which has never at any period been spoken in England." But he went on to point out that, "The question about Morris's style is not whether it is an artificial language—all endurable language in longer works must be that—but whether it is a good one."

Lewis, a great writer in his own right, believed Morris had succeeded marvelously. Morris' style, he wrote, "is incomparably easier and clearer than any 'natural' style could possibly be, and the 'dull finish,' the careful avoidance of rhetoric, gloss and decoration, is of its very essence." In words that apply equally well to Tolkien, Lewis said that it was the very "matter-of-factness" of the tales, that make them seem true. "Other stories have only scenery: his have geography. He is not concerned with 'painting' landscapes; he tells you the lie of the land, and then you paint the landscape for yourself. To a reader long fed on the almost botanical and entomological niceties of much modern fiction—where, indeed, we mostly skip if the characters go through a jungle—the effect is at first very pale and cold, but also very fresh and spacious. We begin to relish what my friend called the 'Northerness.' No mountains in literature are as far away as distant mountains in Morris."

There is also, Lewis said, a remarkable vividness in Morris' descriptions of human society. Unlike many other romantic writers, Morris did not glorify the individual, making him almost God-like in his independence. Morris, Lewis wrote, "immerses the individual completely in the society. 'If thou diest today, where then shall our love be?' asks the heroine in the *House of the Wolfings*. 'It shall abide with the soul of the Wolfings,' comes the answer."

Lewis points out that many writers who have tried to describe an ideal society are "dull" because they fail to define the value of "*x*" that describes what is Good. But he goes on, "The tribal communities which Morris paints in *The House of the Wolfings* or *The Roots of the Mountains* are such attempts, perhaps the most successful attempts ever made, to give *x* a value. . . . A modern poet of the Left, praising that same solidarity with the group which Morris praises, invites a man to be 'one cog in the singing golden hive.' Morris, on the other hand, paints the actual goings on of the communal life, the sowing, planting, begetting, building, ditching, eating and conversation. . . . Morris . . . brings back a sentiment that a man could really live by."

Lewis could have said much the same of the imaginary communities that his friend Tolkien created. The Shire, Rivendell and Rohan have ways of life many find appealing, however different they may be from modern life. Each sets before us what seems to be a reasonable standard by which we might live. All are places we can imagine as our home.

Lewis also believed that Morris might bridge a gap he saw developing in 1939 society which has grown even wider since. "The old indeterminate, half-Christian, half-Pantheistic, piety of the last century is gone," he wrote. "The modern literary world is increasingly divided into two camps, that of the positive, militant Christians and that of the convinced materialists." Both camps, Lewis noted, can "find in him something that they need."

As a Pagan poet, Morris was "content to merely state the [ultimate human] question . . . uncontaminated by theorizing." Within his tales we sense the great Pagan "thirst for immortality, tingling alive," but also totally devoid of the answers that Christianity would later bring to a Pagan Europe. As a "prophet as unconscious, and therefore as far beyond suspicion as Balaam's ass," he testifies to the importance of that thirst in itself and not merely as a prelude to a presentation of the Christian gospel.

Because Morris considered himself a socialist, many on the Left consider him one of them. But Lewis saw a critical difference between Morris and his political allies. He believed that Morris might force an increasingly secular and politicized Left to face a question it would rather ignore. "The Left agrees with Morris that it is an absolute duty to labour for human happiness in this world," he wrote. "But the Left is deceiving itself if it thinks that any zeal for this object can permanently silence the reflection that every moment of this happiness must be lost as soon as gained, that all who enjoy it will die, that the race and the planet themselves must one day follow the individual into a state of being which has no significance—a universe of inorganic homogeneous matter moving at uniform speed in a low temperature. Hitherto the Left has been content, as far as I know, to pretend that this does not matter." Morris makes clear that such things do matter.

Morris can do this because of a peculiarity in his writings. Like Tolkien, the fact that he wrote of a long-ago world has led some to accuse him of being escapist. Not so, says Lewis. Morris (and by implication Tolkien) has "faced the facts" of modern life. "This is the paradox of him. He seems to retire far from the real world and to build a world out of his wishes; but when he has finished the result stands out as a picture of experience ineluctably true." Morris presents, "in one vision the ravishing sweetness and the heart-breaking melancholy of our experience." He shows, "how the one continually passes over into the other." Most important of all, he combines everything into "a stirring practical creed," that "all our adventures, worldly and other-worldly alike, must take into account." The same can be said of Tolkien.

Tolkien recognized the literary debt he owned to those ancient tales and to Morris himself in a letter he wrote to his future wife in the fall of 1914 (now the first letter in *The Letters of J. R. R. Tolkien*). There he spoke of introducing a fellow student to the delights of "Kalevala the Finnish ballads." Tolkien went on to say that he was trying to turn one of those ballads, "which is really a great story and most tragic—into a short story somewhat on the lines of Morris' romances with chunks of poetry in between."

Forty-six years later, in a letter written at the very end of 1960, Tolkien continued to honor his literary debt to Morris when he wrote that the landscape of "The Dead Marshes and the approaches to the Morannon owe something to Northern France after the Battle of the Somme [where Tolkien fought in World War I]. They owe more to William Morris and his Huns and Romans, as in *The House of the Wolfings* or *The Roots of the Mountains*." That remark became the inspiration for this book, combining those two closely related tales under one title, *More to William Morris*, its title derived from Tolkien's own praise for Morris.

After Tolkien died in 1973, many of his admirers hoped stories similar to *The Lord of the Rings* existed in manuscript form among the author's large collection of papers. Unfortunately, time has demonstrated that was only partly true. Fragments of tales and plots that might have become great epics do exist and have been published in *The Silmarillion* and *Unfinished Tales*. In addition, many of the attempted plots and variations in plot that lie behind *The Lord of Rings* have been included in his son Christopher Tolkien's "History of Middle-earth" series. But almost all that material lacks the wide appeal of Tolkien's masterpiece. What Tolkien left behind is simply too fragmentary and incomplete. For tales like Tolkien's, we must go to one of Tolkien's richest literary sources, William Morris.

C. S. Lewis would have agreed. Morris' stories, he wrote, provide readers with "a pleasure so inexhaustible that after twenty or fifty years of reading they find it worked so deeply into all their emotions as to defy analysis." Morris's stories were almost certainly among those Lewis meant when he told Tolkien, "if they won't write the kind of books we want to read, we shall have to write them ourselves."

Readers, however, should keep one thing in mind. In these two tales by Morris, you won't find an epic as broad or as extraordinarily complex as Tolkien's story of the Ring. Instead you will find stories having much the same literary flavor, with heroes and heroines from long ago fighting to keep their freedom in a hostile and dangerous world. You'll also find descriptions of forests and nature every bit as marvelous as anything in Tolkien and stories that stresses the importance of personal choice and the need to remain loyal to those close to us, whatever the cost. Finally, you'll find something Tolkien is often accused of neglecting, warm romances between men and women.

Getting specific, if you like what Tolkien wrote about Aragorn and his Rangers, if you admire the bravery of the Riders of Rohan, if you long for more tales of travel in an unspoiled wilderness, and if you wish that Tolkien had more to say about the courage of women or about romance between men and women, then you'll be delighted by these two marvelous tales from the pen of William Morris.

We should always remember that William Morris, the writer who delighted and inspired Tolkien, can still delight and inspire those who love the stories Tolkien wrote.

—Michael W. Perry, Seattle, Washington, October 3, 2003,
    The 107th anniversary of the death of William Morris

A TALE OF THE HOUSE OF THE WOLFINGS

AND ALL THE KINDREDS OF THE MARK WRITTEN IN PROSE AND IN VERSE

BY WILLIAM MORRIS

Whiles in the early Winter eve
We pass amid the gathering night
Some homestead that we had to leave
Years past; and see its candles bright
Shine in the room beside the door
Where we were merry years agone
But now must never enter more,
As still the dark road drives us on.
E'en so the world of men may turn
At even of some hurried day
And see the ancient glimmer burn
Across the waste that hath no way;
Then with that faint light in its eyes
A while I bid it linger near
And nurse in wavering memories
The bitter-sweet of days that were.

INTRODUCTION

In J. R. R. Tolkien's great epic, *The Lord of the Rings,* the climax of the Council of Elrond comes when a consensus is reached that "the Ruling Ring must be destroyed." When the noon-bell then rings, a silence falls on the group as they ponder who will take up the seemingly impossible task. At that moment the central character in the tale, Frodo, is filled with dread, "A overwhelming longing to rest and remain at peace by Bilbo's side in Rivendell filled all his heart." With much effort, he makes his choice, "I will take the Ring," he said, "though I do not know the way."

In this earlier tale by Morris, the central actor, Thiodolf, faces a similar choice, one linked to a magical hauberk (a coat of chain mail). Like Frodo, he must choose to live and remain close to someone he loves (Wood-Sun) or face the near certainty that he will die protecting his people.

Morris himself said as much in a 1888 letter when he wrote that *The House of the Wolfings* "is a story of the life of the Gothic tribes on their way through Middle Europe, and their first meeting with the Romans in war. It is meant to illustrate the melting of the individual into the society of the tribes: I mean apart from the artistic side of things that is its moral—if it has one."

Though it is probably no more than a coincidence, both Frodo and Thiodolf see in its starkness the decision they must make in the fourteenth chapter of their respective tales. For Frodo the choice is clear beyond doubt. He must carry the Ring to Mordor. But for Thiodolf, the choice remains a dark suspicion, "that a curse goeth with the hauberk, then either for the sake of the folk I will not wear the gift and the curse, and I shall die in great glory, and because of me the House shall live; or else for thy sake I shall bear it and live, and the House shall live or die as may be, but I not helping, nay I no longer of the House nor in it."

Though there is no exact parallel between Morris' tale and any particular historical event, the great struggle between Rome's drive to civilize and enslave their way into central Europe and the Germanic tribes willingness to fight for their independence is a fact of history.

Perhaps the most important battle in that struggle between Romans and Germans was one in A.D. 9 between the Roman general Varus and Gothic soldiers led by Arminius, a German whose talent had been recognized the Romans, who had attempted to buy his allegiance by giving him Roman citizenship and military training. He would use that training against them.

Knowing that troop strength and military skill gave the advantage to Rome, in September Arminius lured Varus out of his Westphalian fortress to put down what was thought to be a minor revolt. The Romans were tricked into entering a wooded and hilly region, where heavy rains made movement difficult. Arminius then launched a series of lightning attacks on the Roman army, using every advantage imaginable. (One key battle took place, much as in Morris' tale, on a forested ridge.) In the end, Varus committed suicide to avoid capture and most of his army was either killed in battle or sacrificed later to blood-thirsty pagan gods. Rome was left angry and bitter by the defeat, but in the end was forced to come to an uneasy truce with the Germanic tribes, with the Rhine River serving as a boundary line. Later, barbarian tribes coming out of central Europe (much like the Huns in *The Roots of the Mountains*) will first weaken and then destroy the Roman empire.

Why would an Englishman like Morris take pride in a long-ago victory by a distant tribe when his own homeland, England, had been successfully occupied and colonized by Rome? The reason is simple. In his day, many educated Englishmen believed that their racial ('blood') roots lay in the Germanic tribes of this era. In the often-reprinted 1851 *Fifteen Decisive Battles of the World,* Edward S. Creasy made the bold claim that, "an Englishman is entitled to claim a closer degree of relationship with Arminius than can be claimed by any German of modern Germany." So the Englishmen of Morris' day would have no problem imagining themselves as brave and fierce Wolfing warriors, even as the British then ruled a Rome-like empire that bore little resemblance to a Gothic village.

Those who have read Tolkien's *The Lord of the Rings* will notice similarities. There is a forest named Mirkwood in Morris, although it is not as dark and mysterious as Tolkien's. In Chapter 2, a messenger brings to the Wolfings (as to Rohan) a "war-arrow ragged and burnt and bloody." And, much like Bilbo and Frodo, Thiodolf acquires a protective coat of mail (hauberk) made by dwarves and having, in addition, dangerous and hidden powers much like Tolkien's Ring. But while the Ring bestows unimaginable power on its possessor, the hauberk has a far different effect. In both tales, however, the plot hinges on the hero making the right choice about the use of the powerful tool he has been given.

—Michael W. Perry, Seattle, Washington, October 3, 2003,
The 107th anniversary of the death of William Morris

1. THE DWELLINGS OF MID-MARK

The tale tells that in times long past there was a dwelling of men beside a great wood. Before it lay a plain, not very great, but which was, as it were, an isle in the sea of woodland, since even when you stood on the flat ground, you could see trees everywhere in the offing, though as for hills, you could scarce say that there were any; only swellings-up of the earth here and there, like the upheavings of the water that one sees at whiles going on amidst the eddies of a swift but deep stream.

On either side, to right and left the tree-girdle reached out toward the blue distance, thick close and unsundered, save where it and the plain which it begirdled was cleft amidmost by a river about as wide as the Thames at Sheene when the flood-tide is at its highest, but so swift and full of eddies, that it gave token of mountains not so far distant, though they were hidden. On each side moreover of the stream of this river was a wide space of stones, great and little, and in most places above this stony waste were banks of a few feet high, showing where the yearly winter flood was most commonly stayed.

You must know that this great clearing in the woodland was not a matter of haphazard; though the river had driven a road whereby men might fare on each side of its hurrying stream. It was men who had made that Isle in the woodland.

For many generations the folk that now dwelt there had learned the craft of iron-founding, so that they had no lack of wares of iron and steel, whether they were tools of handicraft or weapons for hunting and for war. It was the men of the Folk, who coming adown by the river-side had made that clearing. The tale tells not whence they came, but belike from the dales of the distant mountains, and from dales and mountains and plains further aloof and yet further.

Anyhow they came adown the river; on its waters on rafts, by its shores in wains or bestriding their horses or their kine, or afoot, till they had a mind to abide; and there as it fell they stayed their travel, and spread from each side of the river, and fought with the wood and its wild things, that they might make to themselves a dwelling-place on the face of the earth.

So they cut down the trees, and burned their stumps that the grass might grow sweet for their kine and sheep and horses; and they diked the river where need was all through the plain, and far up into the wild-wood to bridle the winter floods: and they made them boats to ferry them over, and to float down stream and track up-stream: they fished the river's eddies also with net and with line; and drew drift from out of it of far-travelled wood and other matters; and the gravel of its shallows they washed for gold; and it became their friend, and they loved it, and gave it a name, and called it the Dusky, and the Glassy, and the Mirkwood-water; for the names of it changed with the generations of man.

There then in the clearing of the wood that for many years grew greater yearly they drave their beasts to pasture in the new-made meadows, where year by year the grass grew sweeter as the sun shone on it and the standing waters went from it; and now in the year whereof the tale telleth it was a fair and smiling plain, and no folk might have a better meadow.

But long before that had they learned the craft of tillage and taken heed to the acres and begun to grow wheat and rye thereon round about their roofs; the spade came into their hands, and they bethought them of the plough-share, and the tillage spread and grew, and there was no lack of bread.

In such wise that Folk had made an island amidst of the Mirkwood, and established a home there, and upheld it with manifold toil too long to tell of. And from the beginning this clearing in the wood they called the Mid-mark: for you shall know that men might journey up and down the Mirkwood-water, and half a day's ride up or down they would come on another clearing or island in the woods, and these were the Upper-mark and the Nether-mark: and all these three were inhabited by men of one folk and one kindred, which was called the Markmen, though of many branches was that stem of folk, who bore divers signs in battle and at the council whereby they might be known.

Now in the Mid-mark itself were many Houses of men; for by that word had they called for generations those who dwelt together under one token of kinship. The river ran from South to North, and both on the East side and on the West were there Houses of the Folk, and their habitations were shouldered up nigh unto the wood, so that ever betwixt them and the river was there a space of tillage and pasture.

Tells the tale of one such House, whose habitations were on the west side of the water, on a gentle slope of land, so that no flood higher than common might reach them. It was straight down to the river mostly that the land fell off, and on its downward-reaching slopes was the tillage, "the Acres," as the men of that time always called tilled land; and beyond that was the meadow going fair and smooth, though with here and there a rising in it, down to the lips of the stony waste of the winter river.

Now the name of this House was the Wolfings, and they bore a Wolf on their banners, and their warriors were marked on the breast with the image of the Wolf, that they might be known for what they were if they fell in battle, and were stripped.

The house, that is to say the Roof, of the Wolfings of the Mid-mark stood on the topmost of the slope aforesaid with its back to the wild-wood and its face to the acres and the water. But you must know that in those days the men of one branch of kindred dwelt under one roof together, and had therein their place and dignity; nor were there many degrees amongst them as hath befallen afterwards, but all they of one blood were brethren and of equal dignity. Howbeit they had servants or thralls, men taken in battle, men of alien blood, though true it is that from time to time were some of such men taken into the House, and hailed as brethren of the blood.

Also (to make an end at once of these matters of kinship and affinity) the men of one House might not wed the women of their own House: to the Wolfing men all Wolfing women were as sisters: they must needs wed with the Hartings or the Elkings or the Bearings, or other such Houses of the Mark as were not so close akin to the blood of the Wolf; and this was a law that none dreamed of breaking. Thus then dwelt this Folk and such was their Custom.

As to the Roof of the Wolfings, it was a great hall and goodly, after the fashion of their folk and their day; not built of stone and lime, but framed of the goodliest trees of the wild-wood squared with the adze, and betwixt the framing filled with clay wattled with reeds. Long was that house, and at one end anigh the gable was the Man's-door, not so high that a man might stand on the threshold and his helmcrest clear the lintel; for such was the custom, that a tall man must bow himself as he came into the hall; which custom maybe was a memory of the days of onslaught when the foemen were mostly wont to beset the hall; whereas in the days whereof the tale tells they drew out into the fields and fought unfenced; unless at whiles when the odds were over great, and then they drew their wains about them and were fenced by the Wain-burg. At least it was from no niggardry that the door was made thus low, as might be seen by the fair and manifold carving of knots and dragons that was wrought above the lintel of the door for some three foot's space. But a like door was there anigh the other gable-end, whereby the women entered, and it was called the Woman's-door.

Near to the house on all sides except toward the wood were there many bowers and cots round about the penfolds and the byres: and these were booths for the stowage of wares, and for crafts and smithying that were unhandy to do in the house; and withal they were the dwelling-places of the thralls. And the lads and young men often abode there many days and were cherished there of the thralls that loved them, since at whiles they shunned the Great Roof that they might be the freer to come and go at their pleasure, and deal as they would. Thus was there a clustering on the slopes and bents betwixt the acres of the Wolfings and the wild-wood wherein dwelt the wolves.

As to the house within, two rows of pillars went down it endlong, fashioned of the mightiest trees that might be found, and each one fairly wrought with base and chapiter, and wreaths and knots, and fighting men and dragons; so that it was like a church of later days that has a nave and aisles: windows there were above the aisles, and a passage underneath the said windows in their roofs. In the aisles were the sleeping-places of the Folk, and down the nave under the crown of the roof were three hearths for the fires, and above each hearth a luffer or smoke-bearer to draw the smoke up when the fires were lighted. Forsooth on a bright winter afternoon it was strange to see the three columns of smoke going wavering up to the dimness of the mighty roof, and one maybe smitten athwart by the sunbeams. As for the timber of the roof itself and its framing, so exceeding great and high it was, that the tale tells how that none might see the fashion of it from the hall-floor unless he were to raise aloft a blazing faggot on a long pole: since no lack of timber was there among the men of the Mark.

At the end of the hall anigh the Man's-door was the dais, and a table thereon set thwartwise of the hall; and in front of the dais was the noblest and greatest of the hearths; (but of the others one was in the very midmost, and another in the Woman's Chamber) and round about the dais, along the gable-wall, and hung from pillar to pillar were woven cloths pictured with images of ancient tales and the deeds of the Wolfings, and the deeds of the Gods from whence they came. And this was the fairest place of all the house and the best-beloved of the Folk, and especially of the older and the mightier men: and there were tales told, and songs sung, especially if they were new: and thereto also were messengers brought if any tidings were abroad: there also would the elders talk together about matters concerning the House or the Mid-mark or the whole Folk of the Markmen.

Yet you must not think that their solemn councils were held there, the folk-motes whereat it must be determined what to do and what to forbear doing; for according as such councils, (which they called Things) were of the House or of the Mid-mark or of the whole Folk, were they held each at the due Thing-steads in the Wood aloof from either acre or meadow, (as was the custom of our forefathers for long after) and at such Things would all the men of the House or the Mid-mark or the Folk be present man by man. And in each of these steads was there a Doomring wherein Doom was given by the neighbours chosen, (whom now we call the Jury) in matters between man and man; and no such doom of neighbours was given, and no such voice of the Folk proclaimed in any house or under any roof, nor even as aforesaid on the tilled acres or the depastured meadows. This was the custom of our forefathers, in memory, belike, of the days when as yet there was neither house nor tillage, nor flocks and herds, but the Earth's face only and what freely grew thereon.

But over the dais there hung by chains and pulleys fastened to a tie-beam of the roof high aloft a wondrous lamp fashioned of glass; yet of no such glass as the folk made then and there, but of a fair and clear green like an emerald, and all done with figures and knots in gold, and strange beasts, and a warrior slaying a dragon, and the sun rising on the earth: nor did any tale tell whence this lamp came, but it was held as an ancient and holy thing by all the Markmen, and the kindred of the Wolf had it in charge to keep a light burning in it night and day for ever; and they appointed a maiden of their own kindred to that office; which damsel must needs be unwedded, since no wedded woman dwelling under that roof could be a Wolfing woman, but would needs be of the houses wherein the Wolfings wedded.

This lamp which burned ever was called the Hall-Sun, and the woman who had charge of it, and who was the fairest that might be found was called after it the Hall-Sun also.

At the other end of the hall was the Woman's Chamber, and therein were the looms and other gear for the carding and spinning of wool and the weaving of cloth.

Such was the Roof under which dwelt the kindred of the Wolfings; and the other kindreds of the Mid-mark had roofs like to it; and of these the chiefest were the Elkings, the Vallings, the Alftings, the Beamings, the Galtings, and the Bearings; who bore on their banners the Elk, the Falcon, the Swan, the Tree, the Boar, and the Bear. But other lesser and newer kindreds there were than these: as for the Hartings above named, they were a kindred of the Upper-mark.

2. THE FLITTING OF THE WAR-ARROW

Tells the tale that it was an evening of summer, when the wheat was in the ear, but yet green; and the neat-herds were done driving the milch-kine to the byre, and the horseherds and the shepherds had made the night-shift, and the out-goers were riding two by two and one by one through the lanes between the wheat and the rye towards the meadow. Round the cots of the thralls were gathered knots of men and women both thralls and freemen, some talking together, some hearkening a song or a tale, some singing and some dancing together; and the children gambolling about from group to group with their shrill and tuneless voices, like young throstles who have not yet learned the song of their race. With these were mingled dogs, dun of colour, long of limb, sharp-nosed, gaunt and great; they took little heed of the children as they pulled them about in their play, but lay down, or loitered about, as though they had forgotten the chase and the wild-wood.

Merry was the folk with that fair tide, and the promise of the harvest, and the joy of life, and there was no weapon among them so close to the houses, save here and there the boar-spear of some herdman or herd-woman late come from the meadow.

Tall and for the most part comely were both men and women; the most of them light-haired and grey-eyed, with cheek-bones somewhat high; white of skin but for the sun's burning, and the wind's parching, and whereas they were tanned of a very ruddy and cheerful hue. But the thralls were some of them of a shorter and darker breed, black-haired also and dark-eyed, lighter of limb; sometimes better knit, but sometimes crookeder of leg and knottier of arm. But some also were of build and hue not much unlike to the freemen; and

these doubtless came of some other Folk of the Goths which had given way in battle before the Men of the Mark, either they or their fathers.

Moreover some of the freemen were unlike their fellows and kindred, being slenderer and closer-knit, and black-haired, but grey-eyed withal; and amongst these were one or two who exceeded in beauty all others of the House.

Now the sun was set and the glooming was at point to begin and the shadowless twilight lay upon the earth. The nightingales on the borders of the wood sang ceaselessly from the scattered hazel-trees above the greensward where the grass was cropped down close by the nibbling of the rabbits; but in spite of their song and the divers voices of the men-folk about the houses, it was an evening on which sounds from aloof can be well heard, since noises carry far at such tides.

Suddenly they who were on the edges of those throngs and were the less noisy, held themselves as if to listen; and a group that had gathered about a minstrel to hear his story fell hearkening also round about the silenced and hearkening tale-teller: some of the dancers and singers noted them and in their turn stayed the dance and kept silence to hearken; and so from group to group spread the change, till all were straining their ears to hearken the tidings. Already the men of the night-shift had heard it, and the shepherds of them had turned about, and were trotting smartly back through the lanes of the tall wheat: but the horse-herds were now scarce seen on the darkening meadow, as they galloped on fast toward their herds to drive home the stallions. For what they had heard was the tidings of war.

There was a sound in the air as of a humble-bee close to the ear of one lying on a grassy bank; or whiles as of a cow afar in the meadow lowing in the afternoon when milking-time draws nigh: but it was ever shriller than the one, and fuller than the other; for it changed at whiles, though after the first sound of it, it did not rise or fall, because the eve was windless. You might hear at once that for all it was afar, it was a great and mighty sound; nor did any that hearkened doubt what it was, but all knew it for the blast of the great war-horn of the Elkings, whose Roof lay up Mirkwood-water next to the Roof of the Wolfings.

So those little throngs broke up at once; and all the freemen, and of the thralls a good many, flocked, both men and women, to the Man's-door of the hall, and streamed in quietly and with little talk, as men knowing that they should hear all in due season.

Within under the Hall-Sun, amidst the woven stories of time past, sat the elders and chief warriors on the dais, and amidst of all a big strong man of forty winters, his dark beard a little grizzled, his eyes big and grey. Before him on the board lay the great War-horn of the Wolfings carved out of the tusk of a sea-whale of the North and with many devices on it and the Wolf amidst them all; its golden mouth-piece and rim wrought finely with flowers. There it abode the blowing, until the spoken word of some messenger should set forth the tidings borne on the air by the horn of the Elkings.

But the name of the dark-haired chief was Thiodolf (to wit Folk-wolf) and he was deemed the wisest man of the Wolfings, and the best man of his hands, and of heart most dauntless. Beside him sat the fair woman called the Hall-Sun; for she was his foster-daughter before men's eyes; and she was black-haired and grey-eyed like to her fosterer, and never was woman fashioned fairer: she was young of years, scarce twenty winters old.

There sat the chiefs and elders on the dais, and round about stood the kindred intermingled with the thralls, and no man spake, for they were awaiting sure and certain tidings: and when all were come in who had a mind to, there was so great a silence in the hall, that the song of the nightingales on the wood-edge sounded clear and loud therein, and even the chink of the bats about the upper windows could be heard. Then amidst the hush of men-folk, and the sounds of the life of the earth came another sound that made all turn their eyes toward the door; and this was the pad-pad of one running on the trodden and summer-dried ground anigh the hall: it stopped for a moment at the Man's-door, and the door opened, and the throng parted, making way for the man that entered and came hastily up to the midst of the table that stood on the dais athwart the hall, and stood there panting, holding forth in his outstretched hand something which not all could see in the

dimness of the hall-twilight, but which all knew nevertheless. The man was young, lithe and slender, and had no raiment but linen breeches round his middle, and skin shoes on his feet. As he stood there gathering his breath for speech, Thiodolf stood up, and poured mead into a drinking horn and held it out towards the new-comer, and spake, but in rhyme and measure:

Welcome, thou evening-farer, and holy be thine head,
Since thou hast sought unto us in the heart of the Wolfings' stead;
Drink now of the horn of the mighty, and call a health if thou wilt
O'er the eddies of the mead-horn to the washing out of guilt.
For thou com'st to the peace of the Wolfings, and our very guest thou art,
And meseems as I behold thee, that I look on a child of the Hart.

But the man put the horn from him with a hasty hand, and none said another word to him until he had gotten his breath again; and then he said:

All hail ye Wood-Wolfs' children! nought may I drink the wine,
For the mouth and the maw that I carry this eve are nought of mine;
And my feet are the feet of the people, since the word went forth that tide,
'O Elf here of the Hartings, no longer shalt thou bide
In any house of the Markmen than to speak the word and wend,
Till all men know the tidings and thine errand hath an end.'
Behold, O Wolves, the token and say if it be true!
I bear the shaft of battle that is four-wise cloven through,
And its each end dipped in the blood-stream, both the iron and the horn,
And its midmost scathed with the fire; and the word that I have borne
Along with this war-token is, 'Wolfings of the Mark
Whenso ye see the war-shaft, by the daylight or the dark,
Busk ye to battle faring, and leave all work undone
Save the gathering for the handplay at the rising of the sun.
Three days hence is the hosting, and thither bear along
Your wains and your kine for the slaughter lest the journey should be long.
For great is the Folk, saith the tidings, that against the Markmen come;
In a far off land is their dwelling, whenso they sit at home,
And Welsh[1] *is their tongue, and we wot not of the word that is in their mouth,*
As they march a many together from the cities of the South.'

Therewith he held up yet for a minute the token of the war-arrow ragged and burnt and bloody; and turning about with it in his hand went his ways through the open door, none hindering; and when he was gone, it was as if the token were still in the air there against the heads of the living men, and the heads

---

1. Welch with these men means Foreign, and is used for all people of Europe who are not of Gothic or Teutonic blood.

of the woven warriors, so intently had all gazed at it; and none doubted the tidings or the token. Then said Thiodolf:

Forth will we Wolfing children, and cast a sound abroad:
The mouth of the sea-beast's weapon shall speak the battle-word;
And ye warriors hearken and hasten, and dight the weed of war,
And then to acre and meadow wend ye adown no more,
For this work shall be for the women to drive our neat from the mead,
And to yoke the wains, and to load them as the men of war have need.

Out then they streamed from the hall, and no man was left therein save the fair Hall-Sun sitting under the lamp whose name she bore. But to the highest of the slope they went, where was a mound made higher by man's handiwork; thereon stood Thiodolf and handled the horn, turning his face toward the downward course of Mirkwood-water; and he set the horn to his lips, and blew a long blast, and then again, and yet again the third time; and all the sounds of the gathering night were hushed under the sound of the roaring of the war-horn of the Wolfings; and the Kin of the Beamings heard it as they sat in their hall, and they gat them ready to hearken to the bearer of the tidings who should follow on the sound of the war-blast.

But when the last sound of the horn had died away, then said Thiodolf:

Now Wolfing children hearken, what the splintered War-shaft saith,
The fire scathed blood-stained aspen! we shall ride for life or death,
We warriors, a long journey with the herd and with the wain;
But unto this our homestead shall we wend us back again,
All the gleanings of the battle; and here for them that live
Shall stand the Roof of the Wolfings, and for them shall the meadow thrive,
And the acres give their increase in the harvest of the year;
Now is no long departing since the Hall-Sun bideth here
'Neath the holy Roof of the Fathers, and the place of the Wolfing kin,

And the feast of our glad returning shall yet be held therein
Hear the bidding of the War-shaft! All men, both thralls and free,
'Twixt twenty winters and sixty, beneath the shield shall be,
And the hosting is at the Thing-stead, the Upper-mark anigh;
And we wend away to-morrow ere the Sun is noon-tide high.

Therewith he stepped down from the mound, and went his way back to the hall; and manifold talk arose among the folk; and of the warriors some were already dight for the journey, but most not, and a many went their ways to see to their weapons and horses, and the rest back again into the hall.

By this time night had fallen, and between then and the dawning would be no darker hour, for the moon was just rising; a many of the horse-herds had done their business, and were now making their way back again through the lanes of the wheat, driving the stallions before them, who played together kicking, biting and squealing, paying but little heed to the standing corn on either side. Lights began to glitter now in the cots of the thralls, and brighter still in the stithies where already you might hear the hammers clinking on the anvils, as men fell to looking to their battle gear.

But the chief men and the women sat under their Roof on the eve of departure: and the tuns of mead were broached, and the horns filled and borne round by young maidens, and men ate and drank and were merry; and from time to time as some one of the warriors had done with giving heed to his weapons, he entered into the hall and fell into the company of those whom he loved most and by whom he was best beloved; and whiles they talked, and whiles they sang to the harp up and down that long house; and the moon risen high shone in at the windows, and there was much laughter and merriment, and talk of deeds of arms of the old days on the eve of that departure: till little by little weariness fell on them, and they went their ways to slumber, and the hall was fallen silent.

3. THIODOLF TALKETH WITH THE WOOD-SUN

But yet sat Thiodolf under the Hall-Sun for a while as one in deep thought; till at last as he stirred, his sword clattered on him; and then he lifted up his eyes and looked down the hall and saw no man stirring, so he stood up and settled his raiment on him, and went forth, and so took his ways through the hall-door, as one who hath an errand.

The moonlight lay in a great flood on the grass without, and the dew was falling in the coldest hour of the night, and the earth smelled sweetly: the whole habitation was asleep now, and there was no sound to be known as the sound of any creature, save that from the distant meadow came the lowing of a cow that had lost her calf, and that a white owl was flitting about near the eaves of the Roof with her wild cry that sounded like the mocking of merriment now silent.

Thiodolf turned toward the wood, and walked steadily through the scattered hazel-trees, and thereby into the thick of the beech-trees, whose boles grew smooth and silver-grey, high and close-set: and so on and on he went as one going by a well-known path, though there was no path, till all the moonlight was quenched under the close roof of the beech-leaves, though yet for all the darkness, no man could go there and not feel that the roof was green above him. Still he went on in despite of the darkness, till at last there was a glimmer before him, that grew greater till he came unto a small wood-lawn whereon the turf grew again, though the grass was but thin, because little sunlight got to it, so close and thick were the tall trees round about it. In the heavens above it by now there was a light that was not all of the moon, though it might scarce be told whether that light were the memory of yesterday or the promise of to-morrow, since little of the heavens could be seen thence, save the crown of them, because of the tall tree-tops.

Nought looked Thiodolf either at the heavens above, or the trees, as he strode from off the husk-strewn floor of the beech wood on to the scanty grass of the lawn, but his eyes looked straight before him at that which was amidmost of the lawn: and little wonder was that; for there on a stone chair sat a woman exceeding fair, clad in glittering raiment, her hair lying as pale in the moonlight on the grey stone as the barley acres in the August night before the reaping-hook goes in amongst them. She sat there as though she were awaiting someone, and he made no stop nor stay, but went straight up to her, and took her in his arms, and kissed her mouth and her eyes, and she him again; and then he sat himself down beside her. But her eyes looked kindly on him as she said:

"O Thiodolf, hardy art thou, that thou hast no fear to take me in thine arms and to kiss me, as though thou hadst met in the meadow with a maiden of the Elkings: and I, who am a daughter of the Gods of thy kindred, and a Chooser of the Slain! Yea, and that upon the eve of battle and the dawn of thy departure to the stricken field!"

"O Wood-Sun," he said "thou art the treasure of life that I found when I was young, and the love of life that I hold, now that my beard is grizzling. Since when did I fear thee, Wood-Sun? Did I fear thee when first I saw thee, and we stood amidst the hazelled field, we twain living amongst the slain? But my sword was red with the blood of the foe, and my raiment with mine own blood; and I was a-weary with the day's work, and sick with many strokes, and methought I was fainting into death. And there thou wert before me, full of life and ruddy and smiling both lips and eyes; thy raiment clean and clear, thine hands unstained with blood: then didst thou take me by my bloody and weary hand, and didst kiss my lips grown ashen pale, and thou saidst 'Come with me.' And I strove to go, and might not; so many and sore were my hurts. Then amidst my sickness and my weariness was I merry; for I said to myself, This is the death of the warrior, and it is exceeding sweet. What meaneth it? Folk said of me; he is over young to meet the foeman; yet am I not over young to die?"

Therewith he laughed out amid the wild-wood, and his speech became song, and he said:

We wrought in the ring of the hazels, and the wine of war we drank;
From the tide when the sun stood highest to the hour wherein she sank;

And three kings came against me, the mightiest of the Huns,
The evil-eyed in battle, the swift-foot wily ones;
And they gnashed their teeth against me, and they gnawed on the
shield-rims there,
On that afternoon of summer, in the high-tide of the year.
Keen-eyed I gazed about me, and I saw the clouds draw up
Till the heavens were dark as the hollow of a wine-stained iron cup,
And the wild-deer lay unfeeding on the grass of the forest glades,
And all earth was scared with the thunder above our clashing blades.

Then sank a King before me, and on fell the other twain,
And I tossed up the reddened sword-blade in the gathered rush of the
rain
And the blood and the water blended, and fragrant grew the earth.

There long I turned and twisted within the battle-girth
Before those bears of onset: while out from the grey world streamed
The broad red lash of the lightening and in our byrnies gleamed.
And long I leapt and laboured in that garland of the fight
'Mid the blue blades and the lightening; but ere the sky grew light
The second of the Hun-kings on the rain-drenched daisies lay;
And we twain with the battle blinded a little while made stay,
And leaning on our sword-hilts each on the other gazed.

Then the rain grew less, and one corner of the veil of clouds was raised,
And as from the broidered covering gleams out the shoulder white
Of the bed-mate of the warrior when on his wedding night
He layeth his hand to the linen; so, down there in the west
Gleamed out the naked heaven: but the wrath rose up in my breast,
And the sword in my hand rose with it, and I leaped and hewed at the
Hun;
And from him too flared the war-flame, and the blades danced bright in
the sun
Come back to the earth for a little before the ending of day.

There then with all that was in him did the Hun play out the play,
Till he fell, and left me tottering, and I turned my feet to wend
To the place of the mound of the mighty, the gate of the way without
end.
And there thou wert. How was it, thou Chooser of the Slain,
Did I die in thine arms, and thereafter did thy mouth-kiss wake me
again?

Ere the last sound of his voice was done she turned and kissed him; and then she said; "Never hadst thou a fear and thine heart is full of hardihood."

Then he said:

'Tis the hardy heart, beloved, that keepeth me alive,
As the king-leek in the garden by the rain and the sun doth thrive,
So I thrive by the praise of the people; it is blent with my drink and my
meat;

More to William Morris—The House of the Wolfings

As I slumber in the night-tide it laps me soft and sweet;
And through the chamber window when I waken in the morn
With the wind of the sun's arising from the meadow is it borne
And biddeth me remember that yet I live on earth:
Then I rise and my might is with me, and fills my heart with mirth,
As I think of the praise of the people; and all this joy I win
By the deeds that my heart commandeth and the hope that lieth therein.

"Yea," she said, "but day runneth ever on the heels of day, and there are many and many days; and betwixt them do they carry eld."

"Yet art thou no older than in days bygone," said he. "Is it so, O Daughter of the Gods, that thou wert never born, but wert from before the framing of the mountains, from the beginning of all things?"

But she said:

Nay, nay; I began, I was born; although it may be indeed
That not on the hills of the earth I sprang from the godhead's seed.
And e'en as my birth and my waxing shall be my waning and end.
But thou on many an errand, to many a field dost wend
Where the bow at adventure bended, or the fleeing dastard's spear
Oft lulleth the mirth of the mighty. Now me thou dost not fear,
Yet fear with me, beloved, for the mighty Maid I fear;
And Doom is her name, and full often she maketh me afraid
And even now meseemeth on my life her hand is laid.

But he laughed and said:

In what land is she abiding? Is she near or far away?
Will she draw up close beside me in the press of the battle play?
And if then I may not smite her 'midst the warriors of the field
With the pale blade of my fathers, will she bide the shove of my shield?

But sadly she sang in answer:

In many a stead Doom dwelleth, nor sleepeth day nor night:
The rim of the bowl she kisseth, and beareth the chambering light
When the kings of men wend happy to the bride-bed from the board.
It is little to say that she wendeth the edge of the grinded sword,
When about the house half builded she hangeth many a day;
The ship from the strand she shoveth, and on his wonted way
By the mountain-hunter fareth where his foot ne'er failed before:
She is where the high bank crumbles at last on the river's shore:
The mower's scythe she whetteth; and lulleth the shepherd to sleep
Where the deadly ling-worm wakeneth in the desert of the sheep.
Now we that come of the God-kin of her redes for ourselves we wot,
But her will with the lives of men-folk and their ending know we not.
So therefore I bid thee not fear for thyself of Doom and her deed,
But for me: and I bid thee hearken to the helping of my need.

Or else—Art thou happy in life, or lusteth thou to die
In the flower of thy days, when thy glory and thy longing bloom on high?

But Thiodolf answered her:

I have deemed, and long have I deemed that this is my second life,
That my first one waned with my wounding when thou cam'st to the ring of strife.
For when in thine arms I wakened on the hazelled field of yore,
Meseemed I had newly arisen to a world I knew no more,
So much had all things brightened on that dewy dawn of day.
It was dark dull death that I looked for when my thought had died away.
It was lovely life that I woke to; and from that day henceforth
My joy of the life of man-folk was manifolded of worth.
Far fairer the fields of the morning than I had known them erst,
And the acres where I wended, and the corn with its half-slaked thirst;
And the noble Roof of the Wolfings, and the hawks that sat thereon;
And the bodies of my kindred whose deliverance I had won;
And the glimmering of the Hall-Sun in the dusky house of old;
And my name in the mouth of the maidens, and the praises of the bold,
As I sat in my battle-raiment, and the ruddy spear well steeled
Leaned 'gainst my side war-battered, and the wounds thine hand had healed.
Yea, from that morn thenceforward has my life been good indeed,
The gain of to-day was goodly, and good to-morrow's need,
And good the whirl of the battle, and the broil I wielded there,
Till I fashioned the ordered onset, and the unhoped victory fair.
And good were the days thereafter of utter deedless rest
And the prattle of thy daughter, and her hands on my unmailed breast.
Ah good is the life thou hast given, the life that mine hands have won.
And where shall be the ending till the world is all undone?
Here sit we twain together, and both we in Godhead clad,
We twain of the Wolfing kindred, and each of the other glad.

But she answered, and her face grew darker withal:

O mighty man and joyous, art thou of the Wolfing kin?
'Twas no evil deed when we mingled, nor lieth doom therein.
Thou lovely man, thou black-haired, thou shalt die and have done no ill.
Fame-crowned are the deeds of thy doing, and the mouths of men they fill.
Thou betterer of the Godfolk, enduring is thy fame:
Yet as a painted image of a dream is thy dreaded name.
Of an alien folk thou comest, that we twain might be one indeed.
Thou shalt die one day. So hearken, to help me at my need.

His face grew troubled and he said: "What is this word that I am no chief of the Wolfings?"

"Nay," she said, "but better than they. Look thou on the face of our daughter the Hall-Sun, thy daughter and mine: favoureth she at all of me?"

He laughed: "Yea, whereas she is fair, but not otherwise. This is a hard saying, that I dwell among an alien kindred, and it wotteth not thereof. Why hast thou not told me hereof before?"

She said: "It needed not to tell thee because thy day was waxing, as now it waneth. Once more I bid thee hearken and do my bidding though it be hard to thee."

He answered: "Even so will I as much as I may; and thus wise must thou look upon it, that I love life, and fear not death."

Then she spake, and again her words fell into rhyme:

In forty fights hast thou foughten, and been worsted but in four;
And I looked on and was merry; and ever more and more
Wert thou dear to the heart of the Wood-Sun, and the Chooser of the
*   Slain.*
But now whereas ye are wending with slaughter-herd and wain
To meet a folk that ye know not, a wonder, a peerless foe,
I fear for thy glory's waning, and I see thee lying alow.

Then he brake in: "Herein is little shame to be worsted by the might of the mightiest: if this so mighty folk sheareth a limb off the tree of my fame, yet shall it wax again."

But she sang:

In forty fights hast thou foughten, and beside thee who but I
Beheld the wind-tossed banners, and saw the aspen fly?
But to-day to thy war I wend not, for Weird withholdeth me
And sore my heart forebodeth for the battle that shall be.
To-day with thee I wend not; so I feared, and lo my feet,
That are wont to the woodland girdle of the acres of the wheat,
For thee among strange people and the foeman's throng have trod,
And I tell thee their banner of battle is a wise and a mighty God.
For these are the folk of the cities, and in wondrous wise they dwell
'Mid confusion of heaped houses, dim and black as the face of hell;
Though therefrom rise roofs most goodly, where their captains and their
*   kings*
Dwell amidst the walls of marble in abundance of fair things;
And 'mid these, nor worser nor better, but builded otherwise
Stand the Houses of the Fathers, and the hidden mysteries.
And as close as are the tree-trunks that within the beech-wood thrive
E'en so many are their pillars; and therein like men alive
Stand the images of god-folk in such raiment as they wore
In the years before the cities and the hidden days of yore.
Ah for the gold that I gazed on! and their store of battle gear,
And strange engines that I knew not, or the end for which they were.
Ah for the ordered wisdom of the war-array of these,

And the folks that are sitting about them in dumb down-trodden peace!
So I thought now fareth war-ward my well-beloved friend,
And the weird of the Gods hath doomed it that no more with him may I
*   wend!*
Woe's me for the war of the Wolfings wherefrom I am sundered apart,
And the fruitless death of the war-wise, and the doom of the hardy
*   heart!"*

Then he answered, and his eyes grew kind as he looked on her:

For thy fair love I thank thee, and thy faithful word, O friend!
But how might it otherwise happen but we twain must meet in the end,
The God of this mighty people and the Markmen and their kin?
Lo, this is the weird of the world, and what may we do herein?

Then mirth came into her face again as she said:

"Who wotteth of Weird, and what she is till the weird is accomplished? Long hath it been my weird to love thee and to fashion deeds for thee as I may; nor will I depart from it now." And she sang:

Keen-edged is the sword of the city, and bitter is its spear,
But thy breast in the battle, beloved, hath a wall of the stithy's gear.
What now is thy wont in the handplay with the helm and the hauberk
*   of rings?*
Farest thou as the thrall and the cot-carle, or clad in the raiment of
*   kings?*

He started, and his face reddened as he answered:

O Wood-Sun thou wottest our battle and the way wherein we fare:
That oft at the battle's beginning the helm and the hauberk we bear;
Lest the shaft of the fleeing coward or the bow at adventure bent
Should slay us ere the need be, ere our might be given and spent.
Yet oft ere the fight is over, and Doom hath scattered the foe,
No leader of the people by his war-gear shall ye know,
But by his hurts the rather, from the cot-carle and the thrall:
For when all is done that a man may, 'tis the hour for a man to fall.

She yet smiled as she said in answer:

O Folk-wolf, heed and hearken; for when shall thy life be spent
And the Folk wherein thou dwellest with thy death be well content?
Whenso folk need the fire, do they hew the apple-tree,
And burn the Mother of Blossom and the fruit that is to be?
Or me wilt thou bid to thy grave-mound because thy battle-wrath
May nothing more be bridled than the whirl wind on his path?
So hearken and do my bidding, for the hauberk shalt thou bear
E'en when the other warriors cast off their battle-gear.
So come thou, come unwounded from the war-field of the south,
And sit with me in the beech-wood, and kiss me, eyes and mouth.

More to William Morris—The House of the Wolfings

And she kissed him in very deed, and made much of him, and fawned on him, and laid her hand on his breast, and he was soft and blithe with her, but at last he laughed and said:

God's Daughter, long hast thou lived, and many a matter seen,
And men full often grieving for the deed that might have been;
But here my heart thou wheedlest as a maid of tender years
When first in the arms of her darling the horn of war she hears.
Thou knowest the axe to be heavy, and the sword, how keen it is;
But that Doom of which thou hast spoken, wilt thou not tell of this,
God's Daughter, how it sheareth, and how it breaketh through
Each wall that the warrior buildeth, yea all deeds that he may do?
What might in the hammer's leavings, in the fire's thrall shall abide
To turn that Folks' o'erwhelmer from the fated warrior's side?

Then she laughed in her turn, and loudly; but so sweetly that the sound of her voice mingled with the first song of a newly awakened wood-thrush sitting on a rowan twig on the edge of the Wood-lawn. But she said:

Yea, I that am God's Daughter may tell thee never a whit
From what land cometh the hauberk nor what smith smithied it,
That thou shalt wear in the handplay from the first stroke to the last;
But this thereof I tell thee, that it holdeth firm and fast
The life of the body it lappeth, if the gift of the Godfolk it be.
Lo this is the yoke-mate of doom, and the gift of me unto thee.

Then she leaned down from the stone whereon they sat, and her hand was in the dewy grass for a little, and then it lifted up a dark grey rippling coat of rings; and she straightened herself in the seat again, and laid that hauberk on the knees of Thiodolf, and he put his hand to it, and turned it about, while he pondered long: then at last he said:

What evil thing abideth with this warder of the strife,
This burg and treasure chamber for the hoarding of my life?
For this is the work of the dwarfs, and no kindly kin of the earth;

And all we fear the dwarf-kin and their anger and sorrow and mirth.

She cast her arms about him and fondled him, and her voice grew sweeter than the voice of any mortal thing as she answered:

No ill for thee, beloved, or for me in the hauberk lies;
No sundering grief is in it, no lonely miseries.
But we shall abide together, and that new life I gave,
For a long while yet henceforward we twain its joy shall have.
Yea, if thou dost my bidding to wear my gift in the fight
No hunter of the wild-wood at the changing of the night
Shall see my shape on thy grave-mound or my tears in the morning find
With the dew of the morning mingled; nor with the evening wind
Shall my body pass the shepherd as he wandereth in the mead
And fill him with forebodings on the eve of the Wolfings' need.
Nor the horse-herd wake in the midnight and hear my fateful cry;
Nor yet shall the Wolfing women hear words on the wind go by
As they weave and spin the night down when the House is gone to the war,
And weep for the swains they wedded and the children that they bore.
Yea do my bidding, O Folk-wolf, lest a grief of the Gods should weigh
On the ancient House of the Wolfings and my death o'ercloud its day.

And still she clung about him, while he spake no word of yea or nay: but at the last he let himself glide wholly into her arms, and the dwarf-wrought hauberk fell from his knees and lay on the grass.

So they abode together in that wood-lawn till the twilight was long gone, and the sun arisen for some while. And when Thiodolf stepped out of the beech-wood into the broad sunshine dappled with the shadow of the leaves of the hazels moving gently in the fresh morning air, he was covered from the neck to the knee by a hauberk of rings dark and grey and gleaming, fashioned by the dwarfs of ancient days.

4. THE HOUSE FARETH TO THE WAR

Now when Thiodolf came back to the habitations of the kindred the whole House was astir, both thrall-men and women, and free women hurrying from cot to stithy, and from stithy to hall bearing the last of the war-gear or raiment for the fighting-men. But they for their part were some standing about anigh the Man's-door, some sitting gravely within the hall, some watching the hurry of the thralls and women from the midmost of the open space amidst of the habitations, whereon there stood yet certain wains which were belated: for the most of the wains were now standing with the oxen already yoked to them down in the meadow past the acres, encircled by a confused throng of kine and horses and thrall-folk, for thither had all the beasts for the slaughter, and the horses for the warriors been brought; and there were the horses tethered or held by the thralls; some indeed were already saddled and bridled, and on others were the thralls doing the harness.

But as for the wains of the Markmen, they were stoutly framed of ash-tree with panels of aspen, and they were broad-wheeled so that they might go over rough and smooth. They had high tilts over them well framed of willow-poles covered over with squares of black felt over-lapping like shingles; which felt they made of the rough of their fleeces, for they had many sheep. And these wains were to them for houses upon the way if need were, and therein as now were stored their meal and their war-store and after fight they would flit their wounded men in them, such as were too sorely hurt to back a horse: nor must it be hidden that whiles they looked to bring back with them the treasure of the south. Moreover the folk if they were worsted in any battle, instead of fleeing without more done, would often draw back fighting into a garth made by these wains, and guarded by some of their thralls; and there would abide the onset of those who had thrust them back in the field. And this garth they called the Wain-burg.

So now stood three of these wains aforesaid belated amidst of the habitations of the House, their yoke-beasts standing or lying down unharnessed as yet to them: but in the very midst of that place was a wain unlike to them; smaller than they but higher; square of shape as to the floor of it; built lighter than they, yet far stronger; as the warrior is stronger than the big carle and trencher-licker that loiters about the hall; and from the midst of this wain arose a mast made of a tall straight fir-tree, and thereon hung the banner of the Wolfings, wherein was wrought the image of the Wolf, but red of hue as a token of war, and with his mouth open and gaping upon the foemen. Also whereas the other wains were drawn by mere oxen, and those of divers colours, as chance would have it, the wain of the banner was drawn by ten black bulls of the mightiest of the herd, deep-dewlapped, high-crested and curly-browed; and their harness was decked with gold, and so was the wain itself, and the woodwork of it painted red with vermilion. There then stood the Banner of the House of the Wolfings awaiting the departure of the warriors to the hosting.

So Thiodolf stood on the top of the bent beside that same mound wherefrom he had blown the War-horn yester-eve, and which was called the Hill of Speech, and he shaded his eyes with his hand and looked around him; and even therewith the carles fell to yoking the beasts to the belated wains, and the warriors gathered together from out of the mixed throngs, and came from the Roof and the Man's-door and all set their faces toward the Hill of Speech.

So Thiodolf knew that all was ready for departure, and it wanted but an hour of high-noon; so he turned about and went into the Hall, and there found his shield and his spear hanging in his sleeping place beside the hauberk he was wont to wear; then he looked, as one striving with thought, at his empty hauberk and his own body covered with the dwarf-wrought rings; nor did his face change as he took his shield and his spear and turned away. Then he went to the dais and there sat his foster-daughter (as men deemed her) sitting amidst of it as yester-eve, and now arrayed in a garment of fine white wool, on the breast whereof were wrought in gold two beasts ramping up against a fire-altar whereon a flame flickered; and on the skirts and the hems were other devices, of wolves chasing deer, and men shooting with the bow; and that garment was an ancient treasure; but she had a broad girdle of gold and gems about her middle, and on her arms and neck she wore great gold rings wrought delicately. By then there were few save the Hall-Sun under the Roof, and they but the oldest of the women, or a few very old men, and some who were ailing and might not go abroad. But before her on the thwart table lay the Great War-horn awaiting the coming of Thiodolf to give signal of departure.

Then went Thiodolf to the Hall-Sun and kissed and embraced her fondly, and she gave the horn into his hands, and he went forth and up on to the Hill of Speech, and blew thence a short blast on the horn, and then came all the Warriors flocking to the Hill of Speech, each man stark in his harness, alert and joyous.

Then presently through the Man's-door came the Hall-Sun in that ancient garment, which fell straight and stiff down to her ancles as she stepped lightly and slowly along, her head crowned with a garland of eglantine. In her right hand also she held a great torch of wax lighted, whose flame amidst the bright sunlight looked like a wavering leaf of vermilion.

The warriors saw her, and made a lane for her, and she made her way through it up to the Hill of Speech, and she went up to the top of it and stood there holding the lighted candle in her hand, so that all might see it. Then suddenly was there as great a silence as there may be on a forenoon of summer; for even the thralls down in the meadow had noted what was toward, and ceased their talking and shouting, for as far off as they were, since they could see that the Hall-Sun stood on the Hill of Speech, for the wood was dark behind her; so they knew the Farewell Flame was lighted, and that the maiden would speak; and to all men her speech was a boding of good or of ill.

So she began in a sweet voice yet clear and far-reaching:

O Warriors of the Wolfings by the token of the flame
That here in my right hand flickers, come aback to the House of the
  Name!
For there yet burneth the Hall-Sun beneath the Wolfing roof,
And this flame is litten from it, nor as now shall it fare aloof
Till again it seeth the mighty and the men to be gleaned from the fight.
So wend ye as weird willeth and let your hearts be light;
For through your days of battle all the deeds of our days shall be fair.
To-morrow beginneth the haysel, as if every carle were here;
And who knoweth ere your returning but the hook shall smite the corn?
But the kine shall go down to the meadow as their wont is every morn,
And each eve shall come back to the byre; and the mares and foals afield
Shall ever be heeded duly; and all things shall their increase yield.
And if it shall befal us that hither cometh a foe
Here have we swains of the shepherds good players with the bow,

And old men battle-crafty whose might is nowise spent,
And women fell and fearless well wont to tread the bent
Amid the sheep and the oxen; and their hands are hard with the spear
And their arms are strong and stalwart the battle shield to bear;
And store of weapons have we and the mighty walls of the stead;
And the Roof shall abide you steadfast with the Hall-Sun overhead.
Lo here I quench this candle that is lit from the Hall-Sun's flame
Which unto the Wild-wood clearing with the kin of the Wolfings came
And shall wend with their departure to the limits of the earth;
Nor again shall the torch be lighted till in sorrow or in mirth,
Overthrown or overthrowing, ye come aback once more,
And bid me bear the candle before the Wolf of War.

As she spake the word she turned the candle downward, and thrust it against the grass and quenched it indeed; but the whole throng of warriors turned about, for the bulls of the banner-wain lowered their heads in the yokes and began to draw, lowing mightily; and the wain creaked and moved on, and all the men-at-arms followed after, and down they went through the lanes of the corn, and a many women and children and old men went down into the mead with them.

In their hearts they all wondered what the Hall-Sun's words might signify; for she had told them nought about the battles to be, saving that some should come back to the Mid-mark; whereas aforetime somewhat would she foretell to them concerning the fortune of the fight, and now had she said to them nothing but what their own hearts told them. Nevertheless they bore their crests high as they followed the Wolf down into the meadow, where all was now ready for departure. There they arrayed themselves and went down to the lip of Mirkwood-water; and such was their array that the banner went first, save that a band of fully armed men went before it; and behind it and about were the others as well arrayed as they. Then went the wains that bore their munition, with armed carles of the thrall-folk about them, who were ever the guard of the wains, and should never leave them night or day; and lastly went the great band of the warriors and the rest of the thralls with them.

As to their war-gear, all the freemen had helms of some kind, but not all of iron or steel; for some bore helms fashioned of horse-hide and bull-hide covered over with the similitude of a Wolf's muzzle; nor were these ill-defence against a sword-stroke. Shields they all had, and all these had the image of the Wolf marked on them, but for many their thralls bore them on the journey. As to their body-armour some carried long byrnies of ring-mail, some coats of leather covered with splinters of horn laid like the shingles of a roof, and some skin-coats only: whereof indeed there were some of which tales went that they were better than the smith's hammer-work, because they had had spells sung over them to keep out steel or iron.

But for their weapons, they bore spears with shafts not very long, some eight feet of our measure; and axes heavy and long-shafted; and bills with great and broad heads; and some few, but not many of the kindred were bowmen, and every freeman was girt with a sword; but of the swords some were long and two-edged, some short and heavy, cutting on one edge, and these were of the kind which they and our forefathers long after called 'sax.' Thus were the freemen arrayed.

But for the thralls, there were many bows among them, especially among those who were of blood alien from the Goths; the others bore short spears, and feathered broad arrows, and clubs bound with iron, and knives and axes, but not every man of them had a sword. Few iron helms they had and no ringed byrnies, but most had a buckler at their backs with no sign or symbol on it.

Thus then set forth the fighting men of the House of the Wolf toward the Thing-stead of the Upper-mark where the hosting was to be, and by then they were moving up along the side of Mirkwood-water it was somewhat past high-noon.

But the stay-at-home people who had come down with them to the meadow lingered long in that place; and much foreboding there was among them of evil to come; and of the old folk, some remembered tales of the past days of the Markmen, and how they had come from the ends of the earth, and the mountains where none dwell now but the Gods of their kindreds; and many of these tales told of their woes and their wars as they went from river to river and from wild-wood to wild-wood before they had established their Houses in the Mark, and fallen to dwelling there season by season and year by year whether the days were good or ill. And it fell into their hearts that now at last mayhappen was their abiding wearing out to an end, and that the day should soon be when they should have to bear the Hall-Sun through the wild-wood, and seek a new dwelling-place afar from the troubling of these newly arisen Welsh foemen.

And so those of them who could not rid themselves of this foreboding were somewhat heavier of heart than their wont was when the House went to the War. For long had they abided there in the Mark, and the life was sweet to them which they knew, and the life which they knew not was bitter to them: and Mirkwood-water was become as a God to them no less than to their fathers of old time; nor lesser was the mead where fed the horses that they loved and the kine that they had reared, and the sheep that they guarded from the Wolf of the Wild-wood: and they worshipped the kind acres which they themselves and their fathers had made fruitful, wedding them to the seasons of seed-time and harvest, that the birth that came from them might become a part of the kindred of the Wolf, and the joy and might of past springs and summers might run in the blood of the Wolfing children. And a dear

God indeed to them was the Roof of the Kindred, that their fathers had built and that they yet warded against the fire and the lightening and the wind and the snow, and the passing of the days that devour and the years that heap the dust over the work of men. They thought of how it had stood, and seen so many generations of men come and go; how often it had welcomed the new-born babe, and given farewell to the old man: how many secrets of the past it knew; how many tales which men of the present had forgotten, but which yet mayhap men of times to come should learn of it; for to them yet living it had spoken time and again, and had told them what their fathers had not told them, and it held the memories of the generations and the very life of the Wolfings and their hopes for the days to be.

Thus these poor people thought of the Gods whom they worshipped, and the friends whom they loved, and could not choose but be heavy-hearted when they thought that the wildwood was awaiting them to swallow all up, and take away from them their Gods and their friends and the mirth of their life, and burden them with hunger and thirst and weariness, that their children might begin once more to build the House and establish the dwelling, and call new places by old names, and worship new Gods with the ancient worship.

Such imaginations of trouble then were in the hearts of the stay-at-homes of the Wolfings; the tale tells not indeed that all had such forebodings, but chiefly the old folk who were nursing the end of their life-days amidst the cherishing Kindred of the House.

But now they were beginning to turn them back again to the habitations, and a thin stream was flowing through the acres, when they heard a confused sound drawing near blended of horns and the lowing of beasts and the shouting of men; and they looked and saw a throng of brightly clad men coming up stream alongside of Mirkwood-water; and they were not afraid, for they knew that it must be some other company of the Markmen journeying to the hosting of the Folk: and presently they saw that it was the House of the Beamings following their banner on the way to the Thing-stead. But when the new-comers saw the throng out in the meads, some of their young men pricked on their horses and galloped on past the women and old men, to whom they threw a greeting, as they ran past to catch up with the bands of the Wolfings; for between the two houses was there affinity, and much good liking lay between them; and the stay-at-homes, many of them, lingered yet till the main body of the Beamings came with their banner: and their array was much like to that of the Wolfings, but gayer; for whereas it pleased the latter to darken all their wargear to the colour of the grey Wolf, the Beamings polished all their gear as bright as might be, and their raiment also was mostly bright green of hue and much beflowered; and the sign on their banner was a green leafy tree, and the wain was drawn by great white bulls.

So when their company drew anear to the throng of the stay-at-homes they went to meet and greet each other, and tell tidings to each other; but their banner held steadily onward amidst their converse, and in a little while they followed it, for the way was long to the Thing-stead of the Upper-mark.

So passed away the fighting men by the side of Mirkwood-water, and the throng of the stay-at-homes melted slowly from the meadow and trickled along through the acres to the habitations of the Wolfings, and there they fell to doing whatso of work or play came to their hands.

5. CONCERNING THE HALL-SUN

When the warriors and the others had gone down to the mead, the Hall-Sun was left standing on the Hill of Speech, and she stood there till she saw the host in due array going on its ways dark and bright and beautiful; then she made as if to turn aback to the Great Roof; but all at once it seemed to her as if something held her back, as if her will to move had departed from her, and that she could not put one foot before the other. So she lingered on the Hill, and the quenched candle fell from her hand, and presently she sank adown on the grass and sat there with the face of one thinking intently. Yet was it with her that a thousand thoughts were in her mind at once and no one of them uppermost, and images of what had been and what then was flickered about in her brain, and betwixt them were engendered images of things to be, but unstable and not to be trowed in. So sat the Hall-Sun on the Hill of Speech lost in a dream of the day, whose stories were as little clear as those of a night-dream.

But as she sat musing thus, came to her a woman exceeding old to look on, whom she knew not as one of the kindred or a thrall; and this carline greeted her by the name of Hall-Sun and said:

Hail, Hall-Sun of the Markmen! how fares it now with thee
When the whelps of the Woodbeast wander with the Leafage of the
* Tree*
All up the Mirkwood-water to seek what they shall find,
The oak-boles of the battle and the war-wood stark and blind?

Then answered the maiden:

It fares with me, O mother, that my soul would fain go forth

To behold the ways of the battle, and the praise of the warriors' worth.
But yet is it held entangled in a maze of many a thing,
As the low-grown bramble holdeth the brake-shoots of the Spring.
I think of the thing that hath been, but no shape is in my thought;
I think of the day that passeth, and its story comes to nought.
I think of the days that shall be, nor shape I any tale.
I will hearken thee, O mother, if hearkening may avail.

The Carline gazed at her with dark eyes that shone brightly from amidst her brown wrinkled face: then she sat herself down beside her and spake:

From a far folk have I wandered and I come of an alien blood,
But I know all tales of the Wolfings and their evil and their good;
And when I heard of thy fairness, thereof I heard it said,
That for thee should be never a bridal nor a place in the warrior's bed.

The maiden neither reddened nor paled, but looking with calm steady eyes into the Carline's face she answered:

Yea true it is, I am wedded to the mighty ones of old,
And the fathers of the Wolfings ere the days of field and fold.

Then a smile came into the eyes of the old woman and she said.

How glad shall be thy mother of thy worship and thy worth,
And the father that begat thee if yet they dwell on earth!

But the Hall-Sun answered in the same steady manner as before:

None knoweth who is my mother, nor my very father's name;
But when to the House of the Wolfings a wild-wood waif I came,
They gave me a foster-mother an ancient dame and good,
And a glorious foster-father the best of all the blood.

Spake the Carline.

Yea, I have heard the story, but scarce therein might I trow
That thou with all thy beauty wert born 'neath the oaken bough,
And hast crawled a naked baby o'er the rain-drenched autumn-grass;
Wilt thou tell the wandering woman what wise it cometh to pass
That thou art the Mid-mark's Hall-Sun, and the sign of the Wolfings'
  gain?
Thou shalt pleasure me much by the telling, and there of shalt thou be
  fain.

Then answered the Hall-Sun.

Yea; thus much I remember for the first of my memories;
That I lay on the grass in the morning and above were the boughs of the
  trees.
But nought naked was I as the wood-whelp, but clad in linen white,
And adown the glades of the oakwood the morning sun lay bright.
Then a hind came out of the thicket and stood on the sunlit glade,

And turned her head toward the oak tree and a step on toward me
  made.
Then stopped, and bounded aback, and away as if in fear,
That I saw her no more; then I wondered, though sitting close anear
Was a she-wolf great and grisly. But with her was I wont to play,
And pull her ears, and belabour her rugged sides and grey,
And hold her jaws together, while she whimpered, slobbering
For the love of my love; and nowise I deemed her a fearsome thing.
There she sat as though she were watching, and o'er head a blue-winged
  jay
Shrieked out from the topmost oak-twigs, and a squirrel ran his way
Two tree-trunks off. But the she-wolf arose up suddenly
And growled with her neck-fell bristling, as if danger drew anigh;
And therewith I heard a footstep, for nice was my ear to catch
All the noises of the wild-wood; so there did we sit at watch
While the sound of feet grew nigher: then I clapped hand on hand
And crowed for joy and gladness, for there out in the sun did stand
A man, a glorious creature with a gleaming helm on his head,
And gold rings on his arms, in raiment gold-broidered crimson-red.
Straightway he strode up toward us nor heeded the wolf of the wood
But sang as he went in the oak-glade, as a man whose thought is good,
And nought she heeded the warrior, but tame as a sheep was grown,
And trotted away through the wild-wood with her crest all laid adown.
Then came the man and sat down by the oak-bole close unto me
And took me up nought fearful and set me on his knee.
And his face was kind and lovely, so my cheek to his cheek I laid
And touched his cold bright war-helm and with his gold rings played,
And hearkened his words, though I knew not what tale they had to tell,
Yet fain was my heart of their music, and meseemed I loved him well.
So we fared for a while and were fain, till he set down my feet on the
  grass,
And kissed me and stood up himself, and away through the wood did he
  pass.
And then came back the she-wolf and with her I played and was fain.
Lo the first thing I remember: wilt thou have me babble again?

Spake the Carline and her face was soft and kind:

Nay damsel, long would I hearken to thy voice this summer day.
But how didst thou leave the wild-wood, what people brought thee
  away?

Then said the Hall-Sun:

I awoke on a time in the even, and voices I heard as I woke;
And there was I in the wild-wood by the bole of the ancient oak,
And a ring of men was around me, and glad was I indeed
As I looked upon their faces and the fashion of their weed.
For I gazed on the red and the scarlet and the beaten silver and gold,
And blithe were their noble faces and kindly to behold,

And nought had I seen of such-like since that hour of the other day
When that warrior came to the oak glade with the little child to play.
And forth now he came, with the face that my hands had fondled
    before,
And a battle shield wrought fairly upon his arm he bore,
And thereon the wood-wolf's image in ruddy gold was done.
Then I stretched out my little arms towards the glorious shining one
And he took me up and set me on his shoulder for a while
And turned about to his fellows with a blithe and joyous smile;
And they shouted aloud about me and drew forth gleaming swords
And clashed them on their bucklers; but nought I knew of the words
Of their shouting and rejoicing. So thereafter was I laid
And borne forth on the warrior's warshield, and our way through the
    wood we made
'Midst the mirth and great contentment of those fair-clad shielded men.

But no tale of the wolf and the wild-wood abides with me since then,
And the next thing I remember is a huge and dusky hall,
A world for my little body from ancient wall to wall;
A world of many doings, and nought for me to do,
A world of many noises, and known to me were few.

Time wore, and I spoke with the Wolfings and knew the speech of the
    kin,
And was strange 'neath the roof no longer, as a lonely waif therein;
And I wrought as a child with my playmates and every hour looked on,
Unto the next hour's joyance till the happy day was done.
And going and coming amidst us was a woman tall and thin
With hair like the hoary barley and silver streaks therein.
And kind and sad of visage, as now I remember me,
And she sat and told us stories when we were aweary with glee,
And many of us she fondled, but me the most of all.

And once from my sleep she waked me and bore me down the hall,
In the hush of the very midnight, and I was feared thereat.
But she brought me unto the dais, and there the warrior sat,
Who took me up and kissed me, as erst within the wood;
And meseems in his arms I slumbered: but I wakened again and stood
Alone with the kindly woman, and gone was the goodly man,
And athwart the hush of the Folk-hall the moon shone bright and wan,
And the woman dealt with a lamp hung up by a chain aloft,
And she trimmed it and fed it with oil, while she chanted sweet and
    soft
A song whose words I knew not: then she ran it up again,
And up in the darkness above us died the length of its wavering chain.

"Yea," said the carline, "this woman will have been the
Hall-Sun that came before thee. What next dost thou remember?"

Said the maiden:

Next I mind me of the hazels behind the People's Roof,
And the children running thither and the magpie flitting aloof,
And my hand in the hand of the Hall-Sun, as after the others we went,
And she soberly hearkening my prattle and the words of my intent.
And now would I call her 'Mother,' and indeed I loved her well.

So I waxed; and now of my memories the tale were long to tell;
But as the days passed over, and I fared to field and wood,
Alone or with my playmates, still the days were fair and good.
But the sad and kindly Hall-Sun for my fosterer now I knew,
And the great and glorious warrior that my heart clung sorely to
Was but my foster-father; and I knew that I had no kin
In the ancient House of the Wolfings, though love was warm therein.

Then smiled the carline and said: "Yea, he is thy foster-father, and yet a fond one."

"Sooth is that," said the Hall-Sun. "But wise art thou by seeming. Hast thou come to tell me of what kindred I am, and who is my father and who is my mother?"

Said the carline: "Art thou not also wise? Is it not so that the Hall-Sun of the Wolfings seeth things that are to come?"

"Yea," she said, "yet have I seen waking or sleeping no other father save my foster-father; yet my very mother I have seen, as one who should meet her in the flesh one day."

"And good is that," said the carline; and as she spoke her face waxed kinder, and she said:

"Tell us more of thy days in the House of the Wolfings and how thou faredst there."

Said the Hall-Sun:

I waxed 'neath the Roof of the Wolfings, till now to look upon
I was of sixteen winters, and the love of the Folk I won,
And in lovely weed they clad me like the image of a God:
And lonely now full often the wild-wood ways I trod,
And I feared no wild-wood creature, and my presence scared them
    nought;
And I fell to know of wisdom, and within me stirred my thought,
So that oft anights would I wander through the mead and far away,
And swim the Mirkwood-water, and amidst his eddies play
When earth was dark in the dawn-tide; and over all the folk
I knew of the beasts' desires, as though in words they spoke.

So I saw of things that should be, were they mighty things or small,
And upon a day as it happened came the war-word to the hall,
And the House must wend to the warfield, and as they sang, and
    played
With the strings of the harp that even, and the mirth of the war-eve
    made,
Came the sight of the field to my eyes, and the words waxed hot in me,

And I needs must show the picture of the end of the fight to be.
Then I showed them the Red Wolf bristling o'er the broken fleeing foe;
And the war-gear of the fleers, and their banner did I show,
To wit the Ling-worm's image with the maiden in his mouth;
There I saw my foster-father 'mid the pale blades of the South,
Till aloof swept all the handplay and the hurry of the chase,
And he lay along by an ash-tree, no helm about his face,
No byrny on his body; and an arrow in his thigh,
And a broken spear in his shoulder. Then I saw myself draw nigh
To sing the song blood-staying. Then saw I how we twain
Went 'midst of the host triumphant in the Wolfings' banner-wain,
The black bulls lowing before us athwart the warriors' song,
As up from Mirkwood-water we went our ways along
To the Great Roof of the Wolfings, whence streamed the women out
And the sound of their rejoicing blent with the warriors' shout.

They heard me and saw the picture, and they wotted how wise I was
    grown,
And they loved me, and glad were their hearts at the tale my lips had
    shown;
And my body clad as an image of a God to the field they bore,
And I held by the mast of the banner as I looked upon their war,
And endured to see unblenching on the wind-swept sunny plain
All the picture of my vision by the menfolk done again.
And over my Foster-father I sang the staunching-song,
Till the life-blood that was ebbing flowed back to his heart the strong,
And we wended back in the war-wain 'midst the gleanings of the fight
Unto the ancient dwelling and the Hall-Sun's glimmering light.

So from that day henceforward folk hung upon my words,
For the battle of the autumn, and the harvest of the swords;
And e'en more was I loved than aforetime.
So wore a year away, And heavy was the burden of the lore that on me
    lay.

But my fosterer the Hall-Sun took sick at the birth of the year,
And changed her life as the year changed, as summer drew anear.
But she knew that her life was waning, and lying in her bed
She taught me the lore of the Hall-Sun, and every word to be said
At the trimming in the midnight and the feeding in the morn,
And she laid her hands upon me ere unto the howe she was borne
With the kindred gathered about us; and they wotted her weird and her
    will,
And hailed me for the Hall-Sun when at last she lay there still.
And they did on me the garment, the holy cloth of old,
And the neck-chain wrought for the goddess, and the rings of the
    hallowed gold.
So here am I abiding, and of things to be I tell,

Yet know not what shall befall me nor why with the Wolfings I dwell.

    Then said the carline:

What seest thou, O daughter, of the journey of to-day?
And why wendest thou not with the war-host on the battle-echoing
    way?

    Said the Hall-Sun.

O mother, here dwelleth the Hall-Sun while the kin hath a dwelling-
    place,
Nor ever again shall I look on the onset or the chase,
Till the day when the Roof of the Wolfings looketh down on the girdle
    of foes,
And the arrow singeth over the grass of the kindred's close;
Till the pillars shake with the shouting and quivers the roof-tree dear,
When the Hall of the Wolfings garners the harvest of the spear.

Therewith she stood on her feet and turned her face to the
Great Roof, and gazed long at it, not heeding the crone by her
side; and she muttered words of whose signification the other
knew not, though she listened intently, and gazed ever at her
as closely as might be.

Then fell the Hall-Sun utterly silent, and the lids closed over
her eyes, and her hands were clenched, and her feet pressed
hard on the daisies: her bosom heaved with sore sighs, and
great tear-drops oozed from under her eyelids and fell on to
her raiment and her feet and on to the flowery summer grass;
and at the last her mouth opened and she spake, but in a voice
that was marvellously changed from that she spake in before:

Why went ye forth, O Wolfings, from the garth your fathers built,
And the House where sorrow dieth, and all unloosed is guilt?
Turn back, turn back, and behold it! lest your feet be over slow
When your shields are heavy-burdened with the arrows of the foe;
How ye totter, how ye stumble on the rough and corpse-strewn way!
And lo, how the eve is eating the afternoon of day!
O why are ye abiding till the sun is sunk in night
And the forest trees are ruddy with the battle-kindled light?
O rest not yet, ye Wolfings, lest void be your resting-place,
And into lands that ye know not the Wolf must turn his face,
And ye wander and ye wander till the land in the ocean cease,
And your battle bring no safety and your labour no increase.

Then was she silent for a while, and her tears ceased to flow;
but presently her eyes opened once more, and she lifted up her
voice and cried aloud -

I see, I see! O Godfolk behold it from aloof,
How the little flames steal flickering along the ridge of the Roof!
They are small and red 'gainst the heavens in the summer afternoon;
But when the day is dusking, white, high shall they wave to the moon.
Lo, the fire plays now on the windows like strips of scarlet cloth

Wind-waved! but look in the night-tide on the onset of its wrath,
How it wraps round the ancient timbers and hides the mighty roof
But lighteth little crannies, so lost and far aloof,
That no man yet of the kindred hath seen them ere to-night,
Since first the builder builded in loving and delight!

Then again she stayed her speech with weeping and sobbing, but after a while was still again, and then she spoke pointing toward the roof with her right hand.

I see the fire-raisers and iron-helmed they are,
Brown-faced about the banners that their hands have borne afar.
And who in the garth of the kindred shall bear adown their shield
Since the onrush of the Wolfings they caught in the open field,
As the might of the mountain lion falls dead in the hempen net?
O Wolfings, long have ye tarried, but the hour abideth yet.
What life for the life of the people shall be given once for all,
What sorrow shall stay sorrow in the half-burnt Wolfing Hall?
There is nought shall quench the fire save the tears of the Godfolk's kin,
And the heart of the life-delighter, and the life-blood cast therein.

Then once again she fell silent, and her eyes closed again, and the slow tears gushed out from them, and she sank down sobbing on the grass, and little by little the storm of grief sank and her head fell back, and she was as one quietly asleep. Then the carline hung over her and kissed her and embraced her; and then through her closed eyes and her slumber did the Hall-Sun see a marvel; for she who was kissing her was young in semblance and unwrinkled, and lovely to look on, with plenteous long hair of the hue of ripe barley, and clad in glistening raiment such as has been woven in no loom on earth.

And indeed it was the Wood-Sun in the semblance of a crone, who had come to gather wisdom of the coming time from the foreseeing of the Hall-Sun; since now at last she herself foresaw nothing of it, though she was of the kindred of the Gods and the Fathers of the Goths. So when she had heard the Hall-Sun she deemed that she knew but too well what her words meant, and what for love, what for sorrow, she grew sick at heart as she heard them.

So at last she arose and turned to look at the Great Roof; and strong and straight, and cool and dark grey showed its ridge against the pale sky of the summer afternoon all quivering with the heat of many hours' sun: dark showed its windows as she gazed on it, and stark and stiff she knew were its pillars within.

Then she said aloud, but to herself: "What then if a merry and mighty life be given for it, and the sorrow of the people be redeemed; yet will not I give the life which is his; nay rather let him give the bliss which is mine. But oh! how may it be that he shall die joyous and I shall live unhappy!"

Then she went slowly down from the Hill of Speech, and whoso saw her deemed her but a gangrel carline. So she went her ways and let the wood cover her.

But in a little while the Hall-Sun awoke alone, and sat up with a sigh, and she remembered nothing concerning her sight of the flickering flame along the hall-roof, and the fire-tongues like strips of scarlet cloth blown by the wind, nor had she any memory of her words concerning the coming day. But the rest of her talk with the carline she remembered, and also the vision of the beautiful woman who had kissed and embraced her; and she knew that it was her very mother. Also she perceived that she had been weeping, therefore she knew that she had uttered words of wisdom. For so it fared with her at whiles, that she knew not her own words of foretelling, but spoke them out as if in a dream.

So now she went down from the Hill of Speech soberly, and turned toward the Woman's-door of the hall, and on her way she met the women and old men and youths coming back from the meadow with little mirth: and there were many of them who looked shyly at her as though they would gladly have asked her somewhat, and yet durst not. But for her, her sadness passed away when she came among them, and she looked kindly on this and that one of them, and entered with them into the Woman's Chamber, and did what came to her hand to do.

6. THEY TALK ON THE WAY TO THE FOLK-THING

All day long one standing on the Speech-hill of the Wolfings might have seen men in their war-array streaming along the side of Mirkwood-water, on both sides thereof; and the last comers from the Nether-mark came hastening all they might; for they would not be late at the trysting-place. But these were of a kindred called the Laxings, who bore a salmon on their banner; and they were somewhat few in number, for they had but of late years become a House of the Markmen. Their banner-wain was drawn by white horses, fleet and strong, and they were no great band, for they had but few thralls with them, and all, free men and thralls, were a-horseback; so they rode by hastily with their banner-wain, their few munition-wains following as they might.

Now tells the tale of the men-at-arms of the Wolfings and the Beamings, that soon they fell in with the Elking host, which was journeying but leisurely, so that the Wolfings might catch up with them: they were a very great kindred, the most numerous of all Mid-mark, and at this time they had affinity with the Wolfings. But old men of the House remembered how they had heard their grandsires and very old men tell that there had been a time when the Elking House had been established by men from out of the Wolfing kindred, and how they had wandered away from the Mark in the days when it had been first settled, and had abided aloof for many generations of men; and so at last had come back again to the Mark, and had taken up their habitation at a place in Mid-mark where was dwelling but a remnant of a House called the Thyrings, who had once been exceeding mighty, but had by that time almost utterly perished in a great sickness which befell in those days. So then these two Houses, the wanderers come back and the remnant left by the sickness of the Gods, made one House together, and increased and throve after their coming together, and wedded with the Wolfings, and became a very great House.

Gallant and glorious was their array now, as they marched along with their banner of the Elk, which was drawn by the very beasts themselves tamed to draught to that end through many generations; they were fatter and sleeker than their wild-wood brethren, but not so mighty.

So were the men of the three kindreds somewhat mingled together on the way. The Wolfings were the tallest and the biggest made; but of those dark-haired men aforesaid, were there fewest amongst the Beamings, and most among the Elkings, as though they had drawn to them more men of alien blood during their wanderings aforesaid. So they talked together and made each other good cheer, as is the wont of companions in arms on the eve of battle; and the talk ran, as may be deemed, on that journey and what was likely to come of it: and spake an Elking warrior to a Wolfing by whom he rode:

"O Wolfkettle, hath the Hall-Sun had any foresight of the day of battle?"

"Nay," said the other, "when she lighted the farewell candle, she bade us come back again, and spoke of the day of our return; but that methinks, as thou and I would talk of it, thinking what would be likely to befal. Since we are a great host of valiant men, and these Welshmen[2] most valiant, and as the rumour runneth bigger-bodied men than the Hun-folk, and so well ordered as never folk have been. So then if we overthrow them we shall come back again; and if they overthrow us, the remnant of us shall fall back before them till we come to our habitations; for it is not to be looked for that they will fall in upon our rear and prevent us, since we have the thicket of the wild-wood on our flanks."

"Sooth is that," said the Elking; "and as to the mightiness of this folk and their customs, ye may gather somewhat from the songs which our House yet singeth, and which ye have heard wide about in the Mark; for this is the same folk of which a

2. i.e. Foreigners: see note [in Chapter 2].

many of them tell, making up that story-lay which is called the South-Welsh Lay; which telleth how we have met this folk in times past when we were in fellowship with a folk of the Welsh of like customs to ourselves: for we of the Elkings were then but a feeble folk. So we marched with this folk of the Kymry and met the men of the cities, and whiles we overthrew and whiles were overthrown, but at last in a great battle were overthrown with so great a slaughter, that the red blood rose over the wheels of the wains, and the city-folk fainted with the work of the slaughter, as men who mow a match in the meadows when the swathes are dry and heavy and the afternoon of midsummer is hot; and there they stood and stared on the field of the slain, and knew not whether they were in Home or Hell, so fierce the fight had been."

Therewith a man of the Beamings, who was riding on the other side of the Elking, reached out over his horse's neck and said:

"Yea friend, but is there not some telling of a tale concerning how ye and your fellowship took the great city of the Welshmen of the South, and dwelt there long."

"Yea," said the Elking, "Hearken how it is told in the South-Welsh Lay:

> 'Have ye not heard
> Of the ways of Weird?
> How the folk fared forth
> Far away from the North?
> And as light as one wendeth
> Whereas the wood endeth,
> When of nought is our need,
> And none telleth our deed,
> So Rodgeir unwearied and Reidfari wan
> The town where none tarried the shield-shaking man.
> All lonely the street there, and void was the way
> And nought hindered our feet but the dead men that lay
> Under shield in the lanes of the houses heavens-high,
> All the ring-bearing swains that abode there to die.'

"Tells the Lay, that none abode the Goths and their fellowship, but such as were mighty enough to fall before them, and the rest, both man and woman, fled away before our folk and before the folk of the Kymry, and left their town for us to dwell in; as saith the Lay:

> 'Glistening of gold
> Did men's eyen behold;
> Shook the pale sword
> O'er the unspoken word,
> No man drew nigh us
> With weapon to try us,

For the Welsh-wrought shield
Lay low on the field.
By man's hand unbuilded all seemed there to be,
The walls ruddy gilded, the pearls of the sea:
Yea all things were dead there save pillar and wall,
But they lived and they said us the song of the hall;
The dear hall left to perish by men of the land,
For the Goth-folk to cherish with gold gaining hand.'

"See ye how the Lay tells that the hall was bolder than the men, who fled from it, and left all for our fellowship to deal with in the days gone by?"

Said the Wolfing man:

"And as it was once, so shall it be again. Maybe we shall go far on this journey, and see at least one of the garths of the Southlands, even those which they call cities. For I have heard it said that they have more cities than one only, and that so great are their kindreds, that each liveth in a garth full of mighty houses, with a wall of stone and lime around it; and that in every one of these garths lieth wealth untold heaped up. And wherefore should not all this fall to the Markmen and their valiancy?"

Said the Elking:

"As to their many cities and the wealth of them, that is sooth; but as to each city being the habitation of each kindred, it is otherwise: for rather it may be said of them that they have forgotten kindred, and have none, nor do they heed whom they wed, and great is the confusion amongst them. And mighty men among them ordain where they shall dwell, and what shall be their meat, and how long they shall labour after they are weary, and in all wise what manner of life shall be amongst them; and though they be called free men who suffer this, yet may no house or kindred gainsay this rule and order. In sooth they are a people mighty, but unhappy."

Said Wolfkettle:

"And hast thou learned all this from the ancient story lays, O Hiarandi? For some of them I know, though not all, and therein have I noted nothing of all this. Is there some new minstrel arisen in thine House of a memory excelling all those that have gone before? If that be so, I bid him to the Roof of the Wolfings as soon as may be; for we lack new tales."

"Nay," said Hiarandi, "This that I tell thee is not a tale of past days, but a tale of to-day. For there came to us a man from out of the wild-wood, and prayed us peace, and we gave it him; and he told us that he was of a House of the Gael, and that his House had been in a great battle against these Welshmen, whom he calleth the Romans; and that he was taken in the battle, and sold as a thrall in one of their garths; and howbeit, it was not their master-garth, yet there he learned of their customs: and sore was the lesson! Hard was his life amongst

them, for their thralls be not so well entreated as their draught-beasts, so many do they take in battle; for they are a mighty folk; and these thralls and those aforesaid unhappy freemen do all tilling and herding and all deeds of craftsmanship: and above these are men whom they call masters and lords who do nought, nay not so much as smithy their own edge-weapons, but linger out their days in their dwellings and out of their dwellings, lying about in the sun or the hall-cinders, like cur-dogs who have fallen away from kind.

"So this man made a shift to flee away from out of that garth, since it was not far from the great river; and being a valiant man, and young and mighty of body, he escaped all perils and came to us through the Mirkwood. But we saw that he was no liar, and had been very evilly handled, for upon his body was the mark of many a stripe, and of the shackles that had been soldered on to his limbs; also it was more than one of these accursed people whom he had slain when he fled. So he became our guest and we loved him, and he dwelt among us and yet dwelleth, for we have taken him into our House. But yesterday he was sick and might not ride with us; but may be he will follow on and catch up with us in a day or two. And if he come not, then will I bring him over to the Wolfings when the battle is done."

Then laughed the Beaming man, and spake:

"How then if ye come not back, nor Wolfkettle, nor the Welsh Guest, nor I myself? Meseemeth no one of these Southland Cities shall we behold, and no more of the Southlanders than their war-array."

"These are evil words," said Wolfkettle, "though such an outcome must be thought on. But why deemest thou this?"

Said the Beaming: "There is no Hall-Sun sitting under our Roof at home to tell true tales concerning the Kindred every day. Yet forsooth from time to time is a word said in our Folk-hall for good or for evil; and who can choose but hearken thereto? And yestereve was a woeful word spoken, and that by a man-child of ten winters."

Said the Elking: "Now that thou hast told us thus much, thou must tell us more, yea, all the word which was spoken; else belike we shall deem of it as worse than it was."

Said the Beaming: "Thus it was; this little lad brake out weeping yestereve, when the Hall was full and feasting; and he wailed, and roared out, as children do, and would not be pacified, and when he was asked why he made that to do, he said: 'Well away! Raven hath promised to make me a clay horse and to bake it in the kiln with the pots next week; and now he goeth to the war, and he shall never come back, and never shall my horse be made.' Thereat we all laughed as ye may well deem. But the lad made a sour countenance on us and said, 'why do ye laugh? look yonder, what see ye?' 'Nay,' said one, 'nought but the Feast-hall wall and the hangings of the

High-tide thereon.' Then said the lad sobbing: 'Ye see ill: further afield see I: I see a little plain, on a hill top, and fells beyond it far bigger than our speech-hill: and there on the plain lieth Raven as white as parchment; and none hath such hue save the dead.' Then said Raven, (and he was a young man, and was standing thereby). 'And well is that, swain, to die in harness! Yet hold up thine heart; here is Gunbert who shall come back and bake thine horse for thee.' 'Nay never more,' quoth the child, 'For I see his pale head lying at Raven's feet; but his body with the green gold-broidered kirtle I see not.' Then was the laughter stilled, and man after man drew near to the child, and questioned him, and asked, 'dost thou see me?' 'dost thou see me?' And he failed to see but few of those that asked him. Therefore now meseemeth that not many of us shall see the cities of the South, and those few belike shall look on their own shackles therewithal."

"Nay," said Hiarandi, "What is all this? heard ye ever of a company of fighting men that fared afield, and found the foe, and came back home leaving none behind them?"

Said the Beaming: "Yet seldom have I heard a child foretell the death of warriors. I tell thee that hadst thou been there, thou wouldst have thought of it as if the world were coming to an end."

"Well," said Wolfkettle, "let it be as it may! Yet at least I will not be led away from the field by the foemen. Oft may a man be hindered of victory, but never of death if he willeth it."

Therewith he handled a knife that hung about his neck, and went on to say: "But indeed, I do much marvel that no word came into the mouth of the Hall-Sun yestereven or this morning, but such as any woman of the kindred might say."

Therewith fell their talk awhile, and as they rode they came to where the wood drew nigher to the river, and thus the Mid-mark had an end; for there was no House had a dwelling in the Mid-mark higher up the water than the Elkings, save one only, not right great, who mostly fared to war along with the Elkings: and this was the Oselings, whose banner bore the image of the Wood-ousel, the black bird with the yellow neb; and they had just fallen into the company of the greater House.

So now Mid-mark was over and past, and the serried trees of the wood came down like a wall but a little way from the lip of the water; and scattered trees, mostly quicken-trees, grew here and there on the very water side. But Mirkwood-water ran deep, swift and narrow between high clean-cloven banks, so that none could dream of fording, and not so many of swimming its dark green dangerous waters. And the day wore on towards evening and the glory of the western sky was unseen because of the wall of high trees. And still the host made on, and because of the narrowness of the space between river and wood it was strung out longer and looked a very great company of men. And moreover the men of the eastern-lying part of Mid-mark, were now marching thick and close on the other side of the river but a little way from the Wolfings and their fellows; for nothing but the narrow river sundered them.

So night fell, and the stars shone, and the moon rose, and yet the Wolfings and their fellows stayed not, since they wotted that behind them followed a many of the men of the Mark, both the Mid and the Nether, and they would by no means hinder their march.

So wended the Markmen between wood and stream on either side of Mirkwood-water, till now at last the night grew deep and the moon set, and it was hard on midnight, and they had kindled many torches to light them on either side of the water. So whereas they had come to a place where the trees gave back somewhat from the river, which was well-grassed for their horses and neat, and was called Baitmead, the companies on the western side made stay there till morning. And they drew the wains right up to the thick of the wood, and all men turned aside into the mead from the beaten road, so that those who were following after might hold on their way if so they would. There then they appointed watchers of the night, while the rest of them lay upon the sward by the side of the trees, and slept through the short summer night.

The tale tells not that any man dreamed of the fight to come in such wise that there was much to tell of his dream on the morrow; many dreamed of no fight or faring to war, but of matters little, and often laughable, mere mingled memories of bygone time that had no waking wits to marshal them.

But that man of the Beamings dreamed that he was at home watching a potter, a man of the thralls of the House working at his wheel, and fashioning bowls and ewers: and he had a mind to take of his clay and fashion a horse for the lad that had bemoaned the promise of his toy. And he tried long and failed to fashion anything; for the clay fell to pieces in his hands; till at last it held together and grew suddenly, not into an image of a horse, but of the Great Yule Boar, the similitude of the Holy Beast of Frey. So he laughed in his sleep and was glad, and leaped up and drew his sword with his clay-stained hands that he might wave it over the Earth Boar, and swear a great oath of a doughty deed. And therewith he found himself standing on his feet indeed, just awakened in the cold dawn, and holding by his right hand to an ash-sapling that grew beside him. So he laughed again, and laid him down, and leaned back and slept his sleep out till the sun and the voices of his fellows stirring awakened him.

7. THEY GATHER TO THE FOLK-MOTE

When it was the morning, all the host of the Markmen was astir on either side of the water, and when they had broken their fast, they got speedily into array, and were presently on the road again; and the host was now strung out longer yet, for the space between water and wood once more diminished till at last it was no wider than ten men might go abreast, and looking ahead it was as if the wild-wood swallowed up both river and road.

But the fighting-men hastened on merrily with their hearts raised high, since they knew that they would soon be falling in with more of their people, and the coming fight was growing a clearer picture to their eyes; so from side to side of the river they shouted out the cries of their Houses, or friend called to friend across the eddies of Mirkwood-water, and there was game and glee enough.

So they fared till the wood gave way before them, and lo, the beginning of another plain, somewhat like the Mid-mark. There also the water widened out before them, and there were eyots in it with stony shores crowned with willow or with alder, and aspens rising from the midst of them.

But as for the plain, it was thus much different from Mid-mark, that the wood which begirt it rose on the south into low hills, and away beyond them were other hills blue in the distance, for the most bare of wood, and not right high, the pastures of the wild-bull and the bison, whereas now dwelt a folk somewhat scattered and feeble; hunters and herdsmen, with little tillage about their abodes, a folk akin to the Markmen and allied to them. They had come into those parts later than the Markmen, as the old tales told; which said moreover that in days gone by a folk dwelt among those hills who were alien from the Goths, and great foes to the Markmen; and how that on a time they came down from their hills with a great host, together with new-comers of their own blood, and made their way through the wild-wood, and fell upon the Upper-mark; and how that there befel a fearful battle that endured for three days; and the first day the Aliens worsted the Markmen, who were but a few, since they were they of the Upper-mark only. So the Aliens burned their houses and slew their old men, and drave off many of their women and children; and the remnant of the men of the Upper-mark with all that they had, which was now but little, took refuge in an island of Mirkwood-water, where they fenced themselves as well as they could for that night; for they expected the succour of their kindred of the Mid-mark and the Nether-mark, unto whom they had sped the war-arrow when they first had tidings of the onset of the Aliens.

So at the sun-rising they sacrificed to the Gods twenty chieftains of the Aliens whom they had taken, and therewithal a maiden of their own kindred, the daughter of their war-duke, that she might lead that mighty company to the House of the Gods; and thereto was she nothing loth, but went right willingly.

There then they awaited the onset. But the men of Mid-mark came up in the morning, when the battle was but just joined, and fell on so fiercely that the aliens gave back, and then they of the Upper-mark stormed out of their eyot, and fell on over the ford, and fought till the water ran red with their blood, and the blood of the foemen. So the Aliens gave back before the onset of the Markmen all over the meads; but when they came to the hillocks and the tofts of the half-burned habitations, and the wood was on their flank, they made a stand again, and once more the battle waxed hot, for they were very many, and had many bow-men: there fell the War-duke of the Markmen, whose daughter had been offered up for victory, and his name was Agni, so that the tofts where he fell have since been called Agni's Tofts. So that day they fought all over the plain, and a great many died, both of the Aliens and the Markmen, and though these last were victorious, yet when the sun went down there still were the Aliens abiding in the Upper-mark, fenced by their Wain-burg, beaten, and much diminished in number, but still a host of men: while of the Markmen many had fallen, and many more were hurt, because the Aliens were good bow-men.

But on the morrow again, as the old tale told, came up the men of the Nether-mark fresh and unwounded; and so the battle began again on the southern limit of the Upper-mark where the Aliens had made their Wain-burg. But not long did it endure; for the Markmen fell on so fiercely, that they stormed over the Wain-burg, and slew all before them, and there was a very great slaughter of the Aliens; so great, tells the old tale, that never again durst they meet the Markmen in war.

Thus went forth the host of the Markmen, faring along both sides of the water into the Upper-mark; and on the west side, where went the Wolfings, the ground now rose by a long slope into a low hill, and when they came unto the brow thereof, they beheld before them the whole plain of the Upper-mark, and the dwellings of the kindred therein all girdled about by the wild-wood; and beyond, the blue hills of the herdsmen, and beyond them still, a long way aloof, lying like a white cloud on the verge of the heavens, the snowy tops of the great mountains. And as they looked down on to the plain they saw it embroidered, as it were, round about the habitations which lay within ken by crowds of many people, and the banners of the kindreds and the arms of men; and many a place they saw named after the ancient battle and that great slaughter of the Aliens.

On their left hand lay the river, and as it now fairly entered with them into the Upper-mark, it spread out into wide rippling shallows beset with yet more sandy eyots, amongst which was one much greater, rising amidmost into a low hill, grassy and bare of tree or bush; and this was the island whereon the Markmen stood on the first day of the Great Battle, and it was now called the Island of the Gods.

Thereby was the ford, which was firm and good and changed little from year to year, so that all Markmen knew it well and it was called Battleford: thereover now crossed all the eastern companies, footmen and horsemen, freemen and thralls, wains and banners, with shouting and laughter, and the noise of horns and the lowing of neat, till all that plain's end was flooded with the host of the Markmen.

But when the eastern-abiders had crossed, they made no stay, but went duly ordered about their banners, winding on toward the first of the abodes on the western side of the water; because it was but a little way south-west of this that the Thing-stead of the Upper-mark lay; and the whole Folk was summoned thither when war threatened from the South, just as it was called to the Thing-stead of the Nether-mark, when the threat of war came from the North. But the western companies stayed on the brow of that low hilt till all the eastern men were over the river, and on their way to the Thing-stead, and then they moved on.

So came the Wolfings and their fellows up to the dwellings of the northernmost kindred, who were called the Daylings, and bore on their banner the image of the rising sun. Thereabout was the Mark somewhat more hilly and broken than in the Mid-mark, so that the Great Roof of the Daylings, which was a very big house, stood on a hillock whose sides had been cleft down sheer on all sides save one (which was left as a bridge) by the labour of men, and it was a very defensible place.

Thereon were now gathered round about the Roof all the stay-at-homes of the kindred, who greeted with joyous cries the men-at-arms as they passed. Albeit one very old man, who sat in a chair near to the edge of the sheer hill looking on the war array, when he saw the Wolfing banner draw near, stood up to gaze on it, and then shook his head sadly, and sank back again into his chair, and covered his face with his hands: and when the folk saw that, a silence bred of the coldness of fear fell on them, for that elder was deemed a foreseeing man.

But as those three fellows, of whose talk of yesterday the tale has told, drew near and beheld what the old carle did (for they were riding together this day also) the Beaming man laid his hand on Wolfkettle's rein and said:

"Lo you, neighbour, if thy Vala hath seen nought, yet hath this old man seen somewhat, and that somewhat even as the little lad saw it. Many a mother's son shall fall before the Welshmen."

But Wolfkettle shook his rein free, and his face reddened as of one who is angry, yet he kept silence, while the Elking said:

"Let be, Toti! for he that lives shall tell the tale to the foreseers, and shall make them wiser than they are to-day."

Then laughed Toti, as one who would not be thought to be too heedful of the morrow. But Wolfkettle brake out into speech and rhyme, and said:

O warriors, the Wolfing kindred shall live or it shall die;
And alive it shall be as the oak-tree when the summer storm goes by;
But dead it shall be as its bole, that they hew for the corner-post
Of some fair and mighty folk-hall, and the roof of a war-fain host.

So therewith they rode their ways past the abode of the Daylings.

Straight to the wood went all the host, and so into it by a wide way cleft through the thicket, and in some thirty minutes they came thereby into a great wood-lawn cleared amidst of it by the work of men's hands. There already was much of the host gathered, sitting or standing in a great ring round about a space bare of men, where amidmost rose a great mound raised by men's hands and wrought into steps to be the sitting-places of the chosen elders and chief men of the kindred; and atop the mound was flat and smooth save for a turf bench or seat that went athwart it whereon ten men might sit.

All the wains save the banner-wains had been left behind at the Dayling abode, nor was any beast there save the holy beasts who drew the banner-wains and twenty white horses, that stood wreathed about with flowers within the ring of warriors, and these were for the burnt offering to be given to the Gods for a happy day of battle. Even the war-horses of the host they must leave in the wood without the wood-lawn, and all men were afoot who were there.

For this was the Thing-stead of the Upper-mark, and the holiest place of the Markmen, and no beast, either neat, sheep, or horse might pasture there, but was straightway slain and burned if he wandered there; nor might any man eat therein save at the holy feasts when offerings were made to the Gods.

So the Wolfings took their place there in the ring of men with the Elkings on their right hand and the Beamings on their left. And in the midst of the Wolfing array stood Thiodolf clad in the dwarf-wrought hauberk: but his head was bare; for he had sworn over the Cup of Renown that he would fight unhelmed throughout all that trouble, and would bear no shield in any battle thereof however fierce the onset might be.

Short, and curling close to his head was his black hair, a little grizzled, so that it looked like rings of hard dark iron: his forehead was high and smooth, his lips full and red, his eyes steady and wide-open, and all his face joyous with the thought of the fame of his deeds, and the coming battle with a foeman whom the Markmen knew not yet.

He was tall and wide-shouldered, but so exceeding well fashioned of all his limbs and body that he looked no huge man. He was a man well beloved of women, and children would mostly run to him gladly and play with him. A most fell warrior was he, whose deeds no man of the Mark could equal, but blithe of speech even when he was sorrowful of mood, a man that knew not bitterness of heart: and for all his exceeding might and valiancy, he was proud and high to no man; so that the very thralls loved him.

He was not abounding in words in the field; nor did he use much the custom of those days in reviling and defying with words the foe that was to be smitten with swords.

There were those who had seen him in the field for the first time who deemed him slack at the work: for he would not always press on with the foremost, but would hold him a little aback, and while the battle was young he forbore to smite, and would do nothing but help a kinsman who was hard pressed, or succour the wounded. So that if men were dealing with no very hard matter, and their hearts were high and overweening, he would come home at whiles with unbloodied blade. But no man blamed him save those who knew him not: for his intent was that the younger men should win themselves fame, and so raise their courage, and become high-hearted and stout.

But when the stour was hard, and the battle was broken, and the hearts of men began to fail them, and doubt fell upon the Markmen, then was he another man to see: wise, but swift and dangerous, rushing on as if shot out by some mighty engine: heedful of all, on either side and in front; running hither and thither as the fight failed and the fire of battle faltered; his sword so swift and deadly that it was as if he wielded the very lightening of the heavens: for with the sword it was ever his wont to fight.

But it must be said that when the foemen turned their backs, and the chase began, then Thiodolf would nowise withhold his might as in the early battle, but ever led the chase, and smote on the right hand and on the left, sparing none, and crying out to the men of the kindred not to weary in their work, but to fulfil all the hours of their day.

For thuswise would he say and this was a word of his:

Let us rest to-morrow, fellows, since to-day we have fought amain!
Let not these men we have smitten come aback on our hands again,
And say 'Ye Wolfing warriors, ye have done your work but ill,
Fall to now and do it again, like the craftsman who learneth his skill.'

Such then was Thiodolf, and ever was he the chosen leader of the Wolfings and often the War-duke of the whole Folk.

By his side stood the other chosen leader, whose name was Heriulf; a man well stricken in years, but very mighty and valiant; wise in war and well renowned; of few words save in battle, and therein a singer of songs, a laugher, a joyous man, a merry companion. He was a much bigger man than Thiodolf; and indeed so huge was his stature, that he seemed to be of the kindred of the Mountain Giants; and his bodily might went with his stature, so that no one man might deal with him body to body. His face was big; his cheek-bones high; his nose like an eagle's neb, his mouth wide, his chin square and big; his eyes light-grey and fierce under shaggy eyebrows: his hair white and long.

Such were his raiment and weapons, that he wore a coat of fence of dark iron scales sewn on to horse-hide, and a dark iron helm fashioned above his brow into the similitude of the Wolf's head with gaping jaws; and this he had wrought for himself with his own hands, for he was a good smith. A round buckler he bore and a huge twibill, which no man of the kindred could well wield save himself; and it was done both blade and shaft with knots and runes in gold; and he loved that twibill well, and called it the Wolf's Sister.

There then stood Heriulf, looking no less than one of the forefathers of the kindred come back again to the battle of the Wolfings.

He was well-beloved for his wondrous might, and he was no hard man, though so fell a warrior, and though of few words, as aforesaid, was a blithe companion to old and young. In numberless battles had he fought, and men deemed it a wonder that Odin had not taken to him a man so much after his own heart; and they said it was neighbourly done of the Father of the Slain to forbear his company so long, and showed how well he loved the Wolfing House.

For a good while yet came other bands of Markmen into the Thing-stead; but at last there was an end of their coming. Then the ring of men opened, and ten warriors of the Daylings made their way through it, and one of them, the oldest, bore in his hand the War-horn of the Daylings; for this kindred had charge of the Thing-stead, and of all appertaining to it. So while his nine fellows stood round about the Speech-Hill, the old warrior clomb up to the topmost of it, and blew a blast on the horn. Thereon they who were sitting rose up, and they who were talking each to each held their peace, and the whole ring drew nigher to the hill, so that there was a clear space behind them 'twixt them and the wood, and a space before them between them and the hill, wherein were those nine warriors, and the horses for the burnt-offering, and the altar of the Gods; and now were all well within ear-shot of a man speaking amidst the silence in a clear voice.

But there were gathered of the Markmen to that place some four thousand men, all chosen warriors and doughty men; and of the thralls and aliens dwelling with them they were leading two thousand. But not all of the freemen of the Upper-mark could be at the Thing; for needs must there be some guard to the passes of the wood toward the south and the hills of the herdsmen, whereas it was no wise impassable to a wisely led host: so five hundred men, what of freemen, what of thralls, abode there to guard the wild-wood; and these looked to have some helping from the hill-men.

Now came an ancient warrior into the space between the men and the wild-wood holding in his hand a kindled torch; and first he faced due south by the sun, then, turning, he slowly paced the whole circle going from east to west, and so on till he had reached the place he started from: then he dashed the torch to the ground and quenched the fire, and so went his ways to his own company again.

Then the old Dayling warrior on the mound-top drew his sword, and waved it flashing in the sun toward the four quarters of the heavens; and thereafter blew again a blast on the War-horn. Then fell utter silence on the whole assembly, and the wood was still around them, save here and there the stamping of a war-horse or the sound of his tugging at the woodland grass; for there was little resort of birds to the depths of the thicket, and the summer morning was windless.

8. THE FOLK-MOTE OF THE MARKMEN

So the Dayling warrior lifted up his voice and said:

O kindreds of the Markmen, hearken the words I say;
For no chancehap assembly is gathered here to-day.
The fire hath gone around us in the hands of our very kin,
And twice the horn hath sounded, and the Thing is hallowed in.
Will ye hear or forbear to hearken the tale there is to tell?
There are many mouths to tell it, and a many know it well.
And the tale is this, that the foemen against our kindreds fare
Who eat the meadows desert, and burn the desert bare.

Then sat he down on the turf seat; but there arose a murmur in the assembly as of men eager to hearken; and without more ado came a man out of a company of the Upper-mark, and clomb up to the top of the Speech-Hill, and spoke in a loud voice:

"I am Bork, a man of the Geirings of the Upper-mark: two days ago I and five others were in the wild-wood a-hunting, and we wended through the thicket, and came into the land of the hill-folk; and after we had gone a while we came to a long dale with a brook running through it, and yew-trees scattered about it and a hazel copse at one end; and by the copse was a band of men who had women and children with them, and a few neat, and fewer horses; but sheep were feeding up and down the dale; and they had made them booths of turf and boughs, and were making ready their cooking fires, for it was evening. So when they saw us, they ran to their arms, but we cried out to them in the tongue of the Goths and bade them peace. Then they came up the bent to us and spake to us in the Gothic tongue, albeit a little diversely from us; and when we had told them what and whence we were, they were glad of us, and bade us to them, and we went, and they entreated us kindly, and made us such cheer as they might, and gave us mutton to eat, and we gave them venison of the wild-wood which we had taken, and we abode with them there that night.

"But they told us that they were a house of the folk of the herdsmen, and that there was war in the land, and that the people thereof were fleeing before the cruelty of a host of warriors, men of a mighty folk, such as the earth hath not heard of, who dwell in great cities far to the south; and how that this host had crossed the mountains, and the Great Water that runneth from them, and had fallen upon their kindred, and overcome their fighting-men, and burned their dwellings, slain their elders, and driven their neat and their sheep, yea, and their women and children in no better wise than their neat and sheep.

"And they said that they had fled away thus far from their old habitations, which were a long way to the south, and were now at point to build them dwellings there in that Dale of the Hazels, and to trust to it that these Welshmen, whom they called Romans, would not follow so far, and that if they did, they might betake them to the wild-wood, and let the thicket cover them, they being so nigh to it.

"Thus they told us; wherefore we sent back one of our fellowship, Birsti of the Geirings, to tell the tale; and one of the herdsmen folk went with him, but we ourselves went onward to hear more of these Romans; for the folk when we asked them, said that they had been in battle against them, but had fled away for fear of their rumour only. Therefore we went on, and a young man of this kindred, who named themselves the Hrutings of the Fell-folk, went along with us. But the others were sore afeard, for all they had weapons.

"So as we went up the land we found they had told us the very sooth, and we met divers Houses, and bands, and broken men, who were fleeing from this trouble, and many of them poor and in misery, having lost their flocks and herds as well as their roofs; and this last be but little loss to them, as their dwellings are but poor, and for the most part they have no tillage. Now of these men, we met not a few who had been in battle with the Roman host, and much they told us of their might not to be dealt with, and their mishandling of those whom they took, both men and women; and at the last we heard true tidings how they had raised them a garth, and made a stronghold in the midst of the land, as men who meant abiding there, so that neither might the winter drive them aback, and that they might be succoured by their people on the other side of the Great River; to which end they have made other garths, though not so great, on the road to that water, and all these well and wisely warded by tried men. For as to the Folks on the other side of the Water, all these lie under their hand already, what by fraud what by force, and their warriors go with them to the battle and help them; of whom we met bands now and again, and fought with them, and took men of them, who told us all this and much more, over long to tell of here."

He paused and turned about to look on the mighty assembly, and his ears drank in the long murmur that followed his speaking, and when it had died out he spake again, but in rhyme:

Lo thus much of my tidings! But this too it behoveth to tell,
That these masterful men of the cities of the Markmen know full well:
And they wot of the well-grassed meadows, and the acres of the Mark,
And our life amidst of the wild-wood like a candle in the dark;
And they know of our young men's valour and our women's loveliness,
And our tree would they spoil with destruction if its fruit they may
*   never possess.*
For their lust is without a limit, and nought may satiate
Their ravening maw; and their hunger if ye check it turneth to hate,
And the blood-fever burns in their bosoms, and torment and anguish
*   and woe*
O'er the wide field ploughed by the sword-blade for the coming years
*   they sow;*
And ruth is a thing forgotten and all hopes they trample down;
And whatso thing is steadfast, whatso of good renown,
Whatso is fair and lovely, whatso is ancient sooth
In the bloody marl shall they mingle as they laugh for lack of ruth.
Lo the curse of the world cometh hither; for the men that we took in the
*   land*
Said thus, that their host is gathering with many an ordered band
To fall on the wild-wood passes and flood the lovely Mark,
As the river over the meadows upriseth in the dark.
Look to it, O ye kindred! availeth now no word
But the voice of the clashing of iron, and the sword-blade on the sword.

Therewith he made an end, and deeper and longer was the murmur of the host of freemen, amidst which Bork gat him down from the Speech-Hill, his weapons clattering about him, and mingled with the men of his kindred.

Then came forth a man of the kin of the Shieldings of the Upper-mark, and clomb the mound; and he spake in rhyme from beginning to end; for he was a minstrel of renown:

Lo I am a man of the Shieldings and Geirmund is my name;
A half-moon back from the wild-wood out into the hills I came,
And I went alone in my war-gear; for we have affinity
With the Hundings of the Fell-folk, and with them I fain would be;
For I loved a maid of their kindred. Now their dwelling was not far
From the outermost bounds of the Fell-folk, and bold in the battle they
*   are,*
And have met a many people, and held their own abode.
Gay then was the heart within me, as over the hills I rode
And thought of the mirth of to-morrow and the sweet-mouthed
*   Hunding maid*
And their old men wise and merry and their young men unafraid,
And the hall-glee of the Hundings and the healths o'er the guesting cup.
But as I rode the valley, I saw a smoke go up
O'er the crest of the last of the grass-hills 'twixt me and the Hunding
*   roof,*
And that smoke was black and heavy: so a while I bided aloof,
And drew my girths the tighter, and looked to the arms I bore
And handled my spear for the casting; for my heart misgave me sore,
For nought was that pillar of smoke like the guest-fain cooking-fire.
I lingered in thought for a minute, then turned me to ride up higher,
And as a man most wary up over the bent I rode,
And nigh hid peered o'er the hill-crest adown on the Hunding abode;
And forsooth 'twas the fire wavering all o'er the roof of old,
And all in the garth and about it lay the bodies of the bold;
And bound to a rope amidmost were the women fair and young,
And youths and little children, like the fish on a withy strung
As they lie on the grass for the angler before the beginning of night.
Then the rush of the wrath within me for a while nigh blinded my sight;
Yet about the cowering war-thralls, short dark-faced men I saw,
Men clad in iron armour, this way and that way draw,
As warriors after the battle are ever wont to do.
Then I knew them for the foemen and their deeds to be I knew,
And I gathered the reins together to ride down the hill amain,
To die with a good stroke stricken and slay ere I was slain.
When lo, on the bent before me rose the head of a brown-faced man,
Well helmed and iron-shielded, who some Welsh speech began
And a short sword brandished against me; then my sight cleared and I
*   saw*
Five others armed in likewise up hill and toward me draw,
And I shook the spear and sped it and clattering on his shield
He fell and rolled o'er smitten toward the garth and the Fell-folk's
*   field.*

More to William Morris—The House of the Wolfings

But my heart changed with his falling and the speeding of my stroke,
And I turned my horse; for within me the love of life awoke,
And I spurred, nor heeded the hill-side, but o'er rough and smooth I
*   rode*
Till I heard no chase behind me; then I drew rein and abode.
And down in a dell was I gotten with a thorn-brake in its throat,
And heard but the plover's whistle and the blackbird's broken note
'Mid the thorns; when lo! from a thorn-twig away the blackbird swept,
And out from the brake and towards me a naked man there crept,
And straight I rode up towards him, and knew his face for one
I had seen in the hall of the Hundings ere its happy days were done.
I asked him his tale, but he bade me forthright to bear him away;
So I took him up behind me, and we rode till late in the day,
Toward the cover of the wild-wood, and as swiftly as we might.
But when yet aloof was the thicket and it now was moonless night,
We stayed perforce for a little, and he told me all the tale:
How the aliens came against them, and they fought without avail
Till the Roof o'er their heads was burning and they burst forth on the
*   foe,*
And were hewn down there together; nor yet was the slaughter slow.
But some they saved for thralldom, yea, e'en of the fighting men,
Or to quell them with pains; so they stripped them; and this man
*   espying just then*
Some chance, I mind not whatwise, from the garth fled out and away.

Now many a thing noteworthy of these aliens did he say,
But this I bid you hearken, lest I wear the time for nought,
That still upon the Markmen and the Mark they set their thought;
For they questioned this man and others through a go-between in words
Of us, and our lands and our chattels, and the number of our swords;
Of the way and the wild-wood passes and the winter and his ways.
Now look to see them shortly; for worn are fifteen days
Since in the garth of the Hundings I saw them dight for war,
And a hardy folk and ready and a swift-foot host they are.

Therewith Geirmund went down clattering from the Hill and stood with his company. But a man came forth from the other side of the ring, and clomb the Hill: he was a red-haired man, rather big, clad in a skin coat, and bearing a bow in his hand and a quiver of arrows at his back, and a little axe hung by his side. He said:

"I dwell in the House of the Hrossings of the Mid-mark, and I am now made a man of the kindred: howbeit I was not born into it; for I am the son of a fair and mighty woman of a folk of the Kymry, who was taken in war while she went big with me; I am called Fox the Red.

"These Romans have I seen, and have not died: so hearken! for my tale shall be short for what there is in it.

"I am, as many know, a hunter of Mirkwood, and I know all its ways and the passes through the thicket somewhat better than most.

"A moon ago I fared afoot from Mid-mark through Upper-mark into the thicket of the south, and through it into the heath country; and I went over a neck and came in the early dawn into a little dale when somewhat of mist still hung over it. At the dale's end I saw a man lying asleep on the grass under a quicken tree, and his shield and sword hanging over his head to a bough thereof, and his horse feeding hoppled higher up the dale.

"I crept up softly to him with a shaft nocked on the string, but when I drew near I saw him to be of the sons of the Goths. So I doubted nothing, but laid down my bow, and stood upright, and went to him and roused him, and he leapt up, and was wroth.

"I said to him, 'Wilt thou be wroth with a brother of the kindred meeting him in unpeopled parts?'

"But he reached out for his weapons; but ere he could handle them I ran in on him so that he gat not his sword, and had scant time to smite at me with a knife which he drew from his waist.

"I gave way before him for he was a very big man, and he rushed past me, and I dealt him a blow on the side of the head with my little axe which is called the War-babe, and gave him a great wound: and he fell on the grass, and as it happened that was his bane.

"I was sorry that I had slain him, since he was a man of the Goths: albeit otherwise he had slain me, for he was very wroth and dazed with slumber.

"He died not for a while; and he bade me fetch him water; and there was a well hard by on the other side of the tree; so I fetched it him in a great shell that I carry, and he drank. I would have sung the blood-staunching song over him, for I know it well. But he said, 'It availeth nought: I have enough: what man art thou?'

"I said, 'I am a fosterling of the Hrossings, and my mother was taken in war: my name is Fox.'

"Said he; 'O Fox, I have my due at thy hands, for I am a Markman of the Elkings, but a guest of the Burgundians beyond the Great River; and the Romans are their masters and they do their bidding: even so did I who was but their guest: and I a Markman to fight against the Markmen, and all for fear and for gold! And thou an alien-born hast slain their traitor and their dastard! This is my due. Give me to drink again.'

"So did I; and he said; 'Wilt thou do an errand for me to thine own house?' 'Yea,' said I.

"Said he, 'I am a messenger to the garth of the Romans, that I may tell the road to the Mark, and lead them through the thicket; and other guides are coming after me: but not yet for three days or four. So till they come there will be no man in the Roman garth to know thee that thou art not even I myself. If thou art doughty, strip me when I am dead and do my raiment on thee, and take this ring from my neck, for that is my token, and when they ask thee for a word say, '*no limit;*' for that is the token-word. Go south-east over the dales keeping Broadshield-fell square with thy right hand, and let thy wisdom, O Fox, lead thee to the Garth of the Romans, and so back to thy kindred with all tidings thou hast gathered—for indeed they come—a many of them. Give me to drink.'

"So he drank again, and said, 'The bearer of this token is called Hrosstyr of the River Goths. He hath that name among dastards. Thou shalt lay a turf upon my head. Let my death pay for my life.'

"Therewith he fell back and died. So I did as he bade me and took his gear, worth six kine, and did it on me; I laid turf upon him in that dale, and hid my bow and my gear in a blackthorn brake hard by, and then took his horse and rode away.

"Day and night I rode till I came to the garth of the Romans; there I gave myself up to their watchers, and they brought me to their Duke, a grim man and hard. He said in a terrible voice, 'Thy name?' I said, 'Hrosstyr of the River Goths.' He said, '*What limit?*' I answered, '*No limit.*' 'The token!' said he, and held out his hand. I gave him the ring. 'Thou art the man,' said he.

"I thought in my heart, 'thou liest, lord,' and my heart danced for joy.

"Then he fell to asking me questions a many, and I answered every one glibly enough, and told him what I would, but no word of truth save for his hurt, and my soul laughed within me at my lies; thought I, the others, the traitors, shall come, and they shall tell him the truth, and he will not trow it, or at the worst he will doubt them. But me he doubted nothing, else had he called in the tormentors to have the truth of me by pains; as I well saw afterwards, when they questioned with torments a man and a woman of the hill-folk whom they had brought in captive.

"I went from him and went all about that garth espying everything, fearing nothing; albeit there were divers woful captives of the Goths, who cursed me for a dastard, when they saw by my attire that I was of their blood.

"I abode there three days, and learned all that I might of the garth and the host of them, and the fourth day in the morning I went out as if to hunt, and none hindered me, for they doubted me not.

"So I came my ways home to the Upper-mark, and was guested with the Geirings. Will ye that I tell you somewhat of the ways of these Romans of the garth? The time presses, and my tale runneth longer than I would. What will ye?"

Then there arose a murmur, "Tell all, tell all." "Nay," said the Fox, "All I may not tell; so much did I behold there during the three days' stay; but this much it behoveth you to know: that these men have no other thought save to win the Mark and waste it, and slay the fighting men and the old carles, and enthrall such as they will, that is, all that be fair and young, and they long sorely for our women either to have or to sell.

"As for their garth, it is strongly walled about with a dyke newly dug; on the top thereof are they building a wall made of clay, and burned like pots into ashlar stones hard and red, and these are laid in lime.

"It is now the toil of the thralls of our blood whom they have taken, both men and women, to dig that clay and to work it, and bear it to kilns, and to have for reward scant meat and many stripes. For it is a grim folk, that laugheth to see others weep.

"Their men-at-arms are well dight and for the most part in one way: they are helmed with iron, and have iron on their breasts and reins, and bear long shields that cover them to the knees. They are girt with a sax and have a heavy casting-spear. They are dark-skinned and ugly of aspect, surly and of few words: they drink little, and eat not much.

"They have captains of tens and of hundreds over them, and that War-duke over all; he goeth to and fro with gold on his head and his breast, and commonly hath a cloak cast over him of the colour of the crane's-bill blossom.

"They have an altar in the midst of their burg, and thereon they sacrifice to their God, who is none other than their banner of war, which is an image of the ravening eagle with outspread wings; but yet another God they have, and look you! it is a wolf, as if they were of the kin of our brethren; a she-wolf and two man-children at her dugs; wonderful is this.

"I tell you that they are grim; and know it by this token: those captains of tens, and of hundreds, spare not to smite the warriors with staves even before all men, when all goeth not as they would; and yet, though they be free men, and mighty warriors, they endure it and smite not in turn. They are a most evil folk.

"As to their numbers, they of the burg are hard on three thousand footmen of the best; and of horsemen five hundred, nowise good; and of bowmen and slingers six hundred or more: their bows weak; their slingers cunning beyond measure. And the talk is that when they come upon us they shall have with them some five hundred warriors of the Over River Goths, and others of their own folk."

Then he said:

O men of the Mark, will ye meet them in the meadows and the field,
Or will ye flee before them and have the wood for a shield?
Or will ye wend to their war-burg with weapons cast away,

With your women and your children, a peace of them to pray?
So doing, not all shall perish; but most shall long to die
Ere in the garths of the Southland two moons have loitered by.

Then rose the rumour loud and angry mingled with the rattle of swords and the clash of spears on shields; but Fox said:

"Needs must ye follow one of these three ways. Nay, what say I? there are but two ways and not three; for if ye flee they shall follow you to the confines of the earth. Either these Welsh shall take all, and our lives to boot, or we shall hold to all that is ours, and live merrily. The sword doometh; and in three days it may be the courts shall be hallowed: small is the space between us."

Therewith he also got him down from the Hill, and joined his own house: and men said that he had spoken well and wisely. But there arose a noise of men talking together on these tidings; and amidst it an old warrior of the Nether-mark strode forth and up to the Hill-top. Gaunt and stark he was to look on; and all men knew him and he was well-beloved, so all held their peace as he said:

"I am Otter of the Laxings: now needeth but few words till the War-duke is chosen, and we get ready to wend our ways in arms. Here have ye heard three good men and true tell of our foes, and this last, Fox the Red, hath seen them and hath more to tell when we are on the way; nor is the way hard to find. It were scarce well to fall upon these men in their garth and warburg; for hard is a wall to slay. Better it were to meet them in the Wild-wood, which may well be a friend to us and a wall, but to them a net. O Agni of the Daylings, thou warder of the Thing-stead, bid men choose a War-duke if none gainsay it."

And without more words he clattered down the Hill, and went and stood with the Laxing band. But the old Dayling arose and blew the horn, and there was at once a great silence, amidst which he said:

"Children of Slains-father, doth the Folk go to the war?"

There was no voice but shouted "yea," and the white swords sprang aloft, and the westering sun swept along a half of them as they tossed to and fro, and the others showed dead-white and fireless against the dark wood.

Then again spake Agni:

"Will ye choose the War-duke now and once, or shall it be in a while, after others have spoken?"

And the voice of the Folk went up, "Choose! Choose!"

Said Agni: "Sayeth any aught against it?" But no voice of a gainsayer was heard, and Agni said:

"Children of Tyr, what man will ye have for a leader and a duke of war?"

Then a great shout sprang up from amidst the swords: "We will have Thiodolf; Thiodolf the Wolfing!"

Said Agni: "I hear no other name; are ye of one mind? hath any aught to say against it? If that be so, let him speak now, and not forbear to follow in the wheatfield of the spears. Speak, ye that will not follow Thiodolf!"

No voice gainsaid him: then said the Dayling: "Come forth thou War-duke of the Markmen! take up the gold ring from the horns of the altar, set it on thine arm and come up hither!"

Then came forth Thiodolf into the sun, and took up the gold ring from where it lay, and did it on his arm. And this was the ring of the leader of the folk whenso one should be chosen: it was ancient and daintily wrought, but not very heavy: so ancient it was that men said it had been wrought by the dwarfs.

So Thiodolf went up on to the hill, and all men cried out on him for joy, for they knew his wisdom in war. Many wondered to see him unhelmed, but they had a deeming that he must have made oath to the Gods thereof and their hearts were glad of it. They took note of the dwarf-wrought hauberk, and even from a good way off they could see what a treasure of smith's work it was, and they deemed it like enough that spells had been sung over it to make it sure against point and edge: for they knew that Thiodolf was well beloved of the Gods.

But when Thiodolf was on the Hill of Speech, he said:

"Men of the kindreds, I am your War-duke to-day; but it is oftenest the custom when ye go to war to choose you two dukes, and I would it were so now. No child's play is the work that lies before us; and if one leader chance to fall let there be another to take his place without stop or stay. Thou Agni of the Daylings, bid the Folk choose them another duke if so they will."

Said Agni: "Good is this which our War-duke hath spoken; say then, men of the Mark, who shall stand with Thiodolf to lead you against the Aliens?"

Then was there a noise and a crying of names, and more than two names seemed to be cried out; but by far the greater part named either Otter of the Laxings, or Heriulf of the Wolfings. True it is that Otter was a very wise warrior, and well known to all the men of the Mark; yet so dear was Heriulf to them, that none would have named Otter had it not been mostly their custom not to choose both War-dukes from one House.

Now spake Agni: "Children of Tyr, I hear you name more than one name: now let each man cry out clearly the name he nameth.

So the Folk cried the names once more, but this time it was clear that none was named save Otter and Heriulf; so the Dayling was at point to speak again, but or ever a word left his lips, Heriulf the mighty, the ancient of days, stood forth: and when men saw that he would take up the word there was a great silence. So he spake:

"Hearken, children! I am old and war-wise; but my wisdom is the wisdom of the sword of the mighty warrior, that knoweth which way it should wend, and hath no thought of turning back till it lieth broken in the field. Such wisdom is good against Folks that we have met heretofore; as when we have fought with the Huns, who would sweep us away from the face of the earth, or with the Franks or the Burgundians, who would quell us into being something worser than they be. But here is a new foe, and new wisdom, and that right shifty, do we need to meet them. One wise duke have ye gotten, Thiodolf to wit; and he is young beside me and beside Otter of the Laxings. And now if ye must needs have an older man to stand beside him, (and that is not ill) take ye Otter; for old though his body be, the thought within him is keen and supple like the best of Welsh-wrought blades, and it liveth in the days that now are: whereas for me, meseemeth, my thoughts are in the days bygone. Yet look to it, that I shall not fail to lead as the sword of the valiant leadeth, or the shaft shot by the cunning archer. Choose ye Otter; I have spoken over long."

Then spoke Agni the Dayling, and laughed withal: "One man of the Folk hath spoken for Otter and against Heriulf—now let others speak if they will!"

So the cry came forth, "Otter let it be, we will have Otter!"

"Speaketh any against Otter?" said Agni. But there was no voice raised against him.

Then Agni said: "Come forth, Otter of the Laxings, and hold the ring with Thiodolf."

Then Otter went up on to the hill and stood by Thiodolf, and they held the ring together; and then each thrust his hand and arm through the ring and clasped hands together, and stood thus awhile, and all the Folk shouted together.

Then spake Agni: "Now shall we hew the horses and give the gifts to the Gods."

Therewith he and the two War-dukes came down from the hill; and stood before the altar; and the nine warriors of the Daylings stood forth with axes to hew the horses and with copper bowls wherein to catch the blood of them, and each hewed down his horse to the Gods, but the two War-dukes slew the tenth and fairest: and the blood was caught in the bowls, and Agni took a sprinkler and went round about the ring of men,

and cast the blood of the Gods'-gifts over the Folk, as was the custom of those days.

Then they cut up the carcases and burned on the altar the share of the Gods, and Agni and the War-dukes tasted thereof, and the rest they bore off to the Daylings' abode for the feast to be holden that night.

Then Otter and Thiodolf spake apart together for awhile, and presently went up again on to the Speech-Hill, and Thiodolf said:

O kindreds of the Markmen; to-morrow with the day
We shall wend up Mirkwood-water to bar our foes the way;
And there shall we make our Wain-burg on the edges of the wood,
Where in the days past over at last the aliens stood,
The Slaughter Tofts ye call it. There tidings shall we get
If the curse of the world is awakened, and the serpent crawleth yet
Amidst the Mirkwood thicket; and when the sooth we know,
Then bearing battle with us through the thicket shall we go,
The ancient Wood-wolf's children, and the People of the Shield,
And the Spear-kin and the Horse-kin, while the others keep the field
About the warded Wain-burg; for not many need we there
Where amidst of the thickets' tangle and the woodland net they fare,
And the hearts of the aliens falter and they curse the fight ne'er done,
And wonder who is fighting and which way is the sun.

Thus he spoke; then Agni took up the war-horn again, and blew a blast, and then he cried out:

Now sunder we the Folk-motel and the feast is for to-night,
And to-morrow the Wayfaring; But unnamed is the day of the fight;
O warriors, look ye to it that not long we need abide
'Twixt the hour of the word we have spoken, and our fair-fame's
blooming-tide!
For then 'midst the toil and the turmoil shall we sow the seeds of peace,
And the Kindreds' long endurance, and the Gothfolk's great increase.

Then arose the last great shout, and soberly and in due order, kindred by kindred, they turned and departed from the Thing-stead and went their way through the wood to the abode of the Daylings.

9. THE ANCIENT MAN OF THE DAYLINGS

There still hung the more part of the stay-at-homes round about the Roof. But on the plain beneath the tofts were all the wains of the host drawn up round about a square like the streets about a market-place; all these now had their tilts rigged over them, some white, some black, some red, some tawny of hue; and some, which were of the Beamings, green like the leafy tree.

The warriors of the host went down into this wain-town, which they had not fenced in any way, since they in no wise looked for any onset there; and there were their thralls dighting the feast for them, and a many of the Dayling kindred, both men and women, went with them; but some men did the Daylings bring into their Roof, for there was room for a good many besides their own folk. So they went over the Bridge of turf into the garth and into the Great Roof of the Daylings; and amongst these were the two War-dukes.

So when they came to the dais it was as fair all round about there as might well be; and there sat elders and ancient warriors to welcome the guests; and among them was the old carle who had sat on the edge of the burg to watch the faring of the host, and had shuddered back at the sight of the Wolfing Banner.

And when the old carle saw the guests, he fixed his eyes on Thiodolf, and presently came up and stood before him; and Thiodolf looked on the old man, and greeted him kindly and smiled on him; but the carle spake not till he had looked on him a while; and at last he fell a-trembling, and reached his hands out to Thiodolf's bare head, and handled his curls and caressed them, as a mother does with her son, even if he be a grizzled-haired man, when there is none by: and at last he said:

How dear is the head of the mighty, and the apple of the tree
That blooms with the life of the people which is and yet shall be!
It is helmed with ancient wisdom, and the long remembered thought,
That liveth when dead is the iron, and its very rust but nought.
Ah! were I but young as aforetime, I would fare to the battle-stead
And stand amidst of the spear-hail for the praise of the hand and the head!

Then his hands left Thiodolf's head, and strayed down to his shoulders and his breast, and he felt the cold rings of the hauberk, and let his hands fall down to his side again; and the tears gushed out of his old eyes and again he spake:

O house of the heart of the mighty, O breast of the battle-lord
Why art thou coldly hidden from the flickering flame of the sword?
I know thee not, nor see thee; thou art as the fells afar
Where the Fathers have their dwelling, and the halls of Godhome are:
The wind blows wild betwixt us, and the cloud-rack flies along,
And high aloft enfoldeth the dwelling of the strong;
They are, as of old they have been, but their hearths flame not for me;
And the kindness of their feast-halls mine eyes shall never see.

Thiodolf's lips still smiled on the old man, but a shadow had come over his eyes and his brow; and the chief of the Daylings and their mighty guests stood by listening intently with the knit brows of anxious men; nor did any speak till the ancient man again betook him to words:

I came to the house of the foeman when hunger made me a fool;
And the foeman said, 'Thou art weary, lo, set thy foot on the stool;'
And I stretched out my feet,—and was shackled: and he spake with a dastard's smile,

'O guest, thine hands are heavy; now rest them for a while!'
So I stretched out my hands, and the hand-gyves lay cold on either wrist:
And the wood of the wolf had been better than that feast-hall, had I wist
That this was the ancient pit-fall, and the long expected trap,
And that now for my heart's desire I had sold the world's goodhap.

Therewith the ancient man turned slowly away from Thiodolf, and departed sadly to his own place. Thiodolf changed countenance but little, albeit those about him looked strangely on him, as though if they durst they would ask him what these words might be, and if he from his hidden knowledge might fit a meaning to them. For to many there was a word of warning in them, and to some an evil omen of the days soon to be; and scarce anyone heard those words but he had a misgiving in his heart, for the ancient man was known to be foreseeing, and wild and strange his words seemed to them.

But Agni would make light of it, and he said: "Asmund the Old is of good will, and wise he is; but he hath great longings for the deeds of men, when he hath tidings of battle; for a great warrior and a red-hand hewer he hath been in times past; he loves the Kindred, and deems it ill if he may not fare afield with them; for the thought of dying in the straw is hateful to him."

"Yea," said another, "and moreover he hath seen sons whom he loved slain in battle; and when he seeth a warrior in his prime he becometh dear to him, and he feareth for him."

"Yet," said a third, "Asmund is foreseeing; and may be, Thiodolf, thou wilt wot of the drift of these words, and tell us thereof."

But Thiodolf spake nought of the matter, though in his heart he pondered it.

So the guests were led to table, and the feast began, within the hall and without it, and wide about the plain; and the Dayling maidens went in bands trimly decked out throughout all the host and served the warriors with meat and drink, and sang the overword to their lays, and smote the harp, and drew the bow over the fiddle till it laughed and wailed and chuckled, and were blithe and merry with all, and great was the glee on the eve of battle. And if Thiodolf's heart were overcast, his face showed it not, but he passed from hall to Wain-burg and from Wain-burg to hall again blithe and joyous with all men. And thereby he raised the hearts of men, and they deemed it good that they had gotten such a War-duke, meet to uphold all hearts of men both at the feast and in the fray.

10. THAT CARLINE COMETH TO THE ROOF OF THE WOLFINGS

Now it was three days after this that the women were gathering to the Women's-Chamber of the Roof of the Wolfings a little before the afternoon changes into evening. The hearts of most were somewhat heavy, for the doubt wherewith they had watched the departure of the fighting-men still hung about them; nor had they any tidings from the host (nor was it like that they should have). And as they were somewhat downhearted, so it seemed by the aspect of all things that afternoon. It was not yet the evening, as is aforesaid, but the day was worn and worsened, and all things looked weary. The sky was a little clouded, but not much; yet was it murky down in the south-east, and there was a threat of storm in it, and in the air close round each man's head, and in the very waving of the leafy boughs. There was by this time little doing in field and fold (for the kine were milked), and the women were coming up from the acres and the meadow and over the open ground anigh the Roof; there was the grass worn and dusty, and the women that trod it, their feet were tanned and worn, and dusty also; skin-dry and weary they looked, with the sweat dried upon them; their girt-up gowns grey and lightless, their half-unbound hair blowing about them in the dry wind, which had in it no morning freshness, and no evening coolness.

It was a time when toil was well-nigh done, but had left its aching behind it; a time for folk to sleep and forget for a little while, till the low sun should make it evening, and make all things fair with his level rays; no time for anxious thoughts concerning deeds doing, wherein the anxious ones could do nought to help. Yet such thoughts those stay-at-homes needs must have in the hour of their toil scarce over, their rest and mirth not begun.

Slowly one by one the women went in by the Women's-door, and the Hall-Sun sat on a stone hard by, and watched them as they passed; and she looked keenly at all persons and all things. She had been working in the acres, and her hand was yet on the hoe she had been using, and but for her face her body was as of one resting after toil: her dark blue gown was ungirded, her dark hair loose and floating, the flowers that had wreathed it, now faded, lying strewn upon the grass before her: her feet bare for coolness' sake, her left hand lying loose and open upon her knee.

Yet though her body otherwise looked thus listless, in her face was no listlessness, nor rest: her eyes were alert and clear, shining like two stars in the heavens of dawntide; her lips were set close, her brow knit, as of one striving to shape thoughts hard to understand into words that all might understand.

So she sat noting all things, as woman by woman went past her into the hall, till at last she slowly rose to her feet; for there came two young women leading between them that same old carline with whom she had talked on the Hill-of-Speech. She looked on the carline steadfastly, but gave no token of knowing her; but the ancient woman spoke when she came near to the Hall-Sun, and old as her semblance was, yet did her speech sound sweet to the Hall-Sun, and indeed to all those that heard it: and she said:

"May we be here to-night, O Hall-Sun, thou lovely Seeress of the mighty Wolfings? may a wandering woman sit amongst you and eat the meat of the Wolfings?"

Then spake the Hall-Sun in a sweet measured voice: "Surely mother: all men who bring peace with them are welcome guests to the Wolfings: nor will any ask thine errand, but we will let thy tidings flow from thee as thou wilt. This is the custom of the kindred, and no word of mine own; I speak to thee because thou hast spoken to me, but I have no authority here, being myself but an alien. Albeit I serve the House of the Wolfings, and I love it as the hound loveth his master who feedeth him, and his master's children who play with him. Enter, mother, and be glad of heart, and put away care from thee."

Then the old woman drew nigher to her and sat down in the dust at her feet, for she was now sitting down again, and took her hand and kissed it and fondled it, and seemed loth to leave handling the beauty of the Hall-Sun; but she looked kindly on the carline, and smiled on her, and leaned down to her, and kissed her mouth, and said:

"Damsels, take care of this poor woman, and make her good cheer; for she is wise of wit, and a friend of the Wolfings; and I have seen her before, and spoken with her; and she loveth us. But as for me I must needs be alone in the meads for a while; and it may be that when I come to you again, I shall have a word to tell you."

Now indeed it was in a manner true that the Hall-Sun had no authority in the Wolfing House; yet was she so well beloved for her wisdom and beauty and her sweet speech, that all hastened to do her will in small matters and in great, and now as they looked at her after the old woman had caressed her, it seemed to them that her fairness grew under their eyes, and that they had never seen her so fair; and the sight of her seemed so good to them, that the outworn day and its weariness changed to them, and it grew as pleasant as the first hours of the sunlight, when men arise happy from their rest, and look on the day that lieth hopeful before them with all its deeds to be.

So they grew merry, and they led the carline into the Hall with them, and set her down in the Women's-Chamber, and washed her feet, and gave her meat and drink, and bade her rest and think of nothing troublous, and in all wise made her good cheer; and she was merry with them, and praised their fairness and their deftness, and asked them many questions about their weaving and spinning and carding; (howbeit the looms were idle as then because it was midsummer, and the men gone to the war). And this they deemed strange, as it seemed to them that all women should know of such things; but they thought it was a token that she came from far away.

But afterwards she sat among them, and told them pleasant tales of past times and far countries, and was blithe to them and they to her and the time wore on toward nightfall in the Women's-Chamber.

11. THE HALL-SUN SPEAKETH

But for the Hall-Sun; she sat long on that stone by the Women's-door; but when the evening was now come, she arose and went down through the cornfields and into the meadow, and wandered away as her feet took her.

Night was falling by then she reached that pool of Mirk-wood-water, whose eddies she knew so well. There she let the water cover her in the deep stream, and she floated down and sported with the ripples where the river left that deep to race over the shallows; and the moon was casting shadows by then she came up the bank again by the shallow end bearing in her arms a bundle of the blue-flowering mouse-ear. Then she clad herself at once, and went straight as one with a set purpose toward the Great Roof, and entered by the Man's-door; and there were few men within and they but old and heavy with the burden of years and the coming of night-tide; but they wondered and looked to each other and nodded their heads as she passed them by, as men who would say, There is something toward.

So she went to her sleeping-place, and did on fresh raiment, and came forth presently clad in white and shod with gold and having her hair wreathed about with the herb of wonder, the blue-flowering mouse-ear of Mirkwood-water. Thus she passed through the Hall, and those elders were stirred in their hearts when they beheld her beauty. But she opened the door of the Women's-Chamber, and stood on the threshold; and lo, there sat the carline amidst a ring of the Wolfing women, and she telling them tales of old time such as they had not yet heard; and her eyes were glittering, and the sweet words were flowing from her mouth; but she sat straight up like a young woman; and at whiles it seemed to those who hearkened, that she was no old and outworn woman, but fair and strong, and of much avail. But when she heard the Hall-Sun she turned and saw her on the threshold, and her speech fell suddenly, and all that might and briskness faded from her, and she fixed her eyes on the Hall-Sun and looked wistfully and anxiously on her.

Then spake the Hall-Sun standing in the doorway:

Hear ye a matter, maidens, and ye Wolfing women all,
And thou alien guest of the Wolfings! But come ye up the hall,
That the ancient men may hearken: for methinks I have a word
Of the battle of the Kindreds, and the harvest of the sword.

Then all arose up with great joy, for they knew that the tidings were good, when they looked on the face of the Hall-Sun and beheld the pride of her beauty unmarred by doubt or pain.

She led them forth to the dais, and there were the sick and the elders gathered and some ancient men of the thralls: so she stepped lightly up to her place, and stood under her namesake, the wondrous lamp of ancient days. And thus she spake:

On my soul there lies no burden, and no tangle of the fight
In plain or dale or wild-wood enmeshes now my sight.
I see the Markmen's Wain-burg, and I see their warriors go
As men who wait for battle and the coming of the foe.
And they pass 'twixt the wood and the Wain-burg within earshot of
*   the horn,*
But over the windy meadows no sound thereof is borne,
And all is well amongst them. To the burg I draw anigh
And I see all battle-banners in the breeze of morning fly,
But no Wolfings round their banner and no warrior of the Shield,
No Geiring and no Hrossing in the burg or on the field.

She held her peace for a little while, and no one dared to speak; then she lifted up her head and spake:

Now I go by the lip of the wild-wood and a sound withal I hear,
As of men in the paths of the thicket, and a many drawing anear.
Then, muffled yet by the tree-boles, I hear the Shielding song,
And warriors blithe and merry with the battle of the strong.
Give back a little, Markmen, make way for men to pass
To your ordered battle-dwelling o'er the trodden meadow-grass,
For alive with men is the wild-wood and shineth with the steel,
And hath a voice most merry to tell of the Kindreds' weal
'Twixt each tree a warrior standeth come back from the spear-strewn
*   way,*

And forth they come from the wild-wood and a little band are they.

Then again was she silent; but her head sank not, as of one thinking, as before it did, but she looked straight forward with bright eyes and smiling, as she said:

Lo, now the guests they are bringing that ye have not seen before;
Yet guests but ill-entreated; for they lack their shields of war,
No spear in the hand they carry and with no sax are girt.
Lo, these are the dreaded foemen, these once so strong to hurt;
The men that all folk fled from, the swift to drive the spoil,
The men that fashioned nothing but the trap to make men toil.
They drew the sword in the cities, they came and struck the stroke
And smote the shield of the Markmen, and point and edge they broke.
They drew the sword in the war-garth, they swore to bring aback
God's gifts from the Markmen houses where the tables never lack.
O Markmen, take the God-gifts that came on their own feet
O'er the hills through the Mirkwood thicket the Stone of Tyr to meet!

Again she stayed her song, which had been loud and joyous, and they who heard her knew that the Kindreds had gained the day, and whilst the Hall-Sun was silent they fell to talking of this fair day of battle and the taking of captives. But presently she spread out her hands again and they held their peace, and she said:

I see, O Wolfing women, and many a thing I see,
But not all things, O elders, this eve shall ye learn of me,
For another mouth there cometh: the thicket I behold
And the Sons of Tyr amidst it, and I see the oak-trees old,
And the war-shout ringing round them; and I see the battle-lord
Unhelmed amidst of the mighty; and I see his leaping sword;
Strokes struck and warriors falling, and the streaks of spears I see,
But hereof shall the other tell you who speaketh after me.
For none other than the Shieldings from out the wood have come,
And they shift the turn with the Daylings to drive the folk-spear home,
And to follow with the Wolfings and thrust the war-beast forth.
And so good men deem the tidings that they bid them journey north
On the feet of a Shielding runner, that Gisli hath to name;
And west of the water he wendeth by the way that the Wolfings came;
Now for sleep he tarries never, and no meat is in his mouth
Till the first of the Houses hearkeneth the tidings of the south;
Lo, he speaks, and the mead-sea sippeth, and the bread by the way doth eat,
And over the Geiring threshold and outward pass his feet;
And he breasts the Burg of the Daylings and saith his happy word,
And stayeth to drink for a minute of the waves of Battle-ford.
Lone then by the stream he runneth, and wendeth the wild-wood road,
And dasheth through the hazels of the Oselings' fair abode,
And the Elking women know it, and their hearts are glad once more,
And ye—yea, hearken, Wolfings, for his feet are at the door.

12. TIDINGS OF THE BATTLE IN MIRKWOOD

As the Hall-Sun made an end they heard in good sooth the feet of the runner on the hard ground without the hall, and presently the door opened and he came leaping over the threshold, and up to the table, and stood leaning on it with one hand, his breast heaving with his last swift run. Then he spake presently:

"I am Gisli of the Shieldings: Otter sendeth me to the Hall-Sun; but on the way I was to tell tidings to the Houses west of the Water: so have I done. Now is my journey ended; for Otter saith: 'Let the Hall-Sun note the tidings and send word of them by four of the lightest limbed of the women, or by lads a-horseback, both west and east of the Water; let her send the word as it seemeth to her, whether she hath seen it or not. I will drink a short draught since my running is over."

Then a damsel brought him a horn of mead and let it come into his hand, and he drank sighing with pleasure, while the damsel for pleasure of him and his tidings laid her hand on his shoulder. Then he set down the horn and spake:

"We, the Shieldings, with the Geirings, the Hrossings, and the Wolfings, three hundred warriors and more, were led into the Wood by Thiodolf the War-duke, beside whom went Fox, who hath seen the Romans. We were all afoot; for there is no wide way through the Wood, nor would we have it otherwise, lest the foe find the thicket easy. But many of us know the thicket and its ways; so we made not the easy hard. I was near the War-duke, for I know the thicket and am light-foot: I am a bowman. I saw Thiodolf that he was unhelmed and bore no shield, nor had he any coat of fence; nought but a deer-skin frock."

As he said that word, the carline, who had drawn very near to him and was looking hard at his face, turned and looked on the Hall-Sun and stared at her till she reddened under those keen eyes: for in her heart began to gather some knowledge of the tale of her mother and what her will was.

But Gisli went on: "Yet by his side was his mighty sword, and we all knew it for Throng-plough, and were glad of it and of him and the unfenced breast of the dauntless. Six hours we went spreading wide through the thicket, not always seeing one another, but knowing one another to be nigh; those that knew the thicket best led, the others followed on. So we went till it was high noon on the plain and glimmering dusk in the thicket, and we saw nought, save here and there a roe, and here and there a sounder of swine, and coneys where it was opener, and the sun shone and the grass grew for a little space. So came we unto where the thicket ended suddenly, and there was a long glade of the wild-wood, all set about with great oak-trees and grass thereunder, which I knew well; and thereof the tale tells that it was a holy place of the folk who abided in these parts before the Sons of the Goths. Now will I drink."

So he drank of the horn and said: "It seemeth that Fox had a deeming of the way the Romans should come; so now we abided in the thicket without that glade and lay quiet and hidden, spreading ourselves as much about that lawn of the oak-trees as we might, the while Fox and three others crept through the wood to espy what might be toward: not long had they been gone ere we heard a war-horn blow, and it was none of our horns: it was a long way off, but we looked to our weapons: for men are eager for the foe and the death that cometh, when they lie hidden in the thicket. A while passed, and again we heard the horn, and it was nigher and had a marvellous voice; then in a while was a little noise of men, not their voices, but footsteps going warily through the brake to the south, and twelve men came slowly and warily into that oak-lawn, and lo, one of them was Fox; but he was clad in the raiment of the dastard of the Goths whom he had slain. I tell you my heart beat, for I saw that the others were Roman men, and one of them seemed to be a man of authority, and he held Fox by the shoulder, and pointed to the thicket where we lay, and something he said to him, as we saw by his gesture and face, but his voice we heard not, for he spake soft.

"Then of those ten men of his he sent back two, and Fox going between them, as though he should be slain if he misled them; and he and the eight abided there wisely and warily, standing silently some six feet from each other, moving scarce at all, but looking like images fashioned of brown copper and iron; holding their casting-spears (which be marvellous heavy weapons) and girt with the sax.

"As they stood there, not out of earshot of a man speaking in his wonted voice, our War-duke made a sign to those about him, and we spread very quietly to the right hand and the left of him once more, and we drew as close as might be to the thicket's edge, and those who had bows the nighest thereto. Thus then we abided a while again; and again came the horn's voice; for belike they had no mind to come their ways covertly because of their pride.

"Soon therewithal comes Fox creeping back to us, and I saw him whisper into the ear of the War-duke, but heard not the word he said. I saw that he had hanging to him two Roman saxes, so I deemed he had slain those two, and so escaped the Romans. Maidens, it were well that ye gave me to drink again, for I am weary and my journey is done."

So again they brought him the horn, and made much of him; and he drank, and then spake on.

"Now heard we the horn's voice again quite close, and it was sharp and shrill, and nothing like to the roar of our battle-horns: still was the wood and no wind abroad, not even down the oak-lawn; and we heard now the tramp of many men as they thrashed through the small wood and bracken of the thicket-way; and those eight men and their leader came forward, moving like one, close up to the thicket where I lay, just where the path passed into the thicket beset by the Sons of the Goths: so near they were that I could see the dints upon their armour, and the strands of the wire on their sax-handles. Down then bowed the tall bracken on the further side of the wood-lawn, the thicket crashed before the march of men, and on they strode into the lawn, a goodly band, wary, alert, and silent of cries.

"But when they came into the lawn they spread out somewhat to their left hands, that is to say on the west side, for that way was the clear glade; but on the east the thicket came close up to them and edged them away. Therein lay the Goths.

"There they stayed awhile, and spread out but a little, as men marching, not as men fighting. A while we let them be; and we saw their captain, no big man, but dight with very fair armour and weapons; and there drew up to him certain Goths armed, the dastards of the folk, and another unarmed, an old man bound and bleeding. With these Goths had the captain some converse, and presently he cried out two or three words of Welsh in a loud voice, and the nine men who were ahead shifted them somewhat away from us to lead down the glade westward.

"The prey had come into the net, but they had turned their faces toward the mouth of it.

"Then turned Thiodolf swiftly to the man behind him who carried the war-horn, and every man handled his weapons: but that man understood, and set the little end to his mouth, and loud roared the horn of the Markmen, and neither friend nor foe misdoubted the tale thereof. Then leaped every man to his feet, all bow-strings twanged and the cast-spears flew; no man forebore to shout; each as he might leapt out of the thicket and fell on with sword and axe and spear, for it was from the bow-men but one shaft and no more.

"Then might you have seen Thiodolf as he bounded forward like the wild-cat on the hare, how he had no eyes for any save the Roman captain. Foemen enough he had round about him after the two first bounds from the thicket; for the Romans were doing their best to spread, that they might handle those heavy cast-spears, though they might scarce do it, just come out of the thicket as they were, and thrust together by that onslaught of the kindreds falling on from two sides and even somewhat from behind. To right and left flashed Throng-plough, while Thiodolf himself scarce seemed to guide it: men fell before him at once, and close at his heels poured the Wolfing kindred into the gap, and in a minute of time was he amidst of the throng and face to face with the gold-dight captain.

"What with the sweep of Throng-plough and the Wolfing onrush, there was space about him for a great stroke; he gave a side-long stroke to his right and hewed down a tall Burgundian, and then up sprang the white blade, but ere its edge fell he turned his wrist, and drove the point through that Captain's throat just above the ending of his hauberk, so that he fell dead amidst of his folk.

"All the four kindreds were on them now, and amidst them, and needs must they give way: but stoutly they fought; for surely no other warriors might have withstood that onslaught of the Markmen for the twinkling of an eye: but had the Romans had but the space to have spread themselves out there, so as to handle their shot-weapons, many a woman's son of us had fallen; for no man shielded himself in his eagerness, but let the swiftness of the Onset of point-and-edge shield him; which, sooth to say, is often a good shield, as here was found.

"So those that were unslain and unhurt fled west along the glade, but not as dastards, and had not Thiodolf followed hard in the chase according to his wont, they might even yet have made a fresh stand and spread from oak-tree to oak-tree across the glade: but as it befel, they might not get a fair offing so as to disentangle themselves and array themselves in good order side by side; and whereas the Markmen were fleet of foot, and in the woods they knew, there were a many aliens slain in the chase or taken alive unhurt or little hurt: but the rest fled this way and that way into the thicket, with whom were some of the Burgundians; so there they abide now as outcasts and men unholy, to be slain as wild-beasts one by one as we meet them.

"Such then was the battle in Mirkwood. Give me the mead-horn that I may drink to the living and the dead, and the memory of the dead, and the deeds of the living that are to be."

So they brought him the horn, and he waved it over his head and drank again and spake:

"Sixty and three dead men of the Romans we counted there up and down that oak-glade; and we cast earth over them; and three dead dastards of the Goths, and we left them for the wolves to deal with. And twenty-five men of the Romans we took alive to be for hostages if need should be, and these did we Shielding men, who are not very many, bring aback to the Wain-burg; and the Daylings, who are a great company, were appointed to enter the wood and be with Thiodolf; and me did Otter bid to bear the tidings, even as I have told you. And I have not loitered by the way."

Great then was the joy in the Hall; and they took Gisli, and made much of him, and led him to the bath, and clad him in fine raiment taken from the coffer which was but seldom opened, because the cloths it held were precious; and they set a garland of green wheat-ears on his head. Then they fell to and spread the feast in the hall; and they ate and drank and were merry.

But as for speeding the tidings, the Hall-Sun sent two women and two lads, all a-horseback, to bear the words: the women to remember the words which she taught them carefully, the lads to be handy with the horses, or in the ford, or the swimming of the deeps, or in the thicket. So they went their ways, down the water: one pair went on the western side, and the other crossed Mirkwood-water at the shallows (for being Midsummer the water was but small), and went along the east side, so that all the kindred might know of the tidings and rejoice.

Great was the glee in the Hall, though the warriors of the House were away, and many a song and lay they sang: but amidst the first of the singing they bethought them of the old woman, and would have bidden her tell them some tale of times past, since she was so wise in the ancient lore. But when they sought for her on all sides she was not to be found, nor could anyone remember seeing her depart from the Hall. But this had they no call to heed, and the feast ended, as it began, in great glee.

Albeit the Hall-Sun was troubled about the carline, both that she had come, and that she had gone: and she determined that the next time she met her she would strive to have of her a true tale of what she was, and of all that was toward.

13. THE HALL-SUN SAITH ANOTHER WORD

It was no later than the next night, and a many of what thralls were not with the host were about in the feast-hall with the elders and lads and weaklings of the House; for last night's tidings had drawn them thither. Gisli had gone back to his kindred and the Wain-burg in the Upper-mark, and the women were sitting, most of them, in the Women's-Chamber, some of them doing what little summer work needed doing about the looms, but more resting from their work in field and acre.

Then came the Hall-Sun forth from her room clad in glittering raiment, and summoned no one, but went straight to her place on the dais under her namesake the Lamp, and stood there a little without speaking. Her face was pale now, her lips a little open, her eyes set and staring as if they saw nothing of all that was round about her.

Now went the word through the Hall and the Women's-Chamber that the Hall-Sun would speak again, and that great tidings were toward; so all folk came flock-meal to the dais, both thralls and free; and scarce were all gathered there, ere the Hall-Sun began speaking, and said:

The days of the world thrust onward, and men are born therein
A many and a many, and divers deeds they win
In the fashioning of stories for the kindreds of the earth,
A garland interwoven of sorrow and of mirth.
To the world a warrior cometh; from the world he passeth away,
And no man then may sunder his good from his evil day.
By the Gods hath he been tormented, and been smitten by the foe:
He hath seen his maiden perish, he hath seen his speech-friend go:
His heart hath conceived a joyance and hath brought it unto birth:
But he hath not carried with him his sorrow or his mirth.
He hath lived, and his life hath fashioned the outcome of the deed,
For the blossom of the people, and the coming kindreds' seed.

Thus-wise the world is fashioned, and the new sun of the morn
Where earth last night was desert beholds a kindred born,
That to-morrow and to-morrow blossoms all gloriously
With many a man and maiden for the kindreds yet to be,
And fair the Goth-folk groweth. And yet the story saith
That the deeds that make the summer make too the winter's death,
That summer-tides unceasing from out the grave may grow
And the spring rise up unblemished from the bosom of the snow.

Thus as to every kindred the day comes once for all
When yesterday it was not, and to-day it builds the hall,
So every kindred bideth the night-tide of the day,
Whereof it knoweth nothing, e'en when noon is past away.
E'en thus the House of the Wolfings 'twixt dusk and dark doth stand,
And narrow is the pathway with the deep on either hand.
On the left are the days forgotten, on the right the days to come,
And another folk and their story in the stead of the Wolfing home.
Do the shadows darken about it, is the even here at last?
Or is this but a storm of the noon-tide that the wind is driving past?

Unscathed as yet it standeth; it bears the stormy drift,
Nor bows to the lightening flashing adown from the cloudy lift.

I see the hail of battle and the onslaught of the strong,
And they go adown to the folk-mote that shall bide there over long.
I see the slain-heaps rising and the alien folk prevail,
And the Goths give back before them on the ridge o'er the treeless vale.
I see the ancient fallen, and the young man smitten dead,
And yet I see the War-duke shake Throng-plough o'er his head,
And stand unhelmed, unbyrnied before the alien host,
And the hurt men rise around him to win back battle lost;
And the wood yield up her warriors, and the whole host rushing on,
And the swaying lines of battle until the lost is won.
Then forth goes the cry of triumph, as they ring the captives round
And cheat the crow of her portion and heap the warriors' mound.
There are faces gone from our feast-hall not the least beloved nor worst,
But the wane of the House of the Wolfings not yet the world hath cursed.
The sun shall rise to-morrow on our cold and dewy roof,
For they that longed for slaughter were slaughtered far aloof.

She ceased for a little, but her countenance, which had not changed during her song, changed not at all now: so they all kept silence although they were rejoicing in this new tale of victory; for they deemed that she was not yet at the end of her speaking. And in good sooth she spake again presently, and said:

I wot not what hath befallen nor where my soul may be,
For confusion is within me and but dimly do I see,
As if the thing that I look on had happed a while ago.
They stand by the tofts of a war-garth, a captain of the foe,
And a man that is of the Goth-folk, and as friend and friend they speak,
But I hear no word they are saying, though for every word I seek,
And now the mist flows round me and blind I come aback
To the House-roof of the Wolfings and the hearth that hath no lack.

Her voice grew weaker as she spake the last words, and she sank backward on to her chair: her clenched hands opened, the lids fell down over her bright eyes, her breast heaved no more as it had done, and presently she fell asleep.

The folk were doubtful and somewhat heavy-hearted because of those last words of hers; but they would not ask her more, or rouse her from her sleep, lest they should grieve her; so they departed to their beds and slept for what was yet left of the night.

14. THE HALL-SUN IS CAREFUL CONCERNING THE PASSES OF THE WOOD

In the morning early folk arose; and the lads and women who were not of the night-shift got them ready to go to the mead and the acres; for the sunshine had been plenty these last days and the wheat was done blossoming, and all must be got ready for harvest. So they broke their fast, and got their tools into their hands: but they were somewhat heavy-hearted because of those last words of the Hall-Sun, and the doubt of last night still hung about them, and they were scarcely as merry as men are wont to be in the morning.

As for the Hall-Sun, she was afoot with the earliest, and was no less, but mayhap more merry than her wont was, and was blithe with all, both old and young.

But as they were at the point of going she called to them, and said:

"Tarry a little, come ye all to the dais and hearken to me."

So they all gathered thereto, and she stood in her place and spake.

"Women and elders of the Wolfings, is it so that I spake somewhat of tidings last night?"

"Yea," said they all.

She said, "And was it a word of victory?"

They answered "yea" again.

"Good is that," she said; "doubt ye not! there is nought to unsay. But hearken! I am nothing wise in war like Thiodolf or Otter of the Laxings, or as Heriulf the Ancient was, though he was nought so wise as they be. Nevertheless ye shall do well to take me for your captain, while this House is bare of warriors."

"Yea, yea," they said, "so will we."

And an old warrior, hight Sorli, who sat in his chair, no longer quite way-worthy, said:

"Hall-Sun, this we looked for of thee; since thy wisdom is not wholly the wisdom of a spae-wife, but rather is of the children of warriors: and we know thine heart to be high and proud, and that thy death seemeth to thee a small matter beside the life of the Wolfing House."

Then she smiled and said, "Will ye all do my bidding?"

And they all cried out heartily, "Yea, Hall-Sun, that will we."

She said: "Hearken then; ye all know that east of Mirkwood-water, when ye come to the tofts of the Bearings, and their Great Roof, the thicket behind them is close, but that there is a wide way cut through it; and often have I gone there: if ye go by that way, in a while ye come to the thicket's end and to bare places where the rocks crop up through the gravel and the woodland loam. There breed the coneys without number; and wild-cats haunt the place for that sake, and foxes; and the wood-wolf walketh there in summer-tide, and hard by the she-wolf hath her litter of whelps, and all these have enough; and the bald-head erne hangeth over it and the kite, and also the kestril, for shrews and mice abound there. Of these things there is none that feareth me, and none that maketh me afraid. Beyond this place for a long way the wood is nowise thick, for first grow ash-trees about the clefts of the rock and also quicken-trees, but not many of either; and here and there a hazel brake easy to thrust through; then comes a space of oak-trees scattered about the lovely wood-lawn, and then at last the beech-wood close above but clear beneath. This I know well, because I myself have gone so far and further; and by this easy way have I gone so far to the south, that I have come out into the fell country, and seen afar off the snowy mountains beyond the Great Water.

"Now fear ye not, but pluck up a heart! For either I have seen it or dreamed it, or thought it, that by this road easy to wend the Romans should come into the Mark. For shall not those dastards and traitors that wear the raiment and bodies of the Goths over the hearts and the lives of foemen, tell them hereof? And will they not have heard of our Thiodolf, and this my holy namesake?

"Will they not therefore be saying to themselves, 'Go to now, why should we wrench the hinges off the door with plenteous labour, when another door to the same chamber standeth open before us? This House of the Wolfings is the door to the treasure chamber of the Markmen; let us fall on that at once rather than have many battles for other lesser matters, and then at last have to fight for this also: for having this we have all, and they shall be our thralls, and we may slaughter what we will, and torment what we will and deflower what we will, and make our souls glad with their grief and anguish, and take aback with us to the cities what we will of the thralls, that their anguish and our joy may endure the longer.' Thus will they say: therefore is it my rede that the strongest and hardiest of you women take horse, a ten of you and one to lead besides, and ride the shallows to the Bearing House, and tell them of our rede; which is to watch diligently the ways of the wood; the outgate to the Mark, and the places where the wood is thin and easy to travel on: and ye shall bid them give you of their folk as many as they deem fittest thereto to join your company, so that ye may have a chain of watchers stretching far into the wilds; but two shall lie without the wood, their horses ready for them to leap on and ride on the spur to the Wain-burg in the Upper-mark if any tidings befal.

"Now of these eleven I ordain Hrosshild to be the leader and captain, and to choose for her fellows the stoutest-limbed and heaviest-handed of all the maidens here: art thou content Hrosshild?"

Then stood Hrosshild forth and said nought, but nodded yea; and soon was her choice made amid jests and laughter, for this seemed no hard matter to them.

So the ten got together, and the others fell off from them, and there stood the ten maidens with Hrosshild, well nigh as strong as men, clean-limbed and tall, tanned with sun and wind; for all these were unwearied afield, and oft would lie out a-nights, since they loved the lark's song better than the mouse's squeak; but as their kirtles shifted at neck and wrist, you might see their skins as white as privet-flower where they were wont to be covered.

Then said the Hall-Sun: "Ye have heard the word, see ye to it, Hrosshild, and take this other word also: Bid the Bearing stay-at-homes bide not the sword and the torch at home if the Romans come, but hie them over hither, to hold the Hall or live in the wild-wood with us, as need may be; for might bides with many.

"But ye maidens, take this counsel for yourselves; do ye each bear with you a little keen knife, and if ye be taken, and it seem to you that ye may not bear the smart of the Roman torments (for they be wise in tormenting), but will speak and bewray us under them, then thrust this little edge tool into the place of your bodies where the life lieth closest, and so go to the Gods with a good tale in your mouths: so may the Almighty God of Earth speed you, and the fathers of the kindred!"

So she spoke; and they made no delay but each one took what axe or spear or sword she liked best, and two had their bows and quivers of arrows; and so all folk went forth from the Hall.

Soon were the horses saddled and bridled, and the maidens bestrode them joyously and set forth on their way, going down the lanes of the wheat, and rode down speedily toward the shallows of the water, and all cried good speed after them. But the others would turn to their day's work, and would go about their divers errands. But even as they were at point to sunder, they saw a swift runner passing by those maidens just where the acres joined the meadow, and he waved his hand aloft and shouted to them, but stayed not his running for them, but came up the lanes of the wheat at his swiftest: so they knew at once that this was again a messenger from the host, and they stood together and awaited his coming; and as he drew near they knew him for Egil, the swiftest-footed of the Wolfings; and he gave a great shout as he came among them; and he was dusty and wayworn, but eager; and they received him with all love, and would have brought him to the Hall to wash him and give him meat and drink, and cherish him in all ways.

But he cried out, "To the Speech-Hill first, to the Speech-Hill first! But even before that, one word to thee, Hall-Sun! Saith Thiodolf, Send ye watchers to look to the entrance into Mid-mark, which is by the Bearing dwelling; and if aught untoward befalleth let one ride on the spur with the tidings to the Wain-burg. For by that way also may peril come."

Then smiled some of the bystanders, and the Hall-Sun said: "Good is it when the thought of a friend stirreth betimes in one's own breast. The thing is done, Egil; or sawest thou not those ten women, and Hrosshild the eleventh, as thou camest up into the acres?"

Said Egil; "Fair fall thine hand, Hall-Sun! thou art the Wolfings' Ransom. Wend we now to the Speech-Hill."

So did they, and every thrall that was about the dwellings, man, woman, and child fared with them, and stood about the Speech-Hill: and the dogs went round about the edge of that assembly, wandering in and out, and sometimes looking hard on some one whom they knew best, if he cried out aloud.

But the men-folk gave all their ears to hearkening, and stood as close as they might.

Then Egil clomb the Speech-Hill, and said.

15. THEY HEAR TELL OF THE BATTLE ON THE RIDGE

"Ye have heard how the Daylings were appointed to go to help Thiodolf in driving the folk-spear home to the heart of the Roman host. So they went; but six hours thereafter comes one to Otter bidding him send a great part of the kindreds to him; for that he had had tidings that a great host of Romans were drawing near the wood-edge, but were not entered therein, and that fain would he meet them in the open field.

"So the kindreds drew lots, and the lot fell first to the Elkings, who are a great company, as ye know; and then to the Hartings, the Beamings, the Alftings, the Vallings (also a great company), the Galtings, (and they no lesser) each in their turn; and last of all to the Laxings; and the Oselings prayed to go with the Elkings, and this Otter deemed good, whereas a many of them be bowmen.

"All these then to the number of a thousand or more entered the wood; and I was with them, for in sooth I was the messenger.

"No delay made we in the wood, nor went we over warily, trusting to the warding of the wood by Thiodolf; and there were men with us who knew the paths well, whereof I was one; so we speedily came through into the open country.

"Shortly we came upon our folk and the War-duke lying at the foot of a little hill that went up as a buttress to a long ridge high above us, whereon we set a watch; and a little brook came down the dale for our drink.

"Night fell as we came thither; so we slept for a while, but abode not the morning, and we were afoot (for we had no horses with us) before the moon grew white. We took the road in good order, albeit our folk-banners we had left behind in the burg; so each kindred raised aloft a shield of its token to be for a banner. So we went forth, and some swift footmen, with Fox, who hath seen the Roman war-garth, had been sent on before to spy out the ways of the foemen.

"Two hours after sunrise cometh one of these, and telleth how he hath seen the Romans, and how that they are but a short mile hence breaking their fast, not looking for any onslaught; 'but,' saith he, 'they are on a high ridge whence they can see wide about, and be in no danger of ambush, because the place is bare for the most part, nor is there any cover except here and there down in the dales a few hazels and blackthorn bushes, and the rushes of the becks in the marshy bottoms, wherein a snipe may hide, or a hare, but scarce a man; and note that there is no way up to that ridge but by a spur thereof as bare as my hand; so ye will be well seen as ye wend up thereto.'

"So spake he in my hearing. But Thiodolf bade him lead on to that spur, and old Heriulf, who was standing nigh, laughed merrily and said: 'Yea, lead on, and speedily, lest the day wane and nothing done save the hunting of snipes.'

"So on we went, and coming to the hither side of that spur beheld those others and Fox with them; and he held in his hand an arrow of the aliens, and his face was all astir with half-hidden laughter, and he breathed hard, and pointed to the ridge, and somewhat low down on it we saw a steel cap and three spear-heads showing white from out a little hollow in its side, but the men hidden by the hollow: so we knew that Fox had been chased, and that the Romans were warned and wary.

"No delay made the War-duke, but led us up that spur, which was somewhat steep; and as we rose higher we saw a band of men on the ridge, a little way down it, not a many; archers and slingers mostly, who abode us till we were within shot, and then sent a few shots at us, and so fled. But two men were hurt with the sling-plummets, and one, and he not grievously, with an arrow, and not one slain.

"Thus we came up on to the ridge, so that there was nothing between us and the bare heavens; thence we looked south-east and saw the Romans wisely posted on the ridge not far from where it fell down steeply to the north; but on the south, that is to say on their left hands, and all along the ridge past where we were stayed, the ground sloped gently to the south-west for a good way, before it fell, somewhat steeply, into another long dale. Looking north we saw the outer edge of Mirkwood but a little way from us, and we were glad thereof; because ere we left our sleeping-place that morn Thiodolf had sent to Otter another messenger bidding him send yet more men on to us in case we should be hard-pressed in the battle; for he had had a late rumour that the Romans were many. And now when he had looked on the Roman array and noted how wise it was, he sent three swift-foot ones to take stand on a high knoll which we had passed on the way, that they might take heed where our folk came out from the wood and give signal to them by the horn, and lead them to where the battle should be.

"So we stood awhile and breathed us, and handled our weapons some half a furlong from the alien host. They had no earth rampart around them, for that ridge is waterless, and they could not abide there long, but they had pitched sharp pales in front of them and they stood in very good order, as if abiding an onslaught, and moved not when they saw us; for that band of shooters had joined themselves to them already. Taken one with another we deemed them to be more than we were; but their hauberked footmen with the heavy cast-spears not so many as we by a good deal.

"Now we were of mind to fall on them ere they should fall on us; so all such of us as had shot-weapons spread out from our company and went forth a little; and of the others Heriulf stood foremost along with the leaders of the Beamings and the Elkings; but as yet Thiodolf held aback and led the midmost company, as his wont was, and the more part of the Wolfings were with him.

"Thus we ordered ourselves, and awaited a little while yet what the aliens should do; and presently a war-horn blew amongst them, and from each flank of their mailed footmen came forth a many bowmen and slingers and a band of horsemen; and drew within bowshot, the shooters in open array yet wisely, and so fell to on us, and the horsemen hung aback a little as yet.

"Their arrow-shot was of little avail, their bowmen fell fast before ours; but deadly was their sling-shot, and hurt and slew many and some even in our main battle; for they slung round leaden balls and not stones, and they aimed true and shot quick; and the men withal were so light and lithe, never still, but crouching and creeping and bounding here and there, that they were no easier to hit than coneys amidst of the fern, unless they were very nigh.

"Howbeit when this storm had endured a while, and we moved but little, and not an inch aback, and gave them shot for shot, then was another horn winded from amongst the aliens; and thereat the bowmen cast down their bows, and the slingers wound their slings about their heads, and they all came on with swords and short spears and feathered darts, running and leaping lustily, making for our flanks, and the horsemen set spurs to their horses and fell on in the very front of our folk like good and valiant men-at-arms.

"That saw Heriulf and his men, and they set up the war-whoop, and ran forth to meet them, axe and sword aloft, terribly yet maybe somewhat unwarily. The archers and slingers never came within sword-stroke of them, but fell away before them on all sides; but the slingers fled not far, but began again with their shot, and slew a many. Then was a horn winded, as if to call back the horsemen, who, if they heard, heeded not, but rode hard on our kindred like valiant warriors who feared not death. Sooth to say, neither were the horses big or good, nor the men fit for the work, saving for their hardihood; and their spears were short withal and their bucklers unhandy to wield.

"Now could it be seen how the Goths gave way before them to let them into the trap, and then closed around again, and the axes and edge weapons went awork hewing as in a wood; and Heriulf towered over all the press, and the Wolf's-sister flashed over his head in the summer morning.

"Soon was that storm over, and we saw the Goths tossing up their spears over the slain, and horses running loose and masterless adown over the westward-lying slopes, and a few with their riders still clinging to them. Yet some, sore hurt by seeming, galloping toward the main battle of the Romans.

"Unwarily then fared the children of Tyr that were with Heriulf; for by this time they were well nigh within shot of the spears of those mighty footmen of the Romans: and on their flanks were the slingers, and the bowmen, who had now gotten their bows again; and our bowmen, though they shot well and strong, were too few to quell them; and indeed some of them had cast by their bows to join in Heriulf's storm. Also the lie of the ground was against us, for it sloped up toward the Roman array at first very gently, but afterwards steeply enough to breathe a short-winded man. Also behind them were we of the other kindreds, whom Thiodolf had ordered into the wedge-array; and we were all ready to move forward, so that had they abided somewhat, all had been well and better.

"So did they not, but straightway set up the Victory-whoop and ran forward on the Roman host. And these were so ordered that, as aforesaid, they had before them sharp piles stuck into the earth and pointed against us, as we found afterwards to our cost; and within these piles stood the men some way apart from each other, so as to handle their casting spears,

and in three ranks were they ordered and many spears could be cast at once, and if any in the front were slain, his fellow behind him took his place.

"So now the storm of war fell at once upon our folk, and swift and fierce as was their onslaught yet were a many slain and hurt or ever they came to the piles aforesaid. Then saw they death before them and heeded it nought, but tore up the piles and dashed through them, and fell in on those valiant footmen. Short is the tale to tell: wheresoever a sword or spear of the Goths was upraised there were three upon him, and saith Toti of the Beamings, who was hurt and crawled away and yet lives, that on Heriulf there were six at first and then more; and he took no thought of shielding himself, but raised up the Wolf's-sister and hewed as the woodman in the thicket, when night cometh and hunger is on him. There fell Heriulf the Ancient and many a man of the Beamings and the Elkings with him, and many a Roman.

"But amidst the slain and the hurt our wedge-array moved forward slowly now, warily shielded against the plummets and shafts on either side; and when the Romans saw our unbroken array, and Thiodolf the first with Throng-plough naked in his hand, they chased not such men of ours unhurt or little hurt, as drew aback from before them: so these we took amongst us, and when we had gotten all we might, and held a grim face to the foe, we drew aback little by little, still facing them till we were out of shot of their spears, though the shot of the arrows and the sling-plummets ceased not wholly from us. Thus ended Heriulf's Storm."

Then he rested from his speaking for a while, and none said aught, but they gazed on him as if he bore with him a picture of the battle, and many of the women wept silently for Heriulf, and yet more of the younger ones were wounded to the heart when they thought of the young men of the Elkings, and the Beamings, since with both those houses they had affinity; and they lamented the loves that they had lost, and would have asked concerning their own speech-friends had they durst. But they held their peace till the tale was told out to an end.

Then Egil spake again:

"No long while had worn by in Heriulf's Storm, and though men's hearts were nothing daunted, but rather angered by what had befallen, yet would Thiodolf wear away the time somewhat more, since he hoped for succour from the Wain-burg and the Wood; and he would not that any of these Romans should escape us, but would give them all to Tyr, and to be a following to Heriulf the Old and the Great.

"So there we abided a while moving nought, and Thiodolf stood with Throng-plough on his shoulder, unhelmed, unbyrnied, as though he trusted to the kindred for all defence. Nor for their part did the Romans dare to leave their vantage-ground, when they beheld what grim countenance we made them.

"Albeit, when we had thrice made as if we would fall on, and yet they moved not, whereas it trieth a man sorely to stand long before the foeman, and do nought but endure, and whereas many of our bowmen were slain or hurt, and the rest too few to make head against the shot-weapons of the aliens, then at last we began to draw nearer and a little nearer, not breaking the wedge-array; and at last, just before we were within shot of the cast-spears of their main battle, loud roared our war-horn: then indeed we broke the wedge-array, but orderly as we knew how, spreading out from right and left of the War-duke till we were facing them in a long line: one minute we abode thus, and then ran forth through the spear-storm: and even therewith we heard, as it were, the echo of our own horn, and whoso had time to think betwixt the first of the storm and the handstrokes of the Romans deemed that now would be coming fresh kindreds for our helping.

"Not long endured the spear-rain, so swift we were, neither were we in one throng as betid in Heriulf's Storm, but spread abroad, each trusting in the other that none thought of the backward way.

"Though we had the ground against us we dashed like fresh men at their pales, and were under the weapons at once. Then was the battle grim; they could not thrust us back, nor did we break their array with our first storm; man hewed at man as if there were no foes in the world but they two: sword met sword, and sax met sax; it was thrusting and hewing with point and edge, and no long-shafted weapons were of any avail; there we fought hand to hand and no man knew by eyesight how the battle went two yards from where he fought, and each one put all his heart in the stroke he was then striking, and thought of nothing else.

"Yet at the last we felt that they were faltering and that our work was easier and our hope higher; then we cried our cries and pressed on harder, and in that very nick of time there arose close behind us the roar of the Markmen's horn and the cries of the kindreds answering ours. Then such of the Romans as were not in the very act of smiting, or thrusting, or clinging or shielding, turned and fled, and the whoop of victory rang around us, and the earth shook, and past the place of the slaughter rushed the riders of the Goths; for they had sent horsemen to us, and the paths were grown easier for our much treading of them. Then I beheld Thiodolf, that he had just slain a foe, and clear was the space around him, and he rushed sideways and caught hold of the stirrup of Angantyr of the Bearings, and ran ten strides beside him, and then bounded on afoot swifter than the red horses of the Bearings, urging on the chase, as his wont was.

"But we who were wearier, when we had done our work, stood still between the living and the dead, between the freemen of the Mark and their war-thralls. And in no long while there came back to us Thiodolf and the chasers, and we made a great ring on the field of the slain, and sang the Song of Triumph; and it was the Wolfing Song that we sang.

"Thus then ended Thiodolf's Storm."

When he held his peace there was but little noise among the stay-at-homes, for still were they thinking about the deaths of their kindred and their lovers. But Egil spoke again.

"Yet within that ring lay the sorrow of our hearts; for Odin had called a many home, and there lay their bodies; and the mightiest was Heriulf; and the Romans had taken him up from where he fell, and cast him down out of the way, but they had not stripped him, and his hand still gripped the Wolf's-sister. His shield was full of shafts of arrows and spears; his byrny was rent in many places, his helm battered out of form. He had been grievously hurt in the side and in the thigh by cast-spears or ever he came to hand-blows with the Romans, but moreover he had three great wounds from the point of the sax, in the throat, in the side, in the belly, each enough for his bane. His face was yet fair to look on, and we deemed that he had died smiling.

"At his feet lay a young man of the Beamings in a gay green coat, and beside him was the head of another of his House, but his green-clad body lay some yards aloof. There lay of the Elkings a many. Well may ye weep, maidens, for them that loved you. Now fare they to the Gods a goodly company, but a goodly company is with them.

"Seventy and seven of the Sons of the Goths lay dead within the Roman battle, and fifty-four on the slope before it; and to boot there were twenty-four of us slain by the arrows and plummets of the shooters, and a many hurt withal.

"But there were no hurt men inside the Roman array or before it. All were slain outright, for the hurt men either dragged themselves back to our folk, or onward to the Roman ranks, that they might die with one more stroke smitten.

"Now of the aliens the dead lay in heaps in that place, for grim was the slaughter when the riders of the Bearings and the Wormings fell on the aliens; and a many of the foemen scorned to flee, but died where they stood, craving no peace; and to few of them was peace given. There fell of the Roman footmen five hundred and eighty and five, and the remnant that fled was but little: but of the slingers and bowmen but eighty and six were slain, for they were there to shoot and not to stand; and they were nimble and fleet of foot, men round of limb, very dark-skinned, but not foul of favour."

Then he said:

There are men through the dusk a-faring, our speech-fiends and our kin,
No more shall they crave our helping, nor ask what work to win;
They have done their deeds and departed when they had holpen the
House,

So high their heads are holden, and their hurts are glorious
With the story of strokes stricken, and new weapons to be met,
And new scowling of foes' faces, and new curses unknown yet.
Lo, they dight the feast in Godhome, and fair are the tables spread,
Late come, but well-beloved is every war-worn head,
And the God-folk and the Fathers, as these cross the tinkling bridge,
Crowd round and crave for stories of the Battle on the Ridge.

Therewith he came down from the Speech-Hill and the women-folk came round about him, and they brought him to the Hall, and washed him, and gave him meat and drink; and then would he sleep, for he was weary.

Howbeit some of the women could not refrain themselves, but must needs ask after their speech-friends who had been in the battle; and he answered as he could, and some he made glad, and some sorry; and as to some, he could not tell them whether their friends were alive or dead. So he went to his place and fell asleep and slept long, while the women went down to acre and meadow, or saw to the baking of bread or the sewing of garments, or went far afield to tend the neat and the sheep.

Howbeit the Hall-Sun went not with them; but she talked with that old warrior, Sorli, who was now halt and grown unmeet for the road, but was a wise man; and she and he together with some old carlines and a few young lads fell to work, and saw to many matters about the Hall and the garth that day; and they got together what weapons there were both for shot and for the hand-play, and laid them where they were handy to come at, and they saw to the meal in the hall that there was provision for many days; and they carried up to a loft above the Women's-Chamber many great vessels of water, lest the fire should take the Hall; and they looked everywhere to the entrances and windows and had fastenings and bolts and bars fashioned and fitted to them; and saw that all things were trim and stout. And so they abided the issue.

16. HOW THE DWARF-WROUGHT HAUBERK WAS BROUGHT AWAY FROM THE HALL OF THE DAYLINGS

Now it must be told that early in the morning, after the night when Gisli had brought to the Wolfing Stead the tidings of the Battle in the Wood, a man came riding from the south to the Dayling abode. It was just before sunrise, and but few folk were stirring about the dwellings. He rode up to the Hall and got off his black horse, and tied it to a ring in the wall by the Man's-door, and went in clashing, for he was in his battle-gear, and had a great wide-rimmed helm on his head.

Folk were but just astir in the Hall, and there came an old woman to him, and looked on him and saw by his attire that he was a man of the Goths and of the Wolfing kindred; so she greeted him kindly: but he said:

"Mother, I am come hither on an errand, and time presses."

Said she: "Yea, my son, or what tidings bearest thou from the south? for by seeming thou art new-come from the host."

Said he: "The tidings are as yesterday, save that Thiodolf will lead the host through the wild-wood to look for the Romans beyond it: therefore will there soon be battle again. See ye, Mother, hast thou here one that knoweth this ring of Thiodolf's, if perchance men doubt me when I say that I am sent on my errand by him?"

"Yea," she said, "Agni will know it; since he knoweth all the chief men of the Mark; but what is thine errand, and what is thy name?"

"It is soon told," said he, "I am a Wolfing hight Thorkettle, and I come to have away for Thiodolf the treasure of the world, the Dwarf-wrought Hauberk, which he left with you when we fared hence to the south three days ago. Now let Agni come, that I may have it, for time presses sorely."

There were three or four gathered about them now, and a maiden of them said: "Shall I bring Agni hither, mother?"

"What needeth it?" said the carline, "he sleepeth, and shall be hard to awaken; and he is old, so let him sleep. I shall go fetch the hauberk, for I know where it is, and my hand may come on it as easily as on mine own girdle."

So she went her ways to the treasury where were the precious things of the kindred; the woven cloths were put away in fair coffers to keep them clean from the whirl of the Hall-dust and the reek; and the vessels of gold and some of silver were standing on the shelves of a cupboard before which hung a veil of needlework: but the weapons and war-gear hung upon pins along the wall, and many of them had much fair work on them, and were dight with gold and gems: but amidst them all was the wondrous hauberk clear to see, dark grey and thin, for it was so wondrously wrought that it hung in small compass. So the carline took it down from the pin, and handled it, and marvelled at it, and said:

"Strange are the hands that have passed over thee, sword-rampart, and in strange places of the earth have they dwelt! For no smith of the kindreds hath fashioned thee, unless he had for his friend either a God or a foe of the Gods. Well shalt thou wot of the tale of sword and spear ere thou comest back hither! For Thiodolf shall bring thee where the work is wild."

Then she went with the hauberk to the new-come warrior, and made no delay, but gave it to him, and said:

"When Agni awaketh, I shall tell him that Thorkettle of the Wolfings hath borne aback to Thiodolf the Treasure of the World, the Dwarf-wrought Hauberk."

Then Thorkettle took it and turned to go; but even therewith came old Asmund from out of his sleeping-place, and gazed around the Hall, and his eyes fell on the shape of the Wolfing as he was going out of the door, and he asked the carline.

"What doeth he here? What tidings is there from the host? For my soul was nought unquiet last night."

"It is a little matter," she said; "the War-duke hath sent for the wondrous Byrny that he left in our treasury when he departed to meet the Romans. Belike there shall be a perilous battle, and few hearts need a stout sword-wall more than Thiodolf's."

As she spoke, Thorkettle had passed the door, and got into his saddle, and sat his black horse like a mighty man as he slowly rode down the turf bridge that led into the plain. And Asmund went to the door and stood watching him till he set spurs to his horse, and departed a great gallop to the south. Then said Asmund:

What then are the Gods devising, what wonders do they will?
What mighty need is on them to work the kindreds ill,
That the seed of the Ancient Fathers and a woman of their kin
With her all unfading beauty must blend herself therein?
Are they fearing lest the kindreds should grow too fair and great,
And climb the stairs of God-home, and fashion all their fate,
And make all earth so merry that it never wax the worse,
Nor need a gift from any, nor prayers to quench the curse?
Fear they that the Folk-wolf, growing as the fire from out the spark,
Into a very folk-god, shall lead the weaponed Mark
From wood to field and mountain, to stand between the earth
And the wrights that forge its thraldom and the sword to slay its
mirth?
Fear they that the sons of the wild-wood the Loathly Folk shall quell,
And grow into Gods thereafter, and aloof in God-home dwell?

Therewith he turned back into the Hall, and was heavy-hearted and dreary of aspect; for he was somewhat foreseeing; and it may not be hidden that this seeming Thorkettle was no warrior of the Wolfings, but the Wood-Sun in his likeness; for she had the power and craft of shape-changing.

17. THE WOOD-SUN SPEAKETH WITH THIODOLF

Now the Markmen laid Heriulf in howe on the ridge-crest where he had fallen, and heaped a mighty howe over him that could be seen from far, and round about him they laid the other warriors of the kindreds. For they deemed it was fittest that they should lie on the place whose story they had fashioned. But they cast earth on the foemen lower down on the west-ward-lying bents.

The sun set amidst their work, and night came on; and Thiodolf was weary and would fain rest him and sleep: but he had many thoughts, and pondered whitherward he should lead the folk, so as to smite the Romans once again, and he had a mind to go apart and be alone for rest and slumber; so he spoke to a man of the kindred named Solvi in whom he put all trust, and then he went down from the ridge, and into a little dale on the southwest side thereof, a furlong from the place of the battle. A beck ran down that dale, and the further end of it was closed by a little wood of yew trees, low, but growing thick together, and great grey stones were scattered up and down on the short grass of the dale. Thiodolf went down to the brook-side, and to a place where it trickled into a pool, whence it ran again in a thin thread down the dale, turning aside before it reached the yew-wood to run its ways under low ledges of rock into a wider dale. He looked at the pool and smiled to himself as if he had thought of something that pleased him; then he drew a broad knife from his side, and fell to cutting up turfs till he had what he wanted; and then he brought stones to the place, and built a dam across the mouth of the pool, and sat by on a great stone to watch it filling.

As he sat he strove to think about the Roman host and how he should deal with it; but despite himself his thoughts wandered, and made for him pictures of his life that should be when this time of battle was over; so that he saw nothing of the troubles that were upon his hands that night, but rather he saw himself partaking in the deeds of the life of man. There he was between the plough-stilts in the acres of the kindred when the west wind was blowing over the promise of early spring; or smiting down the ripe wheat in the hot afternoon amidst the laughter and merry talk of man and maid; or far away over Mirkwood-water watching the edges of the wood against the prowling wolf and lynx, the stars just beginning to shine over his head, as now they were; or wending the windless woods in the first frosts before the snow came, the hunter's bow or jave-lin in hand: or coming back from the wood with the quarry on the sledge across the snow, when winter was deep, through the biting icy wind and the whirl of the drifting snow, to the lights and music of the Great Roof, and the merry talk therein and the smiling of the faces glad to see the hunting-carles come back; and the full draughts of mead, and the sweet rest a night-tide when the north wind was moaning round the ancient home.

All seemed good and fair to him, and whiles he looked around him, and saw the long dale lying on his left hand and the dark yews in its jaws pressing up against the rock-ledges of the brook, and on his right its windings as the ground rose up to the buttresses of the great ridge. The moon was rising over it, and he heard the voice of the brook as it tinkled over the stones above him; and the whistle of the plover and the laugh of the whimbrel came down the dale sharp and clear in the calm evening; and sounding far away, because the great hill muffled them, were the voices of his fellows on the ridge, and the songs of the warriors and the high-pitched cries of the watch. And this also was a part of the sweet life which was, and was to be; and he smiled and was happy and loved the days that were coming, and longed for them, as the young man longs for the feet of his maiden at the try sting-place.

So as he sat there, the dreams wrapping him up from troublous thoughts, at last slumber overtook him, and the great warrior of the Wolfings sat nodding like an old carle in the chimney ingle, and he fell asleep, his dreams going with him, but all changed and turned to folly and emptiness.

He woke with a start in no long time; the night was deep, the wind had fallen utterly, and all sounds were stilled save the voice of the brook, and now and again the cry of the watchers of the Goths. The moon was high and bright, and the little pool beside him glittered with it in all its ripples; for it was full now and trickling over the lip of his dam. So he arose from the stone and did off his war-gear, casting Throng-plough down into the grass beside him, for he had been minded to bathe him, but the slumber was still on him, and he stood musing while the stream grew stronger and pushed off first one of his turfs and then another, and rolled two or three of the stones over, and then softly thrust all away and ran with a gush down the dale, filling all the little bights by the way for a minute or two; he laughed softly thereat, and stayed the undoing of his kirtle, and so laid himself down on the grass beside the stone looking down the dale, and fell at once into a dreamless sleep.

When he awoke again, it was yet night, but the moon was getting lower and the first beginnings of dawn were showing in the sky over the ridge; he lay still a moment gathering his thoughts and striving to remember where he was, as is the wont of men waking from deep sleep; then he leapt to his feet, and lo, he was face to face with a woman, and she who but the Wood-Sun? and he wondered not, but reached out his hand to touch her, though he had not yet wholly cast off the heaviness of slumber or remembered the tidings of yesterday.

She drew aback a little from him, and his eyes cleared of the slumber, and he saw her that she was scantily clad in black raiment, barefoot, with no gold ring on her arms or necklace on her neck, or crown about her head. But she looked so fair and lovely even in that end of the night-tide, that he remembered all her beauty of the day and the sunshine, and he laughed aloud for joy of the sight of her, and said:

"What aileth thee, O Wood-Sun, and is this a new custom of thy kindred and the folk of God-home that their brides array themselves like thralls new-taken, and as women who have lost their kindred and are outcast? Who then hath won the Burg of the Anses, and clomb the rampart of God-home?"

But she spoke from where she stood in a voice so sweet, that it thrilled to the very marrow of his bones.

I have dwelt a while with sorrow since we met, we twain, in the wood:
I have mourned, while thou hast been merry, who deemest the war-play good.
For I know the heart of the wilful and how thou wouldst cast away
The rampart of thy life-days, and the wall of my happy day.
Yea I am the thrall of Sorrow; she hath stripped my raiment off
And laid sore stripes upon me with many a bitter scoff.
Still bidding me remember that I come of the God-folk's kin,
And yet for all my godhead no love of thee may win.

Then she looked longingly at him a while and at last could no longer refrain her, but drew nigh him and took his hands in hers, and kissed his mouth, and said as she caressed him:

O where are thy wounds, beloved? how turned the spear from thy
*   breast,*
When the storm of war blew strongest, and the best men met the best?
Lo, this is the tale of to-day: but what shall to-morrow tell?
That Thiodolf the Mighty in the fight's beginning fell;
That there came a stroke ill-stricken, there came an aimless thrust,
And the life of the people's helper lay quenched in the summer dust.

He answered nothing, but smiled as though the sound of her voice and the touch of her hand were pleasant to him, for so much love there was in her, that her very grief was scarcely grievous. But she said again:

Thou sayest it: I am outcast; for a God that lacketh mirth
Hath no more place in God-home and never a place on earth.
A man grieves, and he gladdens, or he dies and his grief is gone;
But what of the grief of the Gods, and the sorrow never undone?
Yea verily I am the outcast. When first in thine arms I lay
On the blossoms of the woodland my godhead passed away;
Thenceforth unto thee was I looking for the light and the glory of life
And the Gods' doors shut behind me till the day of the uttermost strife.

And now thou hast taken my soul, thou wilt cast it into the night,
And cover thine head with the darkness, and turn thine eyes from the light.
Thou wouldst go to the empty country where never a seed is sown
And never a deed is fashioned, and the place where each is alone;
But I thy thrall shall follow, I shall come where thou seemest to lie,
I shall sit on the howe that hides thee, and thou so dear and nigh!
A few bones white in their war-gear that have no help or thought,
Shall be Thiodolf the Mighty, so nigh, so dear—and nought.

His hands strayed over her shoulders and arms, caressing them, and he said softly and lovingly:

I am Thiodolf the Mighty: but as wise as I may be
No story of that grave-night mine eyes can ever see,
But rather the tale of the Wolfings through the coming days of earth,
And the young men in their triumph and the maidens in their mirth;
And morn's promise every evening, and each day the promised morn,
And I amidst it ever reborn and yet reborn.
This tale I know, who have seen it, who have felt the joy and pain,
Each fleeing, each pursuing, like the links of the draw-well's chain:
But that deedless tide of the grave-mound, and the dayless nightless day,
E'en as I strive to see it, its image wanes away.
What say'st thou of the grave-mound? shall I be there at all
When they lift the Horn of Remembrance, and the shout goes down the hall,
And they drink the Mighty War-duke and Thiodolf the old?
Nay rather; there where the youngling that longeth to be bold
Sits gazing through the hall-reek and sees across the board
A vision of the reaping of the harvest of the sword,
There shall Thiodolf be sitting; e'en there shall the youngling be
That once in the ring of the hazels gave up his life to thee.

She laughed as he ended, and her voice was sweet, but bitter was her laugh. Then she said:

Nay thou shalt be dead, O warrior, thou shalt not see the Hall
Nor the children of thy people 'twixt the dais and the wall.
And I, and I shall be living; still on thee shall waste my thought:
I shall long and lack thy longing; I shall pine for what is nought.

But he smiled again, and said:

Not on earth shall I learn this wisdom; and how shall I learn it then
When I lie alone in the grave-mound, and have no speech with men?
But for thee,—O doubt it nothing that my life shall live in thee,
And so shall we twain be loving in the days that yet shall be.

It was as if she heard him not; and she fell aback from him a little and stood silently for a while as one in deep thought; and then turned and went a few paces from him, and stooped down and came back again with something in her arms (and it was the hauberk once more), and said suddenly:

O Thiodolf, now tell me for what cause thou wouldst not bear
This grey wall of the hammer in the tempest of the spear?
Didst thou doubt my faith, O Folk-wolf, or the counsel of the Gods,
That thou needs must cast thee naked midst the flashing battle-rods,
Or is thy pride so mighty that it seemed to thee indeed
That death was a better guerdon than the love of the God-head's seed?

But Thiodolf said: "O Wood-Sun, this thou hast a right to ask of me, why I have not worn in the battle thy gift, the Treasure of the World, the Dwarf-wrought Hauberk! And what is this that thou sayest? I doubt not thy faith towards me and thine abundant love: and as for the rede of the Gods, I know it not, nor may I know it, nor turn it this way nor that: and as for thy love and that I would choose death sooner, I know not what thou meanest; I will not say that I love thy love better than life itself; for these two, my life and my love, are blended together and may not be sundered.

"Hearken therefore as to the Hauberk: I wot well that it is for no light matter that thou wouldst have me bear thy gift, the wondrous hauberk, into battle; I deem that some doom is wrapped up in it; maybe that I shall fall before the foe if I wear it not; and that if I wear it, somewhat may betide me which is unmeet to betide a warrior of the Wolfings. Therefore will I tell thee why I have fought in two battles with the Romans with unmailed body, and why I left the hauberk, (which I see that thou bearest in thine arms) in the Roof of the Daylings. For when I entered therein, clad in the hauberk, there came to meet me an ancient man, one of the very valiant of days past, and he looked on me with the eyes of love, as though he had been the very father of our folk, and I the man that was to come after him to carry on the life thereof. But when he saw the hauberk and touched it, then was his love smitten cold with sadness and he spoke words of evil omen; so that putting this together with thy words about the gift, and that thou didst in a manner compel me to wear it, I could not but deem that this mail is for the ransom of a man and the ruin of a folk.

"Wilt thou say that it is not so? then will I wear the hauberk, and live and die happy. But if thou sayest that I have deemed aright, and that a curse goeth with the hauberk, then either for the sake of the folk I will not wear the gift and the curse, and I shall die in great glory, and because of me the House shall live; or else for thy sake I shall bear it and live, and the House shall live or die as may be, but I not helping, nay I no longer of the House nor in it. How sayest thou?"

Then she said:

Hail be thy mouth, beloved, for that last word of thine,
And the hope that thine heart conceiveth and the hope that is born in mine.

Yea, for a man's delivrance was the hauberk born indeed
That once more the mighty warrior might help the folk at need.
And where is the curse's dwelling if thy life be saved to dwell
Amidst the Wolfing warriors and the folk that loves thee well
And the house where the high Gods left thee to be cherished well
*   therein?*

Yea more: I have told thee, beloved, that thou art not of the kin;
The blood in thy body is blended of the wandering Elking race,
And one that I may not tell of, who in God-home hath his place,
And who changed his shape to beget thee in the wild-wood's leafy roof.
How then shall the doom of the Wolfings be woven in the woof
Which the Norns for thee have shuttled? or shall one man of war
Cast down the tree of the Wolfings on the roots that spread so far?
O friend, thou art wise and mighty, but other men have lived
Beneath the Wolfing roof-tree whereby the folk has thrived.

He reddened at her word; but his eyes looked eagerly on her. She cast down the hauberk, and drew one step nigher to him. She knitted her brows, her face waxed terrible, and her stature seemed to grow greater, as she lifted up her gleaming right arm, and cried out in a great voice.

Thou Thiodolf the Mighty! Hadst thou will to cast the net
And tangle the House in thy trouble, it is I would slay thee yet;
For 'tis I and I that love them, and my sorrow would I give,
And thy life, thou God of battle, that the Wolfing House might live.

Therewith she rushed forward, and cast herself upon him, and threw her arms about him, and strained him to her bosom, and kissed his face, and he her in likewise, for there was none to behold them, and nought but the naked heaven was the roof above their heads.

And now it was as if the touch of her face and her body, and the murmuring of her voice changed and soft close to his ear, as she murmured mere words of love to him, drew him away from the life of deeds and doubts and made a new world for him, wherein he beheld all those fair pictures of the happy days that had been in his musings when first he left the field of the dead.

So they sat down on the grey stone together hand in hand, her head laid upon his shoulder, no otherwise than if they had

been two lovers, young and without renown in days of deep peace.

So as they sat, her foot smote on the cold hilts of the sword, which Thiodolf had laid down in the grass; and she stooped and took it up, and laid it across her knees and his as they sat there; and she looked on Throng-plough as he lay still in the sheath, and smiled on him, and saw that the peace-strings were not yet wound about his hilts. So she drew him forth and raised him up in her hand, and he gleamed white and fearful in the growing dawn, for all things had now gotten their colours again, whereas amidst their talking had the night worn, and the moon low down was grown white and pale.

But she leaned aside, and laid her cheek against Thiodolf's, and he took the sword out of her hand and set it on his knees again, and laid his right hand on it, and said:

Two things by these blue edges in the face of the dawning I swear;
And first this warrior's ransom in the coming fight to bear,
And evermore to love thee who hast given me second birth.
And by the sword I swear it, and by the Holy Earth,
To live for the House of the Wolfings, and at last to die for their need.
For though I trow thy saying that I am not one of their seed,
Nor yet by the hand have been taken and unto the Father shown
As a very son of the Fathers, yet mid them hath my body grown;
And I am the guest of their Folk-Hall, and each one there is my friend.
So with them is my joy and sorrow, and my life, and my death in the
*   end.*
Now whatso doom hereafter my coming days shall bide,
Thou speech-friend, thou deliverer, thine is this dawning-tide.

She spoke no word to him; but they rose up and went hand in hand down the dale, he still bearing his naked sword over his shoulder, and thus they went together into the yew-copse at the dale's end. There they abode till after the rising of the sun, and each to each spake many loving words at their departure; and the Wood-Sun went her ways at her will.

But Thiodolf went up the dale again, and set Throng-plough in his sheath, and wound the peace-strings round him. Then he took up the hauberk from the grass whereas the Wood-Sun had cast it, and did it on him, as it were of the attire he was wont to carry daily. So he girt Throng-plough to him, and went soberly up to the ridge-top to the folk, who were just stirring in the early morning.

18. TIDINGS BROUGHT TO THE WAIN-BURG

Now it must be told of Otter and they of the Wain-burg how they had the tidings of the overthrow of the Romans on the Ridge, and that Egil had left them on his way to Wolfstead.

They were joyful of the tale, as was like to be, but eager also to strike their stroke at the foe-men, and in that mood they abode fresh tidings.

It has been told how Otter had sent the Bearings and the Wormings to the aid of Thiodolf and his folk, and these two were great kindreds, and they being gone, there abode with Otter, one man with another, thralls and freemen, scant three thousand men: of these many were bowmen good to fight from behind a wall or fence, or some such cover, but scarce meet to withstand a shock in the open field. However it was deemed at this time in the Wain-burg that Thiodolf and his men would soon return to them; and in any case, they said, he lay between the Romans and the Mark, so that they had but little doubt; or rather they feared that the Romans might draw aback from the Mark before they could be met in battle again, for as aforesaid they were eager for the fray.

Now it was in the cool of the evening two days after the Battle on the Ridge, that the men, both freemen and thralls, had been disporting themselves in the plain ground without the Burg in casting the spear and putting the stone, and running races a-foot and a-horseback, and now close on sunset three young men, two of the Laxings and one of the Shieldings, and a grey old thrall of that same House, were shooting a match with the bow, driving their shafts at a rushen roundel hung on a pole which the old thrall had dight. Men were peaceful and happy, for the time was fair and calm, and, as aforesaid, they dreaded not the Roman Host any more than if they were Gods dwelling in God-home. The shooters were deft men, and they of the Burg were curious to note their deftness, and many were breathed with the games wherein they had striven, and thought it good to rest, and look on the new sport: so they sat and stood on the grass about the shooters on three sides, and the mead-horn went briskly from man to man; for there was no lack of meat and drink in the Burg, whereas the kindreds that lay nighest to it had brought in abundant provision, and women of the kindreds had come to them, and not a few were there scattered up and down among the carles.

Now the Shielding man, Geirbald by name, had just loosed at the mark, and had shot straight and smitten the roundel in the midst, and a shout went up from the onlookers thereat; but that shout was, as it were, lined with another, and a cry that a messenger was riding toward the Burg: thereat most men looked round toward the wood, because their minds were set on fresh tidings from Thiodolf's company, but as it happened it was from the north and the side toward Mid-mark that they on the outside of the throng had seen the rider coming; and presently the word went from man to man that so it was, and that the new comer was a young man on a grey horse, and would speedily be amongst them; so they wondered what the tidings might be, but yet they did not break up the throng, but abode in their places that they might receive the messenger more orderly; and as the rider drew near, those who were nighest to him perceived that it was a woman.

So men made way before the grey horse, and its rider, and the horse was much spent and travel-worn. So the woman rode right into the ring of warriors, and drew rein there, and lighted down slowly and painfully, and when she was on the ground could scarce stand for stiffness; and two or three of the swains drew near her to help her, and knew her at once for Hrosshild of the Wolfings, for she was well-known as a doughty woman.

Then she said: "Bring me to Otter the War-duke; or bring him hither to me, which were best, since so many men are gathered together; and meanwhile give me to drink; for I am thirsty and weary."

So while one went for Otter, another reached to her the mead-horn, and she had scarce done her draught, ere Otter was there, for they had found him at the gate of the Burg. He had many a time been in the Wolfing Hall, so he knew her at once and said:

"Hail, Hrosshild! how farest thou?"

She said: "I fare as the bearer of evil tidings. Bid thy folk do on their war-gear and saddle their horses, and make no delay; for now presently shall the Roman host be in Mid-mark!"

Then cried Otter: "Blow up the war-horn! get ye all to your weapons and be ready to leap on your horses, and come ye to the Thing in good order kindred by kindred: later on ye shall hear Hrosshild's story as she shall tell it to me!"

Therewith he led her to a grassy knoll that was hard by, and set her down thereon and himself beside her, and said:

"Speak now, damsel, and fear not! For now shall one fate go over us all, either to live together or die together as the free children of Tyr, and friends of the Almighty God of the Earth. How camest thou to meet the Romans and know of their ways and to live thereafter?"

She said: "Thus it was: the Hall-Sun bethought her how that the eastern ways into Mid-mark that bring a man to the thicket behind the Roof of the Bearings are nowise hard, even for an host; so she sent ten women, and me the eleventh to the Bearing dwelling and the road through the thicket aforesaid; and we were to take of the Bearing stay-at-homes whomso we would that were handy, and then all we to watch the ways for fear of the Romans. And methinks she has had some vision of their ways, though mayhap not altogether clear.

"Anyhow we came to the Bearing dwellings, and they gave us of their folk eight doughty women and two light-foot lads, and so we were twenty and one in all.

"So then we did as the Hall-Sun bade us, and ordained a chain of watchers far up into the waste; and these were to sound a point of war upon their horns each to each till the sound thereof should come to us who lay with our horses hoppled ready beside us in the fair plain of the Mark outside the thicket.

"To be short, the horns waked us up in the midst of yestern-ight, and of the watches also came to us the last, which had heard the sound amidst the thicket, and said that it was certainly the sound of the Goths' horn, and the note agreed on. Therefore I sent a messenger at once to the Wolfing Roof to say what was toward; but to thee I would not ride until I had made surer of the tidings; so I waited awhile, and then rode into the wild-wood; and a long tale I might make both of the waiting and the riding, had I time thereto; but this is the end of it; that going warily a little past where the thicket thinneth and the road endeth, I came on three of those watches or links in the chain we had made, and half of another watch or link; that is to say six women, who were come together after having blown their horns and fled (though they should rather have abided in some lurking-place to espy whatever might come that way) and one other woman, who had been one of the watch much further off, and had spoken with the furthest of all, which one had seen the faring of the Roman Host, and that it was very great, and no mere band of pillagers or of scouts. And, said this fleer (who was indeed half wild with fear), that while they were talking together, came the Romans upon them, and saw them; and a band of Romans beat the wood for them when they fled, and she, the fleer, was at point to be taken, and saw two taken indeed, and haled off by the Roman scourers of the wood. But she escaped and so came to the others on the skirts of the thicket, having left of her skin and blood on many a thornbush and rock by the way.

"Now when I heard this, I bade this fleer get her home to the Bearings as swiftly as she might, and tell her tale; and she went away trembling, and scarce knowing whether her feet were on earth or on water or on fire; but belike failed not to come there, as no Romans were before her.

"But for the others, I sent one to go straight to Wolf-stead on the heels of the first messenger, to tell the Hall-Sun what had befallen, and other five I set to lurk in the thicket, whereas none could lightly lay hands on them, and when they had new tidings, to flee to Wolf-stead as occasion might serve them; and for myself I tarried not, but rode on the spur to tell thee hereof.

"But my last word to thee, Otter, is that by the Hall-Sun's bidding the Bearings will not abide fire and steel at their own stead, but when they hear true tidings of the Romans being hard at hand, will take with them all that is not too hot or too heavy to carry, and go their ways unto Wolf-stead: and the tidings will go up and down the Mark on both sides of the water, so that whatever is of avail for defence will gather there at our dwelling, and if we fall, goodly shall be the howe heaped over us, even if ye come not in time.

"Now have I told thee what I needs must and there is no need to question me more, for thou hast it all—do thou what thou hast to do!"

With that word she cast herself down on the grass by the mound-side, and was presently asleep, for she was very weary.

But all the time she had been telling her tale had the horn been sounding, and there were now a many warriors gathered and more coming in every moment: so Otter stood up on the mound after he had bidden a man of his House to bring him his horse and war-gear, and abided a little, till, as might be said, the whole host was gathered: then he bade cry silence, and spake:

"Sons of Tyr, now hath an Host of the Romans gotten into the Mark; a mighty host, but not so mighty that it may not be met. Few words are best: let the Steerings, who are not many, but are men well-tried in war and wisdom abide in the Burg along with the fighting thralls: but let the Burg be broken up and moved from the place, and let its warders wend towards Mid-mark, but warily and without haste, and each night let them make the wain-garth and keep good watch.

"But know ye that the Romans shall fall with all their power on the Wolfing dwellings, deeming that when they have that, they shall have all that is ours with ourselves also. For there is the Hall-Sun under the Great Roof, and there hath Thiodolf, our War-duke, his dwelling-place; therefore shall all of us, save those that abide with the wains, take horse, and ride without delay, and cross the water at Battleford, so that we may fall upon the foe before they come west of the water; for as ye know there is but one ford whereby a man wending straight from the Bearings may cross Mirkwood-water, and it is like that the foe will tarry at the Bearing stead long enough to burn and pillage it.

"So do ye order yourselves according to your kindreds, and let the Shieldings lead. Make no more delay! But for me I will now send a messenger to Thiodolf to tell him of the tidings, and then speedily shall he be with us. Geirbald, I see thee; come hither!"

Now Geirbald stood amidst the Shieldings, and when Otter had spoken, he came forth bestriding a white horse, and with his bow slung at his back. Said Otter: "Geirbald, thou shalt ride at once through the wood, and find Thiodolf; and tell him the tidings, and that in nowise he follow the Roman fleers away from the Mark, nor to heed anything but the trail of the foemen through the south-eastern heaths of Mirkwood, whether other Romans follow him or not: whatever happens let him lead the Goths by that road, which for him is the shortest, towards the defence of the Wolfing dwellings. Lo thou, my ring for a token! Take it and depart in haste. Yet first take thy fellow Viglund the Woodman with thee, lest if perchance one fall, the other may bear the message. Tarry not, nor rest till thy word be said!"

Then turned Geirbald to find Viglund who was anigh to him, and he took the ring, and the twain went their ways without more ado, and rode into the wild-wood.

But about the Wain-burg was there plenteous stir of men till all was ordered for the departure of the host, which was no long while, for there was nothing to do but on with the war-gear and up on to the horse.

Forth then they went duly ordered in their kindreds towards the head of the Upper-mark, riding as swiftly as they might without breaking their array.

19. THOSE MESSENGERS COME TO THIODOLF

Of Geirbald and Viglund the tale tells that they rode the woodland paths as speedily as they might. They had not gone far, and were winding through a path amidst of a thicket mingled of the hornbeam and holly, betwixt the openings of which the bracken grew exceeding tall, when Viglund, who was very fine-eared, deemed that he heard a horse coming to meet them: so they lay as close as they might, and drew back their horses behind a great holly-bush lest it should be some one or more of the foes who had fled into the wood when the Romans were scattered in that first fight. But as the sound drew nearer, and it was clearly the footsteps of a great horse, they deemed it would be some messenger from Thiodolf, as indeed it turned out: for as the new-comer fared on, somewhat unwarily, they saw a bright helm after the fashion of the Goths amidst of the trees, and then presently they knew by his attire that he was of the Bearings, and so at last they knew him to be Asbiorn of the said House, a doughty man; so they came forth to meet him and he drew rein when he saw armed men, but presently beholding their faces he knew them and laughed on them, and said:

"Hail fellows! what tidings are toward?"

"These," said Viglund, "that thou art well met, since now shalt thou turn back and bring us to Thiodolf as speedily as may be."

But Asbiorn laughed and said: "Nay rather turn about with me; or why are ye so grim of countenance?"

"Our errand is no light one," said Geirbald, "but thou, why art thou so merry?"

"I have seen the Romans fall," said he, "and belike shall soon see more of that game: for I am on an errand to Otter from Thiodolf: the War-duke, when he had questioned some of those whom we took on the Day of the Ridge, began to have a deeming that the Romans had beguiled us, and will fall on the Mark by the way of the south-east heaths: so now is he hastening to fetch a compass and follow that road either to overtake them or prevent them; and he biddeth Otter tarry not, but ride hard along the water to meet them if he may, or ever they have set their hands to the dwellings of my House. And belike when I have done mine errand to Otter I shall ride with

him to look on these burners and slayers once more; therefore am I merry. Now for your tidings, fellows."

Said Geirbald: "Our tidings are that both our errands are prevented, and come to nought: for Otter hath not tarried, but hath ridden with all his folk toward the stead of thine House. So shalt thou indeed see these burners and slayers if thou ridest hard; since we have tidings that the Romans will by now be in Mid-mark. And as for our errand, it is to bid Thiodolf do even as he hath done. Hereby may we see how good a pair of War-dukes we have gotten, since each thinketh of the same wisdom. Now take we counsel together as to what we shall do; whether we shall go back to Otter with thee, or thou go back to Thiodolf with us; or else each go the road ordained for us."

Said Asbiorn: "To Otter will I ride as I was bidden, that I may look on the burning of our roof, and avenge me of the Romans afterwards; and I bid you, fellows, ride with me, since fewer men there are with Otter, and he must be the first to bide the brunt of battle."

"Nay," said Geirbald, "as for me ye must even lose a man's aid; for to Thiodolf was I sent, and to Thiodolf will I go: and bethink thee if this be not best, since Thiodolf hath but a deeming of the ways of the Romans and we wot surely of them. Our coming shall make him the speedier, and the less like to turn back if any alien band shall follow after him. What sayest thou, Viglund?"

Said Viglund: "Even as thou, Geirbald: but for myself I deem I may well turn back with Asbiorn. For I would serve the House in battle as soon as may be; and maybe we shall slaughter these kites of the cities, so that Thiodolf shall have no work to do when he cometh."

Said Asbiorn; "Geirbald, knowest thou right well the ways through the wood and on the other side thereof, to the place where Thiodolf abideth? for ye see that night is at hand."

"Nay, not over well," said Geirbald.

Said Asbiorn: "Then I rede thee take Viglund with thee; for he knoweth them yard by yard, and where they be hard and where they be soft. Moreover it were best indeed that ye meet Thiodolf betimes; for I deem not but that he wendeth leisurely, though always warily, because he deemeth not that Otter will ride before to-morrow morning. Hearken, Viglund! Thiodolf will rest to-night on the other side of the water, nigh to where the hills break off into the sheer cliffs that are called the Kites' Nest, and the water runneth under them, coming from the east: and before him lieth the easy ground of the eastern heaths where he is minded to wend to-morrow betimes in the morning: and if ye do your best ye shall be there before he is upon the road, and sure it is that your tidings shall hasten him."

"Thou sayest sooth," saith Geirbald, "tarry we no longer; here sunder our ways; farewell!"

"Farewell," said he, "and thou, Viglund, take this word in parting, that belike thou shalt yet see the Romans, and strike a stroke, and maybe be smitten. For indeed they be most mighty warriors."

Then made they no delay but rode their ways either side. And Geirbald and Viglund rode over rough and smooth all night, and were out of the thick wood by day-dawn: and whereas they rode hard, and Viglund knew the ways well, they came to Mirkwood-water before the day was old, and saw that the host was stirring, but not yet on the way. And or ever they came to the water's edge, they were met by Wolfkettle of the Wolfings, and Hiarandi of the Elkings, and three others who were but just come from the place where the hurt men lay down in a dale near the Great Ridge; there had Wolfkettle and Hiarandi been tending Toti of the Beamings, their fellow-in-arms, who had been sorely hurt in the battle, but was doing well, and was like to live. So when they saw the messengers, they came up to them and hailed them, and asked them if the tidings were good or evil.

"That is as it may be," said Geirbald, "but they are short to tell; the Romans are in Mid-mark, and Otter rideth on the spur to meet them, and sendeth us to bid Thiodolf wend the heaths to fall in on them also. Nor may we tarry one minute ere we have seen Thiodolf."

Said Wolfkettle, "We will lead you to him; he is on the east side of the water, with all his host, and they are hard on departing."

So they went down the ford, which was not very deep; and Wolfkettle rode the ford behind Geirbald, and another man behind Viglund; but Hiarandi went afoot with the others beside the horses, for he was a very tall man.

But as they rode amidst the clear water Wolfkettle lifted up his voice and sang:

White horse, with what are ye laden as ye wade the shallows warm,
But with tidings of the battle, and the fear of the fateful storm?
What loureth now behind us, what pileth clouds before,
On either hand what gathereth save the stormy tide of war?
Now grows midsummer mirky, and fallow falls the morn,
And dusketh the Moon's Sister, and the trees look overworn;

God's Ash tree shakes and shivers, and the sheer cliff standeth white
As the bones of the giants' father when the Gods first fared to fight.

And indeed the morning had grown mirky and grey and threatening, and from far away the thunder growled, and the face of the Kite's Nest showed pale and awful against a dark steely cloud; and a few drops of rain pattered into the smooth water before them from a rag of the cloud-flock right over head. They were in mid stream now, for the water was wide there; on the eastern bank were the warriors gathering, for they had beheld the faring of those men, and the voice of Wolfkettle came to them across the water, so they deemed that great tidings were toward, and would fain know on what errand those were come.

Then the waters of the ford deepened till Hiarandi was wading more than waist-deep, and the water flowed over Geirbald's saddle; then Wolfkettle laughed, and turning as he sat, dragged out his sword, and waved it from east to west and sang:

O sun, pale up in heaven, shrink from us if thou wilt,
And turn thy face from beholding the shock of guilt with guilt!
Stand still, O blood of summer! and let the harvest fade,
Till there be nought but fallow where once was bloom and blade!
O day, give out but a glimmer of all thy flood of light,
If it be but enough for our eyen to see the road of fight!
Forget all else and slumber, if still ye let us wake,
And our mouths shall make the thunder, and our swords shall the
*   lightening make,*
And we shall be the storm-wind and drive the ruddy rain,
Till the joy of our hearts in battle bring back the day again.

As he spake that word they came up through the shallow water dripping on to the bank, and they and the men who abode them on the bank shouted together for joy of fellowship, and all tossed aloft their weapons. The man who had ridden behind Viglund slipped off on to the ground; but Wolfkettle abode in his place behind Geirbald.

So the messengers passed on, and the others closed up round about them, and all the throng went up to where Thiodolf was sitting on a rock beneath a sole ash-tree, the face of the Kite's Nest rising behind him on the other side of a bight of the river. There he sat unhelmed with the dwarf-wrought hauberk about him, holding Throng-plough in its sheath across his knees, while he gave word to this and that man concerning the order of the host.

So when they were come thither, the throng opened that the messengers might come forward; for by this time had many more drawn near to hearken what was toward. There they sat on their horses, the white and the grey, and Wolfkettle stood by Geirbald's bridle rein, for he had now lighted down; and a little behind him, his head towering over the others, stood Hiarandi great and gaunt. The ragged cloud had drifted down south-east now and the rain fell no more, but the sun was still pale and clouded.

Then Thiodolf looked gravely on them, and spake:

What do ye sons of the War-shield? what tale is there to tell?
Is the kindred fallen tangled in the grasp of the fallow Hell?
Crows the red cock over the homesteads, have we met the foe too late?
For meseems your brows are heavy with the shadowing o'er of fate.

But Geirbald answered:

Still cold with dew in the morning the Shielding Roof-ridge stands,
Nor yet hath grey Hell bounden the Shielding warriors' hands;
But lo, the swords, O War-duke, how thick in the wind they shake,
Because we bear the message that the battle-road ye take,
Nor tarry for the thunder or the coming on of rain,
Or the windy cloudy night-tide, lest your battle be but vain.
And this is the word that Otter yestre'en hath set in my mouth;
Seek thou the trail of the Aliens of the Cities of the South,
And thou shalt find it leading o'er the heaths to the beechen-wood,
And thence to the stony places where the foxes find their food;
And thence to the tangled thicket where the folkway cleaves it through,
To the eastern edge of Mid-mark where the Bearings deal and do.

Then said Thiodolf in a cold voice, "What then hath befallen Otter?"

Said Geirbald:

When last I looked upon Otter, all armed he rode the plain,
With his whole host clattering round him like the rush of the summer rain;
To the right or the left they looked not but they rode through the dusk and the dark
Beholding nought before them but the dream of the foes in the Mark.
So he went; but his word fled from him and on my horse it rode,
And again it saith, O War-duke seek thou the Bear's abode,
And tarry never a moment for ought that seems of worth,
For there shall ye find the sword-edge and the flame of the foes of the earth.

"Tarry not, Thiodolf, nor turn aback though a new foe followeth on thine heels. No need to question me more; I have no more to tell, save that a woman brought these tidings to us, whom the Hall-Sun had sent with others to watch the ways: and some of them had seen the Romans, who are a great host and no band stealing forth to lift the herds."

Now all those round about him heard his words, for he spake with a loud voice; and they knew what the bidding of the War-duke would be; so they loitered not, but each man went about his business of looking to his war-gear and gathering to the appointed place of his kindred. And even while Geirbald had been speaking, had Hiarandi brought up the man who bore the great horn, who when Thiodolf leapt to his feet to find him, was close at hand. So he bade him blow the war-blast, and all men knew the meaning of that voice of the horn, and every man armed him in haste, and they who had horses (and these were but the Bearings and the Warnings), saddled them, and mounted, and from mouth to mouth went the word that the Romans were gotten into Mid-mark, and were burning the Bearing abodes. So speedily was the whole host ready for the way, the Wolfings at the head of all. Then came forth Thiodolf from the midst of his kindred, and they raised him upon a great war-shield upheld by many men, and he stood thereon and spake:

O sons of Tyr, ye have vanquished, and sore hath been your pain;
But he that smiteth in battle must ever smite again;
And thus with you it fareth, and the day abideth yet
When ye shall hold the Aliens as the fishes in the net.
On the Ridge ye slew a many; but there came a many more
From their strongholds by the water to their new-built garth of war,
And all these have been led by dastards o'er the way our feet must tread
Through the eastern heaths and the beechwood to the door of the
    Bearing stead,
Now e'en yesterday I deemed it, but I durst not haste away
Ere the word was borne to Otter and 'tis he bids haste to-day;
So now by day and by night-tide it behoveth us to wend
And wind the reel of battle and weave its web to end.
Had ye deemed my eyes foreseeing, I would tell you of my sight,
How I see the folk delivered and the Aliens turned to flight,
While my own feet wend them onwards to the ancient Father's Home.
But belike these are but the visions that to many a man shall come
When he goeth adown to the battle, and before him riseth high
The wall of valiant foemen to hide all things anigh.
But indeed I know full surely that no work that we may win
To-morrow or the next day shall quench the Markmen's kin.
On many a day hereafter shall their warriors carry shield;
On many a day their maidens shall drive the kine afield,
On many a day their reapers bear sickle in the wheat
When the golden wind-wrought ripple stirs round the feast-hall's feet.
Lo, now is the day's work easy—to live and overcome,
Or to die and yet to conquer on the threshold of the Home.

And therewith he gat him down and went a-foot to the head of the Wolfing band, a great shout going with him, which was mingled with the voice of the war-horn that bade away.

So fell the whole host into due array, and they were somewhat over three thousand warriors, all good and tried men and meet to face the uttermost of battle in the open field; so they went their ways with all the speed that footmen may, and in fair order; and the sky cleared above their heads, but the distant thunder still growled about the world. Geirbald and Viglund joined themselves to the Wolfings and went a-foot along with Wolfkettle; but Hiarandi went with his kindred who were second in the array.

20. OTTER AND HIS FOLK COME INTO MID-MARK

Otter and his folk rode their ways along Mirkwood-water, and made no stay, except now and again to breathe their horses, till they came to Battleford in the early morning; there they baited their horses, for the grass was good in the meadow, and the water easy to come at.

So after they had rested there a short hour, and had eaten what was easy for them to get, they crossed the ford, and wended along Mirkwood-water between the wood and the river, but went slower than before lest they should weary their horses; so that it was high-noon before they had come out of the woodland way into Mid-mark; and at once as soon as the whole plain of the Mark opened out before them, they saw what most of them looked to see (since none doubted Hrosshild's tale), and that was a column of smoke rising high and straight up into the air, for the afternoon was hot and windless. Great wrath rose in their hearts thereat, and many a strong man trembled for anger, though none for fear, as Otter raised his right hand and stretched it out towards that token of wrack and ruin; yet they made no stay, nor did they quicken their pace much; because they knew that they should come to Bearham before night-fall, and they would not meet the Romans way-worn and haggard; but they rode on steadily, a terrible company of wrathful men.

They passed by the dwellings of the kindreds, though save for the Galtings the houses on the east side of the water between the Bearings and the wild-wood road were but small; for the thicket came somewhat near to the water and pinched the meadows. But the Galtings were great hunters and trackers of the wild-wood, and they of the Geddings, the Erings and the Withings, which were smaller Houses, lived somewhat on the take of fish from Mirkwood-water (as did the Laxings also of the Nether-mark), for thereabout were there goodly pools and eddies, and sun-warmed shallows therewithal for the spawning of the trouts; as there were eyots in the water, most of which tailed off into a gravelly shallow at their lower ends.

Now as the riders of the Goths came over against the dwellings of the Withings, they saw people, mostly women, driving up the beasts from the meadow towards the garth; but upon the tofts about their dwellings were gathered many folk, who had their eyes turned toward the token of ravage that hung in the sky above the fair plain; but when these beheld the riding of the host, they tossed up their arms to them and whatever they bore in them, and the sound of their shrill cry (for they were all women and young lads) came down the wind to the ears of the riders. But down by the river on a swell of the ground were some swains and a few thralls, and among them some men armed and a-horseback; and these, when they perceived the host coming on turned and rode to meet them; and as they drew near they shouted as men overjoyed to meet their kindred; and indeed the fighting-men of their own House were riding in the host. And the armed men were three old men, and one very old with marvellous long white hair, and four long lads of some fifteen winters, and four stout carles of the thralls bearing bows and bucklers, and these rode behind the swains; so they found their own kindred and rode amongst them.

But when they were all jingling and clashing on together, the dust arising from the sun-dried turf, the earth shaking with the thunder of the horse-hoofs, then the heart of the long-hoary one stirred within him as he bethought him of the days of his youth, and to his old nostrils came the smell of the horses and the savour of the sweat of warriors riding close together knee to knee adown the meadow. So he lifted up his voice and sang:

> Rideth lovely along
> The strong by the strong;
> Soft under his breath
> Singeth sword in the sheath,
> And shield babbleth oft
> Unto helm-crest aloft;
> How soon shall their words rise mid wrath of the battle
> Into wrangle unheeded of clanging and rattle,
> And no man shall note then the gold on the sword
> When the runes have no meaning, the mouth-cry no word,
> When all mingled together, the war-sea of men
> Shall toss up the steel-spray round fourscore and ten.

> Now as maids burn the weed
> Betwixt acre and mead,
> So the Bearings' Roof
> Burneth little aloof,
> And red gloweth the hall
> Betwixt wall and fair wall,
> Where often the mead-sea we sipped in old days,
> When our feet were a-weary with wending the ways;
> When the love of the lovely at even was born,
> And our hands felt fair hands as they fell on the horn.

There round about standeth the ring of the foe
Tossing babes on their spears like the weeds o'er the low.

     Ride, ride then! nor spare
     The red steeds as ye fare!
     Yet if daylight shall fail,
     By the fire-light of bale
     Shall we see the bleared eyes
     Of the war-learned, the wise.
In the acre of battle the work is to win,
Let us live by the labour, sheaf-smiting therein;
And as oft o'er the sickle we sang in time past
When the crake that long mocked us fled light at the last,
So sing o'er the sword, and the sword-hardened hand
Bearing down to the reaping the wrath of the land.

So he sang; and a great shout went up from his kindred and those around him, and it was taken up all along the host, though many knew not why they shouted, and the whole host quickened its pace, and went a great trot over the smooth meadow.

So in no long while were they come over against the stead of the Erings, and thereabouts were no beasts a-field, and no women, for all the neat were driven into the garth of the House; but all they who were not war-fit were standing without doors looking down the Mark towards the reek of the Bearing dwellings, and these also sent a cry of welcome toward the host of their kindred. But along the river-bank came to meet the host an armed band of two old men, two youths who were their sons, and twelve thralls who were armed with long spears; and all these were a-horseback: so they fell in with their kindred and the host made no stay for them, but pressed on over-running the meadow. And still went up that column of smoke, and thicker and blacker it grew a-top, and ruddier amidmost.

So came they by the abode of the Geddings, and there also the neat and sheep were close in the home-garth: but armed men were lying or standing about the river bank, talking or singing merrily none otherwise than though deep peace were on the land; and when they saw the faring of the host they sprang to their feet with a shout and gat to their horses at once: they were more than the other bands had been, for the Geddings were a greater House; they were seven old men, and ten swains, and ten thralls bearing long spears like to those of the Erings; and no sooner had they fallen in with their kindred, than the men of the host espied a greater company yet coming to meet them: and these were of the folk of the Galtings; and amongst them were ten warriors in their prime, because they had but of late come back from the hunting in the wood and had been belated from the muster of the kindreds; and with

them were eight old men and fifteen lads, and eighteen thralls; and the swains and thralls all bore bows besides the swords that they were girt withal, and not all of them had horses, but they who had none rode behind the others: so they joined themselves to the host, shouting aloud; and they had with them a great horn that they blew on till they had taken their place in the array; and whereas their kindred was with Thiodolf, they followed along with the hinder men of the Shieldings.

So now all the host went on together, and when they had passed the Galting abodes, there was nothing between them and Bearham, nor need they look for any further help of men; there were no beasts afield nor any to herd them, and the stay-at-homes were within doors dighting them for departure into the wild-wood if need should be: but a little while after they had passed these dwellings came into the host two swains of about twenty winters, and a doughty maid, their sister, and they bare no weapons save short spears and knives; they were wet and dripping with the water, for they had just swum Mirk-wood-water. They were of the Wolfing House, and had been shepherding a few sheep on the west side of the water, when they saw the host faring to battle, and might not refrain them, but swam their horses across the swift deeps to join their kindred to live and die with them. The tale tells that they three fought in the battles that followed after, and were not slain there, though they entered them unarmed, but lived long years afterwards: of them need no more be said.

Now, when the host was but a little past the Galting dwellings men began to see the flames mingled with the smoke of the burning, and the smoke itself growing thinner, as though the fire had over-mastered everything and was consuming itself with its own violence; and somewhat afterwards, the ground rising, they could see the Bearing meadow and the foe-men thereon: yet a little further, and from the height of another swelling of the earth they could see the burning houses themselves and the array of the Romans; so there they stayed and breathed their horses a while. And they beheld how of the Romans a great company was gathered together in close array betwixt the ford and the Bearing Hall, but nigher unto the ford, and these were a short mile from them; but others they saw streaming out from the burning dwellings, as if their work were done there, and they could not see that they had any captives with them. Other Romans there were, and amongst them men in the attire of the Goths, busied about the river banks, as though they were going to try the ford.

But a little while abode Otter in that place, and then waved his arm and rode on and all the host followed; and as they drew nigher, Otter, who was wise in war, beheld the Romans and deemed them a great host, and the very kernel and main body of them many more than all his company; and moreover they were duly and well arrayed as men waiting a foe; so he knew that he must be wary or he would lose himself and all his men.

So he stayed his company when they were about two furlongs from them, and the main body of the foe stirred not, but horsemen and slingers came forth from its sides and made on toward the Goths, and in three or four minutes were within bowshot of them. Then the bowmen of the Goths slipped down from their horses and bent their bows and nocked their arrows and let fly, and slew and hurt many of the horsemen, who endured their shot but for a minute or two and then turned rein and rode back slowly to their folk, and the slingers came not on very eagerly whereas they were dealing with men a-horse-back, and the bowmen of the Goths also held them still.

Now turned Otter to his folk and made them a sign, which they knew well, that they should get down from their horses; and when they were afoot the leaders of tens and hundreds arrayed them, into the wedge-array, with the bowmen on either flank: and Otter smiled as he beheld this adoing and that the Romans meddled not with them, belike because they looked to have them good cheap, since they were but a few wild men.

But when they were all arrayed he sat still on his horse and spake to them short and sharply, saying:

"Men of the Goths, will ye mount your horses again and ride into the wood and let it cover you, or will ye fight these Romans?" They answered him with a great shout and the clashing of their weapons on their shields. "That is well," quoth Otter, "since we have come so far; for I perceive that the foe will come to meet us, so that we must either abide their shock or turn our backs. Yet must we fight wisely or we are undone, and Thiodolf in risk of undoing; this have we to do if we may, to thrust in between them and the ford, and if we may do that, there let us fight it out, till we fall one over another. But if we may not do it, then will we not throw our lives away but do the foemen what hurt we may without mingling ourselves amongst them, and so abide the coming of Thiodolf; for if we get not betwixt them and the ford we may in no case hinder them from crossing. And all this I tell you that ye may follow me wisely, and refrain your wrath that ye may live yet to give it the rein when the time comes."

So he spake and got down from his horse and drew his sword and went to the head of the wedge-array and began slowly to lead forth; but the thralls and swains had heed of the horses, and they drew aback with them towards the wood which was but a little way from them.

But for Otter he led his men down towards the ford, and when the Romans saw that, their main body began to move forward, faring slant-wise, as a crab, down toward the ford; then Otter hastened somewhat, as he well might, since his men were well learned in war and did not break their array; but now

by this time were those burners of the Romans come up with the main battle, and the Roman captain sent them at once against the Goths, and they advanced boldly enough, a great cloud of men in loose array who fell to with arrows and slings on the wedge-array and slew and hurt many: yet did not Otter stay his folk; but it was ill going for them, for their unshielded sides were turned to the Romans, nor durst Otter scatter his bowmen out from the wedge-array, lest the Romans, who were more than they, should enter in amongst them. Ever he gazed earnestly on the main battle of the Romans, and what they were doing, and presently it became clear to him that they would outgo him and come to the ford, and then he wotted well that they would set on him just when their light-armed were on his flank and his rearward, and then it would go hard but they would break their array and all would be lost: therefore he slacked his pace and went very slowly and the Romans went none the slower for that; but their light-armed grew bolder and drew more together as they came nigher to the Goths, as though they would give them an onset; but just at that nick of time Otter passed the word down the ranks, and, waving his sword, turned sharply to the right and fell with all the wedge-array on the clustering throng of the light-armed, and his bowmen spread out now from the right flank of the wedge-array, and shot sharp and swift and the bowmen on the left flank ran forward swiftly till they had cleared the wedge-array and were on the flank of the light-armed Romans; and they, what between the onset of the swordsmen and spearmen of the Goths, and their sharp arrows, knew not which way to turn, and a great slaughter befell amongst them, and they of them were the happiest who might save themselves by their feet.

Now after this storm, and after these men had been thrust away, Otter stayed not, but swept round about the field toward the horses; and indeed he looked to it that the main-battle of the Romans should follow him, but they did not, but stayed still to receive the fleers of their light-armed. And this indeed was the goodhap of the Goths; for they were somewhat disordered by their chase of the light-armed, and they smote and spared not, their hearts being full of bitter wrath, as might well be; for even as they turned on the Romans, they beheld the great roof of the Bearings fall in over the burned hall, and a great shower of sparks burst up from its fall, and there were the ragged gables left standing, licked by little tongues of flame which could not take hold of them because of the clay which filled the spaces between the great timbers and was daubed over them. And they saw that all the other houses were either alight or smouldering, down to the smallest cot of a thrall, and even the barns and booths both great and little.

Therefore, whereas the Markmen were far fewer in all than the Roman main-battle, and whereas this same host was in very good array, no doubt there was that the Markmen would have been grievously handled had the Romans fallen on; but the Roman Captain would not have it so: for though he was a bold man, yet was his boldness that of the wolf, that falleth on when he is hungry and skulketh when he is full. He was both young and very rich, and a mighty man among his townsmen, and well had he learned that ginger is hot in the mouth, and though he had come forth to the war for the increasing of his fame, he had no will to die among the Markmen, either for the sake of the city of Rome, or of any folk whatsoever, but was liefer to live for his own sake. Therefore was he come out to vanquish easily, that by his fame won he might win more riches and dominion in Rome; and he was well content also to have for his own whatever was choice amongst the plunder of these wild-men (as he deemed them), if it were but a fair woman or two. So this man thought, It is my business to cross the ford and come to Wolfstead, and there take the treasure of the tribe, and have a stronghold there, whence we may slay so many of these beasts with little loss to us that we may march away easily and with our hands full, even if Maenius with his men come not to our aid, as full surely he will: therefore as to these angry men, who be not without might and conduct in battle, let us remember the old saw that saith 'a bridge of gold to a fleeing foe,' and let them depart with no more hurt of Romans, and seek us afterwards when we are fenced into their stead, which shall then be our stronghold: even so spake he to his Captains about him.

For it must be told that he had no tidings of the overthrow of the Romans on the Ridge; nor did he know surely how many fighting-men the Markmen might muster, except by the report of those dastards of the Goths; and though he had taken those two women in the wastes, yet had he got no word from them, for they did as the Hall-Sun bade them, when they knew that they would be questioned with torments, and smiting themselves each with a little sharp knife, so went their ways to the Gods.

Thus then the Roman Captain let the Markmen go their ways, and turned toward the ford, and the Markmen went slowly now toward their horses. Howbeit there were many of them who murmured against Otter, saying that it was ill done to have come so far and ridden so hard, and then to have done so little, and that were to-morrow come, they would not be led away so easily: but now they said it was ill; for the Romans would cross the water, and make their ways to Wolfstead, none hindering them, and would burn the dwellings and slay the old men and thralls, and have away the women and children and the Hall-Sun the treasure of the Markmen. In sooth, they knew not that a band of the Roman light-armed had already crossed the water, and had fallen upon the dwellings of the Wolfings; but that the old men and younglings and thralls of the House had come upon them as they were entangled amidst the tofts and the garths, and had overcome them and slain many.

Thus went Otter and his men to their horses when it was now drawing toward sunset (for all this was some while adoing), and betook them to a rising ground not far from the wood-side, and there made what sort of a garth they might, with their horses and the limbs of trees and long-shafted spears; and they set a watch and abode in the garth right warily, and lighted no fires when night fell, but ate what meat they had with them, which was but little, and so sleeping and watching abode the morning. But the main body of the Romans did not cross the ford that night, for they feared lest they might go astray therein, for it was an ill ford to those that knew not the water: so they abode on the bank nigh to the water's edge, with the mind to cross as soon as it was fairly daylight.

Now Otter had lost of his men some hundred and twenty slain or grievously hurt, and they had away with them the hurt men and the bodies of the slain. The tale tells not how many of the Romans were slain, but a many of their light-armed had fallen, since the Markmen had turned so hastily upon them, and they had with them many of the best bowmen of the Mark.

21. THEY BICKER ABOUT THE FORD

In the grey of the morning was Otter afoot with the watchers, and presently he got on his horse and peered over the plain, but the mist yet hung low on it, so that he might see nought for a while; but at last he seemed to note something coming toward the host from the upper water above the ford, so he rode forward to meet it, and lo, it was a lad of fifteen winters, naked save his breeches, and wet from the river; and Otter drew rein, and the lad said to him: "Art thou the Ward-uke?" "Yea," said Otter.

Said the lad, "I am Ali, the son of Grey, and the Hall-Sun hath sent me to thee with this word: 'Are ye coming? Is Thiodolf at hand? For I have seen the Roof-ridge red in the sunlight as if it were painted with cinnabar.'"

Said Otter, "Art thou going back to Wolfstead, son?"

"Yea, at once, my father," said Ali.

"Then tell her," said Otter, "that Thiodolf is at hand, and when he cometh we shall both together fall upon the Romans either in crossing the ford or in the Wolfing meadow; but tell her also that I am not strong enough to hinder the Romans from crossing."

"Father," said Ali, "the Hall-Sun saith: Thou art wise in war; now tell us, shall we hold the Hall against the Romans that ye may find us there? For we have discomfited their vanguard already, and we have folk who can fight; but belike the main battle of the Romans shall get the upper hand of us ere ye come to our helping: belike it were better to leave the hall, and let the wood cover us."

"Now is this well asked," said Otter; "get thee back, my son, and bid the Hall-Sun trust not to warding of the Hall, for the Romans are a mighty host: and this day, even when Thiodolf cometh hither, shall be hard for the Gothfolk: let her hasten lest these thieves come upon her hastily; let her take the Hall-Sun her namesake, and the old men and children and the women, and let those fighting folk she hath be a guard to all this in the wood. And hearken moreover; it will, maybe, be six hours ere Thiodolf cometh; tell her I will cast the dice for life or death, and stir up these Romans now at once, that they may have other things to think of than burning old men and women and children in their dwellings; thus may she reach the wood unhindered. Hast thou all this in thine head? Then go thy ways."

But the lad lingered, and he reddened and looked on the ground and then he said: "My father, I swam the deeps, and when I reached this bank, I crept along by the mist and the reeds toward where the Romans are, and I came near to them, and noted what they were doing; and I tell thee that they are already stirring to take the water at the ford. Now then do what thou wilt."

Therewith he turned about, and went his way at once, running like a colt which has never felt halter or bit.

But Otter rode back hastily and roused certain men in whom he trusted, and bid them rouse the captains and all the host and bid men get to horse speedily and with as little noise as might be. So did they, and there was little delay, for men were sleeping with one eye open, as folk say, and many were already astir. So in a little while they were all in the saddle, and the mist yet stretched low over the meadow; for the morning was cool and without wind. Then Otter bade the word be carried down the ranks that they should ride as quietly as may be and fare through the mist to do the Romans some hurt, but in nowise to get entangled in their ranks, and all men to heed well the signal of turning and drawing aback; and therewith they rode off down the meadow led by men who could have led them through the dark night.

But for the Romans, they were indeed getting ready to cross the ford when the mist should have risen; and on the bank it was thinning already and melting away; for a little air of wind was beginning to breathe from the north-east and the sunrise, which was just at hand; and the bank, moreover, was stonier and higher than the meadow's face, which fell away from it as a shallow dish from its rim: thereon yet lay the mist like a white wall.

So the Romans and their friends the dastards of the Goths had well nigh got all ready, and had driven stakes into the water from bank to bank to mark out the safe ford, and some of their light-armed and most of their Goths were by now in the water or up on the Wolfing meadow with the more part of their baggage and wains; and the rest of the host was drawn up in good order, band by band, waiting the word to take the water, and the captain was standing nigh to the river bank beside their God the chief banner of the Host.

Of a sudden one of the dastards of the Goths who was close to the Captain cried out that he heard horse coming; but because he spake in the Gothic tongue, few heeded; but even therewith an old leader of a hundred cried out the same tidings in the Roman tongue, and all men fell to handling their weapons; but before they could face duly toward the meadow, came rushing from out of the mist a storm of shafts that smote many men, and therewithal burst forth the sound of the Markmen's war-horn, like the roaring of a hundred bulls mingled with the thunder of horses at the gallop; and then dark over the wall of mist showed the crests of the riders of the Mark, though scarce were their horses seen till their whole war-rank came dark and glittering into the space of the rising-ground where the mist was but a haze now, and now at last smitten athwart by the low sun just arisen.

Therewith came another storm of shafts, wherein javelins and spears cast by the hand were mingled with the arrows: but the Roman ranks had faced the meadow and the storm which it yielded, swiftly and steadily, and they stood fast and threw their spears, albeit not with such good aim as might have been, because of their haste, so that few were slain by them. And the Roman Captain still loth to fight with the Goths in earnest for no reward, and still more and more believing that this was the only band of them that he had to look to, bade those who were nighest the ford not to tarry for the onset of a few wild riders, but to go their ways into the water; else by a sudden onrush might the Romans have entangled Otter's band in their ranks, and so destroyed all. As it was the horsemen fell not on the Roman ranks full in face, but passing like a storm athwart the ranks to the right, fell on there where they were in thinnest array (for they were gathered to the ford as aforesaid), and slew some and drave some into the deeps and troubled the whole Roman host.

So now the Roman Captain was forced to take new order, and gather all his men together, and array his men for a hard fight; and by now the mist was rolling off from the face of the whole meadow and the sun was bright and hot. His men serried their ranks, and the front rank cast their spears, and slew both men and horses of the Goths as those rode along their front casting their javelins, and shooting here and there from behind their horses if occasion served, or making a shift to send an arrow even as they sat a-horseback; then the second rank of the Romans would take the place of the first, and cast in their turn, and they who had taken the water turned back and took their place behind the others, and many of the light-armed came with them, and all the mass of them flowed forward together, looking as if it might never be broken. But Otter would not abide the shock, since he had lost men and horses, and had no mind to be caught in the sweep of their net; so he made the sign, and his Company drew off to right and left, yet keeping within bow-shot, so that the bowmen still loosed at the Romans.

But they for their part might not follow afoot men on untired horses, and their own horse was on the west side with the baggage, and had it been there would have been but of little avail, as the Roman Captain knew. So they stood awhile making grim countenance, and then slowly drew back to the ford under cover of their light-armed who shot at the Goths as they rode forward, but abode not their shock.

But Otter and his folk followed after the Romans again, and again did them some hurt, and at last drew so nigh, that once more the Romans stormed forth, and once more smote a stroke in the air; nor even so would the Markmen cease to meddle with them, though never would Otter suffer his men to be mingled with them. At the last the Romans, seeing that Otter would not walk into the open trap, and growing weary of this bickering, began to take the water little by little, while a strong Company kept face to the Markmen; and now Otter saw that they would not be hindered any longer, and he had lost many men, and even now feared lest he should be caught in the trap, and so lose all. And on the other hand it was high noon by now, so that he had given respite to the stay-at-homes of the Wolfings, so that they might get them into the wood. So he drew out of bowshot and bade his men breathe their horses and rest themselves and eat something; and they did so gladly, since they saw that they might not fall upon the Romans to live and die for it until Thiodolf was come, or until they knew that he was not coming. But the Romans crossed the ford in good earnest and were soon all gathered together on the western bank making them ready for the march to Wolfstead. And it must be told that the Roman Captain was the more deliberate about this because after the overthrow of his light-armed there the morning before, he thought that the Roof was held by warriors of the kindreds, and not by a few old men, and women, and lads. Therefore he had no fear of their escaping him. Moreover it was this imagination of his, to wit that a strong band of warriors was holding Wolf-stead, that made him deem there were no more worth thinking about of the warriors of the Mark save Otter's Company and the men in the Hall of the Wolfings.

22. OTTER FALLS ON AGAINST HIS WILL

It was with the same imagination working in him belike that the Roman Captain set none to guard the ford on the westward side of Mirkwood-water. The Romans tarried there but a little hour, and then went their ways; but Otter sent a man on a swift horse to watch them, and when they were clean gone for half an hour, he bade his folk to horse, and they departed, all save a handful of the swains and elders, who were left to tell the tidings to Thiodolf when he should come into Mid-mark.

So Otter and his folk crossed the ford, and drew up in good order on the westward bank, and it was then somewhat more than three hours after noon. He had been there but a little while before he noted a stir in the Bearing meadow, and lo, it was the first of Thiodolf's folk, who had gotten out of the wood and had fallen in with the men whom he had left behind. And these first were the riders of the Bearings, and the Wormings, (for they had out-gone the others who were afoot). It may well be thought how fearful was their anger when they set eyes on the smouldering ashes of the dwellings; nor even when those folk of Otter had told them all they had to tell could some of them refrain them from riding off to the burnt houses to seek for the bodies of their kindred. But when they came there, and amidst the ashes could find no bones, their hearts were lightened, and yet so mad wroth they were, that some could scarce sit their horses, and great tears gushed from the eyes of some, and pattered down like hail-stones, so eager were they to see the blood of the Romans. So they rode back to where they had left their folk talking with them of Otter; and the Bearings were sitting grim upon their horses and somewhat scowling on Otter's men. Then the foremost of those who had come back from the houses waved his hand toward the ford, but could say nought for a while; but the captain and chief of the Bearings, a grizzled man very big of body, whose name was Arinbiorn, spake to that man and said; "What aileth thee Sweinbiorn the Black? What hast thou seen?"

He said:

Now red and grey is the pavement of the Bearings' house of old:
Red yet is the floor of the dais, but the hearth all grey and cold.

I knew not the house of my fathers; I could not call to mind
The fashion of the building of that Warder of the Wind.
O wide were grown the windows, and the roof exceeding high!
For nought there was to look on 'twixt the pavement and the sky.
But the tie-beam lay on the dais, and methought its staining fair;
For rings of smoothest charcoal were round it here and there,
And the red flame flickered o'er it, and never a staining wight
Hath red earth in his coffer so clear and glittering bright,
And still the little smoke-wreaths curled o'er it pale and blue
Yea, fair is our hall's adorning for a feast that is strange and new.

Said Arinbiorn: "What sawest thou therein, O Sweinbiorn, where sat thy grandsire at the feast? Where were the bones of thy mother lying?"

Said Sweinbiorn:

We sought the feast-hall over, and nought we found therein
Of the bones of the ancient mothers, or the younglings of the kin.
The men are greedy, doubtless, to lose no whit of the prey,
And will try if the hoary elders may yet outlive the way
That leads to the southland cities, till at last they come to stand
With the younglings in the market to be sold in an alien land.

Arinbiorn's brow lightened somewhat; but ere he could speak again an ancient thrall of the Galtings spake and said:

"True it is, O warriors of the Bearings, that we might not see any war-thralls being led away by the Romans when they came away from the burning dwellings; and we deem it certain that they crossed the water before the coming of the Romans, and that they are now with the stay-at-homes of the Wolfings in the wild-wood behind the Wolfing dwellings, for we hear tell that the War-duke would not that the Hall-Sun should hold the Hall against the whole Roman host."

Then Sweinbiorn tossed up his sword into the air and caught it by the hilts as it fell, and cried out: "On, on to the meadow, where these thieves abide us!" Arinbiorn spake no word, but turned his horse and rode down to the ford, and all men followed him; and of the Bearings there were an hundred warriors save one, and of the Wormings eighty and seven.

So rode they over the meadow and into the ford and over it, and Otter's company stood on the bank to meet them, and shouted to see them; but the others made but little noise as they crossed the water.

So when they were on the western bank Arinbiorn came among them of Otter, and cried out: "Where then is Otter, where is the War-duke, is he alive or dead?"

And the throng opened to him and Otter stood facing him; and Arinbiorn spake and said: "Thou art alive and unhurt, War-duke, when many have been hurt and slain; and methinks thy company is little minished though the kindred of the Bearings lacketh a roof; and its elders and women and children are gone into captivity. What is this? Was it a light thing that gangrel thieves should burn and waste in Mid-mark and depart unhurt, that ye stand here with clean blades and cold bodies?"

Said Otter: "Thou grievest for the hurt of thine House, Arinbiorn; but this at least is good, that though ye have lost the timber of your house ye have not lost its flesh and blood; the shell is gone, but the kernel is saved: for thy folk are by this time in the wood with the Wolfing stay-at-homes, and among these are many who may fight on occasion, so they are safe as for this time: the Romans may not come at them to hurt them."

Said Arinbiorn: "Had ye time to learn all this, Otter, when ye fled so fast before the Romans, that the father tarried not for the son, nor the son for the father?"

He spoke in a loud voice so that many heard him, and some deemed it evil; for anger and dissension between friends seemed abroad; but some were so eager for battle, that the word of Arinbiorn seemed good to them, and they laughed for pride and anger.

Then Otter answered meekly, for he was a wise man and a bold: "We fled not, Arinbiorn, but as the sword fleeth, when it springeth up from the iron helm to fall on the woollen coat. Are we not now of more avail to you, O men of the Bearings, than our dead corpses would have been?"

Arinbiorn answered not, but his face waxed red, as if he were struggling with a weight hard to lift: then said Otter:

"But when will Thiodolf and the main battle be with us?"

Arinbiorn answered calmly: "Maybe in a little hour from now, or somewhat more."

Said Otter: "My rede is that we abide him here, and when we are all met and well ordered together, fall on the Romans at once: for then shall we be more than they; whereas now we are far fewer, and moreover we shall have to set on them in their ground of vantage."

Arinbiorn answered nothing; but an old man of the Bearings, one Thorbiorn, came up and spake:

"Warriors, here are we talking and taking counsel, though this is no Hallowed Thing to bid us what we shall do, and what we shall forbear; and to talk thus is less like warriors than old women wrangling over the why and wherefore of a broken crock. Let the War-duke rule here, as is but meet and right. Yet if I might speak and not break the peace of the Goths, then would I say this, that it might be better for us to fall on these Romans at once before they have cast up a dike about them, as Fox telleth is their wont, and that even in an hour they may do much."

As he spake there was a murmur of assent about him, but Otter spake sharply, for he was grieved.

"Thorbiorn, thou art old, and shouldest not be void of prudence. Now it had been better for thee to have been in the wood to-day to order the women and the swains according to thine ancient wisdom than to egg on my young warriors to fare unwarily. Here will I abide Thiodolf."

Then Thorbiorn reddened and was wroth; but Arinbiorn spake:

"What is this to-do? Let the War-duke rule as is but right: but I am now become a man of Thiodolf's company; and he bade me haste on before to help all I might. Do thou as thou wilt, Otter: for Thiodolf shall be here in an hour's space, and if much diking shall be done in an hour, yet little slaying, forsooth, shall be done, and that especially if the foe is all armed and slayeth women and children. Yea if the Bearing women be all slain, yet shall not Tyr make us new ones out of the stones of the waste to wed with the Galtings and the fish-eating Houses?—this is easy to be done forsooth. Yea, easier than fighting the Romans and overcoming them!"

And he was very wrath, and turned away; and again there was a murmur and a hum about him. But while these had been speaking aloud, Sweinbiorn had been talking softly to some of the younger men, and now he shook his naked sword in the air and spake aloud and sang:

Ye tarry, Bears of Battle! ye linger, Sons of the Worm!
Ye crouch adown, O kindreds, from the gathering of the storm!
Ye say, it shall soon pass over and we shall fare afield
And reap the wheat with the war-sword and winnow in the shield.
But where shall be the corner wherein ye then shall abide,
And where shall be the woodland where the whelps of the bears shall
*   hide*
When 'twixt the snowy mountains and the edges of the sea
These men have swept the wild-wood and the fields where men may be
Of every living sword-blade, and every quivering spear,
And in the southland cities the yoke of slaves ye bear?
Lo ye! whoever follows I fare to sow the seed
Of the days to be hereafter and the deed that comes of deed.

Therewith he waved his sword over his head, and made as if he would spur onward. But Arinbiorn thrust through the press and outwent him and cried out:

"None goeth before Arinbiorn the Old when the battle is pitched in the meadows of the kindred. Come, ye sons of the Bear, ye children of the Worm! And come ye, whosoever hath a will to see stout men die!"

Then on he rode nor looked behind him, and the riders of the Bearings and the Wormings drew themselves out of the throng, and followed him, and rode clattering over the meadow towards Wolfstead. A few of the others rode with them, and yet but a few. For they remembered the holy Folk-mote and the oath of the War-duke, and how they had chosen Otter to be their leader. Howbeit, man looked askance at man, as if in shame to be left behind.

But Otter bethought him in the flash of a moment, "If these men ride alone, they shall die and do nothing; and if we ride with them it may be that we shall overthrow the Romans, and if we be vanquished, it shall go hard but we shall slay many of them, so that it shall be the easier for Thiodolf to deal with them."

Then he spake hastily, and bade certain men abide at the ford for a guard; then he drew his sword and rode to the front of his folk, and cried out aloud to them:

"Now at last has come the time to die, and let them of the Markmen who live hereafter lay us in howe. Set on, Sons of Tyr, and give not your lives away, but let them be dearly earned of our foemen."

Then all shouted loudly and gladly; nor were they otherwise than exceeding glad; for now had they forgotten all other joys of life save the joy of fighting for the kindred and the days to be.

So Otter led them forth, and when he heard the whole company clattering and thundering on the earth behind him and felt their might enter into him, his brow cleared, and the anxious lines in the face of the old man smoothed themselves out, and as he rode along the soul so stirred within him that he sang out aloud:

Time was when hot was the summer and I was young on the earth,
And I grudged me every moment that lacked its share of mirth.
I woke in the morn and was merry and all the world methought
For me and my heart's deliverance that hour was newly wrought.
I have passed through the halls of manhood, I have reached the doors of
*   eld,*
And I have been glad and sorry, but ever have upheld
My heart against all trouble that none might call me sad,
But ne'er came such remembrance of how my heart was glad
In the afternoon of summer 'neath the still unwearied sun
Of the days when I was little and all deeds were hopes to be won,
As now at last it cometh when e'en in such-like tide,
For the freeing of my trouble o'er the fathers' field I ride.

Many men perceived that he sang, and saw that he was merry, howbeit few heard his very words, and yet all were glad of him.

Fast they rode, being wishful to catch up with the Bearings and the Wormings, and soon they came anigh them, and they, hearing the thunder of the horse-hoofs, looked and saw that it was the company of Otter, and so slacked their speed till they were all joined together with joyous shouting and laughter. So then they ordered the ranks anew and so set forward in great joy without haste or turmoil toward Wolfstead and the

Romans. For now the bitterness of their fury and the sourness of their abiding wrath were turned into the mere joy of battle; even as the clear red and sweet wine comes of the ugly ferment and rough trouble of the must.

23. THIODOLF MEETETH THE ROMANS IN THE WOLFING MEADOW

It was scarce an hour after this that the footmen of Thiodolf came out of the thicket road on to the meadow of the Bearings; there saw they men gathered on a rising ground, and they came up to them and saw how some of them were looking with troubled faces towards the ford and what lay beyond it, and some toward the wood and the coming of Thiodolf. But these were they whom Otter had bidden abide Thiodolf there, and he had sent two messengers to them for Thiodolf's behoof that he might have due tidings so soon as he came out of the thicket: the first told how Otter had been compelled in a manner to fall on the Romans along with the riders of the Bearings and the Wormings, and the second who had but just then come, told how the Markmen had been worsted by the Romans, and had given back from the Wolfing dwellings, and were making a stand against the foemen in the meadow betwixt the ford and Wolfstead.

Now when Thiodolf heard of these tidings he stayed not to ask long questions, but led the whole host straightway down to the ford, lest the remnant of Otter's men should be driven down there, and the Romans should hold the western bank against him.

At the ford there was none to withstand them, nor indeed any man at all; for the men whom Otter had set there, when they heard that the battle had gone against their kindred, had ridden their ways to join them. So Thiodolf crossed over the ford, he and his in good order all afoot, he like to the others; but for him he was clad in the Dwarf-wrought Hauberk, but was unhelmeted and bare no shield. Throng-plough was naked in his hand as he came up all dripping on to the bank and stood in the meadow of the Wolfings; his face was stern and set as he gazed straight onward to the place of the fray, but he did not look as joyous as his wont was in going down to the battle.

Now they had gone but a short way from the ford before the noise of the fight and the blowing of horns came down the wind to them, but it was a little way further before they saw the fray with their eyes; because the ground fell away from the river somewhat at first, and then rose and fell again before it went up in one slope toward the Wolfing dwellings.

But when they were come to the top of the next swelling of the ground, they beheld from thence what they had to deal with; for there round about a ground of vantage was the field black with the Roman host, and in the midst of it was a tangle of struggling men and tossing spears, and glittering swords.

So when they beheld the battle of their kindred they gave a great shout and hastened onward the faster; and they were ordered into the wedge-array and Thiodolf led them, as meet it was. And now even as they who were on the outward edge of the array and could see what was toward were looking on the battle with eager eyes, there came an answering shout down the wind, which they knew for the voice of the Goths amid the foemen, and then they saw how the ring of the Romans shook and parted, and their array fell back, and lo the company of the Markmen standing stoutly together, though sorely minished; and sure it was that they had not fled or been scattered, but were ready to fall one over another in one band, for there were no men straggling towards the ford, though many masterless horses ran here and there about the meadow. Now, therefore, none doubted but that they would deliver their friends from the Romans, and overthrow the foemen.

But now befel a wonder, a strange thing to tell of. The Romans soon perceived what was adoing, whereupon the half of them turned about to face the new comers, while the other half still withstood the company of Otter: the wedge-array of Thiodolf drew nearer and nearer till it was hard on the place where it should spread itself out to storm down on the foe, and the Goths beset by the Romans made them ready to fall on from their side. There was Thiodolf leading his host, and all men looking for the token and sign to fall on; but even as he lifted up Throng-plough to give that sign, a cloud came over his eyes and he saw nought of all that was before him, and he staggered back as one who hath gotten a deadly stroke, and so fell swooning to the earth, though none had smitten him. Then stayed was the wedge-array even at the very point of onset, and the hearts of the Goths sank, for they deemed that their leader was slain, and those who were nearest to him raised him up and bore him hastily aback out of the battle; and the Romans also had beheld him fall, and they also deemed him dead or sore hurt, and shouted for joy and loitered not, but stormed forth on the wedge-array like valiant men; for it must be told that they, who erst out-numbered the company of Otter, were now much out-numbered, but they deemed it might well be that they could dismay the Goths since they had been stayed by the fall of their leader; and Otter's company were wearied with sore fighting against a great host. Nevertheless these last, who had not seen the fall of Thiodolf (for the Romans were thick between him and them) fell on with such exceeding fury that they drove the Romans who faced them back on those who had set on the wedge-array, which also stood fast undismayed; for he who stood next to Thiodolf, a man big of body, and stout of heart, bight Thorolf, hove up a great axe and cried out aloud:

"Here is the next man to Thiodolf! here is one who will not fall till some one thrusts him over, here is Thorolf of the Wolfings! Stand fast and shield you, and smite, though Thiodolf be gone untimely to the Gods!"

So none gave back a foot, and fierce was the fight about the wedge-array; and the men of Otter—but there was no Otter there, and many another man was gone, and Arinbiorn the Old led them—these stormed on so fiercely that they cleft their way through all and joined themselves to their kindred, and the battle was renewed in the Wolfing meadow. But the Romans had this gain, that Thiodolf's men had let go their occasion for falling on the Romans with their line spread out so that every man might use his weapons; yet were the Goths strong both in valiancy and in numbers, nor might the Romans break into their array, and as aforesaid the Romans were the fewer, for it was less than half of their host that had pursued the Goths when they had been thrust back from their fierce onset: nor did more than the half seem needed, so many of them had fallen along with Otter the War-duke and Sweinbiorn of the Bearings, that they seemed to the Romans but a feeble band easy to overcome.

So fought they in the Wolfing meadow in the fifth hour after high-noon, and neither yielded to the other: but while these things were a-doing, men laid Thiodolf adown aloof from the battle under a doddered oak half a furlong from where the fight was a-doing, round whose bole clung flocks of wool from the sheep that drew around it in the hot summer-tide and rubbed themselves against it, and the ground was trodden bare of grass round the bole, and close to the trunk was worn into a kind of trench. There then they laid Thiodolf, and they wondered that no blood came from him, and that there was no sign of a shot-weapon in his body.

But as for him, when he fell, all memory of the battle and what had gone before it faded from his mind, and he passed into sweet and pleasant dreams wherein he was a lad again in the days before he had fought with the three Hun-Kings in the hazelled field. And in these dreams he was doing after the manner of young lads, sporting in the meadows, backing unbroken colts, swimming in the river, going a-hunting with the elder carles. And especially he deemed that he was in the company of one old man who had taught him both wood-craft and the handling of weapons: and fair at first was his dream of his doings with this man; he was with him in the forge smithy-ing a sword-blade, and hammering into its steel the thin golden wires; and fishing with an angle along with him by the eddies of Mirkwood-water; and sitting with him in an ingle of the Hall, the old man telling a tale of an ancient warrior of the Wolfings hight Thiodolf also: then suddenly and without going there, they were in a little clearing of the woods resting after hunting, a roe-deer with an arrow in her lying at their feet, and the old man was talking, and telling Thiodolf in what wise it was best to go about to get the wind of a hart; but all the while there was going on the thunder of a great gale of wind through the woodland boughs, even as the drone of a bag-pipe cleaves to the tune. Presently Thiodolf arose and would go about his hunting again, and stooped to take up his spear, and even therewith the old man's speech stayed, and Thiodolf looked up, and lo, his face was white like stone, and he touched him, and he was hard as flint, and like the image of an ancient god as to his face and hands, though the wind stirred his hair and his raiment, as they did before. Therewith a great pang smote Thiodolf in his dream, and he felt as if he also were stiffening into stone, and he strove and struggled, and lo, the wild-wood was gone, and a white light empty of all vision was before him, and as he moved his head this became the Wolfing meadow, as he had known it so long, and thereat a soft pleasure and joy took hold of him, till again he looked, and saw there no longer the kine and sheep, and the herdwomen tending them, but the rush and turmoil of that fierce battle, the confused thundering noise of which was going up to the heavens; for indeed he was now fully awake again.

So he stood up and looked about; and around him was a ring of the sorrowful faces of the warriors, who had deemed that he was hurt deadly, though no hurt could they find upon him. But the Dwarf-wrought Hauberk lay upon the ground beside him; for they had taken it off him to look for his hurts.

So he looked into their faces and said: "What aileth you, ye men? I am alive and unhurt; what hath betided?"

And one said: "Art thou verily alive, or a man come back from the dead? We saw thee fall as thou wentest leading us against the foe as if thou hadst been smitten by a thunder-bolt, and we deemed thee dead or grievously hurt. Now the carles are fighting stoutly, and all is well since thou livest yet."

So he said: "Give me the point and edges that I know, that I may smite myself therewith and not the foemen; for I have feared and blenched from the battle."

Said an old warrior: "If that be so, Thiodolf, wilt thou blench twice? Is not once enough? Now let us go back to the hard handplay, and if thou wilt, smite thyself after the battle, when we have once more had a man's help of thee."

Therewith he held out Throng-plough to him by the point, and Thiodolf took hold of the hilts and handled it and said:

"Let us hasten, while the Gods will have it so, and while they are still suffering me to strike a stroke for the kindred."

And therewith he brandished Throng-plough, and went forth toward the battle, and the heart grew hot within him, and the joy of waking life came back to him, the joy which but erewhile he had given to a mere dream.

But the old man who had rebuked him stooped down and lifted the Hauberk from the ground, and cried out after him, "O Thiodolf, and wilt thou go naked into so strong a fight? and thou with this so goodly sword-rampart?"

Thiodolf stayed a moment, and even therewith they looked, and lo! the Romans giving back before the Goths and the Goths following up the chase, but slowly and steadily. Then Thiodolf heeded nothing save the battle, but ran forward hast-ily, and those warriors followed him, the old man last of all holding the Hauberk in his hand, and muttering:

So fares hot blood to the glooming and the world beneath the grass;
And the fruit of the Wolfings' orchard in a flash from the world must pass.
Men say that the tree shall blossom in the garden of the folk,
And the new twig thrust him forward from the place where the old one broke,
And all be well as aforetime: but old and old I grow,
And I doubt me if such another the folk to come shall know.

And he still hurried forward as fast as his old body might go, so that he might wrap the safeguard of the Hauberk round Thiodolf's body.

24. THE GOTHS ARE OVERTHROWN BY THE ROMANS

Now rose up a mighty shout when Thiodolf came back to the battle of the kindreds, for many thought he had been slain; and they gathered round about him, and cried out to him joyously out of their hearts of good-fellowship, and the old man who had rebuked Thiodolf, and who was Jorund of the Wolfings, came up to him and reached out to him the Hauberk, and he did it on scarce heeding; for all his heart and soul was turned toward the battle of the Romans and what they were a-doing; and he saw that they were falling back in good order, as men out-numbered, but undismayed. So he gathered all his men together and ordered them afresh; for they were somewhat dis-arrayed with the fray and the chase: and now he no longer ordered them in the wedge array, but in a line here three deep, here five deep, or more, for the foes were hard at hand, and outnumbered, and so far overcome, that he and all men deemed it a little matter to give these their last overthrow, and then onward to Wolf-stead to storm on what was left there and purge the house of the foemen. Howbeit Thiodolf bethought him that succour might come to the Romans from their main-battle, as they needed not many men there, since there was nought to fear behind them: but the thought was dim within him, for once more since he had gotten the Hauberk on him the earth was wavering and dream-like: he looked about him, and nowise was he as in past days of battle when he saw nought but the foe before him, and hoped for nothing save the victory. But now indeed the Wood-Sun seemed to him to be beside him, and not against his will, as one besetting and hindering him, but as though his own longing had drawn her thither and would not let her depart; and whiles it seemed to him that her beauty was clearer to be seen than the bodies of the warriors round about him. For the rest he seemed to be in a dream indeed, and, as men do in dreams, to be for ever striving to be doing something of more moment than anything which he did, but which he must ever leave undone. And as the dream gathered and thickened about him the foe before him changed to his eyes, and seemed no longer the stern brown-skinned smooth-faced men under their crested iron helms with their iron-covered shields before them, but rather, big-headed men, small of stature, long-bearded, swart, crooked of body, exceeding foul of aspect. And he looked on and did nothing for a while, and his head whirled as though he had been griev-ously smitten.

Thus tarried the kindreds awhile, and they were bewildered and their hearts fell because Thiodolf did not fly on the foe-men like a falcon on the quarry, as his wont was. But as for the Romans, they had now stayed, and were facing their foes again, and that on a vantage-ground, since the field sloped up toward the Wolfing dwelling; and they gathered heart when they saw that the Goths tarried and forbore them. But the sun was sinking, and the evening was hard at hand.

So at last Thiodolf led forward with Throng-plough held aloft in his right hand; but his left hand he held out by his side, as though he were leading someone along. And as he went, he muttered: "When will these accursed sons of the nether earth leave the way clear to us, that we may be alone and take plea-sure each in each amidst of the flowers and the sun?"

Now as the two hosts drew near to one another, again came the sound of trumpets afar off, and men knew that this would be succour coming to the Romans from their main-battle, and the Romans thereon shouted for joy, and the host of the kin-dreds might no longer forbear, but rushed on fiercely against them; and for Thiodolf it was now come to this, that so entan-gled was he in his dream that he rather went with his men than led them. Yet had he Throng-plough in his right hand, and he muttered in his beard as he went, "Smite before! smite behind! and smite on the right hand! but never on the left!"

Thus then they met, and as before, neither might the Goths sweep the Romans away, nor the Romans break the Goths into flight; yet were many of the kindred anxious and troubled, since they knew that aid was coming to the Romans, and they heard the trumpets sounding nearer and more joyous; and at last, as the men of the kindreds were growing a-wearied with fighting, they heard those horns as it were in their very ears, and the thunder of the tramp of footmen, and they knew that a fresh host of men was upon them; then those they had been fighting with opened before them, falling aside to the right and the left, and the fresh men passing between them, fell on the Goths like the waters of a river when a sluice-gate is opened. They came on in very good order, never breaking their ranks, but swift withal, smiting and pushing before them, and so brake through the array of the Goth-folk, and drave them this way and that way down the slopes.

Yet still fought the warriors of the kindred most valiantly, making stand and facing the foe again and again in knots of a score or two score, or maybe ten score; and though many a man was slain, yet scarce any one before he had slain or hurt a Roman; and some there were, and they the oldest, who fought as if they and the few about them were all the host that was left to the folk, and heeded not that others were driven back, or that the Romans gathered about them, cutting them off from all succour and aid, but went on smiting till they were felled with many strokes.

Howbeit the array of the Goths was broken and many were slain, and perforce they must give back, and it seemed as if they would be driven into the river and all be lost.

But for Thiodolf, this befell him: that at first, when those fresh men fell on, he seemed, as it were, to wake unto himself again, and he cried aloud the cry of the Wolf, and thrust into the thickest of the fray, and slew many and was hurt of none, and for a moment of time there was an empty space round about him, such fear he cast even into the valiant hearts of the foemen. But those who had time to see him as they stood by him noted that he was as pale as a dead man, and his eyes set and staring; and so of a sudden, while he stood thus threatening the ring of doubtful foemen, the weakness took him again, Throng-plough tumbled from his hand, and he fell to earth as one dead.

Then of those who saw him some deemed that he had been striving against some secret hurt till he could do no more; and some that there was a curse abroad that had fallen upon him and upon all the kindreds of the Mark; some thought him dead and some swooning. But, dead or alive, the warriors would not leave their War-duke among the foemen, so they lifted him, and gathered about him a goodly band that held its own

against all comers, and fought through the turmoil stoutly and steadily; and others gathered to them, till they began to be something like a host again, and the Romans might not break them into knots of desperate men any more.

Thus they fought their way, Arinbiorn of the Bearings leading them now, with a mind to make a stand for life or death on some vantage-ground; and so, often turning upon the Romans, they came in array ever growing more solid to the rising ground looking one way over the ford and the other to the slopes where the battle had just been. There they faced the foe as men who may be slain, but will be driven no further; and what bowmen they had got spread out from their flanks and shot on the Romans, who had with them no light-armed, or slingers or bowmen, for they had left them at Wolf-stead. So the Romans stood a while, and gave breathing-space to the Markmen, which indeed was the saving of them: for if they had fallen on hotly and held to it steadily, it is like that they would have passed over all the bodies of the Markmen: for these had lost their leader, either slain, as some thought, or, as others thought, banned from leadership by the Gods; and their host was heavy-hearted; and though it is like that they would have stood there till each had fallen over other, yet was their hope grown dim, and the whole folk brought to a perilous and fearful pass, for if these were slain or scattered there were no more but they, and nought between fire and the sword and the people of the Mark.

But once again the faint-heart folly of the Roman Captain saved his foes: for whereas he once thought that the whole power of the Markmen lay in Otter and his company, and deemed them too little to meddle with, so now he ran his head into the other hedge, and deemed that Thiodolf's company was but a part of the succour that was at hand for the Goths, and that they were over-big for him to meddle with.

True it is also that now dark night was coming on, and the land was unknown to the Romans, who moreover trusted not wholly to the dastards of the Goths who were their guides and scouts: furthermore the wood was at hand, and they knew not what it held; and with all this and above it all, it is to be said that over them also had fallen a dread of some doom anear; for those habitations amidst of the wild-woods were terrible to them as they were dear to the Goths; and the Gods of their foemen seemed to be lying in wait to fall upon them, even if they should slay every man of the kindreds.

So now having driven back the Goths to that height over the ford, which indeed was no stronghold, no mountain, scarce a hill even, nought but a gentle swelling of the earth, they forebore them; and raising up the whoop of victory drew slowly aback, picking up their own dead and wounded, and slaying the wounded Markmen. They had with them also some few captives, but not many; for the fighting had been to the death between man and man on the Wolfing Meadow.

25. THE HOST OF THE MARKMEN COMETH INTO THE WILD-WOOD

Yet though the Romans were gone, the Goth-folk were very hard bested. They had been overthrown, not sorely maybe if they had been in an alien land, and free to come and go as they would; yet sorely as things were, because the foeman was sitting in their own House, and they must needs drag him out of it or perish: and to many the days seemed evil, and the Gods fighting against them, and both the Wolfings and the other kindreds bethought them of the Hall-Sun and her wisdom and longed to hear of tidings concerning her.

But now the word ran through the host that Thiodolf was certainly not slain. Slowly he had come to himself, and yet was not himself, for he sat among his men gloomy and silent, clean contrary to his wont; for hitherto he had been a merry man, and a joyous fellow.

Amidst of the ridge whereon the Markmen now abode, there was a ring made of the chief warriors and captains and wise men who had not been slain or grievously hurt in the fray, and amidst them all sat Thiodolf on the ground, his chin sunken on his breast, looking more like a captive than the leader of a host amidst of his men; and that the more as his scabbard was empty; for when Throng-plough had fallen from his hand, it had been trodden under foot, and lost in the turmoil. There he sat, and the others in that ring of men looked sadly upon him; such as Arinbiorn of the Bearings, and Wolfkettle and Thorolf of his own House, and Hiarandi of the Elkings, and Geirbald the Shielding, the messenger of the woods, and Fox who had seen the Roman Garth, and many others. It was night now, and men had lighted fires about the host, for they said that the Romans knew where to find them if they listed to seek; and about those fires were men eating and drinking what they might come at, but amidst of that ring was the biggest fire, and men turned them towards it for counsel and help, for elsewhere none said, "What do we?" for they were heavy-hearted and redeless, since the Gods had taken the victory out of their hands just when they seemed at point to win it.

But amidst all this there was a little stir outside that biggest ring, and men parted, and through them came a swain amongst the chiefs, and said, "Who will lead me to the War-duke?"

Thiodolf, who was close beside the lad, answered never a word; but Arinbiorn said; "This man here sitting is the War-duke: speak to him, for he may hearken to thee: but first who art thou?"

Said the lad; "My name is Ali the son of Grey, and I come with a message from the Hall-Sun and the stay-at-homes who are in the Woodland."

Now when he named the Hall-Sun Thiodolf started and looked up, and turning to his left-hand said, "And what sayeth thy daughter?"

Men did not heed that he said *thy* daughter, but deemed that he said *my* daughter, since he was wont as her would-be foster-father to call her so. But Ali spake:

"War-duke and ye chieftains, thus saith the Hall-Sun: 'I know that by this time Otter hath been slain and many another, and ye have been overthrown and chased by the Romans, and that now there is little counsel in you except to abide the foe where ye are and there to die valiantly. But now do my bidding and as I am bidden, and then whosoever dieth or liveth, the kindreds shall vanquish that they may live and grow greater. Do ye thus: the Romans think no otherwise but to find you here to-morrow or else departed across the water as broken men, and they will fall upon you with their whole host, and then make a war-garth after their manner at Wolf-stead and carry fire and the sword and the chains of thralldom into every House of the Mark. Now therefore fetch a compass and come into the wood on the north-west of the houses and make your way to the Thing-stead of the Mid-mark. For who knoweth but that to-morrow we may fall upon these thieves again? Of this shall ye hear more when we may speak together and take counsel face to face; for we stay-at-homes know somewhat closely of the ways of these Romans. Haste then! let not the grass grow over your feet!

"'But to thee, Thiodolf, have I a word to say when we meet; for I wot that as now thou canst not hearken to my word.' Thus saith the Hall-Sun."

"Wilt thou speak, War-duke?" said Arinbiorn. But Thiodolf shook his head. Then said Arinbiorn; "Shall I speak for thee?" and Thiodolf nodded yea. Then said Arinbiorn: "Ali son of Grey, art thou going back to her that sent thee?"

"Yea," said the lad, "but in your company, for ye will be coming straightway and I know all the ways closely; and there is need for a guide through the dark night as ye will see presently."

Then stood up Arinbiorn and said: "Chiefs and captains, go ye speedily and array your men for departure: bid them leave all the fires burning and come their ways as silently as maybe; for now will we wend this same hour before moonrise into the Wild-wood and the Thing-stead of Mid-mark; thus saith the War-duke."

But when they were gone, and Arinbiorn and Thiodolf were left alone, Thiodolf lifted up his head and spake slowly and painfully:

"Arinbiorn, I thank thee: and thou dost well to lead this folk: since as for me that is somewhat that weighs me down, and I know not whether it be life or death; therefore I may no longer be your captain, for twice now have I blenched from the battle. Yet command me, and I will obey, set a sword in my hand and I will smite, till the God snatches it out of my hand, as he did Throng-plough to-day."

"And that is well," said Arinbiorn, "it may be that ye shall meet that God to-morrow, and heave up sword against him, and either overcome him or go to thy fathers a proud and valiant man."

So they spake, and Thiodolf stood up and seemed of better cheer. But presently the whole host was afoot, and they went their ways warily with little noise, and wound little by little about the Wolfing meadow and about the acres towards the wood at the back of the Houses; and they met nothing by the way except an out-guard of the Romans, whom they slew there nigh silently, and bore away their bodies, twelve in number, lest the Romans when they sent to change the guard, should find the slain and have an inkling of the way the Goths were gone; but now they deemed that the Romans might think their guard fled, or perchance that they had been carried away by the Gods of the woodland folk.

So came they into the wood, and Arinbiorn and the chiefs were for striking the All-men's road to the Thing-stead and so coming thither; but the lad Ali when he heard it laughed and said:

"If ye would sleep to-night ye shall wend another way. For the Hall-Sun hath had us at work cumbering it against the foe with great trees felled with limbs, branches, and all. And indeed ye shall find the Thing-stead fenced like a castle, and the in-gate hard to find; yet will I bring you thither."

So did he without delay, and presently they came anigh the Thing-stead; and the place was fenced cunningly, so that if men would enter they must go by a narrow way that had a fence of tree-trunks on each side wending inward like the maze in a pleasance. Thereby now wended the host all afoot, since it was a holy place and no beast must set foot therein, so that the horses were left without it: so slowly and right quietly once more they came into the garth of the Thing-stead; and lo, a many folk there, of the Wolfings and the Bearings and other kindreds, who had gathered thereto; and albeit these were not warriors in their prime, yet were there none save the young

children and the weaker of the women but had weapons of some kind; and they were well ordered, standing or sitting in ranks like folk awaiting battle. There were booths of boughs and rushes set up for shelter of the feebler women and the old men and children along the edges of the fence, for the Hall-Sun had bidden them keep the space clear round about the Doom-ring and the Hill-of-Speech as if for a mighty folk-mote, so that the warriors might have room to muster there and order their array. There were some cooking-fires lighted about the aforesaid booths, but neither many nor great, and they were screened with wattle from the side that lay toward the Romans; for the Hall-Sun would not that they should hold up lanterns for their foemen to find them by. Little noise there was in that stronghold, moreover, for the hearts of all who knew their right hands from their left were set on battle and the destruction of the foe that would destroy the kindreds.

Anigh the Speech-Hill, on its eastern side, had the bole of a slender beech tree been set up, and at the top of it a cross-beam was nailed on, and therefrom hung the wondrous lamp, the Hall-Sun, glimmering from on high, and though its light was but a glimmer amongst the mighty wood, yet was it also screened on three sides from the sight of the chance wanderer by wings of thin plank. But beneath her namesake as before-time in the Hall sat the Hall-Sun, the maiden, on a heap of fag-gots, and she was wrapped in a dark blue cloak from under which gleamed the folds of the fair golden-broidered gown she was wont to wear at folk-motes, and her right hand rested on a naked sword that lay across her knees: beside her sat the old man Sorli, the Wise in War, and about her were slim lads and sturdy maidens and old carles of the thralls or freedmen ready to bear the commands that came from her mouth; for she and Sorli were the captains of the stay-at-homes.

Now came Thiodolf and Arinbiorn and other leaders into the ring of men before her, and she greeted them kindly and said:

"Hail, Sons of Tyr! now that I behold you again it seemeth to me as if all were already won: the time of waiting hath been weary, and we have borne the burden of fear every day from morn till even, and in the waking hour we presently remem-bered it. But now ye are come, even if this Thing-stead were lighted by the flames of the Wolfing Roof instead of by these moonbeams; even if we had to begin again and seek new dwellings, and another water and other meadows, yet great should grow the kindreds of the Men who have dwelt in the Mark, and nought should overshadow them: and though the beasts and the Romans were dwelling in their old places, yet should these kindreds make new clearings in the Wild-wood; and they with their deeds should cause other waters to be famous, that as yet have known no deeds of man; and they should compel the Earth to bear increase round about their dwelling-places for the welfare of the kindreds. O Sons of Tyr, friendly are your faces, and undismayed, and the Terror of the Nations has not made you afraid any more than would the onrush of the bisons that feed adown the grass hills. Happy is the eve, O children of the Goths, yet shall to-morrow morn be happier."

Many heard what she spake, and a murmur of joy ran through the ranks of men: for they deemed her words to forecast victory.

And now amidst her speaking, the moon, which had arisen on Mid-mark, when the host first entered into the wood, had overtopped the tall trees that stood like a green wall round about the Thing-stead, and shone down on that assembly, and flashed coldly back from the arms of the warriors. And the Hall-Sun cast off her dark blue cloak and stood up in her golden-broidered raiment, which flashed back the grey light like as it had been an icicle hanging from the roof of some hall in the midnight of Yule, when the feast is high within, and without the world is silent with the night of the ten-weeks' frost.

Then she spake again: "O War-duke, thy mouth is silent; speak to this warrior of the Bearings that he bid the host what to do; for wise are ye both, and dear are the minutes of this night and should not be wasted; since they bring about the salvation of the Wolfings, and the vengeance of the Bearings, and the hope renewed of all the kindreds."

Then Thiodolf abode a while with his head down cast; his bosom heaved, and he set his left hand to his swordless scabbard, and his right to his throat, as though he were sore troubled with something he might not tell of: but at last he lifted up his head and spoke to Arinbiorn, but slowly and painfully, as he had spoken before:

"Chief of the Bearings, go up on to the Hill of Speech, and speak to the folk out of thy wisdom, and let them know that to-morrow early before the sun-rising those that may, and are not bound by the Gods against it, shall do deeds according to their might, and win rest for themselves, and new days of deeds for the kindreds."

Therewith he ceased, and let his head fall again, and the Hall-Sun looked at him askance. But Arinbiorn clomb the Speech-Hill and said:

"Men of the kindreds, it is now a few days since we first met the Romans and fought with them; and whiles we have had the better, and whiles the worse in our dealings, as oft in war befalleth: for they are men, and we no less than men. But now look to it what ye will do; for we may no longer endure these outlanders in our houses, and we must either die or get our own again: and that is not merely a few wares stored up for use, nor a few head of neat, nor certain timbers piled up into a dwelling, but the life we have made in the land we have made. I show you no choice, for no choice there is. Here are we bare of everything in the wild-wood: for the most part our children are crying for us at home, our wives are longing for us in our houses, and if we come not to them in kindness, the Romans shall come to them in grimness. Down yonder in the plain, moreover, is our Wain-burg slowly drawing near to us, and with it is much livelihood of ours, which is a little thing, for we may get more; but also there are our banners of battle and the tokens of the kindred, which is a great thing. And between all this and us there lieth but little; nought but a band of valiant men, and a few swords and spears, and a few wounds, and the hope of death amidst the praise of the people; and this ye have to set out to wend across within two or three hours. I will not ask if ye will do so, for I wot that even so ye will; therefore when I have done, shout not, nor clash sword on shield, for we are no great way off that house of ours wherein dwells the foe that would destroy us. Let each man rest as he may, and sleep if he may with his war-gear on him and his weapons by his side, and when he is next awakened by the captains and the leaders of hundreds and scores, let him not think that it is night, but let him betake himself to his place among his kindred and be ready to go through the wood with as little noise as may be. Now all is said that the War-duke would have me say, and to-morrow shall those see him who are foremost in falling upon the foemen, for he longeth sorely for his seat on the days of the Wolfing Hall."

So he spake, and even as he bade them, they made no sound save a joyous murmur; and straightway the more part of them betook themselves to sleep as men who must busy themselves about a weighty matter; for they were wise in the ways of war. So sank all the host to the ground save those who were appointed as watchers of the night, and Arinbiorn and Thiodolf and the Hall-Sun; they three yet stood together; and Arinbiorn said:

"Now it seems to me not so much as if we had vanquished the foe and were safe and at rest, but rather as if we had no foemen and never have had. Deep peace is on me, though hitherto I have been deemed a wrathful man, and it is to me as if the kindreds that I love had filled the whole earth, and left no room for foemen: even so it may really be one day. To-night it is well, yet to-morrow it shall be better. What thine errand may be, Thiodolf, I scarce know; for something hath changed in thee, and thou art become strange to us. But as for mine errand, I will tell it thee; it is that I am seeking Otter of the Laxings, my friend and fellow, whose wisdom my foolishness drave under the point and edge of the Romans, so that he is no longer here; I am seeking him, and to-morrow I think I shall find him, for he hath not had time to travel far, and we shall be blithe and merry together. And now will I sleep; for I have bidden the watchers awaken me if any need be. Sleep thou also, Thiodolf! and wake up thine old self when the moon is low."

Therewith he laid himself down under the lee of the pile of faggots, and was presently asleep.

26. THIODOLF TALKETH WITH THE WOOD-SUN

Now were Thiodolf and the Hall-Sun left alone together standing by the Speech-Hill; and the moon was risen high in the heavens above the tree-tops of the wild-wood. Thiodolf scarce stirred, and he still held his head bent down as one lost in thought.

Then said the Hall-Sun, speaking softly amidst the hush of the camp:

"I have said that the minutes of this night are dear, and they are passing swiftly; and it may be that thou wilt have much to say and to do before the host is astir with the dawning. So come thou with me a little way, that thou mayst hear of new tidings, and think what were best to do amidst them."

And without more ado she took him by the hand and led him forth, and he went as he was led, not saying a word. They passed out of the camp into the wood, none hindering, and went a long way where under the beech-leaves there was but a glimmer of the moonlight, and presently Thiodolf's feet went as it were of themselves; for they had hit a path that he knew well and over-well.

So came they to that little wood-lawn where first in this tale Thiodolf met the Wood-Sun; and the stone seat there was not empty now any more than it was then; for thereon sat the Wood-Sun, clad once more in her glittering raiment. Her head was sunken down, her face hidden by her hands; neither did she look up when she heard their feet on the grass, for she knew who they were.

Thiodolf lingered not; for a moment it was to him as if all that past time had never been, and its battles and hurry and hopes and fears but mere shows, and the unspoken words of a dream. He went straight up to her and sat down by her side and put his arm about her shoulders, and strove to take her hand to caress it; but she moved but little, and it was as if she heeded him not. And the Hall-Sun stood before them and looked at them for a little while; and then she fell to speech; but at the first sound of her voice, it seemed that the Wood-Sun trembled, but still she hid her face. Said the Hall-Sun:

Two griefs I see before me in mighty hearts grown great;
And to change both these into gladness out-goes the power of fate.
Yet I, a lonely maiden, have might to vanquish one
Till it melt as the mist of the morning before the summer sun.
O Wood-Sun, thou hast borne me, and I were fain indeed
To give thee back thy gladness; but thou com'st of the Godhead's seed,
And herein my might avails not; because I can but show

Unto these wedded sorrows the truth that the heart should know
Ere the will hath wielded the hand; and for thee, I can tell thee nought
That thou hast not known this long while; thy will and thine hand
*   have wrought,*
And the man that thou lovest shall live in despite of Gods and of men,
If yet thy will endureth. But what shall it profit thee then
That after the fashion of Godhead thou hast gotten thee a thrall
To be thine and never another's, whatso in the world may befall?
Lo! yesterday this was a man, and to-morrow it might have been
The very joy of the people, though never again it were seen;
Yet a part of all they hoped for through all the lapse of years,
To make their laughter happy and dull the sting of tears;
To quicken all remembrance of deeds that never die,
And death that maketh eager to live as the days go by.
Yea, many a deed had he done as he lay in the dark of the mound;
As the seed-wheat plotteth of spring, laid under the face of the ground
That the foot of the husbandman treadeth, that the wind of the winter
*   wears,*
That the turbid cold flood hideth from the constant hope of the years.
This man that should leave in his death his life unto many an one
Wilt thou make him a God of the fearful who live lone under the sun?
And then shalt thou have what thou wouldedst when amidst of the
*   hazelled field*
Thou kissed'st the mouth of the helper, and the hand of the people's
*   shield,*
Shalt thou have the thing that thou wouldedst when thou broughtest
*   me to birth,*
And I, the soul of the Wolfings, began to look on earth?
Wilt thou play the God, O mother, and make a man anew,
A joyless thing and a fearful? Then I betwixt you two
'Twixt your longing and your sorrow will cast the sundering word,
And tell out all the story of that rampart of the sword!
I shall bid my mighty father make choice of death in life,
Or life in death victorious and the crowned end of strife.

Ere she had ended, the Wood-Sun let her hands fall down, and showed her face, which for all its unpaled beauty looked wearied and anxious; and she took Thiodolf's hand in hers, while she looked with eyes of love upon the Hall-Sun, and Thiodolf laid his cheek to her cheek, and though he smiled not, yet he seemed as one who is happy. At last the Wood-Sun spoke and said:

Thou sayest sooth, O daughter: I am no God of might,
Yet I am of their race, and I think with their thoughts and see with
their sight,
And the threat of the doom did I know of, and yet spared not to lie:
For I thought that the fate foreboded might touch and pass us by,
As the sword that heweth the war-helm and cleaveth a cantle away,
And the cunning smith shall mend it and it goeth again to the fray;
If my hand might have held for a moment, yea, even against his will,
The life of my beloved! But Weird is the master still:
And this man's love of my body and his love of the ancient kin
Were matters o'er mighty to deal with and the game withal to win.
Woe's me for the waning of all things, and my hope that needs must
fade
As the fruitless sun of summer on the waste where nought is made!
And now farewell, O daughter, thou mayst not see the kiss
Of the hapless and the death-doomed when I have told of this;
Yet once again shalt thou see him, though I no more again,
Fair with the joy that hopeth and dieth not in vain.

Then came the Hall-Sun close to her, and knelt down by her, and laid her head upon her knees and wept for love of her mother, who kissed her oft and caressed her; and Thiodolf's hand strayed, as it were, on to his daughter's head, and he looked kindly on her, though scarce now as if he knew her. Then she arose when she had kissed her mother once more, and went her ways from that wood-lawn into the woods again, and so to the Folk-mote of her people.

But when those twain were all alone again, the Wood-Sun spoke: "O Thiodolf canst thou hear me and understand?"

"Yea," he said, "when thou speakest of certain matters, as of our love together, and of our daughter that came of our love."

"Thiodolf," she said, "How long shall our love last?"

"As long as our life," he said.

"And if thou diest to-day, where then shall our love be?" said the Wood-Sun.

He said, "I must now say, I wot not; though time was I had said, It shall abide with the soul of the Wolfing Kindred."

She said: "And when that soul dieth, and the kindred is no more?"

"Time agone," quoth he, "I had said, it shall abide with the Kindreds of the Earth; but now again I say, I wot not."

"Will the Earth hide it," said she, "when thou diest and art borne to mound?"

"Even so didst thou say when we spake together that other night," said he; "and now I may say nought against thy word."

"Art thou happy, O Folk-wolf?" she said.

"Why dost thou ask me?" said he; "I know not; we were sundered and I longed for thee; thou art here; it is enough."

"And the people of thy Kindred?" she said, "dost thou not long for them?"

He said; "Didst thou not say that I was not of them? Yet were they my friends, and needed me, and I loved them: but by this evening they will need me no more, or but little; for they will be victorious over their foes: so hath the Hall-Sun foretold. What then! shall I take all from thee to give little to them?"

"Thou art wise," she said; "Wilt thou go to battle to-day?"

"So it seemeth," said he.

She said: "And wilt thou bear the Dwarf-wrought Hauberk? for if thou dost, thou wilt live, and if thou dost not, thou wilt die."

"I will bear it," said he, "that I may live to love thee."

"Thinkest thou that any evil goes with it?" said she.

There came into his face a flash of his ancient boldness as he answered: "So it seemed to me yesterday, when I fought clad in it the first time; and I fell unsmitten on the meadow, and was shamed, and would have slain myself but for thee. And yet it is not so that any evil goes with it; for thou thyself didst say that past night that there was no evil weird in it."

She said: "How then if I lied that night?"

Said he; "It is the wont of the Gods to lie, and be unashamed, and men-folk must bear with it."

"Ah! how wise thou art!" she said; and was silent for a while, and drew away from him a little, and clasped her hands together and wrung them for grief and anger. Then she grew calm again, and said:

"Wouldest thou die at my bidding?"

"Yea," said he, "not because thou art of the Gods, but because thou hast become a woman to me, and I love thee."

Then was she silent some while, and at last she said, "Thiodolf, wilt thou do off the Hauberk if I bid thee?"

"Yea, yea," said he, "and let us depart from the Wolfings, and their strife, for they need us not."

She was silent once more for a longer while still, and at last she said in a cold voice; "Thiodolf, I bid thee arise, and put off the Hauberk from thee."

He looked at her wondering, not at her words, but at the voice wherewith she spake them; but he arose from the stone nevertheless, and stood stark in the moonlight; he set his hand to the collar of the war-coat, and undid its clasps, which were of gold and blue stones, and presently he did the coat from off him and let it slide to the ground where it lay in a little grey heap that looked but a handful. Then he sat down on the stone again, and took her hand and kissed her and caressed her fondly, and she him again, and they spake no word for a while: but at the last he spake in measure and rhyme in a low voice, but so sweet and clear that it might have been heard far in the hush of the last hour of the night:

Dear now are this dawn-dusk's moments as is the last of the light
When the foemen's ranks are wavering, and the victory feareth night;
And of all the time I have loved thee of these am I most fain,
When I know not what shall betide me, nor what shall be my gain.
But dear as they are, they are waning, and at last the time is come
When no more shall I behold thee till I wend to Odin's Home.
Now is the time so little that once hath been so long
That I fain would ask thee pardon wherein I have done thee wrong,
That thy longing might be softer, and thy love more sweet to have.
But in nothing have I wronged thee, there is nought that I may crave.
Strange too! as the minutes fail me, so do my speech-words fail,
Yet strong is the joy within me for this hour that crowns the tale.

Therewith he clipped her and caressed her, and she spake nothing for a while; and he said; "Thy face is fair and bright; art thou not joyous of these minutes?"

She said: "Thy words are sweet; but they pierce my heart like a sharp knife; for they tell me of thy death and the ending of our love."

Said he; "I tell thee nothing, beloved, that thou hast not known: is it not for this that we have met here once more?"

She answered after a while; "Yea, yea; yet mightest thou have lived."

He laughed, but not scornfully or bitterly and said:

"So thought I in time past: but hearken, beloved; If I fall to-day, shall there not yet be a minute after the stroke hath fallen on me, wherein I shall know that the day is won and see the foemen fleeing, and wherein I shall once again deem I shall never die, whatever may betide afterwards, and though the sword lieth deep in my breast? And shall I not see then and know that our love hath no end?"

Bitter grief was in her face as she heard him. But she spake and said: "Lo here the Hauberk which thou hast done off thee, that thy breast might be the nearer to mine! Wilt thou not wear it in the fight for my sake?"

He knit his brows somewhat, and said:

"Nay, it may not be: true it is that thou saidest that no evil weird went with it, but hearken! Yesterday I bore it in the fight, and ere I mingled with the foe, before I might give the token of onset, a cloud came before my eyes and thick dark-ness wrapped me around, and I fell to the earth unsmitten; and so was I borne out of the fight, and evil dreams beset me of evil things, and the dwarfs that hate mankind. Then I came to myself, and the Hauberk was off me, and I rose up and beheld the battle, that the kindreds were pressing on the foe, and I thought not then of any past time, but of the minutes that were passing; and I ran into the fight straightway: but one followed me with that Hauberk, and I did it on, thinking of nought but the battle. Fierce then was the fray, yet I faltered in it; till the fresh men of the Romans came in upon us and broke up our array. Then my heart almost broke within me, and I faltered no more, but rushed on as of old, and smote great strokes all round about: no hurt I got, but once more came that ugly mist over my eyes, and again I fell unsmitten, and they bore me out of battle: then the men of our folk gave back and were over-come; and when I awoke from my evil dreams, we had gotten away from the fight and the Wolfing dwellings, and were on the mounds above the ford cowering down like beaten men. There then I sat shamed among the men who had chosen me for their best man at the Holy Thing, and lo I was their worst! Then befell that which never till then had befallen me, that life seemed empty and worthless and I longed to die and be done with it, and but for the thought of thy love I had slain myself then and there.

"Thereafter I went with the host to the assembly of the stay-at-homes and fleers, and sat before the Hall-Sun our daughter, and said the words which were put into my mouth. But now must I tell thee a hard and evil thing; that I loved them not, and was not of them, and outside myself there was nothing: within me was the world and nought without me. Nay, as for thee, I was not sundered from thee, but thou wert a part of me; whereas for the others, yea, even for our daughter, thine and mine, they were but images and shows of men, and I longed to depart from them, and to see thy body and to feel thine heart beating. And by then so evil was I grown that my very shame had fallen from me, and my will to die: nay, I longed to live, thou and I, and death seemed hateful to me, and the deeds before death vain and foolish.

"Where then was my glory and my happy life, and the hope of the days fresh born every day, though never dying? Where then was life, and Thiodolf that once had lived?

"But now all is changed once more; I loved thee never so well as now, and great is my grief that we must sunder, and the pain of farewell wrings my heart. Yet since I am once more Thiodolf the Mighty, in my heart there is room for joy also. Look at me, O Wood-Sun, look at me, O beloved! tell me, am I not fair with the fairness of the warrior and the helper of the folk? Is not my voice kind, do not my lips smile, and mine eyes shine? See how steady is mine hand, the friend of the folk! For mine eyes are cleared again, and I can see the kin-dreds as they are, and their desire of life and scorn of death, and this is what they have made me myself. Now therefore shall they and I together earn the merry days to come, the win-ter hunting and the spring sowing, the summer haysel, the ingathering of harvest, the happy rest of midwinter, and Yule-tide with the memory of the Fathers, wedded to the hope of the days to be. Well may they bid me help them who have holpen me! Well may they bid me die who have made me live!

"For whereas thou sayest that I am not of their blood, nor of their adoption, once more I heed it not. For I have lived with them, and eaten and drunken with them, and toiled with them, and led them in battle and the place of wounds and slaughter; they are mine and I am theirs; and through them am I of the whole earth, and all the kindreds of it; yea, even of the foemen, whom this day the edges in mine hand shall smite.

"Therefore I will bear the Hauberk no more in battle; and belike my body but once more: so shall I have lived and death shall not have undone me.

"Lo thou, is not this the Thiodolf whom thou hast loved? no changeling of the Gods, but the man in whom men have trusted, the friend of Earth, the giver of life, the vanquisher of death?"

And he cast himself upon her, and strained her to his bosom and kissed her, and caressed her, and awoke the bitter-sweet joy within her, as he cried out:

"O remember this, and this, when at last I am gone from thee!"

But when they sundered her face was bright, but the tears were on it, and she said: "O Thiodolf, thou wert fain hadst thou done a wrong to me so that I might forgive thee; now wilt thou forgive me the wrong I have done thee?"

"Yea," he said, "Even so would I do, were we both to live, and how much more if this be the dawn of our sundering day! What hast thou done?"

She said: "I lied to thee concerning the Hauberk when I said that no evil weird went with it: and this I did for the saving of thy life."

He laid his hand fondly on her head, and spake smiling: "Such is the wont of the God-kin, because they know not the hearts of men. Tell me all the truth of it now at last."

She said:

Hear then the tale of the Hauberk and the truth there is to tell:
There was a maid of the God-kin, and she loved a man right well,
Who unto the battle was wending; and she of her wisdom knew
That thence to the folk-hall threshold should come back but a very few;
And she feared for her love, for she doubted that of these he should not be;
So she wended the wilds lamenting, as I have lamented for thee;
And many wise she pondered, how to bring her will to pass
(E'en as I for thee have pondered), as her feet led over the grass,
Till she lifted her eyes in the wild-wood, and lo! she stood before
The Hall of the Hollow-places; and the Dwarf-lord stood in the door
And held in his hand the Hauberk, whereon the hammer's blow
The last of all had been smitten, and the sword should be hammer now.

Then the Dwarf beheld her fairness, and the wild-wood many-leaved
Before his eyes was reeling at the hope his heart conceived;
So sorely he longed for her body; and he laughed before her and cried,
'O Lady of the Disir, thou farest wandering wide
Lamenting thy beloved and the folkmote of the spear,
But if amidst of the battle this child of the hammer he bear
He shall laugh at the foemen's edges and come back to thy lily breast
And of all the days of his life-time shall his coming years be best.'
Then she bowed adown her godhead and sore for the Hauberk she prayed;
But his greedy eyes devoured her as he stood in the door and said;
'Come lie in mine arms! Come hither, and we twain the night to wake!
And then as a gift of the morning the Hauberk shall ye take.'
So she humbled herself before him, and entered into the cave,
The dusky, the deep-gleaming, the gem-strewn golden grave.
But he saw not her girdle loosened, or her bosom gleam on his love,
For she set the sleep-thorn in him, that he saw, but might not move,
Though the bitter salt tears burned him for the anguish of his greed;
And she took the hammer's offspring, her unearned morning meed,
And went her ways from the rock-hall and was glad for her warrior's sake.
But behind her dull speech followed, and the voice of the hollow spake:
'Thou hast left me bound in anguish, and hast gained thine heart's desire;
Now I would that the dewy night-grass might be to thy feet as the fire,
And shrivel thy raiment about thee, and leave thee bare to the flame,
And no way but a fiery furnace for the road whereby ye came!
But since the folk of God-home we may not slay nor smite,
And that fool of the folk that thou lovest, thou hast saved in my despite,
Take with thee, thief of God-home, this other word I say:
Since the safeguard wrought in the ring-mail I may not do away
I lay this curse upon it, that whoso weareth the same,
Shall save his life in the battle, and have the battle's shame;
He shall live through wrack and ruin, and ever have the worse,
And drag adown his kindred, and bear the people's curse.'

Lo, this the tale of the Hauberk, and I knew it for the truth:
And little I thought of the kindreds; of their day I had no ruth;
For I said, They are doomed to departure; in a little while must they wane,
And nought it helpeth or hindreth if I hold my hand or refrain.
Yea, thou wert become the kindred, both thine and mine; and thy birth
To me was the roofing of heaven, and the building up of earth.
I have loved, and I must sorrow; thou hast lived, and thou must die;
Ah, wherefore were there others in the world than thou and I?

He turned round to her and clasped her strongly in his arms again, and kissed her many times and said:

Lo, here art thou forgiven; and here I say farewell!
Here the token of my wonder which my words may never tell;
The wonder past all thinking, that my love and thine should blend;
That thus our lives should mingle, and sunder in the end!
Lo, this, for the last remembrance of the mighty man I was,
Of thy love and thy forbearing, and all that came to pass!

Night wanes, and heaven dights her for the kiss of sun and earth;
Look up, look last upon me on this morn of the kindreds' mirth!

Therewith he arose and lingered no minute longer, but departed, going as straight towards the Thing-stead and the Folk-mote of his kindred as the swallow goes to her nest in the hall-porch. He looked not once behind him, though a bitter wailing rang through the woods and filled his heart with the bitterness of her woe and the anguish of the hour of sundering.

27. THEY WEND TO THE MORNING BATTLE

Now when Thiodolf came back to the camp the signs of dawn were plain in the sky, the moon was low and sinking behind the trees, and he saw at once that the men were stirring and getting ready for departure. He looked gladly and blithely at the men he fell in with, and they at him, and scarce could they refrain a shout when they beheld his face and the brightness of it. He went straight up to where the Hall-Sun was yet sitting under her namesake, with Arinbiorn standing before her amidst of a ring of leaders of hundreds and scores: but old Sorli sat by her side clad in all his war-gear.

When Thiodolf first came into that ring of men they looked doubtfully at him, as if they dreaded somewhat, but when they had well beheld him their faces cleared, and they became joyous.

He went straight up to Arinbiorn and kissed the old warrior, and said to him, "I give thee good morrow, O leader of the Bearings! Here now is come the War-duke! and meseems that we should get to work as speedily as may be, for lo the dawning!"

"Hail to thine hand, War-duke!" said Arinbiorn joyously; "there is no more to do but to take thy word concerning the order wherein we shall wend; for all men are armed and ready."

Said Thiodolf; "Lo ye, I lack war-gear and weapons! Is there a good sword hereby, a helm, a byrny and a shield? For hard will be the battle, and we must fence ourselves all we may."

"Hard by," said Arinbiorn, "is the war-gear of Ivar of our House, who is dead in the night of his hurts gotten in yesterday's battle: thou and he are alike in stature, and with a good will doth he give them to thee, and they are goodly things, for he comes of smithying blood. Yet is it a pity of Throng-plough that he lieth on the field of the slain."

But Thiodolf smiled and said: "Nay, Ivar's blade shall serve my turn to-day; and thereafter shall it be seen to, for then will be time for many things."

So they went to fetch him the weapons; but he said to Arinbiorn, "Hast thou numbered the host? What are the gleanings of the Roman sword?"

Said Arinbiorn: "Here have we more than three thousand three hundred warriors of the host fit for battle: and besides this here are gathered eighteen hundred of the Wolfings and the Bearings, and of the other Houses, mostly from over the water, and of these nigh upon seven hundred may bear sword or shoot shaft; neither shall ye hinder them from so doing if the battle be joined."

Then said Thiodolf: "We shall order us into three battles; the Wolfings and the Bearings to lead the first, for this is our business; but others of the smaller Houses this side the water to be with us; and the Elkings and Galtings and the other Houses of the Mid-mark on the further side of the water to be in the second, and with them the more part of the Nether-mark; but the men of Up-mark to be in the third, and the stay-at-homes to follow on with them: and this third battle to let the wood cover them till they be needed, which may not be till the day of fight draws to an end, when all shall be needed: for no Roman man must be left alive or untaken by this even, or else must we all go to the Gods together. Hearken, Arinbiorn. I am not called fore-sighted, and yet meseems I see somewhat how this day shall go; and it is not to be hidden that I shall not see another battle until the last of all battles is at hand. But be of good cheer, for I shall not die till the end of the fight, and once more I shall be a man's help unto you. Now the first of the Romans we meet shall not be able to stand before us, for they shall be unready, and when their men are gotten ready and are fighting with us grimly, ye of the second battle shall hear the war-token, and shall fall on, and they shall be dismayed when they see so many fresh men come into the fight; yet shall they stand stoutly; for they are valiant men, and shall not all be taken unawares. Then, if they withstand us long enough, shall the third battle come forth from the wood, and fall on either flank of them, and the day shall be won. But I think not that they shall withstand us so long, but that the men of Up-mark and the stay-at-homes shall have the chasing of them. Now get me my war-gear, and let the first battle get them to the outgate of the garth."

So they brought him his arms; and meanwhile the Hall-Sun spake to one of the Captains, and he turned and went away a little space, and then came back, having with him three strong warriors of the Wolfings, and he brought them before the Hall-Sun, who said to them:

"Ye three, Steinulf, Athalulf, and Grani the Grey, I have sent for you because ye are men both mighty in battle and deft wood-wrights and house-smiths; ye shall follow Thiodolf closely, when he winneth into the Roman garth, yet shall ye fight wisely, so that ye be not slain, or at least not all; ye shall enter the Hall with Thiodolf, and when ye are therein, if need be, ye shall run down the Hall at your swiftest, and mount up into the loft betwixt the Middle-hearth and the Women's-Chamber, and there shall ye find good store of water in vats and tubs, and this ye shall use for quenching the fire of the Hall if the foemen fire it, as is not unlike to be."

Then Grani spoke for the others and said he would pay all heed to her words, and they departed to join their company.

Now was Thiodolf armed; and Arinbiorn, turning about before he went to his place, beheld him and knit his brow, and said: "What is this, Thiodolf? Didst thou not swear to the Gods not to bear helm or shield in the battles of this strife? yet hast thou Ivar's helm on thine head and his shield ready beside thee: wilt thou forswear thyself? so doing shalt thou bring woe upon the House."

"Arinbiorn," said Thiodolf, "where didst thou hear tell of me that I had made myself the thrall of the Gods? The oath that I sware was sworn when mine heart was not whole towards our people; and now will I break it that I may keep what of good intent there was in it, and cast away the rest. Long is the story; but if we journey together to-night I will tell it thee. Likewise I will tell it to the Gods if they look sourly upon me when I see them, and all shall be well."

He smiled as he spake, and Arinbiorn smiled on him in turn and went his ways to array the host. But when he was gone Thiodolf was alone in that place with the Hall-Sun, and he turned to her, and kissed her, and caressed her fondly, and spake and said:

So fare we, O my daughter, to the sundering of the ways;
Short is my journey henceforth to the door that ends my days,
And long the road that lieth as yet before thy feet.
How fain were I that thy journey from day to day were sweet
With peace to thee and pleasure; that a noble warrior's hand
In its early days might lead thee adown the flowery land,
And thy children in its noon-tide cling round about thy gown,
And the wise that thy womb has carried when the sun is going down,

Be thy happy fellow-farers to tell the tale of Earth,
But I wot that for no such sweetness did we bring thee unto birth,
But to be the soul of the Wolfings till the other days should come,
And the fruit of the kindreds' harvest with thee is garnered home.
Yet if for no blithe faring thy life-day is ordained,
Yet peace that long endureth maybe thy soul hath gained;
And thy sorrow of this even thy latest grief shall be,
The grief wherewith thou singest the death-song over me.

She looked up at him and smiled, though the tears were on her face; then she said:

Though to-day the grief beginneth yet the bitterness is done.
Though my body wendeth barren 'neath the beams of the quickening sun,
Yet remembrance still abideth, and long after the days of my life
Shall I live in the tale of the morning, when they tell of the ending of strife;
And the deeds of this little hand, and the thought conceived in my heart,
And never again henceforward from the folk shall I fare apart.
And if of the Earth, my father, thou hast tidings in thy place
Thou shalt hear how they call me the Ransom and the Mother of happy days.

Then she wept outright for a brief space, and thereafter she said:

Keep this in thine heart, O father, that I shall remember all
Since thou liftedst the she-wolf's nursling in the oak-tree's leafy hall.
Yea, every time I remember when hand in hand we went
Amidst the shafts of the beech-trees, and down to the youngling bent
The Folk-wolf in his glory when the eve of fight drew nigh;
And every time I remember when we wandered joyfully
Adown the sunny meadow and lived a while of life
'Midst the herbs and the beasts and the waters so free from fear and strife,
That thy years and thy might and thy wisdom, I had no part therein;
But thou wert as the twin-born brother of the maiden slim and thin,
The maiden shy in the feast-hall and blithe in wood and field.
Thus have we fared, my father; and e'en now when thou bearest shield,
On the last of thy days of mid-earth, twixt us 'tis even so
That the heart of my like-aged brother is the heart of thee that I know.

Then the bitterness of tears stayed her speech, and he spake no word more, but took her in his arms a while and soothed her and fondled her, and then they parted, and he went with great strides towards the outgoing of the Thing-stead.

There he found the warriors of his House and of the Bearings and the lesser Houses of Mid-mark, all duly ordered for wending through the wood. The dawn was coming on apace, but the wood was yet dark. But whereas the Wolfings led, and each man of them knew the wood like his own hand, there was no straying or disarray, and in less than a half-hour's space Thiodolf and the first battle were come to the wood behind the hazel-trees at the back of the hall, and before them was the dawning round about the Roof of the Kindred; the eastern heavens were brightening, and they could see all things clear without the wood.

28. OF THE STORM OF DAWNING

Then Thiodolf bade Fox and two others steal forward, and see what of foemen was before them; so they fell to creeping on towards the open: but scarcely had they started, before all men could hear the tramp of men drawing nigh; then Thiodolf himself took with him a score of his House and went quietly toward the wood-edge till they were barely within the shadow of the beechwood; and he looked forth and saw men coming straight towards their lurking-place. And those he saw were a good many, and they were mostly of the dastards of the Goths; but with them was a Captain of an Hundred of the Romans, and some others of his kindred; and Thiodolf deemed that the Goths had been bidden to gather up some of the night-watchers and enter the wood and fall on the stay-at-homes. So he bade his men get them aback, and he himself abode still at the very wood's edge listening intently with his sword bare in his hand. And he noted that those men of the foe stayed in the daylight outside the wood, but a few yards from it, and, by command as it seemed, fell silent and spake no word; and the morn was very still, and when the sound of their tramp over the grass had ceased, Thiodolf could hear the tramp of more men behind them. And then he had another thought, to wit that the Romans had sent scouts to see if the Goths yet abided on the vantage-ground by the ford, and that when they had found them gone, they were minded to fall on them unawares in the refuge of the Thing-stead and were about to do so by the counsel and leading of the dastard Goths; and that this was one body of the host led by those dastards, who knew somewhat of the woods. So he drew aback speedily, and catching hold of Fox by the shoulder (for he had taken him alone with him) he bade him creep along through the wood toward the Thing-stead, and bring back speedy word whether there were any more foemen near the wood thereaway; and he himself came to his men, and ordered them for onset, drawing them up in a shallow half moon, with the bowmen at the horns thereof, with the word to loose at the Romans as soon as they heard the war-horn blow: and all this was done speedily and with little noise, for they were well nigh so arrayed already.

Thus then they waited, and there was more than a glimmer of light even under the beechen leaves, and the eastern sky was yellowing to sunrise. The other warriors were like hounds in the leash eager to be slipped; but Thiodolf stood calm and high-hearted turning over the memory of past days, and the time he thought of seemed long to him, but happy.

Scarce had a score of minutes passed, and the Romans before them, who were now gathered thick behind those dastards of the Goths, had not moved, when back comes Fox and tells how he has come upon a great company of the Romans led by their thralls of the Goths who were just entering the wood, away there towards the Thing-stead.

"But, War-duke," says he, "I came also across our own folk of the second battle duly ordered in the wood ready to meet them; and they shall be well dealt with, and the sun shall rise for us and not for them."

Then turns Thiodolf round to those nighest to him and says, but still softly:

Hear ye a word, O people, of the wisdom of the foe!
Before us thick they gather, and unto the death they go.
They fare as lads with their cur-dogs who have stopped a fox's earth,
And standing round the spinny, now chuckle in their mirth,
Till one puts by the leafage and trembling stands astare
At the sight of the Wood-wolf's father arising in his lair—
They have come for our wives and our children, and our sword-edge
    shall they meet;
And which of them is happy save he of the swiftest feet?

Speedily then went that word along the ranks of the Kindred, and men were merry with the restless joy of battle: but scarce had two minutes passed ere suddenly the stillness of the dawn was broken by clamour and uproar; by shouts and shrieks, and the clashing of weapons from the wood on their left hand; and over all arose the roar of the Markmen's horn, for the battle was joined with the second company of the Kindreds. But a rumour and murmur went from the foemen before Thiodolf's men; and then sprang forth the loud sharp word of the captains commanding and rebuking, as if the men were doubtful which way they should take.

Amidst all which Thiodolf brandished his sword, and cried out in a great voice:

    Now, now, ye War-sons!
    Now the Wolf waketh!
    Lo how the Wood-beast
    Wendeth in onset.

And he led forth joyously, and terrible rang the long refrained gathered shout of his battle as his folk rushed on together devouring the little space between their ambush and the hazel-beset green-sward.

In the twinkling of an eye the half-moon had lapped around the Roman-Goths and those that were with them; and the dastards made no stand but turned about at once, crying out that the Gods of the Kindreds were come to aid and none could withstand them. But these fleers thrust against the band of Romans who were next to them, and bore them aback, and great was the turmoil; and when Thiodolf's storm fell full upon them, as it failed not to do, so close were they driven together that scarce could any man raise his hand for a stroke. For behind them stood a great company of those valiant spearmen of the Romans, who would not give way if anywise they might hold it out: and their ranks were closely serried, shield nigh touching shield, and their faces turned toward the foe; and so arrayed, though they might die, they scarce knew how to flee. As they might these thrust and hewed at the fleers, and gave fierce words but few to the Roman-Goths, driving them back against their foemen: but the fleers had lost the cunning of their right hands, and they had cast away their shields and could not defend their very bodies against the wrath of the kindreds; and when they strove to flee to the right hand or to the left, they were met by the horns of the half-moon, and the arrows began to rain in upon them, and from so close were they shot at that no shaft failed to smite home.

There then were the dastards slain; and their bodies served for a rampart against the onrush of the Markmen to those Romans who had stood fast. To them were gathering more and more every minute, and they faced the Goths steadily with their hard brown visages and gleaming eyes above their iron-plated shields; not casting their spears, but standing closely together, silent, but fierce. The light was spread now over all the earth; the eastern heavens were grown golden-red, flecked here and there with little crimson clouds: this battle was fallen near silent, but to the North was great uproar of shouts and cries, and the roaring of the war-horns, and the shrill blasts of the brazen trumpets.

Now Thiodolf, as his wont was when he saw that all was going well, had refrained himself of hand-strokes, but was here and there and everywhere giving heart to his folk, and keeping them in due order, and close array, lest the Romans should yet come among them. But he watched the ranks of the foe, and saw how presently they began to spread out beyond his, and might, if it were not looked to, take them in flank; and he was about to order his men anew to meet them, when he looked on his left hand and saw how Roman men were pouring thick from the wood out of all array, followed by a close throng of the kindreds: for on this side the Romans were outnumbered and had stumbled unawares into the ambush of the Markmen, who had fallen on them straightway and disarrayed them from the first. This flight of their folk the Romans saw also, and held their men together, refraining from the onset, as men who deem that they will have enough to do to stand fast.

But the second battle of the Markmen, (who were of the Nether-mark, mingled with the Mid-mark) fought wisely, for they swept those fleers from before them, slaying many and driving the rest scattering, yet held the chase for no long way, but wheeling about came sidelong on toward the battle of the Romans and Thiodolf. And when Thiodolf saw that, he set up the whoop of victory, he and his, and fell fiercely on the Romans, casting everything that would fly, as they rushed on to the handplay; so that there was many a Roman slain with the Roman spears that those who had fallen had left among their foemen.

Now the Roman captains perceived that it availed not to tarry till the men of the Mid and Nether-marks fell upon their flank; so they gave command, and their ranks gave back little by little, facing their foes, and striving to draw themselves within the dike and garth, which, after their custom, they had already cast up about the Wolfing Roof, their stronghold.

Now as fierce as was the onset of the Markmen, the main body of the Romans could not be hindered from doing this much before the men of the second battle were upon them; but Thiodolf and Arinbiorn with some of the mightiest brake their array in two places and entered in amongst them. And wrath so seized upon the soul of Arinbiorn for the slaying of Otter, and his own fault towards him, that he cast away his shield, and heeding no strokes, first brake his sword in the press, and then, getting hold of a great axe, smote at all before him as though none smote at him in turn; yea, as though he were smiting down tree-boles for a match against some other mighty man; and all the while amidst the hurry, strokes of swords and spears rained on him, some falling flatwise and some glancing sideways, but some true and square, so that his helm was smitten off and his hauberk rent adown, and point and edge reached his living flesh; and he had thrust himself so far amidst the foe that none could follow to shield him, so that at last he fell shattered and rent at the foot of the new clayey wall cast up by the Romans, even as Thiodolf and a band with him came cleaving the press, and the Romans closed the barriers against friend and foe, and cast great beams adown, and masses of iron and lead and copper taken from the smithying-booths of the Wolfings, to stay them if it were but a little.

Then Thiodolf bestrode the fallen warrior, and men of his House were close behind him, for wisely had he fought, cleaving the press like a wedge, helping his friends that they might help him, so that they all went forward together. But when he saw Arinbiorn fall he cried out:

"Woe's me, Arinbiorn! that thou wouldest not wait for me; for the day is young yet, and over-young!"

There then they cleared the space outside the gate, and lifted up the Bearing Warrior, and bare him back from the rampart. For so fierce had been the fight and so eager the storm of those that had followed after him that they must needs order their battle afresh, since Thiodolf's wedge which he had driven into the Roman host was but of a few and the foe had been many and the rampart and the shot-weapons were close anigh. Wise therefore it seemed to abide them of the second battle and join with them to swarm over the new-built slippery wall in the teeth of the Roman shot.

In this, the first onset of the Morning Battle, some of the Markmen had fallen, but not many, since but a few had entered outright into the Roman ranks; and when they first rushed on from the wood but three of them were slain, and the slaughter was all of the dastards and the Romans; and afterwards not a few of the Romans were slain, what by Arinbiorn, what by the others; for they were fighting fleeing, and before their eyes was the image of the garth-gate which was behind them; and they stumbled against each other as they were driven sideways against the onrush of the Goths, nor were they now standing fair and square to them, and they were hurried and confused with the dread of the onset of them of the two Marks.

As yet Thiodolf had gotten no great hurt, so that when he heard that Arinbiorn's soul had passed away he smiled and said:

"Yea, yea, Arinbiorn might have abided the end, for ere then shall the battle be hard."

So now the Wolfings and the Bearings met joyously the kindreds of the Nether Mark and the others of the second battle, and they sang the song of victory arrayed in good order hard by the Roman rampart, while bowstrings twanged and arrows whistled, and sling-stones hummed from this side and from that.

And of their song of victory thus much the tale telleth:

Now hearken and hear
Of the day-dawn of fear,
And how up rose the sun
On the battle begun.
All night lay a-hiding,
Our anger abiding,

Dark down in the wood
The sharp seekers of blood;
But ere red grew the heaven we bore them all bare,
For against us undriven the foemen must fare;
They sought and they found us, and sorrowed to find,
For the tree-boles around us the story shall mind,
How fast from the glooming they fled to the light,
Yeasaying the dooming of Tyr of the fight.

Hearken yet and again
How the night gan to wane,
And the twilight stole on
Till the world was well won!
E'en in such wise was wending
A great host for our ending;
On our life-days e'en so
Stole the host of the foe;
Till the heavens grew lighter, and light grew the world,
And the storm of the fighter upon them was hurled,
Then some fled the stroke, and some died and some stood,
Till the worst of the storm broke right out from the wood,
And the war-shafts were singing the carol of fear,
The tale of the bringing the sharp swords anear.

Come gather we now,
For the day doth grow.
Come, gather, ye bold,
Lest the day wax old;
Lest not till to-morrow
We slake our sorrow,
And heap the ground
With many a mound.
Come, war-children, gather, and clear we the land!
In the tide of War-father the deed is to hand.
Clad in gear that we gilded they shrink from our sword;
In the House that we builded they sit at the board;
Come, war-children, gather, come swarm o'er the wall
For the feast of War-father to sweep out the Hall!

Now amidst of their singing the sun rose upon the earth, and gleamed in the arms of men, and lit the faces of the singing warriors as they stood turned toward the east.

In this first onset of battle but twenty and three Markmen were slain in all, besides Arinbiorn; for, as aforesaid, they had the foe at a disadvantage. And this onset is called in the tale the Storm of Dawning.

29. OF THIODOLF'S STORM

The Goths tarried not over their victory; they shot with all the bowmen that they had against the Romans on the wall, and therewith arrayed themselves to fall on once more. And Thiodolf, now that the foe were covered by a wall, though it was but a little one, sent a message to the men of the third battle, them of Up-mark to wit, to come forward in good array and help to make a ring around the Wolfing Stead, wherein they should now take the Romans as a beast is taken in a trap. Meanwhile, until they came, he sent other men to the wood to bring tree-boles to batter the gate, and to make bridges whereby to swarm over the wall, which was but breast-high on the Roman side, though they had worked at it ceaselessly since yesterday morning.

In a long half-hour, therefore, the horns of the men of Up-mark sounded, and they came forth from the wood a very great company, for with them also were the men of the stay-at-homes and the homeless, such of them as were fit to bear arms. Amongst these went the Hall-Sun surrounded by a band of the warriors of Up-mark; and before her was borne her namesake the Lamp as a sign of assured victory. But these stay-at-homes with the Hall-Sun were stayed by the command of Thiodolf on the crown of the slope above the dwellings, and stood round about the Speech-Hill, on the topmost of which stood the Hall-Sun, and the wondrous Lamp, and the men who warded her and it.

When the Romans saw the new host come forth from the wood, they might well think that they would have work enough to do that day; but when they saw the Hall-Sun take her stand on the Speech-Hill with the men-at-arms about her, and the Lamp before her, then dread of the Gods fell upon them, and they knew that the doom had gone forth against them. Nevertheless they were not men to faint and die because the Gods were become their foes, but they were resolved rather to fight it out to the end against whatsoever might come against them, as was well seen afterwards.

Now they had made four gates to their garth according to their custom, and at each gate within was there a company of their mightiest men, and each was beset by the best of the Markmen. Thiodolf and his men beset the western gate where they had made that fierce onset. And the northern gate was beset by the Elkings and some of the kindreds of the Nether-mark; and the eastern gate by the rest of the men of Nether-mark; and the southern gate by the kindreds of Up-mark.

All this the Romans noted, and they saw how that the Mark-men were now very many, and they knew that they were men no less valiant than themselves, and they perceived that Thiodolf was a wise Captain; and in less than two hours' space from the Storm of Dawning they saw those men coming from the wood with plenteous store of tree-trunks to bridge their ditch and rampart; and they considered how the day was yet very young, so that they might look for no shelter from the night-tide; and as for any aid from their own folk at the war-garth aforesaid, they hoped not for it, nor had they sent any messenger to the Captain of the garth; nor did they know as yet of his overthrow on the Ridge.

Now therefore there seemed to be but two choices before them; either to abide within the rampart they had cast up, or to break out like valiant men, and either die in the storm, or cleave a way through, whereby they might come to their kindred and their stronghold south-east of the Mark.

This last way then they chose; or, to say the truth, it was their chief captain who chose it for them, though they were nothing loth thereto: for this man was a mocker, yet hot-headed, unstable, and nought wise in war, and heretofore had his greed minished his courage; yet now, being driven into a corner, he had courage enough and to spare, but utterly lacked patience; for it had been better for the Romans to have abided one or two onsets from the Goths, whereby they who should make the onslaught would at the least have lost more men than they on whom they should fall, before they within stormed forth on them; but their pride took away from the Romans their last chance. But their captain, now that he perceived, as he thought, that the game was lost and his life come to its last hour wherein he would have to leave his treasure and pleasure behind him, grew desperate and therewith most fierce and cruel. So all the captives whom they had taken (they were but two score and two, for the wounded men they had slain) he caused to be bound on the chairs of the high-seat clad in their war-gear with their swords or spears made fast to their right hands, and their shields to their left hands; and he said that the Goths should now hold a Thing wherein they should at last take counsel wisely, and abstain from folly. For he caused store of faggots and small wood smeared with grease and oil to be cast into the hall that it might be fired, so that it and the captives should burn up altogether; "So," said he, "shall we have a fair torch for our funeral fire;" for it was the custom of the Romans to burn their dead.

Thus, then, he did; and then he caused men to do away the barriers and open all the four gates of the new-made garth, after he had manned the wall with the slingers and bowmen, and slain the horses, so that the woodland folk should have no gain of them. Then he arrayed his men at the gates and about them duly and wisely, and bade those valiant footmen fall on the Goths who were getting ready to fall on them, and to do their best. But he himself armed at all points took his stand at the Man's-door of the Hall, and swore by all the Gods of his kindred that he would not move a foot's length from thence either for fire or for steel.

So fiercely on that fair morning burned the hatred of men about the dwellings of the children of the Wolf of the Goths, wherein the children of the Wolf of Rome were shut up as in a penfold of slaughter.

Meanwhile the Hall-Sun standing on the Hill of Speech beheld it all, looking down into the garth of war; for the new wall was no hindrance to her sight, because the Speech-Hill was high and but a little way from the Great Roof; and indeed she was within shot of the Roman bowmen, though they were not very deft in shooting.

So now she lifted up her voice and sang so that many heard her; for at this moment of time there was a lull in the clamour of battle both within the garth and without; even as it happens when the thunder-storm is just about to break on the world, that the wind drops dead, and the voice of the leaves is hushed before the first great and near flash of lightening glares over the fields.

So she sang:

Now the latest hour cometh and the ending of the strife;
And to-morrow and to-morrow shall we take the hand of life,
And wend adown the meadows, and skirt the darkling wood,
And reap the waving acres, and gather in the good.
I see a wall before me built up of steel and fire,
And hurts and heart-sick striving, and the war-wright's fierce desire;
But there-amidst a door is, and windows are therein;
And the fair sun-litten meadows and the Houses of the kin
Smile on me through the terror my trembling life to stay,
That at my mouth now flutters, as fain to flee away.
Lo e'en as the little hammer and the blow-pipe of the wright
About the flickering fire deals with the silver white,
And the cup and its beauty groweth that shall be for the people's feast,
And all men are glad to see it from the greatest to the least;
E'en so is the tale now fashioned, that many a time and oft
Shall be told on the acre's edges, when the summer eve is soft;
Shall be hearkened round the hall-blaze when the mid-winter night
The kindreds' mirth besetteth, and quickeneth man's delight,
And we that have lived in the story shall be born again and again
As men feast on the bread of our earning, and praise the grief-born
*   grain.*

As she made an end of singing, those about her understood her words, that she was foretelling victory, and the peace of the Mark, and for joy they raised a shrill cry; and the warriors who were nighest to her took it up, and it spread through the whole host round about the garth, and went up into the breath of the summer morning and went down the wind along the meadow of the Wolfings, so that they of the Wain-burg, who were now drawing somewhat near to Wolfstead heard it and were glad.

But the Romans when they heard it knew that the heart of the battle was reached, and they cast back that shout wrathfully and fiercely, and made toward the foe.

Therewithal those mighty men fell on each other in the narrow passes of the garth; for fear was dead and buried in that Battle of the Morning.

On the North gate Hiarandi of the Elkings was the point of the Markmen's wedge, and first clave the Roman press. In the Eastern gate it was Valtyr, Otter's brother's son, a young man and most mighty. In the South gate it was Geirbald of the Shieldings, the Messenger.

In the west gate Thiodolf the War-duke gave one mighty cry like the roar of an angry lion, and cleared a space before him for the wielding of Ivar's blade; for at that moment he had looked up to the Roof of the Kindred and had beheld a little stream of smoke curling blue out of a window thereof, and he knew what had betided, and how short was the time before them. But his wrathful cry was taken up by some who had beheld that same sight, and by others who saw nought but the Roman press, and terribly it rang over the swaying struggling crowd.

Then fell the first rank of the Romans before those stark men and mighty warriors; and they fell even where they stood, for on neither side could any give back but for a little space, so close the press was, and the men so eager to smite. Neither did any crave peace if he were hurt or disarmed; for to the Goths it was but a little thing to fall in hot blood in that hour of love of the kindred, and longing for the days to be. And for the Romans, they had had no mercy, and now looked for none: and they remembered their dealings with the Goths, and saw before them, as it were, once more, yea, as in a picture, their slayings and quellings, and lashings, and cold mockings which they had dealt out to the conquered foemen without mercy, and now they longed sore for the quiet of the dark, when their hard lives should be over, and all these deeds forgotten, and they and their bitter foes should be at rest for ever.

Most valiantly they fought; but the fury of their despair could not deal with the fearless hope of the Goths, and as rank after rank of them took the place of those who were hewn down by Thiodolf and the Kindred, they fell in their turn, and slowly the Goths cleared a space within the gates, and then began to spread along the wall within, and grew thicker and thicker. Nor did they fight only at the gates; but made them bridges of those tree-trunks, and fell to swarming over the rampart, till they had cleared it of the bowmen and slingers, and then they leaped down and fell upon the flanks of the

Romans; and the host of the dead grew, and the host of the living lessened.

Moreover the stay-at-homes round about the Speech-Hill, and that band of the warriors of Up-mark who were with them, beheld the Great Roof and saw the smoke come gushing out of the windows, and at last saw the red flames creep out amidst it and waver round the window jambs like little banners of scarlet cloth. Then they could no longer refrain themselves, but ran down from the Speech-Hill and the slope about it with great and fierce cries, and clomb the wall where it was unmanned, helping each other with hand and back, both stark warriors, and old men and lads and women: and thus they gat them into the garth and fell upon the lessening band of the Romans, who now began to give way hither and thither about the garth, as they best might.

Thus it befell at the West-gate, but at the other gates it was no worser, for there was no diversity of valour between the Houses; nay, whereas the more part and the best part of the Romans faced the onset of Thiodolf, which seemed to them the main onset, they were somewhat easier to deal with elsewhere than at the West gate; and at the East gate was the place first won, so that Valtyr and his folk were the first to clear a space within the gate, and to tell the tale shortly (for can this that and the other sword-stroke be told of in such a medley?) they drew the death-ring around the Romans that were before them, and slew them all to the last man, and then fell fiercely on the rearward of them of the North gate, who still stood before Hiarandi's onset. There again was no long tale to tell of, for Hiarandi was just winning the gate, and the wall was cleared of the Roman shot-fighters, and the Markmen were standing on the top thereof, and casting down on the Romans spears and baulks of wood and whatsoever would fly. There again were the Romans all slain or put out of the fight, and the two bands of the kindred joined together, and with what voices the battle-rage had left them cried out for joy and fared on together to help to bind the sheaves of war which Thiodolf's sickle had reaped. And now it was mere slaying, and the Romans, though they still fought in knots of less than a score, yet fought on and hewed and thrust without more thought or will than the stone has when it leaps adown the hill-side after it has first been set agoing.

But now the garth was fairly won and Thiodolf saw that there was no hope for the Romans drawing together again; so while the kindreds were busied in hewing down those knots of desperate men, he gathered to him some of the wisest of his warriors, amongst whom were Steinulf and Grani the Grey, the deft wood-wrights (but Athalulf had been grievously hurt by a spear and was out of the battle), and drave a way through the confused turmoil which still boiled in the garth there, and made straight for the Man's-door of the Hall. Soon he was close thereto, having hewn away all fleers that hindered him, and the doorway was before him. But on the threshold, the fire and flames of the kindled hall behind him, stood the Roman Captain clad in gold-adorned armour and surcoat of sea-born purple; the man was cool and calm and proud, and a mocking smile was on his face: and he bore his bright blade unbloodied in his hand.

Thiodolf stayed a moment of time, and their eyes met; it had gone hard with the War-duke, and those eyes glittered in his pale face, and his teeth were close set together; though he had fought wisely, and for life, as he who is most valiant ever will do, till he is driven to bay like the lone wood-wolf by the hounds, yet had he been sore mishandled. His helm and shield were gone, his hauberk rent; for it was no dwarf-wrought coat, but the work of Ivar's hand: the blood was running down from his left arm, and he was hurt in many places: he had broken Ivar's sword in the medley, and now bore in his hand a strong Roman short-sword, and his feet stood bloody on the worn earth anigh the Man's-door.

He looked into the scornful eyes of the Roman lord for a little minute and then laughed aloud, and therewithal, leaping on him with one spring, turned sideways, and dealt him a great buffet on his ear with his unarmed left hand, just as the Roman thrust at him with his sword, so that the Captain staggered forward on to the next man following, which was Wolfkettle the eager warrior, who thrust him through with his sword and shoved him aside as they all strode into the hall together. Howbeit no sword fell from the Roman Captain as he fell, for Thiodolf's side bore it into the Hall of the Wolfings.

Most wrathful were those men, and went hastily, for their Roof was full of smoke, and the flames flickered about the pillars and the wall here and there, and crept up to the windows aloft; yet was it not wholly or fiercely burning; for the Roman fire-raisers had been hurried and hasty in their work. Straightway then Steinulf and Grani led the others off at a run towards the loft and the water; but Thiodolf, who went slowly and painfully, looked and beheld on the dais those men bound for the burning, and he went quietly, and as a man who has been sick, and is weak, up on to the dais, and said:

"Be of good cheer, O brothers, for the kindreds have vanquished the foemen, and the end of strife is come."

His voice sounded strange and sweet to them amidst the turmoil of the fight without; he laid down his sword on the table, and drew a little sharp knife from his girdle and cut their bonds one by one and loosed them with his blood-stained hands; and each one as he loosed him he kissed and said to him, "Brother, go help those who are quenching the fire; this is the bidding of the War-duke."

But as he loosed one after other he was longer and longer about it, and his words were slower. At last he came to the man who was bound in his own high-seat close under the place of the wondrous Lamp, the Hall-Sun, and he was the only one left bound; that man was of the Wormings and was named Elfric; he loosed him and was long about it; and when he was done he smiled on him and kissed him, and said to him:

"Arise, brother! go help the quenchers of the fire, and leave to me this my chair, for I am weary: and if thou wilt, thou mayst bring me of that water to drink, for this morning men have forgotten the mead of the reapers!"

Then Elfric arose, and Thiodolf sat in his chair, and leaned back his head; but Elfric looked at him for a moment as one scared, and then ran his ways down the hall, which now was growing noisy with the hurry and bustle of the quenchers of the fire, to whom had divers others joined themselves.

There then from a bucket which was still for a moment he filled a wooden bowl, which he caught up from the base of one of the hall-pillars, and hastened up the Hall again; and there was no man nigh the dais, and Thiodolf yet sat in his chair, and the hall was dim with the rolling smoke, and Elfric saw not well what the War-duke was doing. So he hastened on, and when he was close to Thiodolf he trod in something wet, and his heart sank for he knew that it was blood; his foot slipped therewith and as he put out his hand to save himself the more part of the water was spilled, and mingled with the blood. But he went up to Thiodolf and said to him, "Drink, War-duke! here hath come a mouthful of water."

But Thiodolf moved not for his word, and Elfric touched him, and he moved none the more.

Then Elfric's heart failed him and he laid his hand on the War-duke's hand, and looked closely into his face; and the hand was cold and the face ashen-pale; and Elfric laid his hand on his side, and he felt the short-sword of the Roman leader thrust deep therein, besides his many other hurts.

So Elfric knew that he was dead, and he cast the bowl to the earth, and lifted up his hands and wailed out aloud, like a woman who hath come suddenly on her dead child, and cried out in a great voice:

"Hither, hither, O men in this hall, for the War-duke of the Markmen is dead! O ye people, Hearken! Thiodolf the Mighty, the Wolfing is dead!"

And he was a young man, and weak with the binding and the waiting for death, and he bowed himself adown and crouched on the ground and wept aloud.

But even as he cried that cry, the sunlight outside the Man's-door was darkened, and the Hall-Sun came over the threshold in her ancient gold-embroidered raiment, holding in her hand her namesake the wondrous Lamp; and the spears and the war-gear of warriors gleamed behind her; but the men tarried on the threshold till she turned about and beckoned to them, and then they poured in through the Man's-door, their war-gear rent and they all befouled and disarrayed with the battle, but with proud and happy faces: as they entered she waved her hand to them to bid them go join the quenchers of the fire; so they went their ways.

But she went with unfaltering steps up to the dais, and the place where the chain of the Lamp hung down from amidst the smoke-cloud wavering a little in the gusts of the hall. Straightway she made the Lamp fast to its chain, and dealt with its pulleys with a deft hand often practised therein, and then let it run up toward the smoke-hidden Roof till it gleamed in its due place once more, a token of the salvation of the Wolfings and the welfare of all the kindreds.

Then she turned toward Thiodolf with a calm and solemn face, though it was very pale and looked as if she would not smile again. Elfric had risen up and was standing by the board speechless and the passion of sobs still struggling in his bosom. She put him aside gently, and went up to Thiodolf and stood above him, and looked down on his face a while: then she put forth her hand and closed his eyes, and stooped down and kissed his face. Then she stood up again and faced the Hall and looked and saw that many were streaming in, and that though the smoke was still eddying overhead, the fire was well nigh quenched within; and without the sound of battle had sunk and died away. For indeed the Markmen had ended their day's work before noontide that day, and the more part of the Romans were slain, and to the rest they had given peace till the Folk-mote should give Doom concerning them; for pity of these valiant men was growing in the hearts of the valiant men who had vanquished them, now that they feared them no more.

And this second part of the Morning Battle is called Thiodolf's Storm.

So now when the Hall-Sun looked and beheld that the battle was done and the fire quenched, and when she saw how every man that came into the Hall looked up and beheld the wondrous Lamp and his face quickened into joy at the sight of it; and how most looked up at the high-seat and Thiodolf lying leaned back therein, her heart nigh broke between the thought of her grief and of the grief of the Folk that their mighty friend was dead, and the thought of the joy of the days to be and all the glory that his latter days had won. But she gathered heart, and casting back the dark tresses of her hair, she lifted up her voice and cried out till its clear shrillness sounded throughout all the Roof:

"O men in this Hall the War-duke is dead! O people hearken! for Thiodolf the Mighty hath changed his life: Come hither, O men, Come hither, for this is true, that Thiodolf is dead!"

30. THIODOLF IS BORNE OUT OF THE HALL AND OTTER IS LAID BESIDE HIM

So when they heard her voice they came thither flockmeal, and a great throng mingled of many kindreds was in the Hall, but with one consent they made way for the Children of the Wolf to stand nearest to the dais. So there they stood, the warriors mingled with the women, the swains with the old men, the freemen with the thralls: for now the stay-at-homes of the House were all gotten into the garth, and the more part of them had flowed into the feast-hall when they knew that the fire was slackening.

All these now had heard the clear voice of the Hall-Sun, or others had told them what had befallen; and the wave of grief had swept coldly over them amidst their joy of the recoverance of their dwelling-place; yet they would not wail nor cry aloud, even to ease their sorrow, till they had heard the words of the Hall-Sun, as she stood facing them beside their dead War-duke.

Then she spake: "O Sorli the Old, come up hither! thou hast been my fellow in arms this long while."

So the old man came forth, and went slowly in his clashing war-gear up on to the dais. But his attire gleamed and glittered, since over-old was he to thrust deep into the press that day, howbeit he was wise in war. So he stood beside her on the dais holding his head high, and proud he looked, for all his thin white locks and sunken eyes.

But again said the Hall-Sun: "Canst thou hear me, Wolfkettle, when I bid thee stand beside me, or art thou, too, gone on the road to Valhall?"

Forth then strode that mighty warrior and went toward the dais: nought fair was his array to look on; for point and edge had rent it and stained it red, and the flaring of the hall-flames had blackened it; his face was streaked with black withal, and his hands were as the hands of a smith among the thralls who hath wrought unwashen in the haste and hurry when men look to see the war-arrow abroad. But he went up on to the dais and held up his head proudly, and looked forth on to the hall-crowd with eyes that gleamed fiercely from his stained and blackened face.

Again the Hall-Sun said: "Art thou also alive, O Egil the messenger? Swift are thy feet, but not to flee from the foe: Come up and stand with us!"

Therewith Egil clave the throng; he was not so roughly dealt with as was Wolfkettle, for he was a bowman, and had this while past shot down on the Romans from aloft; and he yet held his bended bow in his hand. He also came up on to the dais and stood beside Wolfkettle glancing down on the hall-crowd, looking eagerly from side to side.

Yet again the Hall-Sun spake: "No aliens now are dwelling in the Mark; come hither, ye men of the kindreds! Come thou, our brother Hiarandi of the Elkings, for thy sisters, our wives, are fain of thee. Come thou, Valtyr of the Laxings, brother's son of Otter; do thou for the War-duke what thy father's brother had done, had he not been faring afar. Come thou, Geirbald of the Shieldings the messenger! Now know we the deeds of others and thy deeds. Come, stand beside us for a little!"

Forth then they came in their rent and battered war-gear: and the tall Hiarandi bore but the broken truncheon of his sword; and Valtyr a woodman's axe notched and dull with work; and Geirbald a Roman cast-spear, for his own weapons had been broken in the medley; and he came the last of the three, going as a belated reaper from the acres. There they stood by the others and gazed adown the hall-throng.

But the Hall-Sun spake again: "Agni of the Daylings, I see thee now. How camest thou into the hard hand-play, old man? Come hither and stand with us, for we love thee. Angantyr of the Bearings, fair was thy riding on the day of the Battle on the Ridge! Come thou, be with us. Shall the Beamings whose daughters we marry fail the House of the Wolf to-day? Geirodd, thou hast no longer a weapon, but the fight is over, and this hour thou needest it not. Come to us, brother! Gunbald of the Vallings, the Falcon on thy shield is dim with the dint of point and edge, but it hath done its work to ward thy valiant heart: Come hither, friend! Come all ye and stand with us!"

As she named them so they came, and they went up on to the dais and stood altogether; and a terrible band of warriors they looked had the fight been to begin over again, and they to meet death once more. And again spake the Hall-Sun:

"Steinulf and Grani, deft are your hands! Take ye the stalks of the war blossoms, the spears of the kindreds, and knit them together to make a bier for our War-duke, for he is weary and may not go afoot. Thou Ali, son of Grey; thou hast gone errands for me before; go forth now from the garth, and wend thy ways toward the water, and tell me when thou comest back what thou hast seen of the coming of the Wain-burg. For by this time it should be drawing anigh."

So Ali went forth, and there was silence of words for a while in the Hall; but there arose the sound of the wood-wrights busy with the wimble and the hammer about the bier. No long space had gone by when Ali came back into the hall panting with his swift running; and he cried out:

"O Hall-Sun, they are coming; the last wain hath crossed the ford, and the first is hard at hand: bright are their banners in the sun."

Then said the Hall-Sun: "O warriors, it is fitting that we go to meet our banners returning from the field, and that we do the Gods to wit what deeds we have done; fitting is it also that Thiodolf our War-duke wend with us. Now get ye into your ordered bands, and go we forth from the fire-scorched hall, and out into the sunlight, that the very earth and the heavens may look upon the face of our War-duke, and bear witness that he hath played his part as a man.

Then without more words the folk began to stream out of the Hall, and within the garth which the Romans had made they arrayed their companies. But when they were all gone from the Hall save they who were on the dais, the Hall-Sun took the waxen torch which she had litten and quenched at the departure of the host to battle, and now she once more kindled it at the flame of the wondrous Lamp, the Hall-Sun. But the wood-wrights brought the bier which they had made of the spear-shafts of the kindred, and they laid thereon a purple cloak gold-embroidered of the treasure of the Wolfings, and thereon was Thiodolf laid.

Then those men took him up; to wit, Sorli the Old, and Wolfkettle and Egil, all these were of the Wolfing House; Hiarandi of the Elkings also, and Valtyr of the Laxings, Geirbald of the Shieldings, Agni of the Daylings, Angantyr of the Bearings, Geirodd of the Beamings, Gunbald of the Vallings: all these, with the two valiant wood-wrights, Steinulf and Grani, laid hand to the bier.

So they bore it down from the dais, and out at the Man's-door into the sunlight, and the Hall-Sun followed close after it, holding in her hand the Candle of Returning. It was an hour after high-noon of a bright midsummer day when she came out into the garth; and the smoke from the fire-scorched hall yet hung about the trees of the wood-edge. She looked neither down towards her feet nor on the right side or the left, but straight before her. The ordered companies of the kindreds hid the sight of many fearful things from her eyes; though indeed the thralls and women had mostly gleaned the dead from the living both of friend and foe, and were tending the hurt of either host. Through an opening in the ranks moreover could they by the bier behold the scanty band of Roman captives, some standing up, looking dully around them, some sitting or lying on the grass talking quietly together, and it seemed by their faces that for them the bitterness of death was passed.

Forth then fared the host by the West gate, where Thiodolf had done so valiantly that day, and out on to the green amidst the booths and lesser dwellings. Sore then was the heart of the Hall-Sun, as she looked forth over dwelling, and acre, and meadow, and the blue line of the woods beyond the water, and bethought her of all the familiar things that were within the compass of her eyesight, and remembered the many days of her father's loving-kindness, and the fair words wherewith he had solaced her life-days. But of the sorrow that wrung her heart nothing showed in her face, nor was she paler now than her wont was. For high was her courage, and she would in no wise mar that fair day and victory of the kindreds with grief for what was gone, whereas so much of what once was, yet abided and should abide for ever.

Then fared they down through the acres, where what was yet left of the wheat was yellowing toward harvest, and the rye hung grey and heavy; for bright and hot had the weather been all through these tidings. Howbeit much of the corn was spoiled by the trampling of the Roman bands.

So came they into the fair open meadow and saw before them the wains coming to meet them with their folk; to wit a throng of stout carles of the thrall-folk led by the war-wise and ripe men of the Steerings. Bright was the gleaming of the banner-wains, though for the lack of wind the banners hung down about their staves; the sound of the lowing of the bulls and the oxen, the neighing of horses and bleating of the flocks came up to the ears of the host as they wended over the meadow.

They made stay at last on the rising ground, all trampled and in parts bloody, where yesterday Thiodolf had come on the fight between the remnant of Otter's men and the Romans: there they opened their ranks, and made a ring round about a space, amidmost of which was a little mound whereon was set the bier of Thiodolf. The wains and their warders came up with them and drew a garth of the wains round about the ring of men with the banners of the kindreds in their due places.

There was the Wolf and the Elk, the Falcon, the Swan, the Boar, the Bear, and the Green-tree: the Willow-bush, the Gedd, the Water-bank and the Wood-Ousel, the Steer, the Mallard and the Roe-deer: all these were of the Mid-mark. But of the Upper-mark were the Horse and the Spear, and the Shield, and the Daybreak, and the Dale, and the Mountain, and the Brook, and the Weasel, and the Cloud, and the Hart.

Of the Nether-mark were the Salmon, and the Lynx, and the Ling worm, the Seal, the Stone, and the Sea-mew; the Buck-goat, the Apple-tree, the Bull, the Adder, and the Crane.

There they stood in the hot sunshine three hours after noon; and a little wind came out of the west and raised the pictured cloths upon the banner-staves, so that the men could now see the images of the tokens of their Houses and the Fathers of old time.

Now was there silence in the ring of men; but it opened presently and through it came all-armed warriors bearing another bier, and lo, Otter upon it, dead in his war-gear with many a grievous wound upon his body. For men had found him in an ingle of the wall of the Great Roof, where he had been laid yesterday by the Romans when his company and the Bearings with the Wormings made their onset: for the Romans had noted his exceeding valour, and when they had driven off the Goths some of them brought him dead inside their garth, for they would know the name and dignity of so valorous a man.

So now they bore him to the mound where Thiodolf lay and set the bier down beside Thiodolf's, and the two War-dukes of the Markmen lay there together: and when the warriors beheld that sight, they could not forbear, but some groaned aloud, and some wept great tears, and they clashed their swords on their shields and the sound of their sorrow and their praise went up to the summer heavens.

Now the Hall-Sun holding aloft the waxen torch lifted up her voice and said:

O warriors of the Wolfings, by the token of the flame
That here in my right hand flickers, ye are back at the House of the
* Name,*
And there yet burneth the Hall-Sun beneath the Wolfing Roof,
And the flame that the foemen quickened hath died out far aloof.
Ye gleanings of the battle, lift up your hearts on high,
For the House of the War-wise Wolfings and the Folk undoomed to
* die.*
But ye kindreds of the Markmen, the Wolfing guests are ye,
And to-night we hold the high-tide, and great shall the feasting be,
For to-day by the road that we know not a many wend their ways
To the Gods and the ancient Fathers, and the hope of the latter days.
And how shall their feet be cumbered if we tangle them with woe,
And the heavy rain of sorrow drift o'er the road they go?
They have toiled, and their toil was troublous to make the days to come;

Use ye their gifts in gladness, lest they grieve for the Ancient Home!
Now are our maids arraying that fire-scorched Hall of ours
With the treasure of the Wolfings and the wealth of summer flowers,
And this eve the work before you will be the Hall to throng
And purge its walls of sorrow and quench its scathe and wrong.

She looked on the dead Thiodolf a moment, and then glanced from him to Otter and spake again:

O kindreds, here before you two mighty bodies lie;
Henceforth no man shall see them in house and field go by
As we were used to behold them, familiar to us then
As the wind beneath the heavens and the sun that shines on men;
Now soon shall there be nothing of their dwelling-place to tell,
Save the billow of the meadows, the flower-grown grassy swell!
Now therefore, O ye kindreds, if amidst you there be one
Who hath known the heart of the War-dukes, and the deeds their
* hands have done,*
Will not the word be with him, while yet your hearts are hot,
Of our praise and long remembrance, and our love that dieth not?
Then let him come up hither and speak the latest word
O'er the limbs of the battle-weary and the hearts outworn with the
* sword.*

She held her peace, and there was a stir in the ring of men: for they who were anigh the Dayling banner saw an old warrior sitting on a great black horse and fully armed. He got slowly off his horse and walked toward the ring of warriors, which opened before him; for all knew him for Asmund the old, the war-wise warrior of the Daylings, even he who had lamented over the Hauberk of Thiodolf. He had taken horse the day before, and had ridden toward the battle, but was belated, and had come up with them of the Wain-burg just as they had crossed the water.

31. OLD ASMUND SPEAKETH OVER THE WAR-DUKES: THE DEAD ARE LAID IN MOUND

Now while all looked on, he went to the place where lay the bodies of the War-dukes, and looked down on the face of Otter and said:

O Otter, there thou liest! and thou that I knew of old,
When my beard began to whiten, as the best of the keen and the bold,
And thou wert as my youngest brother, and thou didst lead my sons
When we fared forth over the mountains to meet the arrowy Huns,
And I smiled to see thee teaching the lore that I learned thee erst.
O Otter, dost thou remember how the Goth-folk came by the worst,
And with thee in mine arms I waded the wide shaft-harrowed flood

That lapped the feet of the mountains with its water blent with blood;
And how in the hollow places of the mountains hidden away
We abode the kindreds' coming as the wet night bideth day?
Dost thou remember, Otter, how many a joy we had,
How many a grief remembered has made our high-tide glad?
O fellow of the hall-glee! O fellow of the field!
Why then hast thou departed and left me under shield?
I the ancient, I the childless, while yet in the Laxing hall
Are thy brother's sons abiding and their children on thee call.

O kindreds of the people! the soul that dwelt herein,

This goodly way-worn body, was keen for you to win
Good days and long endurance. Who knoweth of his deed
What things for you it hath fashioned from the flame of the fire of
*   need?*
But of this at least well wot we, that forth from your hearts it came
And back to your hearts returneth for the seed of thriving and fame.
In the ground wherein ye lay it, the body of this man,
No deed of his abideth, no glory that he wan,
But evermore the Markmen shall bear his deeds o'er earth,
With the joy of the deeds that are coming, the garland of his worth.

He was silent a little as he stood looking down on Otter's face with grievous sorrow, for all that his words were stout. For indeed, as he had said, Otter had been his battle-fellow and his hall-fellow, though he was much younger than Asmund; and they had been standing foot to foot in that battle wherein old Asmund's sons were slain by his side.

After a while he turned slowly from looking at Otter to gaze upon Thiodolf, and his body trembled as he looked, and he opened his mouth to speak; but no word came from it; and he sat down upon the edge of the bier, and the tears began to gush out of his old eyes, and he wept aloud. Then they that saw him wondered; for all knew the stoutness of his heart, and how he had borne more burdens than that of eld, and had not cowered down under them. But at last he arose again, and stood firmly on his feet, and faced the Folk-mote, and in a voice more like the voice of a man in his prime than of an old man, he sang:

Wild the storm is abroad
Of the edge of the sword!
Far on runneth the path
Of the war-stride of wrath!
The Gods hearken and hear
The long rumour of fear
From the meadows beneath
Running fierce o'er the heath,
Till it beats round their dwelling-place builded aloof
And at last all up-swelling breaks wild o'er their roof,
And quencheth their laughter and crieth on all,
As it rolleth round rafter and beam of the Hall,
Like the speech of the thunder-cloud tangled on high,
When the mountain-halls sunder as dread goeth by.

So they throw the door wide
Of the Hall where they bide,
And to murmuring song
Turns that voice of the wrong,
And the Gods wait a-gaze
For that Wearer of Ways:
For they know he hath gone

A long journey alone.
Now his feet are they hearkening, and now is he come,
With his battle-wounds darkening the door of his home,
Unbyrnied, unshielded, and lonely he stands,
And the sword that he wielded is gone from his hands—
Hands outstretched and bearing no spoil of the fight,
As speechless, unfearing, he stands in their sight.

War-father gleams
Where the white light streams
Round kings of old
All red with gold,
And the Gods of the name
With joy aflame.
All the ancient of men
Grown glorious again:
Till the Slains-father crieth aloud at the last:
'Here is one that believeth no hope of the past!
No weapon, no treasure of earth doth he bear,
No gift for the pleasure of Godhome to share;
But life his hand bringeth, well cherished, most sweet;
And hark! the Hall singeth the Folk-wolf to greet!'

As the rain of May
On earth's happiest day,
So the fair flowers fall
On the sun-bright Hall
As the Gods rise up
With the greeting-cup,
And the welcoming crowd
Falls to murmur aloud.
Then the God of Earth speaketh; sweet-worded he saith,
'Lo, the Sun ever seeketh Life fashioned of death;
And to-day as he turneth the wide world about
On Wolf-stead he yearneth; for there without doubt
Dwells the death-fashioned story, the flower of all fame.
Come hither new Glory, come Crown of the Name!'

All men's hearts rose high as he sang, and when he had ended arose the clang of sword and shield and went ringing down the meadow, and the mighty shout of the Markmen's joy rent the heavens: for in sooth at that moment they saw Thiodolf, their champion, sitting among the Gods on his golden chair, sweet savours around him, and sweet sound of singing, and he himself bright-faced and merry as no man on earth had seen him, for as joyous a man as he was.

But when the sound of their exultation sank down, the Hall-Sun spake again:

Now wendeth the sun westward, and weary grows the Earth

Of all the long day's doings in sorrow and in mirth;
And as the great sun waneth, so doth my candle wane,
And its flickering flame desireth to rest and die again.
Therefore across the meadows wend we aback once more
To the holy Roof of the Wolfings, the shrine of peace and war.
And these that once have loved us, these warriors images,
Shall sit amidst our feasting, and see, as the Father sees
The works that menfolk fashion and the rest of toiling hands,
When his eyes look down from the mountains and the heavens above all lands,
And up from the flowery meadows and the rolling deeps of the sea.
There then at the feast with our champions familiar shall we be
As oft we are with the Godfolk, when in story-rhymes and lays
We laugh as we tell of their laughter, and their deeds of other days.

Come then, ye sons of the kindreds who hither bore these twain!
Take up their beds of glory, and fare we home again,
And feast as men delivered from toil unmeet to bear,
Who through the night are looking to the dawn-tide fresh and fair
And the morn and the noon to follow, and the eve and its morrow morn,
All the life of our deliv'rance and the fair days yet unborn.

So she spoke, and a murmur arose as those valiant men came forth again. But lo, now were they dight in fresh and fair raiment and gleaming war-array. For while all this was a-doing and a-saying, they had gotten them by the Hall-Sun's bidding unto the wains of their Houses, and had arrayed them from the store therein.

So now they took up the biers, and the Hall-Sun led them, and they went over the meadow before the throng of the kindreds, who followed them duly ordered, each House about its banner; and when they were come through the garth which the Romans had made to the Man's-door of the Hall, there were the women of the House freshly attired, who cast flowers on the living men of the host, and on the dead War-dukes, while they wept for pity of them. So went the freemen of the Houses into the Hall, following the Hall-Sun, and the bearers of the War-dukes; but the banners abode without in the garth made by the Romans; and the thralls arrayed a feast for themselves about the wains of the kindreds in the open place before their cots and the smithying booths and the byres.

And as the Hall-Sun went into the Hall, she thrust down the candle against the threshold of the Man's-door, and so quenched it.

Long were the kindreds entering, and when they were under the Roof of the Wolfings, they looked and beheld Thiodolf set in his chair once more, and Otter set beside him; and the chiefs and leaders of the House took their places on the dais, those to whom it was due, and the Hall-Sun sat under the wondrous Lamp her namesake.

Now was the glooming falling upon the earth; but the Hall was bright within even as the Hall-Sun had promised. Therein was set forth the Treasure of the Wolfings; fair cloths were hung on the walls, goodly broidered garments on the pillars: goodly brazen cauldrons and fair-carven chests were set down in nooks where men could see them well, and vessels of gold and silver were set all up and down the tables of the feast. The pillars also were wreathed with flowers, and flowers hung garlanded from the walls over the precious hangings; sweet gums and spices were burning in fair-wrought censers of brass, and so many candles were alight under the Roof, that scarce had it looked more ablaze when the Romans had litten the faggots therein for its burning amidst the hurry of the Morning Battle.

There then they fell to feasting, hallowing in the high-tide of their return with victory in their hands: and the dead corpses of Thiodolf and Otter, clad in precious glistering raiment, looked down on them from the High-seat, and the kindreds worshipped them and were glad; and they drank the Cup to them before any others, were they Gods or men.

But before the feast was hallowed in, came Ali the son of Grey up to the High-seat, bearing something in his hand: and lo! it was Throng-plough, which he had sought all over the field where the Markmen had been overcome by the Romans, and had found it at last. All men saw him how he held it in his hand now as he went up to the Hall-Sun and spake to her. But she kissed the lad on the forehead, and took Throng-plough, and wound the peace-strings round him and laid him on the board before Thiodolf; and then she spake softly as if to herself, yet so that some heard her:

"O father, no more shalt thou draw Throng-plough from the sheath till the battle is pitched in the last field of fight, and the sons of the fruitful Earth and the sons of Day meet Swart and his children at last, when the change of the World is at hand. Maybe I shall be with thee then: but now and in meanwhile, farewell, O mighty hand of my father!"

Thus then the Houses of the Mark held their High-tide of Returning under the Wolfing Roof with none to blame them or make them afraid: and the moon rose and the summer night wore on towards dawn, and within the Roof and without was there feasting and singing and harping and the voice of abundant joyance: for without the Roof feasted the thralls and the strangers, and the Roman war-captives.

But on the morrow the kindreds laid their dead men in mound betwixt the Great Roof and the Wild-wood. In one mound they laid them with the War-dukes in their midst, and Arinbiorn by Otter's right side; and Thiodolf bore Throng-plough to mound with him.

But a little way from the mound of their own dead, toward the south they laid the Romans, a great company, with their Captain in the midst: and they heaped a long mound over them not right high; so that as years wore, and the feet of men and beasts trod it down, it seemed a mere swelling of the earth not made by men's hands; and belike men knew not how many bones of valiant men lay beneath; yet it had a name which endured for long, to wit, the Battle-toft.

But the mound whereunder the Markmen were laid was called Thiodolf's Howe for many generations of men, and many are the tales told of him; for men were loth to lose him and forget him: and in the latter days men deemed of him that he sits in that Howe not dead but sleeping, with Throng-plough laid before him on the board; and that when the sons of the Goths are at their sorest need and the falcons cease to sit on the ridge of the Great Roof of the Wolfings, he will wake and come forth from the Howe for their helping. But none have dared to break open that Howe and behold what is therein.

But that swelling of the meadow where the Goths had their overthrow at the hands of the Romans, and Thiodolf fell to earth unwounded, got a name also, and was called the Swooning Knowe; and it kept that name long after men had forgotten wherefore it was so called.

Now when all this was done, and the warriors of the kindreds were departed each to his own stead, the Wolfings gathered in wheat-harvest, and set themselves to make good all that the Romans had undone; and they cleansed and mended their Great Roof and made it fairer than before, and took from it all signs of the burning, save that they left the charring and marks of the flames on one tie-beam, the second from the dais, for a token of the past tidings. Also when Harvest was over the Wolfings, the Beamings, the Galtings, and the Elkings, set to work with the Bearings to rebuild their Great Roof and the other dwellings and booths which the Romans had burned; and right fair was that house.

But the Wolfings throve in field and fold, and they begat children who grew up to be mighty men and deft of hand, and the House grew more glorious year by year.

The tale tells not that the Romans ever fell on the Mark again; for about this time they began to stay the spreading of their dominion, or even to draw in its boundaries somewhat.

And this is all that the tale has to tell concerning the House of the Wolfings and the Kindreds of the Mark.

The End

THE ROOTS OF THE MOUNTAINS

WHEREIN IS TOLD SOMEWHAT
OF THE LIVES OF THE MEN
OF THE BURGDALE,
THEIR FRIENDS,
THEIR NEIGHBOURS,
THEIR FOEMEN AND
THEIR FELLOWS
IN ARMS

Whiles carried o'er the iron road,
We hurry by some fair abode;
The garden bright amidst the hay,
The yellow wain upon the way,
The dining men, the wind that sweeps
Light locks from off the sun-sweet heaps—
The gable grey, the hoary roof,
Here now—and now so far aloof.
How sorely then we long to stay
And midst its sweetness wear the day,
And 'neath its changing shadows sit,
And feel ourselves a part of it.
Such rest, such stay, I strove to win
With these same leaves that lie herein.

INTRODUCTION

Move forward hundreds of years from the time of *The House of the Wolfings,* and you arrive at the setting for *The Roots of the Mountains.* The tribe in the former tale has moved and now lives in the foothills of a large mountain chain, though we cannot be certain if it is the Alps in Western Europe or the Carpathians of Eastern Europe. Morris clearly wants us to focus on the lives and the personal dilemmas his characters face rather than the broader historical context. This is a tale of Everyman living in Anytime.

As the tale progresses, we discover that these people are threatened by a cruel, fierce and ugly (for them) people called the Dusky Men or Huns. Like Rome in the previous tale, the Dusky Men want to enslave them and destroy their harmonious culture. Unlike Rome, they seem to have no particular talent for warfare or ruling. Instead, they rely on sheer numbers and raw terror to conquer and dominate. In *The House of the Wolfings,* some readers may feel that the Wolfings, with a religion that involved the sacrifice of prisoners of war, might have benefited from more contact with the civilized and literate Rome. It is unlikely any reader will feel that these Dusky Men have anything to teach.

Again, the plot contains romance, including one with two women, the unfortunately named Bride and the mysterious Sun-beam. As sometimes happens, both want to wed Burgstead's most eligible bachelor, the heart-stoppingly handsome Gold-mane. (As in Tolkien, major characters often have more than one name. Gold-mane's other name is Face-of-god.) The parallels to J. R. R. Tolkien's *The Lord of the Rings* and to Éowyn and Arwen's romantic interest in Aragorn should be obvious. There is even a father who tries to block the marriage, although in Morris, the unhappy father is that of the groom-to-be.

Much as in *The House of the Wolfings,* in this tale Morris wrestled with the conflict that can exist between an individual and his society. But in this tale, that conflict took a different twist.

In *The House of the Wolfings.* Thiodolf had to choose between serving his people and following the desires of the woman he loves, a goddess who is willing to do almost anything to make sure he does not die in battle. Gold-mane faces a different conflict. When he eventually learns of the threat the Dusky Men pose to Sun-beam's tiny people and the role she wants him to play in protecting them, it is clear at almost the same time that the Dusky Men pose the same threat to his own people. By making war on them, he can serve his people *and* possess Sun-beam.

This tale is more personal and emotional. Instead of facing a conflict between himself and his society, Thiodolf is the romantic victim of another's choice to serve her society. As Sun-beam eventually admits, her romantic pursuit of him began as a carefully planned scheme by her people to win the support his much more numerous people in their struggle with the Dusky Men. When Gold-mane realizes that, he is torn inside. Is he being loved or merely used? In Chapter 20, he puts those doubts into a painful question: "But tell me this if thou wilt: dost thou desire me as I desire thee? or is it that thou wilt suffer me to wed thee and bed thee at last as mere payment for the help that I shall give to thee and thine?"

Gold-mane will have no peace in his heart until he resolves that conflict and another that is linked to obligations placed on him by his people. Unlike many, he is as kind and honorable as he is handsome. He must find a way to ease the hurt that his sudden love for Sun-beam has inflicted upon Bride, the woman his community has long expected him to marry.

As you read this story, keep in mind a major difference between Morris and Tolkien. Morris not only had no personal experience with warfare, he lived in an England and a Europe that was in the midst of an extraordinarily lengthy period free of extended, violent warfare at home (the century from the Napoleonic Wars until World War I). Tolkien, on the other hand, experienced first hand what war could be like in World War I trenches. As a result, while both men attach a high value to bravery in combat, Morris seems less aware of what war demands physically, particularly in the age of sword and spear (hence his pretty young maiden warriors). He also does not seem to grasp the tremendous psychological costs of war. In this tale you will find no equivalent to Tolkien's deeply wounded Frodo.

One final note. Some may wonder what a poem about riding the railroad ("the iron road") is doing at the start of a story that takes place many hundreds of years before its invention. Morris included it, as he put it, "just to fill up the great white lower half" of the title page. Interestingly, when faced with what to do with that odd little poem, I placed it in the same place and for that same purpose *before* discovering Morris' rationale. Think of it as a poem for readers in an age when people often read while traveling by train. *The House of the Wolfings* opened with a similar poem directed at his present-day readers rather than his story.

Morris planned to create a trilogy of historical novels with similar themes, but he never completed the third, one his daughter entitled *The Story of Desiderius.* So regrettably, the tale of the Wolfings must end here.

—Michael W. Perry, Seattle, Washington, October 3, 2003,
The 107th anniversary of the death of William Morris

More to William Morris—The Roots of the Mountains

1. OF BURGSTEAD AND ITS FOLK AND ITS NEIGHBOURS

Once upon a time amidst the mountains and hills and falling streams of a fair land there was a town or thorp in a certain valley. This was well-nigh encompassed by a wall of sheer cliffs; toward the East and the great mountains they drew together till they went near to meet, and left but a narrow path on either side of a stony stream that came rattling down into the Dale: toward the river at that end the hills lowered somewhat, though they still ended in sheer rocks; but up from it, and more especially on the north side, they swelled into great shoulders of land, then dipped a little, and rose again into the sides of huge fells clad with pine-woods, and cleft here and there by deep ghylls: thence again they rose higher and steeper, and ever higher till they drew dark and naked out of the woods to meet the snow-fields and ice-rivers of the high mountains. But that was far away from the pass by the little river into the valley; and the said river was no drain from the snow-fields white and thick with the grinding of the ice, but clear and bright were its waters that came from wells amidst the bare rocky heaths.

The upper end of the valley, where it first began to open out from the pass, was rugged and broken by rocks and ridges of water-borne stones, but presently it smoothed itself into mere grassy swellings and knolls, and at last into a fair and fertile plain swelling up into a green wave, as it were, against the rock-wall which encompassed it on all sides save where the river came gushing out of the strait pass at the east end, and where at the west end it poured itself out of the Dale toward the lowlands and the plain of the great river.

Now the valley was some ten miles of our measure from that place of the rocks and the stone-ridges, to where the faces of the hills drew somewhat anigh to the river again at the west, and then fell aback along the edge of the great plain; like as when ye fare a-sailing past two nesses of a river-mouth, and the main-sea lieth open before you.

Besides the river afore-mentioned, which men called the Weltering Water, there were other waters in the Dale. Near the eastern pass, entangled in the rocky ground was a deep tarn full of cold springs and about two acres in measure, and therefrom ran a stream which fell into the Weltering Water amidst the grassy knolls. Black seemed the waters of that tarn which on one side washed the rocks-wall of the Dale; ugly and aweful it seemed to men, and none knew what lay beneath its waters save black mis-shapen trouts that few cared to bring to net or angle: and it was called the Death-Tarn.

Other waters yet there were: here and there from the hills on both sides, but especially from the south side, came trickles of water that ran in pretty brooks down to the river; and some of these sprang bubbling up amidst the foot-mounds of the sheer-rocks; some had cleft a rugged and strait way through them, and came tumbling down into the Dale at diverse heights from their faces. But on the north side about halfway down the Dale, one stream somewhat bigger than the others, and dealing with softer ground, had cleft for itself a wider way; and the folk had laboured this way wider yet, till they had made them a road running north along the west side of the stream. Sooth to say, except for the strait pass along the river at the eastern end, and the wider pass at the western, they had no other way (save one of which a word anon) out of the Dale but such as mountain goats and bold cragsmen might take; and even of these but few.

This midway stream was called the Wildlake, and the way along it Wildlake's Way, because it came to them out of the wood, which on that north side stretched away from nigh to the lip of the valley-wall up to the pine woods and the high fells on the east and north, and down to the Plain-country on the west and south.

Now when the Weltering Water came out of the rocky tangle near the pass, it was turned aside by the ground till it swung right up to the feet of the Southern crags; then it turned and slowly bent round again northward, and at last fairly doubled back on itself before it turned again to run westward; so that when, after its second double, it had come to flowing softly westward under the northern crags, it had cast two thirds of a girdle round about a space of land a little below the grassy knolls and tofts aforesaid; and there in that fair space between the folds of the Weltering Water stood the Thorp whereof the tale hath told.

The men thereof had widened and deepened the Weltering Water about them, and had bridged it over to the plain meads; and athwart the throat of the space left clear by the water they had built them a strong wall though not very high, with a gate amidst and a tower on either side thereof. Moreover, on the face of the cliff which was but a stone's throw from the gate they had made them stairs and ladders to go up by; and on a knoll nigh the brow had built a watch-tower of stone strong and great, lest war should come into the land from over the hills. That tower was ancient, and therefrom the Thorp had its name and the whole valley also; and it was called Burgstead in Burgdale.

So long as the Weltering Water ran straight along by the northern cliffs after it had left Burgstead, betwixt the water and the cliffs was a wide flat way fashioned by man's hand. Thus was the water again a good defence to the Thorp, for it ran slow and deep there, and there was no other ground betwixt it and the cliffs save that road, which was easy to bar across so that no foemen might pass without battle, and this road was called the Portway. For a long mile the river ran under the northern cliffs, and then turned into the midst of the Dale, and went its way westward a broad stream winding in gentle laps and folds here and there down to the out-gate of the Dale. But the Portway held on still underneath the rock-wall, till the sheer-rocks grew somewhat broken, and were cumbered with certain screes, and at last the wayfarer came upon the break in them, and the ghyll through which ran the Wildlake with Wildlake's Way beside it, but the Portway still went on all down the Dale and away to the Plain-country.

That road in the ghyll, which was neither wide nor smooth, the wayfarer into the wood must follow, till it lifted itself out of the ghyll, and left the Wildlake coming rattling down by many steps from the east; and now the way went straight north through the woodland, ever mounting higher, (because the whole set of the land was toward the high fells,) but not in any cleft or ghyll. The wood itself thereabout was thick, a blended growth of diverse kinds of trees, but most of oak and ash; light and air enough came through their boughs to suffer the holly and bramble and eglantine and other small wood to grow together into thickets, which no man could pass without hewing a way. But before it is told whereto Wildlake's Way led, it must be said that on the east side of the ghyll, where it first began just over the Portway, the hill's brow was clear of wood for a certain space, and there, overlooking all the Dale, was the Mote-stead of the Dalesmen, marked out by a great ring of stones, amidst of which was the mound for the Judges and the Altar of the Gods before it. And this was the holy place of the men of the Dale and of other folk whereof the tale shall now tell.

For when Wildlake's Way had gone some three miles from the Mote-stead, the trees began to thin, and presently afterwards was a clearing and the dwellings of men, built of timber as may well be thought. These houses were neither rich nor great, nor was the folk a mighty folk, because they were but a few, albeit body by body they were stout carles enough. They had not affinity with the Dalesmen, and did not wed with them, yet it is to be deemed that they were somewhat akin to them. To be short, though they were freemen, yet as regards the Dalesmen were they well-nigh their servants; for they were but poor in goods, and had to lean upon them somewhat. No tillage they had among those high trees; and of beasts nought save some flocks of goats and a few asses. Hunters they were, and charcoal-burners, and therein the deftest of men, and they could shoot well in the bow withal: so they trucked their charcoal and their smoked venison and their peltries with the Dalesmen for wheat and wine and weapons and weed; and the Dalesmen gave them main good pennyworths, as men who

had abundance wherewith to uphold their kinsmen, though they were but far-away kin. Stout hands had these Woodlanders and true hearts as any; but they were few-spoken and to those that needed them not somewhat surly of speech and grim of visage: brown-skinned they were, but light-haired; well-eyed; with but little red in their cheeks: their women were not very fair, for they toiled like the men, or more. They were thought to be wiser than most men in foreseeing things to come. They were much given to spells, and songs of wizardry, and were very mindful of the old story-lays, wherein they were far more wordy than in their daily speech. Much skill had they in runes, and were exceeding deft in scoring them on treen bowls, and on staves, and door-posts and roof-beams and standing-beds and such like things. Many a day when the snow was drifting over their roofs, and hanging heavy on the tree-boughs, and the wind was roaring through the trees aloft and rattling about the close thicket, when the boughs were clattering in the wind, and crashing down beneath the weight of the gathering freezing snow, when all beasts and men lay close in their lairs, would they sit long hours about the house-fire with the knife or the gouge in hand, with the timber twixt their knees and the whetstone beside them, hearkening to some tale of old times and the days when their banner was abroad in the world; and they the while wheedling into growth out of the tough wood knots and blossoms and leaves and the images of beasts and warriors and women.

They were called nought save the Woodland-Carles in that day, though time had been when they had borne a nobler name: and their abode was called Carlstead. Shortly, for all they had and all they had not, for all they were and all they were not, they were well-beloved by their friends and feared by their foes.

Now when Wildlake's Way was gotten to Carlstead, there was an end of it toward the north; though beyond it in a right line the wood was thinner, because of the hewing of the Carles. But the road itself turned west at once and went on through the wood, till some four miles further it first thinned and then ceased altogether, the ground going down-hill all the way: for this was the lower flank of the first great upheaval toward the high mountains. But presently, after the wood was ended, the land broke into swelling downs and winding dales of no great height or depth, with a few scattered trees about the hillsides, mostly thorns or scrubby oaks, gnarled and bent and kept down by the western wind: here and there also were yew-trees, and whiles the hillsides would be grown over with box-wood, but none very great; and often juniper grew abundantly. This then was the country of the Shepherds, who were friends both of the Dalesmen and the Woodlanders. They dwelt not in any fenced town or thorp, but their homesteads were scattered about as was handy for water and shelter. Nevertheless they had their own stronghold; for amidmost of their country, on the highest of a certain down above a bottom where a willowy stream winded, was a great earthwork: the walls thereof were high and clean and overlapping at the entering in, and amidst of it was a deep well of water, so that it was a very defensible place: and thereto would they drive their flocks and herds when war was in the land, for nought but a very great host might win it; and this stronghold they called Greenbury.

These Shepherd-Folk were strong and tall like the Woodlanders, for they were partly of the same blood, but burnt they were both ruddy and brown: they were of more words than the Woodlanders but yet not many-worded. They knew well all those old story-lays, (and this partly by the minstrelsy of the Woodlanders,) but they had scant skill in wizardry, and would send for the Woodlanders, both men and women, to do whatso they needed therein. They were very hale and long-lived, whereas they dwelt in clear bright air, and they mostly went light-clad even in the winter, so strong and merry were they. They wedded with the Woodlanders and the Dalesmen both; at least certain houses of them did so. They grew no corn; nought but a few pot-herbs, but had their meal of the Dalesmen; and in the summer they drave some of their milch-kine into the Dale for the abundance of grass there; whereas their own hills and bents and winding valleys were not plenteously watered, except here and there as in the bottom under Greenbury. No swine they had, and but few horses, but of sheep very many, and of the best both for their flesh and their wool. Yet were they nought so deft craftsmen at the loom as were the Dalesmen, and their women were not very eager at the weaving, though they loathed not the spindle and rock. Shortly, they were merry folk well-beloved of the Dalesmen, quick to wrath, though it abode not long with them; not very curious in their houses and halls, which were but little, and were decked mostly with the handiwork of the Woodland-Carles their guests; who when they were abiding with them, would oft stand long hours nose to beam, scoring and nicking and hammering, answering no word spoken to them but with aye or no, desiring nought save the endurance of the daylight. Moreover, this Shepherd-folk heeded not gay raiment over-much, but commonly went clad in white woollen or sheep-brown weed.

But beyond this Shepherd-folk were more downs and more, scantily peopled, and that after a while by folk with whom they had no kinship or affinity, and who were at whiles their foes. Yet was there no enduring enmity between them; and ever after war and battle came peace; and all blood-wites were duly paid and no long feud followed: nor were the Dalesmen and the Woodlanders always in these wars, though at whiles they were. Thus then it fared with these people.

But now that we have told of the folks with whom the Dalesmen had kinship, affinity, and friendship, tell we of their chief abode, Burgstead to wit, and of its fashion. As hath been told, it lay upon the land made nigh into an isle by the folds of the Weltering Water towards the uppermost end of the Dale; and it was warded by the deep water, and by the wall aforesaid with its towers. Now the Dale at its widest, to wit where Wildlake fell into it, was but nine furlongs over, but at Burgstead it was far narrower; so that betwixt the wall and the wandering stream there was but a space of fifty acres, and therein lay Burgstead in a space of the shape of a sword-pommel: and the houses of the kinships lay about it, amidst of gardens and orchards, but little ordered into streets and lanes, save that a way went clean through everything from the tower-warded gate to the bridge over the Water, which was warded by two other towers on its hither side.

As to the houses, they were some bigger, some smaller, as the housemates needed. Some were old, but not very old, save two only, and some quite new, but of these there were not many: they were all built fairly of stone and lime, with much fair and curious carved work of knots and beasts and men round about the doors; or whiles a wale of such-like work all along the house-front. For as deft as were the Woodlanders with knife and gouge on the oaken beams, even so deft were the Dalesmen with mallet and chisel on the face of the hewn stone; and this was a great pastime about the Thorp. Within these houses had but a hall and solar, with shut-beds out from the hall on one side or two, with whatso of kitchen and buttery and out-bower men deemed handy. Many men dwelt in each house, either kinsfolk, or such as were joined to the kindred.

Near to the gate of Burgstead in that street aforesaid and facing east was the biggest house of the Thorp; it was one of the two abovesaid which were older than any other. Its door-posts and the lintel of the door were carved with knots and twining stems fairer than other houses of that stead; and on the wall beside the door carved over many stones was an image wrought in the likeness of a man with a wide face, which was terrible to behold, although it smiled: he bore a bent bow in his hand with an arrow fitted to its string, and about the head of him was a ring of rays like the beams of the sun, and at his feet was a dragon, which had crept, as it were, from amidst of the blossomed knots of the door-post wherewith the tail of him was yet entwined. And this head with the ring of rays about it was wrought into the adornment of that house, both within and without, in many other places, but on never another house of the Dale; and it was called the House of the Face. Thereof hath the tale much to tell hereafter, but as now it goeth on to tell of the ways of life of the Dalesmen.

In Burgstead was no Mote-hall or Town-house or Church, such as we wot of in these days; and their market-place was wheresoever any might choose to pitch a booth: but for the most part this was done in the wide street betwixt the gate and the bridge. As to a meeting-place, were there any small matters between man and man, these would the Alderman or one of the Wardens deal with, sitting in Court with the neighbours on the wide space just outside the Gate: but if it were to do with greater matters, such as great manslayings and blood-wites, or the making of war or ending of it, or the choosing of the Alderman and the Wardens, such matters must be put off to the Folk-mote, which could but be held in the place aforesaid where was the Doom-ring and the Altar of the Gods; and at that Folk-mote both the Shepherd-Folk and the Woodland-Carles foregathered with the Dalesmen, and duly said their say. There also they held their great casts and made offerings to the Gods for the Fruitfulness of the Year, the ingathering of the increase, and in Memory of their Forefathers. Natheless at Yule-tide also they feasted from house to house to be glad with the rest of Midwinter, and many a cup drank at those feasts to the memory of the fathers, and the days when the world was wider to them, and their banners fared far afield.

But besides these dwellings of men in the field between the wall and the water, there were homesteads up and down the Dale whereso men found it easy and pleasant to dwell: their halls were built of much the same fashion as those within the Thorp; but many had a high garth-wall cast about them, so that they might make a stout defence in their own houses if war came into the Dale.

As to their work afield; in many places the Dale was fair with growth of trees, and especially were there long groves of sweet chestnut standing on the grass, of the fruit whereof the folk had much gain. Also on the south side nigh to the western end was a wood or two of yew-trees very great and old, whence they gat them bow-staves, for the Dalesmen also shot well in the bow. Much wheat and rye they raised in the Dale, and especially at the nether end thereof. Apples and pears and cherries and plums they had in plenty; of which trees, some grew about the borders of the acres, some in the gardens of the Thorp and the homesteads. On the slopes that had grown from the breaking down here and there of the Northern cliffs, and which faced the South and the Sun's burning, were rows of goodly vines, whereof the folk made them enough and to spare of strong wine both white and red.

As to their beasts; swine they had a many, but not many sheep, since herein they trusted to their trucking with their friends the Shepherds; they had horses, and yet but a few, for they were stout in going afoot; and, had they a journey to make with women big with babes, or with children or outworn elders, they would yoke their oxen to their wains, and go fair and softly whither they would. But the said oxen and all their neat were exceeding big and fair, far other than the little beasts of the Shepherd-Folk; they were either dun of colour, or white with black horns (and those very great) and black tail-tufts and ear-tips. Asses they had, and mules for the paths of the mountains to the east; geese and hens enough, and dogs not a few, great hounds stronger than wolves, sharp-nosed, long-jawed, dun of colour, shag-haired.

As to their wares; they were very deft weavers of wool and flax, and made a shift to dye the thrums in fair colours; since both woad and madder came to them good cheap by means of the merchants of the Plain-country, and of greening weeds was abundance at hand. Good smiths they were in all the metals: they washed somewhat of gold out of the sands of the Weltering Water, and copper and tin they fetched from the rocks of the eastern mountains; but of silver they saw little, and iron they must buy of the merchants of the plain, who came to them twice in the year, to wit in the spring and the late autumn just before the snows. Their wares they bought with wool spun and in the fleece, and fine cloth, and skins of wine and young neat both steers and heifers, and wrought copper bowls, and gold and copper by weight, for they had no stamped money. And they guested these merchants well, for they loved them, because of the tales they told them of the Plain and its cities, and the manslayings therein, and the fall of Kings and Dukes, and the uprising of Captains.

Thus then lived this folk in much plenty and ease of life, though not delicately nor desiring things out of measure. They wrought with their hands and wearied themselves; and they rested from their toil and feasted and were merry: to-morrow was not a burden to them, nor yesterday a thing which they would fain forget: life shamed them not, nor did death make them afraid.

As for the Dale wherein they dwelt, it was indeed most fair and lovely, and they deemed it the Blessing of the Earth, and they trod its flowery grass beside its rippled streams amidst its green tree-boughs proudly and joyfully with goodly bodies and merry hearts.

THE ROOTS OF THE MOUNTAINS

2. OF FACE-OF-GOD AND HIS KINDRED

Tells the tale, that on an evening of late autumn when the weather was fair, calm, and sunny, there came a man out of the wood hard by the Mote-stead aforesaid, who sat him down at the roots of the Speech-mound, casting down before him a roe-buck which he had just slain in the wood. He was a young man of three and twenty summers; he was so clad that he had on him a sheep-brown kirtle and leggings of like stuff bound about with white leather thongs; he bore a short-sword in his

More to William Morris—The Roots of the Mountains

girdle and a little axe withal; the sword with fair wrought gilded hilts and a dew-shoe of like fashion to its sheath. He had his quiver at his back and bare in his hand his bow unstrung. He was tall and strong, very fair of fashion both of limbs and face, white-skinned, but for the sun's tanning, and ruddy-cheeked: his beard was little and fine, his hair yellow and curling, cut somewhat close, but for its length so plenteous, and so thick, that none could fail to note it. He had no hat nor hood upon his head, nought but a fillet of golden beads.

As he sat down he glanced at the dale below him with a well-pleased look, and then cast his eyes down to the grass at his feet, as though to hold a little longer all unchanged the image of the fair place he had just seen. The sun was low in the heavens, and his slant beams fell yellow all up the dale, gilding the chestnut groves grown dusk and grey with autumn, and the black masses of the elm-boughs, and gleaming back here and there from the pools of the Weltering Water. Down in the midmost meadows the long-horned dun kine were moving slowly as they fed along the edges of the stream, and a dog was bounding about with exceeding swiftness here and there among them. At a sharply curved bight of the river the man could see a little vermilion flame flickering about, and above it a thin blue veil of smoke hanging in the air, and clinging to the boughs of the willows anear; about it were a dozen menfolk clear to see, some sitting, some standing, some walking to and fro, but all in company together: four of were brown-clad and short-skirted like himself, and from above the hand of one came a flash of light as the sun smote upon the steel of his spear. The others were long-skirted and clad gayer, and amongst them were red and blue and green and white garments, and they were clear to be seen for women. Just as the young man looked up again, those of them who were sitting down rose up, and those that were strolling drew nigh, and they joined hands together, and fell to dancing on the grass, and the dog and another one with him came up to the dancers and raced about and betwixt them; and so clear to see were they all and so little, being far away, that they looked like dainty well-wrought puppets.

The young man sat smiling at it for a little, and then rose up and shouldered his venison, and went down into Wildlake's Way, and presently was fairly in the Dale and striding along the Portway beside the northern cliffs, whose greyness was gilded yet by the last rays of the sun, though in a minute or two it would go under the western rim. He went fast and cheerily, murmuring to himself snatches of old songs; none overtook him on the road, but he overtook divers folk going alone or in company toward Burgstead; swains and old men, mothers and maidens coming from the field and the acre, or going from house to house; and one or two he met but not many. All these greeted him kindly, and he them again; but he stayed not to speak with any, but went as one in haste.

It was dusk by then he passed under the gate of Burgstead; he went straight thence to the door of the House of the Face, and entered as one who is at home, and need go no further, nor abide a bidding.

The hall he came into straight out of the open air was long and somewhat narrow and not right high; it was well-nigh dark now within, but since he knew where to look, he could see by the flicker that leapt up now and then from the smouldering brands of the hearth amidmost the hall under the luffer, that there were but three men therein, and belike they were even they whom he looked to find there, and for their part they looked for his coming, and knew his step.

He set down his venison on the floor, and cried out in a cheery voice: "Ho, Kettel! Are all men gone without doors to sleep so near the winter-tide, that the Hall is as dark as a cave? Hither to me! Or art thou also sleeping?"

A voice came from the further side of the hearth: "Yea, lord, asleep I am, and have been, and dreaming; and in my dream I dealt with the flesh-pots and the cake-board, and thou shalt see my dream come true presently to thy gain."

Quoth another voice: "Kettel hath had out that share of his dream already belike, if the saw sayeth sooth about cooks. All ye have been away, so belike he hath done as Rafe's dog when Rafe ran away from the slain buck."

He laughed therewith, and Kettel with him, and a third voice joined the laughter. The young man also laughed and said: "Here I bring the venison which my kinsman desired; but as ye see I have brought it over-late: but take it, Kettel. When cometh my father from the stithy?"

Quoth Kettel: "My lord hath been hard at it shaping the Yule-tide sword, and doth not lightly leave such work, as ye wot, but he will be here presently, for he has sent to bid us dight for supper straightway."

Said the young man: "Where are there lords in the dale, Kettel, or hast thou made some thyself, that thou must be always throwing them in my teeth?"

"Son of the Alderman," said Kettel, "ye call me Kettel, which is no name of mine, so why should I not call thee lord, which is no dignity of thine, since it goes well over my tongue from old use and wont? But here comes my mate of the kettle, and the women and lads. Sit down by the hearth away from their hurry, and I will fetch thee the hand-water."

The young man sat down, and Kettel took up the venison and went his ways toward the door at the lower end of the hall; but ere he reached it it opened, and a noisy crowd entered of men, women, boys, and dogs, some bearing great wax candles, some bowls and cups and dishes and trenchers, and some the boards for the meal.

2. Of Face-of-god and his Kindred

The young man sat quiet smiling and winking his eyes at the sudden flood of light let into the dark place; he took in without looking at this or the other thing the aspect of his Fathers'' House, so long familiar to him; yet to-night he had a pleasure in it above his wont, and in all the stir of the household; for the thought of the wood wherein he had wandered all day yet hung heavy upon him. Came one of the girls and cast fresh brands on the smouldering fire and stirred it into a blaze, and the wax candles were set up on the dais, so that between them and the mew-quickened fire every corner of the hall was bright. As aforesaid it was long and narrow, over-arched with stone and not right high, the windows high up under the springing of the roof-arch and all on the side toward the street; over against them were the arches of the shut-beds of the housemates. The walls were bare that evening, but folk were wont to hang up hallings of woven pictures thereon when feasts and high-days were toward; and all along the walls were the tenter-hooks for that purpose, and divers weapons and tools were hanging from them here and there. About the dais behind the thwart-table were now stuck for adornment leavy boughs of oak now just beginning to turn with the first frosts. High up on the gable wall above the tenter-hooks for the hangings were carven fair imagery and knots and twining stems; for there in the hewn atone was set forth that same image with the rayed head that was on the outside wall, and he was smiting the dragon and slaying him; but here inside the house all this was stained in fair and lively colours, and the sun-like rays round the head of the image were of beaten gold. At the lower end of the hall were two doors going into the butteries, and kitchen, and other out-bowers; and above these doors was a loft upborne by stone pillars, which loft was the sleeping chamber of the goodman of the house; but the outward door was halfway between the said loft and the hearth of the hall.

So the young man took the shoes from his feet and then sat watching the women and lads arraying the boards, till Kettel came again to him with an old woman bearing the ewer and basin, who washed his feet and poured the water over his hands, and gave him the towel with fair-broidered ends to dry them withal.

Scarce had he made an end of this ere through the outer door came in three men and a young woman with them; the foremost of these was a man younger by some two years than the first-comer, but so like him that none might misdoubt that he was his brother; the next was an old man with a long white beard, but hale and upright; and lastly came a man of middle-age, who led the young woman by the hand. He was taller than the first of the young men, though the other who entered with him outwent him in height; a stark carle he was, broad across the shoulders, thin in the flank, long-armed and big-handed; very noble and well-fashioned of countenance, with a straight nose and grey eyes underneath a broad brow: his hair grown somewhat scanty was done about with a fillet of golden beads like the young men his sons. For indeed this was their father, and the master of the House.

His name was Iron-face, for he was the deftest of weapon-smiths, and he was the Alderman of the Dalesmen, and well-beloved of them; his kindred was deemed the noblest of the Dale, and long had they dwelt in the House of the Face. But of his sons the youngest, the new-comer, was named Hall-face, and his brother the elder Face-of-god; which name was of old use amongst the kindred, and many great men and stout warriors had borne it aforetime: and this young man, in great love had he been gotten, and in much hope had he been reared, and therefore had he been named after the best of the kindred. But his mother, who was hight the Jewel, and had been a very fair woman, was dead now, and Iron-face lacked a wife.

Face-of-god was well-beloved of his kindred and of all the Folk of the Dale, and he had gotten a to-name, and was called Gold-mane because of the abundance and fairness of his hair.

As for the young woman that was led in by Iron-face, she was the betrothed of Face-of-god, and her name was the Bride. She looked with such eyes of love on him when she saw him in the hall, as though she had never seen him before but once, nor loved him but since yesterday; though in truth they had grown up together and had seen each other most days of the year for many years. She was of the kindred with whom the chiefs and great men of the Face mostly wedded, which was indeed far away kindred of them. She was a fair woman and strong: not easily daunted amidst perils she was hardy and handy and light-foot: she could swim as well as any, and could shoot well in the bow, and wield sword and spear: yet was she kind and compassionate, and of great courtesy, and the very dogs and kine trusted in her and loved her. Her hair was dark red of hue, long and fine and plenteous, her eyes great and brown, her brow broad and very fair, her lips fine and red: her cheek not ruddy, yet nowise sallow, but clear and bright: tall she was and of excellent fashion, but well-knit and well-measured rather than slender and wavering as the willow-bough. Her voice was sweet and soft, her words few, but exceeding dear to the listener. In short, she was a woman born to be the ransom of her Folk.

Now as to the names which the menfolk of the Face bore, and they an ancient kindred, a kindred of chieftains, it has been said that in times past their image of the God of the Earth had over his treen face a mask of beaten gold fashioned to the shape of the image; and that when the Alderman of the Folk died, he to wit who served the God and bore on his arm the gold-ring between the people and the altar, this visor or face of God was laid over the face of him who had been in a manner his priest, and therewith he was borne to mound; and the new

Alderman and priest had it in charge to fashion a new visor for the God; and whereas for long this great kindred had been chieftains of the people, they had been, and were all so named, that the word Face was ever a part of their names.

3. THEY TALK OF DIVERS MATTERS IN THE HALL

Now Face-of-god, who is also called Gold-mane, rose up to meet the new-comers, and each of them greeted him kindly, and the Bride kissed him on the cheek, and he her in likewise; and he looked kindly on her, and took her hand, and went on up the hall to the dais, following his father and the old man; as for him, he was of the kindred of the House, and was foster-father of Iron-face and of his sons both; and his name was Stone-face: a stark warrior had he been when he was young, and even now he could do a man's work in the battlefield, and his understanding was as good as that of a man in his prime. So went these and four others up on to the dais and sat down before the thwart-table looking down the hall, for the meat was now on the board; and of the others there were some fifty men and women who were deemed to be of the kindred and sat at the endlong tables.

So then the Alderman stood up and made the sign of the Hammer over the meat, the token of his craft and of his God. Then they fell to with good hearts, for there was enough and to spare of meat and drink. There was bread and flesh (though not Gold-mane's venison), and leeks and roasted chestnuts of the grove, and red-cheeked apples of the garth, and honey enough of that year's gathering, and medlars sharp and mellow: moreover, good wine of the western bents went up and down the hall in great gilded copper bowls and in mazers girt and lipped with gold.

But when they were full of meat, and had drunken somewhat, they fell to speech, and Iron-face spake aloud to his son, who had but been speaking softly to the Bride as one playmate to the other: but the Alderman said: "Scarce are the wood-deer grown, kinsman, when I must needs eat sheep's flesh on a Thursday, though my son has lain abroad in the woods all night to hunt for me."

And therewith he smiled in the young man's face; but Gold-mane reddened and said: "So is it, kinsman, I can hit what I can see; but not what is hidden."

Iron-face laughed and said: "Hast thou been to the Woodland-Carles? are their women fairer than our cousins?"

Face-of-god took up the Bride's hand in his and kissed it and laid it to his cheek; and then turned to his father and said: "Nay, father, I saw not the Wood-carles, nor went to their abode; and on no day do I lust after their women. Moreover, I brought home a roebuck of the fattest; but I was over-late for Kettel, and the flesh was ready for the board by then I came."

"Well, son," quoth Iron-face, for he was merry, "a roebuck is but a little deer for such big men as are thou and I. But I rede thee take the Bride along with thee the next time; and she shall seek whilest thou sleepest, and hit when thou missest."

Then Face-of-god smiled, but he frowned somewhat also, and he said: "Well were that, indeed! But if ye must needs drag a true tale out of me: that roebuck I shot at the very edge of the wood nigh to the Mote-stead as I was coming home: harts had I seen in the wood and its lawns, and boars, and bucks, and loosed not at them: for indeed when I awoke in the morning in that wood-lawn ye wot of, I wandered up and down with my bow unbent. So it was that I fared as if I were seeking something, I know not what, that should fill up something lacking to me, I know not what. Thus I felt in myself even so long as I was underneath the black boughs, and there was none beside me and before me, and none to turn aback to: but when I came out again into the sunshine, and I saw the fair dale, and the happy abode lying before me, and folk abroad in the meads merry in the eventide; then was I full fain of it, and loathed the wood as an empty thing that had nought to give me; and lo you! all that I had been longing for in the wood, was it not in this House and ready to my hand?—and that is good meseemeth."

Therewith he drank of the cup which the Bride put into his hand after she had kissed the rim, but when he had set it down again he spake once more:

"And yet now I am sitting honoured and well-beloved in the House of my Fathers, with the holy hearth sparkling and gleaming down there before me; and she that shall bear my children sitting soft and kind by my side, and the bold lads I shall one day lead in battle drinking out of my very cup: now it seems to me that amidst all this, the dark cold wood, wherein abide but the beasts and the Foes of the Gods, is bidding me to it and drawing me thither. Narrow is the Dale and the World is wide; I would it were dawn and daylight, that I might be afoot again."

And he half rose up from his place. But his father bent his brow on him and said: "Kinsman, thou hast a long tongue for a half-trained whelp: nor see I whitherward thy mind is wandering, but if it be on the road of a lad's desire to go further and fare worse. Hearken then, I will offer thee somewhat! Soon shall the West-country merchants be here with their winter truck. How sayest thou? hast thou a mind to fare back with them, and look on the Plain and its Cities, and take and give with the strangers? To whom indeed thou shalt be nothing save a purse with a few lumps of gold in it, or maybe a spear in the stranger's band on the stricken field, or a bow on the wall of an alien city. This is a craft which thou mayst well learn, since thou shalt be a chieftain; a craft good to learn, however grievous it be in the learning. And I myself have been there; for in my youth I desired sore to look on the world beyond the mountains; so I went, and I filled my belly with the fruit of my own desires, and a bitter meat was that; but now that it has passed through me, and I yet alive, belike I am more of a grown man for having endured its gripe. Even so may it well be with thee, son; so go if thou wilt; and thou shalt go with my blessing, and with gold and wares and wain and spearmen."

"Nay," said Face-of-god, "I thank thee, for it is well offered; but I will not go, for I have no lust for the Plain and its Cities; I love the Dale well, and all that is round about it; therein will I live and die."

Therewith he fell a-musing; and the Bride looked at him anxiously, but spake not. Sooth to say her heart was sinking, as though she foreboded some new thing, which should thrust itself into their merry life.

But the old man Stone-face took up the word and said:

"Son Gold-mane, it behoveth me to speak, since belike I know the Wild-wood better than most, and have done for these three-score and ten years; to my cost. Now I perceive that thou longest for the wood and the innermost of it; and wot ye what? This longing will at whiles entangle the sons of our chieftains, though this Alderman that now is hath been free therefrom, which is well for him. For, time was this longing came over me, and I went whither it led me: overlong it were to tell of all that befell me because of it, and how my heart bled thereby. So sorry were the tidings that came of it, that now meseemeth my heart should be of stone and not my face, had it not been for the love wherewith I have loved the sons of the kindred. Therefore, son, it were not ill if ye went west away with the merchants this winter, and learned the dealings of the cities, and brought us back tales thereof."

But Gold-mane cried out somewhat angrily, "I tell thee, foster-father, that I have no mind for the cities and their men and their fools and their whores and their runagates. But as for the wood and its wonders, I have done with it, save for hunting there along with others of the Folk. So let thy mind be at ease; and for the rest, I will do what the Alderman commandeth, and whatso my father craveth of me."

"And that is well, son," said Stone-face, "if what ye say come to pass, as sore I misdoubt me it will not. But well it were, well it were! For such things are in the wood, yea and before ye come to its innermost, as may well try the stoutest heart. Therein are Kobbolds, and Wights that love not men, things unto whom the grief of men is as the sound of the fiddle-bow unto us. And there abide the ghosts of those that may not rest; and there wander the dwarfs and the mountain-dwellers, the dealers in marvels, the givers of gifts that destroy Houses; the forgers of the curse that clingeth and the murder that flitteth to and fro. There moreover are the lairs of Wights in the shapes of women, that draw a young man's heart out of his body, and fill up the empty place with desire never to be satisfied, that they may mock him therewith and waste his manhood and destroy him. Nor say I much of the strong-thieves that dwell there, since thou art a valiant sword; or of them who have been made Wolves of the Holy Places; or of the Murder-Carles, the remnants and off-scourings of wicked and wretched Folks—men who think as much of the life of a man as of the life of a fly. Yet happiest is the man whom they shall tear in pieces, than he who shall live burdened by the curse of the Foes of the Gods."

The housemaster looked on his son as the old carle spake, and a cloud gathered on his face a while; and when Stone-face had made an end he spake:

"This is long and evil talk for the end of a merry day, O fosterer! Wilt thou not drink a draught, O Redesman, and then stand up and set thy fiddle-bow a-dancing, and cause it draw some fair words after it? For my cousin's face hath grown sadder than a young maid's should be, and my son's eyes gleam with thoughts that are far away from us and abroad in the Wild-wood seeking marvels."

Then arose a man of middle-age from the top of the endlong bench on the east side of the hall: a man tall, thin and scant-haired, with a nose like an eagle's neb: he reached out his hand for the bowl, and when they had given to him he handled it, and raised it aloft and cried:

"Here I drink a double health to Face-of-god and the Bride, and the love that lieth between them, and the love betwixt them twain and us."

He drank therewith, and the wine went up and down the hall, and all men drank, both carles and queens, with shouting and great joy. Then Redesman put down the cup (for it had come into his hands again), and reached his hand to the wall behind him, and took down his fiddle hanging there in its case, and drew it out and fell to tuning it, while the hall grew silent to hearken: then he handled the bow and laid it on the strings till they wailed and chuckled sweetly, and when the song was well awake and stirring briskly, then he lifted up his voice and sang:

The Minstrel Saith:

O why on this morning, ye maids, are ye tripping
  Aloof from the meadows yet fresh with the dew,
Where under the west wind the river is lipping
  The fragrance of mint, the white blooms and the blue?

For rough is the Portway where panting ye wander;

On your feet and your gown-hems the dust lieth dun;
Come trip through the grass and the meadow-sweet yonder,
And forget neath the willows the sword of the sun.

The Maidens Answer:

Though fair are the moon-daisies down by the river,
And soft is the grass and the white clover sweet;
Though twixt us and the rock-wall the hot glare doth quiver,
And the dust of the wheel-way is dun on our feet;

Yet here on the way shall we walk on this morning
Though the sun burneth here, and sweet, cool is the mead;
For here when in old days the Burg gave its warning,
Stood stark under weapons the doughty of deed.

Here came on the aliens their proud words a-crying,
And here on our threshold they stumbled and fell;
Here silent at even the steel-clad were lying,
And here were our mothers the story to tell.

Here then on the morn of the eve of the wedding
We pray to the Mighty that we too may bear
Such war-walls for warding of orchard and steading,
That the new days be merry as old days were dear.

Therewith he made an end, and shouts and glad cries arose all about the hall; and an old man arose and cried: "A cup to the memory of the Mighty of the Day of the Warding of the Ways." For you must know this song told of a custom of the Folk, held in memory of a time of bygone battle, wherein they had overthrown a great host of aliens on the Portway betwixt the river and the cliffs, two furlongs from the gate of Burgstead. So now two weeks before Midsummer those maidens who were presently to be wedded went early in the morning to that place clad in very fair raiment, swords girt to their sides and spears in their hands, and abode there on the highway from morn till even as though they were a guard to it. And they made merry there, singing songs and telling tales of times past: and at the sunsetting their grooms came to fetch them away to the Feast of the Eve of the Wedding.

While the song was a-singing Face-of-god took the Bride's hand in his and caressed it, and was soft and blithe with her; and she reddened and trembled for pleasure, and called to mind wedding feasts that had been, and fair brides that she had seen thereat, and she forgot her fears and her heart was at peace again.

And Iron-face looked well-pleased on the two from time to time, and smiled, but forbore words to them.

But up and down the hall men talked with one another about things long ago betid: for their hearts were high and they desired deeds; but in that fair Dale so happy were the years from day to day that there was but little to tell of. So deepened the night and waned, and Gold-mane and the Bride still talked sweetly together, and at whiles kindly to the others; and by seeming he had clean forgotten the wood and its wonders.

Then at last the Alderman called for the cup of good-night, and men drank thereof and went their ways to bed.

4. FACE-OF-GOD FARETH TO THE WOOD AGAIN

When it was the earliest morning and dawn was but just beginning, Face-of-god awoke and rose up from his bed, and came forth into the hall naked in his shirt, and stood by the hearth, wherein the piled-up embers were yet red, and looked about and could see nothing stirring in the dimness: then he fetched water and washed the night-tide off him, and clad himself in haste, and was even as he was yesterday, save that he left his bow and quiver in their place and took instead a short casting-spear; moreover he took a leathern scrip and went therewith to the buttery, and set therein bread and flesh and a little gilded beaker; and all this he did with but little noise; for he would not be questioned, lest he should have to answer himself as well as others.

Thus he went quietly out of doors, for the door was but latched, since no bolts or bars or locks were used in Burgstead, and through the town-gate, which stood open, save when rumours of war were about. He turned his face straight towards Wildlake's Way, walking briskly, but at whiles looking back over his shoulder toward the East to note what way was made by the dawning, and how the sky lightened above the mountain passes.

By then he was come to the place where the Maiden Ward was held in the summer the dawn was so far forward that all things had their due colours, and were clear to see in the shadowless day. It was a bright morning, with an easterly air stirring that drave away the haze and dried the meadows, which had otherwise been rimy; for it was cold. Gold-mane lingered on the place a little, and his eyes fell on the road, as dusty yet as in Redesman's song; for the autumn had been very dry, and the strip of green that edged the outside of the way was worn and dusty also. On the edge of it, half in the dusty road, half on the worn grass, was a long twine of briony red-berried and black-leaved; and right in the midst of the road were two twigs of great-leaved sturdy pollard oak, as though they had been thrown aside there yesterday by women or children a-sporting; and the deep white dust yet held the marks of feet, some bare, some shod, crossing each other here and there. Face-of-god smiled as he passed on, as a man with a happy thought; for his mind showed him a picture of the Bride as she would be leading the Maiden Ward next summer, and singing first among the singers, and he saw her as clearly as he had often seen her verily, and before him was the fashion of her hands and all her body, and the little mark on her right wrist, and the place where her arm whitened, because the sleeve guarded it against the sun, which had long been pleasant unto him, and the little hollow in her chin, and the lock of red-brown hair waving in the wind above her brow, and shining in the sun as brightly as the Alderman's cunningest work of golden wire. Soft and sweet seemed that picture, till he almost seemed to hear her sweet voice calling to him, and desire of her so took hold of the youth, that it stirred him up to go swiftlier as he strode on, the day brightening behind him.

Now was it nigh sunrise, and he began to meet folk on the way, though not many; since for most their way lay afield, and not towards the Burg. The first was a Woodlander, tall and gaunt, striding beside his ass, whose panniers were laden with charcoal. The carle's daughter, a little maiden of seven winters, riding on the ass's back betwixt the panniers, and prattling to herself in the cold morning; for she was pleased with the clear light in the east, and the smooth wide turf of the meadows, as one who had not often been far from the shadow of the heavy trees of the wood, and their dark wall round about the clearing where they dwelt. Face-of-god gave the twain the sele of the day in merry fashion as he passed them by, and the sober dark-faced man nodded to him but spake no word, and the child stayed her prattle to watch him as he went by.

Then came the sound of the rattle of wheels, and, as he doubled an angle of the rock-wall, he came upon a wain drawn by four dun kine, wherein lay a young woman all muffled up against the cold with furs and cloths; beside the yoke-beasts went her man, a well-knit trim-faced Dalesman clad bravely in holiday raiment, girt with a goodly sword, bearing a bright steel helm on his head, in his hand a long spear with a gay red and white shaft done about with copper bands. He looked merry and proud of his wain-load, and the woman was smiling kindly on him from out of her scarlet and fur; but now she turned a weary happy face on Gold-mane, for they knew him, as did all men of the Dale.

So he stopped when they met, for the goodman had already stayed his slow beasts, and the goodwife had risen a little on her cushions to greet him, yet slowly and but a little, for she was great with child, and not far from her time. That knew Gold-mane well, and what was toward, and why the goodman wore his fine clothes, and why the wain was decked with oak-boughs and the yoke-beasts with their best gilded bells and copper-adorned harness. For it was a custom with many of the kindreds that the goodwife should fare to her father's house to lie in with her first babe, and the day of her coming home was made a great feast in the house. So then Face-of-god cried out: "Hail to thee, O Warcliff! Shrewd is the wind this morning, and thou dost well to heed it carefully, this thine orchard, this thy garden, this thy fair apple-tree! To a good hall thou wendest, and the Wine of Increase shall be sweet there this even."

Then smiled Warcliff all across his face, and the goodwife hung her head and reddened. Said the goodman: "Wilt thou not be with us, son of the Alderman, as surely thy father shall be?"

"Nay," said Face-of-god, "though I were fain of it: my own matters carry me away."

"What matters?" said Warcliff; "perchance thou art for the cities this autumn?"

Face-of-god answered somewhat stiffly: "Nay, I am not;" and then more kindly, and smiling, "All roads lead not down to the Plain, friend."

"What road then farest thou away from us?" said the goodwife.

"The way of my will," he answered.

"And what way is that?" said she; "take heed, lest I get a longing to know. For then must thou needs tell me, or deal with the carle there beside thee."

"Nay, goodwife," said Face-of-god, "let not that longing take thee; for on that matter I am even as wise as thou. Now good speed to thee and to the new-comer!"

Therewith he went close up to the wain, and reached out his hand to her, and she gave him hers and he kissed it, and so went his ways smiling kindly on them. Then the carle cried to his kine, and they bent down their heads to the yoke; and presently, as he walked on, he heard the rumble of the wain mingling with the tinkling of their bells, which in a little while became measured and musical, and sounded above the creaking of the axles and the rattle of the gear and the roll of the great wheels over the road: and so it grew thinner and thinner till it all died away behind him.

He was now come to where the river turned away from the sheer rock-wall, which was not so high there as in most other places, as there had been in old time long screes from the cliff, which had now grown together, with the waxing of herbs and the washing down of the earth on to them, and made a steady slope or low hill going down riverward. Over this the road lifted itself above the level of the meadows, keeping a little way from the cliffs, while on the other side its bank was somewhat broken and steep here and there. As Face-of-god came up to one of these broken places, the sun rose over the eastern pass, and the meadows grew golden with its long beams. He lingered, and looked back under his hand, and as he did so heard the voices and laughter of women coming up from the slope below him, and presently a young woman came struggling up the broken bank with hand and knee, and cast herself down on the roadside turf laughing and panting. She was a long-limbed light-made woman, dark-faced and black-haired: amidst her laughter she looked up and saw Gold-mane, who had stopped at once when he saw her; she held out her hands to him, and said lightly, though her face flushed withal:

"Come hither, thou, and help the others to climb the bank; for they are beaten in the race, and now must they do after my will; that was the forfeit."

He went up to her, and took her hands and kissed them, as was the custom of the Dale, and said:

"Hail to thee, Long-coat! who be they, and whither away this morning early?"

She looked hard at him, and fondly belike, as she answered slowly: "They be the two maidens of my father's house, whom thou knowest; and our errand, all three of us, is to Burgstead, the Feast of the Wine of Increase which shall be drunk this even."

As she spake came another woman half up the bank, to whom went Face-of-god, and, taking her hands, drew her up while she laughed merrily in his face: he saluted her as he had Long-coat, and then with a laugh turned about to wait for the third; who came indeed, but after a little while, for she had abided, hearing their voices. Her also Gold-mane drew up, and kissed her hands, and she lay on the grass by Long-coat, but the second maiden stood up beside the young man. She was white-skinned and golden-haired, a very fair damsel, whereas the last-comer was but comely, as were well-nigh all the women of the Dale.

Said Face-of-god, looking on the three: "How comes it, maidens, that ye are but in your kirtles this sharp autumn morning? or where have ye left your gowns or your cloaks?"

For indeed they were clad but in close-fitting blue kirtles of fine wool, embroidered about the hems with gold and coloured threads.

The last-comer laughed and said: "What ails thee, Gold-mane, to be so careful of us, as if thou wert our mother or our nurse? Yet if thou must needs know, there hang our gowns on the thorn-bush down yonder; for we have been running a match and a forfeit; to wit, that she who was last on the highway should go down again and bring them up all three; and now that is my day's work: but since thou art here, Alderman's son, thou shalt go down instead of me and fetch them up."

But he laughed merrily and outright, and said: "That will I not, for there be but twenty-four hours in the day, and what between eating and drinking and talking to fair maidens, I have enough to do in every one of them. Wasteful are ye women, and simple is your forfeit. Now will I, who am the Alderman's son, give forth a doom, and will ordain that one of

you fetch up the gowns yourselves, and that Long-coat be the one; for she is the fleetest-footed and ablest thereto. Will ye take my doom? for later on I shall not be wiser."

"Yea," said the fair woman, "not because thou art the Alderman's son, but because thou art the fairest man of the Dale, and mayst bid us poor souls what thou wilt."

Face-of-god reddened at her words, and the speaker and the last-comer laughed; but Long-coat held her peace: she cast one very sober look on him, and then ran lightly down the bent; he drew near the edge of it, and watched her going; for her light-foot slimness was fair to look on: and he noted that when she was nigh the thorn-bush whereon hung the bright-broidered gowns, and deemed belike that she was not seen, she kissed both her hands where he had kissed them erst.

Thereat he drew aback and turned away shyly, scarce looking at the other twain, who smiled on him with somewhat jeering looks; but he bade them farewell and departed speedily; and if they spoke, it was but softly, for he heard their voices no more.

He went on under the sunlight which was now gilding the outstanding stones of the cliffs, and still his mind was set upon the Bride; and his meeting with the mother of the yet unborn baby, and with the three women with their freshness and fairness, did somehow turn his thought the more upon her, since she was the woman who was to be his amongst all women, for she was far fairer than any one of them; and through all manner of life and through all kinds of deeds would he be with her, and know more of her fairness and kindness than any other could: and him-seemed he could see pictures of her and of him amidst all these deeds and ways.

Now he went very swiftly; for he was eager, though he knew not for what, and he thought but little of the things on which his eyes fell. He met none else on the road till he was come to Wildlake's Way, though he saw folk enough down in the meadows; he was soon amidst the first of the trees, and without making any stay set his face east and somewhat north, that is, toward the slopes that led to the great mountains. He said to himself aloud, as he wended the wood: "Strange! yestereven I thought much of the wood, and I set my mind on not going thither, and this morning I thought nothing of it, and here am I amidst its trees, and wending towards its innermost."

His way was easy at first, because the wood for a little space was all of beech, so that there was no undergrowth, and he went lightly betwixt the tall grey and smooth boles; albeit his heart was nought so gay as it was in the dale amidst the sunshine. After a while the beech-wood grew thinner, and at last gave out altogether, and he came into a space of rough broken ground with nought but a few scrubby oaks and thorn-bushes growing thereon here and there. The sun was high in the heavens now, and shone brightly down on the waste, though there were a few white clouds high up above him. The rabbits scuttled out of the grass before him; here and there he turned aside from a stone on which lay coiled an adder sunning itself; now and again both hart and hind bounded away from before him, or a sounder of wild swine ran grunting away toward closer covert. But nought did he see but the common sights and sounds of the woodland; nor did he look for aught else, for he knew this part of the woodland indifferent well.

He held on over this treeless waste for an hour or more, when the ground began to be less rugged, and he came upon trees again, but thinly scattered, oak and ash and hornbeam not right great, with thickets of holly and blackthorn between them. The set of the ground was still steadily up to the east and north-east, and he followed it as one who wendeth an assured way. At last before him seemed to rise a wall of trees and thicket; but when he drew near to it, lo! an opening in a certain place, and a little path as if men were wont to thread the tangle of the wood thereby; though hitherto he had noted no slot of men, nor any sign of them, since he had plunged into the deep of the beech-wood. He took the path as one who needs must, and went his ways as it led. In sooth it was well-nigh blind, but he was a deft woodsman, and by means of it skirted many a close thicket that had otherwise stayed him. So on he went, and though the boughs were close enough overhead, and the sun came through but in flecks, he judged that it was growing towards noon, and he wotted well that he was growing aweary. For he had been long afoot, and the more part of the time on a rough way, or breasting a slope which was at whiles steep enough.

At last the track led him skirting about an exceeding close thicket into a small clearing, through which ran a little woodland rill amidst rushes and dead leaves: there was a low mound near the eastern side of this wood-lawn, as though there had been once a dwelling of man there, but no other sign or slot of man was there.

So Face-of-god made stay in that place, casting himself down beside the rill to rest him and eat and drink somewhat. Whatever thoughts had been with him through the wood (and they been many) concerning his House and his name, and his father, and the journey he might make to the cities of the Westland, and what was to befall him when he was wedded, and what war or trouble should be on his hands—all this was now mingled together and confused by this rest amidst his weariness. He laid down his scrip, and drew his meat from it and ate what he would, and dipping his gilded beaker into the brook, drank water smacking of the damp musty savour of the woodland; and then his head sank back on a little mound in the short turf, and he fell asleep at once. A long dream he had in short space; and therein were blent his thoughts of the morning with the deeds of yesterday; and other matters long forgotten in his waking hours came back to his slumber in unordered confusion: all which made up for him pictures clear, but of little meaning, save that, as oft befalls in dreams, whatever he was a-doing he felt himself belated.

When he awoke, smiling at something strange in his gone-by dream, he looked up to the heavens, thinking to see signs of the even at hand, for he seemed to have been dreaming so long. The sky was thinly overcast by now, but by his wonted woodcraft he knew the whereabouts of the sun, and that it was scant an hour after noon. He sat there till he was wholly awake, and then drank once more of the woodland water; and he said to himself, but out loud, for he was fain of the sound of a man's voice, though it were but his own:

"What is mine errand hither? Whither wend I? What shall I have done to-morrow that I have hitherto left undone? Or what manner of man shall I be then other than I am now?"

Yet though he said the words he failed to think the thought, or it left him in a moment of time, and he thought but of the Bride and her kindness. Yet that abode with him but a moment, and again he saw himself and those two women on the highway edge, and Long-coat lingering on the slope below, kissing his kisses on her hands; and he was sorry that she desired him over-much, for she was a fair woman and a friendly. But all that also flowed from him at once, and he had no thought in him but that he also desired something that he lacked: and this was a burden to him, and he rose up frowning, and said to himself, "Am I become a mere sport of dreams, whether I sleep or wake? I will go backward—or forward, but will think no more."

Then he ordered his gear again, and took the path onward and upward toward the Great Mountains; and the track was even fainter than before for a while, so that he had to seek his way diligently.

5. FACE-OF-GOD FALLS IN WITH MENFOLK ON THE MOUNTAIN

Now he plodded on steadily, and for a long time the forest changed but little, and of wild things he saw only a few of those that love the closest covert. The ground still went up and up, though at whiles were hollows, and steeper bents out of them again, and the half-blind path or slot still led past the close thickets and fallen trees, and he made way without let or hindrance. At last once more the wood began to thin, and the trees themselves to be smaller and gnarled and ill-grown: therewithal the day was waning, and the sky was quite clear again as the afternoon grew into a fair autumn evening.

Now the trees failed altogether, and the slope grown steeper was covered with heather and ling; and looking up, he saw before him quite near by seeming in the clear even (though indeed they were yet far away) the snowy peaks flushed with the sinking sun against the frosty dark-grey eastern sky; and below them the dark rock-mountains, and below these again, and nigh to him indeed, the fells covered with pine-woods and looking like a wall to the heaths he trod.

He stayed a little while and turned his head to look at the way whereby he had come; but that way a swell of the oak-forest hid everything but the wood itself, making a wall behind him as the pine-wood made a wall before. There came across him then a sharp memory of the boding words which Stoneface had spoken last night, and he felt as if he were now indeed within the trap. But presently he laughed and said: "I am a fool: this comes of being alone in the dark wood and the dismal waste, after the merry faces of the Dale had swept away my foolish musings of yesterday and the day before. Lo! here I stand, a man of the Face, sword and axe by my side; if death come, it can but come once; and if I fear not death, what shall make me afraid? The Gods hate me not, and will not hurt me; and they are not ugly, but beauteous."

Therewith he strode on again, and soon came to a place where the ground sank into a shallow valley and the ling gave place to grass for a while, and there were tall old pines scattered about, and betwixt them grey rocks; this he passed through, climbing a steep bent out of it, and the pines were all about him now, though growing wide apart, till at last he came to where they thickened into a wood, not very close, wherethrough he went merrily, singing to himself and swinging his spear. He was soon through this wood, and came on to a wide well-grassed wood-lawn, hedged by the wood aforesaid on three sides, but sloping up slowly toward the black wall of the thicker pine-wood on the fourth side, and about half a furlong overthwart and endlong. The sun had set while he was in the last wood, but it was still broad daylight on the wood-lawn, and as he stood there he was ware of a house under the pine-wood on the other side, built long and low, much like the houses of the Woodland-Carles, but rougher fashioned and of unhewn trees. He gazed on it, and said aloud to himself as his wont was:

"Marvellous! here is a dwelling of man, scarce a day's journey from Burgstead; yet have I never heard tell of it: may happen some of the Woodland-Carles have built it, and are on some errand of hunting peltries up in the mountains, or maybe are seeking copper and tin among the rocks. Well, at least let

us go see what manner of men dwell there, and if they are minded for a guest to-night; for fain were I of a bed beneath a roof, and of a board with strong meat and drink on it."

Therewith he set forward, not heeding much that the wood he had passed through was hard on his left hand; but he had gone but twenty paces when he saw a red thing at the edge of the wood, and then a glitter, and a spear came whistling forth, and smote his own spear so hard close to the steel that it flew out of his hand; then came a great shout, and a man clad in a scarlet kirtle ran forth on him. Face-of-god had his axe in his hand in a twinkling, and ran at once to meet his foe; but the man had the hill on his side as he rushed on with a short-sword in his hand. Axe and sword clashed together for a moment of time, and then both the men rolled over on the grass together, and Face-of-god as he fell deemed that he heard the shrill cry of a woman. Now Face-of-god found that he was the nethermost, for if he was strong, yet was his foe stronger; the axe had flown out of his hand also, while the strange man still kept a hold of his short-sword; and presently, though he still struggled all he could, he saw the man draw back his hand to smite with the said sword; and at that nick of time the foeman's knee was on his breast, his left hand was doubled back behind him, and his right wrist was gripped hard in the stranger's left hand. Even therewith his ears, sharpened by the coming death, heard the sound of footsteps and fluttering raiment drawing near; something dark came between him and the sky; there was the sound of a great stroke, and the big man loosened his grip and fell off him to one side.

Face-of-god leapt up and ran to his axe and got hold of it; but turning round found himself face to face with a tall woman holding in her hand a stout staff like the limb of a tree. She was calm and smiling, though forsooth it was she who had stricken the stroke and stayed the sword from his throat. His hand and axe dropped down to his side when he saw what it was that faced him, and that the woman was young and fair; so he spake to her and said:

"What aileth, maiden? is this man thy foe? doth he oppress thee? shall I slay him?"

She laughed and said: "Thou art open-handed in thy proffers: he might have asked the like concerning thee but a minute ago."

"Yea, yea," said Gold-mane, laughing also, "but he asked it not of thee."

"That is sooth," she said, "but since thou hast asked me, I will tell thee that if thou slay him it will be my harm as well as his; and in my country a man that taketh a gift is not wont to break the giver's head with it straightway. The man is my brother, O stranger, and presently, if thou wilt, thou mayst be eating at the same board with him. Or if thou wilt, thou mayst go thy ways unhurt into the wood. But I had liefer of the twain that thou wert in our house to-night; for thou hast a wrong against us."

Her voice was sweet and clear, and she spake the last words kindly, and drew somewhat nigher to Gold-mane. Therewithal the smitten man sat up, and put his hand to his head, and quoth he:

"Angry is my sister! good it is to wear the helm abroad when she shaketh the nut-trees."

" Nay," said she, "it is thy luck that thou wert bare-headed, else had I been forced to smite thee on the face. Thou churl, since when hath it been our wont to thrust knives into a guest, who is come of great kin, a man of gentle heart and fair face? Come hither and handsel him self-doom for thy fool's onset!"

The man rose to his feet and said: "Well, sister, least said, soonest mended. A clout on the head is worse than a woman's chiding; but since ye have given me one, ye may forbear the other."

Therewith he drew near to them. He was a very big-made man, most stalwarth, with dark red hair and a thin pointed beard; his nose was straight and fine, his eyes grey and well-opened, but somewhat fierce withal. Yet was he in nowise evil-looking; he seemed some thirty summers old. He was clad in a short scarlet kirtle, a goodly garment, with a hood of like web pulled off his head on to his shoulders: he bore a great gold ring on his left arm, and a collar of gold came down on to his breast from under his hood.

As for the woman, she was clad in a long white linen smock, and over it a short gown of dark blue woollen, and she had skin shoes on her feet.

Now the man came up to Face-of-god, and took his hand and said: "I deemed thee a foe, and I may not have over-many foes alive: but it seems that thou art to be a friend, and that is well and better; so herewith I handsel thee self-doom in the matter of the onslaught."

Then Face-of-god laughed and said: "The doom is soon given forth; against the tumble on the grass I set the clout on the head; there is nought left over to pay to any man's son."

Said the scarlet-clad man: "Belike by thine eyes thou art a true man, and wilt not bewray me. Now is there no foeman here, but rather maybe a friend both now and in time to come." Therewith he cast his arms about Face-of-god and kissed him. But Face-of-god turned about to the woman and said: "Is the peace wholly made?"

She shook her head and said soberly: "Nay, thou art too fair for a woman to kiss."

He flushed red, as his wont was when a woman praised him; yet was his heart full of pleasure and well-liking. But she laid her hand on his shoulder and said: "Now is it for thee to choose betwixt the Wild-wood and the hall, and whether thou wilt be a guest or a wayfarer this night."

As she touched him there took hold of him a sweetness of pleasure he had never felt erst, and he answered: "I will be thy guest and not thy stranger."

"Come then," she said, and took his hand in hers, so that he scarce felt the earth under his feet, as they went all three together toward the house in the gathering dusk, while eastward where the peaks of the great mountains dipped was a light that told of the rising of the moon.

6. OF FACE-OF-GOD AND THOSE MOUNTAIN-DWELLERS

A yard or two from the threshold Gold-mane hung back a moment, entangled in some such misgiving as a man is wont to feel when he is just about to do some new deed, but is not yet deep in the story; his new friends noted that, for they smiled each in their own way, and the woman drew her hand away from his. Face-of-god held out his still as though to take hers again, and therewithal he changed countenance and said as though he had stayed but to ask that question:

"Tell me thy name, tall man; and thou, fair woman, tell me thine; for how can we talk together else?"

The man laughed outright and said: "The young chieftain thinks that this house also should be his! Nay, young man, I know what is in thy thought, be not ashamed that thou art wary; and be assured! We shall hurt thee no more than thou hast been hurt. Now as to my name; the name that was born

with me is gone: the name that was given me hath been taken from me: now I belike must give myself a name, and that shall be Wild-wearer; but it may be that thou thyself shalt one day give me another, and call me Guest."

His sister gazed at him solemnly as he spoke, and Face-of-god beholding her the while, deemed that her beauty grew and grew till she seemed as aweful as a Goddess; and into his mind it came that this over-strong man and over-lovely woman were nought mortal, and they withal dealing with him as father and mother deal with a wayward child: then for a moment his heart failed him, and he longed for the peace of Burgdale, and even the lonely wood. But therewith she turned to him and let her hand come into his again, and looked kindly on him and said: "And as for me, call me the Friend; the name is good and will serve for many things."

He looked down from her face and his eyes lighted on her hand, and when he noted even amid the evening dusk how fair and lovely it was fashioned, and yet as though it were deft in the crafts that the daughters of menfolk use, his fear departed, and the pleasure of his longing filled his heart, and he drew her hand to him to kiss it; but she held it back. Then he said: "It is the custom of the Dale to all women."

So she let him kiss her hand, heeding the kiss nothing, and said soberly:

"Then art thou of Burgdale, and if it were lawful to guess, I would say that thy name is Face-of-god, of the House of the Face."

"Even so it is," said he, "but in the Dale those that love me do mostly call me Gold-mane."

"It is well named," she said, "and seldom wilt thou be called otherwise, for thou wilt be well-beloved. But come in now, Gold-mane, for night is at hand, and here have we meat and lodging such as an hungry and weary man may take; though we be broken people, dwellers in the waste."

Therewith she led him gently over the threshold into the hall, and it seemed to him as if she were the fairest and the noblest of all the Queens of ancient story.

When he was in the house he looked and saw that, rough as it was without it lacked not fairness within. The floor was of hard-trodden earth strewn with pine-twigs, and with here and there brown bearskins laid on it: there was a standing table near the upper end athwart the hall, and a days beyond that, but no endlong table. Gold-mane looked to the shut-beds, and saw that they were large and fair, though there were but a few of them; and at the lower end was a loft for a sleeping chamber dight very fairly with broidered cloths. The hangings on the walls, though they left some places bare which were hung with fresh boughs, were fairer than any he had ever seen, so that he deemed that they must come from far countries and the City of Cities: therein were images wrought of warriors and fair women of old time and their dealings with the Gods and the Giants, and Wondrous wights; and he deemed that this was the story of some great kindred, and that their token and the sign of their banner must needs be the Wood-wolf, for everywhere was it wrought in these pictured webs. Perforce he looked long and earnestly at these fair things, for the hall was not dark yet, because the brands on the hearth were flaming their last, and when Wild-wearer beheld him so gazing, he stood up and looked too for a moment, and then smote his right hand on the hilt of his sword, and turned away and strode up and down the hall as one in angry thought.

But the woman, even the Friend, bestirred herself for the service of the guest, and brought water for his hands and feet, and when she had washed him, bore him the wine of Welcome and drank to him and bade him drink; and he all the while was shamefaced; for it was to him as if one of the Ladies of the Heavenly Burg were doing him service. Then she went away by a door at the lower end of the hall, and Wild-wearer came and sat down by Gold-mane, and fell a-talking with him about the ways of the Dalesmen, and their garths, and the pastures and growths thereof; and what temper the carles themselves were of; which were good men, which were ill, which was loved and which scorned; no otherwise than if he had been the goodman of some neighbouring dale; and Gold-mane told him whatso he knew, for he saw no harm therein.

After a while the outer door opened, and there came in a woman of some five-and-twenty winters, trimly and strongly built; short-skirted she was and clad as a hunter, with a bow in her hand and a quiver at her back: she unslung a pouch, which she emptied at Wild-wearer's feet of a leash of hares and two brace of mountain grouse; of Face-of-god she took but little heed.

Said Wild-wearer: "This is good for to-morrow, not for to-day; the meat is well-nigh on the board."

Then Gold-mane smiled, for he called to mind his home-coming of yesterday. But the woman said:

"The fault is not mine; she told me of the coming guest but three hours agone."

"Ay?" said Wild-wearer, "she looked for a guest then?"

"Yea, certes," said the woman, "else why went I forth this afternoon, as wearied as I was with yesterday?"

"Well, well," said Wild-wearer, "get to thy due work or go play; I meddle not with meat! and for thee all jests are as bitter earnest."

"And with thee, chief," she said, "it is no otherwise; surely I am made on thy model."

"Thy tongue is longer, friend," said he; "now tarry if thou wilt, and if the supper's service craveth thee not."

She turned away with one keen look at Face-of-god, and departed through the door at the lower end of the hall.

By this time the hall was dusk, for there were no candles there, and the hearth-fire was but smouldering. Wild-wearer sat silent and musing now, and Face-of-god spake not, for he was deep in wild and happy dreams. At last the lower door opened and the fair woman came into the hall with a torch in either hand, after whom came the huntress, now clad in a dark blue kirtle, and an old woman yet straight and hale; and these twain bore in the victuals and the table-gear. Then the three fell to dighting the board, and when it was all ready, and Gold-mane and Wild-wearer were set down to it, and with them the fair woman and the huntress, the old woman threw good store of fresh brands on the hearth, so that the light shone into every corner; and even therewith the outer door opened, and four more men entered, whereof one was old, but big and stalwarth, the other three young: they were all clad roughly in sheep-brown weed, but had helms upon their heads and spears in their hands and great swords girt to their sides; and they seemed doughty men and ready for battle. One of the young men cast down by the door the carcass of a big-horned mountain sheep, and then they all trooped off to the out-bower by the lower door, and came back presently fairly clad and without their weapons. Wild-wearer nodded to them kindly, and they sat at table paying no more heed to Face-of-god than to cast him a nod for salutation.

Then said the old woman to them: "Well, lads, have ye been doing or sleeping?"

"Sleeping, mother," said one of the young men, "as was but due after last night was, and to-morrow shall be."

Said the huntress: "Hold thy peace, Wood-wise, and let thy tongue help thy teeth to deal with thy meat; for this is not the talking hour."

"Nay, Bow-may," said another of the swains, "since here is a new man, now is the time to talk to him."

Said the huntress: "'Tis thine hands that talk best, Wood-wont; it is not they that shall bring thee to shame."

Spake the third: "What have we to do with shame here, far away from dooms and doomers, and elders, and wardens, and guarded castles? If the new man listeth to speak, let him speak; or to fight, then let him; it shall ever be man to man."

Then spake the old woman: "Son Wood-wicked, hold thy peace, and forget the steel that ever eggeth thee on to draw."

Therewith she set the last matters on the board, while the three swains sat and eyed Gold-mane somewhat fiercely, now that words had stirred them, and he had sat there saying nothing, as one who was better than they, and contemned them; but now spake Wild-wearer:

"Whoso hungreth let him eat! Whoso would slumber, let him to bed. But he who would bicker, it must needs be with me. Here is a man of the Dale, who hath sought the wood in peace, and hath found us. His hand is ready and his heart is guileless: if ye fear him, run away to the wood, and come back when he is gone; but none shall mock him while I sit by: now, lads, be merry and blithe with the guest."

Then the young men greeted Gold-mane, and the old man said: "Art thou of Burgstead? then wilt thou be of the House of the Face, and thy name will be Face-of-god; for that man is called the fairest of the Dale, and there shall be none fairer than thou."

Face-of-god laughed and said: "There be but few mirrors in Burgdale, and I have no mind to journey west to the cities to see what manner of man I be: that were ill husbandry. But now I have heard the names of the three swains, tell me thy name, father!"

Spake the huntress: "This is my father's brother, and his name is Wood-father; or ye shall call him so: and I am called Bow-may because I shoot well in the bow: and this old carline is my eme's wife, and now belike my mother, if I need one. But thou, fair-faced Dalesman, little dost thou need a mirror in the Dale so long as women abide there; for their faces shall be instead of mirrors to tell thee whether thou be fair and lovely."

Thereat they all laughed and fell to their victual, which was abundant, of wood-venison and mountain-fowl, but of bread was no great plenty; wine lacked not, and that of the best; and Gold-mane noted that the cups and the apparel of the horns and mazers were not of gold nor gilded copper, but of silver; and he marvelled thereat, for in the Dale silver was rare.

So they ate and drank, and Gold-mane looked ever on the Friend, and spake much with her, and he deemed her friendly indeed, and she seemed most pleased when he spoke best, and led him on to do so. Wild-wearer was but of few words, and those somewhat harsh; yet was he as a man striving to be courteous and blithe; but of the others Bow-may was the greatest speaker.

Wild-wearer called healths to the Sun, and the Moon, and the Hosts of Heaven; to the Gods of the Earth; to the Wood-wights; and to the Guest. Other healths also he called, the meaning of which was dark to Gold-mane; to wit, the Jaws of the Wolf; the Silver Arm; the Red Hand; the Golden Bushel; and the Ragged Sword. But when he asked the Friend concerning these names what they might signify, she shook her head and answered not.

At last Wild-wearer cried out: "Now, lads, the night weareth and the guest is weary: therefore whoso of you hath in him any minstrelsy, now let him make it, for later on it shall be over-late."

Then arose Wood-wont and went to his shut-bed and groped therein, and took from out of it a fiddle in its case; and he opened the case and drew from it a very goodly fiddle, and he stood on the floor amidst of the hall and Bow-may his cousin with him; and he laid his bow on the fiddle and woke up song in it, and when it was well awake she fell a-singing, and he to answering her song, and at the last all they of the house sang together; and this is the meaning of the words which they sang:

She singeth.

> *Now is the rain upon the day,*
> *And every water's wide;*
> *Why busk ye then to wear the way,*
> *And whither will ye ride?*

He singeth.

> *Our kine are on the eyot still,*
> *The eddies lap them round;*

> All dykes the wind-worn waters fill,
>> And waneth grass and ground.

She singeth.

> O ride ye to the river's brim
>> In war-weed fair to see?
> Or winter waters will ye swim
>> In hauberks to the knee?

He singeth.

> Wild is the day, and dim with rain,
>> Our sheep are warded ill;
> The wood-wolves gather for the plain,
>> Their ravening maws to fill.

She singeth.

> Nay, what is this, and what have ye,
>> A hunter's band, to bear
> The Banner of our Battle-glee
>> The skulking wolves to scare?

He singeth.

> O women, when we wend our ways
>> To deal with death and dread,
> The Banner of our Fathers' Days
>> Must flap the wind o'erhead.

She singeth.

> Ah, for the maidens that ye leave!
>> Who now shall save the hay?
> What grooms shall kiss our lips at eve,
>> When June hath mastered May?

He singeth.

> The wheat is won, the seed is sown,
>> Here toileth many a maid,
> And ere the hay knee-deep hath grown
>> Your grooms the grass shall wade.

They sing all together.

> Then fair befall the mountain-side
>> Whereon the play shall be!
> And fair befall the summer-tide
>> That whoso lives shall see.

Face-of-god thought the song goodly, but to the others it was well known. Then said Wood-father:

"O foster-son, thy foster-brother hath sung well for a wood abider; but we are deeming that his singing shall be but as a starling to a throstle matched against thy new-come guest. Therefore, Dalesman, sing us a song of the Dale, and if ye will, let it be of gardens and pleasant houses of stone, and fair damsels therein, and swains with them who toil not over-much for a scant livelihood, as do they of the waste, whose heads may not be seen in the Holy Places."

Said Gold-mane: "Father, it is ill to set the words of a lonely man afar from his kin against the song that cometh from the heart of a noble house; yet may I not gainsay thee, but will sing to thee what I may call to mind, and it is called the Song of the Ford."

Therewith he sang in a sweet and clear voice: and this is the meaning of his words:

> In hay-tide, through the day new-born,
>> Across the meads we come;
> Our hauberks brush the blossomed corn
>> A furlong short of home.

> Ere yet the gables we behold
>> Forth flasheth the red sun,
> And smites our fallow helms and cold
>> Though all the fight be done.

> In this last mead of mowing-grass
>> Sweet doth the clover smell,
> Crushed neath our feet red with the pass
>> Where hell was blent with hell.

> And now the willowy stream is nigh,
>> Down wend we to the ford;
> No shafts across its fishes fly,
>> Nor flasheth there a sword.

> But lo! what gleameth on the bank
>> Across the water wan,
> As when our blood the mouse-ear drank
>> And red the river ran?

> Nay, hasten to the ripple clear,
>> Look at the grass beyond!
> Lo ye the dainty band and dear
>> Of maidens fair and fond!

> Lo how they needs must take the stream!
>> The water hides their feet;
> On fair kind arms the gold doth gleam,
>> And midst the ford we meet.

> Up through the garden two and two,
>> And on the flowers we drip;
> Their wet feet kiss the morning dew
>> As lip lies close to lip.

> Here now we sing; here now we stay:

By these grey walls we tell
The love that lived from out the fray,
The love that fought and fell.

When he was done they all said that he had sung well, and that the song was sweet. Yet did Wild-wearer smile somewhat; and Bow-may said outright: "Soft is the song, and hath been made by lads and minstrels rather than by warriors."

"Nay, kinswoman," said Wood-father, "thou art hard to please; the guest is kind, and hath given us that I asked for, and I give him all thanks therefor."

Face-of-god smiled, but he heeded little what they said, for as he sang he had noted that the Friend looked kindly on him; and he thought he saw that once or twice she put out her hand as if to touch him, but drew it back again each time. She spake after a little and said:

"Here now hath been a stream of song running betwixt the Mountain and the Dale even as doth a river; and this is good to come between our dreams of what hath been and what shall be." Then she turned to Gold-mane, and said to him scarce loud enough for all to hear:

"Herewith I bid thee good-night, O Dalesman; and this other word I have to thee: heed not what befalleth in the night, but sleep thy best, for nought shall be to thy scathe. And when thou wakest in the morning, if we are yet here, it is well; but if we are not, then abide us no long while, but break thy fast on the victual thou wilt find upon the board, and so depart and go thy ways home. And yet thou mayst look to it to see us again before thou diest."

Therewith she held out her hand to him, and he took it and kissed it; and she went to her chamber-aloft at the lower end of the hall. And when she was gone, once more he had a deeming of her that she was of the kindred of the Gods. At her departure him-seemed that the hall grew dull and small and smoky, and the night seemed long to him and doubtful the coming of the day.

7. FACE-OF-GOD TALKETH WITH THE FRIEND ON THE MOUNTAIN

So now went all men to bed; and Face-to-god's shut-bed was over against the outer door and toward the lower end of the hall, and on the panel about it hung the weapons and shields of men. Fair was that chamber and roomy, and the man was weary despite his eagerness, so that he went to sleep as soon as his head touched the pillow; but within a while (he deemed about two hours after midnight) he was awaked by the clattering of the weapons against the panel, and the sound of men's hands taking them down; and when he was fully awake, he heard withal men going up and down the house as if on errands: but he called to mind what the Friend had said to him, and he did not so much as turn himself toward the hall; for he said: "Belike these men are outlaws and Wolves of the Holy Places, yet by seeming they are good fellows and nought churlish, nor have I to do with taking up the feud against them. I will abide the morning. Yet meseemeth that she drew me hither: for what cause?"

Therewith he fell asleep again, and dreamed no more. But when he awoke the sun was shining broad upon the hall-floor, and he sat up and listened, but could hear no sound save the moaning of the wind in the pine-boughs and the chatter of the starlings about the gables of the house; and the place seemed so exceeding lonely to him that he was in a manner feared by that loneliness.

Then he arose and clad himself, and went forth into the hall and gazed about him, and at first he deemed indeed that there was no one therein. But at last he looked and beheld the upper gable and there underneath a most goodly hanging was the glorious shape of a woman sitting on a bench covered over with a cloth of gold and silver; and he looked and looked to see if the woman might stir, and if she were alive, and she turned her head toward him, and lo it was the Friend; and his heart rose to his mouth for wonder and fear and desire. For now he doubted whether the other folk were aught save shows and shadows, and she the Goddess who had fashioned them out of nothing for his bewilderment, presently to return to nothing.

Yet whatever he might fear or doubt, he went up the hall towards her till he was quite nigh to her, and there he stood silent, wondering at her beauty and desiring her kindness.

Grey-eyed she was like her brother; but her hair the colour of red wheat: her lips full and red, her chin round, her nose fine and straight. Her hands and all her body fashioned exceeding sweetly and delicately; yet not as if she were an image of which the like might be found if the craftsman were but deft enough to make a perfect thing, but in such a way that there was none like to her for those that had eyes to behold her as she was; and none could ever be made like to her, even by such a master-craftsman as could fashion a body without a blemish.

She was clad in a white smock, whose hems were broidered with gold wire and precious gems of the Mountains, and over that a gown woven of gold and silver: scarce hath the world such another. On her head was a fillet of gold and gems, and there were wondrous gold rings on her arms: her feet lay bare on the dark grey wolf-skin that was stretched before her.

She smiled kindly upon his solemn and troubled face, and her voice sounded strangely familiar to him coming from all that loveliness, as she said: "Hail, Face-of-god! here am I left alone, although I deemed last night that I should be gone with the others. Therefore am I fain to show myself to thee in fairer array than yesternight; for though we dwell in the Wild-wood, from the solace of folk, yet are we not of thralls' blood. But come now, I bid thee break thy fast and talk with me a little while; and then shalt thou depart in peace."

Spake Face-of-god, and his voice trembled as he spake: "What art thou? Last night I deemed at whiles once and again that thou wert of the Gods; and now that I behold thee thus, and it is broad daylight, and of those others is no more to be seen than if they had never lived, I cannot but deem that it is even so, and that thou comest from the City that shall never perish. Now if thou be a goddess, I have nought to pray thee, save to slay me speedily if thou hast a mind for my death. But if thou art a woman—"

She broke in: "Gold-mane, stay thy prayer and hold thy peace for this time, lest thou repent when repentance availeth not. And this I say because I am none of the Gods nor akin to them, save far off through the generations, as art thou also, and all men of goodly kindred. Now I bid thee eat thy meat, since 'tis ill talking betwixt a full man and a fasting; and I have dight it myself with mine own hands; for Bow-may and the Wood-mother went away with the rest three hours before dawn. Come sit and eat as thou hast a hardy heart; as forsooth thou shouldest do if I were a very goddess. Take heed, friend, lest I take thee for some damsel of the lower Dale arrayed in Earl's garments."

She laughed therewith, and leaned toward him and put forth her hand to him, and he took it and caressed it; and the exceeding beauty of her body and of the raiment which was as it were a part of her and her loveliness, made her laughter and her friendly words strange to him, as if one did not belong to the other; as in a dream it might be. Nevertheless he did as she bade him, and sat at the board and ate, while she leaned forward on the arm of her chair and spake to him in friendly wise. And he wondered as she spake that she knew so much of him and his: and he kept saying to himself: "She drew me hither; wherefore did she so?"

But she said: "Gold-mane, how fareth thy father the Alderman? is he as good a wright as ever?"

He told her: Yea, that ever was his hammer on the iron, the copper, and the gold, and that no wright in the Dale was as deft as he.

Said she: "Would he not have had thee seek to the Cities, to see the ways of the outer world?"

"Yea," said he.

She said: "Thou wert wise to naysay that offer; thou shalt have enough to do in the Dale and round about it in twelve months" time."

"Art thou foresighted?" said he.

"Folk have called me so," she said, "but I wot not. But thy brother Hall-face, how fareth he?"

"Well;" said he, "to my deeming he is the Sword of our House, and the Warrior of the Dale, if the days were ready for him."

"And Stone-face, that stark ancient," she said, "doth he still love the Folk of the Dale, and hate all other folks?"

"Nay," he said, "I know not that, but I know that he loveth as, and above all me and my father."

Again she spake: "How fareth the Bride, the fair maid to whom thou art affianced?"

As she spake, it was to him as if his heart was stricken cold; but he put a force upon himself, and neither reddened nor whitened, nor changed countenance in any way; so he answered:

"She was well the eve of yesterday." Then he remembered what she was, and her beauty and valour, and he constrained himself to say: "Each day she groweth fairer; there is no man's son and no daughter of woman that does not love her; yea, the very beasts of field and fold love her."

The Friend looked at him steadily and spake no word, but a red flush mounted to her cheeks and brow and changed her face; and he marvelled thereat; for still he misdoubted that she was a Goddess. But it passed away in a moment, and she smiled and said:

"Guest, thou seemest to wonder that I know concerning thee and the Dale and thy kindred. But now shalt thou wot that I have been in the Dale once and again, and my brother oftener still; and that I have seen thee before yesterday."

"That is marvellous," quoth he, "for sure am I that I have not seen thee."

"Yet thou hast seen me," she said; "yet not altogether as I am now;" and therewith she smiled on him friendly.

"How is this?" said he; "art thou a skin-changer?"

"Yea, in a fashion," she said. "Hearken! dost thou perchance remember a day of last summer when there was a market holden in Burgstead; and there stood in the way over against the House of the Face a tall old carle who was trucking deer-skins for diverse gear; and with him was a queen, tall and dark-skinned, somewhat well-liking, her hair bound up in a white coif so that none of it could be seen; by the token that she had a large stone of mountain blue set in silver stuck in the said coif?"

As she spoke she set her hand to her bosom and drew something from it, and held forth her hand to Gold-mane, and lo amidst the palm the great blue stone set in silver.

"Wondrous as a dream is this," said Face-of-god, "for these twain I remember well, and what followed."

She said: "I will tell thee that. There came a man of the Shepherd-Folk, drunk or foolish, or both, who began to chaffer with the big carle; but ever on the queen were his eyes set, and presently he put forth his hand to her to clip her, whereon the big carle hove up his fist and smote him, so that he fell to earth noseling. Then ran the folk together to hale off the stranger and help the shepherd, and it was like that the stranger should be mishandled. Then there thrust through the press a young man with yellow hair and grey eyes, who cried out, "Fellows, let be! The stranger had the right of it; this is no matter to make a quarrel or a court case of. Let the market go on! This man and maid are true folk." So when the folk heard the young man and his bidding, they forebore and let the carle and the queen be, and the shepherd went his ways little hurt. Now then, who was this young man?"

Quoth Gold-mane: "It was even I, and meseemeth it was no great deed to do."

"Yea," she said, "and the big carle was my brother, and the tall queen, it was myself."

"How then," said he, "for she was as dark-skinned as a dwarf, and thou so bright and fair?"

She said: "Well, if the woods are good for nothing else, yet are they good for the growing of herbs, and I know the craft of simpling; and with one of these herbs had I stained my skin and my brother's also. And it showed the darker beneath the white coif."

"Yea," said he, "but why must ye needs fare in feigned shapes? Ye would have been welcome guests in the Dale howsoever ye had come."

"I may not tell thee hereof as now," said she.

Said Gold-mane: "Yet thou mayst belike tell me wherefore was that thy brother desired to slay me yesterday, if he knew me, who I was."

"Gold-mane," she said, "thou art not slain, so little story need be made of that: for the rest, belike he knew thee not at that moment. So it falls with us, that we look to see foes rather than friends in the Wild-woods. Many uncouth things are therein. Moreover, I must tell thee of my brother that whiles he is as the stalled bull late let loose, and nothing is good to him save battle and onset; and then is he blind and knows not friend from foe." Said Face-of-god: "Thou hast asked of me and mine; wilt thou not tell me of thee and thine?"

"Nay," she said, "not as now; thou must betake thee to the

way. Whither wert thou wending when thou happenedst upon us?"

He said: "I know not; I was seeking something, but I knew not what— meseemeth that now I have found it."

"Art thou for the great mountains seeking gems?" she said. "Yet go not thither to-day: for who knoweth what thou shalt meet there that shall be thy foe?"

He said: "Nay, nay; I have nought to do but to abide here as long as I may, looking upon thee and hearkening to thy voice."

Her eyes were upon his, but yet she did not seem to see him, and for a while she answered not; and still he wondered that mere words should come from so fair a thing; for whether she moved foot, or hand, or knee, or turned this way or that, each time she stirred it was a caress to his very heart.

He spake again: "May I not abide here a while? What scathe may be in that?"

"It is not so," she said; "thou must depart, and that straightway: lo, there lieth thy spear which the Wood-mother hath brought in from the waste. Take thy gear to thee and wend thy ways. Have patience! I will lead thee to the place where we first met and there give thee farewell."

Therewith she arose and he also perforce, and when they came to the doorway she stepped across the threshold and then turned back and gave him her hand and so led him forth, the sun flashing back from her golden raiment. Together they went over the short grey grass of that hillside till they came to the place where he had arisen from that wrestle with her brother. There she stayed him and said:

"This is the place; here must we part."

But his heart failed him and he faltered in his speech as he said:

"When shall I see thee again? Wilt thou slay me if I seek to thee hither once more?"

"Hearken," she said, "autumn is now a-dying into winter: let winter and its snows go past: nor seek to me hither; for me thou should'st not find, but thy death thou mightest well fall in with; and I would not that thou shouldest die. When winter is gone, and spring is on the land, if thou hast not forgotten us thou shalt meet us again. Yet shalt thou go further than this Woodland Hall. In Shadowy Vale shalt thou seek to me then, and there will I talk with thee."

"And where," said he, "is Shadowy Vale? for thereof have I never heard tell."

She said: "The token when it cometh to thee shall show thee thereof and the way thither. Art thou a babbler, Gold-mane?"

He said: "I have won no prize for babbling hitherto."

She said: "If thou listest to babble concerning what hath befallen thee on the Mountain, so do, and repent it once only, that is, thy life long."

"Why should I say any word thereof?" said he. "Dost thou not know the sweetness of such a tale untold?"

He spake as one who is somewhat wrathful, and she answered humbly and kindly:

"Well is that. Bide thou the token that shall lead thee to Shadowy Vale. Farewell now."

She drew her hand from his, and turned and went her ways swiftly to the house: he could not choose but gaze on her as she went glittering-bright and fair in that grey place of the mountains, till the dark doorway swallowed up her beauty. Then he turned away and took the path through the pine-woods, muttering to himself as he went:

"What thing have I done now that hitherto I had not done? What manner of man am I to-day other than the man I was yesterday?"

8. FACE-OF-GOD COMETH HOME AGAIN TO BURGSTEAD

Face-of-god went back through the wood by the way he had come, paying little heed to the things about him. For whatever he thought of strayed not one whit from the image of the Fair Woman of the Mountain-side.

He went through the wood swiftlier than yesterday, and made no stay for noon or aught else, nor did he linger on the road when he was come into the Dale, either to speak to any or to note what they did. So he came to the House of the Face about dusk, and found no man within the hall either carle or queen. So he cried out on the folk, and there came in a damsel of the house, whom he greeted kindly and she him again. He bade her bring the washing-water, and she did so and washed his feet and his hands. She was a fair maid enough, as were most in the Dale, but he heeded her little; and when she was done he kissed not her cheek for her pains, as his wont was, but let her go her ways unthanked. But he went to his shut-bed and opened his chest, and drew fair raiment from it, and did off his wood-gear, and did on him a goodly scarlet kirtle fairly broidered, and a collar with gems of price therein, and other braveries. And when he was so attired he came out into the hall, and there was old Stone-face standing by the hearth, which was blazing brightly with fresh brands, so that things were clear to see.

Stone-face noted Gold-mane's gay raiment, for he was not wont to wear such attire, save on the feasts and high days when he behoved to. So the old man smiled and said:

"Welcome back from the Wood! But what is it? Hast thou been wedded there, or who hath made thee Earl and King?"

Said Face-of-god: "Foster-father, sooth it is that I have been to the wood, but there have I seen nought of manfolk worse than myself. Now as to my raiment, needs must I keep it from the moth. And I am weary withal, and this kirtle is light and easy to me. Moreover, I look to see the Bride here again, and I would pleasure her with the sight of gay raiment upon me."

"Nay," said Stone-face, "hast thou not seen some woman in the wood arrayed like the image of a God? and hath she not bidden thee thus to worship her to-night? For I know that such wights be in the wood, and that such is their wont."

Said Gold-mane: "I worship nought save the Gods and the Fathers. Nor saw I in the wood any such as thou sayest."

Therewith Stone-face shook his head; but after a while he said:

"Art thou for the wood to-morrow?"

"Nay," said Gold-mane angrily, knitting his brows.

"The morrow of to-morrow," said Stone-face, "is the day when we look to see the Westland merchants: after all, wilt thou not go hence with them when they wend their ways back before the first snows fall?"

"Nay," said he, "I have no mind to it, fosterer; cease egging me on hereto."

Then Stone-face shook his head again, and looked on him long, and muttered: "To the wood wilt thou go to-morrow or next day; or some day when doomed is thine undoing."

Therewith entered the service and torches, and presently after came the Alderman with Hall-face; and Iron-face greeted his son and said to him: "Thou hast not hit the time to do on thy gay raiment, for the Bride will not be here to-night; she bideth still at the Feast at the Apple-tree House: or wilt thou be there, son?"

"Nay," said Face-of-god, "I am over-weary. And as for my raiment, it is well; it is for thine honour and the honour of the name."

So to table they went, and Iron-face asked his son of his ways again, and whether he was quite fixed in his mind not to go down to the Plain and the Cities: "For," said he, "the morrow of to-morrow shall the merchants be here, and this were great news for them if the son of the Alderman should be their faring-fellow back."

But Face-of-god answered without any haste or heat: "Nay, father, it may not be: fear not, thou shalt see that I have a good will to work and live in the Dale."

And in good sooth, though he was a young man and loved mirth and the ways of his own will, he was a stalwarth work-man, and few could mow a match with him in the hay-month and win it; or fell trees as certainly and swiftly, or drive as straight and clean a furrow through the stiff land of the lower Dale; and in other matters also was he deft and sturdy.

9. THOSE BRETHREN FARE TO THE YEWWOOD WITH THE BRIDE

Next morning Face-of-god dight himself for work, and took his axe; for his brother Hall-face had bidden him go down with him to the Yew-wood and cut timber there, since he of all men knew where to go straight to the sticks that would quarter best for bow-staves; whereas the Alderman had the right of hewing in that wood. So they went forth, those brethren, from the House of the Face, but when they were gotten to the gate, who should be there but the Bride awaiting them, and she with an ass duly saddled for bearing the yew-sticks. Because Hall-face had told her that he and belike Gold-mane were going to hew in the wood, and she thought it good to be of the company, as oft had befallen erst. When they met she greeted Face-of-god and kissed him as her wont was; and he looked upon her and saw how fair she was, and how kind and friendly were her eyes that beheld him, and how her whole face was eager for him as their lips parted. Then his heart failed him, when he knew that he no longer desired her as she did him, and he said within himself:

"Would that she had been of our nighest kindred! Would that I had had a sister and that this were she!"

So the three went along the highway down the Dale, and Hall-face and the Bride talked merrily together and laughed, for she was happy, since she knew that Gold-mane had been to the wood and was back safe and much as he had been before. So indeed it seemed of him; for though at first he was moody and of few words, yet presently he cursed himself for a mar-sport, and so fell into the talk, and enforced himself to be merry; and soon he was so indeed; for he thought: "She drew me thither: she hath a deed for me to do. I shall do the deed and have my reward. Soon will the spring-tide be here, and I shall be a young man yet when it comes."

So came they to the place where he had met the three maidens yesterday; there they also turned from the highway; and as they went down the bent, Gold-mane could not but turn his eyes on the beauty of the Bride and the lovely ways of her body: but presently he remembered all that had betid, and turned away again as one who is noting what it behoves him not to note. And he said to himself: "Where art thou, Gold-mane? Whose art thou? Yea, even if that had been but a dream that I have dreamed, yet would that this fair woman were my sister!"

So came they to the Yew-wood, and the brethren fell to work, and the Bride with them, for she was deft with the axe and strong withal. But at midday they rested on the green slope without the Yew-wood; and they ate bread and flesh and onions and apples, and drank red wine of the Dale. And while they were resting after their meat, the Bride sang to them, and her song was a lay of time past; and here ye have somewhat of it:

'Tis over the hill and over the dale
   Men ride from the city fast and far,
If they may have a soothfast tale,
   True tidings of the host of war.

And first they hap on men-at-arms,
   All clad in steel from head to foot:
Now tell true tale of the new-come harms,
   And the gathered hosts of the mountain-root.

Fair sirs, from murder-carles we flee,
   Whose fashion is as the mountain-trolls";
No man can tell how many they be,
   And the voice of their host as the thunder rolls.

They were weary men at the ending of day,
   But they spurred nor stayed for longer word.
Now ye, O merchants, whither away?
   What do ye there with the helm and the sword?

O we must fight for life and gear,
   For our beasts are spent and our wains are stayed,
And the host of the Mountain-men draws near,
   That maketh all the world afraid.

They left the chapmen on the hill,
   And through the eve and through the night
They rode to have true tidings still,
   And were there on the way when the dawn was bright.

O damsels fair, what do ye then
   To loiter thus upon the way,
And have no fear of the Mountain-men,
   The host of the carles that strip and slay?

O riders weary with the road,
   Come eat and drink on the grass hereby!
And lay you down in a fair abode

Till the midday sun is broad and high;

Then unto you shall we come aback,
  And lead you forth to the Mountain-men,
To note their plenty and their lack,
  And have true tidings there and then.

'Tis over the hill and over the dale
  They ride from the mountain fast and far;
And now have they learned a soothfast tale,
  True tidings of the host of war.

It was summer-tide and the Month of Hay,
  And men and maids must fare afield;
But we saw the place were the bow-staves lay,
  And the hall was hung with spear and shield.

When the moon was high we drank in the hall,
  And they drank to the guests and were kind and blithe,
And they said: Come back when the chestnuts fall,
  And the wine-carts wend across the hythe.

Come oft and o'er again, they said;
  Wander your ways; but we abide
For all the world in the little stead;

For wise are we, though the world be wide.

Yea, come in arms if ye will, they said;
  And despite your host shall we abide
For life or death in the little stead;
  For wise are we, though the world be wide.

So she made an end and looked at the fairness of the dale spreading wide before her, and a robin came nigh from out of a thorn-bush and sung his song also, the sweet herald of coming winter; and the lapwings wheeled about, black and white, above the meadow by the river, sending forth their wheedling pipe as they hung above the soft turf.

She felt the brothers near her, and knew their friendliness from of old, and she was happy; nor had she looked closer at Gold-mane would she have noted any change in him belike; for the meat and the good wine, and the fair sunny time, and the Bride's sweet voice, and the ancient song softened his heart while it fed the desire therein.

So in a while they arose from their rest and did what was left them of their work, and so went back to Burgstead through the fair afternoon; by seeming all three in all content. But yet Gold-mane, as from time to time he looked upon the Bride, kept saying to himself: "O if she had been but my sister! sweet had the kinship been!"

10. NEW TIDINGS IN THE DALE

It was three days thereafter that Gold-mane, leading an ass, went along the highway to fetch home certain fleeces which were needed for the house from a stead a little west of Wild-lake; but he had gone scant half a mile ere he fell in with a throng of folk going to Burgstead. They were of the Shepherds; they had weapons with them, and some were clad in coats of fence. They went along making a great noise, for they were all talking each to each at the same time, and seemed very hot and eager about some matter. When they saw Gold-mane anigh, they stopped, and the throng opened as if to let him into their midmost; so he mingled with them, and they stood in a ring about him and an old man more ill-favoured than it was the wont of the Dalesmen to be.

For he was long, stooping, gaunt and spindle-shanked, his hands big and crippled with gout: his cheeks were red after an old man's fashion, covered with a crimson network like a pippin; his lips thin and not well hiding his few teeth; his nose long like a snipe's neb. In short, a shame and a laughing-stock to the Folk, and a man whom the kindreds had in small esteem, and that for good reasons.

Face-of-god knew him at once for a notable close-fist and starve-all fool of the Shepherds; and his name was now become Penny-thumb the Lean, whatever it might once have been.

So Face-of-god greeted all men, and they him again; and he said: "What aileth you, neighbours? Your weapons, are bare, but I see not that they be bloody. What is it, goodman Penny-thumb?"

Penny-thumb did but groan for all answer; but a stout carle who stood by with a broad grin on his face answered and said:

"Face-of-god, evil tidings be abroad; the strong-thieves of the wood are astir; and some deem that the wood-wights be helping them."

"Yea, and what is the deed they have done?" said Gold-mane.

Said the carle: "Thou knowest Penny-thumb's abode?"

"Yea surely," said Face-of-god; "fair are the water-meadows about it; great gain of cheese can be gotten thence."

"Hast thou been within the house?" said the carle.

"Nay," said Gold-mane.

Then spake Penny-thumb: "Within is scant gear: we gather for others to scatter; we make meat for others" mouths."

The carle laughed: "Sooth is that," said he, "that there is little gear therein now; for the strong-thieves have voided both hall and bower and byre."

"And when was that?" said Face-of-god.

"The night before last night," said the carle, "the door was smitten on, and when none answered it was broken down."

"Yea," quoth Penny-thumb, "a host entered, and they in arms."

"No host was within," said the carle, "nought but Penny-thumb and his sister and his sister's son, and three carles that work for him; and one of them, Rusty to wit, was the worst man of the hill-country. These then the host whereof the goodman telleth bound, but without doing them any scathe; and they ransacked the house, and took away much gear; yet left some."

"Thou liest," said Penny-thumb; "they took little and left none."

Thereat all men laughed, for this seemed to them good game, and another man said: "Well, neighbour Penny-thumb, if it was so little, thou hast done unneighbourly in giving us such a heap of trouble about it."

And they laughed again, but the first carle said: "True it is, goodman, that thou wert exceeding eager to raise the hue and cry after that little when we happed upon thee and thy housemates bound in your chairs yesterday morning. Well, Alderman's son, short is the tale to tell: we could not fail to follow the gear, and the slot led us into the wood, and ill is the going there for us shepherds, who are used to the bare downs, save Rusty, who was a good woodsman and lifted the slot for us; so he outwent us all, and ran out of sight of us, so presently we came upon him dead-slain, with the manslayer's spear in his breast. What then could we do but turn back again, for now was the wood blind now Rusty was dead, and we knew not whither to follow the fray; and the man himself was but little loss: so back we turned, and told goodman Penny-thumb of all this, for we had left him alone in his hall lamenting his gear; so we bided to-day's morn, and have come out now, with our neighbour and the spear, and the dead corpse of Rusty. Stand aside, neighbours, and let the Alderman's son see it."

They did so, and there was the corpse of a thin-faced tall wiry man, somewhat foxy of aspect, lying on a hand-bier covered with black cloth.

"Yea, Face-of-god," said the carle, "he is not good to see now he is dead, yet alive was he worser: but, look you, though the man was no good man, yet was he of our people, and the feud is with us; so we would see the Alderman, and do him to wit of the tidings, that he may call the neighbours together to seek a blood-wite for Rusty and atonement for the ransacking. Or what sayest thou?"

"Have ye the spear that ye found in Rusty?" quoth Gold-mane.

"Yea verily," said the carle. "Hither with it, neighbours; give it to the Alderman's son."

So the spear came into his hand, and he looked at it and said:

"This is no spear of the smiths' work of the Dale, as my father will tell you. We take but little keep of the forging of spearheads here, so that they be well-tempered and made so as to ride well on the shaft; but this head, daintily is it wrought, the blood-trench as clean and trim as though it were an Earl's sword. See you withal this inlaying of runes on the steel? It is done with no tin or copper, but with very silver; and these bands about the shaft be of silver also. It is a fair weapon, and the owner hath a loss of it greater than his gain in the slaying of Rusty; and he will have left it in the wound so that he might be known hereafter, and that he might be said not to have murdered Rusty but to have slain him. Or how think ye?"

They all said that this seemed like to be; but that if the man who had slain Rusty were one of the ransackers they might have a blood-wite of him, if they could find him. Gold-mane said that so it was, and therewithal he gave the shepherds good-speed and went on his way.

But they came to Burgstead and found the Alderman, and in due time was a Court held, and a finding uttered, and outlawry given forth for the manslaying and the ransacking against certain men unknown. As for the spear, it was laid up in the House of the Face.

But Face-of-god pondered these matters in his mind, for such ransackings there had been none of in late years; and he said to himself that his friends of the Mountain must have other folk, of which the Dalesmen knew nought, whose gear they could lift, or how could they live in that place. And he marvelled that they should risk drawing the Dalesmen's wrath upon them; whereas they of the Dale were strong men not easily daunted, albeit peaceable enough if not stirred to wrath. For in good sooth he had no doubt concerning that spear, whose it was and whence it came: for that very weapon had been leaning against the panel of his shut-bed the night he slept on the Mountain, and all the other spears that he saw there were more or less of the same fashion, and adorned with silver.

Albeit all that he knew, and all that he thought of, he kept in his own heart and said nothing of it.

So wore the autumn into early winter; and the Westland merchants came in due time, and departed without Face-of-god, though his father made him that offer one last time. He went to and fro about his work in the Dale, and seemed to most men's eyes nought changed from what he had been. But the Bride noted that he saw her less often than his wont was, and abode with her a lesser space when he met her; and she could not think what this might mean; nor had she heart to ask him thereof, though she was sorry and grieved, but rather withdrew her company from him somewhat; and when she perceived that he noted it not, and made no question of it, then was she the sorrier.

But the first winter-snow came on with a great storm of wind from the north-east, so that no man stirred abroad who was not compelled thereto, and those who went abroad risked life and limb thereby. Next morning all was calm again, and the snow was deep, but it did not endure long, for the wind shifted to the southwest and the thaw came, and three days after, when folk could fare easily again up and down the Dale, came tidings to Burgstead and the Alderman from the Lower Dale, how a house called Greentofts had been ransacked there, and none knew by whom. Now the goodman of Greentofts was little loved of the neighbours: he was grasping and overbearing, and had often cowed others out of their due: he was very cross-grained, both at home and abroad: his wife had fled from his hand, neither did his sons find it good to abide with him: therewithal he was wealthy of goods, a strong man and a deft man-at-arms. When his sons and his wife departed from him, and none other of the Dalesmen cared to abide with him, he went down into the Plain, and got thence men to be with him for hire, men who were not well seen to in their own land. These to the number of twelve abode with him, and did his bidding whenso it pleased them. Two more had he had who had been slain by good men of the Dale for their masterful ways; and no blood-wite had been paid for them, because of their ill-doings, though they had not been made outlaws. This man of Greentofts was called Harts-bane after his father, who was a great hunter.

Now the full tidings of the ransacking were these: The storm began two hours before sunset, and an hour thereafter, when it was quite dark, for without none could see because the wind was at its height and the drift of the snow was hard and full, the hall-door flew open; and at first men thought it had been the wind, until they saw in the dimness (for all lights but the fire on the hearth had been quenched) certain things tumbling in which at first they deemed were wolves; but when they took swords and staves against them, lo they were met by swords and axes, and they saw that the seeming wolves were men with wolf-skins drawn over them. So the new-comers cowed them that they threw down their weapons, and were bound in their places; but when they were bound, and had had time to note who the ransackers were, they saw that there were but six of them all told, who had cowed and bound Harts-bane and his twelve masterful men; and this they deemed a great shaming to them, as might well be.

So then the stead was ransacked, and those wolves took away what they would, and went their ways through the fierce storm, and none could tell whether they had lived or died in it; but at least neither the men nor their prey were seen again; nor did they leave any slot, for next morning the snow lay deep over everything.

No doubt had Gold-mane but that these ransackers were his friends of the Mountain; but he held his peace, abiding till the winter should be over.

11. MEN MAKE OATH AT BURGSTEAD ON THE HOLY BOAR

A week after the ransacking at Greentofts the snow and the winter came on in earnest, and all the Dale lay in snow, and men went on skids when they fared up and down the Dale or on the Mountain.

All was now tidingless till Yule over, and in Burgstead was there feasting and joyance enough; and especially at the House of the Face was high-tide holden, and the Alderman and his sons and Stone-face and all the kindred and all their men sat in glorious attire within the hall; and many others were there of the best of the kindreds of Burgstead who had been bidden.

Face-of-god sat between his father and Stone-face; and he looked up and down the tables and the hall and saw not the Bride, and his heart misgave him because she was not there, and he wondered what had befallen and if she were sick of sorrow.

But Iron-face beheld him how he gazed about, and he laughed; for he was exceeding merry that night and fared as a young man. Then he said to his son: "Whom seekest thou, son? is there someone lacking?"

Face-of-god reddened as one who lies unused to it, and said:

"Yea, kinsman, so it is that I was seeking the Bride my kinswoman."

"Nay," said Iron-face, "call her not kinswoman: therein is ill-luck, lest it seem that thou art to wed one too nigh thine own blood. Call her the Bride only: to thee and to me the name is good. Well, son, desirest thou sorely to see her?"

"Yea, yea, surely," said Face-of-god; but his eyes went all about the hall still, as though his mind strayed from the place and that home of his.

Said Iron-face: "Have patience, son, thou shalt see her anon, and that in such guise as shall please thee."

Therewithal came the maidens with the ewers of wine, and they filled all horns and beakers, and then stood by the end-long tables on either side laughing and talking with the carles and the older women; and the hall was a fair sight to see, for the many candles burned bright and the fire on the hearth flared up, and those maids were clad in fair raiment, and there was none of them but was comely, and some were fair, and some very fair: the walls also were hung with goodly pictured cloths, and the image of the God of the Face looked down smiling terribly from the gable-end above the high-seat.

Thus as they sat they heard the sound of a horn winded close outside the hall door, and the door was smitten on. Then rose Iron-face smiling merrily, and cried out:

"Enter ye, whether ye be friends or foes: for if ye be foemen, yet shall ye keep the holy peace of Yule, unless ye be the foes of all kindreds and nations, and then shall we slay you."

Threat some who knew what was toward laughed; but Gold-mane, who had been away from Burgstead some days past, marvelled and knit his brows, and let his right hand fall on his sword-hilt. For this folk, who were of merry ways, were wont to deal diversely with the Yule-tide customs in the manner of shows; and he knew not that this was one of them.

Now was the Outer door thrown open, and there entered seven men, whereof two were all-armed in bright war-gear, and two bore slug-horns, and two bore up somewhat on a dish covered over with a piece of rich cloth, and the seventh stood before them all wrapped up in a dark fur mantle.

Thus they stood a moment; and when he saw their number, back to Gold-mane's heart came the thought of those folk on the Mountain: for indeed he was somewhat out of himself for doubt and longing, else would he have deemed that all this was but a Yule-tide play.

Now the men with the slug-horns set them to their mouths and blew a long blast; while the first of the new-comers set hand to the clasps of the fur cloak and let it fall to the ground, and lo! a woman exceeding beauteous, clad in glistering raiment of gold and fine web; her hair wreathed with bay, and in her hand a naked sword with goodly-wrought golden hilt and polished blue-gleaming blade.

Face-of-god started up in his sear, and stared like a man new-wakened from a strange dream: because for one moment he deemed verily that it was the Woman of the Mountain arrayed as he had last seen her, and he cried aloud "The Friend, the Friend!"

His father brake out into loud laughter thereat, and clapped his son on the shoulder and said: "Yea, yea, lad, thou mayst well say the Friend; for this is thine old playmate whom thou hast been looking round the hall for, arrayed this eve in such fashion as is meet for her goodliness and her worthiness. Yea, this is the Friend indeed!"

Then waxed Face-of-god as red as blood for shame, and he sat him down in his place again: for now he wotted what was toward, and saw that this fair woman was the Bride.

But Stone-face from the other side looked keenly on him.

Then blew the horns again, and the Bride stepped daintily up the hall, and the sweet odour of her raiment went from her about the fire-warmed dwelling, and her beauty moved all hearts with love. So stood she at the high-table; and those two who bore the burden set it down thereon and drew off the covering, and lo! there was the Holy Boar of Yule on which men were wont to make oath of deeds that they would do in the coming year, according to the custom of their forefathers. Then the Bride laid the goodly sword beside the dish, and then went round the table and sat down betwixt Face-of-god and Stone-face, and turned kindly to Gold-mane, and was glad; for now was his fair face as its wont was to be. He in turn smiled upon her, for she was fair and kind and his fellow for many a day.

Now the men-at-arms stood each side the Boar, and out from them on each side stood the two hornsmen: then these blew up again, whereon the Alderman stood up and cried:

"Ye sons of the brave who have any deed that ye may be desirous of doing, come up, come lay your hand on the sword, and the point of the sword to the Holy Beast, and swear the oath that lieth on your hearts."

Therewith he sat down, and there strode a man up the hall, strong-built and sturdy, but short of stature; black-haired, red-bearded, and ruddy-faced: and he stood on the dais, and took up the sword and laid its point on the Boar, and said:

"I am Bristler, son of Brightling, a man of the Shepherds. Here by the Holy Boar I swear to follow up the ransackers of Penny-thumb and the slayers of Rusty. And I take this feud upon me, although they be no good men, because I am of the kin and it falleth to me, since others forbear; and when the Court was hallowed hereon I was away out of the Dale and the Downs. So help me the Warrior, and the God of the Earth."

Then the Alderman nodded his head to him kindly, and reached him out a cup of wine, and as he drank there went up a rumour of praise from the hall; and men said that his oath was manly and that he was like to keep it; for he was a good man-at-arms and a stout heart.

Then came up three men of the Shepherds and two of the Dale and swore to help Bristler in his feud, and men thought it well sworn.

After that came up a braggart, a man very gay of his raiment, and swore with many words that if he lived the year through he would be a captain over the men of the Plain, and would come back again with many gifts for his friends in the Dale. This men deemed foolishly sworn, for they knew the man; so they jeered at him and laughed as he went back to his place ashamed.

Then swore three others oaths not hard to be kept, and men laughed and were merry.

At last uprose the Alderman, and said: "Kinsmen, and good fellows, good days and peaceable are in the Dale as now; and of such days little is the story, and little it availeth to swear a deed of derring-do: yet three things I swear by this Beast; and first to gainsay no man's asking if I may perform it; and next to set right above law and mercy above custom; and lastly, if the days change and war cometh to us or we go to meet it, I will be no backwarder in the onset than three fathoms behind the foremost. So help me the Warrior, and the God of the Face and the Holy Earth!"

Therewith he sat down, and all men shouted for joy of him, and said that it was most like that he would keep his oath.

Last of all uprose Face-of-god and took up the sword and looked at it; and so bright was the blade that he saw in it the image of the golden braveries which the Bride bore, and even some broken image of her face. Then he handled the hilt and laid the point on the Boar, and cried:

"Hereby I swear to wed the fairest woman of the Earth before the year is worn to an end; and that whether the Dales-men gainsay me or the men beyond the Dale. So help me the Warrior, and the God of the Face and the Holy Earth!"

Therewith he sat down; and once more men shouted for the love of him and of the Bride, and they said he had sworn well and like a chieftain.

But the Bride noted him that neither were his eyes nor his voice like to their wont as he swore, for she knew him well; and thereat was she ill at ease, for now whatever was new in him was to her a threat of evil to come.

Stone-face also noted him, and he knew the young man better than all others save the Bride, and he saw withal that she was ill-pleased, and he said to himself: "I will speak to my fosterling to-morrow if I may find him alone."

So came the swearing to an end, and they fell to on their meat and feasted on the Boar of Atonement after they had duly given the Gods their due share, and the wine went about the hall and men were merry till they drank the parting cup and fared to rest in the shut-beds, and whereso else they might in the Hall and the House, for there were many men there.

12. STONE-FACE TELLETH CONCERNING THE WOOD-WIGHTS

Early on the morrow Gold-mane arose and clad himself and went out-a-doors and over the trodden snow on to the bridge over the Weltering Water, and there betook himself into one of the coins of safety built over the up-stream piles; there he leaned against the wall and turned his face to the Thorp, and fell to pondering on his case. And first he thought about his oath, and how that he had sworn to wed the Mountain Woman, although his kindred and her kindred should gainsay him, yea and herself also. Great seemed that oath to him, yet at that moment he wished he had made it greater, and made all the kindred, yea and the Bride herself, sure of the meaning of the words of it: and he deemed himself a dastard that he had not done so. Then he looked round him and beheld the winter, and he fell into mere longing that the spring were come and the token from the Mountain. Things seemed too hard for him to deal with, and he between a mighty folk and two wayward women; and he went nigh to wish that he had taken his father's offer and gone down to the Cities; and even had he met his bane: well were that! And, as young folk will, he set to work making a picture of his deeds there, had he been there. He showed himself the stricken fight in the plain, and the press, and the struggle, and the breaking of the serried band, and himself amidst the ring of foemen doing most valiantly, and falling there at last, his shield o'er-heavy with the weight of foemen's spears for a man to uphold it. Then the victory of his folk and the lamentation and praise over the slain man of the Mountain Dales, and the burial of the valiant warrior, the praising weeping folk meeting him at the City-gate, laid stark and cold in his arms on the gold-hung garlanded bier.

There ended his dream, and he laughed aloud and said: "I am a fool! All this were good and sweet if I should see it myself; and forsooth that is how I am thinking of it, as if I still alive should see myself dead and famous!"

Then he turned a little and looked at the houses of the Thorp lying dark about the snowy ways under the starlit heavens of the winter morning: dark they were indeed and grey, save where here and there the half-burned Yule-fire reddened the windows of a hall, or where, as in one place, the candle of some early waker shone white in a chamber window. There was scarce a man astir, he deemed, and no sound reached him save the crowing of the cocks muffled by their houses, and a faint sound of beasts in the byres.

Thus he stood a while, his thoughts wandering now, till presently he heard footsteps coming his way down the street and turned toward them, and lo it was the old man Stone-face. He had seen Gold-mane go out, and had risen and followed him that he might talk with him apart. Gold-mane greeted him kindly, though, sooth to say, he was but half content to see him; since he doubted, what was verily the case, that his foster-father would give him many words, counselling him to refrain from going to the wood, and this was loathsome to him; but he spake and said:

"Meseems, father, that the eastern sky is brightening toward dawn."

"Yea," quoth Stone-face.

"It will be light in an hour," said Face-of-god.

"Even so," said Stone-face.

"And a fair day for the morrow of Yule," said the swain.

"Yea," said Stone-face, "and what wilt thou do with the fair day? Wilt thou to the wood?"

"Maybe, father," said Gold-mane; "Hall-face and some of the swains are talking of elks up the fells which may be trapped in the drifts, and if they go a-hunting them, I may go in their company."

"Ah, son," quoth Stone-face, "thou wilt look to see other kind of beasts than elks. Things may ye fall in with there who may not be impounded in the snow like to elks, but can go light-foot on the top of the soft drift from one place to another."

Said Gold-mane: "Father, fear me not; I shall either refrain me from the wood, or if I go, I shall go to hunt the wood-deer with other hunters. But since thou hast come to me, tell me more about the wood, for thy tales thereof are fair."

"Yea," said Stone-face, "fair tales of foul things, as oft it befalleth in the world. Hearken now! if thou deemest that what thou seekest shall come readier to thine hand because of the winter and the snow, thou errest. For the wights that waylay the bodies and souls of the mighty in the Wild-wood heed such matters nothing; yea and at Yule-tide are they most abroad, and most armed for the fray. Even such an one have I seen time agone, when the snow was deep and the wind was rough; and it was in the likeness of a woman clad in such raiment as the Bride bore last night, and she trod the snow light-foot in thin raiment where it would scarce bear the skids of a deft snow-runner. Even so she stood before me; the icy wind blew her raiment round about her, and drifted the hair from her gar-landed head toward me, and she as fair and fresh as in the mid-summer days. Up the fell she fared, sweetest of all things to look on, and beckoned on me to follow; on me, the Warrior, the Stout-heart; and I followed, and between us grief was born; but I it was that fostered that child and not she. Always when she would be, was she merry and lovely; and even so is she now, for she is of those that be long-lived. And I wot that thou hast seen even such an one!"

"Tell me more of thy tales, foster-father," said Gold-mane, "and fear not for me!"

"Ah, son," he said, "mayst thou have no such tales to tell to those that shall be young when thou art old. Yet hearken! We sat in the hall together and there was no third; and methought that the birds sang and the flowers bloomed, and sweet was their savour, though it was midwinter. A rose-wreath was on her head; grapes were on the board, and fair unwrinkled sum-mer apples on the day that we feasted together. When was the feast? sayst thou. Long ago. What was the hall, thou sayest, wherein ye feasted? I know not if it were on the earth or under it, or if we rode the clouds that even. But on the morrow what was there but the stark wood and the drift of the snow, and the iron wind howling through the branches, and a lonely man, a wanderer rising from the ground. A wanderer through the wood and up the fell, and up the high mountain, and up and up to the edges of the ice-river and the green caves of the ice-hills. A wanderer in spring, in summer, autumn and winter, with an empty heart and a burning never-satisfied desire; who hath seen in the uncouth places many an evil unmanly shape, many a foul hag and changing ugly semblance; who hath suf-fered hunger and thirst and wounding and fever, and hath seen many things, but hath never again seen that fair woman, or that lovely feast-hall.

"All praise and honour to the House of the Face, and the bounteous valiant men thereof! and the like praise and honour to the fair women whom they wed of the valiant and goodly House of the Steer!"

"Even so say I," quoth Gold-mane calmly; "but now wend we aback to the House, for it is morning indeed, and folk will be stirring there."

So they turned from the bridge together; and Stone-face was kind and fatherly, and was telling his foster-son many wise things concerning the life of a chieftain, and the giving-out of dooms and the gathering for battle; to all which talk Face-of-god seemed to hearken gladly, but indeed hearkened not at all; for verily his eyes were beholding that snowy waste, and the fair woman upon it; even such an one as Stone-face had told of.

13. THEY FARE TO THE HUNTING OF THE ELK

When they came into the Hall, the hearth-fire had been quickened, and the sleepers on the floor had been wakened, and all folk were astir. So the old man sat down by the hearth while Gold-mane busied himself in fetching wood and water, and in sweeping out the Hall, and other such works of the early morning. In a little while Hall-face and the other young men and warriors were afoot duly clad, and the Alderman came from his chamber and greeted all men kindly. Soon meat was set upon the boards, and men broke their fast; and day dawned while they were about it, and ere it was all done the sun rose clear and golden, so that all men knew that the day would be fair, for the frost seemed hard and enduring.

Then the eager young men and the hunters, and those who knew the mountain best drew together about the hearth, and fell to talking of the hunting of the elk; and there were three there who knew both the woods and also the fells right up to the ice-rivers better than any other; and these said that they who were fain of the hunting of the elk would have no likelier time than that day for a year to come. Short was the rede betwixt them, for they said they would go to the work at once and make the most of the short winter daylight. So they went each to his place, and some outside that House to their fathers" houses to fetch each man his gear. Face-of-god for his part went to his shut-bed, and stood by his chest, and opened it, and drew out of it a fine hauberk of ring-mail which his father had made for him: for though Face-of-god was a deft wright, he was not by a long way so deft as his father, who was the deftest of all men of that time and country; so that the alien merchants would give him what he would for his hauberks and helms, whenso he would chaffer with them, which was but seldom. So Face-of-god did on this hauberk over his kirtle, and over it he cast his foul-weather weed, so that none might see it: he girt a strong war-sword to his side, cast his quiver over his shoulder, and took his bow in his hand, although he had little lust to shoot elks that day, even as Stone-face had said; therewithal he took his skids, and went forth of the hall to the gate of the Burg; whereto gathered the whole company of twenty-three, and Gold-mane the twenty-fourth. And each man there had his skids and his bow and quiver, and whatso other weapon, as short-sword, or wood-knife, or axe, seemed good to him.

So they went out-a-gates, and clomb the stairway in the cliff which led to the ancient watch-tower: for it was on the lower slopes of the fells which lay near to the Weltering Water that they looked to find the elks, and this was the nighest road thereto. When they had gotten to the top they lost no time, but went their ways nearly due east, making way easily where there were but scattered trees close to the lip of the sheer cliffs.

They went merrily on their skids over the close-lying snow, and were soon up on the great shoulders of the fells that went up from the bank of the Weltering Water: at noon they came into a little dale wherein were a few trees, and there they abided to eat their meat, and were very merry, making for themselves tables and benches of the drifted snow, and piling it up to windward as a defence against the wind, which had now arisen, little but bitter from the south-east; so that some,

and they the wisest, began to look for foul weather: wherefore they tarried the shorter while in the said dale or hollow.

But they were scarcely on their way again before the aforesaid south-east wind began to grow bigger, and at last blew a gale, and brought up with it a drift of fine snow, through which they yet made their way, but slowly, till the drift grew so thick that they could not see each other five paces apart.

Then perforce they made stay, and gathered together under a bent which by good luck they happened upon, where they were sheltered from the worst of the drift. There they abode, till in less than an hour's space the drift abated and the wind fell, and in a little while after it was quite clear, with the sun shining brightly and the young waxing moon white and high up in the heavens; and the frost was harder than ever.

This seemed good to them; but now that they could see each other's faces they fell to telling over their company, and there was none missing save Face-of-god. They were somewhat dismayed thereat, but knew not what to do, and they deemed he might not be far off, either a little behind or a little ahead; and Hall-face said:

"There is no need to make this to-do about my brother; he can take good care of himself; neither does a warrior of the Face die because of a little cold and frost and snow-drift. Withal Gold-mane is a wilful man, and of late days hath been wilful beyond his wont; let us now find the elks."

So they went on their ways hoping to fall in with him again. No long story need be made of their hunting, for not very far from where they had taken shelter they came upon the elks, many of them, impounded in the drifts, pretty much where the deft hunters looked to find them. There then was battle between the elks and the men, till the beasts were all slain and only one man hurt: then they made them sleighs from wood which they found in the hollows thereby, and they laid the carcasses thereon, and so turned their faces homeward, dragging their prey with them. But they met not Face-of-god either there or on the way home; and Hall-face said: "Maybe Gold-mane will lie on the fell to-night; and I would I were with him; for adventures oft befall such folk when they abide in the wilds."

Now it was late at night by then they reached Burgstead, so laden as they were with the dead beasts; but they heeded the night little, for the moon was well-nigh as bright as day for them. But when they came to the gate of the Thorp, there were assembled the goodmen and swains to meet them with torches and wine in their honour. There also was Gold-mane come back before them, yea for these two hours; and he stood clad in his holiday raiment and smiled on them.

Then was there some jeering at him that he was come back empty-handed from the hunting, and that he was not able to abide the wind and the drift; but he laughed thereat, for all this was but game and play, since men knew him for a keen hunter and a stout woodsman; and they had deemed it a heavy loss of him if he had been cast away, as some feared he had been: and his brother Hall-face embraced him and kissed him, and said to him: "Now the next time that thou farest to the wood will I be with thee foot to foot, and never leave thee, and then meseemeth I shall wot of the tale that hath befallen thee, and belike it shall be no sorry one."

Face-of-god laughed and answered but little, and they all betook them to the House of the Face and held high feast therein, for as late as the night was, in honour of this Hunting of the Elk.

No man cared to question Face-of-god closely as to how or where he had strayed from the hunt; for he had told his own tale at once as soon as he came home, to wit, that his right-foot skid-strap had broken, and even while he stopped to mend it

came on that drift and weather; and that he could not move from that place without losing his way, and that when it had cleared he knew not whither they had gone because the snow had covered their slot. So he deemed it not unlike that they had gone back, and that he might come up with one or two on the way, and that in any case he wotted well that they could look after themselves; so he turned back, not going very swiftly. All this seemed like enough, and a little matter except to jest about, so no man made any question concerning it: only old Stone-face said to himself:

"Now were I fain to have a true tale out of him, but it is little likely that anything shall come of my much questioning; and it is ill forcing a young man to tell lies."

So he held his peace, and the feast went on merrily and blithely.

14. CONCERNING FACE-OF-GOD AND THE MOUNTAIN

But it must be told of Gold-mane that what had befallen him was in this wise. His skid-strap brake in good sooth, and he stayed to mend it; but when he had done what was needful, he looked up and saw no man nigh, what for the drift, and that they had gone on somewhat; so he rose to his feet, and without more delay, instead of keeping on toward the elk-ground and the way his face had been set, he turned himself north-and-by-east, and went his ways swiftly towards that airt, because he deemed that it might lead him to the Mountain-hall where he had guested. He abode not for the storm to clear, but swept off through the thick of it; and indeed the wind was somewhat at his back, so that he went the swiftlier. But when the drift was gotten to its very worst, he sheltered himself for a little in a hollow behind a thorn-bush he stumbled upon. As soon as it began to abate he went on again, and at last when it was quite clear, and the sun shone out, he found himself on a long slope of the fells covered deep with smooth white snow, and at the higher end a great crag rising bare fifty feet above the snow, and more rocks, but none so great, and broken ground as he judged (the snow being deep) about it on the hither side; and on the further, three great pine-trees all bent down and mingled together by their load of snow.

Thitherward he made, as a man might, seeing nothing else to note before him; but he had not made many strides when forth from behind the crag by the pine-trees came a man; and at first Face-of-god thought it might be one of his hunting-fellows gone astray, and he hailed him in a loud voice, but as he looked he saw the sun flash back from a bright helm on the new-comer's head; albeit he kept on his way till there was but a space of two hundred yards between them; when lo! the helm-bearer notched a shaft to his bent bow and loosed at

Face-of-god, and the arrow came whistling and passed six inches by his right ear. Then Face-of-god stopped perplexed with his case; for he was on the deep snow in his skids, with his bow unbent, and he knew not how to bend it speedily. He was loth to turn his back and flee, and indeed he scarce deemed that it would help him. Meanwhile of his tarrying the archer loosed again at him, and this time the shaft flew close to his left ear. Then Face-of-god thought to cast himself down into the snow, but he was ashamed; till there came a third shaft which flew over his head amidmost and close to it. "Good shooting on the Mountain!" muttered he; "the next shaft will be amidst my breast, and who knows whether the Alderman's handiwork will keep it out."

So he cried aloud: "Thou shootest well, brother; but art thou a foe? If thou art, I have a sword by my side, and so hast thou; come hither to me, and let us fight it out friendly if we must needs fight."

A laugh came down the wind to him clear but somewhat shrill, and the archer came swiftly towards him on his skids with no weapon in his hand save his bow; so that Face-of-god did not draw his sword, but stood wondering.

As they drew nearer he beheld the face of the new-comer, and deemed that he had seen it before; and soon, for all that it was hooded close by the ill-weather raiment, he perceived it to be the face of Bow-may, ruddy and smiling.

She laughed out loud again, as she stopped herself within three feet of him, and said:

"Yea, friend Yellow-hair, we heard of the elks and looked to see thee hereabouts, and I knew thee at once when I came out from behind the crag and saw thee stand bewildered."

Said Gold-mane: "Hail to thee, Bow-may! and glad am I to

see thee. But thou liest in saying that thou knewest me; else why didst thou shoot those three shafts at me? Surely thou art not so quick as that with all thy friends: these be sharp greetings of you Mountain-folk."

"Thou lad with the sweet mouth," she said, "I like to see thee and hear thee talk, but now must I hasten thy departure; so stand we here no longer. Let us get down into the wood where we can do off our skids and sit down, and then will I tell thee the tidings. Come on!"

And she caught his hand in hers, and they went speedily down the slopes toward the great oak-wood, the wind whistling past their ears.

"Whither are we going?" said he.

Said she: "I am to show thee the way back home, which thou wilt not know surely amidst this snow. Come, no words! thou shalt not have my tale from me till we are in the wood: so the sooner we are there the sooner shalt thou be pleased."

So Face-of-god held his peace, and they went on swiftly side by side. But it was not Bow-may's wont to be silent for long, so presently she said:

"Thou art good so do as I bid thee; but see thou, sweet playmate, for all thou art a chieftain's son, thou wert but featherbrained to ask me why I shot at thee. I shoot at thee! that were a fine tale to tell her this even! Or dost thou think that I could shoot at a big man on the snow at two hundred paces and miss him three times? Unless I aimed to miss."

"Yea, Bow-may," said he, "art thou so deft a Bow-may? Thou shalt be in my company whenso I fare to battle."

"Indeed," she said, "therein thou sayest but the bare truth: nowhere else shall I be, and thou shalt find my bow no worse than a good shield."

He laughed somewhat lightly; but she looked on him soberly and said: "Laugh in that fashion on the day of battle, and we shall be well content with thee!"

So on they sped very swiftly, for their way was mostly down hill, so that they were soon amongst the outskirting trees of the wood, and presently after reached the edge of the thicket, beyond which the ground was but thinly covered with snow.

There they took off their skids, and went into the thick wood and sat down under a hornbeam tree; and ere Gold-mane could open his mouth to speak Bow-may began and said:

"Well it was that I fell in with thee, Dalesman, else had there been murders of men to tell of; but ever she ordereth all things wisely, though unwisely hast thou done to seek to her. Hearken! dost thou think that thou hast done well that thou hast me here with my tale? Well, hadst thou busied thyself with the slaying of elks, or with sitting quietly at home, yet shouldest thou have heard my tale, and thou shouldest have seen me in Burgstead in a day or two to tell thee concerning the flitting of

the token. And ill it is that I have missed it, for fain had I been to behold the House of the Face, and to have seen thee sitting there in thy dignity amidst the kindred of chieftains."

And she sighed therewith. But he said: "Hold up thine heart, Bow-may! On the word of a true man that shall befall thee one day. But come, playmate, give me thy tale!"

"Yea," she said, "I must now tell thee in the Wild-wood what else I had told thee in the Hall. Hearken closely, for this is the message:

"Seek not to me again till thou hast the token; else assuredly wilt thou be slain, and I shall be sorry for many a day. Thereof as now I may not tell thee more. Now as to the token: When March is worn two weeks fail not to go to and fro on the place of the Maiden Ward for an hour before sunrise every day till thou hear tidings."

"Now," quoth Bow-may, "hast thou hearkened and understood?"

"Yea," said he.

She said: "Then tell me the words of my message concerning the token." And he did so word for word. Then she said:

"It is well, there is no more to say. Now must I lead thee till thou knowest the wood; and then mayst thou get on to the smooth snow again, and so home merrily. Yet, thou grey-eyed fellow, I will have my pay of thee before I do that last work."

Therewith she turned about to him and took his head between her hands, and kissed him well favouredly both cheeks and mouth; and she laughed, albeit the tears stood in her eyes as she said: "Now smelleth the wood sweeter, and summer will come back again. And even thus will I do once more when we stand side by side in battle array."

He smiled kindly on her and nodded as they both rose up from the earth: she had taken off her foul-weather gloves while they spake, and he kissed her hand, which was shapely of fashion albeit somewhat brown, and hard of palm, and he said in friendly wise:

"Thou art a merry faring-fellow, Bow-may, and belike shalt be withal a true fighting-fellow. Come now, thou shalt be my sister and I thy brother, in despite of those three shafts across the snow."

He laughed therewith; she laughed not, but seemed glad, and said soberly:

"Yea, I may well be thy sister; for belike I also am of the people of the Gods, who have come into these Dales by many far ways. I am of the House of the Ragged Sword of the Kindred of the Wolf. Come, brother, let us toward Wildlake's Way."

Therewith she went before him and led through the thicket as by an assured and wonted path, and he followed hard at heel; but his thought went from her for a while; for those words of brother and sister that he had spoken called to his mind the Bride, and their kindness of little children, and the days when they seemed to have nought to do but to make the sun brighter, and the flowers fairer, and the grass greener, and the birds happier each for the other; and a hard and evil thing it seemed to him that now he should be making all these things nought and dreary to her, now when he had become a man and deeds lay before him. Yet again was he solaced by what Bow-may had said concerning battle to come; for he deemed that she must have had this from the Friend's foreseeing; and he longed sore for deeds to do, wherein all these things might be cleared up and washen clean as it were.

So passed they through the wood a long way, and it was getting dark therein, and Gold-mane said:

"Hold now, Bow-may, for I am at home here."

She looked around and said: "Yea, so it is: I was thinking of many things. Farewell and live merrily till March comes and the token!"

Therewith she turned and went her ways and was soon out of sight, and he went lightly through the wood, and then on skids over the hard snow along the Dale's edge till he was come to the watch-tower, when the moon was bright in heaven.

Thus was he at Burgstead and the House of the Face betimes, and before the hunters were gotten back.

15. MURDER AMONGST THE FOLK OF THE WOODLANDERS

So wore away midwinter tidingless. Stone-face spake no more to Face-of-god about the wood and its wights, when he saw that the young man had come back hale and merry, seemed not to crave over-much to go back thither. As for the Bride, she was sad, and more than misdoubted all; but dauntless as she was in matters that try men's hardihood, she yet lacked heart to ask of Face-of-god what had befallen him since the autumn-tide, or where he was with her. So she put a force upon herself not to look sad or craving when she was in his company, as full oft she was; for he rather sought her than shunned her. For when he saw her thus, he deemed things were changing with her as they had changed with him, and he bethought him of what he had spoken to Bow-may, and deemed that even so he might speak with the Bride when the time came, and that she would not be grieved beyond measure, and all would be well.

Now came on the thaw, and the snow went, and the grass grew all up and down the Dale, and all waters were big. And about this time arose rumours of strange men in the wood, uncouth, vile, and murderous, and many of the feebler sort were made timorous thereby.

But a little before March was born came new tidings from the Woodlanders; to wit: There came on a time to the house of a woodland carle, a worthy goodman well renowned of all, two wayfarers in the first watch of the night; and these men said that they were wending down to the Plain from a far-away dale, Rosedale to wit, which all men had heard of, and that they had strayed from the way and were exceeding weary, and they craved a meal's meat and lodging for the night.

This the goodman might nowise gainsay, and he saw no harm in it, wherefore he bade them abide and be merry.

These men, said they who told the tidings, were outlanders, and no man had seen any like them before: they were armed, and bore short bows made of horn, and round targets, and coats-of-fence done over with horn scales; they had crooked swords girt to their sides, and axes of steel forged all in one piece, right good weapons. They were clad in scarlet and had much silver on their raiment and about their weapons, and great rings of the same on their arms; and all this silver seemed brand-new.

Now the Woodland Carle gave them of such things as he had, and was kind and blithe to them: there were in his house besides himself five men of his sons and kindred, and his wife and three daughters and two other maids. So they feasted after the Woodlanders" fashion, and went to bed a little before midnight. Two hours after, the carle awoke and heard a little stir, and he looked and saw the guests on their feet amidst the hall clad in all their war-gear; and they had betwixt them his two youngest daughters, maids of fifteen and twelve winters, and had bound their hands and done clouts over their mouths, so that they might not cry out; and they were just at point to carry them off. Thereat the goodman, naked as he was, caught up his sword and made at these murder-carles, and or ever they were ware of him he had hewn down one and turned to face the other, who smote at him with his steel axe and gave him a great wound on the shoulder, and therewithal fled out at the open door and forth into the wood.

The Woodlander made no stay to raise the cry (there was no need, for the hall was astir now from end to end, and men getting to their weapons), but ran out after the felon even as he was; and, in spite of his grievous hurt, overran him no long way from the house before he had gotten into the thicket. But the man was nimble and strong, and the goodman unsteady from his wound, and by then the others of the household came up with the hue and cry he had gotten two more sore wounds and was just making an end of throttling the felon with his bare hands. So he fell into their arms fainting from weakness, and for all they could do he died in two hours" time from that axe-wound in his shoulder, and another on the side of the head, and a knife-thrust in his side; and he was a man of sixty winters.

But the stranger he had slain outright; and the one whom he had smitten in the hall died before the dawn, thrusting all help aside, and making no sound of speech.

When these tidings came to Burgstead they seemed great to men, and to Gold-mane more than all. So he and many others took their weapons and fared up to Wildlake's Way, and so came to the Woodland-Carles. But the Woodlanders had borne out the carcasses of those felons and laid them on the green before Wood-grey's door (for that was the name of the dead goodman), and they were saying that they would not bury such accursed folk, but would bear them a little way so that they should not be vexed with the stink of them, and cast them into the thicket for the wolf and the wild-cat and the stoat to deal with; and they should lie there, weapons and silver and all; and they deemed it base to strip such wretches, for who would wear their raiment or bear their weapons after them.

There was a great ring of folk round about them when they of Burgstead drew near, and they shouted for joy to see their neighbours, and made way before them. Then the Dalesmen cursed these murderers who had slain so good a man, and they all praised his manliness, whereas he ran out into the night naked and wounded after his foe, and had fallen like his folk of old time.

It was a bright spring afternoon in that clearing of the Wood, and they looked at the two dead men closely; and Gold-mane, who had been somewhat silent and moody till then, became merry and wordy; for he beheld the men and saw that they were utterly strange to him: they were short of stature, crooked-legged, long-armed, very strong for their size: with small blue eyes, snubbed-nosed, wide-mouthed, thin-lipped, very swarthy of skin, exceeding foul of favour. He and all others wondered who they were, and whence they came, for never had they seen their like; and the Woodlanders, who often guested outlanders strayed from the way of divers kindreds and nations, said also that none such had they ever seen. But Stone-face, who stood by Gold-mane, shook his head and quoth he:

"The Wild-wood holdeth many marvels, and these be of them: the spawn of evil wights quickeneth therein, and at other whiles it melteth away again like the snow; so may it be with these carcasses."

And some of the older folk of the Woodlanders who stood by hearkened what he said, and deemed his words wise, for they remembered their ancient lore and many a tale of old time.

Thereafter they of Burgstead went into Wood-grey's hall, or as many of them as might, for it was but a poor place and not right great. There they saw the goodman laid on the dais in all his war-gear, under the last tie-beam of his hall, whereon was carved amidst much goodly work of knots and flowers and twining stems the image of the Wolf of the Waste, his jaws open and gaping: the wife and daughters of the goodman and other women of the folk stood about the bier singing some old song in a low voice, and some sobbing therewithal, for the man was much beloved: and much people of the Woodlanders was in the hall, and it was somewhat dusk within.

So the Burgstead men greeted that folk kindly and humbly, and again they fell to praising the dead man, saying how his deed should long be remembered in the Dale and wide about; and they called him a fearless man and of great worth. And the women hearkened, and ceased their crooning and their sobbing, and stood up proudly and raised their heads with gleaming eyes; and as the words of the Burgstead men ended, they lifted up their voices and sang loudly and clearly, standing together in a row, ten of them, on the dais of that poor hall, facing the gable and the wolf-adorned tie-beam, heeding nought as they sang what was about or behind them.

And this is some of what they sang:

Why sit ye bare in the spinning-room?
Why weave ye naked at the loom?

Bare and white as the moon we be,
That the Earth and the drifting night may see.

Now what is the worst of all your work?
What curse amidst the web shall lurk?

The worst of the work our hands shall win
Is wrack and ruin round the kin.

Shall the woollen yarn and the flaxen thread
Be gear for living men or dead?

The woollen yarn and the flaxen thread
Shall flare "twixt living men and dead.

O what is the ending of your day?
When shall ye rise and wend away?

Our day shall end to-morrow morn,
When we hear the voice of the battle-horn.

Where first shall eyes of men behold
This weaving of the moonlight cold?

There where the alien host abides

The gathering on the Mountain-sides.

How long aloft shall the fair web fly
When the bows are bent and the spears draw nigh?

From eve to morn and morn till eve
Aloft shall fly the work we weave.

What then is this, the web ye win?
What wood-beast waxeth stark therein?

We weave the Wolf and the gift of war
From the men that were to the men that are.

So sang they: and much were all men moved at their singing, and there was none but called to mind the old days of the Fathers, and the years when their banner went wide in the world.

But the Woodlanders feasted them of Burgstead what they might, and then went the Dalesmen back to their houses; but on the morrow's morrow they fared thither again, and Wood-grey was laid in mound amidst a great assemblage of the Folk.

Many men said that there was no doubt that those two felons were of the company of those who had ransacked the steads of Penny-thumb and Harts-bane; and so at first deemed Bristler the son of Brightling: but after a while, when he had had time to think of it, he changed his mind; for he said that such men as these would have slain first and ransacked afterwards: and some who loved neither Penny-thumb nor Harts-bane said that they would not have been at the pains to choose for ransacking the two worst men about the Dale, whose loss was no loss to any but themselves.

As for Gold-mane he knew not what to think, except that his friends of the Mountain had had nought to do with it.

So wore the days awhile.

16. THE BRIDE SPEAKETH WITH FACE-OF-GOD

February had died into March, and March was now twelve days old, on a fair and sunny day an hour before noon; and Face-of-god was in a meadow a scant mile down the Dale from Burgstead. He had been driving a bull into a goodman's byre nearby, and had had to spend toil and patience both in getting him out of the fields and into the byre; for the beast was hot with the spring days and the new grass. So now he was resting himself in happy mood in an exceeding pleasant place, a little meadow to wit, on one side whereof was a great orchard or grove of sweet chestnuts, which went right up to the feet of the Southern Cliffs: across the meadow ran a clear brook towards the Weltering Water, free from big stones, in some places dammed up for the flooding of the deep pasture-meadow, and with the grass growing on its lips down to the very water. There was a low bank just outside the chestnut trees, as if someone had raised a dyke about them when they were young, which had been trodden low and spreading through the lapse of years by the faring of many men and beasts. The primroses bloomed thick upon it now, and here and there along it was a low blackthorn bush in full blossom; from the mid-meadow and right down to the lip of the brook was the grass well nigh hidden by the blossoms of the meadow-saffron, with daffodils sprinkled about amongst them, and in the trees and bushes the birds, and chiefly the blackbirds, were singing their loudest.

There sat Face-of-god on the bank resting after his toil, and happy was his mood; since in two days" wearing he should be pacing the Maiden Ward awaiting the token that was to lead him to Shadowy Vale; so he sat calling to mind the Friend as he had last seen her, and striving as it were to set her image standing on the flowery grass before him, till all the beauty of the meadow seemed bare and empty to him without her. Then it fell into his mind that this had been a beloved trysting-place betwixt him and the Bride, and that often when they were little would they come to gather chestnuts in the grove, and thereafter sit and prattle on the old dyke; or in spring when the season was warm would they go barefoot into the brook, seeking its treasures of troutlets and flowers and clean-washed agate pebbles. Yea, and time not long ago had they met here to talk as lovers, and sat on that very bank in all the kindness of good days without a blemish, and both he and she had loved the place well for its wealth of blossoms and deep grass and goodly trees and clear running stream

As he thought of all this, and how often there he had praised to himself her beauty, which he scarce dared praise to her, he frowned and slowly rose to his feet, and turned toward the chestnut-grove, as though he would go thence that way; but or ever he stepped down from the dyke he turned about again, and even therewith, like the very image and ghost of his thought, lo! the Bride herself coming up from out the brook and wending toward him, her wet naked feet gleaming in the sun as they trod down the tender meadow-saffron and brushed past the tufts of daffodils. He stood staring at her discomforted, for on that day he had much to think of that seemed happy to him, and he deemed that she would now question him, and his mind pondered divers ways of answering her, and none seemed good to him. She drew near and let her skirts fall over her feet, and came to him, her gown hem dragging over the flowers: then she stood straight up before him and greeted him, but reached not forth her hand to him nor touched him. Her face was paler that its wont, and her voice trembled as she spake to him and said:

"Face-of-god, I would ask thee a gift."

"All gifts," he said, "that thou mayest ask, and I may give, lie open to thee."

She said: "If I be alive when the time comes this gift thou mayst well give me."

"Sweet kinswoman," said he, "tell me what it is that thou wouldest have of me." And he was ill-at-ease as he waited for her answer.

She said: "Ah, kinsman, kinsman! Woe on the day that maketh kinship accursed to me because thou desirest it!"

He held his peace and was exceeding sorry; and she said:

"This is the gift that I ask of thee, that in the days to come when thou art wedded, thou wilt give me the second man-child whom thou begettest."

He said: "This shalt thou have, and would that I might give thee much more. Would that we were little children together other again, as when we played here in other days."

She said: "I would have a token of thee that thou shalt show to the God, and swear on it to give me the gift. For the times change."

"What token wilt thou have?" said he.

She said: "When next thou farest to the Wood, thou shalt bring me back, it maybe a flower from the bank ye sit upon, or a splinter from the dais of the hall wherein ye feast, or maybe a ring or some matter that the strangers are wont to wear. That shall be the token."

She spoke slowly, hanging her head adown, but she lifted it presently and looked into his face and said:

"Woe's me, woe's me, Gold-mane! How evil is this day, when bewailing me I may not bewail thee also! For I know that thine heart is glad. All through the winter have I kept this hidden in my heart, and durst not speak to thee. But now the spring-tide hath driven me to it. Let summer come, and who shall say?"

Great was his grief, and his shame kept him silent, and he had no word to say; and again she said:

"Tell me, Gold-mane, when goest thou thither?"

He said: "I know not surely, may happen in two days, may happen in ten. Why askest thou?"

"O friend!" she said, "is it a new thing that I should ask thee whither thou goest and whence thou comest, and the times of thy coming and going. Farewell to-day! Forget not the token. Woe's me, that I may not kiss thy fair face!"

She spread her arms abroad and lifted up her face as one who waileth, but no sound came from her lips; then she turned about and went away as she had come.

But as for him he stood there after she was gone in all confusion, as if he were undone: for he felt his manhood lessened that he should thus and so sorely have hurt a friend, and in a manner against his will. And yet he was somewhat wroth with her, that she had come upon him so suddenly, and spoken to him with such mastery, and in so few words, and he with none to make answer to her, and that she had so marred his pleasure and his hope of that fair day. Then he sat him down again on the flowery bank, and little by little his heart softened, and he once more called to mind many a time when they had been there before, and the plays and the games they had had together there when they were little. And he bethought him of the days that were long to him then, and now seemed short to him, and as if they were all grown together into one story, and that a sweet one. Then his breast heaved with a sob, and the tears rose to his eyes and burned and stung him, and he fell a-weeping for that sweet tale, and wept as he had wept once before on that old dyke when there had been some child's quarrel between them, and she had gone away and left him.

Then after a while he ceased his weeping, and looked about him lest anyone might be coming, and then he arose and went to and fro in the chestnut-grove for a good while, and afterwards went his ways from that meadow, saying to himself: "Yet remaineth to me the morrow of to-morrow, and that is the first of the days of the watching for the token."

But all that day he was slow to meet the eyes of men; and in the hall that eve he was silent and moody; for from time to time it came over him that some of his manhood had departed from him.

17. THE TOKEN COMETH FROM THE MOUNTAIN

The next day wore away tidingless; and the day after Face-of-god arose betimes; for it was the first day of his watch, and he was at the Maiden Ward before the time appointed on a very fair and bright morning, and he went to and fro on that place, and had no tidings. So he came away somewhat cast down, and said within himself: "Is it but a lie and a mocking when all is said?"

On the morrow he went thither again, and the morn was wild and stormy with drift of rain, and low clouds hurrying over the earth, though for the sunrise they lifted a little in the east, and the sun came up over the passes, amidst the red and angry rack of clouds. This morn also gave him no tidings of the token, and he was wroth and perturbed in spirit: but towards evening he said:

"It is well: ten days she gave me, so that she might be able to send without fail on one of them; she will not fail me."

So again on the morrow he was there betimes, and the morn was windy as on the day before, but the clouds higher and of better promise for the day. Face-of-god walked to and fro on the Maiden Ward, and as he turned toward Burgstead for the tenth time, he heard, as he deemed, a bow-string twang afar off, and even therewith came a shaft flying heavily like a winged bird, which smote a great standing stone on the other side of the way, where of old some chieftain had been buried, and fell to earth at its foot. He went up to it and handled it, and saw that there was a piece of thin parchment wrapped about it, which indeed he was eager to unwrap at once, but forebore; because he was on the highway, and people were already astir, and even then passed by him a goodman of the Dale with a man of his going afield together, and they gave him the sele of the day. So he went along the highway a little till he came to a place where was a footbridge over into the meadow. He crossed thereby and went swiftly till he reached a rising ground grown over with hazel-trees; there he sat down among the rabbit-holes, the primrose and wild-garlic blooming about him, and three blackbirds answering one another from the edges of the coppice. Straightway when he had looked and seen none coming he broke the threads that were wound about the scroll and the arrow, and unrolled the parchment; and there was writing thereon in black ink of small letters, but very fair, and this is what he read therein:

Come thou to the Mountain Hall by the path which thou knowest of, on the morrow of the day whereon thou readest this. Rise betimes and come armed, for there are other men than we in the wood; to whom thy death should be a gain. When thou art come to the Hall, thou shalt find no man therein; but a great hound only, tied to a bench nigh the dais. Call him by his name, Sure-foot to wit, and give him to eat from the meat upon the board, and give him water to drink. If the day is then far spent, as it is like to be, abide thou with the hound in the hall through the night, and eat of what thou shalt find there; but see that the hound fares not abroad till the morrow's morn: then lead him out and bring him to the north-east corner of the Hall, and he shall lift the slot for thee that leadeth to the Shadowy Yale. Follow him and all good go with thee.

Now when he had read this, earth seemed fair indeed about him, and he scarce knew whither to turn or what to do to make the most of his joy. He presently went back to Burgstead and into the House of the Face, where all men were astir now, and

the day was clearing. He hid the shaft under his kirtle, for he would not that any should see it; so he went to his shut-bed and laid it up in his chest, wherein he kept his chiefest treasures; but the writing on the scroll he set in his bosom and so hid it. He went joyfully and proudly, as one who knoweth more tidings and better than those around him. But Stone-face beheld him, and said "Foster-son, thou art happy. Is it that the spring-tide is in thy blood, and maketh thee blithe with all things, or hast thou some new tidings? Nay, I would not have an answer out of thee; but here is good rede: when next thou goest into the wood, it were nought so ill for thee to have a valiant old carle by thy side; one that loveth thee, and would die for thee if need were; one who might watch when thou wert seeking. Or else beware! for there are evil things abroad in the Wood, and moreover the brethren of those two felons who were slain at Carlstead."

Then Gold-mane constrained himself to answer the old carle softly; and he thanked him kindly for his offer, and said that so it should be before long. So the talk between them fell, and Stone-face went away somewhat well-pleased.

And now was Face-of-god become wary; and he would not draw men's eyes and speech on him; so he went afield with Hall-face to deal with the lambs and the ewes, and did like other men. No less wary was he in the hall that even, and neither spake much nor little; and when his father spake to him concerning the Bride, and made game of him as a somewhat sluggish groom, he did not change countenance, but answered lightly what came to hand.

On the morrow ere the earliest dawn he was afoot, and he clad himself and did on his hauberk, his father's work, which was fine-wrought and a stout defence, and reached down to his knees; and over that he did on a goodly green kirtle well embroidered: he girt his war-sword to his side, and it was the work of his father's father, and a very good sword: its name was Dale-warden. He did a good helm on his head, and slung a targe at his back, and took two spears in his hand, short but strong-shafted and well-steeled. Thus arrayed he left Burgstead before the dawn, and came to Wildlake's Way and betook him to the Woodland. He made no stop or stay on the path, but ate his meat standing by an oak-tree close by the half-blind track. When he came to the little wood-lawn, where was the toft of the ancient house, he looked all round about him, for he deemed that a likely place for those ugly wood-wights to set on him; but nought befell him, though he stooped and drank of the woodland rill warily enough. So he passed on; and there were other places also where he fared warily, because they seemed like to hold lurking felons; though forsooth the whole wood might well serve their turn. But no evil befell him, and at last, when it yet lacked an hour to sunset, he came to the wood-lawn where Wild-wearer had made his onset that other eve.

He went straight up to the house, his heart beating, and he scarce believing but that he should find the Friend abiding him there: but when he pushed the door it gave way before him at once, and he entered and found no man therein, and the walls stripped bare and no shield or weapon hanging on the panels. But the hound he saw tied to a bench nigh the dais, and the bristles on the beast's neck arose, and he snarled on Face-of-god, and strained on his leathern leash. Then Face-of-god went up to him and called him by his name, Sure-foot, and gave him his hand to lick, and he brought him water, and fed him with flesh from the meat on the board; so the beast became friendly and wagged his tail and whined and slobbered his hand.

Then he went all about the house, and saw and heard no living thing therein save the mice in the panels and Sure-foot. So he came back to the dais, and sat him down at the board and ate his fill, and thought concerning his case. And it came into his mind that the Woman of the Mountain had some deed for him to do which would try his manliness and exalt his fame; and his heart rose high and he was glad, and he saw himself sitting beside her on the dais of a very fair hall beloved and honoured of all the folk, and none had aught to say against him or owed him any grudge. Thus he pleased himself in thinking of the good days to come, sitting there till the hall grew dusk and dark and the night-wind moaned about it.

Then after a while he arose and raked together the brands on the hearth, and made light in the hall and looked to the door. And he found there were bolts and bars thereto, so he shot the bolts and drew the bars into their places and made all as sure as might be. Then he brought Sure-foot down from the dais, and tied him up so that he might lie down athwart the door, and then lay down his hauberk with his naked sword ready to his hand, and slept long while.

When he awoke it was darker than when he had lain him for the moon had set; yet he deemed that the day was at point of breaking. So he fetched water and washed the night off him, and saw a little glimmer of the dawn. Then he ate somewhat of the meat on the board, and did on his helm and his other gear, and unbarred the door, and led Sure-foot without, and brought him to the north-east corner of the house, and in a little while he lifted the slot and they departed, the man and the hound, just as dawn broke from over the mountains.

Sure-foot led right into the heart of the pine-wood, and it was dark enough therein, with nought but a feeble glimmer for some while, and long was the way therethrough; but in two hours" space was there something of a break, and they came to the shore of a dark deep tarn on whose windless and green waters the daylight shone fully. The hound skirted the water, and led on unchecked till the trees began to grow smaller and the air colder for all that the sun was higher; for they had been going up and up all the way.

So at last after a six hours" journey they came clean out of the pine-wood, and before them lay the black wilderness of the bare mountains, and beyond them, looking quite near now, the great ice-peaks, the wall of the world. It was but an hour short of noon by this time, and the high sun shone down on a barren boggy moss which lay betwixt them and the rocky waste. Sure-foot made no stay, but threaded the ways that went betwixt the quagmires, and in another hour led Face-of-god into a winding valley blinded by great rocks, and everywhere stony and rough, with a trickle of water running amidst of it. The hound fared on up the dale to where the water was bridged by a great fallen stone, and so over it and up a steep bent on the further side, on to a marvellously rough mountain-neck, whiles mere black sand cumbered with scattered rocks and stones, whiles beset with mires grown over with the cottony mire-grass; here and there a little scanty grass growing; otherwhere nought but dwarf willow ever dying ever growing, mingled with moss or red-blossomed sengreen; and all blending together into mere desolation.

Few living things they saw there; up on the neck a few sheep were grazing the scanty grass, but there was none to tend them; yet Face-of-god deemed the sight of them good, for there must be men anigh who owned them. For the rest, the whimbrel laughed across the mires; high up in heaven a great eagle was hanging; once and again a grey fox leapt up before them, and the heath-fowl whirred up from under Face-of-god's feet. A raven who was sitting croaking on a rock in that first dale stirred uneasily on his perch as he saw them, and when they were passed flapped his wings and flew after them croaking still.

Now they fared over that neck somewhat east, making but slow way because the ground was so broken and rocky; and in another hour's space Sure-foot led down-hill due east to where the stony neck sank into another desolate miry heath still falling toward the east, but whose further side was walled by a rampart of crags cleft at their tops into marvellous-shapes, coal-black, ungrassed and unmossed. Thitherward the hound led straight, and Gold-mane followed wondering: as he drew near them he saw that they were not very high, the tallest peak scant fifty feet from the face of the heath.

They made their way through the scattered rocks at the foot of these crags, till, just where the rock-wall seemed the closest, the way through the stones turned into a path going through it skew-wise; and it was now so clear a path that belike it had been bettered by men's hands. Down thereby Face-of-god followed the hound, deeming that he was come to the gates of the Shadowy Vale, and the path went down steeply and swiftly. But when he had gone down a while, the rocks on his right hand sank lower for a space, so that he could look over and see what lay beneath.

There lay below him a long narrow vale quite plain at the bottom, walled on the further side as on the hither by sheer rocks of black stone. The plain was grown over with grass, but he could see no tree therein: a deep river, dark and green, ran through the vale, sometimes through its midmost, sometimes lapping the further rock-wall: and he thought indeed that on many a day in the year the sun would never shine on that valley.

Thus much he saw, and then the rocks rose again and shut it from his sight; and at last they drew so close together over head that he was in a way going through a cave with little daylight coming from above, and in the end he was in a cave indeed and mere darkness: but with the last feeble glimmer of light he thought he saw carved on a smooth space of the living rock at his left hand the image of a wolf.

This cave lasted but a little way, and soon the hound and the man were going once more between sheer black rocks, and the path grew steeper yet and was cut into steps. At last there was a sharp turn, and they stood on the top of a long stony scree, down which Sure-foot bounded eagerly, giving tongue as he went; but Face-of-god stood still and looked, for now the whole Dale lay open before him.

That river ran from north to south, and at the south end the cliffs drew so close to it that looking thence no outgate could be seen; but at the north end there was as it were a dreary street of rocks, the river flowing amidmost and leaving little foot-hold on either side, somewhat as it was with the pass leading from the mountains into Burgdale.

Amidmost of the Dale a little toward the north end he saw a doom-ring of black stones, and hard by it an ancient hall builded of the same black stone both wall and roof, and thitherward was Sure-foot now running. Face-of-god looked up and down the Dale and could see no break in the wall of sheer rock: toward the southern end he saw a few booths and cots built roughly of stone and thatched with turf; thereabout he saw a few folk moving about, the most of whom seemed to be women and children; there were some sheep and lambs near these cots, and a herd of fifty or so of somewhat goodly mountain-kine were feeding higher up the valley. He could look down into the river from where he stood, and he saw that it ran between rocky banks going straight down from the face of the meadow, which was rather high above the water, so that it seemed little likely that the water should rise over its banks, either in summer or winter; and in summer was it like to be highest, because the vale was so near to the high mountains and their snows.

18. FACE-OF-GOD TALKETH WITH THE FRIEND IN SHADOWY VALE

It was now about two hours after noon, and a broad band of sunlight lay upon the grass of the vale below Gold-mane's feet; he went lightly down the scree, and strode forward over the level grass toward the Doom-ring, his helm and war-gear glittering bright in the sun. He must needs go through the Doom-ring to come to the Hall, and as he stepped out from behind the last of the big upright-stones, he saw a woman standing on the threshold of the Hall-door, which was but some score of paces from him, and knew her at once for the Friend.

She was clad like himself in a green kirtle gaily embroidered and fitting close to her body, and had no gown or cloak over it; she had a golden fillet on her head beset with blue mountain stones, and her hair hung loose behind her.

Her beauty was so exceeding, and so far beyond all memory of her that his mind had held, that once more fear of her fell upon Face-of-god, and he stood still with beating heart till she should speak to him. But she came forward swiftly with both her hands held out, smiling and happy-faced, and looking very kindly on him, and she took his hands and said to him:

"Now welcome, Gold-mane, welcome, Face-of-god! and twice welcome art thou and threefold. Lo! this is the day that thou asked for: art thou happy in it?"

He lifted her hands to his lips and kissed them timorously, but said nought; and therewithal Sure-foot came running forth from the Hall, and fell to bounding round about them, barking noisily after the manner of dogs who have met their masters again; and still she held his hands and beheld him kindly. Then she called the hound to her, and patted him on the neck and quieted him, and then turned to Face-of-god and laughed happily and said:

"I do not bid thee hold thy peace; yet thou sayest nought. Is it well with thee?"

"Yea," he said, "and more than well."

"Thou seemest to me a goodly warrior," she said; "hast thou met any foemen yesterday or this morning?"

"Nay," said he, "none hindered me; thou hast made the ways easy to me."

She said soberly, "Such as I might do, I did. But we may not wield everything, for our foes are many, and I feared for thee.

But come thou into our house, which is ours, and far more ours than the booth before the pine-wood."

She took his hand again and led him toward the door, but Face-of-god looked up, and above the lintel he saw carved on the dark stone that image of the Wolf, even as he had seen it carved on Wood-grey's tie-beam; and therewith such thoughts came into his mind that he stopped to look, pressing the Friend's hand hard as though bidding her note it. The stone wherein the image was carved was darker than the other building-stones, and might be called black; the jaws of the wood-beast were open and gaping, and had been painted with cinnabar, but wind and weather had worn away the most of the colour.

Spake the Friend: "So it is: thou beholdest the token of the God and Father of out Fathers, that telleth the tale of so many days, that the days which now pass by us be to them but as the drop in the sea of waters. Thou beholdest the sign of our sorrow, the memory of our wrong; yet is it also the token of our hope. Maybe it shall lead thee far."

"Whither?" said he. But she answered not a great while, and he looked at her as she stood a-gazing on the image, and saw how the tears stole out of her eyes and ran adown her cheeks. Then again came the thought to him of Wood-grey's hall, and the women of the kindred standing before the Wolf and singing of him; and though there was little comeliness in them and she was so exceeding beauteous, he could not but deem that they were akin to her.

But after a while she wiped the tears from her face and turned to him and said: "My friend, the Wolf shall lead thee no-whither but where I also shall be, whatsoever peril or grief may beset the road or lurk at the ending thereof. Thou shalt be no thrall, to labour while I look on."

His heart swelled within him as she spoke, and he was at point to beseech her love that moment; but now her face had grown gay and bright again, and she said while he was gathering words to speak withal:

"Come in, Gold-mane, come into our house; for I have many things to say to thee. And moreover thou art so hushed, and so fearsome in thy mail, that I think thou yet deemest me to be a Wight of the Waste, such as Stone-face thy Fosterer told thee tales of, and forewarned thee. So would I eat before thee, and sign the meat with the sign of the Earth-god's Hammer, to show thee that he is in error concerning me, and that I am a very woman flesh and fell, as my kindred were before me."

He laughed and was exceeding glad, and said: "Tell me now, kind friend, dost thou deem that Stone-face's tales are mere mockery of his dreams, and that he is beguiled by empty semblances or less? Or are there such Wights in the Waste."

"Nay," she said, "the man is a true man; and of these things are there many ancient tales which we may not doubt. Yet so it is that such wights have I never yet seen, nor aught to scare me save evil men: belike it is that I have been over-much busied in dealing with sorrow and ruin to look after them: or it may be that they feared me and the wrath-breeding grief of the kindred."

He looked at her earnestly, and the wisdom of her heart seemed to enter into his; but she said: "It is of men we must talk, and of me and thee. Come with me, my friend."

And she stepped lightly over the threshold and drew him in. The Hall was stern and grim and somewhat dusky, for its windows were but small: it was all of stone, both walls and roof. There was no timber-work therein save the benches and chairs, a little about the doors at the lower end that led to the buttery and out-bowers; and this seemed to have been wrought of late years; yea, the chairs against the gable on the dais were of stone built into the wall, adorned with carving somewhat sparingly, the image of the Wolf being done over the midmost of them. He looked up and down the Hall, and deemed it some seventy feet over all from end to end; and he could see in the dimness those same goodly hangings on the wall which he had seen in the woodland booth.

She led him up to the dais, and stood there leaning up against the arm of one of those stone seats silent for a while; then she turned and looked at him, and said:

"Yea, thou lookest a goodly warrior; yet am I glad that thou camest hither without battle. Tell me, Gold-mane," she said, taking one of his spears from his hand, "art thou deft with the spear?"

"I have been called so," said he.

She looked at him sweetly and said: "Canst thou show me the feat of spear-throwing in this Hall, or shall we wend outside presently that I may see thee throw?"

"The Hall sufficeth," he said. "Shall I set this steel in the lintel of the buttery door yonder?"

"Yea, if thou canst," she said.

He smiled and took the spear from her, and poised it and shook it till it quivered again, then suddenly drew back his arm and cast, and the shaft sped whistling down the dim hall, and smote the aforesaid door-lintel and stuck there quivering: then he sprang down from the dais, and ran down the hall, and put forth his hand and pulled it forth from the wood, and was on the dais again in a trice, and cast again, and the second time set the spear in the same place, and then took his other spear from the board and cast it, and there stood the two staves in the wood side by side; then he went soberly down the hall and drew them both out of the wood and came back to her, while she stood watching him, her cheek flushed, her lips a little parted.

She said: "Good spear-casting, forsooth! and far above what our folk can do, who be no great throwers of the spear."

Gold-mane laughed: "Sooth is that," said he, "or hardly were I here to teach thee spear-throwing."

"Wilt thou *never* be paid for that simple onslaught?" she said.

"Have I been paid then?" said he.

She reddened, for she remembered her word to him on the mountain; and he put his hand on her shoulder and kissed her cheek, but timorously; nor did she withstand him or shrink aback, but said soberly:

"Good indeed is thy spear-throwing, and meseems my brother will love thee when he hath seen thee strike a stroke or two in wrath. But, fair warrior, there be no foemen here: so get thee to the lower end of the Hall, and in the bower beyond shalt thou find fresh water; there wash the waste from off thee, and do off thine helm and hauberk, and come back speedily and eat with me; for I hunger, and so dost thou."

He did as she bade him, and came back presently bearing in his hand both helm and hauberk, and he looked light-limbed and trim and lissome, an exceeding goodly man.

19. THE FAIR WOMAN TELLETH FACE-OF-GOD OF HER KINDRED

When he came back to the dais he saw that there was meat upon the board, and the Friend said to him:

"Now art thou Gold-mane indeed: but come now, sit by me and eat, though the Wood-woman giveth thee but a sorry banquet, O guest; but from the Dale it is, and we be too far now from the dwellings of men to have delicate meat on the board, though to-night when they come back thy cheer shall be better. Yet even then thou shalt have no such dainties as Stone-face hath imagined for thee at the hands of the Wood-wight."

She laughed therewith, and he no less; and in sooth the meat was but simple, of curds and new cheese, meat of the herdsmen. But Face-of-god said gaily: "Sweet it shall be to me; good is all that the Friend giveth."

Then she raised her hand and made the sign of the Hammer over the board, and looked up at him and said:

"Hath the Earth-god changed my face, Gold-mane, to what I verily am?"

He held his face close to hers and looked into it, and himseemed it was as pure as the waters of a mountain lake, and as fine and well-wrought every deal of it as when his father had wrought in his stithy many days and fashioned a small piece of great mastery. He was ashamed to kiss her again, but he said to himself, "This is the fairest woman of the world, whom I have sworn to wed this year." Then he spake aloud and said:

"I see the face of the Friend, and it will not change to me."

Again she reddened a little, and the happy look in her face seemed to grow yet sweeter, and he was bewildered with longing and delight.

But she stood up and went to an ambrye in the wall and brought forth a horn shod and lipped with silver of ancient fashion, and she poured wine into it and held it forth and said:

"O guest from the Dale, I pledge thee! and when thou hast drunk to me in turn we will talk of weighty matters. For indeed I bear hopes in my hands too heavy for the daughters of men to bear; and thou art a chieftain's son, and mayst well help me to bear them; so let us talk simply and without guile, as folk that trust one another."

So she drank and held out the horn to him, and he took the horn and her hand both, and he kissed her hand and said:

"Here in this Hall I drink to the Sons of the Wolf, whosoever they be." Therewith he drank and he said: "Simply and guilelessly indeed will I talk with thee; for I am weary of lies, and for thy sake have I told a many."

"Thou shalt tell no more," she said; "and as for the health thou hast drunk, it is good, and shall profit thee. Now sit we here in these ancient seats and let us talk."

So they sat them down while the sun was westering in the March afternoon, and she said:

"Tell me first what tidings have been in the Dale."

So he told her of the ransackings and of the murder at Carlstead.

She said: "These tidings have we heard before, and some deal of them we know better than ye do, or can; for we were the ransackers of Penny-thumb and Harts-bane. Thereof will I say more presently. What other tidings hast thou to tell of? What oaths were sworn upon the Boar last Yule?"

So he told her of the oath of Bristler the son of Brightling. She smiled and said: "He shall keep his oath, and yet redden no blade."

Then he told of his father's oath, and she said:

"It is good; but even so would he do and no oath sworn. All men may trust Iron-face. And thou, my friend, what oath didst thou swear?"

His face grew somewhat troubled as he said: "I swore to wed the fairest woman in the world, though the Dalesmen gainsaid me, and they beyond the Dale."

"Yea," she said, "and there is no need to ask thee whom thou didst mean by thy "fairest woman," for I have seen that thou deemest me fair enough. My friend, maybe thy kindred will be against it, and the kindred of the Bride; and it might be that my kindred would have gainsaid it if things were not as they are. But though all men gainsay it, yet will not I. It is meet and right that we twain wed."

She spake very soberly and quietly, but when she had spoken there was nothing in his heart but joy and gladness: yet shame of her loveliness refrained him, and he cast down his eyes before hers. Then she said in a kind voice:

"I know thee, how glad thou art of this word of mine, because thou lookest on me with eyes of love, and thinkest of me as better than I am; though I am no ill woman and no beguiler. But this is not all that I have to say to thee, though it be much; for there are more folk in the world than thou and I only. But I told thee this first, that thou mightest trust me in all things. So, my friend, if thou canst, refrain thy joy and thy longing a little, and hearken to what concerneth thee and me, and thy people and mine."

"Fair woman and sweet friend," he said, "thou knowest of a gladness which is hard to bear if one must lay it aside for a while; and of a longing which is hard to refrain if it mingle with another longing— knowest thou not?"

"Yea," she said, "I know it."

"Yet," said Face-of-god, "I will forbear as thou biddest me. Tell me, then, what were the felons who were slain at Carlstead? Knowest thou of them?"

"Over well," she said, "they are our foes this many a year; and since we met last autumn they have become foes of you Dalesmen also. Soon shall ye have tidings of them; and it was against them that I bade thee arm yesterday."

Said Face-of-god: "Is it against them that thou wouldst have us do battle along with thy folk?"

"So it is," she said; "no other foemen have we. And now, Gold-mane, thou art become a friend of the Wolf, and shalt before long be of affinity with our House; that other day thou didst ask me to tell thee of me and mine, and now will I do according to thine asking. Short shall my tale be; because maybe thou shalt hear it told again, and in goodly wise, before thine whole folk.

"As thou wottest we be now outlaws and Wolves' Heads; and whiles we lift the gear of men, but ever if we may of ill men and not of good; there is no worthy goodman of the Dale from whom we would take one hoof, or a skin of wine, or a cake of wax.

"Wherefore are we outlaws? Because we have been driven from our own, and we bore away our lives and our weapons, and little else; and for our lands, thou seest this Vale in the howling wilderness and how narrow and poor it is, though it hath been the nurse of warriors in time past.

"Hearken! Time long ago came the kindred of the Wolf to these Mountains of the World; and they were in a pass in the stony maze and the utter wilderness of the Mountains, and the foe was behind them in numbers not to be borne up against. And so it befell that the pass forked, and there were two ways before our Folk; and one part of them would take the way to the north and the other the way to the south; and they could not agree which way the whole Folk should take. So they sundered into two companies, and one took one way and one another. Now as to those who fared by the southern road, we knew not what befell them, nor for long and long had we any tale of them.

"But we who took the northern road, we happened on this Vale amidst the wilderness, and we were weary of fleeing from the over-mastering foe; and the dale seemed enough, and a refuge, and a place to dwell in, and no man was there before us, and few were like to find it, and we were but a few. So we dwelt here in this Vale for as wild as it is, the place where the sun shineth never in the winter, and scant is the summer sunshine therein. Here we raised a Doom-ring and builded us a Hall, wherein thou now sittest beside me, O friend, and we dwelt here many seasons.

"We had a few sheep in the wilderness, and a few neat fed down the grass of the Vale; and we found gems and copper in the rocks about us wherewith at whiles to chaffer with the aliens, and fish we drew from our river the Shivering Flood. Also it is not to be hidden that in those days we did not spare to lift the goods of men; yea, whiles would our warriors fare down unto the edges of the Plain and lie in wait there till the time served, and then drive the spoil from under the very walls of the Cities. Our men were not little-hearted, nor did our women lament the death of warriors over-much, for they were there to bear more warriors to the Folk.

"But the seasons passed, and the Folk multiplied in Shadowy Vale, and livelihood seemed like to fail them, and needs must they seek wider lands. So by ways which thou wilt one day wot of, we came into a valley that lieth north-west of Shadowy Vale: a land like thine of Burgdale, or better; wide it was, plenteous of grass and trees, well watered, full of all things that man can desire.

"Were there men before us in this Dale? sayest thou. Yea, but not very many, and they feeble in battle, weak of heart, though strong of body. These, when they saw the Sons of the Wolf with weapons in their hands, felt themselves puny before us, and their hearts failed them; and they came to us with gifts, and offered to share the Dale between them and us, for they said there was enough for both folks. So we took their offer and became their friends; and some of our Houses wedded wives of the strangers, and gave them our women to wife. Therein they did amiss; for the blended Folk as the generations passed became softer than our blood, and many were untrusty and greedy and tyrannous, and the days of the whoredom fell upon us, and when we deemed ourselves the mightiest then were we the nearest to our fall. But the House whereof I am would never wed with these Westlanders, and other Houses there were who had affinity with us who chiefly wedded with us of the Wolf, and their fathers had come with ours into that fruitful Dale; and these were called the Red Hand, and the Silver Arm, and the Golden Bushel, and the Ragged Sword. Thou hast heard those names once before, friend?"

"Yea," he said, and as he spoke the picture of that other day came back to him, and he called to mind all that he had said, and his happiness of that hour seemed the more and the sweeter for that memory.

She went on: "Fair and goodly is that Dale as mine own eyes have seen, and plentiful of all things, and up in its mountains to the east are caves and pits whence silver is digged abundantly; therefore is the Dale called Silverdale. Hast thou heard thereof, my friend?"

"Nay," said Face-of-god, "though I have marvelled whence ye gat such foison of silver."

He looked on her and marvelled, for now she seemed as if it were another woman: her eyes were gleaming bright, her lips were parted; there was a bright red flush on the pommels of her two cheeks as she spake again and said:

"Happy lived the Folk in Silverdale for many and many winters and summers: the seasons were good and no lack was there: little sickness there was and less war, and all seemed better than well. It is strange that ye Dalesmen have not heard of Silverdale."

"Nay," said he, "but I have not; of Rosedale have I heard, as a land very far away: but no further do we know of toward that airt. Lieth Silverdale anywhere nigh to Rosedale?"

She said: "It is the next dale to it, yet is it a far journey betwixt the two, for the ice-sea pusheth a horn in betwixt them; and even below the ice the mountain-neck is passable to none save a bold crag-climber, and to him only bearing his life in his hands. But, my friend, I am but lingering over my tale, because it grieveth me sore to have to tell it. Hearken then! In the days when I had seen but ten summers, and my brother was a very young man, but exceeding strong, and as beautiful as thou art now, war fell on us without rumour or warning; for there swarmed into Silverdale, though not by the ways whereby we had entered it, a host of aliens, short of stature, crooked of limb, foul of aspect, but fierce warriors and armed full well: they were men having no country to go back to, though they had no women or children with them, as we had when we were young in these lands, but used all women whom they took as their beastly lust bade them, making them their thralls if they slew them not. Soon we found that these foemen

asked no more of us than all we had, and therewithal our lives to be cast away or used for their service as beasts of burden or pleasure. There then we gathered our fighting-men and withstood them; and if we had been all of the kindreds of the Wolf and the fruit of the wives of warriors, we should have driven back these felons and saved the Dale, though it maybe more than half ruined: but the most part of us were of that mingled blood, or of the generations of the Dalesmen whom we had conquered long ago, and stout as they were of body their hearts failed them, and they gave themselves up to the aliens to be as their oxen and asses.

"Why make a long tale of it? We who were left, and could brook death but not thraldom, fought it out together, women as well as men, till the sweetness of life and a happy chance for escape bid us flee, vanquished but free men. For at the end of three days" fight we had been driven up to the easternmost end of the Dale, and up anigh to the jaws of the pass whereby the Folk had first come into Silverdale, and we had those with us who knew every cranny of that way, while to strangers who knew it not it was utterly impassable; night was coming on also, and even those murder-carles were weary with slaying; and, moreover, on this last day, when they saw that they had won all, they were fighting to keep, and not to slay, and a few stubborn carles and queens, of what use would they be, or where was the gain of risking life to win them?

"So they forbore us, and night came on moonless and dark; and it was the early spring season, when the days are not yet long, and so by night and cloud we fled away, and back again to Shadowy Vale.

"Forsooth, we were but a few; for when we were gotten into this Vale, this strip of grass and water in the wilderness, and had told up our company, we were but two hundred and thirty and five of men and women and children. For there were an hundred and thirty and three grown men of all ages, and of women grown seventy and five, and one score and seven children, whereof I was one; for, as thou mayst deem, it was easier for grown men with weapons in their hands to escape from that slaughter than for women and children.

"There sat we in yonder Doom-ring and took counsel, and to some it seemed good that we should all dwell together in Shadowy Vale, and beset the skirts of the foemen till the days should better; but others deemed that there was little avail therein; and there was a mighty man of the kindred, Stonewolf by name, a man of middle-age, and he said, that late in life had he tasted of war, and though the banquet was made bitter with defeat, yet did the meat seem wholesome to him. "Come down with me to the Cities of the Plain," said he, "all you who are stout warriors; and leave we here the old men and the swains and the women and children. Hateful are the folk there, and full of malice, but soft withal and dastardly. Let us go down thither and make ourselves strong amongst them, and sell our valour for their wealth till we come to rule them, and they make us their kings, and we establish the Folk of the Wolf amongst the aliens; then will we come back hither and bring away that which we have left."

"So he spake, and the more part of the warriors yea said his rede, and they went with him to the Westland, and amongst these was my brother Folk-might (for that is his name in the kindred). And I sorrowed at his departure, for he had borne me thither out of the flames and the clash of swords and the press of battle, and to me had he ever been kind and loving, albeit he hath had the Words of hard and froward used on him full oft.

"So in this Vale abode we that were left, and the seasons passed; some of the elders died, and some of the children also; but more children were born, for amongst us were men and women to whom it was lawful to wed with each other. Even with this scanty remnant was left some of the life of the kindred of old days; and after we had been here but a little while, the young men, yea and the old also, and even some of the women, would steal through passes that we, and we only, knew of, and would fall upon the Aliens in Silverdale as occasion served, and lift their goods both live and dead; and this became both a craft and a pastime amongst us. Nor may I hide that we sometimes went lifting otherwhere; for in the summer and autumn we would fare west a little and abide in the woods the season through, and hunt the deer thereof, and whiles would we drive the spoil from the scattered folk not far from your Shepherd-Folk; but with the Shepherds themselves and with you Dalesmen we meddled not.

"Now that little wood-lawn with the toft of an ancient dwelling in it, wherein, saith Bow-may, thou didst once rest, was one of our summer abodes; and later on we built the hall under the pine-wood that thou knowest.

"Thus then grew up our young men; and our maids were little softer; e'en such as Bow-may is (and kind is she withal), and it seemed in very sooth as if the Spirit of the Wolf was with us, and the roughness of the Waste made us fierce; and law we had not and heeded not, though love was amongst us."

She stopped awhile and fell a-musing, and her face softened, and she turned to him with that sweet happy look upon it and said:

"Desolate and dreary is the Dale, thou deemest, friend; and yet for me I love it and its dark-green water, and it is to me as if the Fathers of the kindred visit it and hold converse with us; and there I grew up when I was little, before I knew what a woman was, and strange communings had I with the wilderness. Friend, when we are wedded, and thou art a great chieftain, as thou wilt be, I shall ask of thee the boon to suffer me to abide here at whiles that I may remember the days when I was little and the love of the kindred waxed in me."

"This is but a little thing to ask," said Face-of-god; "I would thou hadst asked me more."

"Fear not," she said, "I shall ask thee for much and many things; and some of them belike thou shalt deny me."

He shook his head; but she smiled in his face and said:

"Yea, so it is, friend; but hearken. The seasons passed, and six years wore, and I was grown a tall slim maiden, fleet of foot and able to endure toil enough, though I never bore weapons, nor have done. So on a fair even of midsummer when we were together, the most of us, round about this Hall and the Doom-ring, we saw a tall man in bright war-gear come forth into the Dale by the path that thou camest, and then another and another till there were two score and seven men-at-arms standing on the grass below the scree yonder; by that time had we gotten some weapons in our hands, and we stood together to meet the new-comers, but they drew no sword and notched no shaft, but came towards us laughing and joyous, and lo! it was my brother Folk-might and his men, those that were left of them, come back to us from the Westland.

"Glad indeed was I to behold him; and for him when he had taken me in his arms and looked up and down the Dale, he cried out: "In many fair places and many rich dwellings have I been; but this is the hour that I have looked for."

"Now when we asked him concerning Stone-wolf and the others who were missing (for ten tens of stalwarth men had fared to the Westland), he swept out his hand toward the west and said with a solemn face: "There they lie, and grass groweth over their bones, and we who have come aback, and ye who have abided, these are now the children of the Wolf: there are no more now on the earth."

"Let be! It was a fair even and high was the feast in the Hall that night, and sweet was the converse with our folk come back. A glad man was my brother Folk-might when he heard that for years past we had been lifting the gear of men, and chiefly of the Aliens in Silverdale: and he himself was become learned in war and a deft leader of men.

"So the days passed and the seasons, and we lived on as we might; but with Folk-might's return there began to grow up in all our hearts what had long been flourishing in mine, and that was the hope of one day winning back our own again, and dying amidst the dear groves of Silverdale. Within these years we had increased somewhat in number; for if we had lost those warriors in the Westland, and some old men who had died in the Dale, yet our children had grown up (I have now seen twenty and one summers) and more were growing up. Moreover, after the first year, from the time when we began to fall upon the Dusky Men of Silverdale, from time to time they who went on such adventures set free such thralls of our blood as they could fall in with and whom they could trust in, and they dwelt (and yet dwell) with us in the Dale: first and last we have taken in three score and twelve of such men, and a score of women-thralls withal.

"Now during these seasons, and not very long ago, after I was a woman grown, the thought came to me, and to Folk-might also, that there were kindreds of the people dwelling anear us whom we might so deal with that they should become our friends and brothers in arms, and that through them we might win back Silverdale.

"Of Rosedale we wotted already that the Folk were nought of our blood, feeble in the field, cowed by the Dusky Men, and at last made thralls to them; so nought was to do there. But Folk-might went to and fro to gather tidings: at whiles I with him, at whiles one or more of Wood-father's children, who with their father and mother and Bow-may have abided in the Vale ever since the Great Undoing.

"Soon he fell in with thy Folk, and first of all with the Woodlanders, and that was a joy to him; for wot ye what? He got to know that these men were the children of those of our Folk who had sundered from us in the mountain passes time long and long ago; and he loved them, for he saw that they were hardy and trusty, and warriors at heart.

"Then he went amongst the Shepherd-Folk, and he deemed them good men easily stirred, and deemed that they might soon be won to friendship; and he knew that they were mostly come from the Houses of the Woodlanders, so that they also were of the kindred.

"And last he came into Burgdale, and found there a merry and happy Folk, little wont to war, but stout-hearted, and now-ise puny either of body or soul; he went there often and learned much about them, and deemed that they would not be hard to win to fellowship. And he found that the House of the Face was the chiefest house there; and that the Alderman and his sons were well beloved of all the folk, and that they were the men to be won first, since through them should all others be won. I also went to Burgstead with him twice, as I told thee erst; and I saw thee, and I deemed that thou wouldest lightly become our friend; and it came into my mind that I myself might wed thee, and that the House of the Face thereby might have affinity thenceforth with the Children of the Wolf."

He said: "Why didst thou deem thus of me, O friend?"

She laughed and said: "Dost thou long to hear me say the words when thou knowest my thought well? So be it. I saw thee both young and fair; and I knew thee to be the son of a noble, worthy, guileless man and of a beauteous woman of great wits and good rede. And I found thee to be kind and open-handed and simple like thy father, and like thy mother wiser than thou thyself knew of thyself; and that thou wert desirous of deeds and fain of women."

She was silent for a while, and he also: then he said: "Didst thou draw me to the woods and to thee?"

She reddened and said: "I am no spell-wife: but true it is that Wood-mother made a waxen image of thee, and thrust through the heart thereof the pin of my girdle-buckle, and stroked it every morning with an oak-bough over which she had sung spells. But dost thou not remember, Gold-mane, how that one day last Hay-month, as ye were resting in the meadows in the cool of the evening, there came to you a minstrel that played to you on the fiddle, and therewith sang a song that melted all your hearts, and that this song told of the Wild-wood, and what was therein of desire and peril and beguiling and death, and love unto Death itself? Dost thou remember, friend?"

"Yea," he said, "and how when the minstrel was done Stone-face fell to telling us more tales yet of the woodland, and the minstrel sang again and yet again, till his tales had entered into my very heart."

"Yea," she said, "and that minstrel was Wood-wont; and I sent him to sing to thee and thine, deeming that if thou didst hearken, thou would'st seek the woodland and happen upon us."

He laughed and said: "Thou didst not doubt but that if we met, thou mightest do with me as thou wouldest?"

"So it is," she said, "that I doubted it little."

"Therein wert thou wise," said Face-of-god; "but now that we are talking without guile to each other, mightest thou tell me wherefore it was that Folk-might made that onslaught upon me? For certain it is that he was minded to slay me."

She said: "It was sooth what I told thee, that whiles he groweth so battle-eager that whatso edge-tool he beareth must needs come out of the scabbard; but there was more in it than that, which I could not tell thee erst. Two days before thy coming he had been down to Burgstead in the guise of an old carle such as thou sawest him with me in the market-place. There was he guested in your Hall, and once more saw thee and the Bride together; and he saw the eyes of love wherewith she looked on thee (for so much he told me), and deemed that thou didst take her love but lightly. And he himself looked on her with such love (and this he told me not) that he deemed nought good enough for her, and would have had thee give thyself up wholly to her; for my brother is a generous man, my friend. So when I told him on the morn of that day whereon we met that we looked to see thee that eve (for indeed I am somewhat fore-seeing), he said: "Look thou, Sun-beam, if he cometh, it is not unlike that I shall drive a spear through him." "Wherefore?" said I; "can he serve our turn when he is dead?" Said he: "I care little. Mine own turn will I serve. Thou sayest *wherefore?* I tell thee this stripling beguileth to her torment the fairest woman that is in the world—such an one as is meet to be the mother of chieftains, and to stand by warriors in their day of peril. I have seen her; and thus have I seen her." Then said I: "Greatly forsooth shalt thou pleasure her by slaying him!""

And he answered: "I shall pleasure myself. And one day she shall thank me, when she taketh my hand in hers and we go together to the Bride-bed." Therewith came over me a clear foresight of the hours to come, and I said to him: "Yea, Folk-might, cast the spear and draw the sword; but him thou shalt not slay: and thou shalt one day see him standing with us before the shafts of the Dusky Men." So I spake; but he looked fiercely at me, and departed and shunned me all that day, and by good hap I was hard at hand when thou drewest nigh our abode. Nay, Gold-mane, what would'st thou with thy sword? Why art thou so red and wrathful? Would'st thou fight with my brother because he loveth thy friend, thine old playmate, thy kinswoman, and thinketh pity of her sorrow?"

He said, with knit brow and gleaming eyes: "Would the man take her away from me perforce?"

"My friend," she said, "thou art not yet so wise as not to be a fool at whiles. Is it not so that she herself hath taken herself from thee, since she hath come to know that thou hast given thyself to another? Hath she noted nought of thee this winter and spring? Is she well pleased with the ways of thee?"

He said: "Thou hast spoken simply with me, and I will do no less with thee. It was but four days agone that she did me to wit that she knew of me how I sought my love on the Mountain; and she put me to sore shame, and afterwards I wept for her sorrow."

Therewith he told her all that the Bride had said to him, as he well might, for he had forgotten no word of it.

Then said the Friend: "She shall have the token that she craveth, and it is I that shall give it to her."

Therewith she took from her finger a ring wherein was set a very fair changeful mountain-stone, and gave it to him, and said:

"Thou shalt give her this and tell her whence thou hadst it; and tell her that I bid her remember that To-morrow is a new day."

20. THOSE TWO TOGETHER HOLD THE RING OF THE EARTH-GOD

And now they fell silent both of them, and sat hearkening the sounds of the Dale, from the whistle of the plover down by the water-side to the far-off voices of the children and maidens about the kine in the lower meadows. At last Gold-mane took up the word and said:

"Sweet friend, tell me the uttermost of what thou would'st have of me. Is it not that I should stand by thee and thine in the Folk-mote of the Dalesmen, and speak for you when ye pray us for help against your foemen; and then again that I do my best when ye and we are arrayed for battle against the Dusky Men? This is easy to do, and great is the reward thou offerest me."

"I look for this service of thee," she said, "and none other."

"And when I go down to the battle," said he, "shalt thou be sorry for our sundering?"

She said: "There shall be no sundering; I shall wend with thee."

Said he: "And if I were slain in the battle, would'st thou lament me?"

"Thou shalt not be slain," she said.

Again was there silence betwixt them, till at last he said:

"This then is why thou didst draw me to thee in the Wild-wood?"

"Yea," said she.

Again for a while no word was spoken, and Face-of-god looked on her till she cast her eyes down before him.

Then at last he spake, and the colour came and went in his face as he said: "Tell me thy name what it is."

She said: "I am called the Sun-beam."

Then he said, and his voice trembled therewith: "O Sun-beam, I have been seeking pleasant and cunning words, and can find none such. But tell me this if thou wilt: dost thou desire me as I desire thee? or is it that thou wilt suffer me to wed thee and bed thee at last as mere payment for the help that I shall give to thee and thine? Nay, doubt it not that I will take the payment, if this is what thou wilt give me and nought else. Yet tell me."

Her face grew troubled, and she said:

"Gold-mane, maybe that thou hast now asked me one question too many; for this is no fair game to be played between us. For thee, as I deem, there are this day but two people in the world, and that is thou and I, and the earth is for us two alone. But, my friend, though I have seen but twenty and one summers, it is nowise so with me, and to me there are many in the world; and chiefly the Folk of the Wolf, amidst whose very heart I have grown up. Moreover, I can think of her whom I have supplanted, the Bride to wit; and I know her, and how bitter and empty her days shall be for a while, and how vain all our redes for her shall seem to her. Yea, I know her sorrow, and see it and grieve for it: so canst not thou, unless thou verily see her before thee, her face unhappy, and her voice changed and hard. Well, I will tell thee what thou askest.

When I drew thee to me on the Mountain I thought but of the friendship and brotherhood to be knitted up between our two Folks, nor did I anywise desire thy love of a young man. But when I saw thee on the heath and in the Hall that day, it pleased me to think that a man so fair and chieftain-like should one day lie by my side; and again when I saw that the love of me had taken hold of thee, I would not have thee grieved because of me, but would have thee happy. And now what shall I say?—I know not; I cannot tell. Yet am I the Friend, as erst I called myself.

"And, Gold-mane, I have seen hitherto but the outward show and image of thee, and though that be goodly, how would it be if thou didst shame me with little-heartedness and evil deeds? Let me see thee in the Folk-mote and the battle, and then may I answer thee."

Then she held her peace, and he answered nothing; and she turned her face from him and said:

"Out on it! have I beguiled myself as well as thee? These are but empty words I have been saying. If thou wilt drag the truth out of me, this is the very truth: that to-day is happy to me as it is to thee, and that I have longed sore for its coming. O Gold-mane, O speech-friend, if thou wert to pray me or command me that I lie in thine arms to-night, I should know not how to gainsay thee. Yet I beseech thee to forbear, lest thy death and mine come of it. And why should we die, O friend, when we are so young, and the world lies so fair before us, and the happy days are at hand when the Children of the Wolf and the kindreds of the Dale shall deliver the Folk, and all days shall be good and all years?"

They had both risen up as she spake, and now he put forth his hands to her and took her in his arms, wondering the while, as he drew her to him, how much slenderer and smaller and weaker she seemed in his embrace than he had thought of her; and when their lips met, he felt that she kissed him as he her. Then he held her by the shoulders at arms" length from him, and beheld her face how her eyes were closed and her lips quivering. But before him, in a moment of time, passed a picture of the life to be in the fair Dale, and all she would give him there, and the days good and lovely from morn to eve and eve to morn; and though in that moment it was hard for him to speak, at last he spoke in a voice hoarse at first, and said:

"Thou sayest sooth, O friend; we will not die, but live; I will not drag our deaths upon us both, nor put a sword in the hands of Folk-might, who loves me not."

Then he kissed her on the brow and said: "Now shalt thou take me by the hand and lead me forth from the Hall. For the day is waxing old, and here meseemeth in this dim hall there are words crossing in the air about us—words spoken in days long ago, and tales of old time, that keep egging me on to do my will and die, because that is all that the world hath for a valiant man; and to such words I would not hearken, for in this hour I have no will to die, nor can I think of death."

She took his hand and led him forth without more words, and they went hand in hand and paced slowly round the Doom-ring, the light air breathing upon them till their faces were as calm and quiet as their wont was, and hers especially as bright and happy as when he had first seen her that day.

The sun was sinking now, and only sent one golden ray into the valley through a cleft in the western rock-wall, but the sky overhead was bright and clear; from the meadows came the sound of the lowing of kine and the voices of children a-sporting, and it seemed to Gold-mane that they were drawing nigher, both the children and the kine, and somewhat he begrudged it that he should not be alone with the Friend.

Now when they had made half the circuit of the Doom-ring, the Sun-beam stopped him, and then led him through the Ring of Stones, and brought him up to the altar which was amidst of it; and the altar was a great black stone hewn smooth and clean, and with the image of the Wolf carven on the front thereof; and on its face lay the gold ring which the priest or captain of the Folk bore on his arm between the God and the people at all folk-motes.

So she said: "This is the altar of the God of Earth, and often hath it been reddened by mighty men; and thereon lieth the Ring of the Sons of the Wolf; and now it were well that we swore troth on that ring before my brother cometh; for now will he soon be here."

Then Gold-mane took the Ring and thrust his right hand through it, and took her right hand in his; so that the Ring lay on both their hands, and therewith he spake aloud:

"I am Face-of-god of the House of the Face, and I do thee to wit, O God of the Earth, that I pledge my troth to this woman, the Sun-beam of the Kindred of the Wolf, to beget my offspring on her, and to live with her, and to die with her: so help me, thou God of the Earth, and the Warrior and the God of the Face!"

Then spake the Sun-beam: "I, the Sun-beam of the Children of the Wolf, pledge my troth to Face-of-god to lie in his bed and to bear his children and none other's, and to be his speech-friend till I die: so help me the Wolf and the Warrior and the God of the Earth!"

Then they laid the Ring on the altar again, and they kissed each other long and sweetly, and then turned away from the altar and departed from the Doom-ring, going hand in hand together down the meadow, and as they went, the noise of the kine and the children grew nearer and nearer, and presently came the whole company of them round a ness of the rock-wall; there were some thirty little lads and lasses driving on the milch-kine, with half a score of older maids and grown women, one of whom was Bow-may, who was lightly and scantily clad, as one who heeds not the weather, or deems all months midsummer.

The children came running up merrily when they saw the Sun-beam, but stopped short shyly when they noted the tall fair stranger with her. They were all strong and sturdy children, and some very fair, but brown with the weather, if not with the sun. Bow-may came up to Gold-mane and took his hand and greeted him kindly and said:

"So here thou art at last in Shadowy Vale; and I hope that thou art content therewith, and as happy as I would wish thee to be. Well, this is the first time; and when thou comest the second time it may well be that the world shall be growing better."

She held the distaff which she bore in her hand (for she had been spinning) as if it were a spear; her limbs were goodly and shapely, and she trod the thick grass of the Vale with a kind of wary firmness, as though foemen might be lurking nearby. The Sun-beam smiled upon her kindly and said:

"That shall not fail to be, Bow-may: ye have won a new friend to-day. But tell me, when dost thou look to see the men here, for I was down by the water when they went away yesterday?"

"They shall come into the Dale a little after sunset," said Bow-may.

"Shall I abide them, my friend?" said Gold-mane, turning to the Sun-beam.

"Yea," she said; "for what else art thou come hither? or art thou so pressed to depart from us? Last time we met thou wert not so hasty to sunder."

They smiled on each other; and Bow-may looked on them and laughed outright; then a flush showed in her cheeks through the tan of them, and she turned toward the children and the other women who were busied about the milking of the kine.

But those two sat down together on a bank amidst the plain meadow, facing the river and the eastern rock-wall, and the Sun-beam said:

"I am fain to speak to thee and to see thine eyes watching me while I speak; and now, my friend, I will tell thee something unasked which has to do with what e'en now thou didst ask me; for I would have thee trust me wholly, and know me for what I am. Time was I schemed and planned for this day of betrothal; but now I tell thee it has become no longer needful for bringing to pass our fellowship in arms with thy people. Yea yesterday, ere he went on a hunt, whereof he shall tell thee, Folk-might was against it, in words at least; and yet as one who would have it done if he might have no part in it. So, in good sooth, this hand that lieth in thine is the hand of a wilful woman, who desireth a man, and would keep him for her speech-friend. Now art thou fond and happy; yet bear in mind

that there are deeds to be done, and the troth we have just plighted must be paid for. So hearken, I bid thee. Dost thou care to know why the wheedling of thee is no longer needful to us?"

He said: "A little while ago I should have said, Yea, If thy lips say the words. But now, O friend, it seemeth as if thine heart were already become a part of mine, and I feel as if the chieftain were growing up in me and the longing for deeds: so I say, Tell me, for I were fain to hear what toucheth the welfare of thy Folk and their fellowship with my Folk; for on that also have I set my heart?"

She said gravely and with solemn eyes:

"What thou sayest is good: full glad am I that I have not plighted my troth to a mere goodly lad, but rather to a chieftain and a warrior. Now then hearken! Since I saw thee first in the autumn this hath happened, that the Dusky Men, increasing both in numbers and insolence, have it in their hearts to win more than Silverdale, and it is years since they have fallen upon Rosedale and conquered it, rather by murder than by battle, and made all men thralls there, for feeble were the Folk thereof; and doubt it not but that they will look into Burgdale before long. They are already abroad in the woods, and were it not for the fear of the Wolf they would be thicker therein, and faring wider; for we have slain many of them, coming upon them unawares; and they know not where we dwell, nor who we be: so they fear to spread about over-much and pry into unknown places lest the Wolf howl on them. Yet beware! for they will gather in numbers that we may not meet, and then will they swarm into the Dale; and if ye would live your happy life that ye love so well, ye must now fight for it; and in that battle must ye needs join yourselves to us, that we may help each other. Herein have ye nought to choose, for now with you it is no longer a thing to talk of whether ye will help certain strangers and guests and thereby win some gain to yourselves, but whether ye have the hearts to fight for yourselves, and the wits to be the fellows of tall men and stout warriors who have pledged their lives to win or die for it."

She was silent a little and then turned and looked fondly on Face-of-god and said:

"Therefore, Gold-mane, we need thee no longer; for thou must needs fight in our battle. I have no longer aught to do to wheedle thee to love me. Yet if thou wilt love me, then am I a glad woman."

He said: "Thou wottest well that thou hast all my love, neither will I fail thee in the battle. I am not little-hearted, though I would have given myself to thee for no reward."

"It is well," said the Sun-beam; "nought is undone by that which I have done. Moreover, it is good that we have plighted troth to-day. For Folk-might will presently hear thereof, and he must needs abide the thing which is done. Hearken! he cometh."

For as she spoke there came a glad cry from the women and children, and those two stood up and turned toward the west and beheld the warriors of the Wolf coming down into the Dale by the way that Gold-mane had come.

"Come," said the Sun-beam, "here are your brethren in arms, let us go greet them; they will rejoice in thee."

So they went thither, and there stood eighty and seven men on the grass below the scree and Folk-might their captain; and besides some valiant women, and a few carles who were on watch on the waste, and a half score who had been left in the Dale, these were all the warriors of the Wolf. They were clad in no holiday raiment, not even Folk-might, but were in sheep-brown gear of the coarsest, like to husbandmen late come from the plough, but armed well and goodly.

But when the twain drew near, the men clashed their spears on their shields, and cried out for joy of them, for they all knew what Face-of-god's presence there betokened of fellow-ship with the kindreds; but Folk-might came forward and took Face-of-god's hand and greeted him and said:

"Hail, son of the Alderman! Here hast thou come into the ancient abode of chieftains and warriors, and belike deeds await thee also."

Yet his brow was knitted as he said these words, and he spake slowly, as one that constraineth himself; but presently his face cleared somewhat and he said:

"Dalesman, it behoveth thy people to bestir them if ye would live and see good days. Hath my sister told thee what is toward? Or what sayest thou?"

"Hail to thee, son of the Wolf!" said Face-of-god. "Thy sis-ter hath told me all; and even if these Dusky Felons were not our foe-men also, yet could I have my way, we should have given thee all help, and should have brought back peace and good days to thy folk."

Then Folk-might flushed red and spake, as he cast out his hand towards the warriors and up and down toward the Dale:

"These be my folk, and these only: and as to peace, only those of us know of it who are old men. Yet is it well; and if we and ye together be strong enough to bring back good days to the feeble men whom the Dusky Ones torment in Silverdale it shall be better yet."

Then he turned about to his sister, and looked keenly into her eyes till she reddened, and took her hand and looked at the wrist and said:

"O sister, see I not the mark on thy wrist of the Ring of the God of the Earth? Have not oaths been sworn since yester-day?"

"True it is," she said, "that this man and I have plighted troth together at the altar of the Doom-ring."

Said Folk-might: "Thou wilt have thy will, and I may not amend it." Therewith he turned about to Face-of-god and said:

"Thou must look to it to keep this oath, whatever other one thou hast failed in."

Said Face-of-god somewhat wrathfully: "I shall keep it, whether thou biddest me to keep it or break it."

"That is well," said Folk-might, "and then for all that hath gone before thou mayest in a manner pay, if thou art dauntless before the foe."

"I look to be no blencher in the battle," said Face-of-god; "that is not the fashion of our kindred, whosoever may be before us. Yea, and even were it thy blade, O mighty warrior of the Wolf, I would do my best to meet it in manly fashion."

As he spake he half drew forth Dale-warden from his sheath, looking steadily into the eyes of Folk-might; and the Sun-beam looked upon him happily. But Folk-might laughed and said:

"Thy sword is good, and I deem that thine heart will not fail thee; but it is by my side and not in face of me that thou shalt redden the good blade: I see not the day when we twain shall hew at each other."

Then in a while he spake again:

"Thou must pardon us if our words are rough; for we have stood in rough places, where we had to speak both short and loud, whereas there was much to do. But now will we twain talk of matters that concern chieftains who are going on a hard adventure. And ye women, do ye dight the Hall for the evening feast, which shall be the feast of the troth-plight for you twain. This indeed we owe thee, O guest; for little shall be thine heritage which thou shalt have with my sister, over and above that thy sword winneth for thee."

But the Sun-beam said: "Hast thou any to-night?"

"Yea," he said; "Spear-god, how many was it?"

There came forward a tall man bearing an axe in his right hand, and carrying over his shoulder by his left hand a bundle of silver arm-rings just such as Gold-mane had seen on the fel-ons who were slain by Wood-grey's house. The carle cast them on the ground and then knelt down and fell to telling them over; and then looked up and said: "Twelve yesterday in the wood where the battle was going on; and this morning seven by the tarn in the pine-wood and six near this eastern edge of the wood: one score and five all told. But, Folk-might, they are coming nigh to Shadowy Vale."

"Sooth is that," said Folk-might; "but it shall be looked to. Come now apart with me, Face-of-god."

So the others went their ways toward the Hall, while Folk-might led the Burgdaler to a sheltered nook under the sheer rocks, and there they sat down to talk, and Folk-might asked Gold-mane closely of the muster of the Dalesmen and the

Shepherds and the Woodland Caries, and he was well pleased when Face-of-god told him of how many could march to a stricken field, and of their archery, and of their weapons and their goodness.

All this took some time in the telling, and now night was coming on apace, and Folk-might said:

"Now will it be time to go to the Hall; but keep in thy mind that these Dusky Men will overrun you unless ye deal with them betimes. These are of the kind that ye must cast fear into their hearts by falling on them; for if ye abide till they fall upon you, they are like the winter wolves that swarm on and on, how many soever ye slay. And this above all things shall help you, that we shall bring you whereas ye shall fall on them unawares and destroy them as boys do with a wasp's nest. Yet shall many a mother's son bite the dust.

"Is it not so that in four weeks' time is your spring-feast and market at Burgstead, and thereafter the great Folk-mote?"

"So it is," said Gold-mane.

"Thither shall I come then," said Folk-might, "and give myself out for the slayer of Rusty and the ransacker of Harts-bane and Penny-thumb; and therefor shall I offer good blood-wite and theft-wite; and thy father shall take that; for he is a just man. Then shall I tell my tale. Yet it may be thou shalt see us before if battle betide. And now fair befall this new year; for soon shall the scabbards be empty and the white swords be dancing in the air, and spears and axes shall be the growth of this spring-tide."

And he leaped up from his seat and walked to and fro before Gold-mane, and now was it grown quite dark. Then Folk-might turned to Face-of-god and said:

"Come, guest, the windows of the Hall are yellow; let us to the feast. To-morrow shalt thou get thee to the beginning of this work. I hope of thee that thou art a good sword; else have I done a folly and my sister a worse one. But now forget that, and feast."

Gold-mane arose, not very well at ease, for the man seemed overbearing; yet how might he fall upon the Sun-beam's kindred, and the captain of these new brethren in arms? So he spake not. But Folk-might said to him:

"Yet I would not have thee forget that I was wroth with thee when I saw thee to-day; and had it not been for the coming battle I had drawn sword upon thee."

Then Face-of-god's wrath was stirred, and he said:

"There is yet time for that! but why art thou wroth with me? And I shall tell thee that there is little manliness in thy chiding. For how may I fight with thee, thou the brother of my plighted speech-friend and my captain in this battle?"

"Therein thou sayest sooth," said Folk-might; "but hard it was to see you two standing together; and thou canst not give the Bride to me as I give my sister to thee. For I have seen her, and I have seen her looking at thee; and I know that she will not have it so."

Then they went on together toward the Hall, and Face-of-god was silent and somewhat troubled; and as they drew near to the Hall, Folk-might spake again:

"Yet time may amend it; and if not, there is the battle, and maybe the end. Now be we merry!"

So they went into the Hall together, and there was the Sun-beam gloriously arrayed, as erst in the woodland bower, and Face-of-god sat on the dais beside her, and the uttermost sweetness of desire entered into his soul as he noted her eyes and her mouth, that were grown so kind to him, and her hand that strayed toward his.

The Hall was full of folk, and all those warriors were there with Wood-father and his sons, and Wood-mother, and Bow-may and many other women; and Gold-mane looked down the Hall and deemed that he had never seen such stalwarth bodies of men, or so bold and meet for battle: as for the women he had seen fairer in Burgdale, but these were fair of their own fashion, shapely and well-knit, and strong-armed and large-limbed, yet sweet-voiced and gentle withal. Nay, the very lads of fifteen winters or so, whereof a few were there, seemed bold and bright-eyed and keen of wit, and it seemed like that if the warriors fared afield these would be with them.

So wore the feast; and Folk-might as aforetime amongst the healths called on men to drink to the Jaws of the Wolf, and the Red Hand, and the Silver Arm, and the Golden Bushel, and the Ragged Sword. But now had Face-of-god no need to ask what these meant, since he knew that they were the names of the kindreds of the Wolf. They drank also to the troth-plight and to those twain, and shouted aloud over the health and clashed their weapons: and Gold-mane wondered what echo of that shout would reach to Burgstead.

Then sang men songs of old time, and amongst them Wood-wont stood with his fiddle amidst the Hall and Bow-may beside him, and they sang in turn to it sweetly and clearly; and this is some of what they sang:

She singeth.

Wild is the waste and long leagues over;
Whither then wend ye spear and sword,
Where nought shall see your helms but the plover,
Far and far from the dear Dale's sward?

He singeth.

Many a league shall we wend together
With helm and spear and bended bow.
Hark! how the wind blows up for weather:
Dark shall the night be whither we go.

Dark shall the night be round the byre,
  And dark as we drive the brindled kine;
Dark and dark round the beacon-fire,
  Dark down in the pass round our wavering line.

Turn on thy path, O fair-foot maiden,
  And come our ways by the pathless road;
Look how the clouds hang low and laden
  Over the walls of the old abode!

She singeth.

Bare are my feet for the rough waste's wending,
  Wild is the wind, and my kirtle's thin;
Faint shall I be ere the long way's ending
  Drops down to the Dale and the grief therein.

He singeth.
Do on the brogues of the Wild-wood rover,
  Do on the byrnies" ring-close mail;
Take thou the staff that the barbs hang over,
  O'er the wind and the waste and the way to prevail.

Come, for how from thee shall I sunder?
  Come, that a tale may arise in the land;
Come, that the night may be held for a wonder,
  When the Wolf was led by a maiden's hand!

She singeth.
Now will I fare as ye are faring,
  And wend no way but the way ye wend;
And bear but the burdens ye are bearing,
  And end the day as ye shall end.

And many an eve when the clouds are drifting
  Down through the Dale till they dim the roof,
Shall they tell in the Hall of the Maiden's Lifting,
  And how we drave the spoil aloof.

They sing together.
Over the moss through the wind and the weather,
  Through the morn and the eve and the death of the day,
Wend we man and maid together,
  For out of the waste is born the fray.

Then the Sun-beam spake to Gold-mane softly, and told him how this song was made by a minstrel concerning a foray in the early days of their first abode in Shadowy Vale, and how in good sooth a maiden led the fray and was the captain of the warriors:

"Erst," she said, "this was counted as a wonder; but now we are so few that it is no wonder though the women will do whatsoever they may."

So they talked, and Gold-mane was very happy; but ere the good-night cup was drunk, Folk-might spake to Face-of-god and said:

"It were well that ye rose betimes in the morning: but thou shalt not go back by the way thou camest. Wood-wise and another shall go with thee, and show thee a way across the necks and the heaths, which is rough enough as far as toil goes, but where thy life shall be safer; and thereby shalt thou hit the ghyll of the Weltering Water, and so come down safely into Burgdale. Now that we are friends and fellows, it is no hurt for thee to know the shortest way to Shadowy Vale. What thou shalt tell concerning us in Burgdale I leave the tale thereof to thee; yet belike thou wilt not tell everything till I come to Burgstead at the spring market-tide. Now must I presently to bed; for before daylight to-morrow must I be following the hunt along with two score good men of ours."

"What beast is afield then?" said Gold-mane.

Said Folk-might: "The beasts that beset our lives, the Dusky Men. In these days we have learned how to find companies of them; and forsooth every week they draw nigher to this Dale; and some day they should happen upon us if we were not to look to it, and then would there be a murder great and grim; therefore we scour the heaths round about, and the skirts of the woodland, and we fall upon these felons in divers guises, so that they may not know us for the same men; whiles are we clad in homespun, as to-day, and seem like to field-working carles; whiles in scarlet and gold, like knights of the Westland; whiles in wolf-skins; whiles in white glittering gear, like the Wights of the Waste: and in all guises these felons, for all their fierce hearts, fear us, and flee from us, and we follow and slay them, and so minish their numbers somewhat against the great day of battle."

"Tell me," said Gold-mane; "when we fall upon Silverdale shall their thralls, the old Dale-dwellers, fight for them or for us?"

Said Folk-might: "The Dusky Men will not dare to put weapons into the hands of their thralls. Nay, the thralls shall help us; for though they have but small stomach for the fight, yet joyfully when the fight is over shall they cut their masters" throats."

"How is it with these thralls?" said Gold-mane. "I have never seen a thrall."

"But I," said Folk-might, "have seen a many down in the Cities. And there were thralls who were the tyrants of thralls, and held the whip over them; and of the others there were some who were not very hardly entreated. But with these it is otherwise, and they all bear grievous pains daily; for the Dusky Men are as hogs in a garden of lilies. Whatsoever is fair there have they defiled and deflowered, and they wallow in our fair halls as swine strayed from the dunghill. No delight in life, no sweet days do they have for themselves, and they begrudge the delight of others therein. Therefore their thralls know no rest or solace; their reward of toil is many stripes, and the healing of their stripes grievous toil. To many have they appointed to dig and mine in the silver-yielding cliffs, and of all the tasks is that the sorest, and there do stripes abound the most. Such thralls art thou happy not to behold till thou hast set them free; as we shall do."

"Tell me again," said Face-of-god; "Is there no mixed folk between these Dusky Men and the Dalesmen, since they have no women of their own, but lie with the women of the Dale? Moreover, do not the poor folk of the Dale beget and bear children, so that there are thralls born of thralls?"

"Wisely thou askest this," said Folk-might, "but thereof shall I tell thee, that when a Dusky Carle mingles with a woman of the Dale, the child which she beareth shall oftenest favour his race and not hers; or else shall it be witless, a fool natural. But as for the children of these poor thralls; yea, the masters cause them to breed if so their masterships will, and when the children are born, they keep them or slay them as they will, as they would with whelps or calves. To be short,

year by year these vile wretches grow fiercer and more beastly, and their thralls more hapless and down-trodden; and now at last is come the time either to do or to die, as ye men of Burgdale shall speedily find out. But now must I go sleep if I am to be where I look to be at sunrise to-morrow."

Therewith he called for the sleeping-cup, and it was drunk, and all men fared to bed. But the Sun-beam took Gold-mane's hand ere they parted, and said:

"I shall arise betimes on the morrow; so I say not farewell to-night; yea, and after to-morrow it shall not be long ere we meet again."

So Gold-mane lay down in that ancient hall, and it seemed to him ere he slept as if his own kindred were slipping away from him and he were becoming a child of the Wolf. "And yet," said he to himself, "I am become a man; for my Friend, now she no longer telleth me to do or forbear, and I tremble. Nay, rather she is fain to take the word from me; and this great warrior and ripe man, he talketh with me as if I were a chieftain meet for converse with chieftains. Even so it is and shall be."

And soon thereafter he fell asleep in the Hall in Shadowy Vale.

21. FACE-OF-GOD LOOKETH ON THE DUSKY MEN

When he awoke again he saw a man standing over him, and knew him for Wood-wise: he was clad in his war-gear, and had his quiver at his back and his bow in his hand, for Wood-father's children were all good bowmen, though not so sure as Bow-may. He spake to Face-of-god:

"Dawn is in the sky, Dalesman; there is yet time for thee to wash the night off of thee in our bath of the Shivering Flood and to put thy mouth to the milk-bowl; but time for nought else: for I and Bow-may are appointed thy fellows for the road, and it were well that we were back home speedily."

So Face-of-god leapt up and went forth from the Hall, and Wood-wise led to where was a pool in the river with steps cut down to it in the rocky bank.

"This," said Wood-wise, "is the Carle's Bath; but the Queen's is lower down, where the water is wider and shallower below the little mid-dale force."

So Gold-mane stripped off his raiment and leapt into the ice-cold pool; and they had brought his weapons and war-gear with them; so when he came out he clad and armed himself for the road, and then turned with Wood-wise toward the outgate of the Dale; and soon they saw two men coming from lower down the water in such wise that they would presently cross their path, and as yet it was little more than twilight, so that they saw not at first who they were, but as they drew nearer they knew them for the Sun-beam and Bow-may. The Sun-

beam was clad but in her white linen smock and blue gown as he had first seen her, her hair was wet and dripping with the river, her face fresh and rosy: she carried in her two hands a great bowl of milk, and stepped delicately, lest she should spill it. But Bow-may was clad in her war-gear with helm and byrny, and a quiver at her back, and a bended bow in her hand. So they greeted each other kindly, and the Sun-beam gave the bowl to Face-of-god and said:

"Drink, guest, for thou hast a long and thirsty road before thee."

So Face-of-god drank, and gave her the bowl back again, and she smiled on him and drank, and the others after her till the bowl was empty: then Bow-may put her hand on Wood-wise's shoulder, and they led on toward the outgate, while those twain followed them hand in hand. But the Sun-beam said:

"This then is the new day I spoke of, and lo! it bringeth our sundering with it; yet shall it be no longer than a day when all is said, and new days shall follow after. And now, my friend, I shall see thee no later than the April market; for doubt not that I shall go thither with Folk-might, whether he will or not. Also as I led thee out of the house when we last met, so shall I lead thee out of the Dale to-day, and I will go with thee a little way on the waste; and therefore am I shod this morning, as thou seest, for the ways on the waste are rough. And now I bid thee have courage while my hand holdeth thine. For afterwards I need not bid thee anything; for thou wilt have enough to do when thou comest to thy Folk, and must needs think more of warriors then than of maidens."

He looked at her and longed for her, but said soberly: "Thou art kind, O friend, and thinkest kindly of me ever. But methinks it were not well done for thee to wend with me over a deal of the waste, and come back by thyself alone, when ye have so many foemen nearby."

"Nay," she said, "they be nought so near as that yet, and I wot that Folk-might hath gone forth toward the north-west, where he looketh to fall in with a company of the foemen. His battle shall be a guard unto us."

"I pray thee turn back at the top of the outgate," said he, "and be not venturesome. Thou wottest that the pitcher is not broken the first time it goeth to the well, nor maybe the twentieth, but at last it cometh not back."

She said: "Nevertheless I shall have my will herein. And it is but a little way I will wend with thee."

Therewith were they come to the scree, and talk fell down between them as they clomb it; but when they were in the darksome passage of the rocks, and could scarce see one another, Face-of-god said:

"Where then is another outgate from the Dale? Is it not up the water?"

"Yea," she said, "and there is none other: at the lower end the rocks rise sheer from out the water, and a little further down is a great force thundering betwixt them; so that by no boat or raft may ye come out of the Dale. But the outgate up the water is called the Road of War, as this is named the Path of Peace. But now are all ways ways of war."

"There is peace in my heart," said Gold-mane.

She answered not for a while, but pressed his hand, and he felt her breath on his cheek; and even therewithal they came out of the dark, and Gold-mane saw that her cheek was flushed; and now she spake:

"One thing would I say to thee, my friend. Thou hast seen me amongst men of war, amongst outlaws who seek violence; thou hast heard me bid my brother to count the slain, and I shrinking not; thou knowest (for I have told thee) how I have schemed and schemed for victorious battle. Yet I would not have thee think of me as a Chooser of the Slain, a warrior maiden, or as of one who hath no joy save in the battle whereto she biddeth others. O friend, the many peaceful hours that I have had on the grass down yonder, sitting with my rock and spindle in hand, the children round about my knees hearkening to some old story so well remembered by me! or the milking of the kine in the dewy summer even, when all was still but for the voice of the water and the cries of the happy children, and there round about me were the dear and beauteous maidens with whom I had grown up, happy amidst all our troubles, since their life was free and they knew no guile. In such times my heart was at peace indeed, and it seemed to me as if we had won all we needed; as if war and turmoil were over, after they had brought about peace and good days for our little folk.

"And as for the days that be, are they not as that rugged pass, full of bitter winds and the voice of hurrying waters, that leadeth yonder to Silverdale, as thou hast divined? and there is nought good in it save that the breath of life is therein, and that it leadeth to pleasant places and the peace and plenty of the fair dale."

"Sweet friend," he said, "what thou sayest is better than well: for time shall be, if we come alive out of this pass of battle and bitter strife, when I shall lead thee into Burgdale to dwell there. And thou wottest of our people that there is little strife and grudging amongst them, and that they are merry, and fair to look on, both men and women; and no man there lacketh what the earth may give us, and it is a saying amongst us that there may a man have that which he desireth save the sun and moon in his hands to play with: and of this gladness, which is made up of many little matters, what story may be told? Yet amongst it shall I live and thou with me; and ill indeed it were if it wearied thee and thou wert ever longing for some day of victorious strife, and to behold me coming back from battle high-raised on the shields of men and crowned with bay; if thine ears must ever be tickled with the talk of men and their songs concerning my warrior deeds. For thus it shall not be. When I drive the herds it shall be at the neighbours" bidding whereso they will; not necks of men shall I smite, but the stalks of the tall wheat, and the boles of the timber-trees which the woodreeve hath marked for felling; the stilts of the plough rather than the hilts of the sword shall harden my hands; my shafts shall be for the deer, and my spears for the wood-boar, till war and sorrow fall upon us, and I fight for the ceasing of war and trouble. And though I be called a chief and of the blood of chiefs, yet shall I not be masterful to the goodman of the Dale, but rather to my hound; for my chieftainship shall be that I shall be well beloved and trusted, and that no man shall grudge against me. Canst thou learn to love such a life, which to me seemeth lovely? And thou? of whom I say that thou art as if thou wert come down from the golden chairs of the Burg of the Gods."

They were well-nigh out of the steep path by now, and the daylight was bright about them; there she stayed her feet a moment and turned to him and said:

"All this should I love even now, if the grief of our Folk were but healed, and hereafter shall I learn yet more of thy well-beloved face."

Therewith she laid her face to his and kissed him fondly, and put his hand to her side and held it there, saying: "Soon shall we be one in body and in soul."

And he laughed with joy and pride of life, and took her hand and led her on again, and said:

"Yet feel the cold rings of my hauberk, my friend; look at the spears that cumber my hand, and at Dale-warden hanging by my side. Thou shalt yet see me as the Slain's Chooser would see her speech-friend; for there is much to do ere we win wheat-harvest in Burgdale."

Therewith they stepped together on to the level ground of the waste, and saw Bow-may sitting on a stone hard by, and Wood-wise standing beside her bending his bow. Bow-may smiled on Gold-mane and rose up, and they all went on together, turning so that they went nearly alongside the wall of the Vale, but westering a little; then the Sun-beam said:

"Many a time have I trodden this heath alongside our rock-wall; for if ye wend a little further as our faces are turned, ye come to the crags over the place where the Shivering Flood goeth out of Shadowy Vale. There when ye have clomb a little may'st thou stand on the edge of the rock-wall, and look down and behold the Flood swirling and eddying in the black gorge of the rocks, and see presently the reek of the force go up, and hear the thunder of the waters as they pour over it: and all this about us now is as the garden of our house—is it not so, Bow-may?"

"Yea," said she, "and there are goodly cluster-berries to be gotten hereabout in the autumn; many a time have the Sun-beam and I reddened our lips with them. Yet is it best to be wary when war is abroad and hot withal."

"Yea," said the Sun-beam, "and all this place comes into the story of our House: lo! Gold-mane, two score paces before us a little on our right hand those five grey stones. They are called the Rocks of the Elders: for there in the first days of our abiding in Shadowy Vale the Elders were wont to come together to talk privily upon our matters."

Face-of-god looked thither as she spoke, but therewith saw Bow-may, who went on the left hand of the Sun-beam, as Face-of-god on her right hand, notch a shaft on her bent bow, and Wood-wise, who was on his right hand, saw it also and did the like, and therewithal Face-of-god got his target on to his arm, and even as he did so Bow-may cried out suddenly:

"Yea, yea! Cast thyself on to the ground, Sun-beam! Gold-mane, targe and spear, targe and spear! For I see steel gleaming yonder out from behind the Elders" Rocks."

Scarce were the words out of her mouth ere three shafts came flying, and the bow-strings twanged. Gold-mane felt that one smote his helm and glanced from it. Therewithal he saw the Sun-beam fall to earth, though he knew not if she had but cast herself down as Bow-may bade. Bow-may's string twanged at once, and a yell came from the foemen: but Wood-wise loosed not, but set his hand to his mouth and gave a loud

wild cry—Ha! ha! ha! ha! How-ow-ow!—ending in a long and exceeding great whoop like nought but the wolf's howl. Now Gold-mane thinking swiftly, in a moment of time, as war-meet men do, judged that if the Sun-beam were hurt (and she had made no cry), it were yet wiser to fall on the foe before turning to tend her, or else all might be lost; so he rushed forward spear in hand and target on arm, and saw, as he opened up the flank of the Elders" Rocks, six men, whereof one leaned aback on the rock with Bow-may's shaft in his shoulder, and two others were just in act of loosing at him. In a moment, as he rushed at them, one shaft went whistling by him, and the other glanced from off his target; he cast a spear as he bounded on, and saw it smite one of the shooters full in the naked face, and saw the blood spout out and change his face and the man roll over, and then in another moment four men were hewing at him with their short steel axes. He thrust out his target against them, and then let the weight of his body come on his other spear, and drave it through the second shooter's throat, and even therewith was smitten on the helm so hard that, though the Alderman's work held out, he fell to his knees, holding his target over his head and striving to draw forth Dale-warden; in that nick of time a shaft whistled close by his ear, and as he rose to his feet again he saw his foeman rolling over and over, clutching at the ling with both hands. Then rang out again the terrible wolf-whoop from Wood-wise's mouth, and both he and Bow-may loosed a shaft, for the two other foes had turned their backs and were fleeing fast. Again Bow-may hit the clout, and the Dusky Man fell dead at once, but Wood-wise's arrow flew over the felon's shoulder as he ran. Then in a trice was Gold-mane bounding after him like the hare just roused from her form; for it came into his head that these felons had beheld them coming up out of the Vale, and that if even this one man escaped, he would bring his company down upon the Vale-dwellers.

Strong and light-foot as any was Face-of-god, and though he was cumbered with his hauberk, yet was Iron-face's handiwork far lighter than the war-coat of the Dusky Man, and the race was soon over. The felon turned breathless to meet Gold-mane, who drave his target against him and cast him to earth, and as he strove to rise smote off his head at one stroke; for Dale-warden was a good sword and the Dalesman as fierce of mood as might be. There he let the felon lie, and, turning, walked back swiftly toward the Elders" Rocks, and found there Wood-wise and the dead foemen, for the carle had slain the wounded, and he was now drawing the silver arm-rings off the slain men; for all these Dusky Felons bore silver arm-rings. But Bow-may was walking towards the Sun-beam, and thitherward followed Gold-mane speedily.

He found her sitting on a tussock of grass close by where she had fallen, her face pale, her eyes eager and gleaming; she looked up at him as he drew nigher and said:

"Friend, art thou hurt?"

"Nay," he said, "and thou? Thou art pale."

"I am not hurt," she said. Then she smiled and said again:

"Did I not tell thee that I am no warrior like Bow-may here? Such deeds make maidens pale."

Said Bow-may: "If ye will have the truth, Gold-mane, she is not wont to grow pale when battle is nigh her. Look you, she hath had the gift of a new delight, and findeth it sweeter and softer than she had any thought of; and now hath she feared lest it should be taken from her."

"Bow-may saith but the sooth," said the Sun-beam simply, "and kind it is of her to say it. I saw thee, Bow-may, and good was thy shooting, and I love thee for it."

Said Bow-may: "I never shoot otherwise than well. But those idle shooters of the Dusky Ones, whereabouts nigh to thee went their shafts?"

Said the Sun-beam: "One just lifted the hair by my left ear, and that was not so ill-aimed; as for the other, it pierced my raiment by my right knee, and pinned me to the earth, so that I tottered and fell, and my gown and smock are grievously wounded, both of them."

And she took the folds of the garments in her hands to show the rents therein; and her colour was come again, and she was glad.

"What were best to do now?" she said.

Said Face-of-god: "Let us tarry a little; for some of thy carles shall surely come up from the Vale: because they will have heard Wood-wise's whoop, since the wind sets that way."

"Yea, they will come," said the Sun-beam.

"Good is that," said Face-of-god; "for they shall take the dead felons and cast them where they be not seen if perchance any more stray hereby. For if they wind them, they may well happen on the path down to the Vale. Also, my friend, it were well if thou wert to bid a good few of the carles that are in the Vale to keep watch and ward about here, lest there be more foemen wandering about the waste."

She said: "Thou art wise in war, Gold-mane; I will do as thou biddest me. But soothly this is a perilous thing that the Dusky Men are gotten so close to the Vale."

Said Face-of-god: "This will Folk-might look to when he cometh home; and it is most like that he will deem it good to fall on them somewhere a good way aloof, so as to draw them off from wandering over the waste. Also I will do my best to busy them when I am home in Burgdale."

Therewith came up Wood-wise, and fell to talk with them; and his mind it was that these foemen were but a band of stray-ers, and had had no inkling of Shadowy Vale till they had heard them talking together as they came up the path from the Vale, and that then they had made that ambush behind the Elders" Rocks, so that they might slay the men, and then bear off the woman. He said withal that it would be best to carry their corpses further on, so that they might be cast over the cliffs into the fierce stream of the Shivering Flood.

Amidst this talk came up men from the Vale, a score of them, well armed; and they ran to meet the wayfarers; and when they heard what had befallen, they rejoiced exceedingly, and were above all glad that Face-of-god had shown himself doughty and deft; and they deemed his rede wise, to set a watch thereabouts till Folk-might came home, and said that they would do even so.

Then spake the Sun-beam and said:

"Now must ye wayfarers depart; for the road is but rough, and the day not over-long."

Then she turned to Face-of-god and put her hand on his shoulder, and brought her face close to his and spake to him softly:

"Doth this second parting seem at all strange to thee, and that I am now so familiar to thee, I whom thou didst once deem to be a very goddess? And now thou hast seen me red-den before thine eyes because of thee; and thou hast seen me grow pale with fear because of thee; and thou hast felt my caresses which I might not refrain; even as if I were altogether such a maiden as ye warriors hang about for a nine days" won-der, and then all is over save an aching heart—wilt thou do so with me? Tell me, have I not belittled myself before thee as if I asked thee to scorn me? For thus desire dealeth both with maid and man."

He said: "In all this there is but one thing for me to say, and that is that I love thee; and surely none the less, but rather the more, because thou lovest me, and art of my kind, and mayest share in my deeds and think well of them. Now is my heart full of joy, and one thing only weigheth on it; and that is that my kinswoman the Bride begrudgeth our love together. For this is the thing that of all things most misliketh me, that any should bear a grudge against me."

She said: "Forget not the token, and my message to her."

"I will not forget it," said he. "And now I bid thee to kiss me even before all these that are looking on; for there is nought to belittle us therein, since we be troth-plight."

And indeed those folk stood all round about them gazing on them, but a little aloof, that they might not hear their words if they were minded to talk privily. For they had long loved the Sun-beam, and now the love of Face-of-god had begun to spring up in their hearts.

So the twain embraced and kissed one another, and made no haste thereover; and those men deemed that but meet and right, and clashed their weapons on their shields in token of their joy.

Then Face-of-god turned about and strode out of the ring of men, with Bow-may and Wood-wise beside him, and they went on their journey over the necks towards Burgstead. But the Sun-beam turned slowly from that place toward the Vale, and two of the stoutest carles went along with her to guard her from harm, and she went down into the Vale pondering all these things in her heart.

Then the other carles dragged off the corpses of the Dusky Men till they had brought them to the sheer rocks above the Shivering Flood, and there they tossed them over into the boiling caldron of the force, and so departed taking with them the silver arm-rings of the slain to add to the tale.

But when they came back into the Vale the Sun-beam duly ordered that watch and ward to keep the ingate thereto, and note all that should befall till Folk-might came home.

22. FACE-OF-GOD COMETH HOME TO BURGSTEAD

But Face-of-god with Bow-may and Wood-wise fared over the waste, going at first alongside the cliffs of the Shivering Flood, and then afterwards turning somewhat to the west. They soon had to climb a very high and steep bent going up to a mountain-neck; and the way over the neck was rough indeed when they were on it, and they toiled out of it into a barren valley, and out of the valley again on to a rough neck; and such-like their journey the day long, for they were going athwart all those great dykes that went from the ice-mountains toward the lower dales like the outspread fingers of a hand or the roots of a great tree. And the ice-mountains they had on their left hands and whiles at their backs.

They went very warily, with their bows bended and spear in hand, but saw no man, good or bad, and but few living things. At noon they rested in a valley where was a stream, but no grass, nought but stones and sand; but where they were at least sheltered from the wind, which was mostly very great in these high wastes; and there Bow-may drew meat and wine from a wallet she bore, and they ate and drank, and were merry enough; and Bow-may said:

"I would I were going all the way with thee, Gold-mane; for I long sore to let my eyes rest a while on the land where I shall one day live."

"Yea," said Face-of-god, "art thou minded to dwell there? We shall be glad of that."

"Whither are thy wits straying?" said she; "whether I am minded to it or not, I shall dwell there."

And Wood-wise nodded a yea to her. But Face-of-god said:

"Good will be thy dwelling; but wherefore must it be so?"

Then Wood-wise laughed and said: "I shall tell thee in fewer words than she will, and time presses now: Wood-father and Wood-mother, and I and my two brethren and this woman have ever been about and anigh the Sun-beam; and we deem that war and other troubles have made us of closer kin to her than we were born, whether ye call it brotherhood or what not, and never shall we sunder from her in life or in death. So when thou goest to Burgdale with her, there shall we be."

Then was Face-of-god glad when he found that they deemed his wedding so settled and sure; but Wood-wise fell to making ready for the road. And Face-of-god said to him:

"Tell me one thing, Wood-wise; that whoop that thou gavest forth when we were at handy-strokes e'en now—is it but a cry of thine own or is it of thy Folk, and shall I hear it again?"

"Thou may'st look to hear it many a time," said Wood-wise, "for it is the cry of the Wolf. Seldom indeed hath battle been joined where men of our blood are, but that cry is given forth. Come now, to the road!"

So they went their ways and the road worsened upon them, and toilsome was the climbing up steep bents and the scaling of doubtful paths in the cliff-sides, so that the journey, though the distance of it were not so long to the fowl flying, was much eked out for them, and it was not till near nightfall that they came on the ghyll of the Weltering Water some six miles above Burgstead. Forsooth Wood-wise said that the way might be made less toilsome though far longer by turning back eastward a little past the vale where they had rested at midday; and that seemed good to Gold-mane, in case they should be wending hereafter in a great company between Burgdale and Shadowy Vale.

But now those two went with Face-of-god down a path in the side of the cliff whereby him-seemed he had gone before; and they came down into the ghyll and sat down together on a stone by the water-side, and Face-of-god spake to them kindly, for he deemed them good and trusty faring-fellows.

"Bow-may," said he, "thou saidst a while ago that thou wouldst be fain to look on Burgdale; and indeed it is fair and lovely, and ye may soon be in it if ye will. Ye shall both be more than welcome to the house of my father, and heartily I bid you thither. For night is on us, and the way back is long and toilsome and beset with peril. Sister Bow-may, thou wottest that it would be a sore grief to me if thou camest to any harm, and thou also, fellow Wood-wise. Daylight is a good faring-fellow over the waste."

Said Bow-may: "Thou art kind, Gold-mane, and that is thy wont, I know; and fain were I to-night of the candles in thine hall. But we may not tarry; for thou wottest how busy we be at home; and Sun-beam needeth me, if it were only to make her sure that no Dusky Man is bearing off thine head by its lovely locks. Neither shall we journey in the mirk night; for look you, the moon yonder."

"Well," said Face-of-god, "parting is ill at the best, and I would I could give you twain a gift, and especially to thee, my sister Bow-may."

Said Wood-wise: "Thou may'st well do that; or at least promise the gift; and that is all one as if we held it in our hands."

"Yea," said Bow-may, "Wood-wise and I have been thinking in one way belike; and I was at point to ask a gift of thee."

"What is it?" said Gold-mane. "Surely it is thine, if it were but a guerdon for thy good shooting."

She laughed and handled the skirts of his hauberk as she said:

"Show us the dint in thine helm that the steel axe made this morning."

"There is no such great dint," said he; "my father forged that helm, and his work is better than good."

"Yea," said Bow-may, "and might I have hauberk and helm of his handiwork, and Wood-wise a good sword of the same, then were I a glad woman, and this man a happy carle."

Said Gold-mane: "I am well pleased at thine asking, and so shall Iron-face be when he heareth of thine archery; and how that Hall-face were now his only son but for thy close shooting. But now must I to the way; for my heart tells me that there may have been tidings in Burgstead this while I have been aloof."

So they rose all three, and Bow-may said:

"Thou art a kind brother, and soon shall we meet again; and that will be well."

Then he put his hands on her shoulders and kissed both her cheeks; and he kissed Wood-wise, and turned and went his ways, threading the stony tangle about the Weltering Water, which was now at middle height, and running clear and strong; so turning once he beheld Wood-wise and Bow-may climbing the path up the side of the ghyll, and Bow-may turned to him also and waved her bow as token of farewell. Then he went upon his way, which was rough enough to follow by night, though the moon was shining brightly high aloft. Yet as he knew his road he made but little of it all, and in somewhat more than an hour and a half was come out of the pass into the broken ground at the head of the Dale, and began to make his way speedily under the bright moonlight toward the Gate, still going close by the water. But as he went he heard of a sudden cries and rumour not far from him, unwonted in that place, where none dwelt, and where the only folk he might look to

see were those who cast an angle into the pools and eddies of the Water. Moreover, he saw about the place whence came the cries torches moving swiftly hither and thither; so that he looked to hear of new tidings, and stayed his feet and looked keenly about him on every side; and just then, between his rough path and the shimmer of the dancing moonlit water, he saw the moon smite on something gleaming; so, as quietly as he could, he got his target on his arm, and shortened his spear in his right hand, and then turned sharply toward that gleam. Even therewith up sprang a man on his right hand, and then another in front of him just betwixt him and the water; an axe gleamed bright in the moon, and he caught a great stroke on his target, and therewith drave his left shoulder straight forward, so that the man before him fell over into the water with a mighty splash; for they were at the very edge of the deepest eddy of the Water. Then he spun round on his heel, heeding not that another stroke had fallen on his right shoulder, yet ill-aimed, and not with the full edge, so that it ran down his byrny and rent it not. So he sent the thrust of his spear crashing through the face and skull of the smiter, and looked not to him as he fell, but stood still, brandishing his spear and crying out, "For the Burg and the Face! For the Burg and the Face!"

No other foe came against him, but like to the echo of his cry rose a clear shout not far aloof, "For the Face, for the Face! For the Burg and the Face!" He muttered, "So ends the day as it begun," and shouted loud again, "For the Burg and the Face!" And in a minute more came breaking forth from the stone-heaps into the moonlit space before the water the tall shapes of the men of Burgstead, the red torchlight and the moonlight flashing back from their war-gear and weapons; for every man had his sword or spear in hand.

Hall-face was the first of them, and he threw his arms about his brother and said: "Well met, Gold-mane, though thou comest amongst us like Stone-fist of the Mountain. Art thou hurt? With whom hast thou dealt? Where be they? Whence comest thou?"

"Nay, I am not hurt," said Face-of-god. "Stint thy questions then, till thou hast told me whom thou seekest with spear and sword and candle."

"Two felons were they," said Hall-face, "even such as ye saw lying dead at Wood-grey's the other day."

"Then may ye sheathe your swords and go home," said Gold-mane, "for one lieth at the bottom of the eddy, and the other, thy feet are well-nigh treading on him, Hall-face."

Then arose a rumour of praise and victory, and they brought the torches nigh and looked at the fallen man, and found that he was stark dead; so they even let him lie there till the morrow, and all turned about toward the Thorp; and many looked on Face-of-god and wondered concerning him, whence he was and what had befallen him. Indeed, they would have asked him thereof, but could not get at him to ask; but whoso could, went as nigh to Hall-face and him as they might, to hearken to the talk between the brothers.

So as they went along Hall-face did verily ask him whence he came: "For was it not so," said he, "that thou didst enter into the wood seeking some adventure early in the morning the day before yesterday?"

"Sooth is that," said Face-of-god, "and I came to Shadowy Vale, and thence am I come this morning."

Said Hall-face: "I know not Shadowy Vale, nor doth any of us. This is a new word. How say ye, friends, doth any man here know of Shadowy Vale?"

They all said, "Nay."

Then said Hall-face: "Hast thou been amongst mere ghosts and marvels, brother, or cometh this tale of thy minstrelsy?"

"For all your words," said Gold-mane, "to that Vale have I been; and, to speak shortly (for I desire to have your tale, and am waiting for it), I will tell thee that I found there no marvels or strange wights, but a folk of valiant men; a folk small in numbers, but great of heart; a folk come, as we be, from the Fathers and the Gods. And this, moreover, is to be said of them, that they are the foes of these felons of whom ye were chasing these twain. And these same Dusky Men of Silverdale would slay them every man if they might; and if we look not to it they will soon be doing the same by us; for they are many, and as venomous as adders, as fierce as bears, and as foul as swine. But these valiant men, who bear on their banner the image of the Wolf, should be our fellows in arms, and they have good will thereto; and they shall show us the way to Silverdale by blind paths, so that we may fall upon these felons while they dwell there tormenting the poor people of the land, and thus may we destroy them as lads a hornet's nest. Or else the days shall be hard for us."

The men who hung about them drank in his words greedily. But Hall-face was silent a little while, and then he said: "Brother Gold-mane, these be great tidings. Time was when we might have deemed them but a minstrel's tale; for Silverdale we know not, of which thou speakest so glibly, nor the Dusky Men, any more than the Shadowy Vale. Howbeit, things have befallen these two last days so strange and new, that putting them together with the murder at Wood-grey's, and thy words which seem somewhat wild, it may well seem to us that tidings unlooked for are coming our way."

"Come, then," said Face-of-god, "give me what thou hast in thy scrip, and trust me, I shall not jeer at thy tale."

Said Hall-face: "I also will be short with the tale; and that the more, as meseemeth it is not yet done, and that thou thyself shalt share in the ending of it. It was the day before yesterday, that is the day when thou departedst into the woods on that adventure whereof thou shalt one day tell me more, wilt thou

not?"

"Yea, in good time," said Face-of-god.

"Well," quoth Hall-face, "we went into the woods that day and in the morning, but after sunrise, to the number of a score: we looked to meet a bear and a she-bear with cubs in a certain place; for one of the Woodlanders, a keen hunter, had told us of their lair. Also we were wishful to slay some of the wild-swine, the yearlings, if we might. Therefore, though we had no helms or shields or coats of fence, we had bowshot a plenty, and good store of casting-weapons, besides our wood-knives and an axe or so; and some of us, of whom I was one, bore our battle-swords, as we are wont ever to do, be the foe beast or man.

"Thus armed we went up Wildlake's Way and came to Carl-stead, where half-a-score Woodlanders joined themselves to us, so that we became a band. We went up the half-cleared places past Carlstead for a mile, and then turned east into the wood, and went I know not how far, for the Woodlanders led us by crooked paths, but two hours wore away in our going, till we came to the place where they looked to find the bears. It is a place that may well be noted, for it is unlike the wood round about. There is a close thicket some two furlongs about of thorn and briar and ill-grown ash and oak and other trees, planted by the birds belike; and it stands as it were in an island amidst of a wide-spreading woodlawn of fine turf, set about in the most goodly fashion with great tall straight-boled oak-trees, that seem to have been planted of set purpose by man's hand. Yea, dost thou know the place?"

"Methinks I do," said Gold-mane, "and I seem to have heard the Woodlanders give it a name and call it Boars-bait."

"That may be," said Hall-face. "Well, there we were, the dogs and the men, and we drew nigh the thicket and beset it, and doubted not to find prey therein: but when we would set the dogs at the thicket to enter it, they were uneasy, and would not take up the slot, but growled and turned about this way and that, so that we deemed that they winded some fierce beast at our flanks or backs.

"Even so it was, and fierce enough and deadly was the beast; for suddenly we heard bow-strings twang, and shafts came flying; and Iron-shield of the Upper Dale, who was close beside me, leapt up into the air and fell down dead with an arrow through his back. Then I bethought me in the twinkling of an eye, and I cried out, "The foe are on us! take the cover of the tree-boles and be wary! For the Burg and the Face! For the Burg and the Face!"

"So we scattered and covered ourselves with the oak-boles, but besides Iron-shield, who was slain outright, two goodmen were sorely hurt, to wit Bald-face, a man of our house, and Stonyford of the Lower Dale.

"I looked from behind my tree-bole, a great one; and far off down the glades I saw men moving, clad in gay raiment; but nearer to me, not a hundred yards from my cover, I saw an arm clad in scarlet come out from behind a tree-bole, so I loosed at it, and missed not; for straight there tottered out from behind the tree one of those dusky foul-favoured men like to those that were slain by Wood-grey. I had another shaft ready notched, so I loosed and set the shaft in his throat, and he fell.

"Straightway was a yelling and howling about us like the cries of scalded curs, and the oak-wood swarmed thick with these felons rushing on us; for it seems that the man whom I had slain was a chief amongst them, or we judged so by his goodly raiment.

"Methought then our last day was come. What could we do but run together again after we had loosed at a venture, and so withstand them sword and spear in hand? Some fell beneath our shot, but not many, for they came on very swiftly.

"So they fell on us; but for all their fierceness and their numbers they might not break our array, and we slew four and hurt many by sword-hewing and spear-casting and push of spear; and five of us were hurt and one slain by their dart-casting. So they drew off from us a little, and strove to spread out and fall to shooting at us again; but this we would not suffer, but pushed on as they fell back, keeping as close together as we might for the trees. For we said that we would all die together if needs must; and verily the stour was hard.

"Yet hearken! In that nick of time rose up a strange cry not far from us, Ha! ha! ha! ha! How-ow-ow! ending like the howl of a wolf, and then another and another and another, till the whole wood rang again.

"At first we deemed that here were come fresh foemen, and that we were undone indeed; but when they heard it, the foemen before us faltered and gave way, and at last turned their backs and fled, and we followed, keeping well together still: thereby the more part of these men escaped us, for they fled wildly here and there from those who bore that cry with them; so we knew that our work was being done for us; therefore we stood, and saw tall men clad in sheep-brown weed running through the glades pursuing those felons and smiting them down, till both fleers and pursuers passed out of our sight like men in a dream, or as when ye roll up a pictured cloth to lay it in the coffer.

"But to Stone-face's mind those brown-clad men were the Wights of the Wood that be of the Fathers" blood, and our very friends; and when some of us would yet have gone forward and foregathered with them, and followed the chase along with them, Stone-face gainsaid it, bidding us not to run into the arms of a second death, when we had but just escaped from the first. Sooth to say, moreover, we had divers hurt men that needed looking to.

"So what with one thing, what with another, we turned back: but War-cliff's brother, a tall man, had felled two of those felons with an oak sapling which he had torn from the thicket; but he had not slain them, and by now they were just awakening from their swoon, and were sitting up looking round them with fierce rolling eyes, expecting the stroke, for Raven of Longscree was standing over them with a naked war-sword in his hand. But now that our blood was cool, we were loth to slay them as they lay in our hands; so we bound them and brought them away with us; and our own dead we carried also on such biers as we might lightly make there, and with them three that were so grievously hurt that they might not go afoot, these we left at Carlstead: they were Tardy the Son of the Untamed, and Swan of Bull-meadow, both of the Lower Dale, and a Woodlander, Undoomed to wit. But the dead were Iron-shield aforesaid, and Wool-sark, and the Hewer, a Woodlander.

"So came we sadly at eventide to Burgstead with the two dead Burgdalers, and the captive felons, and the wounded of us that might go afoot; and ye may judge that they of Burgdale and our father deemed these tidings great enough, and wotted not what next should befall. Stone-face would have had those two felons slain there and then; for no true tale could we get out of them, nor indeed any word at all. But the Alderman would not have it so; and he deemed they might serve our turn as hostages if any of our folk should be taken: for one and all we deemed, and still deem, that war is on us and that new folk have gathered on our skirts.

"So the captives were shut up in the red out-bower of our house; and our father was minded that thou mightest tell us somewhat of them when thou wert come home. But about dusk to-day the word went that they had broken out and gotten them weapons and fled up the Dale; and so it was.

"But to-morrow morning will a Gate-thing be holden, and there it will be looked for of thee that thou tell us a true tale of thy goings. For it is deemed, and it is my deeming especially, that thou may'st tell us more of these men than thou hast yet told us. Is it not so?"

"Yea, surely," said Gold-mane, "I can make as many words as ye will about it; yet when all is said, it will come to much the same tale as I have already told thee. Yet belike, if ye are minded to take up the sword to defend you, I may tell you in what wise to lay hold on the hilts."

"And that is well," said Hall-face, "and no less do I look for of thee. But lo! here are we come to the Gate of the Burg that abideth battle."

23. TALK IN THE HALL OF THE HOUSE OF THE FACE

In sooth they were come to the very Gate of Burgstead, and the great gates were shut, and only a wicket was open, and a half score of stout men in all their war-gear were holding ward thereby. They gave place to Hall-face and his company, albeit some of the warders followed them through the wicket that they might hear the story told.

The street was full of folk, both men and women, talking together eagerly concerning all these tidings, and when they saw the men of the Hue-and-cry they came thronging about them, so that they might scarce get to the door of the House of the Face because of the press; so Hall-face (who was a very tall man) cried out:

"Good people, all is well! the Runaways are slain, and Face-of-god is come back with us; give place a little, that we may come into our house."

Then the throng set up a shout, and made way a little, so that Hall-face and Gold-mane and the others could get to the door. And they entered into the Hall, and saw much folk therein; and men were sitting at table, for supper was not yet over. But when they saw the new-comers they mostly rose up from the board and stood silent to hear the tale, for they had been talking many together each to each, so that the Hall was full of confused noise.

So Hall-face again cried out: "Men in this hall, good is the tidings. The Runaways are slain; and it was Face-of-god who slew them as he came back safe from the waste."

Then they shouted for joy, and the brethren and Stone-face with them (for he had entered with them from the street) went up on to the dais, while the others of the Hue-and-cry gat them seats where they might at the endlong tables.

But when Face-of-god came up on to the dais, there sat Iron-face looking down on the thronged Hall with a ruddy cheerful countenance, and beside him sat the Bride; for he had caused her to be brought thither when he had heard of the tidings of battle. She was daintily clad in a flame-coloured kirtle embroidered with gold about the bosom and sleeves, and there was a fillet of golden roses on her ruddy hair. Her eyes shone bright and eager, and the pommels of her cheeks were flushed and red contrary to their wont. Needs must Gold-mane sit by her, and when he came close to her he knew not what to do, but he put forth his hand to her, yet with a troubled countenance; for he feared her grief mingled with her beauty: as for her, she wavered in her mind whether she should forbear to touch him or not; but she saw that men about were looking at them, and especially was Iron-face looking on her: therefore she stood up and took Gold-mane's hand and kissed his face as she had been wont to do, and by then was her face as white as paper;

and her anguish pierced his heart, so that he well-nigh groaned for grief of her. But Iron-face looked on her and said kindly:

"Kinswoman, thou art pale; thou hast feared for thy mate amidst all these tidings of war, and still fearest for him. But pluck up a heart; for the man is a deft warrior for all his fair face, which thou lovest as a woman should, and his hands may yet save his head. And if he be slain, yet are there other men of the kindred, and the earth will not be a desert to thee even then."

She looked at Iron-face, and the colour was come back to her face somewhat, and she said:

"It is true; I have feared for him; for he goeth into perilous places. But for thee, thou art kind, and I thank thee for it."

And therewith she kissed Iron-face and sat down in her place, and strove to overmaster her grief, that her face might not be changed by it; for now were thoughts of battle, and valiant hopes arising in men's hearts; and it seemed to her too grievous if she should mar that feast on the eve of battle.

But Iron-face kissed and embraced his son and said: "Art thou late come from the waste? Hast thou seen new things? We look to have a notable tale from thee; though here also have been tidings, and it is not unlike that we shall presently have new work on our hands."

"Father," quoth Face-of-god, "I deem that when thou hast heard my tale thou wilt think no less of it than that there are valiant folk to be holpen, poor folk to be delivered, and evil folk to be swept from off the face of the earth."

"It is well, son," said Iron-face. "I see that thy tale is long; let it alone for to-night. To-morrow shall we hold a Gate-thing, and then shall we hear all that thou hast to tell. Now eat thy meat and drink a bowl of wine, and comfort thy troth-plight maiden."

So Gold-mane sat down by the Bride, and ate and drank as he needs must; but he was ill at ease and he durst not speak to her. For, on the one hand, he thought concerning his love for the Sun-beam, and how sweet and good a thing it was that she should take him by the hand and lead him into noble deeds and great fame, caressing him so softly and sweetly the while; and, on the other hand, there sat the Bride beside him, sorrowful and angry, begrudging all that sweetness of love, as though it were something foul and unseemly; and heavy on him lay the weight of that grudge, for he was a man of a friendly heart.

Stone-face sat outward from him on the other side of the Bride; and he leaned across her towards Gold-mane and said:

"Fair shall be thy tale to-morrow, if thou tellest us all thine adventure. Or wilt thou tell us less than all?"

Said Face-of-god: "In good time shalt thou know it all, foster-father; but it is not unlike that by the time that thou hast heard it, there shall be so many other things to tell of, that my tale shall seem of little account to thee—even as the saw saith that one nail driveth out the other."

"Yea," said Stone-face, "but one tale belike shall be knit up with the others, as it fareth with the figures that come one after other on the weaver's cloth; though one maketh not the other, yet one cometh of the other."

Said Face-of-god: "Wise art thou now, foster-father, but thou shalt be wiser yet in this matter by then a month hath worn: and to-morrow shalt thou know enough to set thine hands a-work."

So the talk fell between them; and the night wore, and the men of Burgdale feasted in their ancient hall with merry hearts, little weighed down by thought of the battle that might be and the trouble to come; for they were valorous and kindly folk.

24. FACE-OF-GOD GIVETH THAT TOKEN TO THE BRIDE

Now on the morrow, when Face-of-god arose and other men with him, and the Hall was astir and there was no little throng therein, the Bride came up to him; for she had slept in the House of the Face by the bidding of the Alderman; and she spake to him before all men, and bade him come forth with her into the garden, because she would speak to him apart. He yea-said her, though with a heavy heart; and to the folk about that seemed meet and due, since those twain were deemed to be troth-plight, and they smiled kindly on them as they went out of the Hall together.

So they came into the garden, where the pear-trees were blossoming over the spring lilies, and the cherries were showering their flowers on the deep green grass, and everything smelled sweetly on the warm windless spring morning.

She led the way, going before him till they came by a smooth grass path between the berry bushes, to a square space of grass about which were barberry trees, their first tender leaves bright green in the sun against the dry yellowish twigs. There was a sundial amidmost of the grass, and betwixt the garden-boughs one could see the long grey roof of the ancient hall; and sweet familiar sounds of the nesting birds and men and women going on their errands were all about in the scented air. She turned about at the sundial and faced Face-of-god, her hand lightly laid on the scored brass, and spake with no anger in her voice:

"I ask thee if thou hast brought me the token whereon thou shalt swear to give me that gift."

"Yea," said he; and therewith drew the ring from his bosom, and held it out to her. She reached out her hand to him slowly and took it, and their fingers met as she did so, and he noted that her hand was warm and firm and wholesome as he well remembered it.

She said: "Whence hadst thou this fair finger-ring?"

Said Face-of-god: "My friend there in the mountain-valley drew it from off her finger for thee, and bade me bear thee a message."

Her face flushed red: "Yea," she said, "and doth she send me a message? Then doth she know of me, and ye have talked of me together. Well, give the message!"

Said Face-of-god: "She saith, that thou shalt bear in mind, That to-morrow is a new day."

"Yea," she said, "for her it is so, and for thee; but not for me. But now I have brought thee here that thou mightest swear thine oath to me; lay thine hand on this ring and on this brazen plate whereby the sun measures the hours of the day for happy folk, and swear by the spring-tide of the year and all glad things that find a mate, and by the God of the Earth that rejoiceth in the life of man."

Then he laid his hand on the finger-ring as it lay on the dial-plate and said:

"By the spring-tide and the live things that long to multiply their kind; by the God of the Earth that rejoiceth in the life of man, I swear to give to my kinswoman the Bride the second man-child that I beget; to be hers, to leave or cherish, to love or hate, as her will may bid her." Then he looked on her soberly and said: "It is duly sworn; is it enough?"

"Yea," she said; but he saw how the tears ran out of her eyes and wetted the bosom of her kirtle, and she hung her head for shame of her grief. And Gold-mane was all abashed, and had no word to say; for he knew that no word of his might comfort her; and he deemed it ill done to stay there and behold her sorrow; and he knew not how to get him gone, and be glad elsewhere, and leave her alone.

Then, as if she had read his thought, she looked up at him and said smiling a little amidst of her tears:

"I bid thee stay by me till the flood is over; for I have yet a word to say to thee."

So he stood there gazing down on the grass in his turn, and not daring to raise his eyes to her face, and the minutes seemed long to him: till at last she said in a voice scarcely yet clear of weeping:

"Wilt thou say anything to me, and tell me what thou hast done, and why, and what thou deemest will come of it?"

He said: "I will tell the truth as I know it, because thou askest it of me, and not because I would excuse myself before thee. What have I done? Yesterday I plighted my troth to wed the woman that I met last autumn in the wood. And why? I wot not why, but that I longed for her. Yet I must tell thee that it seemed to me, and yet seemeth, that I might do no otherwise—that there was nothing else in the world for me to do. What do I deem will come of it, sayest thou? This, that we shall be happy together, she and I, till the day of our death."

She said: "And even so long shall I be sorry: so far are we sundered now. Alas! who looked for it? And whither shall I turn to now?"

Said Gold-mane: "She bade me tell thee that to-morrow is a new day: meseemeth I know her meaning."

"No word of hers hath any meaning to me," said the Bride.

"Nay," said he, "but hast thou not heard these rumours of war that are in the Dale? Shall not these things avail thee? Much may grow out of them; and thou with the mighty heart, so faithful and compassionate!"

She said: "What sayest thou? What may grow out of them? Yea, I have heard those rumours as a man sick to death heareth men talk of their business down in the street while he lieth on his bed; and already he hath done with it all, and hath no world to mend or mar. For me nought shall grow out of it. What meanest thou?"

Said Gold-mane: "Is there nought in the fellowship of Folks, and the aiding of the valiant, and the deliverance of the hapless?"

"Nay," she said, "there is nought to me. I cannot think of it to-day nor yet to-morrow belike. Yet true it is that I may mingle in it, though thinking nought of it. But this shall not avail me."

She was silent a little, but presently spake and said: "Thou sayest right; it is not thou that hast done this, but the woman who sent me the ring and the message of an old saw. O that she should be born to sunder us! How hath it befallen that I am now so little to thee and she so much?"

And again she was silent; and after a while Face-of-god spake kindly and softly and said: "Kinswoman, wilt thou for ever begrudge our love? this grudge lieth heavy on my soul, and it is I alone that have to bear it."

She said: "This is but a light burden for thee to bear, when thou hast nought else to bear! But do I begrudge thee thy love, Gold-mane? I know not that. Rather meseemeth I do not believe in it—nor shall do ever."

Then she held her peace a long while, nor did he speak one word: and they were so still, that a robin came hopping about them, close to the hem of her kirtle, and a starling pitched in the apple-tree hard by and whistled and chuckled, turning about and about, heeding them nought. Then at last she lifted up her face from looking on the grass and said: "These are idle words and avail nothing: one thing only I know, that we are sundered. And now it repenteth me that I have shown thee my tears and my grief and my sickness of the earth and those that dwell thereon. I am ashamed of it, as if thou hadst smitten me, and I had come and shown thee the stripes, and said, See what thou hast done! hast thou no pity? Yea, thou pitiest me, and wilt try to forget thy pity. Belike thou art right when thou sayest, To-morrow is a new day; belike matters will arise that will call me back to life, and I shall once more take heed of the joy and sorrow of my people. Nay, it is most like that this I shall feign to do even now. But if to-morrow be a new day, it is to-day now and not to-morrow, and so shall it be for long. Hereof belike we shall talk no more, thou and I. For as the days wear, the dealings between us shall be that thou shalt but get thee away from my life, and I shall be nought to thee but the name of a kinswoman. Thus should it be even wert thou to strive to make it otherwise; and thou shalt *not* strive. So let all this be; for this is not the word I had to say to thee. But hearken! now are we sundered, and it irketh me beyond measure that folk know it not, and are kind, and rejoice in our love, and deem it a happy thing for the folk; and this burden I may bear no longer. So I shall declare unto men that I will not wed thee; and belike they may wonder why it is, till they see thee wedded to the Woman of the Mountain. Art thou content that so it shall be?"

Said Face-of-god: "Nay, thou shalt not take this all upon thyself; I also shall declare unto the Folk that I will wed none but her, the Mountain-Woman."

She said: "This shalt thou not do; I forbid it thee. And I *will* take it all upon myself. Shall I have it said of me that I am unmeet to wed thee, and that thou hast found me out at last and at latest? I lay this upon thee, that wheresoever I declare this and whatsoever I may say, thou shalt hold thy peace. This at least thou may'st do for me. Wilt thou?"

"Yea," he said, "though it shall put me to shame."

Again she was silent for a little; then she said:

"O Gold-mane, this would I take upon myself not soothly for any shame of seeming to be thy cast-off; but because it is I who needs must bear all the sorrow of our sundering; and I have the will to bear it greater and heavier, that I may be as the women of old time, and they that have come from the Gods, lest I belittle my life with malice and spite and confusion, and it become poisonous to me. Be at peace! be at peace! And leave all to the wearing of the years; and forget not that which thou hast sworn!"

Therewith she turned and went from that green place toward the House of the Face, walking slowly through the garden amongst the sweet odours, beneath the fair blossoms, a body most dainty and beauteous of fashion, but the casket of grievous sorrow, which all that goodliness availed not.

But Face-of-god lingered in that place a little, and for that little while the joy of his life was dulled and overworn; and the days before his wandering on the mountain seemed to him free and careless and happy days that he could not but regret. He was ashamed, moreover, that this so unquenchable grief should come but of him, and the pleasure of his life, which he himself had found out for himself, and which was but such a little portion of the Earth and the deeds thereof. But presently his thought wandered from all this, and as he turned away from the sundial and went his ways through the garden, he called to mind his longing for the day of the spring market, when he should see the Sun-beam again and be cherished by the sweetness of her love.

25. OF THE GATE-THING AT BURGSTEAD

But now must he hasten, for the Gate-thing was to be holden two hours before noon; so he betook him speedily to the Hall, and took his shield and did on a goodly helm and girt his sword to his side, for men must needs go to all folk-motes with their weapons and clad in war-gear. Thus he went forth to the Gate with many others, and there already were many folk assembled in the space aforesaid betwixt the Gate of the Burg and the sheer rocks on the face of which were the steps that led up to the ancient Tower on the height. The Alderman was sitting on the great stone by the Gate-side which was his appointed place, and beside him on the stone bench were the six Wardens of the Burg; but of the six Wardens of the Dale there were but three, for the others had not yet heard tell of the battle or had got the summons to the Thing, since they had been about their business down the Dale.

Face-of-god took his place silently amongst the neighbours, but men made way for him, so that he must needs stand in front, facing his father and the Wardens; and there went up a murmur of expectation round about him, both because the word had gone about that he had a tale of new tidings to tell, and also because men deemed him their best and handiest man, though he was yet so young.

Now the Alderman looked around and beheld a great throng gathered together, and he looked on the shadow of the Gate which the southering sun was casting on the hard white ground of the Thing-stead, and he saw that it had just taken in the standing-stone which was in the midst of the place. On the face of the said stone was carven the image of a fighting man with shield on arm and axe in hand; for it had been set there in old time in memory of the man who had bidden the Folk build the Gate and its wall, and had showed them how to fashion it: for he was a deft house-smith as well as a great warrior; and his name was Iron-hand. So when the Alderman saw that this stone was wholly within the shadow of the Gate he knew that it was the due time for the hallowing-in of the Thing. So he bade one of the wardens who sat beside him and had a great slug-horn slung about him, to rise and set the horn to his mouth.

So that man arose and blew three great blasts that went bellowing about the towers and down the street, and beat back again from the face of the sheer rocks and up them and over into the Wild-wood; and the sound of it went on the light west-wind along the lips of the Dale toward the mountain wastes. And many a goodman, when he heard the voice of the horn in the bright spring morning, left spade or axe or plough-stilts, or the foddering of the ewes and their younglings, and turned back home to fetch his sword and helm and hasten to the Thing, though he knew not why it was summoned: and women wending over the meadows, who had not yet heard of the battle in the wood, hearkened and stood still on the green grass or amidst the ripples of the ford, and the threat of coming trouble smote heavy on their hearts, for they knew that great tidings must be towards if a Thing must needs be summoned so close to the Great Folk-mote.

But now the Alderman stood up and spake amidst the silence that followed the last echoes of the horn:

"Now is hallowed in this Gate-thing of the Burgstead Men and the Men of the Dale, wherein they shall take counsel concerning matters late befallen, that press hard upon them. Let no man break the peace of the Holy Thing, lest he become a man accursed in holy places from the plain up to the mountain, and from the mountain down to the plain; a man not to be cherished of any man of good will, not be holpen with victuals or edge-tool or draught-beast; a man to be sheltered under no roof-tree, and warmed at no hearth of man: so help us the Warrior and the God of the Earth, and Him of the Face, and all the Fathers!"

When he had spoken men clashed their weapons in token of assent; and he sat down again, and there was silence for a space. But presently came thrusting forward a goodman of the Dale, who seemed as if he had come hurriedly to the Thing; for his face was running down with sweat, his wide-rimmed iron cap sat awry over his brow, and he was girt with a rusty sword without a scabbard, and the girdle was ill-braced up about his loins. So he said:

"I am Red-coat of Waterless of the Lower Dale. Early this

morning as I was going afield I met on the way a man akin to me, Fox of Upton to wit, and he told me that men were being summoned to a Gate-thing. So I turned back home, and caught up any weapon that came handy, and here I am, Alderman, asking thee of the tidings which hath driven thee to call this Thing so hard on the Great Folk-mote, for I know them not."

Then stood up Iron-face the Alderman and said: "This is well asked, and soon shall ye be as wise as I am on this matter. Know ye, O men of Burgstead and the Dale, that we had not called this Gate-thing so hard on the Great Folk-mote had not great need been to look into troublous matters. Long have ye dwelt in peace, and it is years on years now since any foeman hath fallen on the Dale: but, as ye will bear in mind, last autumn were there ransackings in the Dale and amidst of the Shepherds after the manner of deeds of war; and it troubleth us that none can say who wrought these ill deeds. Next, but a little while agone, was Wood-grey, a valiant goodman of the Woodlanders, slain close to his own door by evil men. These men we took at first for mere gangrel felons and outcasts from their own folk: though there were some who spoke against that from the beginning.

"But thirdly are new tidings again: for three days ago, while some of the folk were hunting peaceably in the Wild-wood and thinking no evil, they were fallen upon of set purpose by a host of men-at-arms, and nought would serve but mere battle for dear life, so that many of our neighbours were hurt, and three slain outright; and now mark this, that those who there fell upon our folk were clad and armed even as the two felons that slew Wood-grey, and moreover were like them in aspect of body. Now stand forth Hall-face my son, and answer to my questions in a loud voice, so that all may hear thee."

So Hall-face stood forth, clad in gleaming war-gear, with an axe over his shoulder, and seemed a doughty warrior. And Iron-face said to him:

"Tell me, son, those whom ye met in the wood, and of whom ye brought home two captives, how much like were they to the murder-carles at Wood-grey's?"

Said Hall-face: "As like as peas out of the same cod, and to our eyes all those whom we saw in the wood might have been sons of one father and one mother, so much alike were they."

"Yea," said the Alderman; "now tell me how many by thy deeming fell upon you in the wood?"

Said Hall-face: "We deemed that if they were any less than threescore, they were little less."

"Great was the odds," said the Alderman. "Or how many were ye?"

"One score and seven," said Hall-face.

Said the Alderman: "And yet ye escaped with life all save those three?"

Hall-face said: "I deem that scarce one should have come back alive, had it not been that as we fought came a noise like the howling of wolves, and thereat the foemen turned and fled, and there followed on the fleers tall men clad in sheep-brown raiment, who smote them down as they fled."

"Here then is the story, neighbours," said the Alderman, "and ye may see thereby that if those slayers of Wood-grey were outcast, their band is a great one; but it seemeth rather that they were men of a folk whose craft it is to rob with the armed hand, and to slay the robbed; and that they are now gathering on our borders for war. Yet, moreover, they have foemen in the woods who should be fellows-in-arms of us. How sayest thou, Stone-face? Thou art old, and hast seen many wars in the Dale, and knowest the Wild-wood to its innermost.

"Alderman," said Stone-face, "and ye neighbours of the Dale, maybe these foes whom ye have met are not of the race of man, but are trolls and wood-wights. Now if they be trolls it is ill, for then is the world growing worser, and the wood shall be right perilous for those who needs must fare therein. Yet if they be men it is a worse matter; for the trolls would not come out of the waste into the sunlight of the Dale. But these foes, if they be men, are lusting after our fair Dale to eat it up, and it is most like that they are gathering a huge host to fall upon us at home. Such things I have heard of when I was young, and the aspect of the evil men who overran the kindreds of old time, according to all tales and lays that I have heard, is even such as the aspect of those whom we have seen of late. As to those wolves who saved the neighbours and chased their foemen, there is one here who belike knoweth more of all this than we do, and that, O Alderman, is thy son whom I have fostered, Face-of-god to wit. Bid him answer to thy questioning, and tell us what he hath seen and heard of late; then shall we verily know the whole story as far as it can be known."

Then men pressed round, and were eager to hear what Face-of-god would be saying. But or ever the Alderman could begin to question him, the throng was cloven by new-comers, and these were the men who had been sent to bring home the corpses of the Dusky Men: so they had cast loaded hooks into the Weltering Water, and had dragged up him whom Face-of-god had shoved into the eddy, and who had sunk like a stone just where he fell, and now they were bringing him on a bier along with him who had been slain a-land. They were set down in the place before the Alderman, and men who had not seen them before looked eagerly on them that they might behold the aspect of their foemen; and nought lovely were they to look on; for the drowned man was already bleached and swollen with the water, and the other, his face was all wryed and twisted with that spear-thrust in the mouth.

Then the Alderman said: "I would question my son Face-of-god. Let him stand forth!"

And therewith he smiled merrily in his son's face, for he was standing right in front of him; and he said:

"Ask of me, Alderman, and I will answer."

"Kinsman," said Iron-face, "look at these two dead men, and tell me, if thou hast seen any such besides those two murder-carles who were slain at Carlstead; or if thou knowest aught of their folk?"

Said Face-of-god: "Yesterday I saw six others like to these both in array and of body, and three of them I slew, for we were in battle with them early in the morning."

There was a murmur of joy at this word, since all men took these felons for deadly foemen; but Iron-face said: "What meanest thou by "we"?"

"I and the men who had guested me overnight," said Face-of-god, "and they slew the other three; or rather a woman of them slew the felons."

"Valiant she was; all good go with her hand!" said the Alderman. "But what be these people, and where do they dwell?"

Said Face-of-god: "As to what they are, they are of the kindred of the Gods and the Fathers, valiant men, and guest-cherishing: rich have they been, and now are poor: and their poverty cometh of these same felons, who mastered them by numbers not to be withstood. As to where they dwell: when I say the name of their dwelling-place men mock at me, as if I named some valley in the moon: yet came I to Burgdale thence in one day across the mountain-necks led by sure guides, and I tell thee that the name of their abode is Shadowy Vale."

"Yea," said Iron-face, "knoweth any man here of Shadowy Vale, or where it is?"

None answered for a while; but there was an old man who was sitting on the shafts of a wain on the outskirts of the throng, and when he heard this word he asked his neighbour what the Alderman was saying, and he told him. Then said that elder:

"Give me place; for I have a word to say hereon." Therewith he arose, and made his way to the front of the ring of men, and said: "Alderman, thou knowest me?"

"Yea," said Iron-face, "thou art called the Fiddle, because of thy sweet speech and thy minstrelsy; whereof I mind me well in the time when I was young and thou no longer young."

"So it is," said the Fiddle. "Now hearken! When I was very young I heard of a vale lying far away across the mountain-necks; a vale where the sun shone never in winter and scantily in summer; for my sworn foster-brother, Fight-fain, a bold man and a great hunter, had happened upon it; and on a day in full midsummer he brought me thither; and even now I see the Vale before me as in a picture; a marvellous place, well grassed, treeless, narrow, betwixt great cliff-walls of black stone, with a green river running through it towards a yawning gap and a huge force. Amidst that Vale was a doom-ring of black stones, and nigh thereto a feast-hall well builded of the like stones, over whose door was carven the image of a wolf with red gaping jaws, and within it (for we entered into it) were stone benches on the dais. Thence we came away, and thither again we went in late autumn, and so dusk and cold it was at that season, that we knew not what to call it save the valley of deep shade. But its real name we never knew; for there was no man there to give us a name or tell us any tale thereof; but all was waste there; the wimbrel laughed across its water, the raven croaked from its crags, the eagle screamed over it, and the voices of its waters never ceased; and thus we left it. So the seasons passed, and we went thither no more: for Fight-fain died, and without him wandering over the waste was irksome to me; so never have I seen that valley again, or heard men tell thereof.

"Now, neighbours, have I told you of a valley which seemeth to be Shadowy Vale; and this is true and no made-up story."

The Alderman nodded kindly to him, and then said to Face-of-god: "Kinsman, is this word according with what thou knowest of Shadowy Vale?"

"Yea, on all points," said Face-of-god; "he hath put before me a picture of the valley. And whereas he saith, that in his youth it was waste, this also goeth with my knowledge thereof. For once was it peopled, and then was waste, and now again is it peopled."

"Tell us then more of the folk thereof," said the Alderman; "are they many?"

"Nay," said Face-of-god, "they are not. How might they be many, dwelling in that narrow Vale amid the wastes? But they are valiant, both men and women, and strong and well-liking. Once they dwelt in a fair dale called Silverdale, the name whereof will be to you as a name in a lay; and there were they wealthy and happy. Then fell upon them this murderous Folk, whom they call the Dusky Men; and they fought and were overcome, and many of them were slain, and many enthralled, and the remnant of them escaped through the passes of the mountains and came back to dwell in Shadowy Vale, where their forefathers had dwelt long and long ago; and this overthrow befell them ten years agone. But now their old foemen have broken out from Silverdale and have taken to scouring the wood seeking prey; so they fall upon these Dusky Men as occasion serves, and slay them without pity, as if they were adders or evil dragons; and indeed they be worse. And these valiant men know for certain that their foemen are now of mind to fall upon this Dale and destroy it, as they have done with others nigher to them. And they will slay our men, and lie with our women against their will, and enthrall our children, and torment all those that lie under their hands till life shall be worse than death to them. Therefore, O Alderman and Wardens, and ye neighbours all, it behoveth you to take counsel what we shall do, and that speedily."

There was again a murmur, as of men nothing daunted, but intent on taking some way through the coming trouble. But no man said aught till the Alderman spake:

"When didst thou first happen upon this Earl-folk, son?"

"Late last autumn," said Face-of-god.

Said Iron-face: "Then mightest thou have told us of this tale before."

"Yea," said his son, "but I knew it not, or but little of it, till two days agone. In the autumn I wandered in the woodland, and on the fell I happened on a few of this folk dwelling in a booth by the pine-wood; and they were kind and guest-fain with me, and gave me meat and drink and lodging, and bade me come to Shadowy Vale in the spring, when I should know more of them. And that was I fain of; for they are wise and goodly men. But I deemed no more of those that I saw there save as men who had been outlawed by their own folk for deeds that were unlawful belike, but not shameful, and were biding their time of return, and were living as they might meanwhile. But of the whole Folk and their foemen knew I no more than ye did, till two days agone, when I met them again in Shadowy Vale. Also I think before long ye shall see their chieftain in Burgstead, for he hath a word for us. Lastly, my mind it is that those brown-clad men who helped Hall-face and his company in the wood were nought but men of this Earl-kin seeking their foemen; for indeed they told me that they had come upon a battle in the woodland wherein they had slain their foemen. Now have I told you all that ye need to know concerning these matters."

Again was there silence as Iron-face sat pondering a question for his son; then a goodman of the Upper Dale, Gritgarth to wit, spake and said:

"Gold-mane mine, tell us how many is this folk; I mean their fighting-men?"

"Well asked, neighbour," said Iron-face.

Said Face-of-god: "Their fighting-men of full age may be five score; but besides that there shall be some two or three score of women that will fight, whoever says them nay; and many of these are little worse in the field than men; or no worse, for they shoot well in the bow. Moreover, there will be a full score of swains not yet twenty winters old whom ye may not hinder to fight if anything is a-doing."

"This is no great host," said the Alderman; "yet if they deem there is little to lose by fighting, and nought to gain by sitting still, they may go far in winning their desire; and that more especially if they may draw into their quarrel some other val-

iant Folk more in number than they be. I marvel not, though, they were kind to thee, son Gold-mane, if they knew who thou wert."

"They knew it," said Face-of-god.

"Neighbours," said the Alderman, "have ye any rede hereon, and aught to say to back your rede?"

Then spake the Fiddle: "As ye know and may see, I am now very old, and, as the word goes, unmeet for battle: yet might I get me to the field, either on mine own legs or on the legs of some four-foot beast, I would strike, if it were but one stroke, on these pests of the earth. And, Alderman, meseemeth we shall do amiss if we bid not the Earl-folk of Shadowy Vale to be our fellows in arms in this adventure. For look you, how few soever they be, they will be sure to know the ways of our foemen, and the mountain passes, and the surest and nighest roads across the necks and the mires of the waste; and though they be not a host, yet shall they be worth a host to us?"

When men heard his words they shouted for joy of them; for hatred of the Dusky Men who should so mar their happy life in the Dale was growing up in them, and the more that hatred waxed, the more waxed their love of those valiant ones.

Now Red-coat of Waterless spake again: he was a big man, both tall and broad, ruddy-faced and red-haired, some forty winters old. He said:

"Life hath been well with us of the Lower Dale, and we deem that we have much to lose in losing it. Yet ill would the bargain be to buy life with thraldom: we have been over-merry hitherto for that. Therefore I say, to battle! And as to these men, these well-wishers of Face-of-god, if they also are minded for battle with our foes, we were fools indeed if we did not join them to our company, were they but one score instead of six."

Men shouted again, and they said that Red-coat had spoken well. Then one after other the goodmen of the Dale came and gave their word for fellowship in arms with the Men of Shadowy Vale, if there were such as Face-of-god had said, which they doubted not; and amongst them that spake were Fox of Nethertown, and Warwell, and Gritgarth, and Bearswain, and Warcliff, and Hart of Highcliff, and Worm of Willowholm, and Bullsbane, and Highneb of the Marsh: all these were stout men-at-arms and men of good counsel.

Last of all the Alderman spake and said:

"As to the war, that must we needs meet if all be sooth that we have heard, and I doubt it not.

"Now therefore let us look to it like wise men while time yet serves. Ye shall know that the muster of the Dalesmen will bring under shield eight long hundreds of men well-armed, and of the Shepherd-Folk four hundreds, and of the Woodlanders two hundreds; and this is a goodly host if it be well ordered and wisely led. Now am I your Alderman and your

Doomster, and I can heave up a sword as well as another maybe, nor do I think that I shall blench in the battle; yet I misdoubt me that I am no leader or orderer of men-of-war: therefore ye will do wisely to choose a wiser man-at-arms than I be for your War-leader; and if at the Great Folk-mote, when all the Houses and Kindreds are gathered, men yeasay your choosing, then let him abide; but if they naysay it, let him give place to another. For time presses. Will ye so choose?"

"Yea, yea!" cried all men.

"Good is that, neighbours," said the Alderman. "Whom will ye have for War-leader? Consider well."

Short was their rede, for every man opened his mouth and cried out "Face-of-god!" Then said the Alderman:

"The man is young and untried; yet though he is so near akin to me, I will say that ye will do wisely to take him; for he is both deft of his hands and brisk; and moreover, of this matter he knoweth more than all we together. Now therefore I declare him your War-leader till the time of the Great Folk-mote."

Then all men shouted with great glee and clashed their weapons; but some few put their heads together and spake apart a little while, and then one of them, Red-coat of Waterless to wit, came forward and said: "Alderman, some of us deem it good that Stone-face, the old man wise in war and in the ways of the Wood, should be named as a counsellor to the War-leader; and Hall-face, a very brisk and strong young man, to be his right hand and sword-bearer."

"Good is that," said Iron-face. "Neighbours, will ye have it so?" This also they yeasaid without delay, and the Alderman declared Stone-face and Hall-face the helpers of Face-of-god in this business. Then he said:

"If any hath aught to say concerning what is best to be done at once, it were good that he said it now before all and not to murmur and grudge hereafter."

None spake save the Fiddle, who said: "Alderman and War-leader, one thing would I say: that if these foemen are anywise akin to those overrunners of the Folks of whom the tales went in my youth (for I also as well as Stone-face mind me well of those tales concerning them), it shall not avail us to sit still and await their onset. For then may they not be withstood, when they have gathered head and burst out and over the folk that have been happy, even as the waters that overtop a dyke and cover with their muddy ruin the deep green grass and the flower-buds of spring. Therefore my rede is, as soon as may be to go seek these folk in the woodland and wheresoever else they may be wandering. What sayest thou, Face-of-god?"

"My rede is as thine," said he; "and to begin with, I do now call upon ten tens of good men to meet me in arms at the beginning of Wildlake's Way to-morrow morning at daybreak; and I bid my brother Hall-face to summon such as are most meet thereto. For this I deem good, that we scour the wood daily at present till we hear fresh tidings from them of Shadowy Vale, who are nigher than we to the foemen. Now, neighbours, are ye ready to meet me?"

Then all shouted, "Yea, we will go, we will go!"

Said the Alderman: "Now have we made provision for the war in that which is nearest to our hands. Yet have we to deal with the matter of the fellowship with the Folk whom Face-of-god hath seen. This is a matter for thee, son, at least till the Great Folk-mote is holden. Tell me then, shall we send a messenger to Shadowy Vale to speak with this folk, or shall we abide the chieftain's coming?"

"By my rede," said Face-of-god, "we shall abide his coming: for first, though I might well make my way thither, I doubt if I could give any the bearings, so that he could come there without me; and belike I am needed at home, since I am become War-leader. Moreover, when your messenger cometh to Shadowy Vale, he may well chance to find neither the chieftain there, nor the best of his men; for whiles are they here, and whiles there, as they wend following after the Dusky Men."

"It is well, son," said the Alderman, "let it be as thou sayest: soothly this matter must needs be brought before the Great Folk-mote. Now will I ask if any other hath any word to say, or any rede to give before this Gate-thing sundereth?"

But no man came forward, and all men seemed well content and of good heart; and it was now well past noontide.

26. THE ENDING OF THE GATE-THING

But just as the Alderman was on the point of rising to declare the breaking-up of the Thing, there came a stir in the throng and it opened, and a warrior came forth into the innermost of the ring of men, arrayed in goodly glittering War-gear; clad in such wise that a tunicle of precious gold-wrought web covered the hauberk all but the sleeves thereof, and the hem of it beset with blue mountain-stones smote against the ankles and well-nigh touched the feet, shod with sandals gold-embroidered and gemmed. This warrior bore a goodly gilded helm on the head, and held in hand a spear with gold-garlanded shaft, and was girt with a sword whose hilts and scabbard both were adorned with gold and gems: beardless, smooth-cheeked, exceeding fair of face was the warrior, but pale and somewhat haggard-eyed: and those who were nearby beheld and wondered; for they saw that there was come the Bride arrayed for war and battle, as if she were a messenger from the House of the Gods, and the Burg that endureth for ever.

Then she fell to speech in a voice which at first was somewhat hoarse and broken, but cleared as she went on, and she said:

"There sittest thou, O Alderman of Burgdale! Is Face-of-god thy son anywhere nigh, so that he can hear me?"

But Iron-face wondered at her word, and said: "He is beside thee, as he should be." For indeed Face-of-god was touching her, shoulder to shoulder. But she looked not to the right hand nor the left, but said:

"Hearken, Iron-face! Chief of the House of the Face, Alderman of the Dale, and ye also, neighbours and goodmen of the Dale: I am a woman called the Bride, of the House of the Steer, and ye have heard that I have plighted my troth to Face-of-god to wed with him, to love him, and lie in his bed. But it is not so: we are not troth-plight; nor will I wed with him, nor any other, but will wend with you to the war, and play my part therein according to what might is in me; nor will I be worser than the wives of Shadowy Vale."

Face-of-god heard her words with no change of countenance; but Iron-face reddened over all his face, and stared at her, and knit his brows and said:

"Maiden, what are these words? What have we done to thee? Have I not been to thee as a father, and loved thee dearly? Is not my son goodly and manly and deft in arms? Hath it not ever been the wont of the House of the Face to wed in the House of the Steer? and in these two Houses there hath never yet been a goodlier man and a lovelier maiden than are ye two. What have we done then?"

"Ye have done nought against me," she said, "and all that thou sayest is sooth; yet will I not wed with Face-of-god."

Yet fiercer waxed the face of the Alderman, and he said in a loud voice:

"But how if I tell thee that I will speak with thy kindred of the Steer, and thou shalt do after my bidding whether thou wilt or whether thou wilt not?"

"And how will ye compel me thereto?" she said. "Are there thralls in the Dale? Or will ye make me an outlaw? Who shall heed it? Or I shall betake me to Shadowy Vale and become one of their warrior-maidens."

Now was the Alderman's face changing from red to white, and belike he forgat the Thing, and what he was doing there, and he cried out:

"This is an evil day, and who shall help me? Thou, Face-of-god, what hast thou to say? Wilt thou let this woman go without a word? What hath bewitched thee?"

But never a word spake his son, but stood looking straight forward, cold and calm by seeming. Then turned Iron-face again to the Bride, and said in a softer voice:

"Tell me, maiden, whom I erst called daughter, what hath befallen, that thou wilt leave my son; thou who wert once so kind and loving to him; whose hand was always seeking his, whose eyes were ever following his; who wouldst go where he bade, and come when he called. What hath betid that ye have cast him out, and flee from our House?"

She flushed red beneath her helm and said:

"There is war in the land, and I have seen it coming, and that things shall change around us. I have looked about me and seen men happy and women content, and children weary for mere mirth and joy. And I have thought, in a day, or two days or three, all this shall be changed, and the women shall be, some anxious and wearied with waiting, some casting all hope away; and the men, some shall come back to the garth no more, and some shall come back maimed and useless, and there shall be loss of friends and fellows, and mirth departed, and dull days and empty hours, and the children wandering about marvelling at the sorrow of the house. All this I saw before me, and grief and pain and wounding and death; and I said: Shall I be any better than the worst of the folk that loveth me? Nay, this shall never be; and since I have learned to be deft with mine hands in all the play of war, and that I am as strong as many a man, and as hardy-hearted as any, I will give myself to the Warrior and the God of the Face; and the battle-field shall be my home, and the after-grief of the fight my banquet and holiday, that I may bear the burden of my people, in the battle and out of it; and know every sorrow that the Dale hath; and cast aside as a grievous and ugly thing the bed of the warrior that the maiden desires, and the toying of lips and hands and soft words of desire, and all the joy that dwelleth in the Castle of Love and the Garden thereof; while the world outside is sick and sorry, and the fields lie waste and the harvest burneth. Even so have I sworn, even so will I do."

Her eyes glittered and her cheek was flushed, and her voice was clear and ringing now; and when she ended there arose a murmur of praise from the men round about her. But Iron-face said coldly:

"These are great words; but I know not what they mean. If thou wilt to the field and fight among the carles (and that I would not naysay, for it hath oft been done and praised aforetime), why shouldest thou not go side by side with Face-of-god and as his plighted maiden?"

The light which the sweetness of speech had brought into her face had died out of it now, and she looked weary and hapless as she answered him slowly:

"I will not wed with Face-of-god, but will fare afield as a virgin of war, as I have sworn to the Warrior."

Then waxed Iron-face exceeding wroth, and he rose up before all men and cried loudly and fiercely:

"There is some lie abroad, that windeth about us as the gossamers in the lanes of an autumn morning."

And therewith he strode up to Face-of-god as though he had nought to do with the Thing; and he stood before him and cried out at him while all men wondered:

"Thou! what hast thou done to turn this maiden's heart to stone? Who is it that is devising guile with thee to throw aside this worthy wedding in a worthy House, with whom our sons are ever wont to wed? Speak, tell the tale!"

But Face-of-god held his peace and stood calm and proud before all men.

Then the blood mounted to Iron-face's head, and he forgat folk and kindred and the war to come, and he cried so that all the place rang with the words of his anger:

"Thou dastard! I see thee now; it is thou that hast done this, and not the maiden; and now thou hast made her bear a double burden, and set her on to speak for thee, whilst thou standest by saying nought, and wilt take no scruple's weight of her shame upon thee!"

But his son spake never a word, and Iron-face cried: "Out on thee! I know thee now, and why thou wouldest not to the West-land last winter. I am no fool; I know thee. Where hast thou hidden the stranger woman?"

Therewith he drew forth his sword and hove it aloft as if to hew down Face-of-god, who spake not nor flinched nor raised a hand from his side. But the Bride threw herself in front of Gold-mane, while there arose an angry cry of "The Peace of the Holy Thing! Peace-breaking, peace-breaking!" and some cried, "For the War-leader, the War-leader!" and as men could for the press they drew forth their swords, and there was tumult and noise all over the Thing-stead.

But Stone-face caught hold of the Alderman's right arm and dragged down the sword, and the big carle, Red-coat of Waterless, came up behind him and cast his arms about his middle and drew him back; and presently he looked around him, and slowly sheathed his sword, and went back to his place and sat him down; and in a little while the noise abated and swords were sheathed, and men waxed quiet again, and the Alderman arose and said in a loud voice, but in the wonted way of the head man of the Thing:

"Here hath been trouble in the Holy Thing; a violent man hath troubled it, and drawn sword on a neighbour; will the neighbours give the dooming hereof into the hands of the Alderman?"

Now all knew Iron-face, and they cried out, "That will we." So he spake again:

"I doom the troubler of the Peace of the Holy Thing to pay a fine, to wit double the blood-wite that would be duly paid for a full-grown freeman of the kindreds."

Then the cry went up and men yeasaid his doom, and all said that it was well and fairly doomed; and Iron-face sat still.

But Stone-face stood forth and said:

"Here have been wild words in the air; and dreams have taken shape and come amongst us, and have bewitched us, so that friends and kin have wrangled. And meseemeth that this is through the wizardry of these felons, who, even dead as they are, have cast spells over us. Good it were to cast them into the Death Tarn, and then to get to our work; for there is much to do."

All men yeasaid that; and Forkbeard of Lea went with those who had borne the corpses thither to cast them into the black pool.

But the Fiddle spake and said:

"Stone-face sayeth sooth. O Alderman, thou art no young man, yet am I old enough to be thy father; so will I give thee a rede, and say this: Face-of-god thy son is no liar or dastard or beguiler, but he is a young man and exceeding goodly of fashion, well-spoken and kind; so that few women may look on him and hear him without desiring his kindness and love, and to such men as this many things happen. Moreover, he hath now become our captain, and is a deft warrior with his hands, and as I deem, a sober and careful leader of men; therefore we need him and his courage and his skill of leading. So rage not against him as if he had done an ill deed not to be forgiven—whatever he hath done, whereof we know not—for life is long before him, and most like we shall still have to thank him for many good deeds towards us. As for the maiden, she is both lovely and wise. She hath a sorrow at her heart, and we deem that we know what it is. Yet hath she not lied when she said that she would bear the burden of the griefs of the people. Even so shall she do; and whether she will, or whether she will not, that shall heal her own griefs. For to-morrow is a new day. Therefore, if thou do after my rede, thou wilt not meddle betwixt these twain, but wilt remember all that we have to do, and that war is coming upon us. And when that is over, we shall turn round and behold each other, and see that we are not wholly what we were before; and then shall that which were hard to forgive, be forgotten, and that which is remembered be easy to forgive."

So he spake; and Iron-face sat still and put his left hand to his beard as one who pondereth; but the Bride looked in the face of the old man the Fiddle, and then she turned and looked at Gold-mane, and her face softened, and she stood before the Alderman, and bent down before him and held out both her hands to him the palms upward. Then she said: "Thou hast been wroth with me, and I marvel not; for thy hope, and the hope which we all had, hath deceived thee. But kind indeed hast thou been to me ere now: therefore I pray thee take it not amiss if I call to thy mind the oath which thou swearedst on the Holy Boar last Yule, that thou wouldst not gainsay the prayer of any man if thou couldest perform it; therefore I bid thee naysay not mine: and that is, that thou wilt ask me no more about this matter, but wilt suffer me to fare afield like any swain of the Dale, and to deal so with my folk that they shall not hinder me. Also I pray thee that thou wilt put no shame upon Face-of-god my playmate and my kinsman, nor show thine anger to him openly, even if for a little while thy love for him be abated. No more than this will I ask of thee."

All men who heard her were moved to the heart by her kindness and the sweetness of her voice, which was like to the robin singing suddenly on a frosty morning of early winter. But as for Gold-mane, his heart was smitten sorely by it, and her sorrow and her friendliness grieved him out of measure.

But Iron-face answered after a little while, speaking slowly and hoarsely, and with the shame yet clinging to him of a man who has been wroth and has speedily let his wrath run off him. So he said:

"It is well, my daughter. I have no will to forswear myself; nor hast thou asked me a thing which is over-hard. Yet indeed I would that to-day were yesterday, or that many days were worn away."

Then he stood up and cried in a loud voice over the throng:

"Let none forget the muster; but hold him ready against the time that the Warden shall come to him. Let all men obey the War-leader, Face-of-god, without question or delay. As to the fine of the peace-breaker, it shall be laid on the altar of the God at the Great Folk-mote. Herewith is the Thing broken up."

Then all men shouted and clashed their weapons, and so sundered, and went about their business.

And the talk of men it was that the breaking of the troth-plight between those twain was ill; for they loved Face-of-god, and as for the Bride they deemed her the Dearest of the kindreds and the Jewel of the Folk, and as if she were the fairest and the kindest of all the Gods. Neither did the wrath of Iron-face mislike any; but they said he had done well and manly both to be wroth and to let his wrath run off him. As to the war which was to come, they kept a good heart about it, and deemed it as a game to be played, wherein they might show themselves deft and valiant, and so get back to their merry life again.

So wore the day through afternoon to even and night.

27. FACE-OF-GOD LEADETH A BAND THROUGH THE WOOD

Next morning tryst was held faithfully, and an hundred and a half were gathered together on Wildlake's Way; and Face-of-god ordered them into three companies. He made Hall-face leader over the first one, and bade him hold on his way northward, and then to make for Boars-bait and see if he should meet with anything thereabout where the battle had been. Red-coat of Waterless he made captain of the second band; and he had it in charge to wend eastward along the edge of the Dale, and not to go deep into the wood, but to go as far as he might within the time appointed, toward the Mountains. Furthermore, he bade both Hall-face and Red-coat to bring their bands back to Wildlake's Way by the morrow at sunset, where other goodmen should be come to take the places of their men; and then if he and his company were back again, he would bid them further what to do; but if not, as seemed likely, then Hall-face's band to go west toward the Shepherd country half a day's journey, and so back, and Red-coat's east along the Dale's lip again for the like time, and then back, so that there might be a constant watch and ward of the Dale kept against the felons.

All being ordered Gold-mane led his own company northeast through the thick wood, thinking that he might so fare as

to come nigh to Silverdale, or at least to hear tidings thereof. This intent he told to Stone-face, but the old man shook his head and said:

"Good is this if it may be done; but it is not for everyone to go down to Hell in his lifetime and come back safe with a tale thereof. However, whither thou wilt lead, thither will I follow, though assured death waylayeth us."

And the old carle was joyous and proud to be on this adventure, and said, that it was good indeed that his foster-son had with him a man well stricken in years, who had both seen many things, and learned many, and had good rede to give to valiant men.

So they went on their ways, and fared very warily when they were gotten beyond those parts of the wood which they knew well. By this time they were strung out in a long line; and they noted their road carefully, blazing the trees on either side when there were trees, and piling up little stone-heaps where the trees failed them. For Stone-face said that oft it befell men amidst the thicket and the waste to be misled by wights that begrudged men their lives, so that they went round and round in a ring which they might not depart from till they died; and no man doubted his word herein.

All day they went, and met no foe, nay, no man at all; nought but the wild things of the wood; and that day the wood changed little about them from mile to mile. There were many thickets across their road which they had to go round about; so that to the crow flying over the tree-tops the journey had not been long to the place where night came upon them, and where they had to make the wood their bedchamber.

That night they lighted no fire, but ate such cold victual as they might carry with them; nor had they shot any venison, since they had with them more than enough; they made little noise or stir therefore and fell asleep when they had set the watch.

On the morrow they arose betimes, and broke their fast and went their ways till noon: by then the wood had thinned somewhat, and there was little underwood betwixt the scrubby oak and ash which were pretty nigh all the trees about: the ground also was broken, and here and there rocky, and they went into and out of rough little dales, most of which had in them a brook of water running west and southwest; and now Face-of-god led his men somewhat more easterly; and still for some while they met no man.

At last, about four hours after noon, when they were going less warily, because they had hitherto come across nothing to hinder them, rising over the brow of a somewhat steep ridge, they saw down in the valley below them a half score of men sitting by the brook-side eating and drinking, their weapons lying beside them, and along with them stood a woman with her hands tied behind her back.

They saw at once that these men were of the felons, so they that had their bows bent, loosed at them without more ado, while the others ran in upon them with sword and spear. The felons leapt up and ran scattering down the dale, such of them as were not smitten by the shafts; but he who was nighest to the woman, ere he ran, turned and caught up a sword from the ground and thrust it through her, and the next moment fell across the brook with an arrow in his back.

No one of the felons was nimble enough to escape from the fleet-foot hunters of Burgdale, and they were all slain there to the number of eleven.

But when they came back to the woman to tend her, she breathed her last in their hands: she was a young and fair woman, black-haired and dark-eyed. She had on her body a gown of rich web, but nought else: she had been bruised and sore mishandled, and the Burgdale carles wept for pity of her, and for wrath, as they straightened her limbs on the turf of the little valley. They let her lie there a little, whilst they searched round about, lest there should be any other poor soul needing their help, or any felon lurking thereby; but they found nought else save a bundle wherein was another rich gown and divers woman's gear, and sundry rings and jewels, and therewithal

the weapons and war-gear of a knight, delicately wrought after the Westland fashion: these seemed to them to betoken other foul deeds of these murder-carles. So when they had abided a while, they laid the dead woman in mould by the brook-side, and buried with her the other woman's attire and the knight's gear, all but his sword and shield, which they had away with them: then they cast the carcasses of the felons into the brake, but brought away their weapons and the silver rings from their arms, which they wore like all the others of them whom they had fallen in with; and so went on their way to the north-east, full of wrath against those dastards of the Earth.

It was hard on sunset when they left the valley of murder, and they went no long way thence before they must needs make stay for the night; and when they had arrayed their sleeping-stead the moon was up, and they saw that before them lay the close wood again, for they had made their lair on the top of a little ridge.

There then they lay, and nought stirred them in the night, and betimes on the morrow they were afoot, and entered the abovesaid thicket, wherein two of them, keen hunters, had been aforetime, but had not gone deep into it. Through this wood they went all day toward the north-east, and met nought but the wild things therein. At last, when it was near sunset, they came out of the thicket into a small plain, or shallow dale rather, with no great trees in it, but thorn-brakes here and there where the ground sank into hollows; a little river ran through the midst of it, and winded round about a height whose face toward the river went down sheer into the water, but away from it sank down in a long slope to where the thick wood began again: and this height or burg looked well-nigh west.

Thitherward they went; but as they were drawing nigh to the river, and were on the top of a bent above a bushy hollow between them and the water, they espied a man standing in the river near the bank, who saw them not, because he was stooping down intent on something in the bank or under it: so they gat them speedily down into the hollow without noise, that they might get some tidings of the man.

Then Face-of-god bade his men abide hidden under the bushes and stole forward quietly up the further bank of the hollow, his target on his arm and his spear poised. When he was behind the last bush on the top of the bent he was within half a spear-cast of the water and the man; so he looked on him and saw that he was quite naked except for a clout about his middle.

Face-of-god saw at once that he was not one of the Dusky Men; he was a black-haired man, but white-skinned, and of fair stature, though not so tall as the Burgdale folk. He was busied in tickling trouts, and just as Face-of-god came out from the bush into the westering sunlight, he threw up a fish on to the bank, and looked up therewithal, and beheld the weaponed man glittering, and uttered a cry, but fled not when he saw the spear poised for casting.

Then Face-of-god spake to him and said: "Come hither, Woodsman! we will not harm thee, but we desire speech of thee: and it will not avail thee to flee, since I have bowmen of the best in the hollow yonder."

The man put forth his hands towards him as if praying him to forbear casting, and looked at him hard, and then came dripping from out the water, and seemed not greatly afeard; for he stooped down and picked up the trouts he had taken, and came towards Face-of-god stringing the last-caught one through the gills on to the withy whereon were the others: and Face-of-god saw that he was a goodly man of some thirty winters.

Then Face-of-god looked on him with friendly eyes and said:

"Art thou a foemen? or wilt thou be helpful to us?"

He answered in the speech of the kindreds with the hoarse voice of a much weather-beaten man:

"Thou seest, lord, that I am naked and unarmed."

"Yet may'st thou bewray us," said Face-of-god. "What man art thou?"

Said the man: "I am the runaway thrall of evil men; I have fled from Rosedale and the Dusky Men. Hast thou the heart to hurt me?"

"We are the foemen of the Dusky Men," said Face-of-god; "wilt thou help us against them?"

The man knit his brows and said: "Yea, if ye will give me your word not to suffer me to fall into their hands alive. But whence art thou, to be so bold?"

Said Face-of-god: "We are of Burgdale; and I will swear to thee on the edge of the sword that thou shalt not fall alive into the hands of the Dusky Men."

"Of Burgdale have I heard," said the man; "and in sooth thou seemest not such a man as would bewray a hapless man. But now had I best bring you to some lurking-place where ye shall not be easily found of these devils, who now oft-times scour the woods hereabout."

Said Face-of-god: "Come first and see my fellows; and then if thou thinkest we have need to hide, it is well."

So the man went side by side with him towards their lair, and as they went Gold-mane noted marks of stripes on his back and sides, and said: "Sorely hast thou been mishandled, poor man!"

Then the man turned on him and said somewhat fiercely: "Said I not that I had been a thrall of the Dusky Men? how then should I have escaped tormenting and scourging, if I had been with them for but three days?"

As he spake they came about a thorn-bush, and there were the Burgdale men down in the hollow; and the man said: "Are these thy fellows? Call to mind that thou hast sworn by the edge of the sword not to hurt me."

"Poor man!" said Face-of-god; "these are thy friends, unless thou bewrayest us."

Then he cried aloud to his folk: "Here is now a good hap! this is a runaway thrall of the Dusky Men; of him shall we hear tidings; so cherish him all ye may."

So the carles thronged about him and bestirred themselves to help him, and one gave him his surcoat for a kirtle, and another cast a cloak about him; and they brought him meat and drink, such as they had ready to hand: and the man looked as if he scarce believed in all this, but deemed himself to be in a dream. But presently he turned to Face-of-god and said:

"Now I see so many men and weapons I deem that ye have no need to skulk in caves to-night, though I know of good ones: yet shall ye do well not to light a fire till moon-setting; for the flame ye may lightly hide, but the smoke may be seen from far aloof."

But they bade him to meat, and he needed no second bidding but ate lustily, and they gave him wine, and he drank a great draught and sighed as for joy. Then he said in a trembling voice, as though he feared a naysay:

"If ye are from Burgdale ye shall be faring back again presently; and I pray you to take me with you."

Said Face-of-god: "Yea surely, friend, that will we do, and rejoice in thee."

Then he drank another cup which Warcliff held out to him, and spake again: "Yet if ye would abide here till about noon to-morrow, or mayhappen a little later, I would bring other Runaways to see you; and them also might ye take with you: ye may think when ye see them that ye shall have small gain of their company; for poor wretched folk they be, like to myself. Yet since ye seek for tidings, herein might they do you more service than I; for amongst them are some who came out of the hapless Dale within this moon; and it is six months since I escaped. Moreover, though they may look spent and outworn now, yet if ye give them a little rest, and feed them well, they shall yet do many a day's work for you: and I tell you that if ye take them for thralls, and put collars on their necks, and use them no worse than a goodman useth his oxen and his asses, beating them not save when they are idle or at fault, it shall be to them as if they were come to heaven out of hell, and to such goodhap as they have not thought of, save in dreams, for many and many a day. And thus I entreat you to do because ye seem to me to be happy and merciful men, who will not begrudge us this happiness."

The carles of Burgdale listened eagerly to what he said, and they looked at him with great eyes and marvelled; and their hearts were moved with pity towards him; and Stone-face said:

"Herein, O War-leader, need I give thee no rede, for thou mayst see clearly that all we deem that we should lose our manhood and become the dastards of the Warrior if we did not abide the coming of these poor men, and take them back to the Dale, and cherish them."

"Yea," said Wolf of Whitegarth, "and great thanks we owe to this man that he biddeth us this: for great will be the gain to us if we become so like the Gods that we may deliver the poor from misery. Now must I needs think how they shall wonder when they come to Burgdale and find out how happy it is to dwell there."

"Surely," said Face-of-god, "thus shall we do, whatever cometh of it. But, friend of the wood, as to thralls, there be none such in the Dale, but therein are all men friends and neighbours, and even so shall ye be."

And he fell a-musing, when he bethought him of how little he had known of sorrow.

But that man, when he beheld the happy faces of the Burgdalers, and hearkened to their friendly voices, and understood what they said, and he also was become strong with the meat and drink, he bowed his head adown and wept a long while; and they meddled not with him, till he turned again to them and said:

"Since ye are in arms, and seem to be seeking your foemen, I suppose ye wot that these tyrants and man-quellers will fall upon you in Burgdale ere the summer is well worn."

"So much we deem indeed," said Face-of-god, "but we were fain to hear the certainty of it, and how thou knowest thereof."

Said the man: "It was six moons ago that I fled, as I have told you; and even then it was the common talk amongst our masters that there were fair dales to the south which they would overrun. Man would say to man: We were over many in Silverdale, and we needed more thralls, because those we had were lessening, and especially the women; now are we more at ease in Rosedale, though we have sent thralls to Silverdale; but yet we can bear no more men from thence to eat up our stock from us: let them fare south to the happy dales, and conquer them, and we will go with them and help therein, whether we come back to Rosedale or no. Such talk did I hear then with mine own ears: but some of those whom I shall bring to you to-morrow shall know better what is doing, since they have fled from Rosedale but a few days. Moreover, there is a man and a woman who have fled from Silverdale itself, and are but a month from it, journeying all the time save when they must needs hide; and these say that their masters have got to know the way to Burgdale, and are minded for it before the winter, as I said; and nought else but the ways thither do they desire to know, since they have no fear."

By then was night come, and though the moon was high in heaven, and lighted all that waste, the Burgdalers must needs light a fire for cooking their meat, whatsoever that woodsman might say; moreover, the night was cold and somewhat frosty. A little before they had come to that place they had shot a fat buck and some smaller deer, but of other meat they had no great store, though there was wine enough. So they lit their fire in the thickest of the thorn-bush to hide it all they might, and threat they cooked their venison and the trouts which the runaway had taken, and they fell to, and ate and drank and were merry, making much of that poor man till him-seemed he was gotten into the company of the kindest of the Gods.

But when they were full, Face-of-god spake to him, and asked him his name; and he named himself Dallach; but said he: "Lord, this is according to the naming of men in Rosedale before we were enthralled: but now what names have thralls? Also I am not altogether of the blood of them of Rosedale, but of better and more warrior-like kin."

Said Face-of-god: "Thou hast named Silverdale; knowest thou it?"

Dallach answered: "I have never seen it. It is far hence; in a week's journey, making all diligence, and not being forced to hide and skulk like those Runaways, ye shall come to the mouth thereof lying west, where its rock-walls fall off toward the plain."

"But," said Face-of-god, "is there no other way into that Dale?"

"Nay, none that folk wot of," said Dallach, "except to bold cragsmen with their lives in their hands."

"Knowest thou aught of the affairs of Silverdale?" said Face-of-god.

Said Dallach: "Somewhat I know: we wot that but a few years ago there was a valiant folk dwelling therein, who were lords of the whole dale, and that they were vanquished by the Dusky Men: but whether they were all slain and enthralled we wot not; but we deem it otherwise. As for me it is of their blood that I am partly come; for my father's father came thence to settle in Rosedale, and wedded a woman of the Dale, who was my father's mother."

"When was it that ye fell under the Dusky Men?" said Face-of-god.

Said Dallach: "It was five years ago. They came into the Dale a great company, all in arms."

"Was there battle betwixt you?" said Face-of-god.

"Alas! not so," said Dallach. "We were a happy folk there; but soft and delicate: for the Dale is exceeding fertile, and beareth wealth in abundance, both corn and oil and wine and fruit, and of beasts for man's service the best that may be. Would that there had been battle, and that I had died therein with those that had a heart to fight; and even so saith now every man, yea, every woman in the Dale. But it was not so when the elders met in our Council-House on the day when the Dusky Men bade us pay them tribute and give them houses to dwell in and lands to live by. Then had we weapons in our hands, but no hearts to use them."

"What befell then?" said the goodman of Whitegarth.

Said Dallach: "Look ye to it, lords, that it befall not in Burgdale! We gave them all they asked for, and deemed we had much left. What befell, sayst thou? We sat quiet; we went about our work in fear and trembling, for grim and hideous were they to look on. At first they meddled not much with us, save to take from our houses what they would of meat and drink, or raiment, or plenishing. And all this we deemed we might bear, and that we needed no more than to toil a little more each day so as to win somewhat more of wealth. But soon we found that it would not be so; for they had no mind to till the teeming earth or work in the acres we had given them, or to sit at the loom, or hammer in the stithy, or do any man-like work; it was we that must do all that for their behoof, and it was altogether for them that we laboured, and nought for ourselves; and our bodies were only so much our own as they were needful to be kept alive for labour. Herein were our tasks harder than the toil of any mules or asses, save for the younger and goodlier of the women, whom they would keep fair and delicate to be their bed-thralls.

"Yet not even so were our bodies safe from their malice: for these men were not only tyrants, but fools and madmen. Let alone that there were few days without stripes and torments to satiate their fury or their pleasure, so that in all streets and nigh any house might you hear wailing and screaming and groaning; but moreover, though a wise man would not willingly slay his own thrall any more than his own horse or ox, yet did these men so wax in folly and malice, that they would often hew at man or woman as they met them in the way from mere grimness of soul; and if they slew them it was well. Thereof indeed came quarrels enough betwixt master and master, for they are much given to man-slaying amongst themselves: but what profit to us thereof? Nay, if the dead man were a chieftain, then woe betide the thralls! for thereof must many an one be slain on his grave-mound to serve him on the hell-road. To be short: we have heard of men who be fierce, and men who be grim; but these we may scarce believe us to be men at all, but trolls rather; and ill will it be if their race waxeth in the world."

The Burgdale men hearkened with all their ears, and wondered that such things could befall; and they rejoiced at the work that lay before them, and their hearts rose high at the thought of battle in that behalf, and the fame that should come of it. As for the runaway, they made so much of him that the man marvelled; for they dealt with him like a woman cherishing a son, and knew not how to be kind enough to him.

28. THE MEN OF BURGDALE MEET THE RUNAWAYS

Now ere the night was far spent, Dallach arose and said:

"Kind folk, ye will presently be sleeping; but I bid you keep a good watch, and if ye will be ruled by me, ye will kindle no fire on the morrow, for the smoke riseth thick in the morning air, and is as a beacon. As for me, I shall leave you here to rest, and I myself will fare on mine errand."

They bade him sleep and rest him after so many toils and hardships, saying that they were not tied to an hour to be back in Burgdale; but he said: "Nay, the moon is high, and it is as good as daylight to me, who could find my way even by star-light; and your tarrying here is nowise safe. Moreover, if I could find those folk and bring them part of the way by night and cloud it were well; for if we were taken again, burning quick would be the best death by which we should die. As for me, now am I strong with meat and drink and hope; and when I come to Burgdale there will be time enough for resting and slumber."

Said Face-of-god: "Shall I not wend with thee to see these people and the lairs wherein they hide?"

The man smiled: "Nay, earl," said he, "that shall not be. For wot ye what? If they were to see me in company of a man-at-arms they would deem that I was bringing the foe upon them, and would flee, or mayhappen would fall upon us. For as for me, when I saw thee, thou wert close anigh me, so I knew thee to be no Dusky Man; but they would see the glitter of thine arms from afar, and to them all weaponed men are foemen. Thou, lord, knowest not the heart of a thrall, nor the fear and doubt that is in it. Nay, I myself must cast off these clothes that ye have given me, and fare naked, lest they mistrust me. Only I will take a spear in my hand, and sling a knife round my neck, if ye will give them to me; for if the worst happen, I will not be taken alive."

Therewith he cast off his raiment, and they gave him the weapons and wished him good speed, and he went his way twixt moonlight and shadow; but the Burgdalers went to sleep when they had set a watch.

Early in the morning they awoke, and the sun was shining and the thrushes singing in the thorn-brake, and all seemed fair and peaceful, and a little haze still hung about the face of the burg over the river. So they went down to the water and washed the night from off them; and thence the most part of them went back to their lair among the thorn-bushes: but four of them went up the dale into the oak-wood to shoot a buck, and five more they sent out to watch their skirts around them; and Face-of-god with old Stone-face went over a ford of the stream, and came on to the lower slope of the burg, and so went up it to the top. Thence they looked about to see if aught were stirring, but they saw little save the waste and the wood, which on the north-east was thick of big trees stretching out a long way. Their own lair was clear to see over its bank and the bushes thereof, and that misliked Face-of-god, lest any foe should climb the burg that day. The morning was clear, and Face-of-god looking north-and-by-west deemed he saw smoke rising into the air over the tree-covered ridges that hid the further distance toward that airt, though further east uphove the black shoulders of the Great that Waste and the snowy peaks behind them. The said smoke was not such as cometh from one great fire, but was like a thin veil staining the pale blue sky, as when men are burning ling on the heath-side and it is seen aloof.

He showed that smoke to Stone-face, who smiled and said:

"Now will they be lighting the cooking fires in Rosedale: would I were there with a few hundreds of axes and staves at my back!"

"Yea," said Face-of-god, smiling in his face, "but where I pray thee are these elves and wood-wights, that we meet them not? Grim things there are in the woods, and things fair enough also: but meseemeth that the trolls and the elves of thy young years have been frighted away."

Said Stone-face: "Maybe, foster-son; that hath been seen ere now, that when one race of man overrunneth the land inhabited by another, the wights and elves that love the vanquished are seen no more, or get them away far off into the outermost wilds, where few men ever come."

"Yea," said Face-of-god, "that may well be. But deemest thou by that token that we shall be vanquished?"

"As for us, I know not," said Stone-face; "but thy friends of Shadowy Vale have been vanquished. Moreover, concerning these felons whom now we are hunting, are we all so sure that they be men? Certain it is, that when I go into battle with them, I shall smite with no more pity than my sword, as if I were smiting things that may not feel the woes of man."

Said Face-of-god: "Yea, even so shall it be with me. But what thinkest thou of these Runaways? Shall we have tidings of them, or shall Dallach bring the foe upon us? It was for the sake of that question that I have clomb the burg: and that we might watch the land about us."

"Nay," said Stone-face, "I have seen many men, and I deem of Dallach that he is a true man. I deem we shall soon have tidings of his fellows; and they may have seen the elves and wood-wights: I would fain ask them thereof, and am eager to see them."

Said Face-of-god: "And I somewhat dread to see them, and their rags and their misery and the weals of their stripes. It irked me to see Dallach when he first fell to his meat last night, how he ate like a dog for fear and famine. How shall it be, moreover, when we have them in the Dale, and they fall to the deed of kind there, as they needs must. Will they not bear us evil and thrall-like men?"

"Maybe," said Stone-face, "and maybe not; for they have been thralls but for a little while: and I deem that in no long time shall ye see them much bettered by plenteous meat and rest. And after all is said, this Dallach bore him like a valiant man; also it was valiant of him to flee; and of the others may ye say the like. But look you! there are men going down yonder towards our lair: belike those shall be our guests, and there be no Dusky Men amongst them. Come, let us home!"

So Face-of-god looked and beheld from the height of the burg shapes of men grey and colourless creeping toward the lair from sunshine to shadow, like wild creatures shy and fearful of the hunter, or so he deemed of them.

So he turned away, angry and sad of heart, and the twain went down the burg and across the water to their camp, having seen little to tell of from the height.

When they came to their campment there were their folk standing in a ring round about Dallach and the other Runaways. They made way for the War-leader and Stone-face, who came amongst them and beheld the Runaways, that they were many more than they looked to see; for they were of carles one score and three, and of women eighteen, all told save Dallach. When they saw those twain come through the ring of men and perceived that they were chieftains, some of them fell down on their knees before them and held out their joined hands to them, and kissed the Burgdalers" feet and the hems of their garments, while the tears streamed out of their eyes: some stood moving little and staring before them stupidly: and some kept glancing from face to face of the well-liking happy Burgdale carles, though for a while even their faces were sad and downcast at the sight of the poor men: some also kept murmuring one or two words in their country tongue, and Dallach told Face-of-god that these were crying out for victual.

It must be said of these poor folk that they were of divers conditions, and chiefly of three: and first there were seven of Rosedale and five of Silverdale late come to the wood (of these Silverdalers Dallach had told but of two, for the other three were but just come). Of these twelve were seven women, and all, save two of the women, were clad in one scanty kirtle or shirt only; for such was the wont of the Dusky Men with their thralls. They had brought away weapons, and had amongst them six axes and a spear, and a sword, and five knives, and one man had a shield.

Yet though these were clad and armed, yet in some wise were they the worst of all; they were so timorous and cringing, and most of them heavy-eyed and sullen and down-looking. Many of them had been grievously mishandled: one man had had his left hand smitten off; another was docked of three of his toes, and the gristle of his nose slit up; one was halt, and four had been ear-cropped, nor did any lack weals of whipping. Of the Silverdale new-comers the three men were the worst of all the Runaways, with wild wandering eyes, but sullen also, and cringing if any drew nigh, and would not look anyone in the face, save presently Face-of-god, on whom they were soon fond to fawn, as a dog on his master. But the women who were with them, and who were well-nigh as timorous as the men, were those two gaily-dad ones, and they were soft-handed and white-skinned, save for the last days of weather in the wood; for they had been bed-thralls of the Dusky Men.

Such were the new-comers to the wood. But others had been, like Dallach, months therein; it may be said that there were eighteen of these, carles and queens together. Little raiment they had amongst them, and some were all but stark naked, so that on these might well be seen as on Dallach the marks of old stripes, and of these also were there men who had been shorn of some member or other, and they were all burnt and blackened by the weather of the woodland; yet for all their nakedness, they bore themselves bolder and more manlike than the later comers, nor did they altogether lack weapons taken from their foemen, and most of them had some edge-tool or another. Of these folk were four from Silverdale, though Dallach knew it not.

Besides these were a half score and one who had been years in the wood instead of months; weather-beaten indeed were these, shaggy and rough-skinned like wild men of kind. Some of them had made themselves skin breeches or clouts, some went stark naked; of weapons of the Dale had they few, but they bore bows of hazel or wych-elm strung with deer-gut, and shafts headed with flint stones; staves also of the same fashion, and great clubs of oak or holly: some of them also had made them targets of skin and willow-twigs, for these were the warriors of the Runaways: they had a few steel knives amongst them, but had mostly learned the craft of using sharp flints for knives: but four of these were women.

Three of these men were of the kindreds of the Wolf from Silverdale, and had been in the wood for hard upon ten years, and wild as they were, and without hope of meeting their fellows again, they went proudly and boldly amongst the others, overtopping them by the head and more. For the greater part of these men were somewhat short of stature, though by nature strong and stout of body.

It must be told that though Dallach had thus gotten all these many Runaways together, yet had they not been dwelling together as one folk; for they durst not, lest the Dusky Men should hear thereof and fall upon them, but they had kept themselves as best they could in caves and in brakes three together or two, or even faring alone as Dallach did: only as he was a strong and stout-hearted man, he went to and fro and wandered about more than the others, so that he foregathered with most of them and knew them. He said also that he doubted not but that there were more Runaways in the wood, but these were all he could come at. Divers who had fled had died from time to time, and some had been caught and cruelly slain by their masters. They were none of them old; the oldest, said Dallach, scant of forty winters, though many from their aspect might have been old enough.

So Face-of-god looked and beheld all these poor people; and said to himself, that he might well have dreaded that sight. For here was he brought face to face with the Sorrow of the Earth, whereof he had known nought heretofore, save it might be as a tale in a minstrel's song. And when he thought of the minutes that had made the hours, and the hours that had made the days that these men had passed through, his heart failed him, and he was dumb and might not speak, though he perceived that the men of Burgdale looked for speech from him; but he waved his hand to his folk, and they understood him, for they had heard Dallach say that some of them were crying for victual. So they set to work and dighted for them such meat as they had, and they set them down on the grass and made themselves their carvers and serving-men, and bade them eat what they would of such as there was. Yet, indeed, it grieved the Burgdalers again to note how these folk were driven to eat; for they themselves, though they were merry folk, were exceeding courteous at table, and of great observance of manners: whereas these poor Runaways ate, some of them like hungry dogs, and some hiding their meat as if they feared it should be taken from them, and some cowering over it like falcons, and scarce any with a manlike pleasure in their meal. And, their eating over, the more part of them sat dull and mopish, and as if all things were forgotten for the time present.

Albeit presently Dallach bestirred him and said to Face-of-god: "Lord of the Earl-folk, if I might give thee rede, it were best to turn your faces to Burgdale without more tarrying. For we are over-nigh to Rosedale, being but thus many in company. But when we come to our next resting-place, then shall bring thee to speech with the last-comers from Silverdale; for there they talk with the tongue of the kindreds; but we of Rosedale for the more part talk otherwise; though in my house it came down from father to son."

"Yea," said Face-of-god, gazing still on that unhappy folk, as they sat or lay upon the grass at rest for a little while: but him-seemed as he gazed that some memories of past time stirred in some of them; for some, they hung their heads and the tears stole out of their eyes and rolled down their cheeks. But those older Runaways of Silverdale were not crouched down like most of the others, but strode up and down like beasts in a den; yet were the tears on the face of one of these. Then Face-of-god constrained himself, and spake to the folk, and said: "We are now over-nigh to our foes of Rosedale to lie here any longer, being too few to fall upon them. We will come hither again with a host when we have duly questioned these men who have sought refuge with us: and let us call yonder height the Burg of the Runaways, and it shall be a landmark for us when we are on the road to Rosedale."

Then the Burgdalers bade the Runaways courteously and kindly to arise and take the road with them; and by that time were their men all come in; and four of them had venison with them, which was needful, if they were to eat that night or the morrow, as the guests had eaten them to the bone.

So they tarried no more, but set out on the homeward way; and Face-of-god bade Dallach walk beside him, and asked him much concerning Rosedale and its Dusky Men. Dallach told him that these were not so many as they were masterful, not being above eight hundreds of men, all fighting-men. As to women, they had none of their own race, but lay with the Daleswomen at their will, and begat children of them; and all or most of the said children favoured the race of their begetters. Of the men-children they reared most, but the women-children they slew at once; for they valued not women of their own blood: but besides the women of the Dale, they would go at whiles in bands to the edges of the Plain and beguile wayfarers, and bring back with them thence women to be their bed-thralls; albeit some of these were bought with a price from the Westland men.

As to the number of the folk of Rosedale, its own folk, he said they would number some five thousand souls, one with another; of whom some thousand might be fit to bear arms if they had the heart thereto, as they had none. Yet being closely questioned, he deemed that they might fall on their masters from behind, if battle were joined.

He said that the folk of Rosedale had been a goodly folk before they were enthralled, and peaceable with one another, but that now it was a sport of the Dusky Men to set a match between their thralls to fight it out with sword and buckler or otherwise; and the vanquished man, if he were not sore hurt, they would scourge, or shear some member from him, or even slay him outright, if the match between the owners were so made. And many other sad and grievous tales he told to Face-of-god, more than need be told again; so that the War-leader went along sorry and angry, with his teeth set, and his hand on the sword-hilt.

Thus they went till night fell on them, and they could scarce see the signs they had made on their outward journey. Then they made stay in a little valley, having set a watch duly; and since they were by this time far from Rosedale, and were a great company as regarded scattered bands of the foe, they lighted their fires and cooked their venison, and made good cheer to the Runaways, and so went to sleep in the Wild-wood.

When morning was come they gat them at once to the road; and if the Burgdalers were eager to be out of the wood, their eagerness was as nought to the eagerness of the Runaways, most of whom could not be easy now, and deemed every minute lost unless they were wending on to the Dale; so that this day they were willing to get over the more ground, whereas they had not set out on their road till afternoon yesterday.

Howsoever, they rested at noontide, and Face-of-god bade Dallach bring him to speech with others of the Runaways, and first that he might talk with those three men of the kindreds who had fled from Silverdale in early days. So Dallach brought them to him; but he found that though they spake the tongue, they were so few-spoken from wildness and loneliness, at least at first, that nought could come from them that was not dragged from them.

These men said that they had been in the wood more than nine years, so that they knew but little of the conditions of the Dale in that present day. However, as to what Dallach had said concerning the Dusky Men, they strengthened his words; and they said that the Dusky Men took no delight save in beholding torments and misery, and that they doubted if they were men or trolls. They said that since they had dwelt in the wood they had slain not a few of the foemen, waylaying them as occasion served, but that in this warfare they had lost two of their fellows. When Face-of-god asked them of their deeming of the numbers of the Dusky Men, they said that before those bands had broken into Rosedale, they counted them, as far as they could call to mind, at about three thousand men, all warriors; and that somewhat less than one thousand had gone up into Rosedale, and some had died, and many had been cast away in the Wild-wood, their fellows knew not how. Yet had not their numbers in Silverdale diminished; because two years after they (the speakers) had fled, came three more Dusky Companies or Tribes into Silverdale, and each of these tribes was of three long hundreds; and with their coming had the cruelty and misery much increased in the Dale, so that the thralls began to die fast; and that drave the Dusky Men beyond the borders of Silverdale, so that they fell upon Rosedale. When asked how many of the kindreds might yet be abiding in Silverdale, their faces clouded, and they seemed exceeding wroth, and answered, that they would willingly hope that most of those that had not been slain at the time of the overthrow were now dead, yet indeed they feared there were yet some alive, and mayhappen not a few women.

By then must they get on foot again, and so the talk fell between them; but when they made stay for the night, after they had done their meat, Face-of-god prayed Dallach bring to him some of the latest-come folk from Silverdale, and he brought to him the man and the woman who had been in the Dale within that moon. As to the man, if those of the Earl-folk had been few-spoken from fierceness and wildness, he was no less so from mere dulness and weariness of misery; but the woman's tongue went glibly enough, and it seemed to pleasure her to talk about her past miseries. As aforesaid, she was better clad than most of those of Rosedale, and indeed might be called gaily clad, and where her raiment was befouled or rent, it was from the roughness of the wood and its weather, and not from the thralldom. She was a young and fair woman, black-haired and grey-eyed. She had washed herself that day in a woodland stream which they had crossed on the road, and had arrayed her garments as trimly as she might, and had plucked some fumitory, wherewith she had made a garland for her head. She sat down on the grass in front of Face-of-god, while the man her mate stood leaning against a tree and looked on her greedily. The Burgdale carles drew near to her to hearken her story, and looked kindly on the twain. She smiled on them, but especially on Face-of-god, and said:

"Thou hast sent for me, lord, and I wot well thou wouldst hear my tale shortly, for it would be long to tell if I were to tell it fully, and bring into it all that I have endured, which has been bitter enough, for all that ye see me smooth of skin and well-liking of body. I have been the bed-thrall of one of the chieftains of the Dusky Men, at whose house many of their great men would assemble, so that ye may ask me whatso ye will; as I have heard much talk and may call it to mind. Now if ye ask me whether I have fled because of the shame that I, a free woman come of free folk, should be a mere thrall in the bed of the foes of my kin, and with no price paid for me, I must needs say it is not so; since over long have we of the Dale been thralls to be ashamed of such a matter. And again, if ye deem that I have fled because I have been burdened with grievous toil and been driven thereto by the whip, ye may look on my hands and my body and ye will see that I have toiled lit-tle therewith: nor again did I flee because I could not endure a few stripes now and again; for such usage do thralls look for, even when they are delicately kept for the sake of the fairness of their bodies, and this they may well endure; yea also, and the mere fear of death by torment now and again. But before me lay death both assured and horrible; so I took mine own counsel, and told none for fear of bewrayal, save him who guarded me; and that was this man; who fled not from fear, but from love of me, and to him I have given all that I might give. So we got out of the house and down the Dale by night and

cloud, and hid for one whole day in the Dale itself, where I trembled and feared, so that I deemed I should die of fear; but this man was well pleased with my company, and with the lack of toil and beating even for the day. And in the night again we fled and reached the Wild-wood before dawn, and well-nigh fell into the hands of those who were hunting us, and had out-gone us the day before, as we lay hid. Well, what is to say? They saw us not, else had we not been here, but scattered piece-meal over the land. This carle knew the passes of the wood, because he had followed his master therein, who was a great hunter in the wastes, contrary to the wont of these men, and he had lain a night on the burg yonder; therefore he brought me thither, because he knew that thereabout was plenty of prey easy to take, and he had a bow with him; and there we fell in with others of our folk who had fled before, and with Dallach; who e'en now told us what was hard to believe, that there was a fair young man like one of the Gods leading a band of goodly warriors, and seeking for us to bring us into a peaceful and happy land; and this man would not have gone with him because he feared that he might fall into thralldom of other folk, who would take me away from him; but for me, I said I would go in any case, for I was weary of the wood and its roughness and toil, and that if I had a new master he would scarcely be worse than my old one was at his best, and him I could endure. So I went, and glad and glad I am, whatever ye will do with me. And now will I answer whatso ye may ask of me."

She laid her limbs together daintily and looked fondly on Face-of-god, and the carle scowled at her somewhat at first, but presently, as he watched her, his face smoothed itself out of its wrinkles.

But Face-of-god pondered a little while, and then asked the woman if she had heard any words to remember of late days concerning the affairs of the Dusky Men and their intent; and he said:

"I pray thee, sister, be truthful in thine answer, for somewhat lieth on it."

She said: "How could I speak aught but the sooth to thee, O lovely lord? The last word spoken hereof I mind me well: for my master had been mishandling me, and I was sullen to him after the smart, and he mocked and jeered me, and said: Ye women deem we cannot do without you, but ye are fools, and know nothing; we are going to conquer a new land where the women are plenty, and far fairer than ye be; and we shall leave you to fare afield like the other thralls, or work in the digging of silver; and belike ye wot what that meaneth. Also he said that they would leave us to the new tribe of their folk, far wilder than they, whom they looked for in the Dale in about a moon's wearing; so that they needs must seek to other lands. Also this same talk would we hear whenever it pleased any of them to mock us their bed-thralls. Now, my sweet lord, this is nought but the very sooth."

Again spake Face-of-god after a while:

"Tell me, sister, hast thou heard of any of the Dusky Men being slain in the wood?"

"Yea," she said, and turned pale therewith and caught her breath as one choking; but said in a little while:

"This alone was it hard for me to tell thee amongst all the I griefs I have borne, whereof I might have told thee many tales, and will do one day if thou wilt suffer it; but fear makes this hard for me. For in very sooth this was the cause of my fleeing, that my master was brought in slain by an arrow in the wood; and he was to be borne to bale and burned in three days" wearing; and we three bed-thralls of his, and three of the best of the men-thralls, were to be burned quick on his bale-fire after sore torments; therefore I fled, and hid a knife in my bosom, that I might not be taken alive; but sweet was life to me, and belike I should not have smitten myself."

And she wept sore for pity of herself before them all. But Face-of-god said:

"Knowest thou, sister, by whom the man was slain?"

"Nay," she said, still sobbing; "but I heard nought thereof, nor had I noted it in my terror. The death of others, who were slain before him, and the loss of many, we knew not how, made them more bitterly cruel with us."

And again was she weeping; but Face-of-god said kindly to her: "Weep no more, sister, for now shall all thy troubles be over; I feel in my heart that we shall overcome these felons, and make an end of them, and there then is Burgdale for thee in its length and breadth, or thine own Dale to dwell in freely."

"Nay," she said, "never will I go back thither!" and she turned round to him and kissed his feet, and then arose and turned a little toward her mate; and the carle caught her by the hand and led her away, and seemed glad so to do.

So once again they fell asleep in the woods, and again the next morning fared on their way early that they might come into Burgdale before nightfall. When they stayed a while at noontide and ate, Face-of-god again had talk with the Runaways, and this time with those of Rosedale, and he heard much the same story from them that he had heard before, told in divers ways, till his heart was sick with the hearing of it.

On this last day Face-of-god led his men well athwart the wood, so that he hit Wildlake's Way without coming to Carlstead; and he came down into the Dale some four hours after noon on a bright day of latter March. At the ingate to the Dale he found watches set, the men whereof told him that the tidings were not right great. Hall-face's company had fallen in with a band of the felons three score in number in the oakwood nigh to Boars-bait, and had slain some and chased the rest, since they found it hard to follow them home as they ran for the tangled thicket: of the Burgdalers had two been slain and five hurt in this battle.

As for Red-coat's company, they had fallen in with no foemen.

29. THEY BRING THE RUNAWAYS TO BURGSTEAD

So now being out of the wood, they went peaceably and safely along the Portway, the Runaways mingling with the Dalesmen. Strange showed amidst the health and wealth of the Dale the rags and misery and nakedness of the thralls, like a dream amidst the trim gaiety of spring; and whomsoever they met, or came up with on the road, whatso his business might be, could not refrain himself from following them, but mingled with the men-at-arms, and asked them of the tidings; and when they heard who these poor people were, even delivered thralls of the Foemen, they were glad at heart and cried out for joy; and many of the women, nay, of the men also, when they first came across that misery from out the heart of their own pleasant life, wept for pity and love of the poor folk, now at last set free, and blessed the swords that should do the like by the whole people.

They went slowly as men began to gather about them; yea, some of the good folk that lived hard by must needs fare home to their houses to fetch cakes and wine for the guests; and they made them sit down and rest on the green grass by the side of the Portway, and eat and drink to cheer their hearts; others, women and young swains, while they rested went down into the meadows and plucked of the spring flowers, and twined them hastily with deft and well-wont fingers into chaplets and garlands for their heads and bodies. Thus indeed they covered their nakedness, till the lowering faces and weather-beaten skins of those hardly-entreated thralls looked grimly out from amidst the knots of cowslip and oxlip, and the branches of the milk-white blackthorn bloom, and the long trumpets of the daffodils, of the hue that wrappeth round the quill which the webster takes in hand when she would pleasure her soul with the sight of the yellow growing upon the dark green web.

So they went on again as the evening was waning, and when they were gotten within a furlong of the Gate, lo! there was come the minstrelsy, the pipe and the tabor, the fiddle and the harp, and the folk that had learned to sing the sweetest, both men and women, and Redesman at the head of them all.

Then fell the throng into an ordered company; first went the music, and then a score of Face-of-god's warriors with drawn swords and uplifted spears; and then the flower-bedecked misery of the Runaways, men and women going together, gaunt, befouled, and hollow-eyed, with here and there a flushed cheek or gleaming eye, or tear-bedewed face, as the joy and triumph of the eve pierced through their wonted weariness of grief; then the rest of the warriors, and lastly the mingled crowd of Dalesfolk, tall men and fair women gaily arrayed, clean-faced, clear-skinned, and sleek-haired, with glancing eyes and ruddy lips.

And now Redesman turned about to the music and drew his bow across his fiddle, and the other bows ran out in concert, and the harps followed the story of them, and he lifted up his voice and sang the words of an old song, and all the singers joined him and blended their voices with his. And these are some of the words which they sang:

Lo! here is Spring, and all we are living,
We that were wan with Winter's fear;
Reach out your hands to her hands that are giving,
Lest ye lose her love and the light of the year.

Many a morn did we wake to sorrow,
When low on the land the cloud-wrath lay;
Many an eve we feared to-morrow,
The unbegun unfinished day.

Ah we—we hoped not, and thou wert tardy;
Nought wert thou helping; nought we prayed.
Where was the eager heart, the hardy?
Where was the sweet-voiced unafraid?

But now thou lovest, now thou leadest,
Where is gone the grief of our minds?
What was the word of the tale, that thou heedest
E'en as the breath of the bygone winds?

Green and green is thy garment growing
Over thy blossoming limbs beneath;
Up o'er our feet rise the blades of thy sowing,
Pierced are our hearts with thine odorous breath.

But where art thou wending, thou new-comer?
Hurrying on to the Courts of the Sun?
Where art thou now in the House of the Summer?
Told are thy days and thy deed is done.

Spring has been here for us that are living
After the days of Winter's fear;
Here in our hands is the wealth of her giving,
The Love of the Earth, and the Light of the Year.

Thus came they to the Gate, and lo! the Bride thereby, leaning against a buttress, gazing with no dull eyes at the coming throng. She was now clad in her woman's attire again, to wit a light flame-coloured gown over a green kirtle; but she yet bore a gilded helm on her head and a sword girt to her side in token of her oath to the God. She had been in Hall-face's company in that last battle, and had done a man's service there, fighting very valiantly, but had not been hurt, and had come back to Burgstead when the shift of men was.

Now she drew herself up and stood a little way before the Gate and looked forth on the throng, and when her eyes beheld the Runaways amidst of the weaponed carles of Burgdale, her face flushed, and her eyes filled with tears as she stood, partly wondering, partly deeming what they were. She waited till Stone-face came by her, and then she took the old man by the sleeve, and drew him apart a little and said to him: "What meaneth this show, my friend? Who hath clad these folk thus strangely; and who be these three naked tall ones, so fierce-looking, but somewhat noble of aspect?"

For indeed those three men of the kindreds, when they had gotten into the Dale, and had rested them, and drunk a cup of wine, and when they had seen the chaplets and wreaths of the spring-flowers wherewith they were bedecked, and had smelt the sweet savour of them, fell to walking proudly, heeding not their nakedness; for no rag had they upon them save breech-clouts of deer-skin: they had changed weapons with the Burgdale carles; and one had gotten a great axe, which he bore over his shoulder, and the shaft thereof was all done about with copper; and another had shouldered a long heavy thrusting-spear, and the third, an exceeding tall man, bore a long broad-bladed war-sword. Thus they went, brown of skin beneath their flower-garlands, their long hair bleached by the sun falling about their shoulders; high they strode amongst the shuffling carles and tripping women of the later-come thralls. But when they heard the music, and saw that they were coming to the Gate in triumph, strange thoughts of old memories swelled up in their hearts, and they refrained them not from weeping, for they felt that the joy of life had come back to them.

Nor must it be deemed that these were the only ones amongst the Runaways whose hearts were cheered and softened: already were many of them coming back to life, as they felt their worn bodies caressed by the clear soft air of Burgdale, and the sweetness of the flowers that hung about them, and saw all round about the kind and happy faces of their well-willers.

So Stone-face looked on the Bride as she stood with face yet tear-bedewed, awaiting his answer, and said:

"Daughter, thou sayest who clad these folk thus? It was misery that hath so dight them; and they are the images of what we shall be if we love foul life better than fair death, and so fall into the hands of the felons, who were the masters of these men. As for the tall naked men, they are of our own blood, and kinsmen to Face-of-god's new friends; and they are of the best of the vanquished: it was in early days that they fled from thraldom; as we may have to do. Now, daughter, I bid thee be as joyous as thou art valiant, and then shall all be well."

Therewith she smiled on him, and he departed, and she stood a little while, as the throng moved on and was swallowed by the Gate, and looked after them; and for all her pity for the other folk, she thought chiefly of those fearless tall men who were of the blood of those with whom it was lawful to wed.

There she stood as the wind dried the tears upon her cheeks, thinking of the sorrow which these folk had endured, and their stripes and mocking, their squalor and famine; and she wondered and looked on her own fair and shapely hands with the precious finger-rings thereon, and on the dainty cloth and trim broidery of her sleeve; and she touched her smooth cheek with the back of her hand, and smiled, and felt the spring sweet in her mouth, and its savour goodly in her nostrils; and therewith she called to mind the aspect of her lovely body, as whiles she had seen it imaged, all its full measure, in the clear pool at midsummer, or piece-meal, in the shining steel of the Westland mirror. She thought also with what joy she drew the breath of life, yea, even amidst of grief, and of how sweet and pure and well-nurtured she was, and how well beloved of many friends and the whole folk, and she set all this beside those woeful bodies and lowering faces, and felt shame of her sorrow of heart, and the pain it had brought to her; and ever amidst shame and pity of all that misery rose up before her the images of those tall fierce men, and it seemed to her as if she had seen something like to them in some dream or imagination of her mind.

So came the Burgdalers and their guests into the street of Burgstead amidst music and singing; and the throng was great there. Then Face-of-god bade make a ring about the strangers, and they did so, and he and the Runaways alone were in the midst of it; and he spake in a loud voice and said:

"Men of the Dale and the Burg, these folk whom here ye see in such a sorry plight are they whom our deadly foes have rejoiced to torment; let us therefore rejoice to cherish them. Now let those men come forth who deem that they have enough and more, so that they may each take into their houses some two or three of these friends such as would be fain to be together. And since I am War-leader, and have the right hereto, I will first choose them whom I will lead into the House of the Face. And lo you! will I have this man (and he laid his hand on Dallach),who is he whom I first came across, and who found us all these others, and next I will have yonder tall carles, the three of them, because I perceive them to be

men meet to be with a War-leader, and to follow him in battle."

Therewith he drew the three Men of the Wolf towards him, but Dallach already was standing beside him. And folk rejoiced in Face-of-god.

But the Bride came forward next, and spake to him meekly and simply:

"War-leader, let me have of the women those who need me most, that I may bring them to the House of the Steer, and try if there be not some good days yet to be found for them, wherein they shall but remember the past grief as an ugly dream."

Then Face-of-god looked on her, and him-seemed he had never seen her so fair; and all the shame wherewith he had beheld her of late was gone from him, and his heart ran over with friendly love towards her as she looked into his face with kindly eyes; and he said:

"Kinswoman, take thy choice as thy kindness biddeth, and happy shall they be whom thou choosest."

She bowed her head soberly, and chose from among the guests four women of the saddest and most grievous, and no man of their kindred spake for going along with them; then she went her ways home, leading one of them by the hand, and strange was it to see those twain going through sun and shade together, that poor wretch along with the goodliest of women.

Then came forward one after other of the worthy goodmen of the Dale, and especially such as were old, and they led away one one man, and another two, and another three, and often would a man crave to go with a woman or a woman with a man, and it was not gainsaid them. So were all the guests apportioned, and ill-content were those goodmen that had to depart without a guest; and one man would say to another: "Such-an-one, be not downcast; this guest shall be between us, if he will, and shall dwell with thee and me month about; but this first month with me, since I was first comer." And so forth was it said.

Now to prevent the time to come, it may be said about the Runaways, that when they had been a little while amongst the Burgdalers, well fed and well clad and kindly cherished, it was marvellous how they were bettered in aspect of body, and it began to be seen of them that they were well-favoured people, and divers of the women exceeding goodly, black-haired and grey-eyed, and very clear-skinned and white-skinned; most of them were young, and the oldest had not seen above forty winters. They of Rosedale, and especially such as had first fled away to the wood, were very soon seen to be merry and kindly folk; but they who had been longest in captivity, and notably those from Silverdale who were not of the kindreds, were for a long time sullen and heavy, and it availed little to trust to them for the doing of work; albeit they would follow about their friends of Burgdale with the love of a dog; also they were, divers of them, somewhat thievish, and if they lacked anything would liefer take it by stealth than ask for it; which forsooth the Burgdale men took not amiss, but deemed of it as a jest rather.

Very few of the Runaways had any will to fare back to their old homes, or indeed could be got to go into the wood, or, after a day or two, to say any word of Rosedale or Silverdale. In this and other matters the Burgdalers dealt with them as with children who must have their way; for they deemed that their guests had much time to make up; also they were well content when they saw how goodly they were, for these Dalesmen loved to see men goodly of body and of a cheerful countenance.

As for Dallach and the three Silverdale men of the kindred, they went gladly whereas the Burgdale men would have them; and half a score others took weapons in their hands when the war was foughten: concerning which more hereafter.

But on the even whereof the tale now tells, Face-of-god and Stone-face and their company met after nightfall in the Hall of the Face clad in glorious raiment, and therewith were Dallach and the men of Silverdale, washen and docked of their long hair, after the fashion of warriors who bear the helm; and they were clad in gay attire, with battle-swords girt to their sides and gold rings on their arms. Somewhat stern and sad-eyed were those Silverdalers yet, though they looked on those about them kindly and courteously when they met their eyes; and Face-of-god yearned towards them when he called to mind the beauty and wisdom and loving-kindness of the Sun-beam. They were, as aforesaid, strong men and tall, and one of them taller than any amidst that house of tall men. Their names were Wolf-stone, the tallest, and God-swain, and Spear-fist; and God-swain the youngest was of thirty winters, and Wolf-stone of forty. They came into the Hall in such wise, that when they were washed and attired, and all men were assembled in the Hall, and the Alderman and the chieftains sitting on the dais, Face-of-god brought them in from the out-bower, holding Dallach by the right hand and Wolf-stone by the left; and he looked but a stripling beside that huge man.

And when the men in the Hall beheld such goodly warriors, and remembered their grief late past, they all stood up and shouted for joy of them. But Face-of-god passed up the Hall with them, and stood before the dais and said:

"O Alderman of the Dale and Chief of the House of the Face, here I bring to you the foes of our foemen, whom I have met in the Wild-wood, and bidden to our House; and meseemeth they will be our friends, and stand beside us in the day of battle. Therefore I say, take these guests and me together, or put us all to the door together; and if thou wilt take them, then show them to such places as thou deemest meet."

Then stood up the Alderman and said:

"Men of Silverdale and Rosedale, I bid you welcome! Be ye our friends, and abide here with us as long as seemeth good to you, and share in all that is ours. Son Face-of-god, show these warriors to seats on the dais beside thee, and cherish them as well as thou knowest how."

Then Face-of-god brought them up on to the dais and sat down on the right hand of his father, with Dallach on his right hand, and then Wolf-stone out from him; then sat Stone-face, that there might be a man of the Dale to talk with them and serve them; and on his right hand first Spear-fist and then God-swain. And when they were all sat down, and the meat was on the board, Iron-face turned to his son Face-of-god and took his hand, and said in a loud voice, so that many might hear him:

"Son Face-of-god, son Gold-mane, thou bearest with thee both ill luck and good. Erewhile, when thou wanderedst out into the Wild-wood, seeking thou knewest not what from out of the Land of Dreams, thou didst but bring aback to us grief and shame; but now that thou hast gone forth with the neighbours seeking thy foemen, thou hast come aback to us with thine hands full of honour and joy for us, and we thank thee for thy gifts, and I call thee a lucky man. Herewith, kinsman, I drink to thee and the lasting of thy luck."

Therewith he stood up and drank the health of the War-leader and the Guests: and all men were exceeding joyous thereat, when they called to mind his wrath at the Gate-thing, and they shouted for gladness as they drank that health, and the feast became exceeding merry in the House of the Face; and as to the war to come, it seemed to them as if it were over and done in all triumph.

30. HALL-FACE GOETH TOWARD ROSEDALE

On the morrow Face-of-god took counsel with Hall-face and Stone-face as to what were best to be done, and they sat on the dais in the Hall to talk it over.

Short was the time that had worn since that day in Shadowy Vale, for it was but eight days since then; yet so many things had befallen in that time, and, to speak shortly, the outlook for the Burgdalers had changed so much, that the time seemed long to all the three, and especially to Face-of-god.

It was yet twenty days till the Great Folk-mote should beholden, and to Hall-face the time seemed long enough to do somewhat, and he deemed it were good to gather force and fall on the Dusky Men in Rosedale, since now they had gotten men who could lead them the nighest way and by the safest passes, and who knew all the ways of the foemen. But to Stone-face this rede seemed not so good; for they would have to go and come back, and fight and conquer, in less time than twenty days, or be belated of the Folk-mote, and meanwhile much might happen.

"For," said Stone-face, "we may deem the fighting-men of Rosedale to be little less than one thousand, and however we fall on them, even if it be unawares at first, they shall fight stubbornly; so that we may not send against them many less than they be, and that shall strip Burgdale of its fighting-men, so that whatever befalls, we that be left shall have to bide at home."

Now was Face-of-god of the same mind as Stone-face; and he said moreover: "When we go to Rosedale we must abide there a while unless we be overthrown. For if ye conquer it and come away at once, presently shall the tidings come to the ears of the Dusky Men in Silverdale, and they shall join themselves to those of Rosedale who have fled before you, and between them they shall destroy the unhappy people therein; for ye cannot take them all away with you: and that shall they do all the more now, when they look to have new thralls in Burgdale, both men and women. And this we may not suffer, but must abide till we have met all our foemen and have overcome them, so that the poor folk there shall be safe from them till they have learned how to defend their dale. Now my rede is, that we send out the War-arrow at once up and down the Dale, and to the Shepherds and Woodlanders, and appoint a day for the Muster and Weapon-show of all our Folk, and that day to be the day before the Spring Market, that is to say, four days before the Great Folk-mote, and meantime that we keep sure watch about the border of the wood, and now and again scour the wood, so as to clear the Dale of their wandering bands."

"Yea," said Hall-face; "and I pray thee, brother, let me have an hundred of men and thy Dallach, and let us go somewhat deep into the wood towards Rosedale, and see what we may come across; peradventure it might be something better than hart or wild-swine."

Said Face-of-god: "I see no harm therein, if Dallach goeth with thee freely; for I will have no force put on him or any other of the Runaways. Yet meseemeth it were not ill for thee to find the road to Rosedale; for I have it in my mind to send a company thither to give those Rosedale man-quellers somewhat to do at home when we fall upon Silverdale. Therefore go find Dallach, and get thy men together at once; for the sooner thou art gone on thy way the better. But this I bid thee, go no further than three days out, that ye may be back home betimes."

At this word Hall-face's eyes gleamed with joy, and he went out from the Hall straightway and sought Dallach, and found him at the Gate. Iron-face had given him a new sword, a good one, and had bidden him call it Thicket-clearer, and he would not leave it any moment of the day or night, but would lay it under his pillow at night as a child does with a new toy; and now he was leaning against a buttress and drawing the said sword half out of the scabbard and poring over its blade, which was indeed fair enough, being wrought with dark grey waving lines like the eddies of the Weltering Water.

So Hall-face greeted him, and smiled and said:

"Guest, if thou wilt, thou may'st take that new blade of my father's work which thou lovest so, a journey which shall rejoice it."

"Yea," said Dallach, "I suppose that thou wouldest fare on thy brother's footsteps, and deemest that I am the man to lead thee on the road, and even farther than he went; and though it might be thought by some that I have seen enough of Rosedale and the parts thereabout for one while, yet will I go with thee; for now am I a man again, body and soul."

And therewith he drew Thicket-clearer right out of his sheath and waved him in the air. And Hall-face was glad of him and said he was well apaid of his help. So they went away together to gather men, and on the morrow Hall-face departed and went into the Wild-wood with Dallach and an hundred and two score men.

But as for Face-of-god, he fared up and down the Dale following the War-arrow, and went into all houses, and talked with the folk, both young and old, men and women, and told them closely all that had betid and all that was like to betide; and he was well pleased with that which he saw and heard; for all took his words well, and were nought afeard or dismayed by the tidings; and he saw that they would not hang aback. Meantime the days wore, and Hall-face came not back till the seventh day, and he brought with him twelve more Runaways, of whom five were women. But he had lost four men, and had with him Dallach and five others of the Dalesmen borne upon litters sore hurt; and this was his story:

They got to the Burg of the Runaways on the forenoon of the third day, and thereby came on five carles of the Runaways—men who had missed meeting Dallach that other day, but knew what had been done; for one of them had been sick and could not come with him, and he had told the others: so now they were hanging about the Burg of the Runaways hoping somewhat that he might come again; and they met the Burgdalers full of joy, and brought them trouts that they had caught in the river.

As for the other Runaways, namely, five women and two more carles—they had gotten them close to the entrance into Silverdale,[1] where by night and cloud they came on a campment of the Dusky Men, who were leading home these seven poor wretches, Runaways whom they had caught, that they might slay them most evilly in Rose-stead. So Hall-face fell on the Dusky Men, and delivered their captives, but slew not all the foe, and they that fled brought pursuers on them who came up with them the next day, so near was Rosedale, though they made all diligence homeward. The Burgdalers must needs turn and fight with those pursuers, and at last they drave them aback so that they might go on their ways home. They let not the grass grow beneath their feet thereafter, till they were assured by meeting a band of the Woodlanders, who had gone forth to help them, and with whom they rested a little. But neither so were they quite done with the foemen, who came upon them next day a very many: these however they and the Woodlanders, who were all fresh and unwounded and very valiant, speedily put to the worse; and so they came on to Burgstead, leaving those of them who were sorest hurt to be tended by the Woodlanders at Carlstead, who, as might be looked for, deal with them very lovingly.

It was in the first fight that they suffered that loss of slain and wounded; and therein the newly delivered thralls fought valiantly against their masters: as for Dallach, it was no marvel, said Hall-face, that he was hurt; but rather a marvel that he was not slain, so little he recked of point and edge, if he might but slay the foemen.

Such was Hall-face's-tale; and Face-of-god deemed that he had done unwisely to let him go that journey; for the slaying of a few Dusky Men was but a light gain to set against the loss of so many Burgdalers; yet was he glad of the deliverance of those Runaways, and deemed it a gain indeed. But henceforth would he hold all still till he should have tidings of Folk-might; so nought was done thereafter save the warding of the Dale, from the country of the Shepherds to the Waste above the Eastern passes.

But Face-of-god himself went up amongst the Shepherds, and abode with a goodman hight Hound-under-Greenbury, who gathered to him the folk from the country-side, and they went up on to Greenbury, and sat on the green grass while he

1. The distance seems to show that Rosedale is meant.

spoke with them and told them, as he had told the others, what had been done and what should be done. And they heard him gladly, and he deemed that there would be no blenching in them, for they were all in one tale to live and die with their friends of Burgdale, and they said that they would have no other word save that to bear to the Great Folk-mote.

So he went away well-pleased, and he fared on thence to the Woodlanders, and guested at the house of a valiant man hight Wargrove, who on the morrow morn called the folk together to a green lawn of the Wild-wood, so that there was scarce a soul of them that was not there. Then he laid the whole matter before them; and if the Dalesmen had been merry and ready, and the Shepherds stout-hearted and friendly, yet were the Woodlanders more eager still, so that every hour seemed long to them till they stood in their war-gear; and they told him that now at last was the hour drawing nigh which they had dreamed of, but had scarce dared to hope for, when the lost way should be found, and the crooked made straight, and that which had been broken should be mended; that their meat and drink, and sleeping and waking, and all that they did were now become to them but the means of living till the day was come whereon the two remnants of the children of the Wolf should meet and become one Folk to live or die together.

Then went Face-of-god back to Burgstead again, and as he stood anigh the Thing-stead once more, and looked down on the Dale as he had beheld it last autumn, he bethought him that with all that had been done and all that had been promised, the earth was clearing of her trouble, and that now there was nought betwixt him and the happy days of life which the Dale should give to the dwellers therein, save the gathering hosts of the battle-field and the day when the last word should be spoken and the first stroke smitten. So he went down on to the Portway well content.

Thereafter till the day of the Weapon-show there is nought to tell of, save that Dallach and the other wounded men began to grow whole again; and all men sat at home, or went on the woodland ward, expecting great tidings after the holding of the Folk-mote.

31. OF THE WEAPON-SHOW OF THE MEN OF BURGDALE AND THEIR NEIGHBOURS

Now on the day appointed for the Weapon-show came the Folk flock-meal to the great and wide meadow that was cleft by Wildlake as it ran to join the Weltering Water. Early in the morning, even before sunrise, had the wains full of women and children begun to come thither. Also there came little horses and asses from the Shepherd country with one or two or three damsels or children sitting on each, and by wain-side or by beast strode the men of the house, merry and fair in their war-gear. The Woodlanders, moreover, man and woman, elder and swain and young damsel, streamed out of the wood from

Carlstead, eager to make the day begin before the sunrise, and end before his setting.

Then all men fell to pitching of tents and tilting over of wains; for the April sun was hot in the Dale, and when he arose the meads were gay with more than the spring flowers; for the tents and the tilts were stained and broidered with many colours, and there was none who had not furbished up his war-gear so that all shone and glittered. And many wore gay sur-coats over their armour, and the women were clad in all their bravery, and the Houses mostly of a suit; for one bore blue and another corn-colour, and another green, and another brazil, and so forth, and all gleaming and glowing with broidery of gold and bright hues. But the women of the Shepherds were all clad in white, embroidered with green boughs and red blos-soms, and the Woodland women wore dark red kirtles. More-over, the women had set garlands of flowers on their heads and the helms of the men, and for the most part they were slim of body and tall and light-limbed, and as dainty to look upon as the willow-boughs that waved on the brook-side.

Thither had the goodmen who were guesting the Runaways brought their guests, even now much bettered by their new soft days; and much the poor folk marvelled at all this joyance, and they scarce knew where they were; but to some it brought back to their minds days of joyance before the thralldom and all that they had lost, so that their hearts were heavy a while, till they saw the warriors of the kindreds streaming into the mead and bethought them why they carried steel.

Now by then the sun was fully up there was a great throng on the Portway, and this was the folk of the Burg on their way to the Weapon-mead. The men-at-arms were in the midst of the throng, and at the head of them was the War-leader, with the banner of the Face before him, wherein was done the image of the God with the ray-ringed head. But at the rearward of the warriors went the Alderman and the Burg-wardens, before whom was borne the banner of the Burg pictured with the Gate and its Towers; but in the midst betwixt those two was the banner of the Steer, a white beast on a green field.

So when the Dale-wardens who were down in the meadow heard the music and beheld who were coming, they bade the companies of the Dale and the Shepherds and the Wood-landers who were down there to pitch their banners in a half circle about the ingle of the meadow which was made by the streams of Wildlake and the Weltering Water, and gather to them to be ordered there under their leaders of scores and half-hundreds and hundreds; and even so they did. But the banners of the Dale without the Burg were the Bridge, and the Bull, and the Vine, and the Sickle. And the Shepherds had three banners, to wit Greenbury, and the Fleece, and the Thorn.

As for the Woodlanders, they said that they were abiding their great banner, but it should come in good time; "and

meantime," said they, "here are the war-tokens that we shall fight under; for they are good enough banners for us poor men, the remnant of the valiant of time past." Therewith they showed two great spears, and athwart the one was tied an arrow, its point dipped in blood, its feathers singed with fire; and they said, "This is the banner of the War-shaft."

On the other spear there was nought; but the head thereof was great and long, and they had so burnished the steel that the sun smote out a ray of light from it, so that it might be seen from afar. And they said: "This is the Banner of the Spear! Down yonder where the ravens are gathering ye shall see a banner flying over us. There shall fall many a mother's son."

Smiled the Dale-wardens, and said that these were good banners to fight under; and those that stood nearby shouted for the valiancy of the Woodland-Carles.

Now the Dale-wardens went to the entrance from the Port-way to the meadow, and there met the Men of the Burg, and two of them went one on either side of the War-leader to show him to his seat, and the others abode till the Alderman and Burg-wardens came up, and then joined themselves to them, and the horns blew up both in the meadow and on the road, and the new-comers went their ways to their appointed places amidst the shouts of the Dalesmen; and the women and chil-dren and old men from the Burg followed after, till all the mead was covered with bright raiment and glittering gear, save within the ring of men at the further end.

So came the War-leader to his seat of green turf raised in the ingle aforesaid; and he stood beside it till the Alderman and Wardens had taken their places on a seat behind him raised higher than his; below him on the step of his seat sat the Scriv-ener with his pen and ink-horn and scroll of parchment, and men had brought him a smooth shield whereon to write.

On the left side of Face-of-god stood the men of the Face all glittering in their arms, and amongst them were Wolf-stone and his two fellows, but Dallach was not yet whole of his hurts. On his right were the folk of the House of the Steer: the leader of that House was an old white-bearded man, grandfa-ther of the Bride, for her father was dead; and who but the Bride herself stood beside him in her glorious war-gear, look-ing as if she were new come from the City of the Gods, thought most men; but those who beheld her closely deemed that she looked heavy-eyed and haggard, as if she were aweary. Nevertheless, wheresoever she passed, and whosoever looked on her (and all men looked on her), there arose a mur-mur of praise and love; and the women, and especially the young ones, said how fair her deed was, and how meet she was for it; and some of them were for doing on war-gear and faring to battle with the carles; and of these some were sober and sol-emn, as was well seen afterwards, and some spake lightly: some also fell to boasting of how they could run and climb and swim and shoot in the bow, and fell to baring of their arms to show how strong they were: and indeed they were no weaklings, though their arms were fair.

There then stood the ring of men, each company under its banner; and beyond them stood the women and children and men unmeet for battle; and beyond them again the tilted wains and the tents.

Now Face-of-god sat him down on the turf-seat with his bright helm on his head and his naked sword across his knees, while the horns blew up loudly, and when they had done, the elder of the Dale-wardens cried out for silence. Then again arose Face-of-god and said:

"Men of the Dale, and ye friends of the Shepherds, and ye, O valiant Woodlanders; we are not assembled here to take counsel, for in three days" time shall the Great Folk-mote be holden, whereat shall be counsel enough. But since I have been appointed your Chief and War-leader, till such time as the Folk-mote shall either yeasay or naysay my leadership, I have sent for you that we may look each other in the face and number our host and behold our weapons, and see if we be meet for battle and for the dealing with a great host of foemen. For now no longer can it be said that we are going to war, but rather that war is on our borders, and we are blended with it; as many have learned to their cost; for some have been slain and some sorely hurt. Therefore I bid you now, all ye that are weaponed, wend past us that the tale of you may be taken. But first let every hundred-leader and half-hundred-leader and score-leader make sure that he hath his tale aright, and give his word to the captain of his banner that he in turn may give it out to the Scrivener with his name and the House and Company that he leadeth."

So he spake and sat him adown; and the horns blew again in token that the companies should go past; and the first that came was Hall-ward of the House of the Steer, and the first of those that went after him was the Bride, going as if she were his son.

So he cried out his name, and the name of his House, and said, "An hundred and a half," and passed forth, his men following him in most goodly array. Each man was girt with a good sword and bore a long heavy spear over his shoulder, save a score who bare bows; and no man lacked a helm, a shield, and a coat of fence.

Then came a goodly man of thirty winters, and stayed before the Scrivener and cried out:

"Write down the House of the Bridge of the Upper Dale at one hundred, and War-well their leader."

And he strode on, and his men followed clad and weaponed like those of the Steer, save that some had axes hanging to their girdles instead of swords; and most bore casting-spears instead of the long spears, and half a score were bowmen.

Then came Fox of Upton leading the men of the Bull of Middale, an hundred and a half lacking two; very great and tall were his men, and they also bore long spears, and one score and two were bowmen.

Then Fork-beard of Lea, a man well on in years, led on the men of the Vine, an hundred and a half and five men thereto; two score of them bare bow in hand and were girt with sword; the rest bore their swords naked in their right hands, and their shields (which were but small bucklers) hanging at their backs, and in the left hand each bore two casting-spears. With these went two doughty women-at-arms among the bowmen, tall and well-knit, already growing brown with the spring sun, for their work lay among the stocks of the vines on the southward-looking bents.

Next came a tall young man, yellow-haired, with a thin red beard, and gave himself out for Red-beard of the Knolls; he bore his father's name, as the custom of their house was, but the old man, who had long been head man of the House of the Sickle, was late dead in his bed, and the young man had not seen twenty winters. He bade the Scrivener write the tale of the Men of the Sickle at an hundred and a half, and his folk fared past the War-leader joyously, being one half of them bowmen; and fell shooters they were; the other half were girt with swords, and bore withal long ashen staves armed with great blades curved inwards, which weapon they called heft-sax.

All these bands, as the name and the tale of them was declared were greeted with loud shouts from their fellows and the bystanders; but now arose a greater shout still, as Stone-face, clad in goodly glittering array, came forth and said:

"I am Stone-face of the House of the Face, and I bring with me two hundreds of men with their best war-gear and weapons: write it down, Scrivener!"

And he strode on like a young man after those who had gone past, and after him came the tall Hall-face and his men, a gallant sight to see: two score bowmen girt with swords, and the others with naked swords waving aloft, and each bearing two casting-spears in his left hand.

Then came a man of middle age, broad-shouldered, yellow-haired, blue-eyed, of wide and ruddy countenance, and after him a goodly company; and again great was the shout that went up to the heavens; for he said:

"Scrivener, write down that Hound-under-Greenbury, from amongst the dwellers in the hills where the sheep feed, leadeth the men who go under the banner of Greenbury, to the tale of an hundred and four score."

Therewith he passed on, and his men followed, stout, stark, and merry-faced, girt with swords, and bearing over their shoulders long-staved axes, and spears not so long as those which the Dalesmen bore; and they had but a half score of arrow-shot with them.

Next came a young man, blue-eyed also, with hair the colour of flax on the distaff, broad-faced and short-nosed, low of stature, but very strong-built, who cried out in a loud, cheerful voice:

"I am Strongitharm of the Shepherds, and these valiant men are of the Fleece and the Thorn blended together, for so they would have it; and their tale is one hundred and two score and ten."

Then the men of those kindreds went past merry and shouting, and they were clad and weaponed like to them of Greenbury, but had with them a score of bowmen. And all these Shepherd-folk wore over their hauberks white woollen surcoats broidered with green and red.

Now again uprose the cry, and there stood before the War-leader a very tall man of fifty winters, dark-faced and grey-eyed, and he spake slowly and somewhat softly, and said:

"War-leader, this is Red-wolf of the Woodlanders leading the men who go under the sign of the War-shaft, to the number of an hundred and two."

Then he passed on, and his men after him, tall, lean, and silent amidst the shouting. All these men bare bows, for they were keen hunters; each had at his girdle a little axe and a wood-knife, and some had long swords withal. They wore, everyone of the carles, short green surcoats over their coats of fence; but amongst them were three women who bore like weapons to the men, but were clad in red kirtles under their hauberks, which were of good ring-mail gleaming over them from throat to knee.

Last came another tall man, but young, of twenty-five winters, and spake:

"Scrivener, I am Bears-bane of the Woodlanders, and these that come after me wend under the sign of the Spear, and they are of the tale of one hundred and seven."

And he passed by at once, and his men followed him, clad and weaponed no otherwise than they of the War-shaft, and with them were two women.

Now went all those companies back to their banners, and stood there; and there arose among the bystanders much talk concerning the Weapon-show, and who were the best arrayed of the Houses. And of the old men, some spake of past weapon-shows which they had seen in their youth, and they set them beside this one, and praised and blamed. So it went on a little while till the horns blew again, and once more there was silence. Then arose Face-of-god and said:

"Men of Burgdale, and ye Shepherd-folk, and ye of the Woodland, now shall ye wot how many weaponed men we may bring together for this war. Scrivener, arise and give forth the tale of the companies, as they have been told unto you."

Then the Scrivener stood up on the turf-bench beside Face-of-god, and spake in a loud voice, reading from his scroll:

"Of the Men of Burgdale there have passed by me nine hundreds and six; of the Shepherds three hundreds and eight and ten; and of the Woodlanders two hundreds and nine; so that all told our men are fourteen hundreds and thirty and three."

Now in those days men reckoned by long hundreds, so that the whole tale of the host was one thousand, five hundred, and four score and one, telling the tale in short hundreds.

When the tale had been given forth and heard, men shouted again, and they rejoiced that they were so many. For it exceeded the reckoning which the Alderman had given out at the Gate-thing. But Face-of-god said:

"Neighbours, we have held our Weapon-show; but now hold you ready, each man, for the Hosting toward very battle; for belike within seven days shall the leaders of hundreds and twenties summon you to be ready in arms to take whatso fortune may befall. Now is sundered the Weapon-show. Be ye as merry to-day as your hearts bid you to be."

Therewith he came down from his seat with the Alderman and the Wardens, and they mingled with the good folk of the Dale and the Shepherds and the Woodlanders, and merry was their converse there. It yet lacked an hour of noon; so presently they fell to and feasted in the green meadow, drinking from wain to wain and from tent to tent; and thereafter they played and sported in the meads, shooting at the butts and wrestling, and trying other masteries. Then they fell to dancing one and all, and so at last to supper on the green grass in great merriment. Nor might you have known from the demeanour of any that any threat of evil overhung the Dale. Nay, so glad were they, and so friendly, that you might rather have deemed that this was the land whereof tales tell, wherein people die not, but live for ever, without growing any older than when they first come thither, unless they be born into the land itself, and then they grow into fair manhood, and so abide. In sooth, both the land and the folk were fair enough to be that land and the folk thereof.

But a little after sunset they sundered, and some fared home; but many of them abode in the tents and tilted wains, because the morrow was the first day of the Spring Market: and already were some of the Westland chapmen come; yea, two of them were with the bystanders in the meadow; and more were looked for ere the night was far spent.

32. THE MEN OF SHADOWY VALE COME TO THE SPRING MARKET AT BURGSTEAD

On the morrow betimes in the morning the Westland chapmen, who were now all come, went out from the House of the Face, where they were ever wont to be lodged, and set up their booths adown the street betwixt gate and bridge. Gay was the show; for the booths were tilted over with painted cloths, and the merchants themselves were clad in long gowns of fine cloth; scarlet, and blue, and white, and green, and black, with broidered welts of gold and silver; and their knaves were gaily attired in short coats of divers hues, with silver rings about their arms, and short swords girt to their sides. People began to gather about these chapmen at once when they fell to opening their bales and their packs, and unloading their wains. There had they iron, both in pigs and forged scrap and nails; steel they had, and silver, both in ingots and vessel; pearls from over sea; cinnabar and other colours for staining, such as were not in the mountains: madder from the marshes, and purple of the sea, and scarlet grain from the holm-oaks by its edge, and woad from the deep clayey fields of the plain; silken thread also from the outer ocean, and rare webs of silk, and jars of olive oil, and fine pottery, and scented woods, and sugar of the cane. But gold they had none with them, for that they took there; and for weapons, save a few silver-gilt toys, they had no market.

So presently they fell to chaffer; for the carles brought them little bags of the river-borne gold, so that the weights and scales were at work; others had with them scrolls and tallies to tell the number of the beasts which they had to sell, and the chapmen gave them wares therefor without beholding the beasts; for they wotted that the Dalesmen lied not in chaffer. While the day was yet young withal came the Dalesmen from the mid and nether Dale with their wares and set up their booths; and they had with them flasks and kegs of the wine which they had to sell; and bales of the good winter-woven cloth, some grey, some dyed, and pieces of fine linen; and blades of swords, and knives, and axes of such fashion as the Westland men used; and golden cups and chains, and fair rings set with mountain-blue stones, and copper bowls, and vessels gilt and parcel-gilt, and mountain-blue for staining. There were men of the Shepherds also with such fleeces as they could spare from the daily chaffer with the neighbours. And of the Woodlanders were four carles and a woman with peltries and dressed deer-skins, and a few pieces of well-carven woodwork for bedsteads and chairs and such like.

Soon was the Burg thronged with folk in all its open places, and all were eager and merry, and it could not have been told from their demeanour and countenance that the shadow of a grievous trouble hung over them. True it was that every man of the Dale and the neighbours was girt with his sword, or bore spear or axe or other weapon in his hand, and that most had their bucklers at their backs and their helms on their heads; but this was ever their custom at all meetings of men, not because they dreaded war or were fain of strife, but in token that they were free men, from whom none should take the weapons without battle.

Such were the folk of the land: as for the chapmen, they were well-spoken and courteous, and blithe with the folk, as they well might be, for they had good pennyworths of them; yet they dealt with them without using measureless lying, as behoved folk dealing with simple and proud people; and many was the tale they told of the tidings of the Cities and the Plain.

There amongst the throng was the Bride in her maiden's attire, but girt with the sword, going from booth to booth with her guests of the Runaways, and doing those poor people what pleasure she might, and giving them gifts from the goods there, such as they set their hearts on. And the more part of the Runaways were about among the people of the Fair; but Dallach, being still weak, sat on a bench by the door of the House of the Face looking on well-pleased at all the stir of folk.

Hall-face was gone on the woodland ward; while Face-of-god went among the folk in his most glorious attire; but he soon betook him to the place of meeting without the Gate, where Stone-face and some of the elders were sitting along with the Alderman, beside whom sat the head man of the merchants, clad in a gown of fine scarlet embroidered with the best work of the Dale, with a golden chaplet on his head, and a good sword, golden-hilted, by his side, all which the Alderman had given to it him that morning. These chiefs were talking together concerning the tidings of the Plain, and many a tale the guest told to the Dalesmen, some true, some false. For there had been battles down there, and the fall of kings, and destruction of people, as oft befalleth in the guileful Cities. He told them also, in answer to their story of the Dusky Men, of how men even such-like, but riding on horses, or drawn in wains, an host not to be numbered, had erewhile overthrown the hosts of the Cities of the Plain, and had wrought evils scarce to be told of; and how they had piled up the skulls of slaughtered folk into great hills beside the city-gates, so that the sun might no longer shine into the streets; and how because of the death and the rapine, grass had grown in the kings" chambers, and the wolves had chased deer in the Temples of the Gods.

"But," quoth he, "I know you, bold tillers of the soil, valiant scourers of the Wild-wood, that the worst that can befall you will be to die under shield, and that ye shall suffer no torment of the thrall. May the undying Gods bless the threshold of this Gate, and oft may I come hither to taste of your kindness! May your race, the uncorrupt, increase and multiply, till your valiant men and clean maidens make the bitter sweet and purify the earth!"

He spake smooth-tongued and smiling, handling the while the folds of his fine scarlet gown, and belike he meant a full half of what he said; for he was a man very eloquent of speech, and had spoken with kings, uncowed and pleased with his speaking; and for that cause and his riches had he been made chief of the chapmen. As he spake the heart of Face-of-god swelled within him, and his cheek flushed; but Iron-face sat up straight and proud, and a light smile played about his face, as he said gravely:

"Friend of the Westland, I thank thee for the blessing and the kind word. Such as we are, we are; nor do I deem that the very Gods shall change us. And if they will be our friends, it is well; for we desire nought of them save their friendship; and if they will be our foes, that also shall we bear; nor will we curse them for doing that which their lives bid them to do. What sayest thou, Face-of-god, my son?"

"Yea, father," said Face-of-god, "I say that the very Gods, though they slay me, cannot unmake my life that has been. If they do deeds, yet shall we also do."

The Outlander smiled as they spake, and bowed his head to Iron-face and Face-of-god, and wondered at their pride of heart, marvelling what they would say to the great men of the Cities if they should meet them.

But as they sat a-talking, there came two men running to them from the Portway, their weapons all clattering upon them, and they heard withal the sound of a horn winded not far off very loud and clear; and the Chapman's cheek paled: for in sooth he doubted that war was at hand, after all he had heard of the Dalesmen's dealings with the Dusky Men. And all battle was loathsome to him, nor for all the gain of his chaffer had he come into the Dale, had he known that war was looked for.

But the chiefs of the Dalesmen stirred not, nor changed countenance; and some of the goodmen who were in the street nigh the Gate came forth to see what was toward; for they also had heard the voice of the horn.

Then one of those messengers came up breathless, and stood before the chiefs, and said:

"New tidings, Alderman; here be weaponed strangers come into the Dale."

The Alderman smiled on him and said: "Yea, son, and are they a great host of men?"

"Nay," said the man, "not above a score as I deem, and there is a woman with them."

"Then shall we abide them here," said the Alderman, "and thou mightest have saved thy breath, and suffered them to bring tidings of themselves; since they may scarce bring us war. For no man desireth certain and present death; and that is all that such a band may win at our hands in battle to-day; and all who come in peace are welcome to us. What like are they to behold?"

Said the man: "They are tall men gloriously attired, so that they seem like kinsmen of the Gods; and they bear flowering boughs in their hands."

The Alderman laughed, and said: "If they be Gods they are welcome indeed; and they shall grow the wiser for their coming; for they shall learn how guest-fain the Burgdale men may be. But if, as I deem, they be like unto us, and but the children of the Gods, then are they as welcome, and it may be more so, and our greeting to them shall be as their greeting to us would be."

Even as he spake the horn was winded nearer yet, and more loudly, and folk came pouring out of the Gate to learn the tidings. Presently the strangers came from off the Portway into the space before the Gate; and their leader was a tall and goodly man of some thirty winters, in glorious array, helm on head and sword by side, his surcoat green and flowery like the spring meads. In his right hand he held a branch of the blossomed black-thorn (for some was yet in blossom), and his left had hold of the hand of an exceeding fair woman who went beside him: behind him was a score of weaponed men in goodly attire, some bearing bows, some long spears, but each bearing a flowering bough in hand.

The tall man stopped in the midst of the space, and the Alderman and they with him stirred not; though, as for Face-of-god, it was to him as if summer had come suddenly into the midst of winter, and for the very sweetness of delight his face grew pale.

Then the new-comer drew nigh to the Alderman and said:

"Hail to the Gate and the men of the Gate! Hail to the kindred of the children of the Gods!"

But the Alderman stood up and spake: "And hail to thee, tall man! Fair greeting to thee and thy company! Wilt thou name thyself with thine own name, or shall I call thee nought save Guest? Welcome art thou, by whatsoever name thou wilt be called. Here may'st thou and thy folk abide as long as ye will."

Said the new-comer: "Thanks have thou for thy greeting and for thy bidding! And that bidding shall we take, whatsoever may come of it; for we are minded to abide with thee for a while. But know thou, O Alderman of the Dalesmen, that I am not sackless toward thee and thine. My name is Folk-might of the Children of the Wolf, and this woman is the Sun-beam, my sister, and these behind me are of my kindred, and are well beloved and trusty. We are no evil men or wrong-doers; yet have we been driven into sore straits, wherein men must needs at whiles do deeds that make their friends few and their foes many. So it may be that I am thy foeman. Yet, if thou doubtest of me that I shall be a baneful guest, thou shalt have our weapons of us, and then mayest thou do thy will upon us without dread; and here first of all is my sword!"

Therewith he cast down the flowering branch he was bearing, and pulled his sword from out his sheath, and took it by the point, and held out the hilt to Iron-face.

But the Alderman smiled kindly on him and said:

"The blade is a good one, and I say it who know the craft of sword-forging; but I need it not, for thou seest I have a sword by my side. Keep your weapons, one and all; for ye have come amongst many and those no weaklings: and if so be that thy guilt against us is so great that we must needs fall on you, ye will need all your war-gear. But hereof is no need to speak till the time of the Folk-mote, which will be holden in three days" wearing; so let us forbear this matter till then; for I deem we shall have enough to say of other matters. Now, Folk-might, sit down beside me, and thou also, Sun-beam, fairest of women."

Therewith he looked into her face and reddened, and said:

"Yet belike thou hast a word of greeting for my son, Face-of-god, unless it be so that ye have not seen him before?"

Then Face-of-god came forward, and took Folk-might by the hand and kissed him; and he stood before the Sun-beam and took her hand, and the world waxed a wonder to him as he kissed her cheeks; and in no wise did she change countenance, save that her eyes softened, and she gazed at him full kindly from the happiness of her soul.

Then Face-of-god said: "Welcome, Guests, who erewhile guested me so well: now beginneth the day of your well-doing to the men of Burgdale; therefore will we do to you as well as we may."

Then Folk-might and the Sun-beam sat them down with the chieftains, one on either side of the Alderman, but Face-of-god passed forth to the others, and greeted them one by one: of them was Wood-father and his three sons, and Bow-may; and they rejoiced exceedingly to see him, and Bow-may said:

"Now it gladdens my heart to look upon thee alive and thriving, and to remember that day last winter when I met thee on the snow, and turned thee back from the perilous path to thy pleasure, which the Dusky Men were besetting, of whom thou knewest nought. Yea, it was merry that tide; but this is better. Nay, friend," she said, "it availeth thee nought to strive to look out of the back of thine head: let it be enough to thee that she is there. Thou art now become a great chieftain, and she is no less; and this is a meeting of chieftains, and the folk are look-

ing on and expecting demeanour of them as of the Gods; and she is not to be dealt with as if she were the daughter of some little goodman with whom one hath made tryst in the meadows. There! hearken to me for a while; at least till I tell thee that thou seemest to me to hold thine head higher than when last I saw thee; though that is no long time either. Hast thou been in battle again since that day?"

"Nay," he said, "I have stricken no stroke since I slew two felons within the same hour that we parted. And thou, sister, what hast thou done?"

She said: "The grey goose hath been on the wing thrice since that, bearing on it the bane of evil things."

Then said Wood-wise: "Kinswoman, tell him of that battle, since thou art deft with thy tongue."

She said: "Weary on battles! it is nought save this: twelve days agone needs must every fighting-man of the Wolf, carle or of queen, wend away from Shadowy Vale, while those unmeet for battle we hid away in the caves at the nether end of the Dale: but Sun-beam would not endure that night, and fared with us, though she handled no weapon. All this we had to do because we had learned that a great company of the Dusky Men were over-nigh to our Dale, and needs must we fall upon them, lest they should learn too much, and spread the story. Well, so wise was Folk-might that we came on them unawares by night and cloud at the edge of the Pine-wood, and but one of our men was slain, and of them not one escaped; and when the fight was over we counted four score and ten of their arm-rings."

He said: "Did that or aught else come of our meeting with them that morning?"

"Nay," she said, "nought came of it: those we slew were but a straying band. Nay, the four score and ten slain in the Pine-wood knew not of Shadowy Vale belike, and had no intent for it: they were but scouring the wood seeking their warriors that had gone out from Silverdale and came not aback."

"Thou art wise in war, Bow-may," said Face-of-god, and he smiled withal.

Bow-may reddened and said: "Friend Gold-mane, dost thou perchance deem that there is aught ill in my warring? And the Sun-beam, she naysayeth the bearing of weapons; though I deem that she hath little fear of them when they come her way."

Said Face-of-god: "Nay, I deem no ill of it, but much good. For I suppose that thou hast learned overmuch of the wont of the Dusky Men, and hast seen their thralls?"

She knitted her brows, and all the merriment went out of her face at that word, and she answered: "Yea, thou hast it; for I have both seen their thralls and been in the Dale of thralldom; and how then can I do less than I do? But for thee, I perceive that thou hast been nigh unto our foes and hast fallen in with their thralls; and that is well; for whatso tales we had told thee thereof it is like thou wouldst not have trowed in, as now thou must do, since thou thyself hast seen these poor folk. But now I will tell thee, Gold-mane, that my soul is sick of these comings and goings for the slaughter of a few wretches; and I long for the Great Day of Battle, when it will be seen whether we shall live or die; and though I laugh and jest, yet doth the wearing of the days wear me."

He looked kindly on her and said: "I am War-leader of this Folk, and trust me that the waiting-tide shall not be long; wherefore now, sister, be merry to-day, for that is but meet and right; and cast aside thy care, for presently shalt thou behold many new friends. But now meseemeth overlong have ye been standing before our Gate, and it is time that ye should see the inside of our Burg and the inside of our House."

Indeed by this time so many men had come out of the street that the place before the Gate was all thronged, and from where he stood Face-of-god could scarce see his father, or Folk-might and the Sun-beam and the chieftains.

So he took Wood-father by the hand, and close behind him came Wood-wise and Bow-may, and he cried out for way that he might speak with the Alderman, and men gave way to them, and he led those new-comers close up to the gate-seats of the Elders, and as he clove the press smiling and bright-eyed and happy, all gazed on him; but the Sun-beam, who was sitting between Iron-face and the Westland Chapman, and who heretofore had been agaze with eyes beholding little, past whose ears the words went unheard, and whose mind wandered into thoughts of things unfashioned yet, when she beheld him close to her again, then, taken unawares, her eyes caressed him, and she turned as red as a rose, as she felt all the sweetness of desire go forth from her to meet him. So that, he perceiving it, his voice was the clearer and sweeter for the inward joy he felt, as he said:

"Alderman, meseemeth it is now time that we bring our Guests into the House of our Fathers; for since they are in war-like array, and we are no longer living in peace, and I am now War-leader of the Dale, I deem it but meet that I should have the guesting of them. Moreover, when we are come into our House, I will bid thee look into thy treasury, that thou may'st find therein somewhat which it may pleasure us to give to our Guests."

Said Iron-face: "Thou sayest well, son, and since the day is now worn past noon, and these folk are but just come from the Waste, therefore such as we have of meat and drink abideth them. And surely there is within our house a coffer which belongeth to thee and me; and forsooth I know not why we keep the treasures hoarded therein, save that it be for this cause: that if we were to give to our friends that which we ourselves use and love, which would be of all things pleasant to us, if we gave them such goods, they would be worn and worsened by our use of them. For this reason, therefore, do we keep fair things which we use not, so that we may give them to our friends.

"Now, Guests, both of the Waste and the Westland, since here is no Gate-thing or meeting of the Dale-wardens, and we sit here but for our pleasure, let us go take our pleasure within doors for a while, if it seem good to you."

Therewith he arose, and the folk made way for him and his Guests; and Folk-might went on the right hand of Iron-face, and beside him went the Chapman, who looked on him with a half-smile, as though he knew somewhat of him. But on the other side of Iron-face went the Sun-beam, whose hand he held, and after these came Face-of-god, leading in the rest of the New-comers, who yet held the flowery branches in their hands.

Now so much had Face-of-god told the Dalesmen, that they deemed they all knew these men for their battle-fellows of whom they had heard tell; and this the more as the men were so goodly and manly of aspect, especially Folk-might, so that they seemed as if they were nigh akin to the Gods. As for the Sun-beam, they knew not how to praise her beauty enough, but they said that they had never known before how fair the Gods might be. So they raised a great shout of welcome as the men came through the Gate into the Burg, and all men turned their backs on the booths, so eager were they to behold closely these new friends.

But as the Guests went from the Gate to the House of the Face, going very slowly because of the press, there in the front of the throng stood the Bride with the women of the Run-aways, whom she had caused to be clad very fairly; and she was fain to do them a pleasure by bringing them to sight of these new-comers, of whom she had not heard who they were, though she had heard the cry that strangers were at hand. So there she stood smiling a little with the pleasure of showing a fair sight to the poor people, as folk do with children. But when she saw those twain going on each side of the Alderman she knew them at once; and when the Sun-beam, who was on his left side, passed so close to her that she could see the very smoothness and dainty fashion of her skin, then was she astonied, and the world seemed strange to her, and till they were gone by, and for a while afterwards, she knew not where she was nor what she did, though it seemed to her as if she still saw the face of that fair woman as in a picture.

But the Sun-beam had noted her at first, even amongst the fair women of Burgstead, and she so steady and bright beside the wandering timorous eyes and lowering faces of the thralls. But suddenly, as eye met eye, she saw her face change; she saw her cheek whiten, her eyes stare, and her lips quiver, and she knew at once who it was; for she had not seen her before as Folk-might had. Then the Sun-beam cast her eyes adown, lest her compassion might show in her face, and be a fresh grief to her that had lost the wedding and the love; and so she passed on.

As for Folk-might, he had seen her at once amongst all that folk as he came into the street, and in sooth he was looking for her; and when he saw her face change, as the sight of the Sun-beam smote upon her heart, his own face burned with shame and anger, and he looked back at her as he went toward the House. But she saw him not, nor noted him; and none deemed it strange that he looked long on the Bride, the treasure of Burgstead. But for some while Folk-might was few-spoken and sharp-spoken amongst the chieftains; for he was slow to master his longing and his wrath.

So when all the Guests had entered the door of the House of the Face, the Alderman turned back, and, standing on the threshold of his House, spake unto the throng:

"Men of the Dale, and ye Outlanders who may be here, know that this is a happy day; for hither have come to us Guests, men of the kindred of the Gods, and they are even those of whom Face-of-god my son hath told you. And they are friends of our friends and foes of our foes. These men are now in my House, as is but right; but when they come forth I look to you to cherish them in the best way ye know, and make much of them, as of those who may help us and who may by us be holpen."

Therewith he went in again and into the Hall, and bade show the New-comers to the dais; and wine of the best, and meat such as was to hand, was set before them. He bade men also get ready high feast as great as might be against the evening; and they did his bidding straightway.

33. THE ALDERMAN GIVES GIFTS TO THEM OF SHADOWY VALE

In the Hall of the Face Folk-might sat on the dais at the right hand of the Alderman, and the Sun-beam on his left hand. But Iron-face also had beheld the Bride how her face changed, and he knew the cause, and was grieved and angry and ashamed thereof: also he bethought him how this stranger was sitting in the very place where the Bride used to sit, and of all the love, as of a very daughter, that he had had for her; howbeit he constrained himself to talk courteously and kindly both to Folk-might and

the Sun-beam, as behoved the Chief of the House and the Alderman of the Dale. Moreover, he was not a little moved by the goodliness and wisdom of the Sun-beam and the manliness of Folk-might, who was the most chieftain-like of men.

But while they sat there Face-of-god went from man to man of the Guests, and made much of each, but especially of Wood-father and his sons and Bow-may, and they loved him, and praised him, and deemed him the best of hall-mates. Nor might the Sun-beam altogether refrain her from looking lovingly on him, and it could be seen of her that she deemed he was doing well, and like a wise leader and chieftain.

So wore away awhile, and men were fulfilled of meat and drink; so then the Alderman arose and spake, and said:

"Is it not so, Guests, that ye would now gladly behold our market, and the goodly wares which the chapmen have brought us from the Cities?"

Then most men cried out: "Yea, yea!" and Iron-face said:

"Then shall ye go, nor be holden by me from your pleasure. And ye kinsmen who are the most guest-fain and the wisest, go ye with our friends, and make all things easy and happy for them. But first of all, Guests, I were well pleased if ye would take some small matters out of our abundance; for it were well that ye see them ere ye stand before the chapmen's booths, lest ye chaffer with them for what ye have already."

They all praised his bounty and thanked him for his goodwill: so he arose to go to his treasury, and bade certain of his folk go along with him to bear in the gifts. But ere he had taken three steps down the hall, Face-of-god prevented him and said:

"Kinsman, if thou hast anywhere a hauberk somewhat better than folk are wont to bear, such as thine own hand fashioneth, and a sword of the like stuff, I would have thee give them, the sword to my brother-in-arms Wood-wise here, and the war-coat to my sister Bow-may, who shooteth so well in the bow that none may shoot closer, and very few as close; and her shaft it was that delivered me when my skull was amongst the axes of the Dusky Men: else had I not been here."

Thereat Bow-may reddened and looked down, like a scholar who hath been over-praised for his learning and diligence; but the Alderman smiled on her and said:

"I thank thee, son, that thou hast let me know what these our two friends may be fain of: and as for this damsel-at-arms, it is a little thing that thou askest for her, and we might have found her something more worthy of her goodliness; yet forsooth, since we are all bound for the place where shafts and staves shall be good cheap, a greater treasure might be of less avail to her."

Thereat men laughed, and the Alderman went down the Hall with those bearers of gifts, and was away for a space while they drank and made merry: but presently back they came from the treasury bearing loads of goodly things which were laid on one of the endlong boards. Then began the gift-giving: and first he gave unto Folk-might six golden cups marvellously fashioned, the work of four generations of wrights in the Dale, and he himself had wrought the last two thereof. To Sun-beam he gave a girdle of gold, fashioned with great mastery, whereon were images of the Gods and the Fathers, and warriors, and beasts of the field and fowls of the air; and as he girt it about her loins, he said in a soft voice so that few heard:

"Sun-beam, thou fair woman, time has been when thou wert to us as the edge of the poisonous sword or the midnight torch of the murderer; but now I know not how it will be, or if the grief which thou hast given me will ever wear out or not. And now that I have beheld thee, I have little to do to blame my son; for indeed when I look on thee I cannot deem that there is any evil in thee. Yea, however it may be, take thou this gift as the reward of thine exceeding beauty."

She looked on him with kind eyes, and said meekly:

"Indeed, if I have hurt thee unwittingly, I grieve to have hurt so good a man. Hereafter belike we may talk more of this, but now I will but say, that whereas at first I needed but to win thy son's goodwill, so that our Folk might come to life and thriving again, now it is come to this, that he holdeth my heart in his hand and may do what he will with it; therefore I pray thee withhold not thy love either from him or from me."

He looked on her wondering, and said: "Thou art such an one as might make the old man young, and the boy grow into manhood suddenly; and thy voice is as sweet as the voice of the song-birds singing in the dawn of early summer soundeth to him who hath been sick unto death, but who hath escaped it and is mending. And yet I fear thee."

Therewith he kissed her hand and turned unto the others, and he gave unto Bow-may a hauberk of ring-mail of his own fashioning, a sure defence and a wonderful work, and the collar thereof was done with gold and gems.

But he said to her: "Fair damsel-at-arms, faithful is thy face, and the fashion of thee is goodly: now art thou become one of the best of our friends, and this is little enough to give thee; yet would we fain ward thy body against the foeman; so grieve us not by gainsaying us."

And Bow-may was exceeding glad, and scarce knew how to cease handling that marvel of ring-mail.

Then to Wood-wise, Iron-face gave a most goodly sword, the blade all marked with dark lines like the stream of an eddying river, the hilts of steel and gold marvellously wrought; and all the work of a smith who had dwelt in the house of his father's father, and was a great warrior.

Unto Wood-father he gave a very goodly helm parcelgilded; and to his sons and the other folk fair gifts of weapons and jewels and girdles and cups and other good things; so that their hearts were full of joy, and they all praised his open hand.

Then some of the best and merriest of the kinsmen of the Face, and Face-of-god with them, brought the Guests out into the street and among the booths. There Face-of-god beheld the Bride again; and she was standing by the booth of a chapman and dealing with him for a piece of goodly silken cloth to be a gown for one of her guests, and she was talking and smiling as she chaffered with him, as her wont was; for she was ever very friendly of demeanour with all men. But he noted that she was yet exceeding pale, and he was right sorry thereof, for he loved her friendly; yet now had he no shame for all that had befallen, when he bethought him of the Sun-beam and the love she had for him. And also he had a deeming that the Bride would better of her grief.

34. THE CHIEFTAINS TAKE COUNSEL IN THE HALL OF THE FACE

Then turned Face-of-god back into the Hall, and saw where Iron-face sat at the dais, and with him Folk-might and Stone-face and the Elder of the Dale-wardens, and Sun-beam withal; so he went soberly up to the board, and sat himself down thereat beside Stone-face, over against Folk-might and his father, beside whom sat the Sun-beam; and Folk-might looked on him gravely, as a man powerful and trustworthy, yet was his look somewhat sour.

Then the Alderman said: "My son, I said not to thee come back presently, because I wotted that thou wouldst surely do

so, knowing that we have much to speak of. For, whatever these thy friends may have done, or whatsoever thou hast done with them to grieve us, all that must be set aside at this present time, since the matter in hand is to save the Dale and its folk. What sayest thou hereon? Since, young as thou mayst be, thou art our War-leader, and doubtless shalt so be after the Folk-mote hath been holden."

Face-of-god answered not hastily: indeed, as he sat thinking for a minute or two, the fair spring day seemed to darken about them or to glare into the light of flames amidst the night-tide;

and the joyous clamour without doors seemed to grow hoarse and fearful as the sound of wailing and shrieking. But he spake firmly and simply in a clear voice, and said:

"There can be no two words concerning what we have to aim at; these Dusky Men we must slay everyone, though we be fewer than they be."

Folk-might smiled and nodded his head; but the others sat staring down the hall or into the hangings.

Then spake Folk-might: "Thou wert a boy methought when I cast my spear at thee last autumn, Face-of-god, but now hast thou grown into a man. Now tell me, what deemest thou we must do to slay them all?"

Said Face-of-god: "Once again it is clear that we must fall upon them at home in Rosedale and Silverdale."

Again Folk-might nodded: but Iron-face said:

"Needeth this? May we not ward the Dale and send many bands into the wood to fall upon them when we meet them? Yea, and so doing these our guests have already slain many, as this valiant man hath told me e'en now. Will ye not slay so many at last, that they shall learn to fear us, and abide at home and leave us at peace?"

But Face-of-god said: "Meseemeth, father, that this is not thy rede, and that thou sayest this but to try me: and perchance ye have been talking about me when I was without in the street e'en now. Even if it might be that we should thus cow these felons into abiding at home and tormenting their own thralls at their ease, yet how then are our friends of the Wolf holpen to their own again? And I shall tell thee that I have promised to this man and this woman that I will give them no less than a man's help in this matter. Moreover, I have spoken in every house of the Dale, and to the Shepherds and the Woodlanders, and there is no man amongst them but will follow me in the quarrel. Furthermore, they have heard of the thralldom that is done on men no great way from their own houses; yea, they have seen it; and they remember the old saw, "Grief in thy neighbour's hall is grief in thy garth," and sure it is, father, that whether thou or I gainsay them, go they will to deliver the thralls of the Dusky Men, and will leave us alone in the Dale."

"This is no less than sooth," said the Dale-warden, "never have men gone forth more joyously to a merry-making than all men of us shall wend to this war."

"But," said Face-of-god, "of one thing ye may be sure, that these men will not abide our pleasure till we cut them all off in scattered bands, nor will they sit deedless at home. Nor indeed may they; for we have heard from their thralls that they look to have fresh tribes of them come to hand to eat their meat and waste their servants, and these and they must find new abodes and new thralls; and they are now warned by the overthrows and slayings that they have had at our hands that we are astir, and they will not delay long, but will fall upon us with all their host; it might even be to-day or to-morrow."

Said Folk-might: "In all this thou sayest sooth, brother of the Dale; and to cut this matter short, I will tell you all, that yesterday we had with us a runaway from Silverdale (it is overlong to tell how we fell in with her; for it was a woman). But she told us that this very moon is a new tribe come into the Dale, six long hundreds in number, and twice as many more are looked for in two eights of days, and that ere this moon hath waned, that is, in twenty-four days, they will wend their ways straight for Burgdale, for they know the ways thereto. So I say that Face-of-god is right in all wise. But tell me, brother, hast thou thought of how we shall come upon these men?"

"How many men wilt thou lead into battle?" said Face-of-god.

Folk-might reddened, and said: "A few, a few; maybe two-hundreds all told."

"Yea," said Face-of-god, "but some special gain wilt thou be to us."

"So I deem at least," said Folk-might.

Said Face-of-god: "Good is that. Now have we held our Weapon-show in the Dale, and we find that we together with you be sixteen long hundreds of men; and the tale of the foe-men that be now in Silverdale, new-comers and all, shall be three thousands or thereabout, and in Rosedale hard on a thousand."

"Scarce so many," said Folk-might; "some of the felons have died; we told over our silver arm-rings yesterday, and the tale was three hundred and eighty and six. Besides, they were never so many as thou deemest."

"Well," said Face-of-god, "yet at least they shall outnumber us sorely. We may scarce leave the Dale unguarded when our host is gone; therefore I deem that we shall have but one thousand of men for our onslaught on Silverdale."

"How come ye to that?" said Stone-face.

Said Face-of-god: "Abide a while, fosterer! Though the odds between us be great, it is not to be hidden that I wot how ye of the Wolf know of privy passes into Silverdale; yea, into the heart thereof; and this is the special gain ye have to give us. Therefore we, the thousand men, falling on the foe unawares, shall make a great slaughter of them; and if the murder be but grim enough, those thralls of theirs shall fear us and not them, as already they hate them and not us, so that we may look to them for rooting out these sorry weeds after the overthrow. And what with one thing, what with another, we may cherish a good hope of clearing Silverdale at one stroke with the said thousand men.

"There remaineth Rosedale, which will be easier to deal with, because the Dusky Men therein are fewer and the thralls as many: that also would I fall on at the same time as we fall on Silverdale with the men that are left over from the Silverdale onslaught. Wherefore my rede is, that we gather all those unmeet for battle in the field into this Burg, with ten tens of men to strengthen them; which shall be enough for them, along with the old men, and lads, and sturdy women, to defend themselves till help comes, if aught of evil befall, or to flee into the mountains, or at the worst to die valiantly. Then let the other five hundreds fare up to Rosedale, and fall on the Dusky Men therein about the same time, but not before our onslaught on Silverdale: thus shall hand help foot, so that stumbling be not falling; and we may well hope that our rede shall thrive."

Then was he silent, and the Sun-beam looked upon him with gleaming eyes and parted lips, waiting eagerly to hear what Folk-might would say. He held his peace a while, drumming on the board with his fingers, and none else spake a word. At last he said:

"War-leader of Burgdale, all that thou hast spoken likes me well, and even so must it be done, saving that parting of our host and sending one part to fall upon Rosedale. I say, nay; let us put all our might into that one stroke on Silverdale, and then we are undone indeed if we fail; but so shall we be if we fail anywise; but if we win Silverdale, then shall Rosedale lie open before us."

"My brother," said Face-of-god, "thou art a tried warrior, and I but a lad: but dost thou not see this, that whatever we do, we shall not at one onslaught slay all the Dusky Men of Silverdale, and those that flee before us shall betake them to Rosedale, and tell all the tale, and what shall hinder them then from falling on Burgdale (since they are no great way from it) after they have murdered what they will of the unhappy people under their hands?"

Said Folk-might: "I say not but that there is a risk thereof, but in war we must needs run such risks, and all should be risked rather than that our blow on Silverdale be light. For we be the fewer; and if the foemen have time to call that to mind, then are we all lost."

Said Stone-face: "Meseemeth, War-leader, that there is nought much to dread in leaving Rosedale to itself for a while; for not only may we follow hard on the fleers if they flee to Rosedale, and be there no long time after them, before they have time to stir their host but also after the overthrow we shall be free to send men back to Burgdale by way of Shadowy Vale. I deem that herein Folk-might hath the right of it."

"Even so say I," said the Alderman; "besides, we might then leave more folk behind us for the warding of the Dale. So, son, the risk whereof thou speakest groweth the lesser the longer it is looked on."

Then spake the Dale-warden: "Yet saving your wisdom, Alderman, the risk is there yet. For if these felons come into the Dale at all, even if the folk left behind hold the Burg and keep themselves unmurdered, yet may they not hinder the foe from spoiling our homesteads; so that our folk coming back in triumph shall find ruin at home, and spend weary days in hunting their foemen, who shall, many of them, escape into the Wild-wood."

"Yea," said the Sun-beam, "sooth is that; and Face-of-god is wise to think of it and of other matters. Yet one thing we must bear in mind, that all may not go smoothly in our day's work in Silverdale; so we must have force there to fall back on, in case we miss our stroke at first. Therefore, I say, send we no man to Rosedale, and leave we no able man-at-arms behind in the Burg, so that we have with us every blade that may be gathered."

Iron-face smiled and said: "Thou art wise, damsel; and I marvel that so fair-fashioned a thing as thou can think so hardly of the meeting of the fallow blades. But hearken! will not the Dusky Men hear that we have stripped the Dale of fighting-men, and may they not then give our host the go-by and send folk to ruin us?"

There was silence while Face-of-god looked down on the board; but presently he lifted up his face and said:

"Folk-might was right when he said that all must be risked. Let us leave Rosedale till we have overcome them of Silverdale. Moreover, my father, thou must not deem of these felons as if they were of like wits to us, to forecast the deeds to come, and weigh the chances nicely, and unravel tangled clews. Rather they move like to the stares in autumn, or the winter wild-geese, and will all be thrust forward by some sting that entereth into their imaginations. Therefore, if they have appointed one moon to wear before they fall upon us, they will not stir till then, and we have time enough to do what must be done. Wherefore am I now of one mind with the rest of you. Now meseemeth it were well that these things which we have spoken here, and shall speak, should not be noised abroad openly; nay, at the Folk-mote it would be well that nought be said about the day or the way of our onslaught on Silverdale, lest the foe take warning and be on their guard. Though, sooth to say, did I deem that if they had word of our intent they of Rosedale would join themselves to them of Silverdale, and that we should thus have all our foes in one net, then were I fain if the word would reach them. For my soul loathes the hunting that shall befall up and down the wood for the slaying of a man here, and two or three there, and the wearing of the days in wandering up and down with weapons in the hand, and the spinning out of hatred and delaying of peace."

Then Iron-face reached his hand across the board and took his son's hand, and said:

"Hail to thee, son, for thy word! Herein thou speakest as if from my very soul, and fain am I of such a War-leader."

And desire drew the eyes of the Sun-beam to Face-of-god,

and she beheld him proudly. But he said:

"All hath been spoken that the others of us may speak; and now it falleth to the part of Folk-might to order our goings for the tryst for the onslaught, and the trysting-place shall be in Shadowy Vale. How sayest thou, Chief of the Wolf?"

Said Folk-might: "I have little to say; and it is for the War-leader to see to this closely and piecemeal. I deem, as we all deem, that there should be no delay; yet were it best to wend not all together to Shadowy Vale, but in divers bands, as soon as ye may after the Folk-mote, by the sure and nigh ways that we shall show you. And when we are gathered there, short is the rede, for all is ready there to wend by the passes which we know throughly, and whereby it is but two days" journey to the head of Silverdale, nigh to the caves of the silver, where the felons dwell the thickest."

He set his teeth, and his colour came and went: for as constantly as the onslaught had been in his mind, yet whenever he spake of the great day of battle, hope and joy and anger wrought a tumult in his soul; and now that it was so nigh withal, he could not refrain his joy.

But he spake again: "Now therefore, War-leader, it is for thee to order the goings of thy folk. But I will tell thee that they shall not need to take aught with them save their weapons and victual for the way, that is, for thirty hours; because all is ready for them in Shadowy Vale, though it be but a poor place as to victual. Canst thou tell us, therefore, what thou wilt do?"

Face-of-god had knit his brows and become gloomy of countenance; but now his face cleared, and he set his hand to his pouch, and drew forth a written parchment, and said:

"This is the order whereof I have bethought me. Before the Folk-mote I and the Wardens shall speak to the leaders of hundreds, who be mostly here at the Fair, and give them the day and the hour whereon they shall, each hundred, take their weapons and wend to Shadowy Vale, and also the place where they shall meet the men of yours who shall lead them across the Waste. These hundred-leaders shall then go straightway and give the word to the captains of scores, and the captains of scores to the captains of tens; and if, as is scarce doubtful, the Folk-mote yea-says the onslaught and the fellowship with you of the Wolf, then shall those leaders of tens bring their men to the trysting-place, and so go their ways to Shadowy Vale. Now here I have the roll of our Weapon-show, and I will look to it that none shall be passed over; and if ye ask me in what order they had best get on the way, my rede is that a two hundred should depart on the very evening of the day of the Folk-mote, and these to be of our folk of the Upper Dale; and on the morning of the morrow of the Folk-mote another two hundreds from the Dale; and in the evening of the same day the folk of the Shepherds, three hundreds or more, and that will be easy to them; again on the next day two more bands of the Lower Dale, one in the morning, one in the evening. Lastly, in the earliest dawn of the third day from the Folk-mote shall the Woodlanders wend their ways. But one hundred of men let us leave behind for the warding of the Burg, even as we agreed before. As for the place of tryst for the faring over the Waste, let it be the end of the knolls just by the jaws of the pass yonder, where the Weltering Water comes into the Dale from the East. How say ye?"

They all said, and Folk-might especially, that it was right well devised, and that thus it should be done.

Then turned Face-of-god to the Dale-warden, and said:

"It were good, brother, that we saw the other wardens as soon as may be, to do them to wit of this order, and what they have to do."

Therewith he arose and took the Elder of the Dale-wardens away with him, and the twain set about their business straight-way. Neither did the others abide long in the Hall, but went out into the Burg to see the chapmen and their wares. There the Alderman bought what he needed of iron and steel and other matters; and Folk-might cheapened him a dagger curiously wrought, and a web of gold and silk for the Sun-beam, for which wares he paid in silver arm-rings, new-wrought and of strange fashion.

But amidst of the chaffer was now a great ring of men; and in the midst of the ring stood Redesman, fiddle and bow in hand, and with him were four damsels wondrously arrayed; for the first was clad in a smock so craftily wrought with threads of green and many colours, that it seemed like a piece of the green field beset with primroses and cowslips and harebells and windflowers, rather than a garment woven and sewn; and in her hand she bore a naked sword, with golden hilts and gleaming blade. But the second bore on her roses done in like manner, both blossoms and green leaves, wherewith her body was covered decently, which else had been naked. The third was clad as though she were wading the wheat-field to the waist, and above was wrapped in the leaves and bunches of the wine-tree. And the fourth was clad in a scarlet gown flecked with white wool to set forth the winter's snow, and broidered over with the burning brands of the Holy Hearth; and she bore on her head a garland of mistletoe. And these four damsels were clearly seen to image the four seasons of the year— Spring, Summer, Autumn, and Winter. But amidst them stood a fountain or conduit of gilded work cunningly wrought, and full of the best wine of the Dale, and gilded cups and beakers hung about it.

So now Redesman fell to caressing his fiddle with the bow till it began to make sweet music, and therewith the hearts of all danced with it; and presently words come into his mouth, and he fell to singing; and the damsels answered him:

Earth-wielders, that fashion the Dale-dwellers' treasure,

Soft are ye by seeming, yet hardy of heart!
No warrior amongst us withstandeth your pleasure;
  No man from his meadow may thrust you apart.

Fresh and fair are your bodies, but far beyond telling
  Are the years of your lives, and the craft ye have stored.
Come give us a word, then, concerning our dwelling,
  And the days to befall us, the fruit of the sword.

Winter saith:
When last in the feast-hall the Yule-fire flickered,
  The foot of no foeman fared over the snow,
And nought but the wind with the ash-branches bickered:
  Next Yule ye may deem it a long time ago.

Autumn saith:
Loud laughed ye last year in the wheat-field a-smiting;
  And ye laughed as your backs drave the beam of the press.
When the edge of the war-sword the acres are lighting
  Look up to the Banner and laugh ye no less.

Summer saith:
Ye called and I came, and how good was the greeting,
  When ye wrapped me in roses both bosom and side!
Here yet shall I long, and be fain of our meeting,
  As hidden from battle your coming I bide.

Spring saith:
I am here for your comfort, and lo! what I carry;
  The blade with the bright edges bared to the sun.
To the field, to the work then, that e'en I may tarry
  For the end of the tale in my first days begun!

Therewith the throng opened, and a young man stepped
lightly into the ring, clad in very fair armour, with a gilded
helm on his head; and he took the sword from the hand of the
Maiden of Spring, and waved it in the air till the westering sun
flashed back from it. Then each of the four damsels went up to
the swain and kissed his mouth; and Redesman drew the bow
across the strings, and the four damsels sang together, standing
round about the young warrior:

It was but a while since for earth's sake we trembled,
  Lest the increase our life-days had won for the Dale,
All the wealth that the moons and the years had assembled,
  Should be but a mock for the days of your bale.

But now we behold the sun smite on the token
  In the hand of the Champion, the heart of a man;
We look down the long years and see them unbroken;
  Forth fareth the Folk by the ways it began.

So bid ye these chapmen in autumn returning,

To bring iron for ploughshares and steel for the scythe,
And the over-sea oil that hath felt the sun's burning,
  And fair webs for your women soft-spoken and blithe;

And pledge ye your word in the market to meet them,
  As many a man and as many a maid,
As eager as ever, as guest-fain to greet them,
  And bide till the booth from the waggon is made.

Come, guests of our lovers! for we, the year-wielders,
  Bid each man and all to come hither and take
A cup from our hands midst the peace of our shielders,
  And drink to the days of the Dale that we make.

Then went the damsels to that wine-fountain, and drew
thence cups of the best and brightest wine of the Dale, and
went round about the ring, and gave drink to whomsoever
would, both of the chapmen and the others; while the weaponed youth stood in the midst bearing aloft his sword and
shield like an image in a holy place, and Redesman's bow still
went up and down the strings, and drew forth a sweet and
merry tune.

Great game it was now to see the stark Burgdale carles dragging the Men of the Plain, little loth, up to the front of the ring,
that they might stretch out their hands for a cup, and how
many a one, as he took it, took as much as he might of the
damsel's hand withal. As for the damsels, they played the
Holy Play very daintily, neither reddening nor laughing, but
faring so solemnly, and withal so sweetly and bright-faced,
that it might well have been deemed that they were in very
sooth Maidens of the God of Earth sent from the ever-endur-
ing Hall to cheer the hearts of men.

So simply and blithely did the Men of Burgdale disport them
after the manner of their fathers, trusting in their valour and
beholding the good days to be.

So wore the evening, and when night was come, men feasted
throughout the Burg from house to house, and every hall was
full. But the Guests from Shadowy Vale feasted in the Hall of
the Face in all glee and goodwill; and with them were the chief
of the chapmen and two others; but the rest of them had been
laid hold of by goodmen of the Burg, and dragged into their
feast-halls, for they were fain of those guests and their tales.
One of the chapmen in the House of the Face knew Folk-
might, and hailed him by the name he had borne in the Cities,
Regulus to wit; indeed, the chief chapman knew him, and even
somewhat over-well, for he had been held to ransom by Folk-
might in those past days, and even yet feared him, because he,
the chapman, had played somewhat of a dastard's part to him.
But the other was an open-hearted and merry fellow, and no
weakling; and Folk-might was fain of his talk concerning
times bygone, and the fields they had foughten in, and other

adventures that had befallen them, both good and evil.

As for Face-of-god, he went about the Hall soberly, and spake no more than behoved him, so as not to seem a mar-feast; for the image of the slaughter to be yet abode with him, and his heart foreboded the after-grief of the battle. He had no speech with the Sun-beam till men were sundering after the feast, and then he came close to her amidst of the turmoil, and said:

"Time presses on me these days; but if thou wouldest speak with me to-morrow as I would with thee, then mightest thou go on the Bridge of the Burg about sunrise, and I will be there, and we two only."

Her face, which had been somewhat sad that evening (for she had been watching his), brightened at that word, and she took his hand as folk came thronging round about them, and said:

"Yea, friend, I shall be there, and fain of thee." And therewithal they sundered for that night.

And all men went to sleep throughout the Burg: howbeit they set a watch at the Burg-Gate; and Hall-face, when he was coming back from the woodland ward about sunset, fell in with Redcoat of Waterless and four score men on the Portway coming to meet him and take his place. All which was clean contrary to the wont of the Burgdalers, who at most whiles held no watch and ward, not even in Fair-time.

35. FACE-OF-GOD TALKETH WITH THE SUN-BEAM

Face-of-god was at the Bridge on the morrow before sun-rising, and as he turned about at the Bridge-foot he saw the Sun-beam coming down the street; and his heart rose to his mouth at the sight of her, and he went to meet her and took her by the hand; and there were no words between them till they had kissed and caressed each other, for there was no one stirring about them. So they went over the Bridge into the meadows, and eastward of the beaten path thereover.

The grass was growing thick and strong, and it was full of flowers, as the cowslip and the oxlip, and the chequered daffodil, and the wild tulip: the black-thorn was well-nigh done blooming, but the hawthorn was in bud, and in some places growing white. It was a fair morning, warm and cloudless, but the night had been misty, and the haze still hung about the meadows of the Dale where they were wettest, and the grass and its flowers were heavy with dew, so that the Sun-beam went barefoot in the meadow. She had a dark cloak cast over her kirtle, and had left her glittering gown behind her in the House.

They went along hand in hand exceeding fain of each other, and the sun rose as they went, and the long beams of gold shone through the tops of the tall trees across the grass they trod, and a light wind rose up in the north, as Face-of-god stayed a moment and turned toward the Face of the Sun and prayed to Him, while the Sun-beam's hand left the War-leader's hand and stole up to his golden locks and lay amongst them.

Presently they went on, and the feet of Face-of-god led him unwitting toward the chestnut grove by the old dyke where he had met the Bride such a little while ago, till he bethought whither he was going and stopped short and reddened; and the Sun-beam noted it, but spake not; but he said: "Hereby is a fair place for us to sit and talk till the day's work beginneth."

So then he turned aside, and soon they came to a hawthorn brake out of which arose a great tall-stemmed oak, showing no green as yet save a little on its lower twigs; and anigh it, yet with room for its boughs to grow freely, was a great bird-cherry tree, all covered now with sweet-smelling white blossoms. There they sat down on the trunk of a tree felled last year, and she cast off her cloak, and took his face between her two hands and kissed him long and fondly, and for a while their joy had no word. But when speech came to them, it was she that spake first and said:

"Gold-mane, my dear, sorely I wonder at thee and at me, how we are changed since that day last autumn when I first saw thee. Whiles I think, didst thou not laugh when thou wert by thyself that day, and mock at me privily, that I must needs take such wisdom on myself, and lesson thee standing like a stripling before me. Dost thou not call it all to mind and make merry over it, now that thou art become a great chieftain and a wise warrior, and I am yet what I always was, a young maiden of the kindred; save that now I abide no longer for my love?"

Her face was exceeding bright and rippled with joyous smiles, and he looked at her and deemed that her heart was overflowing with happiness, and he wondered at her indeed that she was so glad of him, and he said:

"Yea, indeed, oft do I see that morning in the woodland hall and thee and me therein, as one looketh on a picture; yea verily, and I laugh, yet is it for very bliss; neither do I mock at all. Did I not deem thee a God then? and am I not most happy now when I can call it thus to mind? And as to thee, thou wert wise then, and yet art thou wise now. Yea, I thought thee a God; and if we are changed, is it not rather that thou hast lifted me up to thee, and not come down to me?"

Yet therewithal he knit his brows somewhat and said:

"Yet thou hast not to tell me that all thy love for thy Folk, and thy yearning hope for its recoverance, was but a painted show. Else why shouldst thou love me the better now that I am become a chieftain, and therefore am more meet to understand thy hope and thy sorrow? Did I not behold thee as we stood before the Wolf of the Hall of Shadowy Vale, how the tears stood in thine eyes as thou beheldest him, and thine hand in mine quivered and clung to me, and thou wert all changed in a moment of time? Was all this then but a seeming and a beguilement?"

"O young man," she said, "hast thou not said it, that we stood there close together, and my hand in thine and desire growing up in me? Dost thou not know how this also quickeneth the story of our Folk, and our goodwill towards the living, and remembrance of the dead? Shall they have lived and desired, and we deny desire and life? Or tell me: what was it made thee so chieftain-like in the Hall yesterday, so that thou wert the master of all our wills, for as self-willed as some of us were? Was it not that I, whom thou deemest lovely, was thereby watching thee and rejoicing in thee? Did not the sweetness of thy love quicken thee? Yet because of that was thy warrior's wisdom and thy foresight an empty show? Heedest thou nought the Folk of the Dale? Wouldest thou sunder from the children of the Fathers, and dwell amongst strangers?"

He kissed her and smiled on her and said: "Did I not say of thee that thou wert wiser than the daughters of men? See how wise thou hast made me!"

She spake again: "Nay, nay, there was no feigning in my love for my people. How couldest thou think it, when the Fathers and the kindred have made this body that thou lovest, and the voice of their songs is in the speech thou deemest sweet?"

He said: "Sweet friend, I deemed not that there was feigning in thee: I was but wondering what I am and how I was fashioned, that I should make thee so glad that thou couldst for a while forget thy hope of the days before we met."

She said: "O how glad, how glad! Yet was I nought hapless. In despite of all trouble I had no down-weighing grief, and I had the hope of my people before me. Good were my days; but I knew not till now how glad a child of man may be."

Their words were hushed for a while amidst their caresses. Then she said:

"Gold-mane, my friend, I mocked not my past self because I deem that I was a fool then, but because I see now that all that my wisdom could do, would have come about without my wisdom; and that thou, deeming thyself something less than wise, didst accomplish the thing I craved, and that which thou didst crave also; and withal wisdom embraced thee, along with love."

Therewith she cast her arms about him and said:

"O friend, I mock myself of this: that erst thou deemedst me a God and fearedst me, but now thou seemest to me to be a God, and I fear thee. Yea, though I have longed so sore to be with thee since the day of Shadowy Vale, and though I have wearied of the slow wearing of the days, and it hath tormented me; yet now that I am with thee, I bless the torment of my longing; for it is but my longing that compelleth me to cast away my fear of thee and caress thee, because I have learned how sweet it is to love thee thus."

He wound his arms about her, and sweeter was their longing than mere joy; and though their love was beyond measure, yet was therein no shame to aught, not even to the lovely Dale and that fair season of spring, so goodly they were among the children of men.

In a while they arose and turned homeward, and went over the open meadow, and it was yet early, and the dew was as heavy on the grass as before, though the wide sunlight was now upon it, glittering on the wet blades, and shining through the bells of the chequered daffodils till they looked like gouts of blood.

"Look," said Sun-beam, as they went along by the same way whereas they came, "deemest thou not that other speech-friends besides us have been abroad to talk together apart on this morning of the eve of battle. It is nought unwonted, that we do, even though we forget the trouble of the people to think of our own joy for a while."

The smile died out of her face as she spoke, and she said:

"O friend, this much may I say for myself in all sooth, that indeed I would die for the kindred and its good days, nor falter therein; but if I am to die, might I but die in thine arms!"

He looked very lovingly on her, and put his arm about her and kissed her and said: "What ails us to stand in the doom-ring and bear witness against ourselves before the kindred? Now I will say, that whatsoever the kindred may or can call upon me to do, that will I do, nor grudge the deed: I am sackless before them. But that is true which I spake to thee when we came together up out of Shadowy Vale, to wit, that I am no strifeful man, but a peaceful; and I look to it to win through this war, and find on the other side either death, or life amongst a happy folk; and I deem that this is mostly the mind of our people."

She said: "Thou shalt not die, thou shalt not die!"

"Mayhappen not," he said; "yet yesterday I could not but look into the slaughter to come, and it seemed to me a grim thing, and darkened the day for me; and I grew acold as a man walking with the dead. But tell me: thou sayest I shall not die; dost thou say this only because I am become dear to thee, or dost thou speak it out of thy foresight of things to come?"

She stopped and looked silently a while over the meadows towards the houses of the Thorp: they were standing now on the border of a shallow brook that ran down toward the Wel-tering Water; it had a little strand of fine sand like the sea-shore, driven close together, and all moist, because that brook was used to flood the meadow for the feeding of the grass; and the last evening the hatches which held up the water had been drawn, so that much had ebbed away and left the strand afore-said.

After a while the Sun-beam turned to Face-of-god, and she was become somewhat pale; she said:

"Nay, I have striven to see, and can see nought save the pic-ture of hope and fear that I make for myself. So it oft befalleth foreseeing women, that the love of a man cloudeth their vision. Be content, dear friend; it is for life or death; but whichso it be, the same for me and thee together?"

"Yea," he said, "and well content I am; so now let each of us trust in the other to be both good and dear, even as I trusted in thee the first hour that I looked on thee."

"It is well," she said; "it is well. How fair thou art; and how fair is the morn, and this our Dale in the goodly season; and all this abideth us when the battle is over."

Once more her voice became sweet and wheedling, and the smile lit up her face again, and she pointed down to the sand with her finger, and said:

"See thou! Here indeed have other lovers passed by across the brook. Shall we wish them good luck?"

He laughed and looked down on the sand, and said:

"Thou art in haste to make a story up. Indeed I see that these first footprints are of a woman, for no carle of the Dale has a foot as small; for we be tall fellows; and these others withal are a man's footprints; and if they showed that they had been walking side by side, simple had been thy tale; but so it is not. I cannot say that these two pairs of feet went over the brook within five minutes of each other; but sure it is that they could not have been faring side by side. Well, belike they were lov-ers bickering, and we may wish them luck out of that. Truly it is well seen that Bow-may hath done thine hunting for thee, dear friend; or else wouldest thou have lacked venison; for thou hast no hunter's eye."

"Well," she said, "but wish them luck, and give me thine hand upon it."

He took her hand, and fondled it, and said: "By this hand of my speech-friend, I wish these twain all luck, in love and in leisure, in faring and fighting, in sowing and samming, in get-ting and giving. Is it well enough wished? If so it be, then come thy ways, dear friend; for the day's work is at hand."

"It is well wished," she said. "Now hearken: by the valiant hand of the War-leader, by the hand that shall unloose my gir-dle, I wish these twain to be as happy as we be."

He made as if to draw her away, but she hung aback to set the print of her foot beside the woman's foot, and then they went on together, and soon crossed the Bridge, and came home to the House of the Face.

When they had broken their fast, Face-of-god would straight get to his business of ordering matters for the warfare, and was wishful to speak with Folk-might; but found him not, either in the House or the street. But a man said:

"I saw the tall Guest come abroad from the House and go toward the Bridge very early in the morning."

The Sun-beam, who was anigh when that was spoken, heard it and smiled, and said: "Gold-mane, deemest thou that it was my brother whom we blessed?"

"I wot not," he said; "but I would he were here, for this gear must speedily be looked to."

Nevertheless it was nigh an hour before Folk-might came home to the House. He strode in lightly and gaily, and shaking the crest of his war-helm as he went. He looked friendly on Face-of-god, and said to him:

"Thou hast been seeking me, War-leader; but grudge it not that I have caused thee to tarry. For as things have gone, I am twice the man for thine helping that I was yester-eve; and thou art so ready and deft, that all will be done in due time."

He looked as if he would have had Face-of-god ask of him what made him so fain, but Face-of-god said only:

"I am glad of thy gladness; but now let us dally no longer, for I have many folk to see to-day and much to set a-going."

So therewith they spake together a while, and then went their ways together toward Carlstead and the Woodlanders.

36. FOLK-MIGHT SPEAKETH WITH THE BRIDE

It must be told that those footprints which Face-of-god and the Sun-beam had blessed betwixt jest and earnest had more to do with them than they wotted of. For Folk-might, who had had many thoughts and longings since he had seen the Bride again, rose up early about sunrise, and went out-a-doors, and wandered about the Burg, letting his eyes stray over the goodly stone houses and their trim gardens, yet noting them little, since the Bride was not there.

At last he came to where there was an open place, straight-sided, longer than it was wide, with a wall on each side of it, over which showed the blossomed boughs of pear and cherry and plum-trees: on either hand before the wall was a row of great lindens, now showing their first tender green, especially on their lower twigs, where they were sheltered by the wall. At the nether end of this place Folk-might saw a grey stone house, and he went towards it betwixt the lindens, for it seemed right great, and presently was but a score of paces from its door, and as yet there was no man, carle or queen, stirring about it.

It was a long low house with a very steep roof; but belike the hall was built over some undercroft, for many steps went up to the door on either hand; and the doorway was low, with a straight lintel under its arch. This house, like the House of the Face, seemed ancient and somewhat strange, and Folk-might could not choose but take note of it. The front was all of good ashlar work, but it was carven all over, without heed being paid to the joints of the stones, into one picture of a flowery meadow, with tall trees and bushes in it, and fowl perched in the trees and running through the grass, and sheep and kine and oxen and horses feeding down the meadow; and over the door at the top of the stair was wrought a great steer bigger than all the other neat, whose head was turned toward the sun-rising and uplifted with open mouth, as though he were lowing aloud. Exceeding fair seemed that house to Folk-might, and as though it were the dwelling of some great kindred.

But he had scarce gone over it with his eyes, and was just about to draw nigher yet to it, when the door at the top of those steps opened, and a woman came out of the house clad in a green kirtle and a gown of brazil, with a golden-hilted sword girt to her side. Folk-might saw at once that it was the Bride, and drew aback behind one of the trees so that she might not see him, if she had not already seen him, as it seemed not that she had, for she stayed but for a moment on the top of the stair, looking out down the tree-rows, and then came down the stair and went soberly along the road, passing so close to Folk-might that he could see the fashion of her beauty closely, as one looks into the work of some deftest artificer. Then it came suddenly into his head that he would follow her and see whither she was wending. "At least," said he to himself, "if I come not to speech with her, I shall be nigh unto her, and shall see somewhat of her beauty."

So he came out quietly from behind the tree, and followed her softly; and he was clad in no garment save his kirtle, and bare no weapons to clash and jingle, though he had his helm on his head for lack of a softer hat. He kept her well in sight, and she went straight onward and looked not back. She went by the way whereas he had come, till they were in the main street, wherein as yet was no one afoot; she made her way to the Bridge, and passed over it into the meadows; but when she had gone but a few steps, she stayed a little and looked on the ground, and as she did so turned a little toward Folk-might, who had drawn back into the last of the refuges over the up-stream buttresses. He saw that there was a half-smile on her face, but he could not tell whether she were glad or sorry. A light wind was beginning to blow, that stirred her raiment and raised a lock of hair that had strayed from the golden fillet round about her head, and she looked most marvellous fair.

Now she looked along the grass that glittered under the beams of the newly-risen sun, and noted belike how heavy the dew lay on it; and the grass was high already, for the spring had been hot, and haysel would be early in the Dale. So she put off her shoes, that were of deerskin and broidered with golden threads, and turned somewhat from the way, and hung them up amidst the new green leaves of a hawthorn bush that stood nearby, and so went thwart the meadow somewhat east-ward straight from that bush, and her feet shone out like pearls amidst the deep green grass.

Folk-might followed presently, and she stayed not again, nor turned, nor beheld him; he recked not if she had, for then would he have come up with her and hailed her, and he knew that she was no foolish maiden to start at the sight of a man who was the friend of her Folk.

So they went their ways till she came to the strand of the water-meadow brook aforesaid, and she went through the little ripples of the shallow without staying, and on through the tall deep grass of the meadow beyond, to where they met the brook again; for it swept round the meadow in a wide curve, and turned back toward itself; so it was some half furlong over from water to water.

She stood a while on the brink of the brook here, which was brim-full and nigh running into the grass, because there was a dam just below the place; and Folk-might drew nigher to her under cover of the thorn-bushes, and looked at the place about her and beyond her. The meadow beyond stream was very fair and flowery, but not right great; for it was bounded by a grove of ancient chestnut trees, that went on and on toward the southern cliffs of the Dale: in front of the chestnut wood stood a broken row of black-thorn bushes, now growing green and losing their blossom, and he could see betwixt them that there was a grassy bank running along, as if there had once been a turf-wall and ditch round about the chestnut trees. For indeed this was the old place of tryst between Gold-mane and the Bride, whereof the tale hath told before.

The Bride stayed scarce longer than gave him time to note all this; but he deemed that she was weeping, though he could not rightly see her face; for her shoulders heaved, and she hung her face adown and put up her hands to it. But now she went a little higher up the stream, where the water was shal-lower, and waded the stream and went up over the meadow, still weeping, as he deemed, and went between the black-thorn bushes, and sat her down on the grassy bank with her back to the chestnut trees.

Folk-might was ashamed to have seen her weeping, and was

half-minded to turn him back again at once; but love constrained him, and he said to himself, "Where shall I see her again privily if I pass by this time and place?" So he waited a little till he deemed she might have mastered the passion of tears, and then came forth from his bush, and went down to the water and crossed it, and went quietly over the meadow straight towards her. But he was not half-way across, when she lifted up her face from between her hands and beheld the man coming. She neither started nor rose up; but straightened herself as she sat, and looked right into Folk-might's eyes as he drew near, though the tears were not dry on her cheeks.

Now he stood before her, and said: "Hail to the Daughter of a mighty House! Mayst thou live happy!"

She answered: "Hail to thee also, Guest of our Folk! Hast thou been wandering about our meadows, and happened on me perchance?"

"Nay," he said; "I saw thee come forth from the House of the Steer, and I followed thee hither."

She reddened a little, and knit her brow, and said:

"Thou wilt have something to say to me?"

"I have much to say to thee," he said; "yet it was sweet to me to behold thee, even if I might not speak with thee."

She looked on him with her deep simple eyes, and neither reddened again, nor seemed wroth; then she said:

"Speak what thou hast in thine heart, and I will hearken without anger whatsoever it may be; even if thou hast but to tell me of the passing folly of a mighty man, which in a month or two he will not remember for sorrow or for joy. Sit here beside me, and tell me thy thought."

So he sat him adown and said: "Yea, I have much to say to thee, but it is hard to me to say it. But this I will say: to-day and yesterday make the third time I have seen thee. The first time thou wert happy and calm, and no shadow of trouble was on thee; the second time thine happy days were waning, though thou scarce knewest it; but to-day and yesterday thou art constrained by the bonds of grief, and wouldest loosen them if thou mightest."

She said: "What meanest thou? How knowest thou this? How may a stranger partake in my joy and my sorrow?"

He said: "As for yesterday, all the people might see thy grief and know it. But when I beheld thee the first time, I saw thee that thou wert more fair and lovely than all other women; and when I was away from thee, the thought of thee and thine image were with me, and I might not put them away; and oft at such and such a time I wondered and said to myself, what is she doing now? though god wot I was dealing with tangles and troubles and rough deeds enough. But the second time I beheld thee, when I had looked to have great joy in the sight of thee, my heart was smitten with a pang of grief; for I saw thee hang-

ing on the words and the looks of another man, who was light-minded toward thee, and that thou wert troubled with the anguish of doubt and fear. And he knew it not, nor saw it, though I saw it."

Her face grew troubled, and the tearful passion stirred within her. But she held it aback, and said, as anyone might have said it:

"How wert thou in the Dale, mighty man? We saw thee not."

He said: "I came hither hidden in other semblance than mine own. But meddle not therewith; it availeth nought. Let me say this, and do thou hearken to it. I saw thee yesterday in the street, and thou wert as the ghost of thine old gladness; although belike thou hast striven with sorrow; for I see thee with a sword by thy side, and we have been told that thou, O fairest of women, hast given thyself to the Warrior to be his damsel."

"Yea," she said, "that is sooth."

He went on: "But the face which thou bearedst yesterday against thy will, amidst all the people, that was because thou hadst seen my sister the Sun-beam for the first time, and Face-of-god with her, hand clinging to hand, lip longing for lip, desire unsatisfied, but glad with all hope."

She laid hand upon hand in the lap of her gown, and looked down, and her voice trembled as she said:

"Doth it avail to talk of this?"

He said: "I know not: it may avail; for I am grieved, and shall be whilst thou art grieved; and it is my wont to strive with my griefs till I amend them."

She turned to him with kind eyes and said:

"O mighty man, canst thou clear away the tangle which besetteth the soul of her whose hope hath bewrayed her? Canst thou make hope grow up in her heart? Friend, I will tell thee that when I wed, I shall wed for the sake of the kindred, hoping for no joy therein. Yea, or if by some chance the desire of man came again into my heart, I should strive with it to rid myself of it, for I should know of it that it was but a wasting folly, that should but beguile me, and wound me, and depart, leaving me empty of joy and heedless of life."

He shook his head and said: "Even so thou deemest now; but one day it shall be otherwise. Or dost thou love thy sorrow? I tell thee, as it wears thee and wears thee, thou shalt hate it, and strive to shake it off."

"Nay, nay," she said; "I love it not; for not only it grieveth me, but also it beateth me down and belittleth me."

"Good is that," said he. "I know how strong thine heart is. Now, wilt thou take mine hand, which is verily the hand of thy friend, and remember what I have told thee of my grief which cannot be sundered from thine? Shall we not talk more concerning this? For surely I shall soon see thee again, and often;

since the Warrior, who loveth me belike, leadeth thee into fellowship with me. Yea, I tell thee, O friend, that in that fellowship shalt thou find both the seed of hope, and the sun of desire that shall quicken it."

Therewith he arose and stood before her, and held out to her his hand all hardened with the sword-hilt, and she took it, and stood up facing him, and said:

"This much will I tell thee, O friend; that what I have said to thee this hour, I thought not to have said to any man; or to talk with a man of the grief that weareth me, or to suffer him to see my tears; and marvellous I deem it of thee, for all thy might, that thou hast drawn this speech from out of me, and left me neither angry nor ashamed, in spite of these tears; and thou whom I have known not, though thou knewest me!

"But now it were best that thou depart, and get thee home to the House of the Face, where I was once so frequent; for I wot that thou hast much to do; and as thou sayest, it will be in warfare that I shall see thee. Now I thank thee for thy words and the thought thou hast had of me, and the pain which thou hast taken to heal my hurt: I thank thee, I thank thee, for as grievous as it is to show one's hurts even to a friend."

He said: "O Bride, I thank thee for hearkening to my tale; and one day shall I thank thee much more. Mayest thou fare well in the Field and amidst the Folk!"

Therewith he kissed her hand, and turned away, and went across the meadow and the stream, glad at heart and blithe with everyone; for kindness grew in him as gladness grew.

37. OF THE FOLK-MOTE OF THE DALESMEN, THE SHEPHERD-FOLK, AND THE WOODLAND-CARLES: THE BANNER OF THE WOLF DISPLAYED

Now came the day of the Great Folk-mote, and there was much thronging from everywhere to the Mote-stead, but most from Burgstead itself, whereas few of the Dale-dwellers who had been at the Fair had gone back home. Albeit some of the Shepherds and of the Dalesmen of the westernmost Dale had brought light tents, and tilted themselves in in the night before the Mote down in the meadows below the Mote-stead. From early morning there had been a stream of folk on the Portway setting westward; and many came thus early that they might hold converse with friends and well-wishers; and some that they might disport them in the woods. Men went in no ordered bands, as the Burgstead men at least had done on the day of the Weapon-show, save that a few of them who were arrayed the bravest gathered about the banners, and went with them to the Mote-stead; for all the banners must needs be there.

The Folk-mote was to be hallowed-in three hours before noon, as all men knew; therefore an hour before that time were all men of the Dale and the Shepherds assembled that might be looked for, save the Alderman and the chieftains with the banner of the Burg, and these were not like to come many minutes before the Hallowing. Folk were gathered on the Field in such wise, that the men-at-arms made a great ring round about the Doom-ring, (albeit there were many old men there, girt with swords that they should never heave up again in battle), so that without that ring there was nought save women and children. But when all the other Houses were assembled, men looked around, and beheld the place of the Woodlanders that it was empty; and they marvelled that they were thus belated. For now all was ready, and a watcher had gone up to the Tower on the height, and had with him the great Horn of Warning, which could be heard past the Mote-stead and a great way down the Dale: and if he saw foes coming from the East he should blow one blast; if from the South, two; if from the West, three; if from the North, four.

So half an hour from the appointed time of Hallowing rose the rumour that the Alderman was on the road, and presently they of the women who were on the outside of the throng, by drawing nigh to the edge of the sheer rock, could behold the Banner of the Burg on the Portway, and soon after could see the wain, done about with green boughs, wherein sat the chieftains in their glittering war-gear. Speedily they spread the tidings, and a confused shout went up into the air; and in a little while the wain stayed on Wildlake's Way at the bottom of the steep slope that went up to the Mote-stead, and the banner of the Burg came on proudly up the hill. Soon all men beheld it, and saw that the tall Hall-face bore it in front of his brother Face-of-god, who came on gleaming in war-gear better than most men had seen; which was indeed of his father's fashioning, and his father's gift to him that morning.

After Face-of-god came the Alderman, and with him Folk-might leading the Sun-beam by the hand, and then Stone-face and the Elder of the Dale-wardens; and then the six Burg-wardens: as to the other Dale-wardens, they were in their places on the Field.

So now those who had been standing up turned their faces toward the Altar of the Gods, and those who had been sitting down sprang to their feet, and the confused rumour of the throng rose into a clear shout as the chieftains went to their places, and sat them down on the turf-seats amidst the Doomring facing the Speech-hill and the Altar of the Gods. Amidmost sat the Alderman, on his right hand Face-of-god, and out from him Hall-face, and then Stone-face and three of the Wardens; but on his left hand sat first the two Guests, then the Elder of the Dale-wardens, and then the other three Burg-wardens; as for the Banner of the Burg, its staff was stuck into the earth behind them, and the Banner raised itself in the morning wind and flapped and rippled over their heads.

There then they sat, and folk abided, and it still lacked some minutes of the due time, as the Alderman wotted by the shadow of the great standing-stone betwixt him and the Altar. Therewithal came the sound of a great horn from out of the wood on the north side, and men knew it for the horn of the Woodland-Carles, and were glad; for they could not think why they should be belated; and now men stood up a-tiptoe and on other's shoulders to look over the heads of the women and children to behold their coming; but their empty place was at the southwest corner of the ring of men.

So presently men beheld them marching toward their place, cleaving the throng of the women and children, a great company; for besides that they had with them two score more of men under weapons than on the day of the Weapon-show, all their little ones and women and outworn elders were with them, some on foot, some riding on oxen and asses. In their forefront went the two signs of the Battle-shaft and the War-spear. But moreover, in front of all was borne a great staff with the cloth of a banner wrapped round about it, and tied up with a hempen yarn that it might not be seen.

Stark and mighty men they looked; tall and lean, broad-shouldered, dark-faced. As they came amongst the throng the voice of their horn died out, and for a few moments they fared on with no sound save the tramp of their feet; then all at once the man who bare the hidden banner lifted up one hand, and straightway they fell to singing, and with that song they came to their place. And this is some of what they sang:

O white, white Sun, what things of wonder
  Hast thou beheld from thy wall of the sky!
All the Roofs of the Rich and the grief thereunder,
  As the fear of the Earl-folk flitteth by!

Thou hast seen the Flame steal forth from the Forest
  To slay the slumber of the lands,
As the Dusky Lord whom thou abhorrest
  Clomb up to thy Burg unbuilt with hands.

Thou lookest down from thy door the golden,
  Nor batest thy wide-shining mirth,
As the ramparts fall, and the roof-trees olden
  Lie smouldering low on the burning earth.

When flitteth the half-dark night of summer
  From the face of the murder great and grim,
'Tis thou thyself and no new-comer
  Shines golden-bright on the deed undim.

Art thou our friend, O Day-dawn's Lover?
  Full oft thine hand hath sent aslant
Bright beams athwart the Wood-bear's cover,
  Where the feeble folk and the nameless haunt.

Thou hast seen us quail, thou hast seen us cower,
  Thou hast seen us crouch in the Green Abode,
While for us wert thou slaying slow hour by hour,
  And smoothing down the war-rough road.

Yea, the rocks of the Waste were thy Dawns upheaving,
  To let the days of the years go through;
And thy Noons the tangled brake were cleaving
  The slow-foot seasons" deed to do.

Then gaze adown on this gift of our giving,
  For the WOLF comes wending frith and ford,
And the Folk fares forth from the dead to the living,
  For the love of the Lief by the light of the Sword.

Then ceased the song, and the whole band of the Woodlanders came pouring tumultuously into the space allotted them, like the waters pouring over a river-dam, their white swords waving aloft in the morning sunlight; and wild and strange cries rose up from amidst them, with sobbing and weeping of joy. But soon their troubled front sank back into ordered ranks, their bright blades stood upright in their hands before them, and folk looked on their company, and deemed it the very Terror of battle and Render of the ranks of war. Right well were they armed; for though many of their weapons were ancient and somewhat worn, yet were they the work of good smiths of old days; and moreover, if any of them lacked good war-gear of his own, that had the Alderman and his sons made good to them.

But before the hedge of steel stood the two tall men who held in their hands the war-tokens of the Battle-shaft and the War-spear, and betwixt them stood one who was indeed the tallest man of the whole assembly, who held the great staff of the hidden banner. And now he reached up his hand, and plucked at the yarn that bound it, which of set purpose was but feeble, and tore it off, and then shook the staff aloft with both hands, and shouted, and lo! the Banner of the Wolf with the

Sun-burst behind him, glittering-bright, new-woven by the women of the kindred, ran out in the fresh wind, and flapped and rippled before His warriors there assembled.

Then from all over the Mote-stead arose an exceeding great shout, and all men waved aloft their weapons; but the men of Shadowy Vale who were standing amidst the men of the Face knew not how to demean themselves, and some of them ran forth into the Field and leapt for joy, tossing their swords into the air, and catching them by the hilts as they fell: and amidst it all the Woodlanders now stood silent, unmoving, as men abiding the word of onset.

As for that brother and sister: the Sun-beam flushed red all over her face, and pressed her hands to her bosom, and then the passion of tears over-mastered her, and her breast heaved, and the tears gushed out of her eyes, and her body was shaken with weeping. But Folk-might sat still, looking straight before him, his eyes glittering, his teeth set, his right hand clutching hard at the hilts of his sword, which lay naked across his knees. And the Bride, who stood clad in her begemmed and glittering war-array in the forefront of the Men of the Steer, nigh unto the seats of the chieftains, beheld Folk-might, and her face flushed and brightened, and still she looked upon him. The Alderman's face was as of one pleased and proud; yet was its joy shadowed as it were by a cloud of compassion. Face-of-god sat like the very image of the War-god, and stirred not, nor looked toward the Sun-beam; for still the thought of the after-grief of battle, and the death of friends and folk that loved him, lay heavy on his heart, for all that it beat wildly at the shouting of the men.

38. OF THE GREAT FOLK-MOTE: ATONEMENTS GIVEN, AND MEN MADE SACKLESS

Amidst the clamour uprose the Alderman; for it was clear to all men that the Folk-mote should be holden at once, and the matters of the War, and the Fellowship, and the choosing of the War-leader, speedily dealt with. So the Alderman fell to hallowing in the Folk-mote: he went up to the Altar of the Gods, and took the Gold-ring off it, and did it on his arm; then he drew his sword and waved it toward the four airts, and spake; and the noise and shouting fell, and there was silence but for him:

"Herewith I hallow in this Folk-mote of the Men of the Dale and the Sheepcotes and the Woodland, in the name of the Warrior and the Earth-god and the Fathers of the kindreds. Now let not the peace of the Mote be broken. Let not man rise against man, or bear blade or hand, or stick or stone against any. If any man break the Peace of the Holy Mote, let him be a man accursed, a wild-beast in the Holy Places; an outcast from home and hearth, from bed and board, from mead and acre; not to be holpen with bread, nor flesh, nor wine; nor flax, nor wool, nor any cloth; nor with sword, nor shield, nor axe, nor plough-share; nor with horse, nor ox, nor ass; with no saddle-beast nor draught-beast; nor with wain, nor boat, nor way-leading; nor with fire nor water; nor with any world's wealth. Thus let him who hath cast out man be cast out by man. Now is hallowed-in the Folk-mote of the Men of the Dale and the Sheepcotes and the Woodlands."

Therewith he waved his sword again toward the four airts, and went and sat down in his place. But presently he arose again, and said:

"Now if man hath aught to say against man, and claimeth boot of any, or would lay guilt on any man's head, let him come forth and declare it; and the judges shall be named, and the case shall be tried this afternoon or to-morrow. Yet first I shall tell you that I, the Alderman of the Dalesmen, doomed one Iron-face of the House of the Face to pay a double fine, for that he drew a sword at the Gate-thing of Burgstead with the intent to break the peace thereof. Thou, Green-sleeve, bring forth the peace-breaker's fine, that Iron-face may lay the same on the Altar."

Then came forth a man from the men of the Face bearing a bag, and he brought it to Iron-face, who went up to the Altar and poured forth weighed gold from the bag thereon, and said:

"Warden of the Dale, come thou and weigh it!"

"Nay," quoth the Warden, "it needeth not, no man here doubteth thee, Alderman Iron-face."

A murmur of yeasay went up, and none had a word to say against the Alderman, but they praised him rather: also men were eager to hear of the war, and the fellowship, and to be done with these petty matters. Then the Alderman rose again and said:

"Hath any man a grief against any other of the Kindreds of the Dale, or the Sheepcotes, or the Woodlands?"

None answered or stirred; so after he had waited a while, he said:

"Is there any who hath any guilt to lay against a Stranger, an Outlander, being such a man as he deems we can come at?"

Thereat was a stir amongst the Men of the Fleece of the Shepherds, and their ranks opened, and there came forth an ill-favoured lean old man, long-nebbed, blear-eyed, and bent, girt with a rusty old sword, but not otherwise armed. And all men knew Penny-thumb, who had been ransacked last autumn. As he came forth, it seemed as if his neighbours had been trying to hold him back; but a stout, broad-shouldered man, black-haired and red-bearded, made way for the old man, and led him out of the throng, and stood by him; and this man was well armed at all points, and looked a doughty carle. He stood side by side with Penny-thumb, right in front of the men of his house, and looked about him at first somewhat uneasily, as though he were ashamed of his fellow; but though many smiled, none laughed aloud; and they forbore, partly because they knew the man to be a good man, partly because of the solemn tide of the Folk-mote, and partly in sooth because they wished all this to be over, and were as men who had no time for empty mirth.

Then said the Alderman: "What wouldest thou, Penny-thumb, and thou, Bristler, son of Brightling?"

Then Penny-thumb began to speak in a high squeaky voice: "Alderman, and Lord of the Folk!" But therewithal Bristle, pulled him back, and said:

"I am the man who hath taken this quarrel upon me, and have sworn upon the Holy Boar to carry this feud through; and we deem, Alderman, that if they who slew Rusty and ransacked Penny-thumb be not known now, yet they soon may be."

As he spake, came forth those three men of the Shepherds and the two Dalesmen who had sworn with him on the Holy Boar. Then up stood Folk-might, and came forth into the field, and said:

"Bristler, son of Brightling, and ye other good men and true, it is but sooth that the ransackers and the slayer may soon be known; and here I declare them unto you: I it was and none other who slew Rusty; and I was the leader of those who ransacked Penny-thumb, and cowed Harts-bane of Greentofts. As for the slaying of Rusty, I slew him because he chased me, and would not forbear, so that I must either slay or be slain, as hath befallen me erewhile, and will befall again, methinks. As for the ransacking of Penny-thumb, I needed the goods that I took, and he needed them not, since he neither used them, nor gave them away, and, they being gone, he hath lived no worser than aforetime. Now I say, that if ye will take the outlawry off me, which, as I hear, ye laid upon me, not knowing me, then will I handsel self-doom to thee, Bristler, if thou wilt bear thy grief to purse, and I will pay thee what thou wilt out of hand; or if perchance thou wilt call me to Holm, thither will I go, if thou and I come unslain out of this war. As to the ransacking and cowing of Harts-bane, I say that I am sackless therein, because the man is but a ruffler and a man of violence, and hath cowed many men of the Dale; and if he gainsay me, then do I call him to the Holm after this war is over; either him or any man who

will take his place before my sword."

Then he held his peace, and man spake to man, and a murmur arose, as they said for the more part that it was a fair and manly offer. But Bristler called his fellows and Penny-thumb to him, and they spake together; and sometimes Penny-thumb's shrill squeak was heard above the deep-voiced talk of the others; for he was a man that harboured malice. But at last Bristler spake out and said:

"Tall man, we know that thou art a chieftain and of good will to the men of the Dale and their friends, and that want drave thee to the ransacking, and need to the manslaying, and neither the living nor the dead to whom thou art guilty are to be called good men; therefore will I bring the matter to purse, if thou wilt handsel me self-doom."

"Yea, even so let it be," quoth Folk-might; and stepped forward and took Bristler by the hand, and handselled him self-doom. Then said Bristler:

"Though Rusty was no good man, and though he followed thee to slay thee, yet was he in his right therein, since he was following up his goodman's gear; therefore shalt thou pay a full blood-wite for him, that is to say, the worth of three hundreds in weed-stuff in whatso goods thou wilt. As for the ransacking of Penny-thumb, he shall deem himself well paid if thou give him our hundreds in weed-stuff for that which thou didst borrow of him."

Then Penny-thumb set up his squeak again, but no man hearkened to him, and each man said to his neighbour that it was well doomed of Bristler, and neither too much nor too little. But Folk-might bade Wood-wont to bring thither to him that which he had borne to the Mote; and he brought forth a big sack, and Folk-might emptied it on the earth, and lo! the silver rings of the slain felons, and they lay in a heap on the green field, and they were the best of silver. Then the Elder of the Dale-wardens weighed out from the heap the blood-wite for Rusty, according to the due measure of the hundred in weed-stuff, and delivered it unto Bristler. And Folk-might said:

"Draw nigh now, Penny-thumb, and take what thou wilt of this gear, which I need not, and grudge not at me henceforward."

But Penny-thumb was afraid, and abode where he was; and Bristler laughed, and said: "Take it, goodman, take it; spare not other men's goods as thou dost thine own."

And Folk-might stood by, smiling faintly: so Penny-thumb plucked up a heart, and drew nigh trembling, and took what he durst from that heap; and all that stood by said that he had gotten a full double of what had been awarded to him. But as for him, he went his ways straight from the Mote-stead, and made no stay till he had gotten him home, and laid the silver up in a strong coffer; and thereafter he bewailed him sorely that he had not taken the double of that which he took, since none would have said him nay.

When he was gone, the Alderman arose and said:

"Now, since the fines have been paid duly and freely, according to the dooming of Bristler, take we off the outlawry from Folk-might and his fellows, and account them to be sackless before us."

Then he called for other cases; but no man had aught more to bring forward against any man, either of the kindreds or the Strangers.

39. OF THE GREAT FOLK-MOTE: MEN TAKE REDE OF THE WAR-FARING, THE FELLOWSHIP, AND THE WAR-LEADER. FOLK-MIGHT TELLETH WHENCE HIS PEOPLE CAME. THE FOLK-MOTE SUNDERED.

Now a great silence fell upon the throng, and they stood as men abiding some new matter. Unto them arose the Alderman, and said:

"Men of the Dale, and ye Shepherds and Woodlanders; it is well known to you that we have foemen in the wood and beyond it; and now have we gotten sure tidings, that they will not abide at home or in the wood, but are minded to fall upon us at home. Now therefore I will not ask you whether ye will have peace or war; for with these foemen ye may have peace no otherwise save by war. But if ye think with me, three things have ye to determine: first, whether ye will abide your foes in your own houses, or will go meet them at theirs; next, whether ye will take to you as fellows in arms a valiant folk of the children of the Gods, who are foemen to our foemen; and lastly, what man ye will have to be your War-leader. Now, I bid all those here assembled, to speak hereof, any man of them that will, either what they may have conceived in their own minds, or what their kindred may have put into their mouths to speak."

Therewith he sat down, and in a little while came forth old Hall-ward of the House of the Steer, and stood before the Alderman, and said: "O Alderman, all we say: Since war is awake we will not tarry, but will go meet our foes while it is yet time. The valiant men of whom thou tellest shall be our fellows, were there but three of them. We know no better War-leader than Face-of-god of the House of the Face. Let him lead us."

Therewith he went his ways; and next came forth War-well, and said: "The House of the Bridge would have Face-of-god for War-leader, these tall men for fellows, and the shortest way to meet the foe." And he went back to his place.

Next came Fox of Upton, and said: "Time presses, or much might be spoken. Thus saith the House of the Bull: Let us go meet the foe, and take these valiant strangers for way-leaders, and Face-of-god for War-leader." And he also went back again.

Then came forth two men together, an old man and a young, and the old man spake as soon as he stood still: "The Men of the Vine bid me say their will: They will not stay at home to have their houses burned over their heads, themselves slain on their own hearths, and their wives haled off to thralldom. They will take any man for their fellow in arms who will smite stark strokes on their side. They know Face-of-god, and were liefer of him for War-leader than any other, and they will follow him wheresoever he leadeth. Thus my kindred biddeth me say, and I hight Fork-beard of Lea. If I live through this war, I shall have lived through five."

Therewith he went back to his place; but the young man lifted up his voice and said: "To all this I say yea, and so am I bidden by the kindred of the Sickle. I am Red-beard of the Knolls, the son of my father." And he went to his place again.

Then came forth Stone-face, and said: "The House of the Face saith: Lead us through the wood, O Face-of-god, thou War-leader, and ye warriors of the Wolf. I am Stone-face, as men know, and this word hath been given to me by the kindred." And he took his place again.

Then came forth together the three chiefs of the Shepherds, to wit Hound-under-Greenbury, Strongitharm, and the Hyllier; and Strongitharm spake for all three, and said:

"The Men of Greenbury, and they of the Fleece and the Thorn, are of one accord, and bid us say that they are well pleased to have Face-of-god for War-leader; and that they will follow him and the warriors of the Wolf to live or die with them; and that they are ready to go meet the foe at once, and will not skulk behind the walls of Greenbury."

Therewith the three went back again to their places.

Then came forth that tall man that bare the Banner of the Wolf, when he had given the staff into the hands of him who stood next. He came and stood over against the seat of the chieftains; and for a while he could say no word, but stood struggling with the strong passion of his joy; but at last he lifted his hands aloft, and cried out in a loud voice:

"O war, war! O death! O wounding and grief! O loss of friends and kindred! let all this be rather than the drawing back of meeting hands and the sundering of yearning hearts!" and he went back hastily to his place. But from the ranks of the Woodlanders ran forth a young man, and cried out:

"As is the word of Red-wolf, so is my word, Bears-bane of Carlstead; and this is the word which our little Folk hath put into our mouths; and O! that our hands may show the meaning of our mouths; for nought else can."

Then indeed went up a great shout, though many forebore to cry out; for now were they too much moved for words or sounds. And in special was Face-of-god moved; and he scarce knew which way to look, lest he should break out into sobs and weeping; for of late he had been much among the Woodlanders, and loved them much.

Then all the noise and clamour fell, and it was to men as if they who had come thither a folk, had now become an host of war.

But once again the Alderman rose up and spake:

"Now have ye yeasaid three things: That we take Face-of-god of the House of the Face for our War-leader; that we fare under weapons at once against them who would murder us; and that we take the valiant Folk of the Wolf for our fellows in arms."

Therewith he stayed his speech, and this time the shout arose clear and most mighty, with the tossing up of swords and the clashing of weapons on shields.

Then he said: "Now, if any man will speak, here is the War-leader, and here is the chief of our new friends, to answer to whatso any of the kindred would have answered."

Thereon came forth the Fiddle from amongst the Men of the Sickle, and drew somewhat nigh to the Alderman, and said:

"Alderman, we would ask of the War-leader if he hath devised the manner of our assembling, and the way of our warfaring, and the day of our hosting. More than this I will not ask of him, because we wot that in so great an assembly it may be that the foe may have some spy of whom we wot not; and though this be not likely, yet some folk may babble; therefore it is best for the wise to be wise everywhere and always. Therefore my rede it is, that no man ask any more concerning this, but let it lie with the War-leader to bring us face to face with the foe as speedily as he may."

All men said that this was well counselled. But Face-of-god arose and said: "Ye Men of the Dale, ye Shepherds and Woodlanders, meseemeth the Fiddle hath spoken wisely. Now therefore I answer him and say, that I have so ordered everything since the Gate-thing was holden at Burgstead, that we may come face to face with the foemen by the shortest of roads. Every man shall be duly summoned to the Hosting, and if any man fail, let it be accounted a shame to him for ever."

A great shout followed on his words, and he sat down again. But Fox of Upton came forth and said:

"O Alderman, we have yeasaid the fellowship of the valiant men who have come to us from out of the waste; but this we have done, not because we have known them, otherwise than by what our kinsman Face-of-god hath told us concerning them, but because we have seen clearly that they will be of much avail to us in our warfare. Now, therefore, if the tall chieftain who sitteth beside thee were to do us to wit what he is, and whence he and his are come, it were well, and fain were we thereof; but if he listeth not to tell us, that also shall be well."

Then arose Folk-might in his place; but or ever he could open his mouth to speak, the tall Red-wolf strode forward bearing with him the Banner of the Wolf and the Sun-burst, and came and stood beside him; and the wind ran through the folds of the banner, and rippled it out above the heads of those twain. Then Folk-might spake and said:

O Men of the Dale and the Sheepcotes, I will do as ye bid me do;
And fain were ye of the story if every deal ye knew.
But long, long were its telling, were I to tell it all:
Let it bide till the Cup of Deliverance ye drink from hall to hall.

Like you we be of the kindreds, of the Sons of the Gods we come,
Midst the Mid-earth's mighty Woodland of old we had our home;
But of older time we abided 'neath the mountains of the Earth,
O'er which the Sun ariseth to waken woe and mirth.
Great were we then and many; but the long days wore us thin,
And war, wherein the winner hath weary work to win.
And the woodland wall behind us e'en like ourselves was worn,
And the tramp of the hosts of the foemen adown its glades was borne
On the wind that bent our wheat-fields. So in the morn we rose,
And left behind the stubble and the autumn-fruited close,
And went our ways to the westward, nor turned aback to see
The glare of our burning houses rise over brake and tree.
But the foe was fierce and speedy, nor long they tarried there,
And through the woods of battle our laden wains must fare;
And the Sons of the Wolf were minished, and the maids of the Wolf
*   waxed few,*
As amidst the victory-singing we fared the wild-wood through.

So saith the ancient story, that west and west we went,
And many a day of battle we had in brake, on bent;
Whilst here a while we tarried, and there we hastened on,

And still the battle-harvest from many a folk we won.

Of the tale of the days who wotteth?
Of the years what man can tell,
While the Sons of the Wolf were wandering, and knew not where to
dwell?
But at last we clomb the mountains, and mickle was our toil,
As high the spear-wood clambered of the drivers of the spoil;
And tangled were the passes and the beacons flared behind,
And the horns of gathering onset came up upon the wind.
So saith the ancient story, that we stood in a mountain-cleft,
Where the ways and the valleys sundered to the right hand and the left.
There in the place of sundering all woeful was the rede;
We knew no land before us, and behind was heavy need.
As the sword cleaves through the byrny, so there the mountain flank
Cleft through the God-kin's people; and ne'er again we drank
The wine of war together, or feasted side by side
In the Feast-hall of the Warrior on the fruit of the battle-tide.
For there we turned and sundered; unto the North we went
And up along the waters, and the clattering stony bent;
And unto the South and the Sheepcotes down went our sister's sons;
And O for the years passed over since we saw those valiant ones!

He ceased, and laid his right hand on the banner-staff a little below the left hand of Red-wolf; and men were so keen to hear each word that he spake, that there was no cry nor sound of voices when he had done, only the sound of the rippling banner of the Wolf over the heads of those twain. The Sun-beam bowed her head now, and wept silently. But the Bride, she had drawn her sword, and held it upright in her hand before her, and the sun smote fire from out of it.

Then it was but a little while before Red-wolf lifted up his voice, and sang:

Hearken a wonder, O Folk of the Field,
How they that did sunder stand shield beside shield!

Lo! the old wont and manner by fearless folk made,
On the Bole of the Banner the brothers" hands laid.

Lo! here the token of what hath betid!
Grown whole is the broken, found that which was hid.

Now one way we follow whate'er shall befall;
As seeketh the swallow his yesteryear's hall.

Seldom folk fewer to fight-stead hath fared;
Ne'er have men truer the battle-reed bared.

Grey locks now I carry, and old am I grown,
Nor looked I to tarry to meet with mine own.

For we who remember the deeds of old days

Were nought but the ember of battle ablaze.

For what man might aid us? what deed and what day
Should come where Weird laid us aloof from the way?

What man save that other of Twain rent apart,
Our war-friend, our Brother, the piece of our heart.

Then hearken the wonder how shield beside shield
The twain that did sunder wend down to the Field!

Now when he had made an end, men could no longer forebear the shout; and it went up into the heavens, and was borne by the west-wind down the Dale to the ears of the stay-at-home women and men unmeet to go abroad, and it quickened their blood and the spirits within them as they heard it, and they smiled and were fain; for they knew that their kinsfolk were glad.

But when there was quiet on the Mote-field again, Folk-might spake again and said;

It is sooth that my Brother sayeth, and that now again we wend,
All the Sons of the Wolf together, till the trouble hath an end.
But as for that tale of the Ancients, it saith that we who went
To the northward, climbed and stumbled o'er many a stony bent,
Till we happed on that isle of the waste-land, and the grass of Shadowy
Vale,
Where we dwelt till we throve a little, and felt our might avail.
Then we fared abroad from the shadow and the little-lighted hold,
And the increase fell to the valiant, and the spoil to the battle-bold,
And never a man gainsaid us with the weapons in our hands;
And in Silverdale the happy we gat us life and lands.

So wore the years o'er-wealthy; and meseemeth that ye know
How we sowed and reaped destruction, and the Day of the overthrow:
How we leaned on the staff we had broken, and put our lives in the
hand
Of those whom we had vanquished and the feeble of the land;
And these were the stone of stumbling, and the burden not to be borne,
When the battle-blast fell on us and our day was over-worn.
Thus then did our wealth bewray us, and left us wise and sad;
And to you, bold men, it falleth once more to make us glad,
If so your hearts are bidding, and ye deem the deed of worth.
Such were we; what we shall be, 'tis yours to say henceforth.

He said furthermore: "How great we have been I have told you already; and ye shall see for yourselves how little we be now. Is it enough, and will ye have us for friends and brothers? How say ye?"

They answered with shout upon shout, so that all the place and the Wild-wood round about was full of the voice of their crying; but when the clamour fell, then spake the Alderman and said:

"Friend, and chieftain of the Wolf, thou mayst hear by this shouting of the people that we have no mind to naysay our yea-say. And know that it is not our use and manner to seek the strong for friends, and to thrust aside the weak; but rather to choose for our friends them who are of like mind to us, men in whom we put our trust. From henceforth then there is brotherhood between us; we are yours, and ye are ours; and let this endure for ever!"

Then were all men full of joy; and now at last the battle seemed at hand, and the peace beyond the battle.

Then men brought the hallowed beasts all garlanded with flowers into the Doom-ring, and there were they slain and offered up unto the Gods, to wit the Warrior, the Earth-god, and the Fathers; and thereafter was solemn feast holden on the Field of the Folk-mote, and all men were fain and merry. Nevertheless, not all men abode there the feast through; for or ever the afternoon was well worn, were many men wending along the Portway eastward toward the Upper Dale, each man in his war-gear and with a scrip hung about him; and these were they who were bound for the trysting-place and the journey over the waste.

So the Folk-mote was sundered; and men went to their houses, and there abode in peace the time of their summoning; since they wotted well that the Hosting was afoot.

But as for the Woodlanders, who were at the Mote-stead with all their folk, women, children, and old men, they went not back again to Carlstead; but prayed the neighbours of the Middle Dale to suffer them to abide there awhile, which they yeasaid with a good will. So the Woodlanders tilted themselves in, the more part of them, down in the meadows below the Mote-stead, along either side of Wildlake's Way; but their ancient folk, and some of the women and children, the neighbours would have into their houses, and the rest they furnished with victual and all that they needed without price, looking upon them as their very guests. For indeed they deemed that they could see that these men would never return to Carlstead, but would abide with the Men of the Wolf in Silverdale, once it were won. And this they deemed but meet and right, yet were they sorry thereof; for the Woodlanders were well beloved of all the Dalesmen; and now that they had gotten to know that they were come of so noble a kindred, they were better beloved yet, and more looked upon.

40. OF THE HOSTING IN SHADOWY VALE

It was on the evening of the fourth day after the Folk-mote that there came through the Waste to the rocky edge of Shadowy Vale a band of some fifteen score of men-at-arms, and with them a multitude of women and children and old men, some afoot, some riding on asses and bullocks; and with them were sumpter asses and neat laden with household goods, and a few goats and kine. And this was the whole folk of the Woodlanders come to the Hosting in Shadowy Vale and the Home of the Children of the Wolf. Their leaders of the way were Wood-father and Wood-wont and two other carles of Shadowy Vale; and Red-wolf the tall, and Bears-bane and War-grove were the captains and chieftains of their company.

Thus then they entered into the narrow pass aforesaid, which was the ingate to the Vale from the Waste, and little by little its dimness swallowed up their long line. As they went by the place where the lowering of the rock-wall gave a glimpse of the valley, they looked down into it as Face-of-god had done, but much change was there in little time. There was the black wall of crags on the other side stretching down to the ghyll of the great Force; there ran the deep green waters of the Shivering Flood; but the grass which Face-of-god had seen naked of everything but a few kine, thereon now the tents of men stood thick. Their hearts swelled within them as they beheld it, but they forebore the shout and the cry till they should be well

within the Vale, and so went down silently into the darkness. But as their eyes caught that dim image of the Wolf on the wall of the pass, man pointed it out to man, and not a few turned and kissed it hurriedly; and to them it seemed that many a kiss had been laid on that dear token since the days of old, and that the hard stone had been worn away by the fervent lips of men, and that the air of the mirk place yet quivered with the vows sworn over the sword-blade.

But down through the dark they went, and so came on to the stony scree at the end of the pass and into the Vale; and the whole Folk save the three chieftains flowed over it and stood about it down on the level grass of the Vale. But those three stood yet on the top of the scree, bearing the war-signs of the Shaft and the Spear, and betwixt them the banner of the Wolf and the Sunburst newly displayed to the winds of Shadowy Vale.

Up and down the Vale they looked, and saw before the tents of men the old familiar banners of Burgdale rising and falling in the evening wind. But amidst of the Doom-ring was pitched a great banner, whereon was done the image of the Wolf with red gaping jaws on a field of green; and about him stood other banners, to wit, The Silver Arm on a red field, the Red Hand on a white field, and on green fields both, the Golden Bushel and the Ragged Sword.

All about the plain shone glittering war-gear of men as they moved hither and thither, and a stream of folk began at once to draw toward the scree to look on those new-comers; and amidst the helmed Burgdalers and the white-coated Shepherds went the tall men of the Wolf, bare-headed and unarmed save for their swords, mingled with the fair strong women of the kindred, treading barefoot the soft grass of their own Vale.

Presently there was a great throng gathered round about the Woodlanders, and each man as he joined it waved hand or weapon toward them, and the joy of their welcome sent a confused clamour through the air. Then forth from the throng stepped Folk-might, unarmed save his sword, and behind him was Face-of-god, in his war-gear save his helm, hand in hand with the Sun-beam, who was clad in her goodly flowered green kirtle, her feet naked like her sisters of the kindred.

Then Folk-might cried aloud: "A full and free greeting to our brothers! Well be ye, O Sons of our Ancient Fathers! And to-day are ye the dearer to us because we see that ye have brought us a gift, to wit, your wives and children, and your grandsires unmeet for war. By this token we see how great is your trust in us, and that it is your meaning never to sunder from us again. O well be ye; well be ye!"

Then spake Red-wolf, and said: "Ye Sons of the Wolf, who parted from us of old time in that cleft of the mountains, it is our very selves that we give unto you; and these are a part of ourselves; how then should we leave them behind us? Bear witness, O men of Burgdale and the Sheepcotes, that we have become one Folk with the men of Shadowy Vale, never to be sundered again!"

Then all that multitude shouted with a loud voice; and when the shout had died away, Folk-might spake again:

"O Warriors of the Sundering, here shall your wives and children abide, while we go a little journey to rejoice our hearts with the hard handplay, and take to us that which we have missed: and to-morrow morn is appointed for this same journey, unless ye be over foot-weary with the ways of the Waste."

Red-wolf smiled as he answered: "This ye say in jest, brother; for ye may see that our day's journey hath not been over-much for our old men; how then should it weary those who may yet bear sword? We are ready for the road and eager for the handplay."

"This is well," said Folk-might, "and what was to be looked for. Therefore, brother, do ye and your counsel-mates come straightway to the Hall of the Wolf; wherein, after ye have eaten and drunken, shall we take counsel with our brethren of Burgdale and the Sheepcotes, so that all may be ordered for battle!"

Said Red-wolf: "Good is that, if we must needs abide till to-morrow; for verily we came not hither to eat and drink and rest

our bodies; but it must be as ye will have it."

Then the Sun-beam left the hand of Face-of-god and came forward, and held out both her palms to the Woodland-folk, and spake in a voice that was heard afar, though it were a woman's, so clear and sweet it was; and she said:

"O Warriors of the Sundering, ye who be not needed in the Hall, and ye our sisters with your little ones and your fathers, come now to us and down to the tents which we have arrayed for you, and there think for a little that we are all at our very home that we long for and have yet to win, and be ye merry with us and make us merry."

Therewith she stepped forward daintily and entered into their throng, and took an old man of the Woodlanders by the hand, and kissed his cheek and led him away, and the coming rest seemed sweet to him. And then came other women of the Vale, kind and fair and smiling, and led away, some an old mother of the Woodlanders, some a young wife, some a pair of lads; and not a few forsooth kissed and embraced the stark warriors, and went away with them toward the tents, which stood along the side of the Shivering Flood where it was at its quietest; for there was the grass the softest and most abundant. There on the green grass were tables arrayed, and lamps were hung above them on spears, to be litten when the daylight should fail. And the best of the victual which the Vale could give was spread on the boards, along with wine and dainties, bought in Silverdale, or on the edges of the Westland with sword-strokes and arrow-flight.

There then they feasted and were merry; and the Sun-beam and Bow-may and the other women of the Vale served them at table, and were very blithe with them, caressing them with soft words, and with clipping and kissing, as folk who were grown exceeding dear to them; so that that eve of battle was softer and sweeter to them than any hour of their life. With these feasters were God-swain and Spear-fist of the delivered thralls of Silverdale as glad as glad might be; but Wolf-stone their eldest was gone with Dallach to the Council in the Hall.

The men of Burgdale and the Shepherds feasted otherwhere in all content, nor lacked folk of the Vale to serve them. Amongst the men of the Face were the ten delivered thralls who had heart to meet their masters in arms: seven of them were of Rosedale and three of Silverdale.

The Bride was with her kindred of the Steer, with whom were many men of Shadowy Vale, and she served her friends and fellows clad in her war-gear, save helm and hauberk, bearing herself as one who is serving dear guests. And men equalled her for her beauty to the Gods of the High Place and the Choosers of the Slain; and they who had not beheld her before marvelled at her, and her loveliness held all men's hearts in a net of desire, so that they forebore their meat to gaze upon her; and if perchance her hand touched some young man, or her cheek or sweet-breathed mouth came nigh to his face, he became bewildered and wist not where he was, nor what to do. Yet was she as lowly and simple of speech and demeanour as if she were a gooseherd of fourteen winters.

In the Hall was a goodly company, and all the leaders of the Folk were therein, and Folk-might and the War-leader sitting in the midst of those stone seats on the days. There then they agreed on the whole ordering of the battle and the wending of the host, as shall be told later on; and this matter was long a-doing, and when it was done, men went to their places to sleep, for the night was well worn.

But when men had departed and all was still, Folk-might, light-clad and without a weapon, left the Hall and walked briskly toward the nether end of the Vale. He passed by all the tents, the last whereof were of the House of the Steer, and came to a place where was a great rock rising straight up from the plain like sheaves of black staves standing close together; and it was called Staff-stone, and tales of the elves had been told concerning it, so that Stone-face had beheld it gladly the day before.

The moon was just shining into Shadowy Vale, and the grass was bright wheresoever the shadows of the high cliffs were not, and the face of Staff-stone shone bright grey as Folk-might came within sight of it, and he beheld someone sitting at the base of the rock, and as he drew nigher he saw that it was a woman, and knew her for the Bride; for he had prayed her to abide him there that night, because it was nigh to the tents of the House of the Steer; and his heart was glad as he drew nigh to her.

She sat quietly on a fragment of the black rock, clad as she had been all day, in her glittering kirtle, but without hauberk or helm, a wreath of wind-flowers about her head, her feet crossed over each other, her hands laid palm uppermost in her lap. She moved not as he drew nigh, but said in a gentle voice when he was close to her:

"Chief of the Wolf, great warrior, thou wouldest speak with me; and good it is that friends should talk together on the eve of battle, when they may never meet alive again."

He said: "My talk shall not be long; for thou and I both must sleep to-night, since there is work to hand to-morrow. Now since, as thou sayest, O fairest of women, we may never meet again alive, I ask thee now at this hour, when we both live and are near to one another, to suffer me to speak to thee of my love of thee and desire for thee. Surely thou, who art the sweetest of all things the Gods and the kindreds have made, wilt not gainsay me this?"

She said very sweetly, yet smiling: "Brother of my father's sons, how can I gainsay thee thy speech? Nay, hast thou not said it? What more canst thou add to it that will have fresh meaning to mine ears?"

He said: "Thou sayest sooth: might I then but kiss thine hand?"

She said, no longer smiling: "Yea surely, even so may all men do who can be called my friends—and thou art much my friend."

He took her hand and kissed it, and held it thereafter; nor did she draw it away. The moon shone brightly on them; but by its light he could not see if she reddened, but he deemed that her face was troubled. Then he said: "It were better for me if I might kiss thy face, and take thee in mine arms."

Then said she: "This only shall a man do with me when I long to do the like with him. And since thou art so much my friend, I will tell thee that as for this longing, I have it not. Bethink thee what a little while it is since the lack of another man's love grieved me sorely."

"The time is short," said Folk-might, "if we tell up the hours thereof; but in that short space have a many things betid."

She said: "Dost thou know, canst thou guess, how sorely ashamed I went amongst my people? I durst look no man in the face for the aching of mine heart, which methought all might see through my face."

"I knew it well," he said; "yet of me wert thou not ashamed but a little while ago, when thou didst tell me of thy grief."

She said: "True it is; and thou wert kind to me. Thou didst become a dear friend to me, methought."

"And wilt thou hurt a dear friend?" said he.

"O no," she said, "if I might do otherwise. Yet how if I might not choose? Shall there be no forgiveness for me then?"

He answered nothing; and still he held her hand that strove not to be gone from his, and she cast down her eyes. Then he spake in a while:

"My friend, I have been thinking of thee and of me; and now hearken: if thou wilt declare that thou feelest no sweetness embracing thine heart when I say that I desire thee sorely, as now I say it; or when I kiss thine hand, as now I kiss it; or when I pray thee to suffer me to cast mine arms about thee and kiss thy face, as now I pray it: if thou wilt say this, then will I take thee by the hand straightway, and lead thee to the tents of the House of the Steer, and say farewell to thee till the battle is over. Canst thou say this out of the truth of thine heart?"

She said: "What then if I cannot say this word? What then?"

But he answered nothing; and she sat still a little while, and then arose and stood before him, looking him in the eyes, and said:

"I cannot say it."

Then he caught her in his arms and strained her to him, and then kissed her lips and her face again and again, and she strove not with him. But at last she said:

"Yet after all this shalt thou lead me back to my folk

straight-way; and when the battle is done, if both we are living, then shall we speak more thereof."

So he took her hand and led her on toward the tents of the Steer, and for a while he spake nought; for he doubted himself, what he should say; but at last he spake:

"Now is this better for me than if it had not been, whether I live or whether I die. Yet thou hast not said that thou lovest me and desirest me."

"Wilt thou compel me?" she said. "To-night I may not say it. Who shall say what words my lips shall fashion when we stand together victorious in Silverdale; then indeed may the time seem long from now."

He said: "Yea, true is that; yet once again I say that so measured long and long is the time since first I saw thee in Burgdale before thou knewest me. Yet now I will not bicker with thee, for be sure that I am glad at heart. And lo you! our feet have brought us to the tents of thy people. All good go with thee!"

"And with thee, sweet friend," she said. Then she lingered a little, turning her head toward the tents, and then turned her face toward him and laid her hand on his neck, and drew his head adown to her and kissed his cheek, and therewith swiftly and lightly departed from him.

Now the night wore and the morning came; and Face-of-god was abroad very early in the morning, as his custom was; and he washed the night from off him in the Carles" Bath of the Shivering Flood, and then went round through the encampment of the host, and saw none stirring save here and there the last watchmen of the night. He spake with one or two of these, and then went up to the head of the Vale, where was the pass that led to Silverdale; and there he saw the watch, and spake with them, and they told him that none had as yet come forth from the pass, and he bade them to blow the horn of warning to rouse up the Host as soon as the messengers came thence. For forerunners had been sent up the pass, and had been set to hold watch at divers places therein to pass on the word from place to place.

Thence went Face-of-god back toward the Hall; but when he was yet some way from it, he saw a slender glittering warrior come forth from the door thereof, who stood for a moment looking round about, and then came lightly and swiftly toward him; and lo! it was the Sun-beam, with a long hauberk over her kirtle falling below her knees, a helm on her head and plated shoes on her feet. She came up to him, and laid her hand to his cheek and the golden locks of his head (for he was bare-headed), and said to him, smiling:

"Gold-mane! thou badest me bear arms, and Folk-might also constrained me thereto. Lo thou!"

Said Face-of-god: "Folk-might is wise then, even as I am; and forsooth as thou art. For bethink thee if the bow drawn at a venture should speed the eyeless shaft against thy breast, and send me forth a wanderer from my Folk! For how could I bear the sight of the fair Dale, and no hope to see thee again therein?"

She said: "The heart is light within me to-day. Deemest thou that this is strange? Or dost thou call to mind that which thou spakest the other day, that it was of no avail to stand in the Doom-ring of the Folk and bear witness against ourselves? This will I not. This is no light-mindedness that thou beholdest in me, but the valiancy that the Fathers have set in mine heart. Deem not, O Gold-mane, fear not, that we shall die before they dight the bride-bed for us."

He would have kissed her mouth, but she put him away with her hand, and doffed her helm and laid it on the grass, and said:

"This is not the last time that thou shalt kiss me, Gold-mane, my dear; and yet I long for it as if it were, so high as the Fathers have raised me up this morn above fear and sadness."

He said nought, but drew her to him, and wonder so moved him, that he looked long and closely at her face before he kissed her; and forsooth he could find no blemish in it: it was as if it were but new come from the smithy of the Gods, and exceeding longing took hold of him. But even as their lips met, from the head of the Vale came the voice of the great horn; and it was answered straightway by the watchers all down the tents; and presently arose the shouts of men and the clash of weapons as folk armed themselves, and laughter therewith, for most men were battle-merry, and the cries of women shrilly-clear as they hastened about, busy over the morning meal before the departure of the Host. But Face-of-god said softly, still caressing the Sun-beam, and she him:

"Thus then we depart from this Valley of the Shadows, but as thou saidst when first we met therein, there shall be no sundering of thee and me, but thou shalt go down with me to the battle."

And he led her by the hand into the Hall of the Wolf, and there they ate a morsel, and thereafter Face-of-god tarried not, but busied himself along with Folk-might and the other chieftains in arraying the Host for departure.

41. THE HOST DEPARTETH FROM SHADOWY VALE: THE FIRST DAY'S JOURNEY

It was about three hours before noon that the Host began to enter into the pass out of Shadowy Vale by the river-side; and the women and children, and men unfightworthy, stood on the higher ground at the foot of the cliffs to see the Host wend on the way. Of these a many were of the Woodlanders, who were now one folk with them of Shadowy Vale. And all these had chosen to abide tidings in the Vale, deeming that there was little danger therein, since that last slaughter which Folk-might had made of the Dusky Men; albeit Face-of-god had offered to send them all to Burgstead with two score and ten men-at-arms to guard them by the way and to eke out the warders of the Burg.

Now the fighting-men of Shadowy Vale were two long hundreds lacking five; of whom two score and ten were women, and three score and ten lads under twenty winters; but the women, though you might scarce see fairer of face and body, were doughty in arms, all good shooters in the bow; and the swains were eager and light-foot, cragsmen of the best, wont to scaling the cliffs of the Vale in search of the nests of gerfalcons and such-like fowl, and swimming the strong streams of the Shivering Flood; tough bodies and wiry, stronger than most grown men, and as fearless as the best.

The order of the Departure of the Host was this:

The Woodlanders went first into the pass, and with them were two score of the ripe Warriors of the Wolf. Then came of the kindreds of Burgdale, the Men of the Steer, the Bridge, and the Bull; then the Men of the Vine and the Sickle; then the Shepherd-folk; and lastly, the Men of the Face led by Stoneface and Hall-face. With these went another two score of the dwellers in Shadowy Vale, and the rest were scattered up and down the bands of the Host to guide them into the best paths and to make the way easier to them. Face-of-god was sundered from his kindred, and went along with Folk-might in the forefront of the Host, while his father the Alderman went as a simple man-at-arms with his House in the rearward. The Sunbeam followed her brother and Face-of-god amidst the Warriors of the Wolf, and with her were Bow-may clad in the Alderman's gift, and Wood-father and his children. Bow-may had caused her to doff her hauberk for that day, whereon they looked to fall in with no foeman. As for the Bride, she went with her kindred in all her war-gear; and the morning sun shone in the gems of her apparel, and her jewelled feet fell like flowers upon the deep grass of the upper Vale, and shone strange and bright amongst the black stones of the pass. She bore a quiver at her back and a shining yew bow in her hand,

and went amongst the bowmen, for she was a very deft archer.

So fared they into the pass, leaving peace behind them, with all their banners displayed, and the banner of the Red-mouthed Wolf went with the Wolf and the Sun-burst in the forefront of their battle next after the two captains.

As for their road, the grassy space between the rock-wall and the water was wide and smooth at first, and the cliffs rose up like bundles of spear-shafts high and clear from the green grass with no confused litter of fallen stones; so that the men strode on briskly, their hearts high-raised and full of hope. And as they went, the sweetness of song stirred in their souls, and at last Bow-may fell to singing in a loud clear voice, and her cousin Wood-wise answered her, and all the warriors of the Wolf who were in their band fell into the song at the ending, and the sound of their melody went down the water and reached the ears of those that were entering the pass, and of those who were abiding till the way should be clear of them: and this is some of what they sang:

Bow-may singeth:

Hear ye never a voice come crying
*   Out from the waste where the winds fare wide?*
"Sons of the Wolf, the days are dying,
*   And where in the clefts of the rocks do ye hide?*

"Into your hands hath the Sword been given,
*   Hard are the palms with the kiss of the hilt;*
Through the trackless waste hath the road been riven
*   For the blade to seek to the heart of the guilt.*

"And yet ye bide and yet ye tarry;
*   Dear deem ye the sleep 'twixt hearth and board,*
And sweet the maiden mouths ye marry,
*   And bright the blade of the bloodless sword."*

Wood-wise singeth:

Yea, here we dwell in the arms of our Mother
*   The Shadowy Queen, and the hope of the Waste;*
Here first we came, when never another
*   Adown the rocky stair made haste.*

Far is the foe, and no sword beholdeth
*   What deed we work and whither we wend;*
Dear are the days, and the Year enfoldeth
*   The love of our life from end to end.*

Voice of our Fathers, why will ye move us,

And call up the sun our swords to behold?
Why will ye cry on the foeman to prove us?
Why will ye stir up the heart of the bold?

Bow-may singeth:
Purblind am I, the voice of the chiding;
  Then tell me what is the thing ye bear?
What is the gift that your hands are hiding,
  The gold-adorned, the dread and dear?

Wood-wise singeth:
Dark in the sheath lies the Anvil's Brother,
  Hid is the hammered Death of Men.
Would ye look on the gift of the green-clad Mother?
How then shall ye ask for a gift again?

The Warriors sing:
Show we the Sunlight the Gift of the Mother,
  As foot follows foot to the foeman's den!
Gleam Sun, breathe Wind, on the Anvil's Brother,
  For bare is the hammered Death of Men.

Therewith they shook their naked swords in the air, and fared on eagerly, and as swiftly as the pass would have them fare. But so it was, that when the rearward of the Host was entering the first of the pass, and was going on the wide smooth sward, the vanward was gotten to where there was but a narrow space clear betwixt water and cliff; for otherwhere was a litter of great rocks and small, hard to be threaded even by those who knew the passes well; so that men had to tread along the very verge of the Shivering Flood, and wary must they be, for the water ran swift and deep betwixt banks of sheer rock half a fathom below their very foot-soles, which had but bare space to go on the narrow a way. So it held on for a while, and then got safer, and there was more space for going betwixt cliff and flood; albeit it was toilsome enough, since for some way yet there was a drift of stones to cumber their feet, some big and some little, and some very big. After a while the way grew better, though here and there, where the cliffs lowered, were wide screes of loose stones that they must needs climb up and down. Thereafter for a space was there an end of the stony cumber, but the way betwixt the river and the cliffs narrowed again, and the black crags grew higher, and at last so exceeding high, and the way so narrow, that the sky overhead was to them as though they were at the bottom of a well, and men deemed that thence they could see the stars at noontide. For some time withal had the way been mounting up and up, though the cliffs grew higher over it; till at last they were but going on a narrow shelf, the Shivering Flood swirling and rattling far below them betwixt sheer rock-walls grown exceeding high; and above them the cliffs going up towards the heavens as black as a moonless starless night of winter. And as the flood thundered below, so above them roared the ceaseless thunder of the wind of the pass, that blew exceeding fierce down that strait place; so that the skirts of their garments were wrapped about their knees by it, and their feet were well-nigh stayed at whiles as they breasted the push thereof.

But as they mounted higher and higher yet, the noise of the waters swelled into a huge roar that drowned the bellowing of the prisoned wind, and down the pass came drifting a fine rain that fell not from the sky, for between the clouds of that drift could folk see the heavens bright and blue above them. This rain was but the spray of the great force up to whose steps they were climbing.

Now the way got rougher as they mounted; but this toil was caused by their gain; for the rock-wall, which thrust out a buttress there as if it would have gone to the very edge of the gap where-through the flood ran, and so have cut the way off utterly, was here somewhat broken down, and its stones scattered down the steep bent, so that there was a passage, though a toilsome one.

Thus then through the wind-borne drift of the great force, through which men could see the white waters tossing down below, amidst the clattering thunder of the Shivering Flood and the rumble of the wind of the gap, that tore through their garments and hair as if it would rend all to rags and bear it away, the banners of the Wolf won their way to the crest of the midmost height of the pass, and the long line of the Host came clambering after them; and each band of warriors as it reached the top cast an unheard shout from amidst the tangled fury of wind and waters.

A little further on and all that turmoil was behind them; the sun, now grown low, smote the wavering column of spray from the force at their backs, till the rainbows lay bright across it; and the sunshine lay wide over a little valley that sloped somewhat steeply to the west right up from the edge of the river; and beyond these western slopes could men see a low peak spreading down on all sides to the plain, till it was like to a bossed shield, and the name of it was Shield-broad. Dark grey was the valley everywhere, save that by the side of the water was a space of bright green-sward hedged about toward the mountain by a wall of rocks tossed up into wild shapes of spires and jagged points. The river itself was spread out wide and shallow, and went rattling about great grey rocks scattered here and there amidst it, till it gathered itself together to tumble headlong over three slant steps into the mighty gap below.

From the height in the pass those grey slopes seemed easy to traverse; but the warriors of the Wolf knew that it was far otherwise, for they were but the molten rock-sea that in time long past had flowed forth from Shield-broad and filled up the whole valley endlong and overthwart, cooling as it flowed, and the tumbled hedge of rock round about the green plain by the river was where the said rock-sea had been stayed by meeting with soft ground, and had heaped itself up round about the green-sward. And that great rock-flood as it cooled split in divers fashions; and the rain and weather had been busy on it for ages, so that it was worn into a maze of narrow paths, most of which, after a little, brought the wayfarer to a dead stop, or else led him back again to the place whence he had started; so that only those who knew the passes throughly could thread that maze without immeasurable labour.

Now when the men of the Host looked from the high place whereon they stood toward the green plain by the river, they saw on the top of that rock-wall a red pennon waving on a spear, and beside it three or four weaponed men gleaming bright in the evening sun; and they waved their swords to the Host, and made lightning of the sunbeams, and the men of the Host waved swords to them in turn. For these were the outguards of the Host; and the place whereon they were was at whiles dwelt in by those who would drive the spoil in Silverdale, and midmost of the green-sward was a booth builded of rough stones and turf, a refuge for a score of men in rough weather.

So the men of the vanward gat them down the hill, and made the best of their way toward the grassy plain through that rocky maze which had once been as a lake of molten glass; and as short as the way looked from above, it was two hours or ever they came out of it on to the smooth turf, and it was moonlight and night ere the House of the Face had gotten on to the green-sward.

There then the Host abode for that night, and after they had eaten lay down on the green grass and slept as they might. Bow-may would have brought the Sun-beam into the booth with some others of the women, but she would not enter it, because she deemed that otherwise the Bride would abide without; and the Bride, when she came up, along with the House of the Steer, beheld the Sun-beam, that Wood-father's children had made a lair for her without like a hare's form; and forsooth many a time had she lain under the naked heaven in Shadowy Vale and the waste about it, even as the Bride had in the meadows of Burgdale. So when the Bride was bidden thereto, she went meekly into the booth, and lay there with others of the damsels-at-arms.

42. THE HOST COMETH TO THE EDGES OF SILVERDALE

So wore the night, and when the dawn was come were the two captains afoot, and they went from band to band to see that all was ready, and all men were astir betimes, and by the time that the sun smote the eastern side of Shield-broad ruddy, they had broken their fast and were dight for departure. Then the horns blew up beside the banners, and rejoiced the hearts of men. But by the command of the captains this was the last time that they should sound till they blew for onset in Silverdale, because now would they be drawing nigher and nigher to the foemen, and they wotted not but that wandering bands of them might be hard on the lips of the pass, and might hear the horns" voice, and turn to see what was toward.

Forth then went the banners of the Wolf, and the men of the vanward fell to threading the rock-maze toward the north, and in two hours" time were clear of the Dale under Shield-broad. All went in the same order as yesterday; but on this day the Sun-beam would bear her hauberk, and had a sword girt to her side, and her heart was high and her speech merry.

When they left the Dale under Shield-broad the way was easy and wide for a good way, the river flowing betwixt low banks, and the pass being more like a string of little valleys than a mere gap, as it had been on the other side of the Dale. But when one third of the day was past, the way began to narrow on them again, and to rise up little by little; and at last the rock-walls drew close to the river, and when men looked toward the north they saw no way, and nought but a wall. For the gap of the Shivering Flood turned now to the east, and the Flood came down from the east in many falls, as it were over a fearful stair, through a gap where there was no path between the cliffs and the water, nought but the boiling flood and its turmoil; so that they who knew not the road wondered what they should do.

But Folk-might led the banners to where a great buttress of the cliffs thrust itself into the way, coming well-nigh down to the water, just at the corner where the river turned eastward, and they got them about it as they might, and on the other side thereof lo! another gap exceeding strait, scarce twenty foot over, wall-sided, rugged beyond measure, going up steeply from the great valley: a little water ran through it, mostly filling up the floor of it from side to side; but it was but shallow. This was now the battle-road of the Host, and the vanward entered it at once, turning their backs upon the Shivering Flood.

Full toilsome and dreary was that strait way; often great stones hung above their heads, bridging the gap and hiding the sky from them; nor was there any path for them save the stream itself; so that whiles were they wading its waters to the knee or higher, and whiles were they striding from stone to stone amidst the rattle of the waters, and whiles were they stepping warily along the ledges of rock above the deeper pools, and in all wise labouring in overcoming the rugged road amidst the twilight of the gap.

Thus they toiled till the afternoon was well worn, and so at last they came to where the rock-wall was somewhat broken down on the north side, and great rocks had fallen across the gap, and dammed up the waters, which fell scantily over the dam from stone to stone into a pool at the bottom of it. Up this breach, then, below the force they scrambled and struggled, for rough indeed was the road for them; and so came they up out of the gap on to the open hillside, a great shoulder of the heath sloping down from the north, and littered over with big stones, borne thither belike by some ice-river of the earlier days; and one great rock was in special as great as the hall of a wealthy goodman, and shapen like to a hall with hipped gables, which same the men of the Wolf called House-stone.

There then the noise and clatter of the vanward rose up on the face of the heath, and men were exceeding joyous that they had come so far without mishap. Therewith came weaponed men out from under House-stone, and they came toward the men of the vanward, and they were a half-score of the forerunners of the Wolf; therefore Folk-might and Face-of-god fell at once into speech with them, and had their tidings; and when they had heard them, they saw nought to hinder the host from going on their road to Silverdale forthright; and there were still three hours of daylight before them. So the vanward of the host tarried not, and the captains left word with the men from under House-stone that the rest of the Host should fare on after them speedily, and that they should give this word to each company, as men came up from out the gap. Then they fared speedily up the hillside, and in an hour's wearing had come to the crest thereof, and to where the ground fell steadily toward the north, and hereabout the scattered stones ceased, and on the other side of the crest the heath began to be soft and boggy, and at last so soft, that if they had not been wisely led, they had been bemired oftentimes. At last they came to where the flows that trickled through the mires drew together into a stream, so that men could see it running; and thereon some of the Woodlanders cried out joyously that the waters were running north; and then all knew that they were drawing nigh to Silverdale.

No man they met on the road, nor did they of Shadowy Vale look to meet any; because the Dusky Men were not great hunters for the more part, except it were of men, and especially of women; and, moreover, these hill-slopes of the mountain-necks led no-whither and were utterly waste and dreary, and there was nought to be seen there but snipes and bitterns and whimbrel and plover, and here and there a hill-fox, or the great erne hanging over the heath on his way to the mountain.

When sunset came, they were getting clear of the miry ground, and the stream which they had come across amidst of the mires had got clearer and greater, and rattled down between wide stony sides over the heath; and here and there it deepened as it cleft its way through little knolls that rose out of the face of the mountain-neck. As the Host climbed one of these and was come to its topmost (it was low enough not to turn the stream), Face-of-god looked and beheld dark-blue mountains rising up far off before him, and higher than these, but away to the east, the snowy peaks of the World-mountains. Then he called to mind what he had seen from the Burg of the Runaways, and he took Folk-might by the arm, and pointed toward those far-off mountains.

"Yea," said Folk-might, "so it is, War-leader. Silverdale lieth between us and yonder blue ridges, and it is far nigher to us than to them."

But the Sun-beam came close to those twain, and took Face-of-god by the hand and said: "O Gold-mane, dost thou see?" and he turned about and beheld her, and saw how her cheeks flamed and her eyes glittered, and he said in a low voice: "To-morrow for mirth or silence, for life or death."

But the whole vanward as they came up stayed to behold the sight of the mountains on the other side of Silverdale, and the banners of the Folk hung over their heads, moving but little in the soft air of the evening: so went they on their ways.

The sun sank, and dusk came on them as they followed down the stream, and night came, and was clear and starlit, though the moon was not yet risen. Now was the ground firm and the grass sweet and flowery, and wind-worn bushes were scattered round about them, as they began to go down into the ghyll that cleft the wall of Silverdale, and the night-wind blew in their faces from the very Dale and place of the Battle to be. The path down was steep at first, but the ghyll was wide, and the sides of it no longer straight walls, as in the gaps of their earlier journey, but broken, sloping back, and (as they might see on the morrow) partly of big stones and shaly grit, partly grown over with bushes and rough grass, with here and there a little stream trickling down their sides. As they went, the ghyll widened out, till at last they were in a valley going down to the plain, in places steep, in places flat and smooth, the stream ever rattling down the midst of it, and they on the west side thereof. The vale was well grassed, and oak-trees and ash and holly and hazel grew here and there about it; and at last the Host had before it a wood which filled the vale from side to side, not much tangled with undergrowth, and quite clear of it nigh to the stream-side. Thereinto the vanward entered, but went no long way ere the leaders called a halt and bade pitch the banners, for that there should they abide the daylight. Thus it had been determined at the Council of the Hall of the Wolf; for Folk-might had said: "With an Host as great as ours, and mostly of men come into a land of which they know nought at all, an onslaught by night is perilous: yea, and our foes should be over-much scattered, and we should have to wander about seeking them. Let us rather abide in the wood of Wood-dale till the morning, and then display our banners on the hillside above Silverdale, so that they may gather together to fall upon us: in no case shall they keep us out of the Dale."

There then they stayed, and as each company came up to the wood, they were marshalled into their due places, so that they might set the battle in array on the edge of Silverdale,

43. FACE-OF-GOD LOOKETH ON SILVERDALE: THE BOWMEN'S BATTLE

There then they rested, as folk wearied with the toilsome journey, when they had set sure watches round about their campment; and they ate quietly what meat they had with them, and so gat them to sleep in the wood on the eve of battle.

But not all slept; for the two captains went about amongst the companies, Folk-might to the east, Face-of-god to the west, to look to the watches, and to see that all was ordered duly. Also the Sun-beam slept not, but she lay beside Bow-may at the foot of an oak-tree; she watched Face-of-god as he went away amidst the men of the Host, and watched and waked abiding his returning footsteps.

The night was well worn by then he came back to his place in the vanward, and on his way back he passed through the folk of the Steer laid along on the grass, all save those of the watch, and the light of the moon high aloft was mingled with the light of the earliest dawn; and as it happened he looked down, and lo! close to his feet the face of the Bride as she lay beside her grand-sire, her head pillowed on a bundle of bracken. She was sleeping soundly like a child who has been playing all day, and whose sleep has come to him unsought and happily. Her hands were laid together by her side; her cheek was as fair and clear as it was wont to be at her best; her face looked calm and happy, and a lock of her dark-red hair strayed from her uncovered head over her breast and lay across her wrists, so peacefully she slept.

Face-of-god turned his eyes from her at once, and went by swiftly, and came to his own company. The Sun-beam saw him coming, and rose straightway to her feet from beside Bow-may, who lay fast asleep, and she held out her hands to him; and he took them and kissed them, and he cast his arms about her and kissed her mouth and her face, and she his in likewise; and she said:

"O Gold-mane, if this were but the morrow of to-morrow! Yet shall all be well; shall it not?"

Her voice was low, but it waked Bow-may, who sat up at once broad awake, after the manner of a hunter of the waste ever ready for the next thing to betide, and moreover the Sun-beam had been in her thoughts these two days, and she feared for her, lest she should be slain or maimed. Now she smiled on the Sun-beam and said:

"What is it? Does thy mind forebode evil? That needeth not. I tell thee it is not so ill for us of the sword to be in Silverdale. Thrice have I been there since the Overthrow, and never more than a half-score in company, and yet am I whole to-day."

"Yea, sister," said Face-of-god, "but in past times ye did your deed and then fled away; but now we come to abide here, and this night is the last of lurking."

"Ah," she said, "a little way from this I saw such things that we had good will to abide here longer, few as we were, but that we feared to be taken alive."

"What things were these?" said Face-of-god.

"Nay," she said, "I will not tell thee now; but mayhap in the lighted winter feast-hall, when the kindred are so nigh us and about us that they seem to us as if they were all the world, I may tell it thee; or mayhap I never shall."

Said the Sun-beam, smiling: "Thou wilt ever be talking, Bow-may. Now let the War-leader depart, for he will have much to do."

And she was well at ease that she had seen Face-of-god again; but he said:

"Nay, not so much; all is well-nigh done; in an hour it will be broad day, and two hours thereafter shall the Banner be displayed on the edge of Silverdale."

The cheek of the Sun-beam flushed, and paled again, as she said: "Yea, we shall stand even as our Fathers stood on the day when, coming from off the waste, they beheld it, and knew it would be theirs. Ah me! how have I longed for this morn. But now—Tell me, Gold-mane, dost thou deem that I am afraid? And I whom thou hast deemed to be a God."

Quoth Bow-may: "Thou shalt deem her twice a God ere noon-tide, brother Gold-mane. But come now! the hour of deadly battle is at hand, and we may not laugh that away; and therefore I bid thee remember, Gold-mane, how thou didst promise to kiss me once more on the verge of deadly battle."

Therewith she stood up before him, and he tarried not, but kind and smiling took her face between his two hands and kissed her lips, and she cast her arms about him and kissed him, and then sank down on the grass again, and turned from him, and laid her face amongst the grass and the bracken, and they could see that she was weeping, and her body was shaken with sobs. But the Sun-beam knelt down to her, and caressed her with her hand, and spake kind words to her softly, while Face-of-god went his ways to meet Folk-might.

Now was the dawn fading into full daylight; and between dawn and sunrise were all men stirring; for the watch had waked the hundred-leaders, and they the leaders of scores and half-scores, and they the whole folk; and they sat quietly in the wood and made no noise.

In the night the watch of the Sickle had fallen in with a thrall who had stolen up from the Dale to set gins for hares, and now in the early morning they brought him to the War-leader. He was even such a man as those with whom Face-of-god had fallen in before, neither better nor worse than most of them: he was sore afraid at first, but by then he was come to the captains he understood that he had happened upon friends; but he was dull of comprehension and slow of speech. Albeit Folk-might gathered from him that the Dusky Men had some inkling of the onslaught; for he said that they had been gathering together in the marketplace of Silver-stead, and would do so again soon. Moreover, the captains deemed from his speech that those new tribes had come to hand sooner than was looked for, and were even now in the Dale. Folk-might smiled as one who is not best pleased when he heard these tidings; but Face-of-god was glad to hear thereof; for what he loathed most was that the war should drag out in hunting of scattered bands of the foe. Herewith came Dallach to them as they talked (for Face-of-god had sent for him), and he fell to questioning the man further; by whose answers it seemed that many men also had come into the Dale from Rosedale, so that they of the kindreds were like to have their hands full. Lastly Dallach drew from the thrall that it was on that very morning that the great Folk-mote of the Dusky Men should be holden in the market-place of the Stead, which was right great, and about it were the biggest of the houses wherein the men of the kindred had once dwelt.

So when they had made an end of questioning the thrall, and had given him meat and drink, they asked him if he would take weapons in his hand and lead them on the ways into the Dale, bidding him look about the wood and note how great and mighty an host they were. And the carle yeasaid this, after staring about him a while, and they gave him spear and shield, and he went with the vanward as a way-leader.

Again presently came a watch of the Shepherds, and they had found a man and a woman dead and stark naked hanging to the boughs of a great oak-tree deep in the wood. This men knew for some vengeance of the Dusky Men, for it was clear to see that these poor people had been sorely tormented before they were slain. Also the same watch had stumbled on the dead body of an old woman, clad in rags, lying amongst the rank grass about a little flow; she was exceeding lean and hun-ger-starved, and in her hand was a frog which she had half eaten. And Dallach, when he heard of this, said that it was the wont of the Dusky Men to slay their thralls when they were past work, or to drive them into the wilderness to die.

Lastly came a watch from the men of the Face, having with them two more thralls, lusty young men; these they had come upon in company of their master, who had brought them up into the wood to shoot him a buck, and therefore they bare bows and arrows. The watch had slain the master straightway while the thralls stood looking on. They were much afraid of the weaponed men, but answered to the questioning much readier than the first man; for they were household thralls, and better fed and clad than he, who was but a toiler in the fields. They yeasaid all his tale, and said moreover that the Folk-mote of the Dusky Men should be holden in the market-place that forenoon, and that most of the warriors should be there, both the new-comers and the Rosedale lords, and that without doubt they should be under arms.

To these men also they gave a good sword and a helm each, and bade them be brisk with their bows, and they said yea to marching with the Host; and indeed they feared nothing so much as being left behind; for if they fell into the hands of the Dusky Men, and their master missing, they should first be questioned with torments, and then slain in the evillest manner.

Now whereas things had thus betid, and that they knew thus much of their foemen, Face-of-god called all the chieftains together, and they sat on the green grass and held counsel amongst them, and to one and all it seemed good that they should suffer the Dusky Men to gather together before they meddled with them, and then fall upon them in such order and such time as should seem good to the captains watching how things went; and this would be easy, whereas they were all lying in the wood in the same order as they would stand in battle-array if they were all drawn up together on the brow of the hill. Albeit Face-of-god deemed it good, after he had heard all that they who had been in the Stead could tell him thereof, that the Shepherd-Folk, who were more than three long hundreds, and they of the Steer, the Bridge, and the Bull, four hundreds in all, should take their places eastward of the Woodlanders who had led the vanward.

Straightway the word was borne to these men, and the shift was made: so that presently the Woodlanders were amidmost of the Host, and had with them on their right hands the Men of the Steer, the Bridge, and the Bull, and beyond them the Shepherd-Folk. But on their left hand lay the Men of the Vine, then they of the Sickle, and lastly the Men of the Face, and these three kindreds were over five hundreds of warriors: as for the Men of the Wolf, they abode at first with those companies which they had led through the wastes, though this was changed afterwards.

All this being done, Face-of-god gave out that all men should break their fast in peace and leisure; and while men were at their meat, Folk-might spake to Face-of-god and said: "Come, brother, for I would show thee a goodly thing; and thou, Dallach, come with us."

Then he brought them by paths in the wood till Face-of-god saw the sky shine white between the tree-boles, and in a little while they were come well-nigh out of the thicket, and then they went warily; for before them was nought but the slopes of Wood-dale, going down steeply into Silverdale, with nought to hinder the sight of it, save here and there bushes or scattered trees; and so fair and lovely it was that Face-of-god could scarce forbear to cry out. He saw that it was only at the upper or eastern end, where the mountains of the Waste went round about it, that the Dale was narrow; it soon widened out toward the west, and for the most part was encompassed by no such straight-sided a wall as was Burgdale, but by sloping hills and bents, mostly indeed somewhat higher and steeper than the pass wherein they were, but such as men could well climb if they had a mind to, and there were any end to their journey. The Dale went due west a good way, and then winded about to the southwest, and so was hidden from them thereaway by the bents that lay on their left hand. As it was wider, so it was not so plain a ground as was Burgdale, but rose in knolls and little hills here and there. A river greater than the Weltering Water wound about amongst the said mounds; and along the side of it out in the open dale were many goodly houses and homesteads of stone. The knolls were mostly covered over with vines, and there were goodly and great trees in groves and clumps, chiefly oak and sweet chestnut and linden; many were the orchards, now in blossom, about the homesteads; the pastures of the neat and horses spread out bright green up from the water-side, and deeper green showed the acres of the wheat on the lower slopes of the knolls, and in wide fields away from the river.

Just below the pitch of the hill whereon they were, lay Silver-stead, the town of the Dale. Hitherto it had been an unfenced place; but Folk-might pointed to where on the western side a new white wall was rising, and on which, young as the day yet was, men were busy laying the stones and spreading the mortar. Fair seemed that town to Face-of-god: the houses were all builded of stone, and some of the biggest were roofed with lead, which also as well as silver was dug out of the mountains at the eastern end of the Dale. The market-place was clear to see from where they stood, though there were houses on all sides of it, so wide it was. From their standing-place it was but three furlongs to this heart of Silverdale; and Face-of-god could see brightly-clad men moving about in it already. High above their heads he beheld two great clots of scarlet and yellow raised on poles and pitched in front of a great stone-built hall roofed with lead, which stood amidmost of the west end of the Place, and betwixt those poles he saw on a mound with long slopes at its sides somewhat of white stone, and amidmost of the whole Place a great stack of faggot-wood built up four-square. Those red and yellow things on the poles he deemed would be the banners of the murder-carles; and Folk-might told him that even so it was, and that they were but big bunches of strips of woollen cloth, much like to great rag-mops, save that the rags were larger and longer: no other token of war, said Folk-might, did those folk carry, save a crook-bladed sword, smeared with man's blood, and bigger than any man might wield in battle.

"Art thou far-seeing, War-leader?" quoth he. "What canst thou see in the market-place?"

Said Face-of-god: "Far-seeing am I above most men, and I see in the Place a man in scarlet standing by the banner, which is pitched in front of the great stone hall, near to the mound with the white stone on it; and meseemeth he beareth a great horn in his hand."

Said Folk-might: "Yea, and that stone hall was our Mote-house when we were lords of the Dale, and thence it was that they who are now thralls of the Dusky Men sent to them their message and token of yielding. And as for that white stone, it is the altar of their god; for they have but one, and he is that same crook-bladed sword. And now that I look, I see a great stack of wood amidmost the market-place, and well I know what that betokeneth."

"Lo you!" said Face-of-god, "the man with the horn is gone up on to the altar-mound, and meseemeth he is setting the little end of the horn to his mouth."

"Hearken then!" said Folk-might. And in a moment came the hoarse tuneless sound of the horn down the wind towards them; and Folk-might said:

"I deem I should know what that blast meaneth; and now is it time that the Host drew nigher to set them in array behind these very trees. But if ye will, War-leader, we will abide here and watch the ways of the foemen, and send Dallach with the word to the Host; also I would have thee suffer me to bid hither at once two score and ten of the best of the bowmen of our folk and the Woodlanders, and Wood-wise to lead them, for he knoweth well the land hereabout, and what is good to do."

"It is good," said Face-of-god. "Be speedy, Dallach!"

So Dallach departed, running lightly, and the two chiefs abode there; and the horn in Silver-stead blew at whiles for a little, and then stayed; and Folk-might said:

"Lo you! they come flockmeal to the Mote-stead; the Place will be filled ere long."

Said Face-of-god: "Will they make offerings to their god at

the hallowing in of their Folk-mote? Where then are the slaughter-beasts?"

"They shall not long be lacking," said Folk-might. "See you it is getting thronged about the altar and the Mote-house."

Now there were four ways into the Market-place of Silver-stead turned toward the four airts, and the midmost of the kin-dreds" battle looked right down the southern one, which went up to the wood, but stopped there in a mere woodland path, and the more part of the town lay north and west of this way, albeit there was a way from the east also. But the hillside just below the two captains lay two furlongs west of this southern way; and it went down softly till it was gotten quite near to the backs of the houses on the south side of the Market-place, and was sprinkled scantly with bushes and trees as aforesaid; but at last were there more bushes, which well-nigh made a hedge across it, reaching from the side of the southern way; and a foot or two beyond these bushes the ground fell by a steep and broken bent down to the level of the Market-place, and betwixt that fringe of bushes and the backs of the houses on the south side of the Place was less it maybe than a full furlong: but the southern road aforesaid went down softly into the Market-place, since it had been fashioned so by men.

Now the two chiefs heard a loud blast of horns come up from the town, and lo! a great crowd of men wending their ways down the road from the north, and they came into the market-place with spears and other weapons tossing in the air, and amidst of these men, who seemed to be all of the warriors, they saw as they drew nigher some two score and ten of men clad in long raiment of yellow and scarlet, with tall spiring hats of strange fashion on their heads, and in their hands long staves with great blades like scythes done on to them; and again, in the midst of these yellow and red glaive-bearers, in the very heart of the throng were some score of naked folk, they deemed both men and women, but were not sure, so close was the throng; nor could they see if they were utterly naked.

"Lo you, brother!" quoth Folk-might, "said I not that the beasts for the hewing should not tarry? Yonder naked folk are even they: and ye may well deem that they are the thralls of the Dusky Men; and meseemeth by the whiteness of their skins they be of the best of them. For these felons, it is like, look to winning great plenty of thralls in Burgdale, and so set the less store on them they have, and may expend them freely."

As he spake they heard the sound of men marching in the wood behind them, and they turned about and saw that there was come Wood-wise, and with him upwards of two score and ten of the bowmen of the Woodlanders and the Wolf—hunts-men, cragsmen, and scourers of the Waste; men who could shoot the chaffinch on the twig a hundred yards aloof; who could make a hiding-place of the bennets of the wayside grass,

or the stem of the slender birch-tree. With these must needs be Bow-may, who was the closest shooter of all the kindreds.

So then Wood-wise told the War-leader that Dallach had given the word to the Host, and that all men were astir and would be there presently in their ordered companies; and Face-of-god spake to Folk-might, and said: "Chief of the Wolf, wilt thou not give command to these bowmen, and set them to the work; for thou wottest thereof."

"Yea, that will I," said Folk-might, and turned to Wood-wise, and said: "Wood-wise, get ye down the slope, and loose on these felons, who have a murder on hand, if so be ye have a chance to do it wisely. But in any case come ye all back; for all shall be needed yet to-day. So flee if they pursue, for ye shall have us to flee to. Now be ye wary, nor let the curse of the Wolf and the Face lie on your slothfulness."

Wood-wise did but nod his head and lift his hand to his fel-lows, who set off after him down the slope without more tarry-ing. They went very warily, as if they were hunting a quarry which would flee from them; and they crept amongst the grass and stones from bush to bush like serpents, and so, unseen by the Dusky Men, who indeed were busied over their own mat-ters, they came to the fringe of bushes above the broken ground aforesaid, and there they took their stand, and before them below those steep banks was but the space at the back of the houses. As to the houses, as aforesaid, they were not so high as elsewhere about the Market-place; and at the end of a long low hall there was a gap between its gable and the next house, whereby they had a clear sight of the Place about the god's altar and the banners, and the great hall of Silverdale, with the double stair that went up to the door thereof.

There then they made them ready, and Wood-wise set men to watch that none should come sidelong on them unawares; their bows were bent and their quivers open, and they were eager for the fray.

Thus they beheld the Market-place from their cover, and saw that those folk who were to be hewn to the god were now standing facing the altar in a half-ring, and behind them in another half-ring the glaive-bearers who had brought them thither stood glaive in hand ready to hew them down when the token should be given; and these were indeed the priests of the god.

There was clear space round about these poor slaughter-thralls, so that the bowmen could see them well, and they told up a score of them, half men, half women, and they were all stark naked save for wreaths of flowers about their middles and their necks; and they had shackles of lead about their wrists; which same lead should be taken out of the fire wherein they should be burned, and from the shape it should take after it had passed through the fire would the priests fore-tell the luck of the deed to be done.

It was clear to be seen from thence that Folk-might was right when he said that these slaughter-thralls were of the best of the house-thralls and bed-mates of the Dusky Men, and that these felons were open-handed to their god, and would not cheat him, or withhold from him the best and most delicate of all they had.

Now spake Wood-wise to those about him: "It is sure that Folk-might would have us give these poor thralls a chance, and that we must loose upon the felons who would hew them down; and if we are to come back again, we can go no nigher. What sayest thou, Bow-may? Is it nigh enough? Can aught be done?"

"Yea, yea," she said, "nigh enough it is; but let Gold-ring be with me and half a score of the very best, whether they be of our folk or the Woodlanders, men who cannot miss such a mark; and when we have loosed, then let all loose, and stay not till our shot be spent. Haste, now haste! time presseth; for if the Host showeth on the brow of the hill, these felons will hew down their slaughter-beasts before they turn on their foemen. Let the grey-goose wing speed trouble and confusion amongst them."

But ere she had done her words Wood-wise had got to speaking quietly with the Woodlanders; and Bears-bane, who was amidst them, chose out eight of the best of his folk, men who doubted nothing of hitting whatever they could see in the Market-place; and they took their stand for shooting, and with them besides Bow-may were two women and four men of the Wolf, and Gold-ring withal, a carle of fifty winters, long, lean, and wiry, a fell shooter if ever anyone were.

So all these notched their shafts and laid them on the yew, and each had between the two last fingers of the shaft-hand another shaft ready, and a half score more stuck into the ground before him.

Now giveth Wood-wise the word to these sixteen as to which of the felons with the glaives they shall each one aim at; and he saith withal in a soft voice: "Help cometh from the Hill; soon shall battle be joined in Silverdale."

Thus stand they watching Bow-may and Gold-ring till they draw home the notches; and amidst their waiting the glaive-bearing felons fall a-singing a harsh and ugly hymn to their crooked-sword god, and the Market-stead is thronged endlong and overthwart with the tribes of the Dusky Men.

There now standeth Bow-may far-sighted and keen-eyed, her face as pale as a linen sleeve, an awful smile on her glittering eyes and close-set lips, and she feeling the twisted string of the red yew and the polished sides of the notch, while the yelling song of the Dusky priests quavers now and ends with a wild shrill cry, and she noteth the midmost of the priests beginning to handle his weapon: then swift and steady she draweth home the notches, while the yew bow standeth still as the oak-bole ere the summer storm ariseth, and the twang of the sixteen strings maketh but one fell sound as the feathered bane of men goeth on its way.

There was silence for a moment of time in the Market of Silver-stead, as if the bolt of the Gods had fallen there; and then arose a huge wordless yell from those about the altar, and one of the priests who was left hove up his glaive two-handed to smite the naked slaughter-thralls; but or ever the stroke fell, Bow-may's second shaft was through his throat, and he rolled over amidst his dead fellows; and the other fifteen had loosed with her, and then even as they could Wood-wise and the others of their company; and all they notched and loosed without tarrying, and no shout, no word came from their lips, only the twanging strings spake for them; for they deemed the minutes that hurried by were worth much joy of their lives to be. And few indeed were the passing minutes ere the dead men lay in heaps about the Altar of the Crooked Sword, and the wounded men wallowed amidst them.

44. OF THE ONSLAUGHT OF THE MEN OF THE STEER, THE BRIDGE, AND THE BULL

Wild was the turmoil and confusion in the Market-stead; for the more part of the men therein knew not what had befallen about the altar, though some clomb up to the top of that stack of faggots built for the burning of the thralls, and when they saw what was toward fell to yelling and cursing; and their fellows on the plain Place could not hear their story for the clamour, and they also fell to howling as if a wood full of wild dogs was there.

And still the shafts rained down on that throng from the Bent of the Bowmen, for another two score men of the Woodlanders had crept down the hill to them, and shafts failed them not. But the Dusky Men about the altar, for all their terror, or even maybe because of it, now began to turn upon the scarce-seen foemen, and to press up wildly toward the hillside, though as it were without any order or aim. Every man of them had his weapons, and those no mere gilded toys, but their very tools of battle; and some, but no great number, had their bows with them and a few shafts; and these began to shoot at whatsoever they could see on the hillside, but at first so wildly and hurriedly that they did no harm.

It must be said of them that at first only those about the altar fell on toward the hill; for those about the road that led southward knew not what had betided nor whither to turn. So that at this beginning of the battle, of all the thousands in the great Place it was but a few hundreds that set on the Bent of the Bowmen, and at these the bowmen of the kindreds shot so close and so wholly together that they fell one over another in the narrow ways between the houses whereby they must needs go to gather on the plain ground betwixt the backs of the houses and the break of the hillside. But little by little the archers of the Dusky Men gathered behind the corpses of the slain, and fell to shooting at what they could see of the men of the kindreds, which at that while was not much, for as bold as they were, they fought like wary hunters of the Wood and the Waste.

But now at last throughout all that throng of felons in the Market-place the tale began to spread of foemen come into the Dale and shooting from the Bents, and all they turned their faces to the hill, and the whole set of the throng was thitherward; though they fared but slowly, so evil was the order of them, each man hindering his neighbour as he went. And not only did the Dusky Men come flockmeal toward the Bent of the Bowmen, but also they jostled along toward the road that led southward. That beheld Wood-wise from the Bent, and he was minded to get him and his aback, now that they had made so great a slaughter of the foemen; and two or three of his fellows had been hurt by arrows, and Bow-may, she would have been slain thrice over but for the hammer-work of the Alderman. And no marvel was that; for now she stood on a little mound not half covered by a thin thorn-bush, and notched and loosed at whatever was most notable, as though she were shooting at the mark on a summer evening in Shadowy Vale. But as Wood-wise was at point to give the word to depart, from behind them rang out the merry sound of the Burgdale horns, and he turned to look at the wood-side, and lo! thereunder was the hill bright and dark with men-at-arms, and over them floated the Banners of the Wolf, and the Banners of the Steer, the Bridge, and the Bull. Then gave forth the bowmen of the kindreds their first shout, and they made no stay in their shooting; but shot the eagerer, for they deemed that help would come without their turning about to draw it to them: and even so it was. For straightway down the bent came striding Face-of-god betwixt the two Banners of the Wolf, and beside him were Red-wolf the tall and War-grove, and therewithal Wood-wont and Wood-wicked, and many other men of the Wolf; for now that the men of the kindreds had been brought face to face with the foe, and there was less need of them for way-leaders, the more part of them were liefer to fight under their own banner along with the Woodlanders; so that the

company of those who went under the Wolves was more than three long hundreds and a half; and the bowmen on the edge of the bent shouted again and merrily, when they felt that their brothers were amongst them, and presently was the arrow-storm at its fiercest, and the twanging of bow-strings and the whistle of the shafts was as the wind among the clefts of the mountains; for all the new-comers were bowmen of the best.

But the kindreds of the Steer, the Bridge, and the Bull, they hung yet a while longer on the hills" brow, their banners floating over them and their horns blowing; and the Dusky Felons in the Market-place beheld them, and fear and rage at once filled their hearts, and a fierce and dreadful yell brake out from them, and joyously did the Men of Burgdale answer them, and song arose amongst them even such as this:

The Men of the Bridge sing:
Why stand ye together, why bear ye the shield,
Now the calf straineth tether at edge of the field?

Now the lamb bleateth stronger and waters run clear,
And the day groweth longer and glad is the year?

Now the mead-flowers jostle so thick as they stand,
And singeth the throstle all over the land?

The Men of the Steer sing:
No cloud the day darkened, no thunder we heard,
But the horns" speech we hearkened as men unafeared.

Yea, so merry it sounded, we turned from the Dale,
Where all wealth abounded, to wot of its tale.

The Men of the Bridge sing:
What white boles then bear ye, what wealth of the woods?
What chafferers hear ye bid loud for your goods?

The Men of the Bull sing:
O the bright beams we carry are stems of the steel;
Nor long shall we tarry across them to deal.

Hark the men of the cheaping, how loudly they cry
On the hook for the reaping of men doomed to die!

They all sing:
Heave spear up! fare forward, O Men of the Dale!
For the Warrior, our war-ward, shall hearken the tale.

Therewith they ceased a moment, and then gave a great and hearty shout all together, and all their horns blew, and they moved on down the hill as one man, slowly and with no jostling, the spear-men first, and then they of the axe and the sword; and on their flanks the deft archers loosed on the stumbling jostling throng of the Dusky Men, who for their part came on drifting and surging up the road to the hill.

But when those big spearmen of the Dale had gone a little way the horns' voice died out, and their great-staved spears rose up from their shoulders into the air, and stood so a moment, and then slowly fell forward, as the oars of the long-ship fall into the row-locks, and then over the shoulders of the foremost men showed the steel of the five ranks behind them, and their own spears cast long bars of shadow on the whiteness of the sunny road. No sound came from them now save the rattle of their armour and the tramp of their steady feet; but from the Dusky Men rose up hideous confused yelling, and those that could free themselves from the tangle of the throng rushed desperately against the on-rolling hedge of steel, and the whole throng shoved on behind them. Then met steel and men; here and there an ash-stave broke; here and there a Dusky Felon rolled himself unhurt under the ash-staves, and hewed the knees of the Dalesmen, and a tall man came tottering down; but what men or wood-wights could endure the push of spears of those mighty husbandmen? The Dusky Ones shrunk back yelling, or turned their backs and rushed at their own folk with such fierce agony that they entered into the throng, till the terror of the spear reached to the midmost of it and swayed them back on the hindermost; for neither was there outgate for the felons on the flanks of the spearmen, since there the feathered death beset them, and the bowmen (and the Bride amongst the foremost) shot wholly together, and no shaft flew idly. But the wise leaders of the Dalesmen would not that they should thrust in too far amongst the howling throng of the Dusky Men, lest they should be hemmed in by them; for they were but a handful in regard to them: so there they stayed, barring the way to the Dusky Men, and the bowmen still loosed from the flanks of them, or aimed deftly from betwixt the ranks of the spearmen.

And now was there a space of ten strides or more betwixt the Dalesmen and their foes, over which the spears hung terribly, nor durst the Dusky Men adventure there; and thereon was nought but men dead or sorely hurt. Then suddenly a horn rang thrice shrilly over all the noise and clamour of the throng, and the ranks of the spearmen opened, and forth into that space strode two score of the swordsmen and axe-wielders of the Dale, their weapons raised in their hands, and he who led them was Iron-hand of the House of the Bull: tall he was, wide-shouldered, exceeding strong, but beardless and fair-faced. He bore aloft a two-edged sword, broad-bladed, exceeding heavy, so that few men could wield it in battle, but not right long; it was an ancient weapon, and his father before him had called it the Barley-scythe. With him were some of the best of the kindreds, as Wolf of Whitegarth, Long-hand of Oakholt, Hart of Highcliff, and War-well the captain of the Bridge. These made no tarrying on that space of the dead, but cried aloud their cries: "For the Burg and the Steer! for the Dale and the Bridge!

for the Dale and the Bull!" and so fell at once on the felons; who fled not, nor had room to flee; and also they feared not the edge-weapons so sorely as they feared those huge spears. So they turned fiercely on the swordsmen, and chiefly on Iron-hand, as he entered in amongst them the first of all, hewing to the right hand and the left, and many a man fell before the Barley-scythe; for they were but little before him. Yet as one fell another took his place, and hewed at him with the steel axe and the crooked sword; and with many strokes they clave his shield and brake his helm and rent his byrny, while he heeded little save smiting with the Barley-scythe, and the blood ran from his arm and his shoulder and his thigh.

But War-well had entered in among the foe on his left hand, and unshielded hove up a great broad-bladed axe, that clave the iron helms of the Dusky Men, and rent their horn-scaled byrnies. He was not very tall, but his shoulders were huge and his arms long, and nought could abide his stroke. He cleared a ring round Iron-hand, whose eyes were growing dim as the blood flowed from him, and hewed three strokes before him; then turned and drew the champion out of the throng, and gave him into the arms of his fellows to stanch the blood that drained away the might of his limbs; and then with a great wordless roar leaped back again on the Dusky Men as the lion leapeth on the herd of swine; and they shrank away before him; and all the swordsmen shouted, "For the Bridge, for the Bridge!" and pressed on the harder, smiting down all before them. On his left hand now was Hart of Highcliff wielding a good sword hight Chip-driver, wherewith he had slain and hurt a many, fighting wisely with sword and shield, and driving the point home through the joints of the armour. But even therewith, as he drave a great stroke at a lord of the Dusky Ones, a cast-spear came flying and smote him on the breast, so that he staggered, and the stroke fell flatlings on the shield-boss of his foe, and Chip-driver brake atwain nigh the hilts; but Hart closed with him, and smote him on the face with the pommel, and tore his axe from his hand and clave his skull therewith, and slew him with his own weapon, and fought on valiantly beside War-well.

Now War-well had fought so fiercely that he had rent his own hauberk with the might of his strokes, and as he raised his arm to smite a huge stroke, a deft man of the felons thrust the spike of his war-axe up under his arm; and when War-well felt the smart of the steel, he turned on that man, and, letting his axe fall down to his wrist and hang there by its loop, he caught the foeman up by the neck and the breech, and drave him against the other Dusky Ones before him, so that their weapons pierced and rent their own friend and fellow. Then he put forth the might of his arms and the pith of his body, and hove up that felon and cast him on to the heads of his fellow murder-carles, so that he rent them and was rent by them. Then

War-well fell on again with the axe, and all the champions of the Dale shouted and fell on with him, and the foe shrank away; and the Dalesmen cleared a space five fathoms" length before them, and the spearmen drew onward and stood on the space whereon the first onslaught had been.

Then drew those hewers of the Dale together, and forth from the company came the man that bare the Banner of the Bridget and the champions gathered round him, and they ordered their ranks and strode with the Banner before them three times to and fro across the road athwart the front of the spearmen, and then with a great shout drew back within the spear-hedge. Albeit five of the champions of the Dale had been slain outright there, and the more part of them hurt more or less.

But when all were well within the ranks, once again blew the horn, and all the spears sank to the rest, and the kindreds drave the spear-furrow, and a space was swept clear before them, and the cries and yells of the Dusky Men were so fierce and wild that the rough voices of the Dalesmen were drowned amidst them.

Forth then came every bowman of the kindred that was there and loosed on the Dusky Men; and they forsooth had some bowmen amongst them, but cooped up and jostled as they were they shot but wildly; whereas each shaft of the Dale went home truly.

But amongst the bowmen forth came the Bride in her glittering war-gear, and stepped lightly to the front of the spearmen. Her own yew bow had been smitten by a shaft and broken in her hand: so she had caught up a short horn bow and a quiver from one of the slain of the Dusky Men; and now she knelt on one knee under the shadow of the spears nigh to her grandsire Hall-ward, and with a pale face and knitted brow notched and loosed, and notched and loosed on the throng of foemen, as if she were some daintily fashioned engine of war.

So fared the battle on the road that went from the south into the Market-stead. Valiantly had the kindred fought there, and no man of them had blenched, and much had they won; but the way was perilous before them, for the foe was many and many.

45. OF FACE-OF-GOD'S ONSLAUGHT

Now the banners of the Wolf flapped and rippled over the heads of the Woodlanders and the Men of the Wolf; and the men shot all they might, nor took heed now to cover themselves against the shafts of the Dusky Men. As for these, for all they were so many, their arrow-shot was no great matter, for they were in very evil order, as has been said; and moreover, their rage was so great to come to handy strokes with these foemen, that some of them flung away their bows to brandish the axe or the sword. Nevertheless were some among the kindred hurt or slain by their arrows.

Now stood Face-of-god with the foremost; and from where he stood he could see somewhat of the battle of the Dalesmen, and he wotted that it was thriving; therefore he looked before him and close around him, and noted what was toward there. The space betwixt the houses and the break of the bent was crowded with the fury of the Dusky Men tossing their weapons aloft, crying to each other and at the kindred, and here and there loosing a bow-string on them; but whatever was their rage they might not come a many together past a line within ten fathom of the bent's end; for three hundred of the best of bowmen were shooting at them so ceaselessly that no Dusky man was safe of any bare place of his body, and they fell over one another in that penfold of slaughter, and for all their madness did but little.

Yet was the heart of the War-leader troubled; for he wotted that it might not last for ever, and there seemed no end to the throng of murder-carles; and the time would come when the

arrowshot would be spent, and they must needs come to handy strokes, and that with so many.

Now a voice spake to him as he gazed with knitted brows and careful heart on that turmoil of battle:

"What now hast thou done with the Sun-beam, and where is her brother? Is the Chief of the Wolf skulking when our work is so heavy? And thou meseemeth art overlate on the field: the mowing of this meadow is no sluggard's work."

He turned and beheld Bow-may, and gazed on her face for a moment, and saw her eyes how they glittered, and how the pommels of her cheeks were burning red and her lips dry and grey; but before he answered he looked all round about to see what was to note; and he touched Bow-may on the shoulder and pointed to down below where a man of the felons had just come out of the court of one of the houses: a man taller than most, very gaily arrayed, with gilded scales all over him, so that, with his dark face and blue eyes, he looked like some strange dragon. Bow-may spake not, but stamped her foot with anger. Yet if her heart were hot, her hand was steady; for she notched a shaft, and just as the Dusky Chief raised his axe and brandished it aloft, she loosed, and the shaft flew and smote the felon in the armpit and the default of the armour, and he fell to earth. But even as she loosed, Face-of-god cried out in a loud voice:

"O lads of battle! shoot close and all together. Tarry not, tarry not! for we need a little time ere sword meets sword, and the others of the kindreds are at work!"

But Bow-may turned round to him and said: "Wilt thou not answer me? Where is thy kindness gone?"

Even as she was speaking she had notched and loosed another shaft, speaking as folk do who turn from busy work at loom or bench.

Then said Face-of-god: "Shoot on, sister Bow-may! The Sun-beam is gone with her brother, and he is with the Men of the Face."

He broke off here, for a man fell beside him hurt in the neck, and Face-of-god took his bow from his hands and shot a shaft, while one of the women who had been hurt also tended the newly-wounded man. Then Face-of-god went on speaking:

"She was unwilling to go, but Folk-might and I constrained her; for we knew that this is the most perilous place of the battle—hah! see those three felons, Bow-may! they are aiming hither."

And again he loosed and Bow-may also, but a shaft rattled on his helm withal and another smote a Woodlander beside him, and pierced through the calf of his leg, as he turned and stooped to take fresh arrows from a sheaf that lay there; but the carle took it by the notch and the point, and brake it and drew it out, and then stood up and went on shooting. And Face-of-god spake again:

"Folk-might skulketh not; nor the Men of the Vine, and the Sickle, and the Face, nor the Shepherd-Folk: soon shall they be making our work easy to us, if we can hold our own till then. They are on the other roads that lead into the square. Now suffer me, and shoot on!"

Therewith he looked round about him, and he saw on the left hand that all was quiet; and before him was the confused throng of the Dusky Men trampling their own dead and wounded, and not able as yet to cross that death-line of the arrow so near to them. But on his right hand he saw how they of the kindreds held them firm on the way. Then for a moment of time he considered and thought, till him-seemed he could see the whole battle yet to be foughten; and his face flushed, and he said sharply: "Bow-may, abide here and shoot, and show the others where to shoot, while the arrows hold out; but we will go further for a while, and ye shall follow when we have made the rent great enough."

She turned to him and said: "Why art thou not more joyous? thou art like an host without music or banners."

"Nay," said he, "heed not me, but my bidding!"

She said hastily: "I think I shall die here; since for all we have shot we minish them nowise. Now kiss me this once amidst the battle, and say farewell."

He said: "Nay, nay; it shall not go thus. Abide a little while, and thou shalt see all this tangle open, as the sun cleaveth the clouds on the autumn morning. Yet lo thou! since thou wilt have it so."

And he bent forward and kissed her face, and now the tears ran over it, and she said smiling somewhat: "Now is this more than I looked for, whatso may betide."

But while she was yet speaking he cried in a great voice:

"Ye who have spent your shot, or have nigh spent it, to axe and sword, and follow me to clear the ground 'twixt the bent and the halls. Let each help each, but throng not each other. Shoot wisely, ye bowmen, and keep our backs clear of the foe. On, on! for the Burg and the Face, for the Burg and the Face!"

Therewith he leapt down the steep of the hill, bounding like the hart, with Dale-warden naked in his hand; and they that followed were two score and ten; and the arrows of their bowmen rained over their heads on the Dusky Men, as they smote down the first of the foemen, and the others shrieked and shrank from them, or turned on them smiting wildly and desperately.

But Face-of-god swept round the great sword and plunged into that sea of turmoil and noise and evil sights and savours, and even therewith he heard clearly a voice that said: "Gold-ring, I am hurt; take my bow a while!" and knew it for Bow-may's; but it came to his ears like the song of a bird without meaning; for it was as if his life were changed at once; and in a minute or two he had cut thrice with the edge and thrust twice with the point, eager, but clear-eyed and deft; and he saw as in a picture the foe before him, and the grey roofs of Silver-stead, and through the gap in them the tops of the blue ridges far aloof. And now had three fallen before him, and they feared him, and turned on him, and smote so many together that their strokes crossed each other, and one warded him from the other; and he laughed aloud and shielded himself, and drave the point of Dale-warden amidst the tangle of weapons through the open mouth of a captain of the felons, and slashed a cheek with a back-stroke, and swept round the edge to his right hand and smote off a blue-eyed snub-nosed head; and therewith a pole-axe smote him on the left side of his helm, so that he tottered; but he swung himself round, and stood stark and upright, and gave a short hack with the edge, keeping Dale-warden well in hand, and a gold-clad felon, a champion of them, and their tallest on the ground, fell aback, his throat gaping more than the mouth of him.

Then Face-of-god shouted and waved Dale-warden aloft to the Banner of the Wolf that floated behind and above him, and he cried out: "As I have promised so have I done!" And he looked about, and beheld how valiantly his fellows had been doing; for before him now was a space of earth with no man standing on his feet thereon, like the swathe of the mowers of June; and beyond that was the crowd of the Dusky Men wavering like the tall grass abiding the scythe.

But a minute, and they fell to casting at Face-of-god and his fellows spears and knives and shields and whatsoever would fly; and a spear smote him on the breast, but entered not; and a bossed shield fell over his face withal, and a plummet of sling-lead smote his helm, and he fell to earth; but leapt up again straightway, and heard as he arose a great shout close to him, and a shrill cry, and lo! at his left side Bow-may, her sword in her hand, and the hand red with blood from a shaft-graze on her wrist, and a white cloth stained with blood about her neck; and on his right side Wood-wise bearing the banner and crying the Wolf-whoop; for the whole company was come down from the slope and stood around him.

Then for a little while was there such a stilling of the tumult about him there, that he heard great and glad cries from the Road of the South of "The Burg and the Steer! The Dale and the Bridge! The Dale and the Bull!" And thereafter a terrible great shrieking cry, and a huge voice that cried: "Death, death, death to the Dusky Men!" And thereafter again fierce cries and great tumult of the battle.

Then Face-of-god shook Dale-warden in the air, and strode forward fiercely, but not speedily, and the whole company went foot for foot along with him; and as he went, would he or would he not, song came into his mouth, a song of the mead-ows of the Dale, even such as this:

The wheat is done blooming and rust's on the sickle,
  And green are the meadows grown after the scythe.
Come, hands for the dance! For the toil hath been mickle,
  And 'twixt haysel and harvest 'tis time to be blithe.

And what shall the tale be now dancing is over,
  And kind on the meadow sits maiden by man,
And the old man bethinks him of days of the lover,
  And the warrior remembers the field that he wan?

Shall we tell of the dear days wherein we are dwelling,
  The best days of our Mother, the cherishing Dale,
When all round about us the summer is telling,
  To ears that may hearken, the heart of the tale?

Shall we sing of these hands and these lips that caress us,
  And the limbs that sun-dappled lie light here beside,
When still in the morning they rise but to bless us,
  And oft in the midnight our footsteps abide?

O nay, but to tell of the fathers were better,
  And of how we were fashioned from out of the earth;
Of how the once lowly spurned strong at the fetter;
  Of the days of the deeds and beginning of mirth.

And then when the feast-tide is done in the morning,
  Shall we whet the grey sickle that bideth the wheat,
Till wan grow the edges, and gleam forth a warning

Of the field and the fallow where edges shall meet.

And when cometh the harvest, and hook upon shoulder
  We enter the red wheat from out of the road,
We shall sing, as we wend, of the bold and the bolder,
  And the Burg of their building, the beauteous abode.

As smiteth the sickle amid the sun's burning
  We shall sing how the sun saw the token unfurled,
When forth fared the Folk with no thought of returning,
  In the days when the Banner went wide in the world.

Many saw that he was singing, but heard not the words of his mouth, for great was the noise and clamour. But he heard Bow-may, how she laughed by his side, and cried out:

"Gold-mane, dear-heart, now art thou merry indeed; and glad am I, though they told me that I am hurt.—Ah! now beware, beware!"

For indeed the Dusky Men, seeing the wall of steel rolling down on them, and cooped up by the houses, so that they scarce knew how to flee, turned in the face of death, the fore-most of them, and rushed furiously on the array of the Wood-landers, and all those behind pressed on them like the big wave of the ebbing sea when the gust of the wind driveth it land-ward.

The Woodlanders met them, shouting out: "The Greenwood and the Wolf, the Greenwood and the Wolf!" But not a few of them fell there, though they gave not back a foot; for so fierce now were the Dusky Men, that hewing and thrusting at them availed nought, unless they were slain outright or stunned; and even if they fell they rolled themselves up against their tall foe-men, heeding not death or wounds if they might but slay or wound. There then fell War-grove and ten others of the Wood-landers, and four men of the Wolf, but none before he had slain his foeman; and as each man fell or was hurt grievously, another took his place.

Now a felon leapt up and caught Gold-ring by the neck and drew him down, while another strove to smite his head off; but the stout carle drave a wood-knife into the side of the first felon, and drew it out speedily and smote the other, the smiter, in the face with the same knife, and therewith they all three rolled together on the earth amongst the feet of men. Even so did another felon by Bow-may, and dragged her down to the ground, and smote her with a long knife as she tumbled down; and this was a feat of theirs, for they were long-armed like apes.

But as to this felon, Dale-warden's edge split his skull, and Face-of-god gathered his might together and bestrode Bow-may, till he had hewed a space round about him with great two-handed strokes; and yet the blade brake not. Then he caught up Bow-may from the earth, and the felon's knife had not pierced her hauberk, but she was astonied, and might not stand upon her feet; and Face-of-god turned aside a little with her, and half bore her, half thrust her through the throng to the rearward of his folk, and left her there with two carlines of the Wolf who followed the host for leechcraft's sake, and then turned back shouting: "For the Face, for the Face!" and there followed him back to the battle, a band of those who were fresh as yet, and their blades unbloodied, the young men of the Woodlands.

The wearier fighters made way for them as they came on shouting, and Face-of-god was ahead of them all, and leapt at the foemen as a man unwearied and striking his first stroke, so wondrous hale he was; and they drave a wedge amidst of the Dusky Men, and then turned about and stood back to back hewing at all that drifted on them. But as Face-of-god cleared a space about him, lo! almost within reach of his sword-point up rose a grim shape from the earth, tall, grey-haired, and bloody-faced, who uttered the Wolf-whoop from amidst the terror of his visage, and turned and swung round his head an axe of the Dusky Men, and fell to smiting them with their own weapon. The Dusky Men shrieked in answer to his whoop, and all shrunk from him and Face-of-god; but a cry of joy went up from the kindred, for they knew Gold-ring, whom they deemed had been slain. So they all pressed on together, smiting down the foe before them, and the Dusky Men, some turned their backs and drave those behind them, till they too turned and were strained through the passages and courts of the houses, and some were overthrown and trodden down as they strove to hold face to the Woodlanders, and some were hewn down where they stood; but the whole throng of those that were on their feet drifted toward the Market-place, the Woodlanders following them ever with point and edge, till betwixt the bent and the houses no foeman stood up against them.

Then they stood together, and raised the whoop of victory, and blew their horns long and loud in token of their joy, and the Woodland men lifted up their voices and sang:

> Now far, far aloof
> Standeth lintel and roof,
> The dwelling of days
> Of the Woodland ways:
> Now nought wendeth there

> Save the wolf and the bear,
> And the fox of the waste
> Faring soft without haste.
> No carle the axe whetteth on oak-laden hill;
> No shaft the hart letteth to wend at his will;
> None heedeth the thunder-clap over the glade,
> And the wind-storm thereunder makes no man afraid.
> Is it thus then that endeth man's days on Mid-earth,
> For no man there wendeth in sorrow or mirth?

> Nay, look down on the road
> From the ancient abode!
> Betwixt acre and field
> Shineth helm, shineth shield.
> And high over the heath
> Fares the bane in his sheath;
> For the wise men and bold
> Go their ways o'er the wold.
> Now the Warrior hath given them heart and fair day,
> Unbidden, undriven, they fare to the fray.
> By the rock and the river the banners they bear,
> And their battle-staves quiver 'neath halbert and spear;
> On the hill's brow they gather, and hang o'er the Dale
> As the clouds of the Father hang, laden with bale.

> Down shineth the sun
> On the war-deed half done;
> All the fore-doomed to die,
> In the pale dust they lie.
> There they leapt, there they fell,
> And their tale shall we tell;
> But we, e'en in the gate
> Of the war-garth we wait,
> Till the drift of war-weather shall whistle us on,
> And we tread all together the way to be won,
> To the dear land, the dwelling for whose sake we came
> To do deeds for the telling of song-becrowned fame.
> Settle helm on the head then!
> Heave sword for the Dale!
> Nor be mocked of the dead men for deedless and pale.

46. MEN MEET IN THE MARKET OF SILVER-STEAD

So sang they; but Face-of-god went with Red-wolf, who was hurt sorely, but not deadly, and led him back toward the place just under the break of the bent; and there he found Bow-may in the hands of the women who were tending her hurts. She smiled on him from a pale face as he drew nigh, and he looked kindly at her, but he might not abide there, for haste was in his feet. He left Red-wolf to the tending of the women, and clomb the bent hastily, and when he deemed he was high enough, he looked about him; and somewhat more than half an hour had worn since Bow-may had sped the first shaft against the Dusky Men.

He looked down into the Market-stead, and deemed he could see that nigh the Mote-house the Dusky Men were gathering into some better order; but they were no longer drifting toward the southern bents, but were standing round about the altar as men abiding somewhat; and he deemed that they had gotten more bowshot than before, and that most of them bare bows. Though so many had been slain in the battles of the southern bents, yet was the Market-stead full of them, so to say, for others had come thereto in place of those that had fallen.

But now as he looked arose mighty clamour amongst them; and a little west of the Altar was a stir and a hurrying onward and around as in the eddies of a swift stream. Face-of-god wotted not what was betiding there, but he deemed that they were now ware of the onfall of Folk-might and Hall-face and the men of Burgdale, for their faces were all turned to where that was to be looked for.

So he turned and looked on the road to the east of him, where had been the battle of the Steer, but now it was all gone down toward the Market-place, and he could but hear the clamour of it; but nought he saw thereof, because of the houses that hid it.

Then he cast his eyes on the road that entered the Market-stead from the north, and he saw thereon many men gathered; and he wotted not what they were; for though there were weapons amongst them, yet were they not all weaponed, as far as he could see.

Now as he looked this way and that, and deemed that he must tarry no longer, but must enter into the courts of the houses before him and make his way into the Market-stead, lo! a change in the throng of Dusky Warriors nigh the Mote-house, and the ordered bands about the Altar fell to drifting toward the western way with one accord, with great noise and hurry and fierce cries of wrath. Then made Face-of-god no delay, but ran down the bent at once, and at the break of it came upon Bow-may standing upright and sword in hand; and as he passed, she joined herself to him, and said: "What new tidings now, Gold-mane?"

"Tidings of battle!" he cried; "tidings of victory! Folk-might hath fallen on, and the Dusky Men run hastily to meet him. Hark, hark!"

For as he spoke came a great noise of horns, and Bow-may said: "What horn is that blowing?"

He stayed not, but shouted aloud: "For the Face, for the Face! Now will we fall upon their backs!"

Therewith was he come to his company, and he cried out to them: "Heard ye the horn, heard ye the horn? Now follow me into the Market-place; much is yet to do!"

Even therewith came the sound of other horns, and all men were silent a moment, and then shouted all together, for the Woodlanders knew it for the horn of the Shepherds coming on by the eastward way.

But Face-of-god waved his sword aloft and set on at once, and they followed and gat them through the courts of the houses and their passages into the Market-place. There they found more room than they looked to find; for the foemen had drawn away on the left hand toward the battle of Folk-might, and on the right hand toward the battle of the Steer; and great was the noise and cry that came thence.

Now stood Face-of-god under the two banners of the Wolf in the Market-place of Silver-stead, and scarce had he time to be high-hearted, for needs must he ponder in his mind what thing were best to do. For on the left hand he deemed the foe was the strongest and best ordered; but there also were the kindreds the doughtiest, and it was little like that the felons should overcome the spear-casters of the Face and the glaive-bearers of the Sickle, and the bowmen of the Vine: there also were the wisest leaders, as the stark elder Stone-face, and the tall Hall-face, and his father of the unshaken heart, and above all Folk-might, fierce in his wrath, but his anger burning steady and clear, like the oaken butt on the hearth of the hall.

Then as his mind pictured him amongst the foe, it made therewith another picture of the slender warrior Sun-beam caught in the tangle of battle, and longing for him and calling for him amidst the hard hand-play. And thereat his face flushed, and all his body waxed hot, and he was on the very point of leading the onset against the foe on the left. But therewith he bethought him of the bold men of the Steer and the Bridge and the Bull weary with much fighting; and he remembered also that the Bride was amongst them and fighting, it might be, amidst the foremost, and if she were slain how should he ever hold up his head again. He bethought him also that the Shepherds, who had fallen on by the eastern road, valiant as they were, were scarce so well armed or so well led as the others. Therewithal he bethought him (and again it came like a picture into his mind) of falling on the foemen by whom the southern battle was beset, and then the twain of them meeting the Shepherds, and lastly, all those three companies joined together clearing the Market-place, and meeting the men under Folk-might in the midst thereof.

Therefore, scant had he been pondering these things in his mind for a minute ere he cried out: "Blow up horns, blow up! forward banners, and follow me, O valiant men! to the helping of the Steer, the Bridge, and the Bull; deep have they thrust into the Dusky Throng, and belike are hard pressed. Hark how the clamour ariseth from their besetters! On now, on!"

Therewith hung a star of sunlight on his sword as he raised it aloft, and the Wolf-whoop rang out terribly in the Market-place, for now had the Woodlanders also learned it, and the hearts of the foemen sank as they heard the might and the mass thereof. Then the battle of the Woodlanders swept round and fell upon the flank of them who were besetting the kindreds, as an iron bar smiteth the soft fir-wood; and they of the kindreds heard their cry, but faintly and confusedly, so great was the turmoil of battle about them.

Now once more was Bow-may by the side of Face-of-god; and if she had not the might of the mightiest, yet had she the deftness of the deftest. And now was she calm and cool, shielding herself with a copper-bossed target, and driving home the point of her sharp sword; white was her face, and her eyes glittered amidst it, and she seemed to men like to those on whose heads the Warrior hath laid the Holy Bread.

As to Wood-wise, he had given the Banner of the red-jawed Wolf to Stone-wolf, a huge and dreadful warrior some forty winters old, who had fought in the Great Overthrow, and now hewed down the Dusky Men, wielding a heavy short-sword left-handed. But Wood-wise himself fought with a great sword, giving great strokes to the right hand and the left, and was no more hasty than is the hewer in the winter wood.

Face-of-god fought wisely and coldly now, and looked more to warding his friends than destroying his foes, and both to Bow-may and Wood-wise his sword was a shield; for oft he took the life from the edge of the upraised axe, and stayed the point of the foeman in mid-air.

Even so wisely fought the whole band of the Woodlanders and the Wolves, who got within smiting space of the foe; for they had no will to cast away their lives when assured victory was so nigh to them. Sooth to say, the hand-play was not so hard to them as it had been betwixt the bent and the houses; for the Dusky Men were intent on dealing with the men of the kindreds from the southern road, who stood war-wearied before them; and they were hewing and casting at them, and baying and yelling like dogs; and though they turned about to meet the storm of the Woodlanders, yet their hearts failed them withal, and they strove to edge away from betwixt those two fearful scythes of war, fighting as men fleeing, not as men in onset. But still the Woodlanders and the Wolves came on, hewing and thrusting, smiting down the foemen in heaps, till the Dusky Throng grew thin, and the staves of the Dalesmen and their bright banners in the morning sun were clear to see, and at last their very faces, kindly and familiar, worn and strained with the stress of battle, or laughing wildly, or pale with the fury of the fight. Then rose up to the heavens the blended shout of the Woodlanders and the Dalesmen, and now there was nought of foemen betwixt them save the dead and the wounded.

Then Face-of-god thrust his sword into its sheath all bloody as it was, and strode over the dead men to where Hall-ward stood under the banner of the Steer, and cast his arms about the old carle, and kissed him for joy of the victory. But Hall-ward thrust him aback and looked him in the face, and his cheeks were pale and his lips clenched, and his eyes haggard and staring, and he said in a harsh voice:

"O young man, she is dead! I saw her fall. The Bride is dead, and thou hast lost thy troth-plight maiden. O death, death to the Dusky Men!"

Then grew Face-of-god as pale as a linen sleeve, and all the new-comers groaned and cried out. But a bystander said: "Nay, nay, it is nought so bad as that; she is hurt, and sorely; but she liveth yet."

Face-of-god heard him not. He forgot Dale-warden lying in his sheath, and he saw that the last speaker had a great wood-axe broad and heavy in his hand, so he cried: "Man, man, thine axe!" and snatched it from him, and turned about to the foe again, and thrust through the ranks, suffering none to stay him till all his friends were behind him and all his foes before him. And as he burst forth from the ranks waving his axe aloft, bare-headed now, his yellow hair flying abroad, his mouth crying out, "Death, death, death to the Dusky Men!" fear of him smote their hearts, and they howled and fled before him as they might; for they said that the Dalesmen had prayed their Gods into the battle. But not so fast could they flee but he was presently amidst them, smiting down all about him, and they so terror-stricken that scarce might they raise a hand against him. All that blended host followed him mad with wrath and victory, and as they pressed on, they heard behind them the horns and war-cries of the Shepherds falling on from the east. Nought they heeded that now, but drave on a fearful storm of war, and terrible was the slaughter of the felons.

It was but a few minutes ere they had driven them up against that great stack of faggots that had been dight for the burnt-offering of men, and many of the felons had mounted up on to it, and now in their anguish of fear were shooting arrows and casting spears on all about them, heeding little if they were friend or foe. Now were the men of the kindreds at point to climb this twiggen burg; but by this time the fury of Face-of-god had run clear, and he knew where he was and what he was doing; so he stayed his folk, and cried out to them: "Forbear, climb not! let the torch help the sword!" And therewith he looked about and saw the fire-pot which had been set down there for the kindling of the bale-fire, and the coals were yet red in it; so he snatched up a dry brand and lighted it thereat, and so did divers others, and they thrust them among the faggots, and the fire caught at once, and the tongues of flame began to leap from faggot to faggot till all was in a light low; for the wood had been laid for that very end, and smeared with grease and oil so that the burning to the god might be speedy.

But the fierceness of the kindreds heeded not the fire, nor overmuch the men who leapt down from the stack before it, but they left all behind them, faring straight toward the western outgate from the Market-stead; and Face-of-god still led them on; though by now he was wholly come to his right mind again, albeit the burden of sorrow yet lay heavy on his heart. He had broken his axe, and had once more drawn Dale-warden from his sheath, and many felt his point and edge.

But now, as they chased, came a rush of men upon them again, as though a new onset were at hand. That saw Face-of-god and Hall-ward and War-well, and other wise leaders of men, and they bade their folk forbear the chase, and lock their ranks to meet the onfall of this new wave of foemen. And they did so, and stood fast as a wall; but lo! the onrush that drave up against them was but a fleeing shrieking throng, and no longer an array of warriors, for many had cast away their weapons, and were rushing they knew not whither; for they were being thrust on the bitter edges of Face-of-god's companies by the terror of the fleers from the onset of the men of the Face, the Sickle, and the Vine, whom Hall-face and Stone-face were leading, along with Folk-might. Then once again the men of Face-of-god gave forth the whoop of victory, and pressed forward again, hewing their way through the throng of fleers, but turning not to chase to the right or the left; while at their backs came on the Shepherd-folk, who had swept down all that withstood them; for now indeed was the Market-stead getting thinner of living men.

So led the War-leader his ordered ranks, till at last over the tangled crowd of Runaways he saw the banners of the Burg and the Face flashing against the sun, and heard the roar of the kindreds as they drave the chase towards them. Then he lifted up his sword, and stood still, and all the host behind him stayed and cast a huge shout up to the heavens, and there they abode the coming of the other Dalesmen.

But the War-leader sent a message to Hound-under-Greenbury, bidding him lead the Shepherds to the chase of the Dusky Men, who were now all fleeing toward the northern outgate of the Market. Howbeit he called to mind the throng he had seen on the northern road before they were come into the Market-stead, and deemed that way also death awaited the foemen, even if the men of the kindreds forbore them.

But presently the space betwixt the Woodlanders and the men of the Face was clear of all but the dead, so that friend saw the face of friend; and it could be seen that the warriors of the Face were ruddy and smiling for joy, because the battle had been easy to them, and but few of them had fallen; for the Dusky Men who had left the Market-stead to fall on them, had had room for fleeing behind them, and had speedily turned their backs before the spear-casting of the men of the Face and

the onrush of the swordsmen.

There then stood these victorious men facing one another, and the banner-bearers on either side came through the throng, and brought the banners together between the two hosts; and the Wolf kissed the Face, and the Sickle and the Vine met the Steer and the Bridge and the Bull: but the Shepherds were yet chasing the fleers.

There in the forefront stood Hall-face the tall, with the joy of battle in his eyes. And Stone-face, the wise carle in war, stood solemn and stark beside him; and there was the goodly body and the fair and kindly visage of the Alderman smiling on the faces of his friends. But as for Folk-might, his face was yet white and aweful with anger, and he looked restlessly up and down the front of the kindreds, though he spake no word.

Then Face-of-god could no longer forbear, but he thrust Dale-warden into his sheath, and ran forward and cast his arms about his father's neck and kissed him; and the blood of himself and of the foemen was on him, for he had been hurt in divers places, but not sorely, because of the good hammer-work of the Alderman.

Then he kissed his brother and Stone-face, and he took Folk-might by the hand, and was on the point of speaking some word to him, when the ranks of the Face opened, and lo! the Sun-beam in her bright war-gear, and the sword girt to her side, and she unhurt and unsullied.

Then was it to him as when he met her first in Shadowy Vale, and he thought of little else than her; but she stepped lightly up to him, and unashamed before the whole host she kissed him on the mouth, and he cast his mailed arms about her, and joy made him forget many things and what was next to do, though even at that moment came afresh a great clamour of shrieks and cries from the northern outgate of the Market-stead: and the burning pile behind them cast a great wavering flame into the air, contending with the bright sun of that fair day, now come hard on noontide. But ere he drew away his face from the Sun-beam's, came memory to him, and a sharp pang shot through his heart, as he heard Folk-might say: "Where then is the Shield-may of Burgstead? where is the Bride?"

And Face-of-god said under his breath: "She is dead, she is dead!" And then he stared out straight before him and waited till someone else should say it aloud. But Bow-may stepped forward and said: "Chief of the Wolf, be of good cheer; our kinswoman is hurt, but not deadly."

The Alderman's face changed, and he said: "Hast thou seen her, Bow-may?"

"Nay," she said. "How should I leave the battle? but others have told me who have seen her."

Folk-might stared into the ranks of men before him, but said nothing. Said the Alderman: "Is she well tended?"

"Yea, surely," said Bow-may, "since she is amongst friends, and there are no foemen behind us."

Then came a voice from Folk-might which said: "Now were it best to send good men and deft in arms, and who know Silverdale, from house to house, to search for foemen who may be lurking there."

The Alderman looked kindly and sadly on him and said:

"Kinsman Stone-face, and Hall-face my son, the brunt of the battle is now over, and I am but a simple man amongst you; therefore, if ye will give me leave, I will go see this poor kinswoman of ours, and comfort her."

They bade him go: so he sheathed his sword, and went through the press with two men of the Steer toward the southern road; for the Bride had been brought into a house nigh the corner of the Market-place.

But Face-of-god looked after his father as he went, and remembrance of past days came upon him, and such a storm of grief swept over him, as he thought of the Bride lying pale and bleeding and brought anigh to her death, that he put his hands to his face and wept as a child that will not be comforted; nor had he any shame of all those bystanders, who in sooth were men good and kindly, and had no shame of his grief or marvelled at it, for indeed their own hearts were sore for their lovely kinswoman, and many of them also wept with Face-of-god. But the Sun-beam stood by and looked on her betrothed, and she thought many things of the Bride, and was sorry, albeit no tears came into her eyes; then she looked askance at Folk-might and trembled; but he said coldly, and in a loud voice:

"Needs must we search the houses for the lurking felons, or many a man will yet be murdered. Let Wood-wicked lead a band of men at once from house to house."

Then said a man of the Wolf hight Hardgrip: "Wood-wicked was slain betwixt the bent and the houses."

Said Folk-might: "Let it be Wood-wise then."

But Bow-may said: "Wood-wise is even now hurt in the leg by a wounded felon, and may not go afoot."

Then said Folk-might: "Is Crow the Shaft-speeder anigh?"

"Yea, here am I," quoth a tall man of fifty winters, coming from out the ranks where stood the Wolves.

Said Folk-might: "Kinsman Crow, do thou take two score and ten of doughty men who are not too hot-headed, and search every house about the Market-place; but if ye come on any house that makes a stout defence, send ye word thereof to the Mote-house, where we will presently be, and we shall send you help. Slay every felon that ye fall in with; but if ye find in the houses any of the poor folk crouching and afraid, comfort their hearts all ye may, and tell them that now is life come to them."

So Crow fell to getting his band together, and presently departed with them on his errand.

47. THE KINDREDS WIN THE MOTE-HOUSE

The din and tumult still came from the north side of the Market-place, so that all the air was full of noise; and Face-of-god deemed that the thralls had gotten weapons into their hands and were slaying their masters.

Now he lifted up his face, and put his hand on Folk-might's shoulder, and said in a loud voice:

"Kinsmen, it were well if our brother were to bid the banners into the Mote-house of the Wolf, and let all the Host set itself in array before the said house, and abide till the chasers of the foe come to us thither; for I perceive that they are now become many, and are more than those of our kindred."

Then Folk-might looked at him with kind eyes, and said:

"Thou sayest well, brother; even so let it be!"

And he lifted up his sword, and Face-of-god cried out in a loud voice: "Forward, banners! blow up horns! fare we forth with victory!"

So the Host drew its ranks together in good order, and they all set forward, and old Stone-face took the Sun-beam by the hand and led on behind Folk-might and the War-leader. But when they came to the Hall, then saw they how the steps that led up to the door were high and double, going up from each side without any railing or fool-guard; and crowding the stairs and the platform thereof was a band of the Dusky Men, as many as could stand thereon, who shot arrows at the host of the kindreds, howling like dogs, and chattering like apes; and arrows and spears came from the windows of the Hall; yea, and on the very roof a score of these felons were riding the ridge and mocking like the trolls of old days.

Now when they saw this they stayed a while, and men shielded them against the shafts; but the leaders drew together in front of the Host, and Folk-might fell to speech; and his face was very pale and stern; for now he had had time to think of the case of the Bride, and fierce wrath, and grief unholpen filled his soul. So he said:

"Brothers, this is my business to deal with; for I see before me the stair that leadeth to the Mote-house of my people, and now would I sit there whereas my fathers sat, when peace was on the Dale, as once more it shall be to-morrow. Therefore up this stair will I go, and none shall hinder me; and let no man of the host follow me till I have entered into the Hall, unless perchance I fall dead by the way; but stand ye still and look on."

"Nay," said Face-of-god, "this is partly the business of the War-leader. There are two stairs. Be content to take the southern one, and I will take the northern. We shall meet on the plain stone at the top."

But Hall-face said: "War-leader, may I speak?"

"Speak, brother," said Face-of-god.

Said Hall-face: "I have done but little to-day, War-leader. I would stand by thee on the northern stair; so shall Folk-might be content, if he doeth two men's work who are not little-hearted."

Said Face-of-god: "The doom of the War-leader is that Folk-might shall fall on by the southern stair to slake his grief and increase his glory, and Face-of-god and Hall-face by the northern. Haste to the work, O brothers!"

And he and Hall-face went to their places, while all looked on. But the Sun-beam, with her hand still in Stone-face's, she turned white to the lips, and stared with wild eyes before her, not knowing where she was; for she had deemed that the battle was over, and Face-of-god saved from it.

But Folk-might tossed up his head and laughed, and cried out, "At last, at last!" And his sword was in his hand, the Sleep-thorn to wit, a blade of ancient fame; so now he let it fall and hang to his wrist by the leash, while he clapped his hands together and uttered the Wolf-whoop mightily, and all the men of the Wolf that were in the host, and the Woodlanders withal, uttered it with him. Then he put his shield over his head and stood before the first of the steps, and the Dusky Men laughed to see one man come against them, though there was death in their hearts. But he laughed back at them in triumph, and set his foot on the step, and let Sleep-thorn's point go into the throat of a Dusky lord, and thrust amongst them, hewing right and left, and tumbling men over the edge of the stair, which was to them as the narrow path along the cliff-side that hangeth over the unfathomed sea. They hewed and thrust at him in turn; but so close were they packed that their weapons crossed about him, and one shielded him from the other, and they swayed staggering on that fearful verge, while the Sleep-thorn crept here and there amongst them, lulling their hot fury. For, as desperate as they were, and fighting for death and not for life, they had a horror of him and of the sea of hatred below them, and feared where to set their feet, and he feared nought at all, but from feet to sword-point was but an engine of slaughter, while the heart within him throbbed with fury long held back as he thought upon the Bride and her wounding, and all the wrongs of his people since their Great Undoing.

So he smote and thrust, till him-seemed the throng of foes thinned before him: with his sword-pommel he smote a lord of the Dusky Ones in the face, so that he fell over the edge amongst the spears of the kindred; then he thrust the point of Sleep-thorn towards the Hall-door through the breast of another, and then it seemed to him that he had but one before him; so he hove up the edges to cleave him down, but ere the stroke fell, close to his ears exceeding loud rang out the cry, "For the Burg and the Face! for the Face, for the Face!" and he drew aback a little, and his eyes cleared, and lo! it was Hall-face the tall, his long sword all reddened with battle; and beside him stood Face-of-god, silent and panting, his face pale with the fierce anger of the fight, and the weariness which was now at last gaining upon him. There stood those three with no other living man upon the plain of the stairs.

Then Face-of-god turned shouting to the Folk, and cried:

"Forth now with the banners! For now is the Wolf come home. On into the Hall, O Kindred of the Gods!"

Then poured the Folk up over the stairs and into the Hall of the Wolf, the banners flapping over their heads; and first went the War-leader and Folk-might and Hall-face, and then the three delivered thralls, Wolf-stone, God-swain, and Spear-fist, and Dallach with them, though both he and Wolf-stone had been hurt in the battle; and then came blended together the Men of the Face along with them of the Wolf who had entered the Market-stead with them, and with these were Stone-face and Wood-wont and Bow-may, leading the Sun-beam betwixt them; and now was she come to herself again, though her face was yet pale, and her eyes gleamed as she stepped across the threshold of the Hall.

But when a many were gotten in, and the first-comers had had time to handle their weapons and look about them, a cry of the utmost wrath broke from Folk-might and those others who remembered the Hall from of old. For wretched and befouled was that well-builded house: the hangings rent away; the goodly painted walls daubed and smeared with wicked tokens of the Alien murderers: the floor, once bright with polished stones of the mountain, and strewn with sweet-smelling flowers, was now as foul as the den of the man-devouring troll of the heaths. From the fair-carven roof of oak and chestnut-beams hung ugly knots of rags and shapeless images of the sorcery of the Dusky Men. And furthermore, and above all, from the last tie-beam of the roof over the dais dangled four shapes of men-at-arms, whom the older men of the Wolf knew at once for the embalmed bodies of their four great chieftains, who had been slain on the day of the Great Undoing; and they cried out with horror and rage as they saw them hanging there in their weapons as they had lived.

There was the Hostage of the Earth, his shield painted with the green world circled with the worm of the sea. There was the older Folk-might, the uncle of the living man, bearing a shield with an oak and a lion done thereon. There was Wealth-eker, on whose shield was done a golden sheaf of wheat. There was he who bore a name great from of old, Folk-wolf to wit, bearing on his shield the axe of the hewer. There they hung, dusty, befouled, with sightless eyes and grinning mouths, in the dimmed sunlight of the Hall, before the eyes of that victorious Host, stricken silent at the sight of them.

Underneath them on the dais stood the last remnant of the battle of the Dusky Men; and they, as men mad with coming death, shook their weapons, and with shrieking laughter mocked at the overcomers, and pointed to the long-dead chiefs, and called on them in the tongue of the kindreds to come down and lead their dear kinsmen to the high-seat; and then they cried out to the living warriors of the Wolf, and bade them better their deed of slaying, and set to work to make alive again, and cause their kinsmen to live merry on the earth.

With that last mock they handled their weapons and rushed howling on the warriors to meet their death; nor was it long denied them; for the sword of the Wolf, the axe of the Woodland, and the spear of the Dale soon made an end of the dreadful lives of these destroyers of the Folks.

48. MEN SING IN THE MOTE-HOUSE

Then strode the Warriors of the Wolf over the bodies of the slain on to the dais of their own Hall; and Folk-might led the Sun-beam by the hand, and now was his sword in its sheath, and his face was grown calm, though it was stern and sad. But even as he trod the dais comes a slim swain of the Wolves twisting himself through the throng, and so maketh way to Folk-might, and saith to him:

"Chieftain, the Alderman of Burgdale sendeth me hither to say a word to thee; even this, which I am to tell to thee and the War-leader both: It is most true that our kinswoman the Bride will not die, but live. So help me, the Warrior and the Face! This is the word of the Alderman."

When Folk-might heard this, his face changed and he hung his head; and Face-of-god, who was standing close by, beheld him and deemed that tears were falling from his eyes on to the hall-floor. As for him, he grew exceeding glad, and he turned to the Sun-beam and met her eyes, and saw that she could scarce refrain her longing for him; and he was abashed for the sweetness of his love. But she drew close up to him, and spake to him softly and said:

"This is the day that maketh amends; and yet I long for another day. When I saw thee coming to me that first day in Shadowy Vale, I thought thee so goodly a warrior that my heart was in my mouth. But now how goodly thou art! For the battle is over, and we shall live."

"Yea," said Face-of-god, "and none shall begrudge us our love. Behold thy brother, the hard-heart, the warrior; he weepeth because he hath heard that the Bride shall live. Be sure then that she shall not gainsay him. O fair shall the world be to-morrow!"

But she said: "O Gold-mane, I have no words. Is there no minstrelsy amongst us?"

Now by this time were many of the men of the Wolf and the Woodlanders gathered on the dais of the Hall; and the Dalesmen noting this, and wotting that these men were now in their own Mote-house, withdrew them as they might for the press toward the nether end thereof. That the Sun-beam noted, and that all those about her save the War-leader were of the kindreds of the Wolf and the Woodland, and, still speaking softly, she said to Face-of-god:

"Gold-mane, meseemeth I am now in my wrong place; for now the Wolf raiseth up his head, but I am departing from him. Surely I should now be standing amongst my people of the Face, whereto I am going ere long."

He said: "Beloved, I am now become thy kindred and thine home, and it is meet for thee to stand beside me."

She cast her eyes adown and answered not; and she fell a-pondering of how sorely she had desired that fair dale, and now she would leave it, and be content and more than content.

But now the kindreds had sundered, they upon the dais ranked themselves together there in the House which their fathers had builded; and when they saw themselves so meetly ordered, their hearts being full with the sweetness of hope accomplished and the joy of deliverance from death, song arose amongst them, and they fell to singing together; and this is somewhat of their singing:

> Now raise we the lay
> Of the long-coming day!
> Bright, white was the sun
> When we saw it begun:
> O'er its noon now we live;
> It hath ceased not to give;
> It shall give, and give more
> From the wealth of its store.
> O fair was the yesterday! Kindly and good
> Was the wasteland our guester, and kind was the wood;
> Though below us for reaping lay under our hand
> The harvest of weeping, the grief of the land;
> Dumb covered the sorrow, nought daring to cry
> On the help of to-morrow, the deed drawing nigh.

All increase throve
In the Dale of our love;
There the ox and the steed
Fed down the mead;
The grapes hung high
'Twixt earth and sky,
And the apples fell
Round the orchard well.

Yet drear was the land there, and all was for nought;
None put forth a hand there for what the year wrought,
And raised it o'erflowing with gifts of the earth.
For man's grief was growing beside of the mirth
Of the springs and the summers that wasted their wealth;
And the birds, the new-comers, made merry by stealth.

Yet here of old
Abode the bold;
Nor had they wailed
Though the wheat had failed,
And the vine no more
Gave forth her store.
Yea, they found the waste good
For the fearless of mood.

Then to these, that were dwelling aloof from the Dale,
Fared the wild-wind a-telling the worst of the tale;
As men bathed in the morning they saw in the pool
The image of scorning, the throne of the fool.
The picture was gleaming in helm and in sword,
And shone forth its seeming from cups of the board.

Forth then they came
With the battle-flame;
From the Wood and the Waste
And the Dale did they haste:

They saw the storm rise,
And with untroubled eyes
The war-storm they met;
And the rain ruddy-wet.
O'er the Dale then was litten the Candle of Day,
Night-sorrow was smitten, and gloom fled away.
How the grief-shackles sunder! How many to morn
Shall awaken and wonder how gladness was born!
O wont unto sorrow, how sweet unto you
Shall be pondering to-morrow what deed is to do!

Fell many a man
'neath the edges wan,
In the heat of the play
That fashioned the day.
Praise all ye then
The death of men,
And the gift of the aid
Of the unafraid!

O strong are the living men mighty to save,
And good is their giving, and gifts that we have!
But the dead, they that gave us once, never again;
Long and long shall they save us sore trouble and pain.
O Banner above us, O God of the strong,
Love them as ye love us that bore down our wrong!

So they sang in the Hall; and there was many a man wept, as the song ended, for those that should never see the good days of the Dale, and all the joy that was to be; and men swore, by all that they loved, that they would never forget those that had fallen in the Winning of Silverdale; and that when each year the Cups of Memory went round, they should be no mere names to them, but the very men whom they had known and loved.

49. DALLACH FARETH TO ROSEDALE: CROW TELLETH OF HIS ERRAND: THE KINDREDS EAT THEIR MEAT IN SILVERDALE

Now Dallach, who had gone away for a while, came back again into the Hall; and at his back were a half score of men who bore ladders with them: they were stout men, clad in scanty and ragged raiment, but girt with swords and bearing axes, those of them who were not handling the ladders. Men looked on them curiously, because they saw them to be of the roughest of the thralls. They were sullen and fierce-eyed to behold, and their hands and bare arms were flecked with

blood; and it was easy to see that they had been chasing the fleers, and making them pay for their many torments of past days.

But when Face-of-god beheld this he cried out: "Ho, Dallach! is it so that thou hast bethought thee to bring in hither men to fall to the cleansing of the Hall, and to do away the defiling of the Dusky Men?"

"Even so, War-leader," said Dallach; "also ye shall know

that all battle is over in Silver-stead; for the thralls fell in numbers not to be endured on the Dusky Men who had turned their backs to us, and hindered them from fleeing north. But though they have slain many, they have not slain all, and the remnant have fled by divers ways westaway, that they may gain the wood and the ways to Rosedale; and the stoutest of the thralls are at their heels, and ever as they go fresh men from the fields join in the chase with great joy. I have gathered together of the best of them two hundreds and a half well-armed; and if thou wilt give me leave, I will get to me yet more, and follow hard on the fleers, and so get me home to Rosedale; for thither will these Runaways to meet whatso of their kind may be left there. Also I would fain be there to set some order amongst the poor folk of mine own people, whom this day's work hath delivered from torment. And if thou wilt suffer a few men of the Dalesmen to come along with me, then shall all things be better done there."

"Luck go with thine hands!" said Face-of-god. "Take whomso thou wilt of the Burgdalers that have a mind to fare with thee to the number of five score; and send word of thy thriving to Folk-might, the chieftain of the Dale; as for us, meseemeth that we shall abide here no long while. How sayest thou, Folk-might, shall Dallach go?"

Then Folk-might, who stood close beside him, looked up and reddened somewhat, as a man caught heedless when he should be heedful; but he looked kindly on Face-of-god, and said:

"War-leader, so long as thou art in the Dale which ye kindreds have won back for us, thou art the chieftain, and no other, and I bid thee do as thou wilt in this matter, and in all things; and I hereby give command to all my kindred to do according to thy will everywhere and always, as they love me; and indeed I deem that thy will shall be theirs; since it is only fools who know not their well-wishers. How say ye, kinsmen?"

Then those about cried out: "Hail to Face-of-god! Hail to the Dalesmen! Hail to our friends!"

But Folk-might went up to Face-of-god, and threw his arms about him and kissed him, and he said therewithal, so that most men heard him:

"Herewith I kiss not only thee, thou goodly and glorious warrior! but this kiss and embrace is for all the men of the kindreds of the Dale and the Shepherds; since I deem that never have men more valiant dwelt upon the earth."

Therewith all men shouted for joy of him, and were exceeding glad; but Folk-might spake apart to Face-of-god and said:

"Brother, I suppose that thou wilt deem it good to abide in this Hall or anigh it; for hereabouts now is the heart of the Host. But as for me, I would have leave to depart for a little; since I have an errand, whereof thou mayest wot."

Then Face-of-god smiled on him, and said: "Go, and all good go with thee; and tell my father that I would have tidings, since I may not be there." So he spake; yet in his heart was he glad that he might not go to behold the Bride lying sick and sorry. But Folk-might departed without more words; and in the door of the Hall he met Crow the Shaft-speeder, who would have spoken to him, and given him the tidings; but Folk-might said to him: "Do thine errand to the War-leader, who is within the Hall." And so went on his way.

Then came Crow up the Hall, and stood before Face-of-god and said: "War-leader, we have done that which was to be done, and have cleared all the houses about the Market-stead. Moreover, by the rede of Dallach we have set certain men of the poor folk of the Dale, who are well looked to by the others, to the burying of the slain felons; and they be digging trenches in the fields on the north side of the Market-stead, and carry the carcasses thither as they may. But the slain whom they find of the kindreds do they array out yonder before this Hall. In all wise are these men tame and biddable, save that they rage against the Dusky Men, though they fear them yet. As for us, they deem us Gods come down from heaven to help them. So much for what is good: now have I an ill word to say; to wit, that in the houses whereas we have found many thralls alive, yet also have we found many dead; for amongst these murder-carles were some of an evil sort, who, when they saw that the battle would go against them, rushed into the houses hewing down all before them—man, woman, and child; so that many of the halls and chambers we saw running blood like to shambles. To be short: of them whom they were going to hew to the Gods, we have found thirteen living and three dead, of which latter is one woman; and of the living, seven women; and all these, living and dead, with the leaden shackles yet on them wherein they should be burned. To all these and others whom we have found, we have done what of service we could in the way of victual and clothes, so that they scarce believe that they are on this lower earth. Moreover, I have with me two score of them, who are men of some wits, and who know of the stores of victual and other wares which the felons had, and these will fetch and carry for you as much as ye will. Is all done rightly, War-leader?"

"Right well," said Face-of-god, "and we give thee our thanks therefor. And now it were well if these thy folk were to dight our dinner for us in some green field the nighest that may be, and thither shall all the Host be bidden by sound of horn. Meantime, let us void this Hall till it be cleansed of the filth of the Dusky Ones; but hereafter shall we come again to it, and light a fire on the Holy Hearth, and bid the Gods and the Fathers come back and behold their children sitting glad in the ancient Hall."

Then men shouted and were exceeding joyous; but Face-of-god said once more: "Bear ye a bench out into the Market-place over against the door of this Hall: thereon will I sit with other chieftains of the kindreds, that whoso will may have recourse to us."

So therewith all the men of the kindreds made their ways out of the Hall and into the Market-stead, which was by this time much cleared of the slaughtered felons; and the bale for the burnt-offering was now but smouldering, and a thin column of blue smoke was going up wavering amidst the light airs of the afternoon. Men were somewhat silent now; for they were stiff and weary with the morning's battle; and a many had been hurt withal; and on many there yet rested the after-grief of battle, and sorrow for the loss of friends and well-wishers.

For in the battle had fallen one long hundred and two of the men of the Host; and of these were two score and five of the kindreds of the Steer, the Bull, and the Bridge, who had made such valiant onslaught by the southern road. Of the Shepherds died one score save three; for though they scattered the foe at once, yet they fell on with such headlong valour, rather than wisely, that many were trapped in the throng of the Dusky Men. Of the Woodlanders were slain one score and nine; for hard had been the fight about them, and no man of them spared himself one whit. Of the men of the Wolf, who were but a few, fell sixteen men, and all save two of these in Face-of-god's battle. Of the Burgdale men whom Folk-might led, to wit, them of the Face, the Vine, and the Sickle, were but seven men slain outright. In this tale are told all those who died of their hurts after the day of battle. Therewithal many others were sorely hurt who mended, and went about afterwards hale and hearty.

So as the folk abode in the Market-place, somewhat faint and weary, they heard horns blow up merrily, and Crow the Shaft-speeder came forth and stood on the mound of the altar, and bade men fare to dinner, and therewith he led the way, bearing in his hand the banner of the Golden Bushel, of which House he was; and they followed him into a fair and great mead on the southwest of Silver-stead, besprinkled about with ancient trees of sweet chestnut. There they found the boards spread for them with the best of victual which the poor down-trodden folk knew how to dight for them; and especially was there great plenty of good wine of the sun-smitten bents.

So they fell to their meat, and the poor folk, both men and women, served them gladly, though they were somewhat afeard of these fierce sword-wielders, the Gods who had delivered them. The said thralls were mostly not of those who had fallen so bitterly on their fleeing masters, but were men and women of the households, not so roughly treated as the others, that is to say, those who had been wont to toil under the lash in the fields and the silver-mines, and were as wild as they durst be.

As for these waiting-thralls, the men of the kindreds were gentle and blithe with them, and often as they served them would they stay their hands (and especially if they were women), and would draw down their heads to put a morsel in their mouths, or set the wine-cup to their lips; and they would stroke them and caress them, and treat them in all wise as their dear friends. Moreover, when any man was full, he would arise and take hold of one of the thralls, and set him in his place, and serve him with meat and drink, and talk with him kindly, so that the poor folk were much bewildered with joy. And the first that arose from table were the Sun-beam and Bow-may and Hall-face, with many of the swains and the women of the Woodlanders; and they went from table to table serving the others.

The Sun-beam had done off her armour, and went about exceeding fair and lovely in her kirtle; but Bow-may yet bore her hauberk, for she loved it, and indeed it was so fine and well-wrought that it was no great burden. Albeit she had gone down with the Sun-beam and other women to a fair stream thereby, and there had they bathed and washed themselves; and Bow-may's hurts, which were not great, had been looked to and bound up afresh, and she had come to table unhelmed, with a wreath of wind-flowers round her head.

There then they feasted; and their hearts were strengthened by the meat and drink; and if sorrow were blended with their joy, yet were they high-hearted through both joy and sorrow, looking forward to the good days to be in the Dales at the Roots of the Mountains, and the love and fellowship of Folks and of Houses.

But as for Face-of-god, he went not to the meadow, but abode sitting on the bench in the Market-place, where were none else now of the kindreds save the appointed warders. They had brought him a morsel and a cup of wine, and he had eaten and drunk; and now he sat there with Dale-warden lying sheathed across his knees, and seeming to gaze on the thralls of Silverdale busied in carrying away the bodies of the slain felons, after they had stripped them of their raiment and weapons. Yet indeed all this was before his eyes as a picture which he noted not. Rather he sat pondering many things; wondering at his being there in Silverdale in the hour of victory; longing for the peace of Burgdale and the bride-chamber of the Sun-beam. Then went his thought out toward his old playmate lying hurt in Silverdale; and his heart was grieved because of her, yet not for long, though his thought still dwelt on her; since he deemed that she would live and presently be happy— and happy thenceforward for many years. So pondered Face-of-god in the Market-place of Silverdale.

50. FOLK-MIGHT SEETH THE BRIDE AND SPEAKETH WITH HER

Now tells the tale of Folk-might, that he went his ways from the Hall to the house where the Bride lay; and the swain who had brought the message went along with him, and he was proud of walking beside so mighty a warrior, and he talked to Folk-might as they went; and the sound of his voice was irksome to the chieftain, but he made as though he hearkened. Yet when they came to the door of the house, which was just out of the Place on the Southern road (for thereby had the Bride fallen to earth), he could withhold his grief no longer, but turned on the threshold and laid his head on the door-jamb, and sobbed and wept till the tears fell down like rain. And the boy stood by wondering, and wishing that Folk-might would forbear weeping, but durst not speak to him.

In a while Folk-might left weeping and went in, and found a fair hall sore befouled by the felons, and in the corner on a bed covered with furs the wounded woman; and at first sight he deemed her not so pale as he looked to see her, as she lay with her long dark-red hair strewed over the pillow, her head moving about wearily. A linen cloth was thrown over her body, but her arms lay out of it before her. Beside her sat the Alderman, his face sober enough, but not as one in heavy sorrow; and anigh him was another chair as if someone had but just got up from it. There was no one else in the hall save two women of the Woodlanders, one of whom was cooking some potion on the hearth, and another was sweeping the floor anigh of bran or some such stuff, which had been thrown down to sop up the blood.

So Folk-might went up to the Bride, sorely dreading the image of death which she had grown to be, and sorely loving the woman she was and would be.

He knelt down by the bedside, heeding Iron-face little, though he nodded friendly to him, and he held his face close to hers; but she had her eyes shut and did not open them till he had been there a little while; and then they opened and fixed themselves on his without surprise or change. Then she lifted her right hand (for it was in her left shoulder and side that she had been hurt) and slowly laid it on his head, and drew his face to hers and kissed it fondly, as she both smiled and let the tears run over from her eyes. Then she spake in a weak voice:

"Thou seest, chieftain and dear friend, that I may not stand by thy victorious side to-day. And now, though I were fain if thou wouldst never leave me, yet needs must thou go about thy work, since thou art become the Alderman of the Folk of Silverdale. Yea, and even if thou wert not to go from me, yet in a manner should I go from thee. For I am grievously hurt, and I

know by myself, and also the leeches have told me, that the fever is a-coming on me; so that presently I shall not know thee, but may deem thee to be a woman, or a hound, or the very Wolf that is the image of the Father of thy kindred; or even, it may be, someone else—that I have played with time agone."

Her voice faltered and faded out here, and she was silent a while; then she said:

"So depart, kind friend and dear love, bearing this word with thee, that should I die, I call on Iron-face my kinsman to bear witness that I bid thee carry me to bale in Silverdale, and lay mine ashes with the ashes of thy Fathers, with whom thine own shall mingle at the last, since I have been of the warriors who have helped to bring thee aback to the land of thy folk."

Then she smiled and shut her eyes and said: "And if I live, as indeed I hope, and how glad and glad I shall be to live, then shalt thou bring me to thy house and thy bed, that I may not depart from thee while both our lives last."

And she opened her eyes and looked at him; and he might not speak for a while, so ravished as he was betwixt joy and sorrow. But the Alderman arose and took a gold ring from off his arm, and spake:

"This is the gold ring of the God of the Face, and I bear it on mine arm betwixt the Folk and the God in all man-motes, and I bore it through the battle to-day; and it is as holy a ring as may be; and since ye are plighting troth, and I am the witness thereof, it were good that ye held this ring together and called the God to witness, who is akin to the God of the Earth, as we all be. Take the ring, Folk-might, for I trust thee; and of all women now alive would I have this woman happy."

So Folk-might took the ring and thrust his hand through it, and took her hand, and said:

"Ye Fathers, thou God of the Face, thou Earth-god, thou Warrior, bear witness that my life and my body are plighted to this woman, the Bride of the House of the Steer!"

His face was flushed and bright as he spoke, but as his words ceased he noted how feebly her hand lay in his, and his face fell, and he gazed on her timidly. But she lay quiet, and said softly and slowly:

"O Fathers of my kindred! O Warrior and God of the Earth! bear witness that I plight my troth to this man, to lie in his grave if I die, and in his bed if I live."

And she smiled on him again, and then closed her eyes; but opened them presently once more, and said:

"Dear friend, how fared it with Gold-mane to-day?"

Said Folk-might: "So well he did, that none might have done better. He fared in the fight as if he had been our Father the Warrior: he is a great chieftain."

She said: "Wilt thou give him this message from me, that in no wise he forget the oath which he swore upon the finger-ring as it lay on the sundial of the Garden of the Face? And say, moreover, that I am sorry that we shall part, and have between us such breadth of Wild-wood and mountain-neck."

"Yea, surely will I give thy message," said Folk-might; and in his heart he rejoiced, because he heard her speak as if she were sure of life. Then she said faintly:

"It is now thy work to depart from me, and to do as it behoveth a chieftain of the people and the Alderman of Silver-dale. Depart, lest the leeches chide me: farewell, my dear!"

So he laid his face to hers and kissed her, and rose up and embraced Iron-face, and went his ways without looking back.

But just over the threshold he met old Hall-ward of the House of the Steer, who was at point to enter, and he greeted him kindly. The old man looked on him steadily, and said: "To-morrow or the day after I will utter a word to thee, O Chief of the Wolf."

"In a good hour," said Folk-might, "for all thy words are true." Therewith he gat him away from the house, and came to Face-of-god, where he sat before the altar of the Crooked Sword; and now were the chiefs come back from their meat, and were sitting with him; there also were Wood-father and Wood-wont; but Bow-may was with the Sun-beam, who was resting softly in the fair meadow after all the turmoil.

So men made place for Folk-might beside the War-leader, who looked upon his face, and saw that it was sober and unsmiling, but not heavy or moody with grief. So he deemed that all was as well as it might be with the Bride, and with a good heart fell to taking counsel with the others; and kindly and friendly were the redes which they held there, with no gainsaying of man by man, for the whole folk was glad at heart.

So there they ordered all matters duly for that present time, and by then they had made an end, it was past sunset, and men were lodged in the chief houses about the Market-stead.

Albeit, though they ate their meat with all joy of heart, and were merry in converse one with the other, the men of the Wolf would by no means feast in their Hall again till it had been cleansed and hallowed anew.

51. THE DEAD BORNE TO BALE: THE MOTE-HOUSE RE-HALLOWED

On the morrow they bore to bale their slain men, and there withal what was left of the bodies of the four chieftains of the Great Undoing. They brought them into a most fair meadow to the west of Silver-stead, where they had piled up a very great bale for the burning. In that meadow was the Doom-ring and Thing-stead of the Folk of the Wolf, and they had hallowed it when they had first conquered Silverdale, and it was deemed far holier than the Mote-house aforesaid, wherein the men of the kindred might hold no due court; but rather it was a Feast-hall, and a house where men had converse together, and wherein precious things and tokens of the Fathers were stored up.

The Thing-stead in the meadow was flowery and well-grassed, and a little stream winding about thereby nearly cast a ring around it; and beyond the stream was a full fair grove of oak-trees, very tall and ancient. There then they burned the dead of the Host, wrapped about in exceeding fair raiment. And when the ashes were gathered, the men of Burgdale and the Shepherds left those of their folk for the kindred to bury there in Silverdale; for they said that they had a right to claim such guesting for them that had helped to win back the Dale.

But when the Burning was done and the bale quenched, and

the ashes gathered and buried (and that was on the morrow), then men bore forth the Banners of the Jaws of the Wolf, and the Red Hand, and the Silver Arm, and the Golden Bushel, and the Ragged Sword, and the Wolf of the Woodland; and with great joy and triumph they brought them into the Mote-house and hung them up over the dais; and they kindled fire on the Holy Hearth by holding up a disk of bright glass to the sun; and then they sang before the banners. And this is somewhat of the song that they sang before them:

Why are ye wending? O whence and whither?
  What shineth over the fallow swords?
What is the joy that ye bear in hither?
  What is the tale of your blended words?

No whither we wend, but here have we stayed us,
  Here by the ancient Holy Hearth;
Long have the moons and the years delayed us,
  But here are we come from the heart of the dearth.

We are the men of joy belated;
  We are the wanderers over the waste;
We are but they that sat and waited,

Watching the empty winds make haste.

Long, long we sat and knew no others,
  Save alien folk and the foes of the road;
Till late and at last we met our brothers,
  And needs must we to the old abode.

For once on a day they prayed for guesting;
  And how were we then their bede to do?
Wild was the waste for the people's resting,
  And deep the wealth of the Dale we knew.

Here were the boards that we must spread them
  Down in the fruitful Dale and dear;
Here were the halls where we would bed them:
  And how should we tarry otherwhere?

Over the waste we came together:
  There was the tangle athwart the way;
There was the wind-storm and the weather;
  The red rain darkened down the day.

But that day of the days what grief should let us,
  When we saw through the clouds the dale-glad sun?
We tore at the tangle that beset us,
  And stood at peace when the day was done.

Hall of the Happy, take our greeting!
  Bid thou the Fathers come and see
The Folk-signs on thy walls a-meeting,
  And deem to-day what men we be.

Look on the Holy Hearth new-litten,
  How the sparks fly twinkling up aloof!
How the wavering smoke by the sunlight smitten,
  Curls up around the beam-rich roof!

For here once more is the Wolf abiding,
  Nor ever more from the Dale shall wend,
And never again his head be hiding,
  Till all days be dark and the world have end.

52. OF THE NEW BEGINNING OF GOOD DAYS IN SILVERDALE

On the third day there was high-tide and great joy amongst all men from end to end of the Dale; and the delivered thralls were feasted and made much of by the kindreds, so that they scarce knew how to believe their own five senses that told them the good tidings.

For none strove to grieve them and torment them; what they would, that did they, and they had all things plenteously; since for all was there enough and to spare of goods stored up for the Dusky Men, as corn and wine and oil and spices, and raiment and silver. Horses were there also, and neat and sheep and swine in abundance. Withal there was the good and dear land; the waxing corn on the acres; the blossoming vines on the hillside; and about the orchards and alongside the ways, the plum-trees and cherry-trees and pear-trees that had cast their blossom and were overhung with little young fruit; and the fair apple-trees a-blossoming, and the chestnuts spreading their boughs from their twisted trunks over the green grass. And there was the goodly pasture for the horses and the neat, and the thymy hill-grass for the sheep; and beyond it all, the thicket of the great wood, with its unfailing store of goodly timber of ash and oak and holly and yoke-elm. There need no man lack unless man compelled him, and all was rich enough and wide enough for the waxing of a very great folk.

Now, therefore, men betook them to what was their own before the coming of the Dusky Men; and though at first many of the delivered thrall-folk feasted somewhat above measure, and though there were some of them who were not very brisk at working on the earth for their livelihood; yet were the most part of them quick of wit and deft of hand, and they mostly fell to presently at their cunning, both of husbandry and handicraft. Moreover, they had great love of the kindreds, and especially of the Woodlanders, and strove to do all things that might pleasure them. And as for those who were dull and listless because of their many torments of the last ten years, they would at least fetch and carry willingly for them of the kindreds; and these last grudged them not meat and raiment and house-room, even if they wrought but little for it, because they called to mind the evil days of their thralldom, and bethought them how few are men's days upon the earth.

Thus all things throve in Silverdale, and the days wore on toward the summer, and the Yule-tide rest beyond it, and the years beyond and far beyond the winning of Silverdale.

53. OF THE WORD WHICH HALL-WARD OF THE STEER HAD FOR FOLK-MIGHT

But of the time then passing, it is to be said that the whole host abode in Silverdale in great mirth and good liking, till they should hear tidings of Dallach and his company, who had followed hot-foot on the fleers of the Dusky Men. And on the tenth day after the battle, Iron-face and his two sons and Stone-face were sitting about sunset under a great oak-tree by that stream-side which ran through the Mote-stead; there also was Folk-might, somewhat distraught because of his love for the Bride, who was now mending of her hurts. As they sat there in all content they saw folk coming toward them, three in number, and as they drew nigher they saw that it was old Hall-ward of the Steer, and the Sun-beam and Bow-may following him hand in hand.

When they came to the brook Bow-may ran up to the elder to help him over the stepping-stones; which she did as one who loved him, as the old man was stark enough to have waded the water waist-deep. She was no longer in her war-gear, but was clad after her wont of Shadowy Vale, in nought but a white woollen kirtle. So she stood in the stream beside the stones, and let the swift water ripple up over her ankles, while the elder leaned on her shoulder and looked down upon her kindly. The Sun-beam followed after them, stepping daintily from stone to stone, so that she was a fair sight to see; her face was smiling and happy, and as she stepped forth on to the green grass the colour flushed up in it, but she cast her eyes adown as one somewhat shamefaced.

So the chieftains rose up before the leader of the Steer, and Folk-might went up to him, and greeted him, and took his hand and kissed him on the cheek. And Hall-ward said:

"Hail to the chiefs of the kindred, and my earthly friends!"

Then Folk-might bade him sit down by him, and all the men sat down again; but the Sun-beam leaned her back against a sapling ash hard by, her feet set close together; and Bow-may went to and fro in short turns, keeping well within ear-shot.

Then said Hall-ward: "Folk-might, I have prayed thy kins-woman Bow-may to lead me to thee, that I might speak with thee; and it is good that I find my kinsmen of the Face in thy company; for I would say a word to thee that concerns them somewhat."

Said Folk-might: "Guest, and warrior of the Steer, thy words are ever good; and if this time thou comest to ask aught of me, then shall they be better than good."

Said Hall-ward: "Tell me, Folk-might, hast thou seen my daughter the Bride to-day?"

"Yea," said Folk-might, reddening.

"What didst thou deem of her state?" said Hall-ward.

Said Folk-might: "Thou knowest thyself that the fever hath left her, and that she is mending."

Hall-ward said: "In a few days belike we shall be wending home to Burgdale: when deemest thou that the Bride may travel, if it were but on a litter?"

Folk-might was silent, and Hall-ward smiled on him and said:

"Wouldst thou have her tarry, O chief of the Wolf?"

"So it is," said Folk-might, "that it might be labour lost for her to journey to Burgdale at present."

"Thinkest thou?" said Hall-ward; "hast thou a mind then that if she goeth she shall speedily come back hither?"

"It has been in my mind," said Folk-might, "that I should wed her. Wilt thou gainsay it? I pray thee, Iron-face my friend, and ye Stone-face and Hall-face, and thou, Face-of-god, my brother, to lay thy words to mine in this matter."

Then said Hall-ward stroking his beard: "There will be a seat missing in the Hall of the Steer, and a sore lack in the heart of many a man in Burgdale if the Bride come back to us no more. We looked not to lose the maiden by her wedding; for it is no long way betwixt the House of the Steer and the House of the Face. But now, when I arise in the morning and miss her, I shall take my staff and walk down the street of Burgstead; for I shall say, The Maiden hath gone to see Iron-face my friend; she is well in the House of the Face. And then shall I remember how that the wood and the wastes lie between us. How sayest thou, Alderman?"

"A sore lack it will be," said Iron-face; "but all good go with her! Though whiles shall I go hatless down Burgstead street, and say, Now will I go fetch my daughter the Bride from the House of the Steer; while many a day's journey shall lie betwixt us."

Said Hall-ward: "I will not beat about the bush, Folk-might; what gift wilt thou give us for the maiden?"

Said Folk-might: "Whatever is mine shall be thine; and whatsoever of the Dale the kindred and the poor folk begrudge thee not, that shalt thou have; and deemest thou that they will begrudge thee aught? Is it enough?"

Hall-ward said: "I wot not, chieftain; see thou to it! Bow-may, my friend, bring hither that which I would have from Silverdale for the House of the Steer in payment for our maiden."

Then Bow-may came forward speedily, and went up to the Sun-beam, and led her by the hand in front of Folk-might and Hall-ward and the other chieftains. Then Folk-might started, and leapt up from the ground; for, sooth to say, he had been thinking so wholly of the Bride, that his sister was not in his mind, and he had had no deeming of whither Hall-ward was coming, though the others guessed well enough, and now smiled on him merrily, when they saw how wild Folk-might stared. As for the Sun-beam, she stood there blushing like a rose in June, but looking her brother straight in the face, as Hall-ward said:

"Folk-might, chief of the Wolf, since thou wouldst take our maiden the Bride away from us, I ask thee to make good her place with this maiden; so that the House of the Steer may not lack, when they who are wont to wed therein come to us and pray us for a bedfellow for the best of their kindred."

Then became Folk-might smiling and merry like unto the others, and he said: "Chief of the Steer, this gift is thine, together with aught else which thou mayst desire of us."

Then he kissed the Sun-beam, and said: "Sister, we looked for this to befall in some fashion. Yet we deemed that he that should lead thee away might abide with us for a moon or two. But now let all this be, since if thou art not to bear children to the kindreds of Silverdale, yet shalt thou bear them to their friends and fellows. And now choose what gift thou wilt have of us to keep us in thy memory."

She said: "The memory of my people shall not fade from me; yet indeed I ask thee for a gift, to wit, Bow-may, and the two sons of Wood-father that are left since Wood-wicked was slain; and belike the elder and his wife will be fain to go with their sons, and ye will not hinder them."

"Even so shall it be done," said Folk-might, and he was silent a while, pondering; and then he said:

"Lo you, friends! doth it not seem strange to you that peace sundereth as well as war? Indeed I deem it grievous that ye shall have to miss your well-beloved kinswoman. And for me, I am now grown so used to this woman my sister, though at whiles she hath been masterful with me, that I shall often turn about and think to speak to her, when there lie long days of wood and waste betwixt her voice and mine.

The Sun-beam laughed in his face, though the tears stood in her eyes, as she said: "Keep up thine heart, brother; for at least the way is shorter betwixt Burgdale and Silverdale than betwixt life and death; and the road we shall learn belike."

Said Hall-face: "So it is that my brother is no ill woodman,

as ye learned last autumn."

Iron-face smiled, but somewhat sadly; for he beheld Face-of-god, who had no eyes for anyone save the Sun-beam; and no marvel was that, for never had she looked fairer. And forsooth the War-leader was not utterly well-pleased; for he was deeming that there would be delaying of his wedding, now that the Sun-beam was to become a maid of the Steer; and in his mind he half deemed that it would be better if he were to take her by the hand and lead her home through the Wild-wood, he and she alone; and she looked on him shyly, as though she had a deeming of his thought. Albeit he knew it might not be, that he, the chosen War-leader, should trouble the peace of the kindred; for he wotted that all this was done for peace" sake.

So Hall-ward stood forth and took the Sun-beam's right hand in his, and said:

"Now do I take this maiden, Sun-beam of the kindred of the Wolf, and lead her into the House of the Steer, to be in all ways one of the maidens of our House, and to wed in the blood wherein we have been wont to wed. Neither from henceforth let anyone say that this woman is not of the blood of the Steer; for we have given her our blood, and she is of us duly and truly."

Thereafter they talked together merrily for a little, and then turned toward the houses, for the sun was now down; and as they went Iron-face spake to his son, and said:

"Gold-mane, wilt thou verily keep thine oath to wed the fairest woman in the world? By how much is this one fairer than my dear daughter who shall no more dwell in mine house?"

Said Face-of-god: "Yea, father, I shall keep mine oath; for the Gods, who know much, know that when I swore last Yule I was thinking of the fair woman going yonder beside Hall-ward, and of none other."

"Ah, son!" said Iron-face, "why didst thou beguile us? Hadst thou but told us the truth then!"

"Yea, Alderman," said Face-of-god smiling, "and how thou wouldest have raged against me then, when thou hast scarce forgiven me now! In sooth, father, I feared to tell you all: I was young; I was one against the world. Yea, yea; and even that was sweet to me, so sorely as I loved her—Hast thou forgotten, father?"

Iron-face smiled, and answered not; and so came they to the house wherein they were guested.

54. TIDINGS OF DALLACH: A FOLK-MOTE IN SILVERDALE

Three days thereafter came two swift runners from Rosedale with tidings of Dallach. In all wise had he thriven, and had

slain many of the Runaways, and had come happily to Rosedale: therein by the mere shaking of their swords had they all their will; for there were but a few of the Dusky Warriors in the Dale, since the more part had fared to the slaughter in Silver-stead. Now therefore had Dallach been made Alderman of Rosedale; and the Burgdalers who had gone with him should abide the coming thither of the rest of the Burgdale Host, and meantime of their coming should uphold the new Alderman in Rosedale. Howbeit Dallach sent word that it was not to be doubted but that many of the Dusky Men had escaped to the woods, and should yet be the death of many a mother's son, unless it were well looked to.

And now the more part of the Burgdale men and the Shepherds began to look toward home, albeit some amongst them had not been ill-pleased to abide there yet a while; for life was exceeding soft to them there, though they helped the poor folk gladly in their husbandry. For especially the women of the Dale, of whom many were very goodly, hankered after the fair-faced tall Burgdalers, and were as kind to them as might be. Forsooth not a few, both carles and queens, of the old thrall-folk prayed them of Burgdale to take them home thither, that they might see new things and forget their old torments once for all, yea, even in dreams. The Burgdalers would not gainsay them, and there was no one else to hinder; so that there went with the Burgdale men at their departure hard on five score of the Silverdale folk who were not of the kindreds.

And now was a great Folk-mote holden in Silverdale, whereto the Burgdale men and the Shepherds were bidden; and thereat the War-leader gave out the morrow of the morrow for the day of the departure of the Host. There also were the matters of Silverdale duly ordered: the Men of the Wolf would have had the Woodlanders dwell with them in the fair-builded stead, and take to them of the goodly stone houses there what they would; but this they naysaid, choosing rather to dwell in scattered houses, which they built for themselves at the utmost limit of the tillage.

Indeed, the most abode not even there a long while; for they loved the wood and its deeds. So they went forth into the wood, and cleared them space to dwell in, and builded them halls such as they loved, and fell to their old woodland crafts of charcoal-burning and hunting, wherein they throve well. And good for Silverdale was their abiding there, since they became a sure defence and stout outpost against all foemen. For the rest, wheresoever they dwelt, they were guest-cherishing and blithe, and were well beloved by all people; and they wedded with the other Houses of the Children of the Wolf.

As to the other matters whereof they took rede at this Folk-mote, they had mostly to do with the warding of the Dale, and the learning of the delivered thralls to handle weapons duly. For men deemed it most like that they would have to meet other men of the kindred of the felons; which indeed fell out as the years wore.

Moreover, Folk-might (by the rede of Stone-face) sent messengers to the Plain and the Cities, unto men whom he knew there, doing them to wit of the tidings of Silverdale, and how that a peaceful and guest-loving people, having good store of wares, now dwelt therein, so that chapmen might have recourse thither.

Lastly spake Folk-might and said:

"Guests and brothers-in-arms, we have been looking about our new house, which was our old one, and therein we find great store of wares which we need not, and which we can but use if ye use them. Of your kindness therefore we pray you to take of those things what ye can easily carry. And if ye say the way is long, as indeed it is, since ye are bent on going through the wood to Rosedale, and so on to Burgdale, yet shall we furnish you with beasts to bear your goods, and with such wains as may pass through the woodland ways."

Then rose up Fox of Upton and said: "O Folk-might, and ye men of the Wolf, be it known unto you, that if we have done anything for your help in the winning of Silverdale, we have thus done that we might help ourselves also, so that we might live in peace henceforward, and that we might have your friendship and fellowship therewithal, so that here in Silverdale might wax a mighty folk who joined unto us should be strong enough to face the whole world. Such are the redes of wise men when they go a-warring. But we have no will to go back home again made rich with your wealth; this hath been far from our thought in this matter."

And there went up a murmur from all the Burgdalers yeasaying his word.

But Folk-might took up the word again and spake:

"Men of Burgdale and the Sheepcotes, what ye say is both manly and friendly; yet, since we look to see a road made plain through the woodland betwixt Burgdale and Silverdale, and that often ye shall face us in the feast-hall, and whiles stand beside us in the fray, we must needs pray you not to shame us by departing empty-handed; for how then may we look upon your faces again? Stone-face, my friend, thou art old and wise; therefore I bid thee to help us herein, and speak for us to thy kindred, that they naysay us not in this matter."

Then stood up Stone-face and said: "Forsooth, friends, Folk-might is in the right herein; for he may look for anger from the wights that come and go betwixt his kindred and the Gods, if they see us faring back giftless through the woods. Moreover, now that ye have seen Silverdale, ye may wot how rich a land it is of all good things, and able to bring forth enough and to spare. And now meseemeth the Gods love this Folk that shall dwell here; and they shall become a mighty Folk, and a part of our very selves. Therefore let us take the gifts of our friends, and thank them blithely. For surely, as saith Folk-might, henceforth the wood shall become a road betwixt us, and the thicket a halting-place for friends bearing goodwill in their hands."

When he had spoken, men yeasaid his words and forbore the gifts no longer; and the Folk-mote sundered in all loving-kindness.

55. DEPARTURE FROM SILVERDALE

On morrow of the morrow were the Burgdale men and they of the Shepherds gathered together in the Market-stead early in the morning, and they were all ready for departure; and the men of the Wolf and the Woodlanders, and of the delivered thralls a great many, stood round about them grieving that they must go. There was much talk between the folk of the Dale and the Guests, and many promises were given and taken to come and go betwixt the two Dales. There also were the men of the thrall-folk who were to wend home with the Burgdalers; and they had been stuffed with good things by the men of the kindreds, and were as fain as might be.

As for the Sun-beam, she was somewhat out of herself at first, being eager and restless beyond her wont, and yet at whiles weeping-ripe when she called to mind that she was now leaving all those things, the gain whereof had been a dream to her both waking and sleeping for these years past. But at last, as she stood in the door of the Mote-house, and beheld all the throng of folk happy and friendly, it came over her that she herself had done her full share to bring all this about, and that all those pleasant places of Silverdale now full of the goodly life of man would be there even as she had striven for them, and that they would be a part of her left behind, though she were dwelling otherwhere.

Therewithal she said to herself that it was now her part to wield the life of men in Burgdale, and begin once more her days of a chieftain and a swayer of the Folk, and the life of a stirring woman, which the edge of the sword and the need of the hard hand-play had taken out of her hands for a while, making her as a child in the hands of the strong wielders of the blades.

So now she became calm once more, and her face was clad again with the full measure of that majesty of beauty which had once overawed Face-of-god amidst his love of her; and folk beheld her and marvelled at her fairness, and said: "She hath an inward sorrow at leaving the fair Dale wherein her Fathers dwelt, and where her mother's ashes lie in earth." Albeit now was her sorrow but little, and much was her hope, and her foresight of days to be; though all the Dale, yea, every leaf and twig of it whereby her feet had ever passed, and each stone of the fair houses, was to her as a picture that she could look on from henceforth for ever.

Of the Bride it is to be said that she was now much mended, and she caused men bear her on a litter out into the Market-place, that she might look on the departure of her folk. She had seen Face-of-god once and again since the Day of Battle, and each time had been kind and blithe with him; and for Iron-face, she loved him so well that she was ever loth to let him depart from her, save when Folk-might was with her.

And now was the Alderman standing beside her, and she said to him: "Friend and kinsman, this is the day of departure, and though I must needs abide behind, and am content to abide, yet doth mine heart ache with the sundering; for to-morrow when I wake in the morning there will be no more sending of a messenger to fetch thee to me. Indeed, great hath been the love between me and my people, and nought hath come between us to mar it. Now, kinsman, I would see Gold-mane, my cousin, that I may bid him farewell; for who knoweth if I shall see him again hereafter?"

Then went Iron-face and found Face-of-god where he was speaking with Folk-might and the chieftains, and said to him:

"Come quickly, for thy cousin the Bride would speak with thee."

Face-of-god reddened, and paled afterwards, but he went along with his father silently; and his heart beat as he came and stood before the litter whereas the Bride lay, clad all in white and propped up on fair cushions of red silk. She was frail to look on, and worn and pale yet; but he deemed that she was very happy.

She smiled on him, and reached out her hand and said:

"Welcome once more, cousin!" And he held her hand and kissed it, and was nigh weeping, so sore was he beset by a throng of memories concerning her and him in the days when they were little; and he bethought him of her loving-kindness of past days, beyond that of most children, beyond that of most maidens; and how there was nothing in his life but she had a share in it, till the day when he found the Hall on the Mountain.

So he said to her: "Kinswoman, is it well with thee?"

"Yea," she said, "I am now nigh whole of my hurts."

He was silent a while; then he said:

"And otherwise art thou merry at heart?"

"Yea, indeed," said she; "yet thou wilt not find it hard to deem that I am sorry of the sundering betwixt me and Burgdale."

Again was he silent, and said in a while: "Dost thou deem

that I wrought that sundering?"

She smiled kindly on him and said: "Gold-mane, my play-mate, thou art become a mighty warrior and a great chief; but thou art not so mighty as that. Many things lay behind the sundering which were neither thou nor I."

"Yet," said he, "it was but such a little time agone that all things seemed so sure; and we—to both of us was the outlook happy."

"Let it be happy still," she said, "now begrudging is gone. Belike the sundering came because we were so sure, and had no defence against the wearing of the days; even as it fareth with a folk that hath no foes."

He smiled and said: "Even as it hath befallen THY folk, O Bride, a while ago."

She reddened, and reached her hand to him, and he took it and held it, and said: "Shall I see thee again as the days wear?"

Said she: "O chieftain of the Folk, thou shalt have much to do in Burgdale, and the way is long. Yet would I have thee see my children. Forget not the token on my hand which thou holdest. But now get thee to thy folk with no more words; for after all, playmate, the sundering is grievous to me, and I would not spin out the time thereof. Farewell!"

He said no more, but stooped down and kissed her lips, and then turned from her, and took his ways to the head of the Host, and fell to asking and answering, and bidding and array-ing; and in a little time was his heart dancing with joy to think of the days that lay before him, wherein now all seemed happy.

So was all arrayed for departure when it lacked three hours of noon. As Folk-might had promised, there were certain light wains drawn by bullocks abiding the departure of the Host, and of sumpter bullocks and horses no few; and all these were laden with fair gifts of the Dale, as silver, and raiment, and weapons. There were many things fair-wrought in the time of the Sorrow, that henceforth should see but little sorrow. More-over, there was plenty of provision for the way, both meal and wine, and sheep and neat; and all things as fair as might be, and well-arrayed.

It was the Shepherds who were to lead the way; and after them were arrayed the men of the Vine and the Sickle; then they of the Steer, the Bridge, and the Bull; and lastly the House of the Face, with old Stone-face leading them. The Sun-beam was to journey along with the House of the Steer, which had taken her in as a maiden of their blood; and though she had so much liefer have fared with the House of the Face, yet she went meekly as she was bidden, as one who has gotten a great thing, and will make no stir about a small one.

Along with her were Wood-father and Wood-mother, and Wood-wise, now whole of his hurt, and Wood-wont, and Bow-may. Save Bow-may, they were not very joyous; for they were fain of Silverdale, and it irked them to leave it; moreover, they also had liefer have gone along with the House of the War-leader.

Last of all went those people of the once thralls of the Dusky Men who had cast in their lot with the Burgdalers, and they were exceeding merry; and especially the women of them, they were chattering like the stares in the autumn evening, when they gather from the fields in the tall elm-trees before they go to roost.

Now all the men of the Dale, both of the kindreds and of the thrall-folk, made way for the Host and its havings, that they might go their ways down the Dale; albeit the Woodlanders clung close to the line of their ancient friends, and with them, as men who were sorry for the sundering, were Wolf-stone and God-swain and Spear-fist. But the chiefs, they drew around Folk-might a little beside the way.

Now Red-coat of Waterless, who had been hurt, and was now whole again, cast his arms about Folk-might and kissed him, and said:

"All the way hence to Burgdale will I sow with good wishes for thee and thine, and especially for my dear friend God-swain of the Silver Arm; and I would wish and long that they might turn into spells to draw thy feet to usward; for we love thee well."

In like wise spake other of the Burgdalers; and Folk-might was kind and blithe with them, and he said:

"Friends, forget ye not that the way is no longer from you to us than it is from us to you. One half of this matter it is for you to deal with."

"True is that," said Red-beard of the Knolls, "but look you, Folk-might, we be but simple husbandmen, and may not often stir from our meadows and acres; even now I bethink me that May is amidst us, and I am beginning to be drawn by the thought of the haysel. Whereas thou—" (and therewith he red-dened) "I doubt that thou hast little to do save the work of chieftains, and we know that such work is but little missed if it be undone."

Thereat Folk-might laughed; and when the others saw that he laughed, they laughed also, else had they foreborne for courtesy's sake.

But Folk-might answered: "Nay, chief of the Sickle, I am not altogether a chieftain, now we have gotten us peace; and somewhat of a husbandman shall I be. Moreover, doubt ye not that I shall do my utmost to behold the fair Dale again; for it is but mountains that meet not."

Now spake Face-of-god to Folk-might, smiling and some-what softly, and said: "Is all forgiven now, since the day when we first felt each other's arms?"

"Yea, all," said Folk-might; "now hath befallen what I foretold thee in Shadowy Vale, that thou mightest pay for all that had come and gone, if thou wouldest but look to it. Indeed thou wert angry with me for that saying on that eve of Shadowy Vale; but see thou, in those days I was an older man than thou, and might admonish thee somewhat; but now, though but few days have gone over thine head, yet many deeds have abided in thine hand, and thou art much aged. Anger hath left thee, and wisdom hath waxed in thee. As for me, I may now say this word: May the Folk of Burgdale love the Folk of Silverdale as well as I love thee; then shall all be well."

Then Face-of-god cast his arms about him and kissed him, and turned away toward Stone-face and Hall-face his brother, where they stood at the head of the array of the Face; and even therewith came up the Alderman somewhat sad and sober of countenance, and he pushed by the War-leader roughly and would not speak with him.

And now blew up the horns of the Shepherds, and they began to move on amidst the shouting of the men of Silverdale; yet were there amongst the Woodlanders those who wept when they saw their friends verily departing from them.

But when they of the foremost of the Host were gotten so far forward that the men of the Face could begin to move, lo! there was Redesman with his fiddle amongst the leaders; and he had done a man's work in the day of battle, and all looked kindly on him. About him on this morn were some who had learned the craft of singing well together, and knew his minstrelsy, and he turned to these and nodded as their array moved on, and he drew his bow across the strings, and straightway they fell a-singing, even as it might be thus:

Back again to the dear Dale where born was the kindred,
Here wend we all living, and liveth our mirth.
Here afoot fares our joyance, whatever men hindred,
Through all wrath of the heavens, all storms of the earth.

O true, we have left here a part of our treasure,
The ashes of stout ones, the stems of the shield;
But the bold lives they spended have sown us new pleasure,
Fair tales for the telling in fold and on field.

For as oft as we sing of their edges" upheaving,
When the yellowing windows shine forth o'er the night,
Their names unforgotten with song interweaving
Shall draw forth dear drops from the depths of delight.

Or when down by our feet the grey sickles are lying,
And behind us is curling the supper-tide smoke,
No whit shall they grudge us the joyance undying,
Remembrance of men that put from us the yoke.

When the huddle of ewes from the fells we have driven,
And we see down the Dale the grey reach of the roof,

We shall tell of the gift in the battle-joy given,
All the fierceness of friends that drave sorrow aloof.

Once then we lamented, and mourned them departed;
Once only, no oftener. Henceforth shall we fling
Their names up aloft, when the merriest hearted
To the Fathers unseen of our life-days we sing.

Then was there silence in the ranks of men; and many murmured the names of the fallen as they fared on their way from out the Market-place of Silver-stead. Then once more Redesman and his mates took up the song:

Come tell me, O friends, for whom bideth the maiden
Wet-foot from the river-ford down in the Dale?
For whom hath the goodwife the ox-waggon laden
With the babble of children, brown-handed and hale?

Come tell me for what are the women abiding,
Till each on the other aweary they lean?
Is it loitering of evil that thus they are chiding,
The slow-footed bearers of sorrow unseen?

Nay, yet were they toiling if sorrow had worn them,
Or hushed had they bided with lips parched and wan.
The birds of the air other tidings have borne them—
How glad through the wood goeth man beside man.

Then fare forth, O valiant, and loiter no longer
Than the cry of the cuckoo when May is at hand;
Late waxeth the spring-tide, and daylight grows longer,
And nightly the star-street hangs high o'er the land.

Many lives, many days for the Dale do ye carry;
When the Host breaketh out from the thicket unshorn,
It shall be as the sun that refuseth to tarry
On the crown of all mornings, the Midsummer morn.

Again the song fell down till they were well on the western way down Silverdale; and then Redesman handled his fiddle once more, and again the song rose up, and such-like were the words which were borne back into the Market-place of Silver-stead:

And yet what is this, and why fare ye so slowly,
While our echoing halls of our voices are dumb,
And abideth unlitten the hearth-brand the holy,
And the feet of the kind fare afield till we come?

For not yet through the wood and its tangle ye wander;
Now skirt we no thicket, no path by the mere;
Far aloof for our feet leads the Dale-road out yonder;
Full fair is the morning, its doings all clear.

There is nought now our feet on the highway delaying

Save the friend's loving-kindness, the sundering of speech;
The well-willer's word that ends words with the saying,
The loth to depart while each looketh on each.

Fare on then, for nought are ye laden with sorrow;
The love of this land do ye bear with you still.
In two Dales of the earth for to-day and to-morrow

Is waxing the oak-tree of peace and good-will.

Thus then they departed from Silverdale, even as men who were a portion thereof, and had not utterly left it behind. And that night they lay in the Wild-wood not very far from the Dale's end; for they went softly, faring amongst so many friends.

56. TALK UPON THE WILD-WOOD WAY

On the morrow morning when they were on their way again Face-of-god left his own folk to go with the House of the Steer a while; and amongst them he fell in with the Sun-beam going along with Bow-may. So they greeted him kindly, and Face-of-god fell into talk with the Sun-beam as they went side by side through a great oak-wood, where for a space was plain green-sward bare of all underwood.

So in their talk he said to her: "What deemest thou, my speech-friend, concerning our coming back to guest in Silverdale one day?"

"The way is long," she said.

"That may hinder us but not stay us," said Face-of-god.

"That is sooth," said the Sun-beam.

Said Face-of-god: "What things shall stay us? Or deemest thou that we shall never see Silverdale again?"

She smiled: "Even so I think thou deemest, Gold-mane. But many things shall hinder us besides the long road."

Said he: "Yea, and what things?"

"Thinkest thou," said the Sun-beam, "that the winning of Silver-stead is the last battle which thou shalt see?"

"Nay," said he, "nay."

"Shall thy Dale—our Dale—be free from all trouble within itself henceforward? Is there a wall built round it to keep out for ever storm, pestilence, and famine, and the waywardness of its own folk?"

"So it is as thou sayest," quoth Face-of-god, "and to meet such troubles and overcome them, or to die in strife with them,

this is a great part of a man's life."

"Yea," she said, "and hast thou forgotten that thou art now a great chieftain, and that the folk shall look to thee to use thee many days in the year?"

He laughed and said: "So it is. How many days have gone by since I wandered in the wood last autumn, that the world should have changed so much!"

"Many deeds shall now be in thy days," she said, "and each deed as the corn of wheat from which cometh many corns; and a man's days on the earth are not over many."

"Then farewell, Silverdale!" said he, waving his hand toward the north. "War and trouble may bring me back to thee, but it maybe nought else shall. Farewell!"

She looked on him fondly but unsmiling, as he went beside her strong and warrior-like. Three paces from him went Bow-may, barefoot, in her white kirtle, but bearing her bow in her hand; a leash of arrows was in her girdle, her quiver hung at her back, and she was girt with a sword. On the other side went Wood-wont and Wood-wise, lightly clad but weaponed. Wood-mother was riding in an ox-wain just behind them, and Wood-father went beside her bearing an axe. Scattered all about them were the men of the Steer, gaily clad, bearing weapons, so that the oak-wood was bright with them, and the glades merry with their talk and singing and laughter, and before them down the glades went the banner of the Steer, and the White Beast led them the nearest way to Burgdale.

57. HOW THE HOST CAME HOME AGAIN

It was fourteen days before they came to Rosedale; for they had much baggage with them, and they had no mind to weary themselves, and the wood was nothing loathsome to them, whereas the weather was fair and bright for the more part. They fell in with no mishap by the way. But a score and three of Runaways joined themselves to the Host, having watched their goings and wotting that they were not foemen. Of these,

some had heard of the overthrow of the Dusky Men in Silverdale, and others not. The Burgdalers received them all, for it seemed to them no great matter for a score or so of new-comers to the Dale.

But when the Host was come to Rosedale, they found it fair arid lovely; and there they met with those of their folk who had gone with Dallach. But Dallach welcomed the kindreds with great joy, and bade them abide; for he said that they had the less need to hasten, since he had sent messengers into Burgdale to tell men there of the tidings. Albeit they were mostly loth to tarry; yet when he lay hard on them not to depart as men on the morrow of a gild-feast, they abode there three days, and were as well guested as might be, and on their departure they were laden with gifts from the wealth of Rosedale by Dallach and his folk.

Before they went their ways Dallach spake with Face-of-god and the chiefs of the Dalesmen, and said:

"Ye have given me much from the time when ye found me in the wood a naked wastrel; yet now I would ask you a gift to lay on the top of all that ye have given me."

Said Face-of-god: "Name the gift, and thou shalt have it; for we deem thee our friend."

"I am no less," said Dallach, "as in time to come I may perchance be able to show you. But now I am asking you to suffer a score or two of your men to abide here with me this summer, till I see how this folk new-born again is like to deal with me. For pleasure and a fair life have become so strange to them, that they scarce know what to do with them, or how to live; and unless all is to go awry, I must needs command and forbid; and though belike they love me, yet they fear me not; so that when my commandment pleaseth them, they do as I bid, and when it pleaseth them not, they do contrary to my bidding; for it hath got into their minds that I shall in no case lift a hand against them, which indeed is the very sooth. But your folk they fear as warriors of the world, who have slain the Dusky Men in the Market-place of Silver-stead; and they are of alien blood to them, men who will do as their friend biddeth (think our folk) against them who are neither friends or foes. With such help I shall be well holpen."

In such wise spake Dallach; and Face-of-god and the chiefs said that so it should be, if men could be found willing to abide in Rosedale for a while. And when the matter was put abroad, there was no lack of such men amongst the younger warriors, who had noted that the dale was fair amongst dales and its women fairer yet amongst women.

So two score and ten of the Burgdale men abode in Rosedale, no one of whom was of more than twenty and five winters. Forsooth divers of them set up house in Rosedale, and never came back to Burgdale, save as guests. For a half score were wedded in Rosedale before the year's ending; and seven more, who had also taken to them wives of the goodliest of the Rosedale women, betook them the next spring to the Burg of the Runaways, and there built them a stead, and drew a garth about it, and dug and sowed the banks of the river, which they called Inglebourne. And as years passed, this same stead throve exceedingly, and men resorted thither both from Rosedale and Burgdale; for it was a pleasant place; and the

land, when it was cured, was sweet and good, and the wood thereabout was full of deer of all kinds. So their stead was called Inglebourne after the stream; and in latter days it became a very goodly habitation of men.

Moreover, some of the once-enthralled folk of Rosedale, when they knew that men of their kindred from Silverdale were going home with the men of Burgdale to dwell in the Dale, prayed hard to go along with them; for they looked on the Burgdalers as if they were new Gods of the Earth. The Burgdale chiefs would not gainsay these men either, but took with them three score and ten from Rosedale, men and women, and promised them dwelling and livelihood in Burgdale.

So now with good hearts the Host of Burgdale turned their faces toward their well-beloved Dale; and they made good diligence, so that in three days" time they were come anigh the edge of the woodland wilderness. Thither in the even-tide, as they were making ready for their last supper and bed in the wood, came three men and two women of their folk, who had been abiding their coming ever since they had had the tidings of Silverdale and the battles from Dallach. Great was the joy of these messengers as they went from company to company of the warriors, and saw the familiar faces of their friends, and heard their wonted voices telling all the story of battle and slaughter. And for their part the men of the Host feasted these stay-at-homes, and made much of them. But one of them, a man of the House of the Face, left the Host a little after nightfall, and bore back to Burgstead at once the tidings of the coming home of the Host. Albeit since Dallach's tidings of victory had come to the Dale, the dwellers in the steads of the countryside had left Burgstead and gone home to their own houses; so that there was no great multitude abiding in the Thorp.

So early on the morrow was the Host astir; but ere they came to Wildlake's Way, the Shepherd-folk turned aside westward to go home, after they had bidden farewell to their friends and fellows of the Dale; for their souls longed for the sheep-cotes in the winding valleys under the long grey downs; and the garths where the last year's ricks shouldered up against the old stone gables, and where the daws were busy in the tall unfrequent ash-trees; and the green flowery meadows adown along the bright streams, where the crowfoot and the paigles were blooming now, and the harebells were in flower about the thorn-bushes at the down's foot, whence went the savour of their blossom over sheep-walk and water-meadow.

So these went their ways with many kind words; and two hours afterwards all the rest of the Host stood on the level ground of the Portway; but presently were the ranks of war disordered and broken up by the joy of the women and children, as they fell to drawing goodman or brother or lover out of the throng to the way that led speediest to their homesteads and halls. For the War-leader would not hold the Host together any longer, but suffered each man to go to his home, deeming that the men of Burgstead, and chiefly they of the Face and the Steer, would suffice for a company if any need were, and they would be easily gathered to meet any hap.

So now the men of the Middle and Lower Dale made for their houses by the road and the lanes and the meadows, and the men of the Upper Dale and Burgstead went their ways along the Portway toward their halls, with the throng of women and children that had come out to meet them. And now men came home when it was yet early, and the long day lay before them; and it was, as it were, made giddy and cumbered with the exceeding joy of return, and the thought of the day when the fear of death and sundering had been ever in their hearts. For these new hours were full of the kissing and embracing of lovers, and the sweetness of renewed delight in beholding the fair bodies so sorely desired, and hearkening the soft wheedling of longed-for voices. There were the cups of friends beneath the chestnut trees, and the talk of the deeds of the fighting-men, and of the heavy days of the home-abiders; many a tale told oft and o'er again. There was the singing of old songs and of new, and the beholding the well-loved nook of the pleasant places, which death might well have made nought for them; and they were sweet with the fear of that which was past, and in their pleasantness was fresh promise for the days to come.

So amid their joyance came evening and nightfall; and though folk were weary with the fulness of delight, yet now for many their weariness led them to the chamber of love before the rest of deep night came to them to make them strong for the happy life to be begun again on the morrow.

House by house they feasted, and few were the lovers that sat not together that even. But Face-of-god and the Sun-beam parted at the door of the House of the Face; for needs must she go with her new folk to the House of the Steer, and needs must Face-of-god be amongst his own folk in that hour of high-tide, and sit beside his father beneath the image of the God with the ray-begirt head.

58. HOW THE MAIDEN WARD WAS HELD IN BURGDALE

Now May was well worn when the Host came home to Burgdale; and on the very morrow of men's home-coming they began to talk eagerly of the Midsummer Weddings, and how the Maiden Ward would be the greatest and fairest of all yet seen, whereas battle and the deliverance from battle stir up the longing and love both of men and maidens; much also men spake of the wedding of Face-of-god and the Sun-beam; and needs must their wedding abide to the time of the Maiden Ward at Midsummer, and needs also must the Sun-beam go on the Ward with the other Brides of the Folk. So then must Face-of-god keep his soul in patience till those few days were over, doing what work came to hand; and he held his head high among the people, and was well looked to of every man.

In all matters the Sun-beam helped him, both in doing and in forbearing; and now so wonderful and rare was her beauty, that folk looked on her with somewhat of fear, as though she came from the very folk of the Gods.

Indeed she seemed somewhat changed from what she had been of late; she was sober of demeanour during these last days of her maidenhood, and sat amongst the kindred as one communing with herself: of few words she was and little laughter; but her face clear, not overcast by any gloom or shaken by passion: soft and kind was she in converse with others, and sweet were the smiles that came into her face if others" faces seemed to crave for them. For it must be said that as some folk eat out their hearts with fear of the coming evils, even so was she feeding her soul with the joy of the days to be, whatever trouble might fall upon them, whereof belike she foreboded some.

So wore the days toward Midsummer, when the wheat was getting past the blossoming, and the grass in the mown fields was growing deep green again after the shearing of the scythe; when the leaves were most and biggest; when the roses were beginning to fall; when the apples were reddening, and the skins of the grape-berries gathering bloom. High aloft floated the light clouds over the Dale; deep blue showed the distant fells below the ice-mountains; the waters dwindled; all things sought the shadow by daytime, and the twilight of even and the twilight of dawn were but sundered by three hours of half-dark night.

So in the bright forenoon were seventeen brides assembled in the Gate of Burgstead (but of the rest of the Dale were twenty and three looked for), and with these was the Sun-beam, her face as calm as the mountain lake under a summer sunset, while of the others many were restless, and babbling like April throstles; and not a few talked to her eagerly, and in their restless love of her dragged her about hither and thither.

No men were to be seen that morning; for such was the custom, that the carles either departed to the fields and the acres, or abode within doors on the morn of the day of the Maiden Ward; but there was a throng of women about the Gate and down the street of Burgstead, and it may well be deemed that they kept not silence that hour.

So fared the Brides of Burgstead to the place of the Maiden

Ward on the causeway, whereto were come already the other brides from steads up and down the Dale, or were even then close at hand on the way; and among them were Long-coat and her two fellows, with whom Face-of-god had held converse on that morning whereon he had followed his fate to the Mountain.

There then were they gathered under the cliff-wall of the Portway; and by the road-side had their grooms built them up bowers of green boughs to shelter them from the sun's burning, which were thatched with bulrushes, and decked with garlands of the fairest flowers of the meadows and the gardens.

Forsooth they were a lovely sight to look on, for no fairer women might be seen in the world; and the eldest of them was scant of five and twenty winters. Every maiden was clad in as goodly raiment as she might compass; their sleeves and gown-hems and girdles, yea, their very shoes and sandals were embroidered so fairly and closely, that as they shifted in the sun they changed colour like the king-fisher shooting from shadow to sunshine. According to due custom every maiden bore some weapon. A few had bows in their hands and quivers at their backs; some had nought but a sword girt to their sides; some bore slender-shafted spears, so as not to overburden their shapely hands; but to some it seemed a merry game to carry long and heavy thrust-spears, or to bear great war-axes over their shoulders. Most had their flowing hair coifed with bright helms; some had burdened their arms with shields; some bore steel hauberks over their linen smocks: almost all had some piece of war-gear on their bodies; and one, to wit, Steed-linden of the Sickle, a tall and fair damsel, was so arrayed that no garment could be seen on her but bright steel war-gear.

As for the Sun-beam, she was clad in a white kirtle embroidered from throat to hem with work of green boughs and flowers of the goodliest fashion, and a garland of roses on her head. Dale-warden himself was girt to her side by a girdle fair-wrought of golden wire, and she bore no other weapon or war-gear; and she let him lie quiet in his scabbard, nor touched the hilts once; whereas some of the other damsels would be ever drawing their swords out and thrusting them back. But all noted that goodly weapon, the yoke-fellow of so many great deeds.

There then on the Portway, between the water and the rock-wall, rose up plenteous and gleeful talk of clear voices shrill and soft; and whiles the maidens sang, and whiles they told tales of old days, and whiles they joined hands and danced together on the sweet summer dust of the highway. Then they mostly grew aweary, and sat down on the banks of the road or under their leafy bowers.

Noon came, and therewithal goodwives of the neighbouring Dale, who brought them meat and drink, and fruit and fresh flowers from the teeming gardens; and thereafter for a while they nursed their joy in their bosoms, and spake but little and softly while the day was at its hottest in the early afternoon.

Then came out of Burgstead men making semblance of chapmen with a wain bearing wares, and they made as though they were wending down the Portway westward to go out of the Dale. Then arose the weaponed maidens and barred the way to them, and turned them back amidst fresh-springing merriment.

Again in a while, when the sun was westering and the shadows growing long, came herdsmen from down the Dale driving neat, and making as though they would pass by into Burgstead, but to them also did the maidens gainsay the road, so that needs must they turn back amidst laughter and mockery, they themselves also laughing and mocking.

And so at last, when the maidens had been all alone a while, and it was now hard on sunset, they drew together and stood in a ring, and fell to singing; and one Gold-may of the House of the Bridge, a most sweet singer, stood amidst their ring and led them. And this is somewhat of the meaning of their words:

The sun will not tarry; now changeth the light,
Fail the colours that marry the Day to the Night.

Amid the sun's burning bright weapons we bore,
For this eve of our earning comes once and no more.

For to-day hath no brother in yesterday's tide,
And to-morrow no other alike it doth hide.

This day is the token of oath and behest
That ne'er shall be broken through ill days and best.

Here the troth hath been given, the oath hath been done,
To the Folk that hath thriven well under the sun.

And the gifts of its giving our troth-day shall win
Are the Dale for our living and dear days therein.

O Sun, now thou wanest! yet come back and see
Amidst all that thou gainest how gainful are we.

O witness of sorrow wide over the earth,
Rise up on the morrow to look on our mirth!

Thy blooms art thou bringing back ever for men,
And thy birds are a-singing each summer again.

But to men little-hearted what winter is worse
Than thy summers departed that bore them the curse?

And e'en such art thou knowing where thriveth the year,
And good is all growing save thralldom and fear.

Nought such be our lovers" hearts drawing anigh,
While yet thy light hovers aloft in the sky.

Lo the seeker, the finder of Death in the Blade!

58. How the Maiden Ward Was Held in Burgdale 247

What lips shall be kinder on lips of mine laid?

La he that hath driven back tribes of the South!
Sweet-breathed is thine even, but sweeter his mouth.

Come back from the sea then, O sun! come aback,
Look adown, look on me then, and ask what I lack!

Come many a morrow to gaze on the Dale,
And if e'er thou seest sorrow remember its tale!

For 'twill be of a story to tell how men died
In the garnering of glory that no man may hide.

O sun sinking under! O fragrance of earth! O heart!
O the wonder whence longing has birth!

So they sang, and the sun sank indeed; and amidst their singing the eve was still about them, though there came a happy murmur from the face of the meadows and the houses of the Thorp aloof. But as their song fell they heard the sound of footsteps a many on the road; so they turned and stood with beating hearts in such order as when a band of the valiant draw together to meet many foes coming on them from all sides, and they stand back to back to face all comers. And even therewith, their raiment gleaming amidst the gathering dusk, came on them the young men of the Dale newly delivered from the grief of war.

Then in very deed the fierce mouths of the raisers of the war-shout were kind on the faces of tender maidens. Then went spear and axe and helm and shield clattering to the earth, as the arms of the new-comers went round about the bodies of the Brides, weary with the long day of sunshine, and glee and loving speech, and the maidens suffered the young men to lead them whither they would, and twilight began to draw round about them as the Maiden Band was sundered.

Some, they were led away westward down the Portway to the homesteads thereabout; and for divers of these the way was long to their halls, and they would have to wend over long stretches of dewy meadows, and hear the night-wind whisper in many a tree, and see the east begin to lighten with the dawn before they came to the lighted feast that awaited them. But some turned up the Portway straight towards Burgstead; and short was their road to the halls where even now the lights were being kindled for their greeting.

As for the Sun-beam, she had been very quiet the day long, speaking as little as she might do, laughing not at all, and smiling for kindness" sake rather than for merriment; and when the grooms came seeking their maidens, she withdrew herself from the band, and stood alone amidst the road nigher to Burgstead than they; and her heart beat hard, and her breath came short and quick, as though fear had caught her in its grip; and indeed for one moment of time she feared that he was not coming to her. For he had gone with the other grooms to that gathered band, and had passed from one to the other, not finding her, till he had got him through the whole company, and beheld her awaiting him. Then indeed he bounded toward her, and caught her by the hands, and then by the shoulders, and drew her to him, and she nothing loth; and in that while he said to her:

"Come then, my friend; lo thou! they go each their own way toward the halls of their houses; and for thee have I chosen a way—a way over the foot-bridge yonder, and over the dewy meadows on this best even of the year."

"Nay, nay," she said, "it may not be. Surely the Burgstead grooms look to thee to lead them to the gate; and surely in the House of the Face they look to see thee before any other. Nay, Gold-mane, my dear, we must needs go by the Portway."

He said: "We shall be home but a very little while after the first, for the way I tell of is as short as the Portway. But hearken, my sweet! When we are in the meadows we shall sit down for a minute on a bank under the chestnut trees, and thence watch the moon coming up over the southern cliffs. And I shall behold thee in the summer night, and deem that I see all thy beauty; which yet shall make me dumb with wonder when I see it indeed in the house amongst the candles."

"O nay," she said, "by the Portway shall we go; the torch-bearers shall be abiding thee at the gate."

Spake Face-of-god: "Then shall we rise up and wend first through a wide treeless meadow, wherein amidst the night we shall behold the kine moving about like odorous shadows; and through the greyness of the moonlight thou shalt deem that thou seest the pink colour of the eglantine blossoms, so fragrant they are."

"O nay," she said, "but it is meet that we go by the Portway."

But he said: "Then from the wide meadow come we into a close of corn, and then into an orchard-close beyond it. There in the ancient walnut-tree the owl sitteth breathing hard in the night-time; but thou shalt not hear him for the joy of the nightingales singing from the apple-trees of the close. Then from out of the shadowed orchard shall we come into the open town-meadow, and over its daisies shall the moonlight be lying in a grey flood of brightness.

"Short is the way across it to the brim of the Weltering Water, and across the water lieth the fair garden of the Face; and I have dight for thee there a little boat to waft us across the night-dark waters, that shall be like wavering flames of white fire where the moon smites them, and like the void of all things where the shadows hang over them. There then shall we be in the garden, beholding how the hall-windows are yellow, and hearkening the sound of the hall-glee borne across the flowers and blending with the voice of the nightingales in the trees. There then shall we go along the grass paths whereby the pinks and the cloves and the lavender are sending forth their fragrance, to cheer us, who faint at the scent of the over-worn roses, and the honey-sweetness of the lilies.

"All this is for thee, and for nought but for thee this even; and many a blossom whereof thou knowest nought shall grieve if thy foot tread not thereby to-night; if the path of thy wedding which I have made, be void of thee, on the even of the Chamber of Love.

"But lo! at last at the garden's end is the yew-walk arched over for thee, and thou canst not see whereby to enter it; but I, I know it, and I lead thee into and along the dark tunnel through the moonlight, and thine hand is not weary of mine as we go. But at the end shall we come to a wicket, which shall bring us out by the gable-end of the Hall of the Face. Turn we about its corner then, and there are we blinking on the torches of the torch-bearers, and the candles through the open door, and the hall ablaze with light and full of joyous clamour, like the bale-fire in the dark night kindled on a ness above the sea by fisher-folk remembering the Gods."

"O nay," she said, "but by the Portway must we go; the straightest way to the Gate of Burgstead."

In vain she spake, and knew not what she said; for even as he was speaking he led her away, and her feet went as her will went, rather than her words; and even as she said that last word she set her foot on the first board of the foot-bridge; and she turned aback one moment, and saw the long line of the rock-wall yet glowing with the last of the sunset of midsummer, while as she turned again, lo! before her the moon just begin-

ning to lift himself above the edge of the southern cliffs, and betwixt her and him all Burgdale, and Face-of-god moreover.

Thus then they crossed the bridge into the green meadows, and through the closes and into the garden of the Face and unto the Hall-door; and other brides and grooms were there before them (for six grooms had brought home brides to the House of the Face); but none deemed it amiss in the War-leader of the folk and the love that had led him. And old Stone-face said: "Too many are the rows of bee-skeps in the gardens of the Dale that we should begrudge wayward lovers an hour's waste of candle-light."

So at last those twain went up the sun-bright Hall hand in hand in all their loveliness, and up on to the dais, and stood together by the middle seat; and the tumult of the joy of the kindred was hushed for a while as they saw that there was speech in the mouth of the War-leader.

Then he spread his hands abroad before them all and cried out: "How then have I kept mine oath, whereas I swore on the Holy Boar to wed the fairest woman of the world?"

A mighty shout went rattling about the timbers of the roof in answer to his word; and they that looked up to the gable of the Hall said that they saw the ray-ringed image of the God smile with joy over the gathered folk.

But spake Iron-face unheard amidst the clamour of the Hall: "How fares it now with my darling and my daughter, who dwelleth amongst strangers in the land beyond the Wild-wood?"

59. THE BEHEST OF FACE-OF-GOD TO THE BRIDE ACCOMPLISHED:

A MOTE-STEAD APPOINTED FOR THE THREE FOLKS, TO WIT, THE MEN OF BURGDALE, THE SHEPHERDS, AND THE CHILDREN OF THE WOLF.

Three years and two months thereafter, three hours after noon in the days of early autumn, came a wain tilted over with precious webs of cloth, and drawn by eight white oxen, into the Market-place of Silver-stead: two score and ten of spear-men of the tallest, clad in goodly war-gear, went beside it, and much people of Silverdale thronged about them. The wain stayed at the foot of the stair that led up to the door of the Mote-house, and there lighted down therefrom a woman goodly of fashion, with wide grey eyes, and face and hands brown with the sun's burning. She had a helm on her head and a sword girt to her side, and in her arms she bore a yearling child.

And there was come Bow-may with the second man-child born to Face-of-god.

She stayed not amidst the wondering folk, but hastened up the stair, which she had once seen running with the blood of men: the door was open, and she went in and walked straight-way, with the babe in her arms, up the great Hall to the dais.

There were men on the dais: amidmost sat Folk-might, little changed since the last day she had seen him, yet fairer, she deemed, than of old time; and her heart went forth to meet the Chieftain of her Folk, and the glad tears started in her eyes and ran down her cheeks as she drew near to him.

By his side sat the Bride, and her also Bow-may deemed to have waxed goodlier. Both she and Folk-might knew Bow-may ere she had gone half the length of the hall; and the Bride rose up in her place and cried out Bow-may's name joyously.

With these were sitting the elders of the Wolf and the Woodlanders, the more part of whom Bow-may knew well.

On the dais also stood aside a score of men weaponed, and looking as if they were awaiting the word which should send them forth on some errand.

Now stood up Folk-might and said: "Fair greeting and love to my friend and the daughter of my Folk! How farest thou, Bow-may, best of all friendly women? How fareth my sister, and Face-of-god my brother? and how is it with our friends and helpers in the goodly Dale?"

Said Bow-may: "It is well both with all those and with me; and my heart laughs to see thee, Folk-might, and to look on the elders of the valiant, and our lovely sister the Bride. But I have a message for thee from Face-of-god: wilt thou that I deliver it here?"

"Yea surely," said Folk-might, and came forth. and took her hand, and kissed her cheeks and her mouth. The Bride also came forth and cast her arms about her, and kissed her; and they led her between them to a seat on the dais beside Folk-might.

But all men looked on the child in her arms and wondered what it was. But Bow-may took the babe, which was both fair and great, and set it on the knees of the Bride, and said:

"Thus saith Face-of-god: "Friend and kinswoman, well-beloved playmate, the gift which thou badest of me in sorrow do thou now take in joy, and do all the good thou wouldest to the son of thy friend. The ring which I gave thee once in the garden of the Face, give thou to Bow-may, my trusty and well-beloved, in token of the fulfilment of my behest.""

Then the Bride kissed Bow-may again, and fell to fondling of the child, which was loth to leave Bow-may.

But she spake again: "To thee also, Folk-might, I have a message from Face-of-god, who saith: "Mighty warrior, friend and fellow, all things thrive with us, and we are happy. Yet is there a hollow place in our hearts which grieveth us, and only thou and thine may amend it. Though whiles we hear tell of thee, yet we see thee not, and fain were we, might we see thee, and wot if the said tales be true. Wilt thou help us somewhat herein, or wilt thou leave us all the labour? For sure we be that thou wilt not say that thou rememberest us no more, and that thy love for us is departed." This is his message, Folk-might, and he would have an answer from thee."

Then laughed Folk-might and said: "Sister Bow-may, seest thou these weaponed men hereby?"

"Yea," she said.

Said he: "These men bear a message with them to Face-of-god my brother. Crow the Shaft-speeder, stand forth and tell thy friend Bow-may the message I have set in thy mouth, every word of it."

Then Crow stood forth and greeted Bow-may friendly, and said: "Friend Bow-may, this is the message of our Alderman: "Friend and helper, in the Dale which thou hast given to us do all things thrive; neither are we grown old in three years" wearing, nor are our memories worsened. We long sore to see you and give you guesting in Silverdale, and one day that shall befall. Meanwhile, know this: that we of the Wolf and the Woodland, mindful of the earth that bore us, and the pit whence we were digged, have a mind to go see Shadowy Vale once in every three years, and there to hold high-tide in the ancient Hall of the Wolf, and sit in the Doom-ring of our Fathers. But since ye have joined yourselves to us in battle, and have given us this Dale, our health and wealth, without price and without reward, we deem you our very brethren, and small shall be our hall-glee, and barren shall our Doom-ring seem to us, unless ye sit there beside us. Come then, that we may rejoice each other by the sight of face and sound of voice; that we may speak together of matters that concern our welfare; so that we three Kindreds may become one Folk. And if this seem good to you, know that we shall be in Shadowy Vale in a half-month's wearing. Grieve us not by forbearing to come." Lo, Bow-may, this is the message, and I have learned it well, for well it pleaseth me to bear it."

Then said Folk-might: "What say'st thou to the message, Bow-may?"

"It is good in all ways," said she, "but is it timely? May our folk have the message and get to Shadowy Vale, so as to meet you there?"

"Yea surely," said Folk-might, "for our kinsmen here shall take the road through Shadowy Vale, and in four days" time they shall be in Burgdale, and as thou wottest, it is scant a two days" journey thence to Shadowy Vale."

Therewith he turned to those men again, and said: "Kinsman Crow, depart now, and use all diligence with thy message."

So the messengers began to stir; but Bow-may cried out: "Ho! Folk-might, my friend, I perceive thou art little changed from the man I knew in Shadowy Vale, who would have his dinner before the fowl were plucked. For shall I not go back with these thy messengers, so that I also may get all ready to wend to the Mote-house of Shadowy Vale?"

But the Bride looked kindly on her, and laughed and said: "Sister Bow-may, his meaning is that thou shouldest abide here in Silverdale till we depart for the Folk-thing, and then go thither with us; and this I also pray thee to do, that thou mayst rejoice the hearts of thine old friends; and also that thou mayst teach me all that I should know concerning this fair child of

More to William Morris—The Roots of the Mountains

my brother and my sister."

And she looked on her so kindly as she caressed the babe, that Bow-may's heart melted, and she cried out:

"Would that I might never depart from the house wherein thou dwellest, O Bride of my Kinsman! And this that thou biddest me is easy and pleasant for me to do. But afterwards I must get me back to Burgdale; for I seem to have left much there that calleth for me."

"Yea," said Folk-might, "and art thou wedded, Bow-may? Shalt thou never bend the yew in battle again?"

Said Bow-may soberly: "Who knoweth, chieftain? Yea, I am wedded now these two years; and nought I looked for less when I followed those twain through the Wild-wood to Burgdale."

She sighed therewith, and said: "In all the Dale there is no better man of his hands than my man, nor any goodlier to look on, and he is even that Hart of Highcliff whom thou knowest well, O Bride!"

Said the Bride: "Thou sayest sooth, there is no better man in the Dale."

Said Bow-may: "Sun-beam bade me wed him when he pressed hard upon me." She stayed awhile, and then said: "Face-of-god also deemed I should not naysay the man; and now my son by him is of like age to this little one."

"Good is thy story," said Folk-might; "or deemest thou, Bow-may, that such strong and goodly women as thou, and women so kind and friendly, should forbear the wedding and the bringing forth of children? Yea, and we who may even yet have to gather to another field before we die, and fight for life and the goods of life."

"Thou sayest well," she said; "all that hath befallen me is good since the day whereon I loosed shaft from the break of the bent over yonder."

Therewith she fell a-musing, and made as though she were hearkening to the soft voice of the Bride caressing the new-come baby; but in sooth neither heard nor saw what was going on about her, for her thoughts were in bygone days. Howbeit

presently she came to herself again, and fell to asking many questions concerning Silverdale and the kindred, and those who had once been thralls of the Dusky Men; and they answered all duly, and told her the whole story of the Dale since the Day of the Victory.

So Bow-may and the carles who had come with her abode for that half-month in Silverdale, guested in all love by the folk thereof, both the kindreds and the poor folk. And Bow-may deemed that the Bride loved Face-of-god's child little less than her own, whereof she had two, a man and a woman; and thereat was she full of joy, since she knew that Face-of-god and the Sun-beam would be fain thereof.

Thereafter, when the time was come, fared Folk-might and the Bride, and many of the elders and warriors of the Wolf and the Woodland, to Shadowy Vale; and Dallach and the best of Rosedale went with them, being so bidden; and Bow-may and her following, according to the word of the Bride. And in Shadowy Vale they met Face-of-god and Alderman Iron-face, and the chiefs of Burgdale and the Shepherds, and many others; and great joy there was at the meeting. And the Sun-beam remembered the word which she spoke to Face-of-god when first he came to Shadowy Vale, that she would be wishful to see again the dwelling wherein she had passed through so much joy and sorrow of her younger days. But if anyone were fain of this meeting, the Alderman was glad above all, when he took the Bride once more in his arms, and caressed her whom he had deemed should be a very daughter of his House.

Now telleth the tale of all these kindreds, to wit, the Men of Burgdale and the Sheepcotes; and the Children of the Wolf, and the Woodlanders, and the Men of Rosedale, that they were friends henceforth, and became as one Folk, for better or worse, in peace and in war, in waning and waxing; and that whatsoever befell them, they ever held Shadowy Vale a holy place, and for long and long after they met there in mid-autumn, and held converse and counsel together.

No more as now telleth the tale of these kindreds and folks, but maketh an ending.

CPSIA information can be obtained
at www.ICGtesting.com
Printed in the USA
LVHW04s0922220418
574434LV00004B/137/P